ROOSEVELT RANCH

ELISE FABER

Roosevelt Ranch
by Elise Faber

ROOSEVELT RANCH
Copyright © 2021 ELISE FABER
Paperback ISBN-13: 978-1-63749-021-1
Ebook ISBN-13: 978-1-63749-020-4
Cover Art by Jena Brignola

DISASTER AT ROOSEVELT RANCH

CHAPTER ONE

I HAD NEVER THOUGHT of a plus sign as a bad thing.

Of course, I'd never had one show up on a stick I'd peed on. Kudos to me, that changed today.

My knees wobbled, and the idiotic white piece of plastic rattled as I set it on the scarred Formica countertop.

Brown eyes—mine—stared back at me accusingly in the mirror. "You've done it now."

A baby.

My hand found my stomach. Still flat, still the same.

Even though so much had changed.

The bathroom door rattled as a fist slammed against the thin plank of wood. "Move it, Kel! Food's up and your tables are restless."

"Coming!" I called as I wrapped the test in a paper towel before shoving it deep into my purse.

I couldn't leave it here. Not where anyone—where *Henry*—might see it. He would get his back up, storm out to the ranch where he-who-must-not-be-named lived, and drag the no-good, low down piece of crap into town for a proper whooping.

And I might just want to let him.

With a sigh, I washed my hands and left the bathroom.

It was my own fault. I knew the type of man Rex was.

I'd fallen into his bed anyway.

"Regret never fails to burn like a mother," I muttered as I swept into the kitchen, grabbed the plates from the pass, and started hustling toward my table.

"What was that?" Henry asked as he flipped a burger.

"Nothing." I hefted the tray filled with six plates and various food accessories—ketchup, extra dressing, and napkins—with practiced ease.

Oh, God. I was going to be huge and pregnant and . . . waiting tables.

Good luck to the customers, because I lacked the sincerity and cheerfulness that seemed to come naturally to most waitresses on a normal day. I could only imagine what was going to happen when my hormones raged.

Using my back, I pushed through the swinging door and promptly stumbled to a stop.

He was here. *Rex* was here.

Stupidly, my heart raced. He'd changed his mind. He'd—

The man's eyes flicked to mine, completely unrecognizing and indifferent. My momentary burst of hope disintegrated.

He was going to pretend not to know me? To not *recognize* me?

The jerk! The rotten—

Except . . . there was something off about him. I squinted, trying to discern the change, but the tray was taking its toll on my arms. I tore my gaze away from Rex to practically hurl the dishes at my customers.

"Anything else?" I asked, and was thankful when there weren't any requests.

Two seconds later, I was in front of Rex.

Who wasn't *actually* Rex.

Oh, he was the right height and had the same square jaw and the same gorgeous, sun-kissed skin, but *this* man wasn't the one I'd slept with.

"Hi," he said, his green eyes warm. They were a brilliant emerald and just as inviting as they'd been in the picture I'd seen on Rex's desk. "Can I just sit anywhere?"

My nod was jerky. "I'll get you a menu."

Fingers brushed my arm—calloused fingers that felt both familiar and different.

"You okay?"

I forced a smile, my stomach churning. This could *not* be happening. "Just perfect—"

And that was the moment I puked all over Rex's twin's shoes.

CHAPTER TWO

"Hey, puke monster. How's it hanging?"

My eyes slid closed at my sister's voice. I was cowering in the back office, mortified and disgusted.

I'd puked on a man's shoes.

A man I'd never met, who I'd only seen in a photograph on his brother's desk.

Life was good.

"Henry called you, didn't he?" I said, resigned that I was in for no end of sisterly torture now that she knew.

"Of course he did," Melissa said. "He was worried about you driving home."

"I'm fine." And I was. Aside from the unpleasant aftertaste in my mouth, I felt completely normal.

Which was relative, I supposed, since I had a human being growing inside of me.

"Go away," I told her, pulling a fresh shirt over my head and snagging my purse. Puking on a customer was pretty much a surefire way to end your shift.

Or your job.

Thankfully, Henry had been my best friend for almost twenty years. I figured that gave me one puke pass.

"You look like crap," Melissa said, peeking through the door, her bright blue eyes sweeping over me with razor-sharp focus.

Her perfume hit me like a wave and my stomach began to churn again. This pregnancy stuff blew.

"I *feel* like crap."

"You'd better take off. I'll cover the rest of your shift."

Surprised, I glanced over at her. "*You're* going to?"

"I've waited plenty of tables here, Kel."

"Yeah, like ten years ago."

"I'm not that old."

"You have kids."

Her *pfft* of disgust wasn't unwarranted, given the circumstances. Not that I was going to enlighten her to that fact.

"Kids don't mean my life is over!" she protested as she crossed the room and rifled through the stack of café T-shirts to find one in her size.

Which was a small. Or rather a delicate, curvy, perfect size two.

Ugh.

"Lies," I said, even as part of me persisted in wondering why I was pursuing this particular conversational minefield. Probably because I wanted her to convince me I was wrong.

Melissa sighed and sank down into the chair behind the desk. She reached forward, touching my forehead to check my temperature in that quintessential *mom* way. "You're clammy," she said. "And okay, maybe the kids are driving me nuts, and I jumped for an excuse to get the heck out of the house. But, Max and Allie are still the best things I've ever done."

I smiled. "You're a good mom."

"You think?" The slice of vulnerability in her tone caught me off guard. My sister didn't do vulnerable.

"I *know*," I said, not needing to fake my conviction. Melissa was a fantastic mother, so, *so* much better than our own.

Her eyes warmed and tension seemed to leave her spine. A moment later, any softness was gone. She straightened, clapped her hands once. "Okay then, so get the heck out of here and let me have my fun."

I left her to it and drove home carefully. I lived on the edge of town, just before the main turnoff that led to Rex's ranch.

The close proximity had been convenient for the few weeks we were together. At least until he'd stopped calling. Then—*now*—it remained solely a painful reminder of my idiocy.

"The one time in my life I give into stupidity and this happens." I sighed and bumped my car door closed with one hip. Between digging in my purse for my keys and trying—and failing—to keep the lovely smelling baggy of dirty clothes out of nose-range, my hands were full.

So it was the perfect time for someone to pull into my driveway.

Gravel crunched, and I winced as a cloud of dust wafted forward, coating my clammy skin in a fine layer of the stuff.

The car, an expensive silver sedan, slid to a stop and the driver's side window rolled down with a *whir*. "Excuse me. I wondered if you could direct me to . . ."

Warm honey. The masculine voice was liquid and molten, leaving trail marks of sticky sweetness down my spine. If Rex's voice had been sexy, his twin's was *Magic Mike XL*.

". . . Roosevelt Ranch. I think I missed the turnoff."

I stood there, my gaze on the car, on the driver whose face was both so familiar and so different. I'd always felt out of my depth in Rex's presence. Too short. Too fat. Too ugly.

His twin dwarfed everything. All of the feelings Rex had wrought were magnified by his brother's smooth polish and obvious wealth.

And I'd puked on him.

Not my fault. Not my fault. Not my—

I shored my spine, took a step closer, and met those clear green eyes head-on.

"Oh," he said, surprise filling his voice. Clearly he hadn't known whose driveway he'd parked in. "I didn't mean to bother you." There was a pause, spectacularly awkward. "I'm Justin."

"I'm Kelly."

"Nice to meet you." His voice hit me right in the gut, but instead of making me nauseous like everything else seemed to, the sound of Justin talking settled my insides.

"You too." I bit my lip. "And . . . I'm sorry about earlier. I don't normally . . ."

". . . puke on customers?" One corner of his mouth curved up.

"Yeah. That." I winced and my words came in a flurry. "How're the shoes? I meant what I said. I'll pay to replace them and to get your clothes cleaned."

"They're fine."

My brows pulled together. "Fine?"

He shrugged, and his mouth curved further. My pulse sped up in response, the jerk. "Well, *fine* meaning they're in the trash. But I have more clothes. It was really no big deal."

"Getting *puked on* wasn't a big deal?" If that was true, the man was a saint.

"I'm a doctor," Justin said. "There's not much that grosses me out."

"Oh."

"So, Roosevelt Ranch?" he asked after a beat. "Can you tell me how to get there?"

I shook myself. Big deal, so the man was hotter than pretty much any guy I'd ever been around. Sexiness didn't discount the fact I still had a brain.

I just needed to remember to use it.

"You haven't missed the turn," I said, and started to lift my hand to point down the road before I remembered it held the bag of my dirty clothes. *Ick.* I dropped my arm, inclining my head instead. "It's just past that stand of trees. Turn right and drive down for a mile, then turn left at the red mailbox. You can't miss the entrance to the ranch."

"Okay." He raised a brow. "That's very . . . *informative?*"

I paid his surprise no mind. Instead, lifting my chin, I said, "I know Rex."

"So I surmised."

There was a slender thread of derision in his tone. It sliced deep, and I wanted to shout I wasn't the kind of woman he seemed to be assuming I was. The kind other women looked down their noses at, the kind men only used for sex.

Except evidence seemed to be pointing to the contrary.

"Yeah. Well, drive safe." I turned away from Justin and started up the wooden stairs of my little cottage.

"Okay, thanks." I heard the car's transmission *clink* as he shifted into reverse, then the crunch of gravel as he backed down the driveway. "Hope you feel better," he called.

I didn't bother looking back, but gave a little wave and unlocked my front door. "Nothing nine months won't cure."

CHAPTER THREE

JUSTIN DROVE through the gates of Roosevelt Ranch to find a huge moving truck parked just inside the circular drive.

He sighed. It was exactly as he figured.

His twin brother Rex was always the same. Always declaring he'd found his dream job, only to up and quit a few months in.

He'd bought a luxury cruise line and not followed through on the essentials, like feeding people and providing entertainment, then had jumped ship when the customers were angry.

After that, Rex had bought a production company in Los Angeles and produced two horrifically boring films about the dangers of artificial dye in food.

Things never changed. Investment firms. Gourmet catering companies. Oil fields in Texas.

At least *this* venture—the luxury dude ranch business—hadn't hurt other people.

Justin had phoned the ranch manager and learned that the ranch hadn't received a single booking, probably because Rex was supposed to be taking a course on marketing and, no surprise, hadn't actually finished it.

One of the wide-planked garage doors opened just as Justin got out of his car. A cherry-red Lamborghini backed slowly out.

"Rex, you are an idiot," he muttered, watching as the driver carefully drove it up the ramp and into the back of the truck.

"Really feeling the love, J."

Rex's low rumble made the hairs on Justin's nape stand on edge.

Everything was always a joke to his brother, probably because Justin was *always* the one who cleaned up the messes.

He swept a hand at the ridiculous ranch house, complete with columns, two stupidly oversized front doors, and a manicured lawn. This was supposed to be a dude ranch in the middle of Utah, not the set of *Dallas.* "What are you doing, Rex?"

"Ranching isn't for me."

Justin bit back a retort. He'd known what he was getting into before he'd flown in, but his disappointment was still acute.

He'd spent four years in the Middle East as a flight surgeon, had clocked countless hours taking care of people who were sacrificing life and limb for others.

And his brother was still the same.

"What about the ranch? The people who work and live here?" he asked.

"Dad's sending out someone to evaluate everything." Rex shrugged. "They'll be fine. We'll either sell and they'll go with the new owner, or Dad will find someone to run this place and keep on anyone productive. You know he always finds a way to turn a profit."

That, their father did.

The trouble was, turning profits from Rex's schemes was unnecessary stress on their already health-plagued father.

"Dad doesn't need the extra work." Another heart attack might be the end for him.

"Dad is *retired* and bored out of his mind. I'm just giving him something to do."

Justin mentally counted to ten. "Whatever, Rex," he said, striving to keep his tone neutral. "So where are you heading next?"

Rex slung on a pair of aviator glasses that must have cost more than the entirety of Justin's wardrobe and sighed as if the weight of the world was on his shoulders. "Fiji. I need a vacation after all this stress."

Selfish, no-good son-of-a—

"Have a safe flight," Justin said, instead of giving voice to any of the frustrated thoughts pinging around in his mind.

"Did you bring the plane?" Rex asked.

"Yup."

"Good." He jangled a set of keys in his palm, probably to another freaking Lamborghini. "You don't mind waiting here while I have it drop me off, do you?"

"No." Especially since Justin had already figured as much. "I'm going to take a few days to get my civilian legs back."

Rex clapped him on the shoulder. "Good deal. The movers should take care of everything, and Rosa will cook for you. Just make yourself at home."

"Thanks," he told his brother before walking to the back of his car and pulling out his military-grade duffle.

"Oh," Rex said. "I thought Dad told me you were out for good . . ."

"I am," Justin replied. "Just didn't have a chance to get my"—he nodded at the ridiculous looking man-purse in Rex's hand—"*Gucci* out of storage."

"It's Armani and don't hate. This is a classic."

"It's something, all right," Justin said under his breath.

An uncomfortable moment passed between them. Justin remembered when they'd been close, when things had been different.

Before their mom had died.

Now things were just—

"Okay then. I'll send you pics of all the hot chicks I'll be banging."

—just *that.*

Justin rolled his eyes. "Can't wait," he replied, not bothering to hide his sarcasm. "Safe flight."

A minute later, Rex was in one of the many sports cars still dotting the front yard and tearing off down the road toward the front gate.

"And that folks," Justin said under his breath, "is what happens when your brother is a first-class asshole."

CHAPTER FOUR

I stood in front of the massive wooden doors of Roosevelt Ranch, my throat burning with bile and my knees shaking.

Just get it over with, Kel.

I raised my hand to knock. My fingers trembled and I pressed my lips together. Hard. I'd gotten into the mess, now I'd have to figure a way out of it.

I moved to knock, but before my fist made contact with the thick plank of wood, the door swung open and I fell forward.

"Whoa, there," a deep voice—*Justin*, I thought with a shiver—said as he caught my shoulders and stopped me from landing flat on my face.

It took a minute for me to regain my feet . . . and my senses. I stepped back, put some crucial distance between us, and lifted my chin. "I'm here to see your brother."

His eyes went slightly cold. "He's not here."

Well, then. "Okay," I said. "When will he be back?"

A pause.

"He's not."

My brows pulled down. "Not what?"

"Not coming back."

I tried in vain to produce some rational response, but all that came out of my mouth was, "He left? *Just left?*"

"Yup," Justin said. "I suspect that he's halfway to Fiji by now, already cooking up some new scheme."

Everything inside of me stilled, struggling to fit the pieces together in my mind. "But the ranch. The hands. Who's going to exercise the horses?"

"I am," Justin said, and for the first time, I noticed his clothes. Instead of the expensive slacks and button-down he'd worn at the restaurant the day before, he had on jeans and a T-shirt.

The items should have looked ordinary, but, of course, they didn't. They *wouldn't*. Not on Justin, anyway. The man could have worn one of those hideous banana hammock things and he would have still been delectable.

His jeans were the sinner's version of denim. I wanted to stroke across the paper-thin material—the worn seams on the inside of his thighs, the exposed threads at his knees—just to see if it felt as butter-soft as it looked.

"You're taking care of the horses?" I squeaked, desperate to change the subject, to divert my mind back to what was important.

Namely, the pea-sized human growing in my belly.

Justin sighed but didn't respond, just walked past me and around to the back of the house. I trailed him across the lawn that was so impeccably groomed it could have been hand-cut with scissors, and then down a path I knew like the back of my hand.

It led to a building that was basically my version of catnip.

I couldn't have *not* followed him along the path. Not when he was headed for the stables.

I missed seeing the horses, missed the smell of worn leather and alfalfa, missed hearing their whinnies and the soft clopping of their hooves on the stone floor.

The large barn door slid open silently, and he strode through, his gaze swinging from side to side.

I hardly noticed him. My eyes were on Stella. On *my* horse.

Not mine, I reminded myself.

"Hi, baby," I crooned as I crossed to her. She was beautiful, gentle, and even-tempered. I loved her, though her brown head and white spotted rump, with slightly-too-long legs, made her appear a little mismatched.

Kind of like me.

Stella's ears perked up, and she moved to the front of her stall when she heard my voice. My heart melted, and so much of the stress and angst of the last few days just disappeared. God, I'd missed her . . . a whole hell of a lot more than Rex, actually.

I rubbed the space between her eyes and she worked her chin up over my shoulder in her version of a hug. It was so familiar and painfully reminiscent of all the hours I'd spent in these stables, that I felt tears well up.

Wrapping my arms around her neck, I blinked them away. She chuffed in my ear and I laughed, pulling back. "No apples today, sweetheart. I'm sorry. I wasn't prepared."

She gave me an indignant look before bending to drink some water.

"I know. Total failure."

"You like horses."

I jumped and whirled around at the sound of Justin's voice very close behind me. My cheeks heated and, embarrassed, I bit my lip. "I'm sorry. It's just that I used to work here, and I missed—"

His fingers grasped my arm, a steady touch that somehow managed to both settle my nerves and ramp up my heartbeat. "Easy. It's fine," he said. "I just wanted to see if you could show me where everything is."

"But what about Frank?" I asked of the man in charge of running the stables.

Justin blew out a breath and stepped back, leaning against the stall opposite of Stella's. "He got an offer at another ranch and took most of the hands with him. Said he wanted a job with more stability."

I opened my mouth, pointing behind him to where the very temperamental Appalachian, Theodore, was pawing at the ground. "You'd, uh, better move."

Justin either didn't hear me, or didn't care to acknowledge my warning. "I don't blame him, considering Rex, but—"

"Really. I think you should step away from the stall."

"I could use the help. I'm not—*ouch!*"

There was a *rip,* and Justin jumped away from the stall, rubbing the back of his arm as he cursed a mile a minute. I'd been bitten by Theodore before and knew it hurt like a mother.

So I tried not to laugh.

It didn't work.

The giggles burst free. I laughed until I cried and my knees gave out. I sank to the hay-covered ground, unable to ignore the glare Justin was lobbing my way. Not that it mattered, I was lost to most forms of social niceties.

Like not laughing at people when they got hurt.

"I'm sorry!" A gasp of air as I tried to control myself. "I'm really . . . not . . . laughing . . . at . . . you."

"Yes, you are." He crouched down and studied me intently. "What was a nice girl like you doing with a man like Rex?"

That sobered me right up. I blinked at him and found I couldn't lie, not when his eyes were locked with mine.

"I wanted to have an adventure," I said. "For once in my life I wanted to do something that felt good without thinking about the consequences."

Justin was quiet for a while. Then he asked, "And how'd that work out for you?"

I lifted my chin. "Well, considering I'm pregnant and the father's on a plane halfway around the world, it hasn't gone too well."

CHAPTER FIVE

I WINCED and mentally clapped a palm over my mouth. Apparently, pregnancy had taken away my filter.

Okay, that was a lie. I'd never had much of one anyway.

Which was one of the reasons Rex had said he'd liked me so much. Of course, putting up with me on a daily basis—sans filter—had probably driven him away.

Especially when I'd poo-pooed his idea to refurbish the local mechanic shop for luxury car repairs. I'd simply pointed out that he was the sole owner of any vehicle more expensive than a good ole Chevy truck in the vicinity and that it probably wasn't a sound business idea.

He hadn't talked to me for three days.

The sex had been fine . . . okay, more convenient than fine, but I'd been lonely, and Melissa had her own life, and I was already at the ranch anyway—

"What did you say?"

Crap. Justin and he sounded deadly serious.

"Don't worry about it." I pushed to my feet and brushed past him, my insides all squirrely.

"Kelly."

Ignoring him, I pointed to a door. "All of the tack is in there."

"Tack?"

My brows pulled together, concern twisting my gut further. I was suddenly queasy and it had nothing to do with the baby. "Yeah, you know things like saddles, stirrups, bridles?"

"Gotcha." A pause. "What's a bridle?"

Dear lord, the ranch was going to fall to pieces.

"It's the piece of equipment that helps a rider steer the horse." I opened the door and grabbed one, along with a bit. "This part slips over the horse's head," I said, demonstrating the motion in mid air. "This piece —the bit—goes in their mouth."

"Oh, like the reins."

I stopped, hands dropping to my sides, the metal and leather jangling on impact. Then I caught a twinkle in his green eyes.

"Oh. My. God. You're messing with me."

Justin smiled. "Just a little. I've been riding since I could walk." He crossed to me and ducked slightly, meeting my gaze. "What's this about a baby?"

Crap. Crap. Double crap.

"It's not your problem," I told him. "I'll figure it out."

"It's my *brother's* problem, and since he's not here . . ."

I darted into the tack room—sometimes the best offense was a good defense—and hefted a saddle. "Still not your problem. I'm a grown woman. I'll take care of it."

Justin was very close when I rotated around, the saddle in my arms. "How, exactly, are you going to *take care* of it?"

Blinking, I studied him for a moment, trying to understand where he was going with the question.

Then I got it.

"Not like *that*," I exclaimed. "I'm keeping the baby. I—" I shook my head. "I understand why some women do it, but not me." My voice dropped. "I just . . . couldn't."

Something like relief crossed Justin's features. "Okay."

Edging past him, I spent the next few minutes saddling Stella. Other than asking where the tools were kept, Justin didn't speak again until I slipped the bridle over Stella's head and led her from the barn.

"We need to talk about this." He had a screwdriver in his hand and was adjusting a hinge on one of the sliding doors.

"Me riding?" I hesitated, one foot already in the stirrups. I hadn't been to the doctor yet. Was being on a horse going to hurt the baby?

Justin angled his head, scrutinizing me in a way that made me want to squirm. After a moment he said, "No. I'm not an OB but I think the general consensus is for women to continue their normal activities— within reason, that is—for at least the first trimester."

"O-okay." I blew out a breath and lifted myself into the saddle.

"Kelly?"

"Yeah." My heels were poised on Stella's flanks; she practically quivered with excitement.

"Enjoy your ride, but know I'll still be here when you get back."

Damn.

Not about to admit I'd been hoping to outwait him, I nodded, tapped Stella's side, and off we went riding into the sunset.

Or rather, the early morning sun.

And even though I wanted nothing more than to spend hours on her back, feeling the wind blow through my hair, I kept the ride perfunctory.

I still had to brush her down and exercise the other horses. Then there were stalls to muck out, feed to distribute. I might not work at Roosevelt Ranch any longer, but that didn't mean the animals should suffer.

Less than an hour later, I had Stella groomed and turned out to pasture. Justin was saddling Theodore, the pair of them apparently on much better terms. "How'd you do it?"

He glanced up. "Sugar cubes."

I sputtered. "Wh-what? That's bad for horses."

Justin shrugged. "In moderation it's fine and"—Theodore snuffled at his jeans pocket—"look, he's not even trying to bite me."

"Until you run out of sugar cubes," I muttered, "and he takes a bite out of your—"

He laughed and it prickled the hairs on my arms. Seriously, my body was a hussy. "You've got a mouth on you."

I shrugged and grabbed a shovel. "So what?" I asked, scooping out of some of the dirty straw and unmentionables in the stall. Surprisingly, or maybe not, since I'd been raised alongside these horses, the scent didn't bother me.

It was more like . . . home.

"There's no what," Justin said. "I like a girl with spirit."

"That's what your brother said," I snapped. "At least until he stopped talking to me. It probably runs in the family."

The barn went deathly silent, even the horses seeming to realize that I'd said something both incredibly stupid and far beyond the lines of polite conversation.

Justin turned slowly to face me. His face was blank, but scarily so, as though an entire gamut of emotions were roiling just beneath the surface.

"I'm not my brother." Four words calmly spoken. Four words that scared the crap out of me.

I took a step back. "I-I know."

He closed the distance between us, coming so near that I could see the gold flecks in his eyes, the dark bristles of stubble on his jaw.

"Rex is an idiot."

"Maybe." I blew out a breath. "But I was one too, and that isn't your fault. I'm sorry."

Justin's face softened. "Kelly—"

Theodore bumped against the stall door, impatient as always for his ride now that he was saddled. He was a temperamental horse, and while establishing a hierarchy with him was important, today I just wanted some air.

"You'd better take him out. He's getting restless."

"He can wait." Damn, why'd he have to go and make me like him more? "We need to discuss this. Ignoring the baby won't make it go away."

"No," I agreed. "But it also won't discount the fact that I've still got months to figure it out. The baby will hold, Theodore the Grouch won't. The dirty stalls won't. My shift starting in two hours won't."

"At the restaurant?"

I nodded and Justin frowned, but before he could say anything, Theodore whinnied loudly enough to hurt my ears.

"I'll finish these." I inclined my head to the last two dirty stalls. "You burn off some of his energy."

He opened his mouth, no doubt to press me further.

"Please?" And then when that still didn't budge him, "I promise we'll talk later."

Mossy green eyes connected with mine, and I couldn't look away. "Promise?"

I ground my teeth together. "I said so, didn't I?"

One side of his mouth turned up. "So you did." With that, he left me, leading Theodore from the barn.

I really tried not to stare at his butt as he mounted fluidly and galloped away.

I really did not succeed.

CHAPTER SIX

I MUCKED out the stalls and hurried from the ranch before Justin returned. Cowardly, maybe, but self-preservation was speaking, and I needed some distance.

I didn't like how he made me feel.

Okay, that was a total lie. I *really* liked how Rex's twin made me feel.

The problem was that he was *Rex's twin.*

After buckling my seatbelt, I started my car. Or attempted to, anyway. It took five minutes of coaxing, cursing, and finally opening the hood and banging a screwdriver against random engine components to get my old Toyota running.

I slid back into the driver's seat and thunked my head down onto the steering wheel. Everything would be okay. I would get through this. I—

Enough pep talk.

Time to get moving.

Carefully, I pulled away and drove the short distance to my house. Once inside, I showered, slipped on my uniform, and threw my dirty clothes in the wash.

One glance at my empty fridge told me I'd be eating at the restaurant. I guessed with a baby coming, I should fill the thing with fruits and veggies and . . . my stomach growled loudly.

Lots and lots of ice cream. I wanted—no, *needed* ice cream.

My mind went abruptly from hankering for Rocky Road to churning like a boat on the open ocean.

I barely made it in time.

Christening the porcelain goddess before eleven o'clock. Life goals.

Fifteen minutes later, I'd managed to choke down some slightly stale cereal and a glass of water. I felt better, but apparently thoughts of ice cream were off the table.

I'd better be able to at least eat it. Because taking the frozen deliciousness from a pregnant woman seemed like cruel and unusual punishment.

Thankfully, this go around my car started without trouble, and I was on time for my shift.

Henry was in the pass, organizing tickets on the counter and scrutinizing plates. This was *just* a diner, as he tended to call it, but my friend had major cooking chops and took his food seriously. He'd been to culinary school, had even held the position of sous chef for a very famous restaurant.

Then his dad had died, and Henry had come home to take over the family restaurant.

So, as much as I needed this job, I hoped the diner wouldn't keep him in town forever. He might be Darlington's best chef, but he was slated for so much more.

"Looking awfully grave, kiddo," he said and pressed a kiss to my head. "Feeling better?"

I nodded then impulsively hugged him. "I love you. You know that, right?"

He wrapped his arms around me briefly. "Yes. Because I'm exceptionally loveable." Pulling back, he tugged my ponytail. "Now take these to nineteen before they get cold."

"Tyrant," I said, smiling. "We were having a moment."

He grinned. "And proud of it. Now go, there's plenty of time for *moments* later."

Mock pouting, I stacked the plates on a tray. "Fine."

As I flounced off, his laughter floated through the air. "Love you too, Kel."

The exchange reminded me of the hundreds of others we'd had over the years. Henry and I met in kindergarten after he punched a boy who'd cut off two inches of my ponytail. We'd quickly become inseparable, me the quiet, tomboy cowgirl, him the charming, gregarious class favorite.

No doubt, the pairing had confused everyone in town, but we'd clicked from the beginning. It also helped, I supposed, that our childhood houses were literally across the street from one another.

Forced proximity, similar temperaments, and none of those pesky boy-girl attraction hormones to muck things up.

Not to say we hadn't experimented while we were teenagers, but after one very unappealing—and wet . . . I wrinkled my nose—kiss, our curiosity had been assuaged, and we'd gone back to being friends.

Only friends.

Living in a small town meant we'd been in the same class all the way through high school, after which he'd gone to culinary school in New York, and I was supposed to have gone to college upstate.

My end hadn't worked out, but Henry's had.

And he'd done well for himself, working for several big name chefs before his father suddenly got sick and passed away.

He'd come back and . . . stayed. For four years now, saying his mom wasn't ready to run the restaurant on her own and that there was no chef in town good enough to trust with his dad's recipes.

Of course, *I* thought Henry was running from something back in New York.

Or rather, *someone.*

But that was only my intuition talking. He'd never indicated an issue with his heart, broken or bruised or otherwise.

I might not have even suspected anything if not for the occasionally tortured expressions he wore while cooking one particular dish.

Order a Cobb salad and his jaw would tighten, his knife would be a flash of metal almost too fast to track, and his eyes . . . his eyes overflowed with hurt.

Not that we talked about that.

Because, while Henry could get me to spill my guts like no one's business, in reverse I might as well have been talking to a brick wall.

He'd always been open and affectionate toward me, generous with hugs and sympathy. But *his* emotions? Opening up to share the hidden pieces of himself?

Yeah, no. Henry didn't cave until he was good and ready.

So I didn't push. But I knew I'd drop everything if and when he needed me.

———

MY DAY WAS ACTUALLY GOING PRETTY WELL.

I'd gotten to ride and see the horses, even love on Stella. As a rescue horse, she'd been so terrified and emotionally hurt that it had taken me months to coax her through the worst of her trauma.

Which was why Rex firing me from the ranch had hurt so much.

Stifling a sigh, I double checked the latest order and slid the ticket into the holder. Surprisingly, everyone who'd come into the restaurant that day so far had acted like actual human beings.

No one had been rude or made excessively complicated orders. No one had even spilled anything.

Winning.

"You shouldn't be on your feet all day."

Jumping, I spun around and saw Justin standing less than a foot behind me.

He was just as gorgeous as ever. Which was probably why my brain stopped working. "I'm sorry?"

"You don't have to apologize." He smirked, eyes laughing at his stupid joke. "You shouldn't be working here. It's too hard on you."

"Women do it all the time and anyway, normal activity, remember?" I countered. "Plus, I've got *normal* needs. Like eating and having a place to sleep."

Justin shrugged. "Be that as it may, you don't like it. I can see it in your face, your movements, your fake smile."

I plunked my hands on my hips, unable to deny what was obviously the truth. But that didn't mean I was going to let him have the last word. "You don't even know me. How could you possibly know anything about my smiles?"

"I know because I've seen a real one," he said and I snorted. "When you were with Stella. There."

My gaze flashed up to his.

"There it is again. You love that horse and it shows on your face."

My heart twisted. It actually felt as though it was tying itself into knots inside my chest.

"You love her," he said softly, fingers gently touching my arm.

"It doesn't matter." Brushing him off, I snatched a menu and smacked it onto a nearby empty table.

Good day. Ha. That was toast.

"So speaking of eating and sleeping," Justin said as he slid gracefully into the booth. "You know you could sleep at the ranch."

I snorted. "As much as I like the horses—"

"Not in the barn. In the house."

My jaw fell open, but I managed to close it with an audible *click*. I'd been in the house, of course, but I'd never stayed there.

Rex had needed his *space*.

Holy crapballs. Rex was an asshole. But that was probably less important than— "Why are you doing this?"

Justin's mouth flattened. "Doing what?"

"Pushing. Chasing. Pressing the issue."

"I'm not—"

I whipped out my order pad. "This isn't your problem, and I'm definitely not making it yours. So why are you butting in—"

"I'm not pressing—"

"You *are* pressing." I searched my apron pockets for my pen, but I could never find the damned thing. Especially when I wanted to shove it through the eye of a customer.

Probably a good thing, come to think of it.

"I'm not."

I dropped my arms, tilted my head, and just stared at him. Really?

"Okay fine. I *am* pressing—"

"See?" My fingers slipped back into my pockets and—*aha!*—found it.

"Christ, you're difficult. I'm pressing because you're *pregnant.*"

Of course, the restaurant chose that moment to go completely quiet.

Or maybe it had been silent the whole time, tennis-match-watching my confrontation with Justin.

Regardless, every single person in the restaurant heard. Which meant that every single person in Darlington—all 1,068 of them—would know within the hour.

I sighed and asked resignedly, "What'll you have?"

CHAPTER SEVEN

JUSTIN HAD SERIOUSLY SCREWED UP. He'd be a fool to not realize that. Kelly had closed down after he'd put his foot in his mouth, serving him with determined cheerfulness while not once looking him in the eye.

The food at the little diner was off-the-charts delicious, but it had still been a lesson in futility to shove that burger down, no matter how tasty.

He'd existed on MREs for so long that it should be impossible to not gobble down real food.

His confrontation with the tough, sexy-as-hell waitress had proven him wrong.

Why was his stomach churning over a woman that wasn't even his?

He'd seen so much. Violence. Grievous injuries. Men and woman—hell, some were barely adults—who'd given their lives for their country.

Lives cut too short and yet his heart was aching for the first time in years because of a woman.

It was her eyes. Those chocolate irises that expressed her every emotion.

He could tell Kelly was barely holding it together, but still she lifted her chin and went on.

Which would have been exceptionally admirable if her determination wasn't directed at pushing him away.

Slapping a twenty on the table, Justin stood and headed for the door.

Or started to.

"Roosevelt."

Turning, Justin eyed the man who'd come out of the kitchen. He was smaller than his own six feet three inches and not as muscular, but his tone and stance said he'd be trouble in a fight.

And that he was looking for one.

"Come with me."

Since Justin wasn't hankering for a knockdown drag-out diner version of a bar fight, he followed the other man down a hall and into an office.

Its walls were painted an awful shade of gray and boxes were stacked nearly to the ceiling. A desk was crammed into one corner, a small set of lockers into another. It was tight. Too tight, and Justin didn't like the way it made the hairs on his neck prickle.

The man leaned against the desk and glared at him. "You're not Rex."

Justin snorted. "No."

"But he's your brother."

"Unfortunately."

It was miniscule, but Justin saw the other man's stance relax slightly. "Kelly is pregnant?"

He shrugged. "So I hear."

"Damn. I told her—"

Justin propped himself against the doorframe. "Regrettably, my twin seems to have a knack for seducing woman."

And breaking hearts. And stomping on the shattered pieces. Then, when the devastation was complete, leaving town.

"Kelly—" The man shook his head. "I told her. She's so sweet, I told her Rex would chew her up and spit her out—"

"Henry!"

Her voice hit Justin's ears the same moment that her scent reached his nose. It was jasmine, the exact perfume his mom used to wear. His throat went tight and he stiffened, trying to shove the emotion down.

"Oh, God. It's true." Kelly slid past him and shared her glare between the two of them. "You *are* together and talking about me."

"You can't do this on your own, Kel," Henry said.

"I'm not trying to do it on my own."

Justin stifled a snort. But not very well because Kelly tossed him a look that should have shriveled his balls into—

"This isn't 1864. I have a job. I have a house and savings. I have a sister, and I have friends," she said. Her voice gentled. "I know I'll need help, but *God*, you've got to give me some time to wrap my brain around this. A baby is growing inside me and—"

Her voice wobbled.

Justin stepped forward, the urge to take her in his arms intense. But Henry beat him to it and tugged her into a hug.

"We'll figure it out," her friend said. "It'll be okay."

She sniffled, murmured something that Justin couldn't decipher, and ignoring the way his insides twisted at the sight of her in another man's arms, he left the office.

Trouble.

The woman was trouble.

Unfortunately, he couldn't deny it was the type of trouble he really wanted to jump headfirst into.

That thought left him reeling. He unlocked his car with shaking fingers and took a minute to just breathe.

Leaving the military had softened him, cracked the shield around his emotions. Justin couldn't continue like this, a raw nerve exposed to the air, trying to rescue every woman his brother hurt.

There were just too goddamned many. And he was no hero. He hadn't saved the men who'd protected him, who'd begged him to patch them up and get them home to their wives, their kids.

Shuddering at the memory, Justin focused on breathing.

He understood logically that, as a doctor, he'd never be able to save everyone, especially in a chaotic combat scenario but . . . he wished he'd been able to save Ty and Jace.

They weren't anonymous faces he could compartmentalize away. They were soldiers, fathers.

Friends.

His car started with a smooth rumble, and he pulled carefully onto the road. Once he was on a straightaway, he voice dialed his father.

"Vince Roosevelt."

Justin's lips curved. Nothing screamed familiar when his feelings were spiraling out of control than his father's growling greeting.

"It's me," he said. "I've got a problem."

"You'll handle it," Vince replied before asking, "How's your brother?"

Ice settled over Justin's heart, soothed the aching organ. It hurt, but in a good way.

Because sometimes numb was better.

Sometimes feeling nothing at all made it easier to get through the day . . . because Vince's fatherly concern for Rex reminded Justin of exactly how alone he was.

It made him lash out. Want to destroy his father's golden image of Rex.

"Rex knocked up one of his whores."

The desire to wreck was pointless. Justin should know that by now. Nothing could ruin Rex in Vince's eyes.

His father laughed, the term not bothering him in the least, even though the guilt of using it to describe Kelly was already eating at Justin. She wasn't at all like the girls Rex normally dated.

"Well, that's not so bad. Take care of it." Vince hung up.

And Justin was as alone as ever.

CHAPTER EIGHT

I MANAGED to finish the rest of my shift only to find my phone clogged with texts and voicemails from my sister.

She'd heard the news, obviously, and wanted to talk.

Luckily for me, the kids were napping and she was trapped in the house.

I texted back that I was too tired to come over but promised to allow her a full grilling the next day.

You'd better, had been Melissa's response.

Then a second later, *We'll figure it out.*

Ridiculously, the words made me tear up. Between the hormones and her and Henry being so sweet, I was going to be a weeping mess before long.

I curled up with a blanket, the sandwich Henry had sent me home with in my lap, and lost myself in a marathon of *Tiny House Hunters*. I didn't hear anything further from Justin, and he definitely didn't show up on my porch as I'd half expected—okay, *hoped.*

And so it was barely ten when I clicked off the television and went to bed.

Whether it was going to sleep so early, or perhaps because I'd spent the previous morning with the horses and my brain had clicked back into the lifestyle of a ranch hand, I didn't know, but my wakeup came in the form of the sun's rays barely peeping over the horizon.

On autopilot, I slipped my boots and jacket on and was driving before I realized what I was doing. I'd forgotten I didn't work at Roosevelt Ranch any longer.

Or maybe not *forgotten,* per se, so much as had finally given in.

For a millisecond, I debated turning around, but the ranch's metal gates were just ahead and taking care of six horses was too big of a job for one inexperienced person.

Of course, Justin had told me he wasn't exactly inexperienced, and the way he'd galloped off on Theodore had proven it—

Cursing as the image of all his gorgeousness atop the Appalachian filled my brain, I decided to screw it all and navigated the driveway.

I needed a good, hard ride.

Of the equine variety.

After parking behind the barn, I unlocked the back door and slipped inside, flicking on the lights.

The horses chuffed and moved to the front of their stalls, and I walked to the pieces of scrap wood I'd screwed together into a halfhearted table to cut up the apple burning a hole in my pocket.

Okay, fine. I knew I'd come back today.

Clearly enough that I'd stopped at the store and bought two things the afternoon before: ice cream and a big bag of apples.

Cutting the fruit into six pieces took me approximately four seconds. I'd only done it a thousand or so times before. Shoving the slices into my pockets, I walked to each stall, scratched each pair of ears, and gave each horse one piece of apple.

I reveled in their warm horsey breath, the roughness of their whiskers brushing my hand, the way their ears flicked around, tracking me as I moved through the barn.

Stella, as always, was last.

Last to eat, first out was my rule.

So, I played favorites. It was my barn—

No. It really wasn't. I froze for a heartbeat, reminding myself that *I* was the one trespassing. That I held no claim here.

And so, heart firmly back on terra firma, I saddled Stella and rode out. When I returned a half hour later, I let her and the other horses out to pasture, and logged her ride on the chart hanging on the barn wall.

I'd muck the stalls, lay down fresh hay, and exercise as many of the horses as I could before I had to leave.

Of course, that plan went to total crap when Justin strolled into the barn five minutes later.

I was ankle deep in dirty hay, and my hair was falling over my eyes.

He was . . . hot.

Pregnancy hormones. My reaction had to be chalked up to those pesky, sex-addict-turning endorphins.

Because I could not realistically be attracted to Rex's brother.

Complications. I didn't need any more of them.

Justin raised a brow. "Morning?"

I propped the shovel up against my shoulder and nervously wiped my hands on my jeans. The word was a little sharp, a little cold, and so much like Rex that all the perking my lady bits had done thirty seconds before flattened.

"Morning," I returned cautiously. "Hope it's okay I came. I thought you might need some help . . ." My voice trailed off as he stared at me.

He might as well have been a blank slate for as much as I could read his expression.

"It was probably presumptive," I said and bit my lip. "I just—It's a lot of work—"

"By all means, make yourself at home." Green eyes glittered at me icily.

My eyes welled with tears—because, *of course*, the dumb ass pregnancy hormones were rearing their ugly heads. It wasn't because my feelings were hurt. Definitely not. Hurriedly, I turned away, moving to shovel the back of the stall.

I blinked rapidly, concentrated on breathing in and out. In and out.

Seriously, the sexy-time urges were so much easier to deal with.

Justin cursed, and I felt rather than heard him move toward me. Uh-uh. I wasn't some damsel looking for comfort, trying to manipulate the nice guy.

Straightening my shoulders, I shoveled faster, and if I dashed away a rogue tear from the corner of my eye as I did so, then I sure as hell wasn't going to admit it.

And, look at that, the stall was clean.

"Kelly—"

I brushed past him and moved to the next, raking and scooping with relish, gathering my mad like a shield.

"I'm sorry," he said, his voice directly behind me. I hadn't heard him move that time, and he was close, close enough for me to shiver in anticipation.

Not happening, body.

"It's fine." My voice was light. "I'm cranky in the morning too." More shoveling, and at the rate I was moving, I'd have the stables clean in record time.

"It's not that. Kelly, look at me."

Damn, even the way he said my name was hot.

He didn't give me a chance to move, just snagged my shoulder and tugged until I faced him.

My mouth watered. Actually watered. I wanted to lick him from top to bottom and then right back up.

"I'm sorry," he said, shocking the hell out of me.

In my experience, men didn't apologize.

Not ever.

"I'm in a hell of a mood, and shouldn't have taken it out on you."

I opened my mouth. Closed it. Opened it again. Then I got it together. "It happens to the best of us."

Stepping back, I smiled. It was the light, superficial one I'd perfected with my mother. The one that said it didn't matter she'd spent food money on booze. The one I'd fine-tuned with Melissa, not showing how much I regretted her having to take care of me when she should have just been a kid. The one I'd finessed with Rex, not revealing how deeply his barbed words cut.

I held onto the smile like armor. "Just remember, you don't want to make the help mad. Six horses make a big mess."

"Kel—"

"There are more shovels in the closet."

For a moment, I thought he wouldn't let it go, but then he sighed and walked out of the stall.

When he began cleaning at the opposite end of the barn, what I felt was relief. Definitely relief.

Because it certainly couldn't be disappointment.

CHAPTER NINE

"How can you be pregnant?" my sister asked the moment I walked through the door. I was exhausted after helping with the horses then working my shift at the diner, but I'd promised Melissa her interrogation.

And I kept my promises.

"The usual way," I said. "Hi, Rob."

Melissa's husband waved from his perch on the couch. Max and Allie, my nephew and niece, were piled atop him, attempting to tickle him into submission. "Hi, Kel. You two go out back, I'll wrangle the monsters."

"Monsters?" Allie asked.

"Monsters," Rob said and growled.

The kids shrieked and were off like a shot. Their footsteps pounded through the house, reverberated through the ceiling as they ran upstairs.

"Winding them up before bed," Melissa sighed.

Rob gave her a smacking kiss as he walked by. "Tiring them out."

"Semantics," Melissa countered.

My heart pounded painfully as I watched the exchange. The love in their eyes, good grief, it just took my breath away, reminded me exactly how much I wanted to find the same thing.

And just like that, tears.

"Ugh," I said, rolling my eyes.

The lovebirds swirled to face me. "Not you two, just me and these stupid leaking things."

Rob grimaced and patted my shoulder. "I remember those days. There is no rhyme or reason for it."

Melissa nodded. "I once cried at a Lysol commercial."

"And just remember," Rob said, "we're here for you, kiddo. Doctor's visits, midnight ice cream and pickle runs, and anything else you need."

I sniffled and lost my battle with the tears.

Melissa popped him on the chest.

"*Ow!*" He glared. "What was that for?"

"For being too sweet."

He rubbed the spot. "That doesn't even make sense."

"I'm your wife. I don't have to make sense."

A smirk. "Noted." There was a yell from upstairs and a crash. Rob bussed Melissa's cheek. "I'd better go before they tear apart the house."

"Come on," Melissa said when he'd gone. "This calls for daiquiris."

I rubbed my eyes on my sleeve. "I can't have daiquiris."

"Virgin ones you can," Melissa countered. "Plus it's only the mixer that tastes good anyway."

"Virgin," I muttered, following her into the kitchen. "If only."

"Hush you." She grabbed two tall glasses from the fridge and handed me the one with a purple straw. "And see? I'm prepared. One virgin strawberry daiquiri at the ready. Come on."

I followed her into the back yard. It had been a typical sweltering Utah summer day, but the evening had cooled enough that the warm air felt nice rather than oppressive.

Melissa was Suzy Homemaker on steroids, her house full of Pinterest successes rather than fails, unlike myself and the rest of America. Her plants were lush and green, soft floral scents that somehow didn't make my stomach churn. She even had a cute shabby chic patio set with coordinating placemats, candleholders, and mason jars.

Not to mention the twinkly lights wound through the arbor overhead.

If Melissa wasn't so awesome, I'd hate her.

"The first thing you need to do is make an appointment with Dr. Clark."

I nodded. "Already done. I'm going in on Friday morning."

"Want me to come with?" she asked. "I can get someone to watch Allie while Max is at preschool."

"Not this time. I just—" I stopped, not wanting to hurt my sister's feelings.

"Need to do it by yourself?" Melissa asked. "I understand that. You've always been independent, Kel. Ever since Dad pulled his vanishing act, and Mom . . ." She shook her head. "Well, since Mom lost it. I get it. I understand wanting to be strong. Just don't take it so far that you isolate yourself."

Tilting my head back, I stared at the lights. They were cheerful and bright and sweet, so much like Melissa.

I wasn't bright, or at least not cheerful and sweet.

Fluorescent kitchen lighting, yeah that was me. Functional. Enduring. Resistant.

But that didn't mean the yearning wasn't there.

To be able to trust enough to open up and love a man fully. To have a husband like Rob who was devoted to making me happy . . . and be able to return the favor.

I sighed. So maybe I wouldn't have the man, but I could make sure the kid growing inside me knew that I thought of her first. That I loved her. Or him, I guessed.

"I won't isolate myself," I said and straightened. "I just need to see it, you know?"

Melissa smiled. "You're still in the what-the-hell-is-happening phase. It'll take awhile for it to sink in."

I laughed and took a sip of my drink. It was tangy and sweet and delicious. I almost didn't miss the alcohol. Almost. After I swallowed, I asked the question that had been swirling around in my mind. "So you're not disappointed in me?"

My sister was five years older and had been more of a mom to me than our biological mother had ever been. She'd found the money to feed us, checked my homework, skimped and saved to buy me a new pair of Converse I'd been dying to have.

In return, I'd been a good kid. I'd never acted out and had always tried to find ways to make it easier on her. But it still had to have been hard, taking on all of the responsibility for both of us at such a young age.

Melissa set down her drink and knelt in front of me, her hands on either side of my thighs. "Sometimes you're an idiot, you know that right?"

My eyes narrowed, but at least the giant lump in the back of my throat was gone.

"I love you," she said. "And I'll love the little munchkin when he or she comes. You try so hard to be good, Kel, but sometimes we make mistakes. Maybe this isn't the consequence you or I wanted, but that doesn't mean we can't embrace it." She grabbed my shoulders and shook them lightly. "It doesn't mean we can't love it and count our lucky stars it's here on this Earth."

Then she hugged me.

"Aw, crap," I said. My eyes were dripping again.

"It's okay," Melissa said and sniffed. "I'm crying too."

CHAPTER TEN

APPLE SLICES AND BRUSHING. Checking hooves and tack. Saddles, bits, bridles, blankets, shoes. It was a seemingly endless to do list that flowed through my mind.

But it was horses.

And if there was one thing I knew and loved, it was horses.

Their whiskers, the soft, soft hair between their eyes. Brushing them out, trimming their hooves. Their nudges, puffs of horsey breath in my face, nibbling of flat teeth on my clothes and hair, searching for their apples.

It was dawn on Friday morning and it might as well have been Judgment Day.

My doctor's appointment was in two hours, and my pulse was already hammering.

A part of me hoped that the pregnancy test was wrong, that I'd see Dr. Clark and she would say it was a false positive—I'd read about those all over the Internet.

It could happen. Really. It could.

But another piece of me already loved the little jelly bean in my tummy, was already holding tight.

And that scared me.

Because when I held tight, things slipped through my fingers.

Scholarships. Jobs. Love . . . or what I'd imagined it to be.

A wet smack on my nape made me jump.

"Ugh," I said, wiping it dry and whirling to glare at Theodore. "I have your apple right here." I opened my hand flat and let him take the slice from my palm. "So impatient."

He bobbed his head, flopping his blond mane forward so I'd pet him between his eyes.

Of course, I obliged. "Why are you always such a naughty boy?"

"Now there are some words straight out of every man's biggest fantasy."

Green eyes. My mind conjured the piercing emerald even before I turned and met Justin's gaze.

This morning he wore a T-shirt that should've been illegal. The gray material was skintight and thin, enough that I could see every plane of his muscular chest and abs.

And the way it circled his biceps?

Hot damn. Thor had nothing on him.

But there was something off. Maybe it was the smudge of black beneath those eyes or the mussed hair or maybe it was just the way his shoulders were slightly bent . . . as though his burdens were a little heavier this morning.

I tilted my head and studied him. "You okay?"

Justin smiled. Instinctively, I knew it was as false as mine from the other morning. It was all frosting with no cake beneath.

For some reason that made me sad.

"Great," he said, and tugged on my ponytail as he went by. "Just tired. Not sure I'll ever get used to this rising-before-the-sun nonsense."

More artificial sugar. More false sweet.

But what was it to me?

Justin wasn't mine. He *couldn't* be mine. Not when Rex—

I shook my head, finished distributing apples, and grabbed the rake. By the time I'd turned the first horse to pasture, Justin had saddled Stella.

My heart clenched. But she wasn't my horse, and if he wanted to ride her . . .

After closing the stall door, I loaded a flake of alfalfa and turned to the next compartment, fingers fumbling on the lock. It didn't matter. She wasn't—

"You don't feel up to riding today?"

I stilled, slowly rotated to face him. "What?"

"Don't you usually exercise her first?"

"I—uh. Yes?"

Justin tilted his head. "Is that a question?"

I forced a breath. "No. I mean, yes. I usually take Stella out first. I just—"

He led Stella forward, the *clop-clop* of her footfalls on the barn floor the only sound. "Take her," he said and put the reins in my hands.

There was an entire layer of meaning beneath Justin telling me to take her out for a ride.

It was part peace offering, part something deeper, something softer. He knew I wanted to ride Stella.

And he let me.

No one—aside from Melissa or Henry—had ever given me something I wanted, just because I wanted it.

My life was seriously screwed up.

This was a ride, nothing more.

But it felt like so, *so* much more.

Mechanically, I checked the stirrups, tightened the cinch. Stella usually breathed out the first time anyone saddled her, and the fastening needed to be snugged up so the rider and saddle didn't slip to the side.

I slid one foot into the stirrup and—

"Oh!"

A pair of warm, strong hands on my hips assisted me in mounting.

Mounting. Oh dear lord.

By the time those hands left me, I was gaping down at Justin. Who assumedly took my slack-jawed expression for anger because he stepped back and raised his palms in surrender.

"Sorry. Old habit," he said, all velvet and rasp and man . . . so much man.

I blinked, but didn't have a good response. Not when his palms had scorched straight through my clothes to singe the skin and nerves below. Not when my body was humming like a tuning fork at the simple, platonic touch.

Justin patted Stella's shoulder and turned away, snagging the shovel as he went.

I sat frozen on her back for one long moment. Then I remembered to breathe.

I tapped my heels against Stella's side and we rode out of the barn. The hillside was gilded gold with the first rays of the sun, but for once, I couldn't concentrate on the beauty of the fields.

For once, I wanted the ride to be over.

A half hour later, I returned to the barn. My heart pounded, both wanting and not wanting to see Justin.

Not that it mattered.

Justin was gone. Theodore wasn't in his stall, his hoofy-highness apparently getting his exercise.

And that was good, because the barn was clean, the horses were being cared for. Everything was as it should be.

Unfortunately, all I could think was that Justin was gone.

CHAPTER ELEVEN

I sat on the vinyl table covered in paper. It was freezing. Why did OB-GYNs always keep their exam rooms so freaking cold?

The nurse, Sandy, bustled around the room, rummaging through cupboards, laying things out on the counter. The whole experience was familiar and yet different.

There was a large ultrasound machine in one corner, and I had a feeling the wand that the nurse had *prepared* would soon be going somewhere it had no business traveling.

"The doctor is running just a few minutes behind," Sandy said and wrapped a blood pressure cuff around my arm. As the air-filled sleeve tightened and loosened, she smiled down at me. "It's normal to be nervous."

I released a shuddering breath. "That obvious, huh?"

Sandy pulled off the cuff with a loud *rff!* "That and the fact your blood pressure is 150/90 when I've never seen it higher than 120/70. You'll need to make sure the nerves don't jeopardize your health and the baby's."

The baby's.

Holy crap.

I was having a baby. Was *this* the time to hyperventilate?

"Yup. I was just like you the first go-round. Freaked out and alone." She patted my arm. "But then I found my Bobby, and everything was just better. You'll see. Things will work out."

Sandy finished with the supplies and left the room. I was happy she seemed content. Sandy had been a year ahead of me in school and so quiet I'd barely heard her speak three words in all our younger days. But the bubbly woman in wine-red scrubs wasn't anything like the soft, almost invisible girl from the past.

I was very glad of that fact . . . except I didn't have a Bobby.

But I *did* have a Melissa, and she was pretty great.

I whipped out my phone and sent her a text.

I know you're probably busy and have Allie, but I was wondering if you could come?

Her response came almost immediately.

I'll be there.

Blowing out a breath, I half reclined on the table, its paper cover crinkling loudly with each movement. It was impossible to avoid looking at the posters lining the walls. First, second, third trimester, they were all there in weird see-through profiles that might be fascinating if I were not so on edge.

There was a knock on the door, and I steeled myself for Dr. Clark. Except when the door opened, it wasn't the doctor but rather, my sister.

I didn't even get a chance to question her before she was inside the room and talking a mile a minute.

"Rob switched for late shift today. I've been sitting in my car and then the waiting room. Thank God you texted, I was sure someone was going to arrest me for stalking, and then they'd have to call Rob in anyway, and he'd have to bail me out. The guys would never let him hear the end of it —" She paused and her pale brown eyes glinted with amusement. "*Maybe* that's the perfect plan. Oh, man. That would be—"

Another knock at the door cut her off, and Dr. Clark pushed into the room.

The blond woman was in her mid-forties and had a tough but caring bedside manner. I'd been seeing her since my teen years.

"You," she said to Melissa. "Take a breath and give your sister a chance to get some words in." Then she paused and turned to me, hands going to her hips. "What happened?"

I bit my lip, gave an awkward half-shrug given my position. "Um. I got knocked up."

Dr. Clark tsked. "I know you take your pill regularly. You're the most hyper-vigilant patient I've ever had with regards to that. If it's an effectiveness issue we may consider a different form of birth control after this little one is out."

"I don't think it's that," I said, having read up, almost fanatically, about birth control failures after the pregnancy test had come back positive. "I think it's because I got food poisoning just before the last time Rex and I were together."

Dr. Clark reached up and pulled a pair of gloves from the box near the door. "Ah. That would do it. You should always use an alternate form of birth control after episodes of vomiting."

Yeah. That was helpful *now*.

Her eyes flashed to mine and a corner of her mouth quirked up. "Not real helpful given the circumstances, is it?"

Mutely, I shook my head.

"Okay. But noted for the future?" I nodded as she sat on the stool and rolled it near my feet. "Go ahead and lean back. I'll talk you through everything."

She did so, and I stared at the ceiling, counting tiles as I ignored the feel of her hands. Then it came time for the wand, which wasn't nearly as horrible as I'd imagined.

Especially when I turned my head to see the picture on the monitor.

It was hardly anything, a jelly bean shape, but inside that little oval was a smaller circle and it was moving.

Goose bumps exploded on my skin. "Is that its heart?" I asked softly. Melissa squeezed my hand.

"Yes, and everything looks good." Dr. Clark kept the image in place and printed some shots. Then she pushed back and took off her gloves. "Okay, questions?"

I'd been alternating between stasis and panic too much to have the chance to prepare any questions.

Melissa saved me. "Prenatal vitamins, does she need a prescription? What about her work at the restaurant? Sandy said her blood pressure was high . . ."

And on it went, my sister peppering the doctor, and Dr. Clark answering with surprising patience. I understood that Melissa was asking the questions for my benefit. Having already been through the process twice before, she must have known the answers to most of them.

But there was only one question I was worried about. One I'd bravadoed my way through with Justin, and one I was concerned I shouldn't have.

"Can I ride?"

Melissa's words shut off and she glanced at me, aghast. "Kel—"

"For the first trimester, I have no problem with it. Afterward, I would recommend you abstain."

"What if you fall?" Melissa asked.

"The baby is tiny and well-protected behind the pubic bone at this stage. I wouldn't recommend that a newly pregnant mother take up equestrian sports, but Kelly is experienced and can continue with her normal activities—within reason." She touched my hand and slid the ultrasound pictures into it. "But don't do anything you're uncomfortable with. Listen to your body, okay?"

I nodded. "Okay."

When neither Melissa nor I could scrounge another question, she said to make another appointment for the following month and left.

My eyes were latched on to the grainy black and white images in my fingers. I was having a baby and I already loved it.

So, so much.

CHAPTER TWELVE

JUSTIN STARED at the file on his—formerly Rex's—desk in the lushly appointed office within the ranch house.

It was all leather and dark wood, as cliché *male* as one could find. It also was nowhere near his taste. *He* liked bright and clean, with smooth lines and simple furnishings. Not that he was going to be spending enough time at Roosevelt Ranch to do something about it.

But none of *that* had anything to do with the papers he'd been avoiding.

The report showed nothing he hadn't expected. Kelly had barely enough to rub two pennies together. She'd shown promise in high school, enough to be able to leave the stifling opportunity of small town America behind—she'd had a scholarship to a very exclusive private university for their equestrian team, had even been scouted by the Olympic team.

She hadn't gone.

Why?

Why stay on the ranch? Why stay on when his brother had bought it? Why get involved with Rex in the first place?

None of it made sense.

Kelly was a nice girl, his gut told him that. So why give up her chance at freedom?

Why stay in Nowhere, Utah, fighting to make ends meet?

He tossed the file into a drawer and stood, rubbing a hand over his face.

Justin had barely slept the night before, and now it was nearly dawn, nearly time to head for the barn.

It was too damned early to be up, and yet he couldn't stop himself from wanting to see her. To see Kelly. Curvy, sweet-as-sugar Kelly.

With a curse, he strode past the desk. He'd been stateside for only a few weeks. Pair that with months abroad devoid of companionship of the feminine variety, and his idiotic male brain was malfunctioning.

Translation: he needed sex.

And no matter that his body wanted it with Kelly, that wouldn't happen.

Rex was the one who made shit complicated, not him. And there was no doubt that giving in to her particular brand of temptation—chocolate eyes, wavy brown hair, hips he could grab onto, breasts he wanted to—

Fuck.

So. Not. Helping.

Because she was also wounded.

Anyone could see that.

There was also the other thing. The reason he was investigating. The typical *modus operandi* of the women Rex dated.

Money. Women always wanted money.

Sooner or later, Kelly would ask for it, and he couldn't risk his dick being tied up in the situation and softening his heart.

"Shit," he muttered and pushed through the back door.

The light in the barn was already on. Not that it should surprise him. Kelly seemed inexhaustible. At the ranch before the sun was up, working hard, being efficient.

It was that particular twist that was throwing him for a loop, niggling the back of his mind, and saying that maybe she didn't want something from him or his family.

That maybe Kelly was different.

Which was a highly dangerous direction for his thoughts to take.

He walked into the barn, and time stopped.

Every morning it was the same. His heart skipped a beat, his brain shut down, his eyes couldn't be forced from Kelly.

Today she was stroking Stella, the horse having practically crawled into her arms.

Justin had never been so jealous of another being—horse or otherwise—in all his life.

"Ready, baby?" she murmured, her voice slightly husky and completely bedroom. It made Justin's blood flow to parts south and away from where he needed it: his brain.

He was ready. So damned ready.

Then she turned and caught him looking.

Thirty-three and Justin was staring like a teenager desperate to get laid.

Ignoring the voice reminding him that, yes, he *was* desperate for sex, he grunted and pushed past her.

"Morning," she said, all tentative and cautious and—dammit—he didn't want Kelly to be unsure around him. He didn't exactly understand *why* he felt that way, but they'd already established that he was a freaking idiot.

And she was beautiful when she was furious, sparks of fire in those chocolate eyes, a rosy tint to her cheeks, lush lips pressed together in a way that made him want to kiss her.

The lights flicked on, and Justin blinked, realizing that he'd been standing in the dark tack room for who knew how long.

"You okay?" Kelly asked. She hung up the rake then walked to the opposite wall and began pulling down the necessary equipment to take Stella for a ride.

"Fine."

She nodded and turned for the door, her arms laden with leather and jingling metal. At the threshold, she paused. "I can do this if you've got something you need to do."

Justin shook himself. He pulled his weight. Always. "No. I'm good." He picked up a shovel.

"Okay." Kelly nibbled on the corner of her mouth. "All the stalls are clean. The horses just need to be exercised."

"Already?"

She shrugged, and the tinkling of the buckles somehow fit her personality. Light and gentle, sweet and strong—

He hardly knew the girl.

Biting back a curse, Justin struggled to find some distance. Trouble was, no part of him—body, brain . . . heart—wanted it.

Actions spoke louder than words, he'd always believed that with every fiber of his being.

And Kelly's actions, they were damned good.

"Already," she said and left the room. Five minutes later, he heard her lead Stella from the barn.

The gear was in his hands the next instant, Theodore saddled, and he was riding out into the fields in record time.

He tried to convince himself it was because the horse needed exercise, but that was a lie.

Kelly was out there, and she was a temptation he had no hope of resisting.

CHAPTER THIRTEEN

I sat on Stella's back and watched the sunrise. I loved pausing at the crest of this particular hill, and never felt more settled than when I watched rays of sunlight highlight the crags and undulations of the little valley the ranch was situated in.

This had been my spot since forever. My little slice of peace, heaven, and hell all wrapped in one.

I'd once imagined coming back into town and buying the ranch, had dreamed of owning it and the horses within.

It wasn't to be.

Thoroughbreds were expensive and that didn't include the value of the property and freshly remodeled house.

My childhood dream had been just that: fancies of a ten-year-old girl.

A gust of wind pushed through my hair, streaked across my throat, and I shivered before pulling the hood of my sweatshirt tighter and shrinking down into the warm cotton.

Summer would be over before I knew it, and these sunrises would become few and far between.

Stella shifted beneath me, and I patted the horse's dark brown mane. "One more minute, then we'll ride." Stella's ears perked at the word *ride*, and I laughed. "I know, girl."

I reached into the pocket of my sweatshirt and pulled out the ultrasound picture from a week before. It was going to be worn through if I kept holding it and fondling it and staring at it as though a simple photograph could hold the secrets to the world.

But I couldn't stop from running my fingers over the image one more time.

My baby.

Carefully, I began to tuck it back into my pocket. Except, just as I started to do so, the wind gusted again, and the little square of paper slipped from my hands.

The curse word that crossed my lips was definitely not kid appropriate.

I pulled my foot from the stirrup and slid down. After taking a second to ground tie the reins—so Stella wouldn't run off and leave me with a very long walk back to the stables—I lurched after the picture.

It bobbed through the air, fluttering out of reach and bumping into stalks of the long grass.

But, at last, I snagged it and turned back to Stella. My breath hitched.

Justin was there and, even from ten feet away, I could read the amusement in his green eyes.

"So this is what you do every morning."

I shivered and it didn't have a damn thing to do with the cold.

He jumped down from Theodore, picked up Stella's reins, and led both horses toward me.

"Thanks," I said, taking the straps of leather from his hand and ignoring the zing at the contact of his fingers against mine.

Getting burned by one Roosevelt brother was enough, thank you very much.

"What's that?"

My eyes flashed down and I realized it was the ultrasound. I wanted to shove it deep in my pocket. It was mine, dammit. My picture, my baby, mine, mine, *mine*.

But I could occasionally be an adult, and so I carefully extended the black and white image.

"Jelly Bean," I murmured.

His fingers closed on the edge of the paper, and I had to force myself to release it.

Justin stared at it for a long moment before carefully handing it back. "Jelly Bean?"

I shrugged. "So it's not the most creative nickname, but until I know if it's a boy or girl—"

"It's perfect."

My gaze jumped to his, and there was something intense about the way he was staring at me.

Alarm bells blared in my mind. Too much.

Instinctively, I took a step back and his expression cleared, intensity replaced with placid friendliness.

That wasn't a slice of disappointment I felt. It was fear and self-preservation, not regret that I'd doused the potent heat in his eyes so easily.

"Need a boost?" He laced his hands together in a makeshift step.

"Sure," I said and used his joined palms to mount. Justin was on Theodore a minute later, and we turned as one toward the barn.

Theodore huffed, jostling Justin in impatience.

"Got a live one there."

"Nothing I can't handle," he said.

Arrogance. His. That was what prompted me into action.

"Uh-huh, cowboy." I nodded toward the stables. "Last one back hauls the bales of hay."

He tilted his head. "What?"

I didn't explain. I didn't wait.

I cheated.

With a tap of my heels, I told Stella to *go*.

"Kel—"

I gave Stella her head and we rode.

The wind whipped past my face, blew my hair off my neck. It was cold but exhilarating, and though I wasn't galloping into oblivion at full speed, being atop Stella's back was still the best high around.

I shifted slightly, allowing my body to better align with hers. Our movement was fluid, graceful in a way I could have never been solely on my own.

Home was on horseback. Racing down a dusty path, worn fences decorating the hillside, crisp morning air prickling my skin.

A flash of color caught my eye, and I saw Justin and Theodore draw up next to us.

He felt it too, that mix of peace and adrenaline. I could see it in his expression, read it in the fluidity of his spine as he let his horse do what it did best: run.

And a lack of sleep was clearly making me deranged, if I was starting to write poetry on horseback.

"Slow down," he called, barely audible over the sound of eight pounding hooves.

I don't know what possessed me to do it. Pure defiance, mischief, maybe pent-up sex hormones.

No clue.

All I did *know*, however, was that I didn't want to slow down.

I wasn't stupid, but I didn't need to take it completely easy, either.

"What?" I asked, widening my eyes in false innocence. "Go faster?"

"No!" he yelled. "I *said* slow—"

I kicked my heels into Stella's side and whooped as she went a little faster. It wasn't quite a full gallop, but it wasn't the canter from before.

Which was when I realized *she* was being careful with me. Never had Stella *ever* passed up an opportunity to run full out.

But she had today. She'd sensed something different about me and—
Aw, crap.

My eyes welled up, stupid organs that they were.

Just as well, anyway, we were approaching the barn.

Stella paused near the pasture, her sides heaving, and tossed her head in a proud mama sort of way.

I patted her neck. "Thanks, sweetheart. You did good."

Pulling my foot from one stirrup, I readied to dismount . . . exactly as Justin and Theodore came storming up next to us.

Stella shifted uneasily. "Settle," I told her and started to slide my leg over her back.

"What. The. Hell. Were. You. Doing?"

Gritted out words, pure masculine fury.

I glanced over my shoulder and watched as Justin all but threw himself from the saddle, booted feet colliding with the ground and sending up a cloud of dust.

Ugh. Why did I find that incredibly sexy?

With a sigh, I began to lower myself down.

My breath—every single bit of it—flew out of me in a hiss.

Justin's hands had grabbed my waist. He lifted me off Stella's back and placed my feet on the dirt with the utmost gentleness.

I literally could have been the most priceless piece of crystal with how carefully he handled my body. My throat tightened, the stupid lump returning, but not for long.

Because his words were nowhere near tender.

He got in my face, crouching so his furious green eyes met mine. "You could have hurt yourself, galloping off like that. The baby. Hell, your neck—"

That got my spine up. The one *freaking* thing I knew was horses.

They were animals, they were unpredictable. But I could read them, understand the signs. I hadn't taken unnecessary risks.

I didn't say any of that, however, because I knew it wouldn't do any good. Logical arguments had never worked with Rex.

Not saying I could still work at the ranch, even if he didn't want to be with me any longer.

Not saying he didn't need to pay for my meals, even if he had more money than me.

Roosevelts didn't "go Dutch," he'd said.

Of course, he'd also said, "It's over." And my personal favorite, "It's time for you to move on, Kelly."

Le sigh.

I focused on the present and asked, very softly, "What right do you have to command my life, Justin?"

He stilled, every muscle in his body went ramrod stiff.

I waited for him to tell me that he was in charge of the ranch, to tell me to leave and not come back, like his brother had.

He didn't.

Instead, he cursed, wrapped his hands around my upper arms, and yanked me against his chest. "You were fucking magnificent."

Then he kissed me.

CHAPTER FOURTEEN

His arms were steel bands around my torso, pressing me against a chest that had not an ounce of fat on it.

Justin was all rangy muscle, long, lean strength . . . and intoxicating.

I wanted to crawl up his body, wrap my legs around his waist, and find the nearest wall.

His mouth was the only thing—literally, the *only* thing—that was soft. It pillaged mine, taunting and teasing, and then pressing harder and more ardently, demanding my participation when I normally just went along for the ride.

I opened when his tongue touched the seam of my mouth, and then the kiss took a more devastating turn. It was a battle and a sonnet in one. Poetry of sensation while fighting for control.

Then it was over.

Justin set me away from him. His chest heaved and his mouth was swollen.

No doubt a mirror of mine.

"What was that?" I asked when I could breathe. Kind of. If panting between words was considered normal human exhalations.

"Nothing," he said. "That was nothing."

"Um." I tilted my head at him and found my eyes drifting downward. *"That* really isn't *nothing."*

Justin chuckled, and my cheeks went red hot. I clamped a hand over my mouth. Without another word, I turned, snatched up Stella's reins, and started to hightail it into the stables.

"Hey."

I stopped and my shoulders fell an inch. "Can't we pretend I didn't say that?"

"No."

With a sigh, I rotated to face him fully. "No?"

He plunked my hat on my head, bent, and kissed me in a way that made my knees threaten to buckle. When he pulled back, there wasn't turmoil in his expression, exactly, but it wasn't solely pleasure that I was seeing either.

"No," he murmured and gathered up Theodore's reins, leading the horse into the stables. "Just like we can't pretend that didn't happen either."

As far as exits went, Justin's was damned good.

———

"YOU NEED to marry that boy, honey."

I glanced at the permed, bejeweled, cat-sweatshirt-wearing elderly woman sitting at my table.

"Kind of hard to do, Esther, when he's fled the country."

She put on her glasses to read the menu, even though it hadn't changed in a decade and she always got the same thing.

Esther came in every Monday and ordered the fried chicken sandwich with Brussels sprouts, alongside a glass of water with no ice and two lemon slices.

It was tradition, and we liked tradition in Darlington.

"So marry the other one." She gave a little shrug, the long gemstone necklaces around her neck glittering. "He seems strong and virile."

I shuddered at the sound of the word *virile* coming from Esther's mouth. There were some things that were just wrong.

That was one of them.

"Justin is Rex's twin, and I can't just take up with *brothers*," I said. "Plus, I'm off men."

I'd learned my lesson. You only burned me once.

Even if Justin made me feel a hell of a lot more than Rex ever had, even if the man could kiss like . . . well, I didn't know what exactly, just that I'd bet he could have tied a cherry stem into a knot with only his tongue.

"Off men." Esther snorted. "Now that might be the stupidest thing I've ever heard."

I withheld a sigh. "I'll bring your water out."

Esther turned the menu over. "Two lemons, dear."

"Yes, ma'am."

By the time Esther had eaten her meal, I had reached my quota of unasked-for advice for the day.

I'd gotten a half-dozen "you should sue for child supports," two more "you should marry one of the brothers," and only one "you can do this on your own."

Exhausted, I hung up my apron in the kitchen then walked down the hall to Henry's office. I was hot, sweaty, and in absolutely no mood to put up with anyone's shit. The diner smell did not make Jelly Bean happy and I'd run to the bathroom more times than I could count during my shift to puke my guts up.

So it was a perfect time for my mom to be sitting in the chair across from Henry's desk. Though she lived nearby, I rarely saw her.

Which was a good thing.

The rip of paper echoed across the room, and I watched in horror as I saw my friend hand my mother a check.

What in the freaking hell was he doing?

My mom gripped the paper rectangle like it was life preserver.

"Good-bye, Mrs. Harrison."

She stood and turned, seeing me over her shoulder. Consternation crossed her face for a brief moment before she plastered on a fake smile. "I'm getting married!"

"Again?"

I regretted the question the moment it passed my lips. I was too tired to fight with her, too tired to care about all the new ways my mom wrecked her life.

Her lips tightened, and her light brown eyes—so much like Melissa's, except without any of the warmth and love . . . *that* had been leeched out by all the booze—iced over.

"I mean, congratulations," I hurried to say.

"He's just perfect. He . . ."

I tuned out the soliloquy and flicked my gaze to Henry's. His expression was carefully blank.

Oh, we were so going to have words.

Giving my mother money. He might as well have poured water into her cupped hands, it would flow away so easily.

"That's great, Mom," I interrupted. "But I think Henry and I have a meeting."

She could bristle faster than a porcupine if I dared mention the number of times she'd been married, but my mom couldn't understand a dismissal for anything.

After prattling on obliviously for a few more minutes, she finally left. No hug. No "I love you." Just a whirlwind of color and meaningless words and painful memories.

I closed the door and, on second thought, locked it.

"What the hell were you thinking?" I demanded. "You know she'll bleed you dry. You can't give her money."

Henry sighed, leaned back in his chair, and propped his booted feet on his desk. He wore his chef whites, and there was a spot of red near the breast pocket. But he filled out the uniform well, a confident male. Strong arms, flat stomach, and just enough scruff to add an air of mystery.

Oh, things would be so much less complicated if I could just feel something more than friendship for him.

But we'd gone there once, and there was just no chemistry.

Mutual affection, yes. Love even, but it was of the sibling variety.

Which was the only reason I could come up with for the next words that crossed his lips. He was trying to protect me.

"Marry me, Kel."

"Wh-what?" A wave of dizziness made me grab my head and stagger for something to hold on to.

Henry was there in a heartbeat, steadying me, holding me in arms that had comforted me a thousand times.

And yet my heart didn't beat faster, goose bumps didn't prickle my arms, warmth didn't fill my tummy.

My sister might as well have been hugging me.

"It doesn't have to be complicated. You and me," Henry said. "We've gone through worse than this. You know I'd have your back. You know it would be easy and comfortable and . . ."

And that was the problem.

Because love wasn't supposed to be comfortable.

It was supposed to push you to be better. Force you to feel. Slap you in the face with sensation.

It wasn't supposed to be easy. Or not *only* easy.

Still, his offer was tempting, especially with all the upheaval and turmoil currently taking up residence in my life. I might have even been able to accept it. If only it hadn't been driven by the pain of his past.

I might have screwed up my chance for something, but I wasn't going to take away Henry's permanently.

Wrapping my arms around him, I shook my head. "Henry—"

"Don't say no," he murmured. "Just think about it. We'd be good together, you know that."

I stood on tiptoe and kissed his cheek. "I love you, you big lug. Too much to say yes."

Before he could protest, I stepped free of his arms and unlocked the door.

"See you tomorrow," I said, steeling myself against the hurt in his expression.

It was for his own good.

Not that rejecting him made me feel any better.

CHAPTER FIFTEEN

I ARRIVED at my house in the typical cloud of dust. Even though I was lucky enough to have a decent layer of gravel covering my driveway, that didn't mean it wasn't a mud pit in the winter and the equivalent of a desert sandstorm in the summer.

Coughing as I pushed open the car door, I looked up and saw someone on my porch.

Justin.

Funny how a couple of weeks ago I would have been hoping to see Rex. Today he wasn't even a blip on my personal radar.

Because Justin was . . . what? More? Different? Made my body stand up and take notice?

Yes. To all those things.

Shaking my head at myself, I tried to play it cool. Or ignored him and the fact that he'd kissed me within an inch of my life.

That too.

After stepping around the back of my car, I opened the trunk. I'd stopped for groceries, finally.

I'd even bought vegetables.

Heaven help me.

Reaching in, I started to grab the bag out, but a hand on my arm stopped me.

"Let me get that."

The shock that ran through me at Justin's touch was intense. Every time he was close, I wanted to rub against him like a demanding cat throwing itself against its owner's legs.

But that didn't mean I wasn't also stubborn as hell.

Retreating a pace away was enough to break the contact and clear my head. My lady parts might be chirping at me to do something, *anything*, but at least my mind wasn't hazed over any longer.

I leaned a hip against the bumper. "I should note that bag is one of the lighter things I've carried today."

Justin cocked his head, and there might have been a glimmer of amusement in his expression. "I'm sure." A pause and a softness took hold of his words. "But humor me, okay? I was raised to be a gentleman."

With a sigh, I reached in and grabbed the bag then plunked it into his arms. "Fine then, Mr. Chivalrous, it's all yours."

"My macho heart thanks you."

I snorted. "Did you just say *macho*?"

"Somebody's got to."

My brows came up. "Really? *That's* what you're going with?"

He hefted the bag under one arm then reached the other up to close the trunk. I did my best not to notice the bulge of his biceps under the fitted arms of the T-shirt he wore or the way the hem of that shirt rose a couple inches when he stretched upward.

Two inches of smooth, tanned skin, and I just about lost my mind.

Because he looked, well, not macho exactly, since that word rebelled being uttered, even in my mind, but *male*.

Six feet of lithely muscled male that I wanted to actually lick from head to toe.

"Pregnancy hormones," I muttered and turned for the house.

"What was that?" Justin asked.

"Quiet you." But my cheeks were warm. Unfortunately, the space between my thighs wasn't immune either.

Justin snagged the keys out of my hand and strode toward the front door and—sweet Christ and a bucket of chocolate ice cream, his butt was fabulous. My fingers actually ached with the desire to squeeze it like an orange . . . or a Christmas ham or something.

"You live by yourself?"

I nodded, brushing by him after he'd opened the door and leading the way into the kitchen. I opened the refrigerator door and shifted things around to make room.

He placed the bag on the counter, unpacking the contents with a brisk efficiency that reminded me he'd been in the military.

"How long did you serve?"

Justin froze for a split second before continuing to align the vegetables with precision. Broccoli and carrots, peppers, onions, cucumber. All lined up just so. The silence stretched between us, but I didn't push. I figured if he didn't want to talk about it, he would say so.

I'd give him a minute and, if he didn't answer, then I'd change the subject.

To something innocuous. Like the proper way to prepare broccoli. Ick.

But just as I'd reached a hand forward to start putting the food away, he snagged my wrist.

The zing up my arm was ridiculous, a total delusion.

Except . . . he gently pressed my fingers flat on the counter, cupped his hand over mine. It was warm and rough and made enough sparks explode over the surface of my skin that I shivered.

Justin didn't appear to notice as he closed the distance between us. He didn't quite touch me, but I could feel the heat from his chest as it came very close to my back. I was trapped between him and the counter and, all things considered, it wasn't a bad place to be.

Then he spoke, and I couldn't focus on anything except his voice and the daggers of pain hidden within.

"I was in the Air Force Medical Corps for three years. Then I decided I needed more action, that I wanted to do more than just routine checkups and procedures." His fingers flexed as tension wove its way through his body. "I got my combat training and was assigned to several convoys in Afghanistan. I managed to get everyone out alive until—"

I held my breath, not moving, not talking, not wanting to stopper his words.

Because even though I was getting more story than I bargained for, I felt instinctively that Justin needed to get this out, and I highly doubted that Rex had been open to listening.

"I got everyone out . . . until I didn't."

Air escaped my lungs on a shaky exhale. I didn't know what to say. How I could possibly hope to convey my sympathy in a way that didn't minimize the bone-deep pain laced through his words?

I'm sorry just didn't seem to be enough.

In the end, I opted to forgo words. Justin was behind me, still and stiff as a statue. Not breathing, not moving. I turned, slipping my hand from beneath his, and wrapped my arms around his waist.

At first, he didn't react, but I didn't budge, just held on until I felt it.

The slightest relaxation. A minuscule amount of tension leaving his body before Justin was hugging me back, and it was the best thing ever.

Ever.

I didn't know it was possible to feel so warm, so safe, so—

Beep. Beep. Beep.

With those little piercing sounds—the fridge alarming because the door had been left open—the spell was broken.

I remembered all the reasons why I was keeping my distance, everything that was between us. I was carrying his twin's child, for God's sake.

What the hell was I doing snuggling up with Justin?

I pulled briskly away and snatched up the broccoli, walking over to the refrigerator and practically hurling it into the vegetable drawer, then closing the door so the awful beeping noise would stop.

"Thank you."

Freezing in place with the bag of carrots in my hand, I cautiously met Justin's gaze. My words were soft. "Thank you for serving our country. I'm sorry you had to . . . go through that."

It wasn't exactly what I wanted to say, wasn't right, and didn't capture the breadth of what he probably needed to hear, but I'd felt off my game from the moment Justin had shown up in the restaurant.

He nodded, and I turned to deposit the carrots in the fridge. The bag of lettuce appeared over my shoulder, followed by the remainder of the perishable groceries. We worked with quiet efficiency and everything was tucked away in its proper spot in less than five minutes.

And cue awkward.

I leaned back against the counter. "So was there a reason you decided to show up on my doorstep?"

"I needed to make sure you were okay." Justin mirrored my movement, reclining opposite me in the galley style kitchen.

And *God*. The way he said that. Not wanted to make sure I was fine, but *needed*. He was three feet away, and my body was aching in protest at even that much distance.

Get closer, snuggle up against his chest, and grab a handful . . . or more.

Seriously?

I'd read that an increased sex drive could be a symptom of pregnancy, but this was ridiculous.

"Don't look at me like that, Kel."

Blinking, I tore my eyes from his chest and forced them up. "Like what?" I asked, and if my voice sounded as though I'd taken up fire swallowing then that was its problem.

"Like you want me to kiss you again."

I couldn't even form a rebuke against that. Oh, my mind was easily ramping through all the reasons why Justin was a really bad idea, but my body was forming a really solid argument for the opposite.

Kiss me. Just please kiss me.

He didn't.

Unbidden disappointment swelled within me. "Well, as you can see, I'm fine." *Nope. Too shaky.* Steadying myself with a breath, I said, "But I *am* tired. I'm making dinner then going to bed . . ."

Deliberately, I let the words trail off, hoping he'd take the hint.

Unfortunately—or maybe, *fortunately*—he didn't. "Why don't you go change and I'll cook you something."

"I don't need—"

His eyes flashed in irritation, but one side of his mouth quirked up, tempering the reaction. "Always so stubborn," he muttered. "I'm well aware of what you don't *need*, but how about this once you accept some help without a giant protest? I'll cook something edible with those vegetables you were giving the stink eye earlier. Then I'll leave. Promise," he tacked on when I didn't move.

"I guess—"

He made a shooing motion. "I won't poison you, and I won't burn anything."

Which was probably more than I could say about myself.

"Well . . ."

Justin turned and opened the fridge, summarily dismissing me.

I stood in the kitchen, arms akimbo for a minute, feeling completely and totally at a loss.

But that was me with the Roosevelt men.

I could only hope that round two would have a better result that round one.

CHAPTER SIXTEEN

The food smelled incredible.

At least for a solid minute. The scent of deliciousness trailed down the hall and into the bathroom, drawing me from the shower, rushing me through toweling off and throwing on a pair of sweats and a T-shirt.

But the moment I walked into the kitchen, it all went south.

My mouth filled with saliva, my throat tightened.

Clapping a hand over my mouth, I sprinted down the hall, right back into the bathroom, and bent over the toilet as I lost my lunch . . . and maybe my breakfast too.

Miserable and tired as hell of puking my guts up, I rested my head against the cool iron side of the tub.

Just a few more weeks until I was in my second trimester and the morning—afternoon, evening, bedtime—sickness would go away.

Unless I was one of those lucky ones who got to be sick all nine months.

Moaning, I turned so my forehead got some of the cold.

"Vegetables *really* don't agree with you, do they?" A damp, cool cloth rested on my nape and I almost cried in relief.

Or maybe just almost cried. Especially when he began massaging my shoulders. They were strung tight and aching, and the massage felt like heaven.

A few minutes later, Justin brushed his fingers over my cheek. "All done, you think?"

I nodded.

"Come on." He lifted me up from the floor as effortlessly as a child then tucked a hand around my waist and helped me into the front room.

The couch seemed like the best invention ever when he deposited me on it. "I'll grab you something to settle your stomach."

Before I could tell him that I couldn't eat or drink anything for the next couple of hours, or maybe decades, he was back with a package of saltines and a can of 7Up.

He opened the can and poured it into a glass, stirring it with a spoon until the bubbles disappeared. Then he handed me the cup before opening the crackers and extracting a couple.

"Drink, but only a little and slowly."

If only to rinse the awful aftertaste from my mouth, I followed his instructions and sipped the sugary drink carefully.

"You need to eat smaller meals and not let your stomach get empty," he said, after I drank half the glass. He snagged the cup, swapping me for the saltines.

I held the brittle, tasteless square in my hand, staring at it as though it were a ticking time bomb. And given my track record of being sick every *single* day, multiple times per day, it probably was.

I was so tired of being a puke monster, in Melissa's words.

"It'll help. I promise." Justin curled his fingers around my wrist and brought the cracker up to my mouth. "Trust me?"

Unable to deny him, not when he looked so concerned and earnest and—

I ate the damn cracker.

And I felt better.

Justin smiled at me, and I felt something shift in my heart, shattered pieces coming together, forming an organ that wasn't quite whole. Not yet, it was too damaged for that . . . but at least it wasn't resembling a gaping, oozing wound any longer.

———

I WOKE up tucked in my bed, a glass of water and a Ziploc bag of crackers on my bedside.

A scrap of paper was propped next to the supplies.

Eat these before you get out of bed.

-J

Orders even when he wasn't there.

But I was still smiling after I'd nibbled the little squares. And while I was getting dressed. And while driving to the ranch.

Dew from the grass coating my boots, a cool metal handle beneath my palm, leather and hay and horse. I hardly noticed any of it.

Because of Justin.

I should have noticed, however. I should have paid attention to the sky, darker than normal even though I was running late. I should have noticed the humidity in the air, the crackling intensity that was practically making my hair stand on end. I should have picked up on the horses' nervousness.

I didn't.

Because of Justin.

The first boom of thunder took me by surprise. I was next to Stella's stall and jumped. Her eyes were wide, the whites visible.

"It's okay," I murmured, keeping my voice calm as I offered her the apple again. "It's just a little thunder."

She took it, a little cautious, but she'd relaxed.

"Good girl." I stroked her nose.

Another boom of thunder, this time closer. Theodore made a huffing sound and pawed at the front of his stall.

Damn. I'd forgotten how high-strung he was when it came to the weather.

"Easy," I murmured as I approached his stall. "It's just noise. You won't get hurt."

People said thunder was the part of the storm that made the noise, but no one ever talked about the sound lightning made as it zinged through the air, the hiss as it made contact with the ground.

Or in this case, the stables.

I heard—I *felt* it slam into the roof. The air changed, electrified, lifting the hairs on my arms and nape.

Theodore threw himself against the stall door and then screamed, just as the lights went out. The copper tang of blood filled the air. I could hear him struggling, panicking in his stall, but I couldn't see a damned thing.

"Shit," I muttered and felt my way down the hall for the tack room. There was a flashlight just inside.

Snagging it, I flicked it on and moved back toward Theodore.

His breathing was rapid, his eyes wild.

"Hold on, Theo," I said, careful to keep my voice steady. "Let me see." My breath hitched. "Damn."

He'd cut his flank and blood was dripping out of the wound and down his hair, turning the pale blond color almost black in the dim illumination of the spotlight.

Backtracking, I grabbed the first aid kit and cut another apple. If I could calm him enough to eat, I might be able to dress the wound.

"I'm going to make you feel better, I promise." His eyes met mine, and I gently set the first aid kit on the ground before offering him a slice of apple.

At first, Theodore didn't move, but I continued to talk quietly, inane statements as I held up the piece of fruit. Eventually he came to the front of the stall and sniffed it.

"That's it, bud. All yours, and if you cooperate, I've got more."

Warily, he snagged the apple from my palm. I let him chew for a bit before stroking his nose.

We stood for a few minutes like that, me petting, him chewing through the apple pieces as I offered them up one by one. When he'd quieted, his breathing evening out and his eyes softening, I scooped up the kit and slipped into the stall.

"Oh, Theo."

The wound wasn't deep, but I wasn't sure what he'd cut himself on. I'd inspected his stall the previous day. Had I missed a nail or a sharp corner of the feeder?

Luckily, we had a space free next to Stella. I'd move him there and look for anything dangerous, *after* I'd treated the wound.

I talked to him as I worked, monologuing every step.

Surprisingly, Theodore was almost preternaturally still and very calm as I cleaned and bandaged the cut, even though I fumbled with both the supplies and flashlight more than once. Doctoring wasn't the easiest thing to do one-handed, and I ended up wedging the light between two boards so I'd have both hands free.

I removed my gloves, gathered up the supplies, and slid from his stall. I'd need to get the vet out to take a look later, but my work would do for a few hours. I dropped everything on my little table and snagged a halter from the tack room.

Theodore let me slip it over his head without a fuss.

We were almost in the new stall when I felt it.

That zing in the air, the atmosphere tightening, exciting, until . . . *boom*.

We both jumped, and Theo bumped into me.

It was unfortunate that my shoulder collided right with the cut. He grunted and shied back. The sudden movement—pushing then pulling on the reins I gripped—made me slip.

But I was nothing if not experienced with horses. I recovered quickly, regained my balance.

And that was when the lightning crackled just outside the stables.

A flash of light. Electricity in the air.

Theodore reared. I lost my grip on the halter.

Thankfully, he bolted straight for the open stall. I followed him, intending to close the door, when more thunder reverberated through the stables.

Hooves flying through the air were the last thing I remembered.

CHAPTER SEVENTEEN

JUSTIN GLANCED at the skies and figured that Kelly wouldn't make it in today. A storm was threatening, one that had turned the landscape into an alien place, all dark and shadowed and angry.

He'd never thrown out a meal he'd cooked so quickly before, never held a woman's hair back when she'd been sick, never tended another woman in the way she'd needed.

Justin's specialty wasn't bedside care. It was quick thinking, triaging, and patching soldiers together until they could get to a hospital.

But Kelly hadn't needed patching. She'd needed tender.

And, even though he hadn't thought he had a tender piece left, he'd found one.

For her.

He didn't understand her. Why she was working with the horses for free, why she refused to live at the ranch, why she wasn't clamoring for a handout.

She had so little. The background check had determined that, his visit to her house confirmed it.

Yet . . . what? God, he was being an idiot. Just because he'd felt more at home while spending a couple of hours in her little cottage than he had in the two decades since his mother had died didn't mean anything.

He might not understand Kelly, but he *definitely* didn't understand himself around her.

Groaning, he rubbed a hand over his face and glanced out the window. The storm was going to be a bad one.

A bright flash lit up the landscape for a split second.

It was long enough for him to catch the glint of metal.

Kelly's car was in the drive.

His neck prickled, and he was shoving his feet into boots in the next instant.

The minute it took for him to run through the house felt like an eternity.

Because his instincts—the same ones that had saved his ass in the military—were screaming at him that something was wrong.

He slammed through the front door and sprinted for the stables. Thunder echoed, a crack of lightning hit close enough to make his heart skip a beat.

Then he was inside the darkened stables.

"Kelly?" For a moment, he heard nothing except the scared noises of the horses. "Kel?" he called again, louder.

"Here."

The word was pained, and finally Justin saw a flash of light. He moved toward her.

"What happened?" he asked, crouching next to her and trying to visually assess her condition. There was blood on her shoulder. "You're bleeding."

"Not my blood," she murmured and he noticed that she was gripping her stomach tightly.

His own clenched. Hard. Especially when he saw the tears dripping down her cheeks.

"Sweetheart, tell me what happened."

"Theodore spooked." She wiped her face on one shoulder. "Kicked me."

"Where?"

Kelly struggled to sit up, her face deathly pale. When he helped her, she gripped his hand tight. "The baby. We have to make sure the baby is okay."

Justin didn't think, just reacted.

He scooped her up and booked it to his car, where he carefully laid Kelly across the back seat.

It took two minutes to grab Kelly a blanket, get his wallet, keys, and cell phone from the house.

Then he drove her straight to the emergency room.

Those twenty minutes were the worst of his life.

———

THE TIME PASSED in blurs and snatches. Ultrasounds and blood work, a pelvic exam.

Having not been on the patient side before meant that Justin was overwhelmed and frustrated. He wanted to take over, to demand certain procedures for Kelly . . . and it wasn't his place.

She was scared, needed him to hold her hand, not order perfectly capable doctors around. Not to put his worry about not being able to save another life on her shoulders.

And so he waited. Didn't leave her side.

He stayed.

It was just after noon when a middle-aged doctor came into the room. She was attractive with a short queue of blond hair and sharp blue eyes.

"You've had quite a day."

Kelly's breath hitched. "Dr. Clark."

"I'm sorry it took me so long, I wasn't on rotation today, and the nurses didn't think to call." The doctor pulled on a pair of gloves. "Let's take a look, okay?"

Kelly nodded and Justin squeezed her hand. She squeezed back.

Dr. Clark rolled an ultrasound machine closer and stared at the screen silently as she worked. She'd angled the screen so that it wasn't facing them and the little bit of the image Justin could see was a cloudy mess of splotches and lines.

Then she reached forward and pressed a button.

The air was filled with the best sound ever.

A heartbeat. The healthy *whoosh-whoosh* of a heartbeat.

And the world refocused.

CHAPTER EIGHTEEN

I stared out of the window of Justin's car and watched the sun set. Dark clouds were on the horizon, giving the landscape an otherworldly gloominess.

Another storm was on Mother Nature's agenda for this evening.

The car hit a bump and I winced as I rearranged myself in the seat. Even though the sedan was slick and the ride smooth, the road was still gravel and bumps were inevitable.

"Sorry," he said softly and slowed down further. "How's the pain?"

"Fine."

It was decidedly not fine. My ribs hurt like hell, and the last glance I'd gotten of the bruising was a Van-Gogh-like collection of black and purple swirls and swashes.

Justin shot me a glance, and though his green eyes didn't visibly roll, I could feel his mental one.

"Okay, not fine exactly, and I wouldn't say no to a bed, but it doesn't really matter what I feel so long as the baby is okay—"

I broke off and took a few slow—and, in deference of my ribs, *not* deep—breaths.

Justin's hand on my knee made my eyes widen. His action wasn't laced with any bit of sensuality. His palm wasn't in sexy time territory, and I was in enough discomfort that my body didn't do more than register a blip of surprise.

It was what he said that had a deeper impact.

"You matter."

Two words. Two words no man had ever said to me, two words that somehow changed everything.

Justin put his hand back on the steering wheel and drove carefully in the waning light. It wasn't until we were pulling through the gates at Roosevelt Ranch that I realized he hadn't taken me home.

He parked the car and opened his door.

"What are we—?"

It closed on my question.

"Okaaay," I muttered.

I watched him walk toward the house and prop open the front door. I reached for my purse and froze, hissing out a breath. I was completely at Justin's mercy. Without heavy-duty pain meds, I wouldn't be able to drive, and since I was unwilling to risk the baby any further than I already had . . .

Tylenol it was.

Carefully, I unclicked my seatbelt then reached for the handle.

Justin beat me to it.

"Hold on," he said and pulled the door wide. "Okay, turn your body so your feet and legs are facing me."

He was being bossy, but I let it slide. Sort of. Because even though I did what he ordered, I couldn't keep the retort from passing my lips. "I know you were in the military, but I'm not your lackey."

"I'm well aware of that, I promise." He bent slightly. "Okay, right arm around my neck. Can you lift the left?"

I tried but bit my lip and carefully lowered it back down before it even reached halfway.

"That's fine. Rest it on my hip."

I did so, even though my pulse was pounding behind my eyes, and I was sweating, and I couldn't enjoy the feel of Justin beneath my palms.

"Ready?"

"Always."

He huffed out a breath of laughter as he encircled my waist and tugged gently upward. I did my best to go with the movement, knowing I was no lightweight. "Just relax," he murmured. "I've got you."

And as he carefully maneuvered my body out of the car then up into his arms, I realized that maybe he actually did.

Five minutes later, I was in a bed, boots off, jeans replaced with a pair of gym shorts that were way too big for me. A minute after that, Justin was handing me a pill and a glass of water.

I swallowed it and he took back the cup. "Sleep now," he said, setting the glass on the nightstand.

Since fatigue was already clouding the edges of my vision, I didn't protest. My eyes slid closed and I slept.

———

I WOKE in the middle of the night to a clap of thunder that was loud enough to shake the whole house.

The room was dim, the surroundings unfamiliar, and it took a long moment for me to recall the events of the previous day. Biting my lip against the whimper of pain that wanted to escape, I pushed myself into a seated position and flicked on a light.

Nature was calling and I was not looking forward to heeding its voice.

My eyes took a bit to adjust to the sudden brightness. This room wasn't one I'd been in before. It was small, for one thing, and sparsely furnished.

A bed, a dresser, one nightstand. No fur rugs or gaudy finishes.

Definitely not Rex's style.

My eyes trailed over the furnishings, taking note of the green military bag neatly folded in one corner.

Justin's. Did he store his—?

I swallowed when my brain finally caught up with the evidence of my surroundings.

His room. I was in *his* room.

And he hadn't left me alone.

In a lone chair shoved into one corner, Justin was slumped, arms and booted feet crossed, head resting on his shoulder.

As if feeling my eyes on him, he stretched and sat up.

"You okay?"

His voice was deliciously raspy and his hair was disheveled. He was ridiculously cute . . . not to mention sexy as hell.

"I'm fine. I just—" Thankfully my mouth shut before I started talking about my need to use the facilities.

"Bathroom's through this door."

He stood and opened it, flicking on the light inside.

Before I could protest or deny, he'd come over, pulled the blankets back, and gotten me to my feet in a no-nonsense sort of way.

I was walking—okay hobbling, because *damn*, I'd gotten stiff—into the bathroom a few seconds later. Justin hovered behind me, not touching but close enough that I easily felt his presence.

Which probably should have been annoying. I'd been on my own for a long time, after all. But he managed to stay close enough to help me without imposing.

It was impressive, really.

Once I'd gotten to the edge of the counter, I stopped and wondered how in the heck I was supposed to maneuver and push my pants down when it hurt to bend even a little.

"You're going to hate me," he said and wrapped an arm around my waist. "I'll call your sister in the morning, I just didn't want her rushing over in this weather."

My heart twisted, my eyes stung. "Thank you. For all of it." I paused, waiting for my voice to steady when it began to wobble. "And I couldn't hate you."

"Theodore then?"

I snorted. "Don't look, okay?"

"You do realize I'm a doctor and I've seen—"

"Shh." I dropped my head to his chest. "Just don't look."

His fingers found the waistband of the shorts. My heart pounded, suddenly nervous. Any other time, a man like Justin's fingers in that spot would have been exciting or at least nerve-wracking for a completely different reason.

Dr. Clark had said everything looked fine, that the kick had been centered more on my side and the baby seemed okay.

But she'd also said nothing was certain.

And so I was nervous.

"I won't look."

"Okay." I breathed out. "Go."

He tugged my shorts and underwear down. My tension released. No blood, no cramps, no—

"I totally looked."

My eyes shot up. "You're a pig."

But I wasn't mad, couldn't be mad, especially when I saw the amusement in his expression. I found I liked the mischievousness so much more than the heavy sadness weighing down his expression previously.

"Yup."

He helped me down onto the toilet then stepped out while I did my business. When I was done, he tucked me back into bed. "You hungry?"

Surprisingly, I was.

"Be back in a minute."

While he was gone I tried to get my bearings.

What part of the house was I in? Why had he put me in his room? Why hadn't I demanded he take me home? Why? Why? *Why?*

Because he'd stayed.

Justin had stayed when I'd needed him, and though it was scary as hell, his being there with me in the hospital had meant . . . well, it had meant everything.

A gust of wind rattled the windows, and the lamp's bulb flickered. Seconds later, thunder boomed, followed closely by a flash of lightning.

The storm was uncharacteristically violent for late summer. This time of year, I'd more typically be lamenting about the heat, rather than flinching at thunder.

And I was definitely flinching.

Which hurt because while my ribs weren't broken, they *were* severely contused—a fancy word for very bruised.

I'd been incredibly lucky. My gut clenched, because, no, it wasn't me that was lucky, but my baby.

I touched my stomach as I stared out the window, eyes straining against the flashes of lightning. "I'm sorry," I whispered. "I'll be more careful. Just stay safe and strong, and I won't get near the horses, I promise."

"No, you won't."

My head jerked up, and I watched as Justin walked back into the room, two plates in his hands.

"I won't what?" I asked as he set one on my lap.

He sat on the edge of the bed, the small plate with a sandwich and some fruit almost dwarfed in his large hands. "Won't avoid the horses," he said.

"Oh."

I dropped my gaze to my food, abruptly fascinated by the peanut butter and jelly sandwich. When had watermelon become so incredibly interesting?

"You live and breathe those horses, Kel. Maybe you leave Theodore to me and don't go anywhere near them when a storm's brewing, but it was a freak thing, and you can't—"

"I can't predict when they might spook," I shot back, my heart pounding. It wasn't frustration, necessarily. Though I didn't like Justin telling me what to do. The bigger factor making knots of my insides was fear.

Fear that next time I would do it. That next time I would mess it up and my baby—*my baby*—would be in the crosshairs.

"I understand that it wasn't Theo's fault. I just can't . . ."

Justin was quiet for a long time, long enough for me to glance up and try to discern what the heck was going through his mind.

But I might as well have been staring at a brick wall for all I gleaned. His expression was carefully blank, until finally it wasn't.

"I'm very good at running scared and calling it *safe*," he said. "At keeping distance because it's better. But sometimes creatures—and people —wind their way into your life and that's too precious an opportunity to give up."

"You've lost someone?"

"Many someones. My mom too young, friends I tried to desperately save on a dusty battlefield." A slight hesitation. "And I worried today that I might lose you, that you might lose the baby."

I sucked in a breath. "You make it sound as though that would hurt you."

"Because it *would*, Kelly. I tried to be numb to you, to us, to any vulnerability. But you make it impossible. You make me *feel*."

His words stole the air from my lungs, tied my tongue in knots, and made it impossible for me to speak.

Green eyes caught mine, intensity in their depths. "Those horses need you. You need them. Maybe you don't ride for a while or handle them alone. But if you're not in that barn every day, I worry—" He blew out a breath. "Listen to me. Lack of sleep is making me sentimental. Do what you want, Kelly."

He stood, taking his plate with him to the chair.

I didn't know what to say. There was a great big elephant between us, and I wanted to tell Justin he wasn't alone in his feelings, to thank him for pushing me to not be afraid of something I loved . . . and I couldn't.

Because I couldn't find the strength to be vulnerable.

We ate in silence and PB&J had never been so tasteless. Still, I was hungry and the baby needed food.

And so I ate.

Justin took my empty plate when I'd finished.

Yawning, I slid back down into the bed and carefully tugged the blankets up to my chin.

He was on the threshold when I blurted the question that had been bouncing around in my skull.

"What do you worry?"

If I hadn't been watching him so closely, I might not have noticed it. A slight stiffening of his shoulders, a tightening of his grip on the now empty plates.

But I was and I did.

"Will you tell me?" I asked, when he didn't speak or turn around.

"I worry the light inside of you will go out."

While I was digesting that, he disappeared, a flash of movement that left the dim hallway outside the room empty.

Sleep took a long time coming.

CHAPTER NINETEEN

I woke to the smell of breakfast. Rain pattered against the windows, and it was dark outside, despite the alarm clock on the bedside table reading nine o'clock.

It was the latest I'd slept in years, though I was certain my body deserved the break.

Cautiously, I pushed upward, happy to note that despite some soreness and being stiff enough to rival a plank of oak, I was hurting less than I had expected.

A bottle of Tylenol rested on the nightstand, but I ignored it.

This I could endure.

After tossing back the blankets, I hobbled my way into the bathroom. Fifteen minutes in a warm shower and finger brushing my teeth with some toothpaste went a long way toward making me feel human again.

I wrapped myself in a towel and tried my best to nose my way through Justin's dresser drawers for some clothes without being especially *nosy*. As I was scrounging through a drawer, my towel clutched to my chest, I heard a choking sound.

Whipping around as quickly as I could, I saw Justin standing in the doorway.

Heat.

Instant and all encompassing.

It prickled down my spine, soaked between my thighs, flushed my cheeks.

Emerald eyes had gone liquid, and, *damn*, my insides did too. When he looked at me like that . . .

Then he blinked and the heat cleared. Justin stood staring at me, the nonverbal wall he'd erected no less imposing because it was invisible.

"I was just looking for something to wear." It was an awkward statement as I felt it sounded both uncomfortable and sex-kitten cliché.

"Ah." He cleared his throat then crossed the room in a few steps and pulled out a T-shirt and boxer briefs, which he tucked into my hands. "How are you feeling?"

I stood there, fumbling with the clothes while attempting to keep the towel from slipping. "Like I got kicked by a horse."

He smiled and the world may have gotten a little brighter.

"Need help getting dressed?"

I think he meant undressed, or at least that's what my body wanted. "No."

Justin touched my arm, a brush of his knuckles down my skin that raised gooseflesh in its wake. "You sure?"

I nodded.

"I'm glad you and the baby are okay."

"Why? It would be easier if I wasn't—"

He froze, studying me for a long moment. I alternately wanted to take the words back and was relieved they were out there. If not for the baby, we wouldn't have any ties, and he wouldn't have to put up with me in his life.

But it wasn't *Justin's* baby. So he didn't really have any ties with me, anyway. I certainly hadn't reached out for them.

Which begged the question of precisely why he *was* involved?

Calloused fingers ringed my wrist and he brought my hand up, pressing a kiss to my palm.

It was the most romantic gesture I'd ever been given.

"I have this thing, you see," he said, voice husky.

"What thing?" I whispered.

"This thing about women in trouble. I have to save them."

I pulled back, tried to tug my hand free. I could save myself, thank you very much.

He didn't let me go. "Especially when they're tough, hardworking, sexy-as-hell, gorgeous women who didn't deserve their turn."

That took some of the wind from my sails. Mostly because I didn't view myself as any of those things, or *most* of them, anyway. The exception was hardworking. That I knew I was.

I'd had to be.

But sexy? Gorgeous? Tough?

I didn't feel like any of those things.

Still. "I don't need saving."

He chucked me under the chin. "I know. That's why I like you, Kel."

Turning, he called over his shoulder, "Holler if you need help. I'll wait in the hall."

I waited until Justin had gone before dropping my towel and carefully pulling on the shirt and boxer briefs. Snagging his sweatshirt from the chair, I grimaced and grunted as I slipped it over my head.

Rib injuries sucked.

His scent surrounding me did not. Spicy and salty, with a dash of horse. I wanted to roll around in it.

He didn't give me the chance.

"Move it, Kel. Breakfast is getting cold."

With narrowed eyes, I walked out into the hall. "You shouldn't be rushing the girl who was kicked by a horse *yesterday*."

"You don't do coddling." He grinned, a boyish expression that made him appear ten years younger. "Remember?"

I huffed, starting to put my hands on my hips before dropping them with a wince. "I remember. And if you're so hungry, then why don't you go eat already?"

Justin slid a hand around my waist and I promptly lost every thought in my brain.

He's just playing doctor. He'd do it to anyone.

"Because you wouldn't be there."

Oh.

My heart twisted, softening, exposing its weaknesses, risking itself to allow this man a way in.

But somehow, with Justin, I had a really hard time being afraid of where it might lead.

———

JUSTIN'S DEFINITION of breakfast and mine were very different.

Namely with caloric level.

I usually grabbed a yogurt or a few handfuls of cereal. Justin, however, had decided to butcher the entire farm.

Sausage. Bacon. Ham. Eggs. Cheese. Potatoes. Toast.

"Where's Rosa?"

He shrugged, already halfway through consuming a plate filled to the brim. He was sitting opposite me at the round wooden table that took up most of the kitchen's breakfast nook. "It's her day off."

My dish was overflowing as well. I would barely be able to make a dent, but I wasn't a girl who turned down bacon.

Not ever.

Especially when it was crispy deliciousness that melted on my tongue.

I took a bite and moaned, acutely aware of Justin's eyes flashing to my face. Cheeks hot, I wiped my mouth on a napkin.

"So you can cook?"

"Rosa taught me."

He shrugged at what must have been a surprised expression on my face. "Rosa has worked for my family going on thirty years now. She and her husband wanted a change so she came here about six months ago. Her kitchen skills are off the charts, I'm just lucky to have absorbed some of them."

I was less interested in Rosa and more interested in why his voice went all soft when he talked about the older woman.

It was almost maternal affection and I remembered Justin saying he'd lost his mom too young. I wondered how old he'd been, what kind of impact it'd had on his life.

I was embarrassed to say that I had never thought to ask Rex anything about his family.

Was I so self-absorbed?

But Rex and I had never been like this together. Of course we'd talked, or Rex had, about his plans for the future. He was so energetic that it was easy to just sit back and listen, no matter how far-fetched or superficial.

But with Justin, I wanted to know every detail.

Slippery slopes had nothing on me.

"I—uh . . . did your mom not like to cook?" My eyes flashed to his then down to my plate. It only took that single glance but, instinctively, I knew I shouldn't have asked. "Mine was a terrible cook, she just burnt things into submission. But I like cooking. I just don't usually have the time. Or, you know, groceries. I . . ."

I was totally blabbering. Nonsensical, panicked, trying-to-save-the-conversation babbling.

What I really needed to do was shut the heck up. Of course, that was easier said than done.

"Hey."

I hadn't heard him move, but Justin was suddenly next to me, his palm on my cheek. I met his gaze.

"I'm sorry. I didn't mean to pry."

He sighed and tugged a chair close, sitting in it and turning me so that his legs were on either side of my body.

"It's okay. It's been a long time. I just don't usually talk about it." He tucked a strand of my hair behind my ear. "My mom died in a car accident when Rex and I were nine. My dad—" A sigh. "He worked his grief away. Thankfully Rosa was there to keep me in check."

"And teach you how to fry up perfectly crispy bacon?" I asked tremulously.

Fingers brushing my cheek, a smile that told me everything was fine, that I hadn't ruined what was between us with an insensitive question. "Yes. I can also make a mean grilled cheese sandwich. Just don't ask me for pancakes. For some reason, I'm hopeless at those."

"I'll teach you sometime."

"I'd like that."

I touched his arm. "I'm sorry about your mom."

He stood and crossed back to his plate. "Me too."

CHAPTER TWENTY

"I'm stuffed," I said, ten minutes later. Justin had demolished his plate, and I'd made a surprisingly valiant effort on my own.

After standing, I grabbed my plate and walked to the sink, intending to search out a Tupperware container to save the leftovers.

I was struck frozen by the devastation on that side of the island. A raised counter with barstools had hidden the sink and cooktop.

And they'd hidden a disaster of epic proportions.

Pans were perched around like toadstools. Crumbs were everywhere and what looked to be like every kitchen utensil was scattered about.

Justin came up behind me, visibly chagrined. "Never mastered the art of cleaning as I cooked." He lifted one shoulder. "But I'm good at cleaning afterward."

"I'll help," I said and set my plate next to the sink, before pulling open a drawer in search of plastic wrap or a container. "Let me just get something to store those leftovers—"

Thunk.

My leftovers that were currently in the trash.

Blinking, I closed the drawer and stared at him. Then at the open trashcan, my food inside. Then back at him.

My vision blurred, and—for fuck's sake—tears filled my eyes.

I'd done enough crying over the last weeks to water the ridiculous expanse of grass covering the front of the ranch. And now I was crying over *food*?

Good lord, I was a wreck.

"Sorry. I didn't realize you wanted to save—"

"It's fine." Surreptitiously, I swiped a hand over my eyes and turned to the sink. Oh, look, dishes that needed to be washed. Overreactions that needed to be ignored.

Two arms came to the outside of mine, trapping me against the sink, not letting me succeed with the ignore tactic.

Annoying man.

The only thing more frustrating than overreacting was when someone acknowledged you were being idiotic.

"It's nothing," I said, picking up a plate. "Hormones."

"Kelly."

I scrubbed vigorously. Who knew that eggs were so hard to get off?

"Can you put this in the dishwasher?" I held out the ceramic dish. "I don't think I can bend to do it."

Justin let out a long, slow breath. It tickled my nape, blew through my hair, and I shivered.

He took the proffered plate, set it on the counter. But he didn't move away, and I could feel the heat of him soaking into me.

Straight down to my soul.

Blegh. Now I was talking about *soul?* I needed to get it together.

Lips brushed against my neck and I shivered again.

"You cold?"

I shook my head. Cold wasn't any part of it. I was hot, melting, sweltering. My fingers gripped the edge of the sink and it was purely so I didn't grab Justin, even though every cell in my body was shouting at me to turn in his arms and slant my mouth across his.

He placed his hands on my shoulders and exerted pressure. Careful, but inexorable pressure until I faced him. His chest was barely an inch from mine, his lips even less than that. I could smell the syrup on his breath.

I wanted to taste it.

"This is a really bad idea," I whispered, but somehow I was closing the space between us, letting my body lean against Justin's.

"The worst," he agreed.

But he didn't move back either.

We stayed like that, basically frozen in stasis, for what felt like an eternity.

"Fuck it."

Gravel and roughened need. It matched my own.

And that was the last thought I had before Justin's mouth was on mine.

The kiss was even better than before. There wasn't an ounce of hesitancy. My body reacted instantly, lips parting to welcome his tongue as I plastered myself against him. He was strong and hard and smelled good, and I *needed* so much.

His hands slid down my arms, gently grabbing my wrists. He lifted them so that they were around his neck then carefully—oh so carefully—picked me up and set me on the counter.

My ribs protested slightly, but then his mouth was moving on mine again and the pesky ache was forgotten.

Breathing was overrated, pain was of little consequence. Not when I was being twisted and turned and transformed. Nerves that I'd never been aware of before fired to life, entire sections of my body that I'd never paid any notice to demanded attention.

My neck, my collarbones, the space behind my ears. They all prickled with intense longing.

And that wasn't even a drop in the bucket for what was happening south of the border, so to speak.

I was swollen, wet, *aching*. I wanted him to slide the boxers to the side and—

Justin broke his mouth from mine, leaving me panting as he kissed his way down my neck. He seemed to know every spot that was in need and lavished attention on each of them.

His hands came to my thighs, spreading them as he stepped between my legs, pressing himself against me.

Oh. He was different from Rex in that way too.

Rex.

I stiffened, my arousal blowing away like smoke from a campfire. One second the ashy air was in control and the next it was burning the crap out of my eyes.

What had I been thinking?

Dropping my arms and pulling back, I blinked. For a long time. A really, *really long time.*

I'd already imploded my life once. Was I really going to do it again?

Justin's fingers tightened on my legs for a second before he released me. Or at least, let go of my thighs, because his hands came to my waist.

But he was merely helping me down from the counter.

The feeling coursing through me as he stepped away and sank into a chair at the table wasn't disappointment.

Really, it wasn't.

"I'm not going to apologize," he said.

That settled the coursing mess of regret, arousal, and fear. Surprising myself, I laughed as I turned back to the dishes. "I don't think you have the chromosomes for it."

"Maybe not," he said. "But I do know that until I met you, I hadn't felt alive in years."

The plate I'd begun to wash slid from my hands, clattering to the bottom of the sink. By some miracle it didn't break.

"Sooner or later, you'll realize I'm not Rex." A pause, and I lifted my head, watched as he started to leave the room. "Leave the dishes. I'll get them later."

Then Justin was gone, and I was rocked to the core.

If a single kiss and a few hours together did that to me, what would he do if I actually let him in?

I stared at the clutter on the counter and knew it would be a complete and utter disaster.

With a sigh, I grabbed the sponge and scrubbed.

I scrubbed until all the dishes were clean, until the counters sparkled like diamonds. I cleaned until there wasn't a speck of grime, until dust was threatened into submission and wouldn't dare to make an appearance.

But I couldn't scrub away the sensation of sliding down a really steep cliff.

And not wanting to stop.

CHAPTER TWENTY-ONE

I SEQUESTERED myself in the library, where I could light the fireplace with the flip of a switch and lose myself in a book.

What I *should* have done was drive myself home.

Still, one look out the windows, and I decided to stay until the storm cleared. I was a solid driver, but the storm was a doozy, and I just didn't have complete confidence in navigating the roads with my ribs being as sore as they were.

I'd already had one near miss and didn't need to risk having more.

Then there was Justin.

Who—if I was being truthful—was the real reason I hadn't gone anywhere.

I liked him.

And that scared me.

Just not enough to leave.

With a sigh, I closed the book I was attempting to read and took my blanket to the rug in front of the fireplace. It wasn't the easiest thing, lowering myself down, but my ribs were less sore than that morning and that was something.

I tried to turn the situation with Justin over in my head, but I kept getting stuck on two facts: he was Rex's twin and . . . I wanted him more than I had ever wanted Rex.

We hardly knew each other, and yet, there was a pull I was hard-pressed to ignore.

So I did what I always did when I couldn't make heads or tails of a situation: I called Melissa.

She picked up on the first ring, her "Hello" almost panicked.

Which is when I realized I hadn't talked to her since the accident with Theo. My current crisis might be Justin and everything he invoked in me, but hers was her younger sister being in an accident.

"I'm okay."

Silence.

Which was even more worrying than a verbal vomit of words.

"Dr. Clark did an ultrasound and everything," I assured her. "No bleeding. They said since it's so early and it's my first baby, he or she was protected by my pelvis. My ribs hurt like hell, but there's not even much bruising, and . . ."

I forced myself to stop taking a page out of my sister's playbook and halted the flow of words. "I'm okay."

"I was worried," Melissa said. "When Justin called—"

"I'm sorry," I said. "I just—he was here, and then it was chaos, and by the time I got back to the ranch it was late, and I was exhausted. Now the storm."

"*Kelly*. It's okay."

I released a shuddering breath. "Truth is, I was worried too." Which was a ridiculously underwhelming word when compared to the depths of what I'd been feeling.

"I miss your face," my sister said.

That startled a laugh out of me. "I miss you, too."

"Should I bring you over some soup?"

My eyes flicked to the storm raging outside. "Uh. Have you looked outside?" I paused. "Plus, I'm still at the ranch."

Melissa's eyebrows rose. I couldn't see her, obviously, but I could feel the action right through the airwaves.

"It's not what you think," I hurried to add.

"And what do you think I think?" she asked.

I put the phone on speaker and slowly rolled to my back, staring at the ceiling. "I think it's really freaking complicated."

"You going to make a run at something?"

"Not unless you're talking about trying not to put this baby at risk."

"Justin is a Roosevelt," Melissa said. "You're not going to go another round of stupid with that family, are you?"

"I try not to be stupid in general."

"That's not what—" My sister sighed, the noise rattling through the phone's speakers. "Henry told me he proposed."

"Then you understand why I said no."

There was a beat of quiet. I knew my sister well enough to know she agreed with me . . . even though she didn't want to. "Yes." Melissa's reply was grudging. "But I don't think it would be the worst thing in the world."

"Look," I said. "I love Henry, but it's never been anything more than friendship between us. We'd tried, and it just didn't work out."

"Because he was an idiot and cheated on you."

Here we went.

"We weren't exclusive. We'd hardly even held hands at that point. He had every right to—"

"You've always held a piece of yourself separate, Kel. I get that. Dad leaving hurt you. The revolving door of Mom's boyfriends and her total ineptitude at being a parent exacerbated things. But Henry cemented the distance."

The anger roiled within me, coming to an unexpectedly quick boil . . . that rapidly poured over.

"Since when is it bad to protect yourself? Since when—"

"Since you spend more time with horses than people. Since you never trust anyone," Melissa interrupted. "I worried about you with Rex, but I was happy to see you step out of your comfort zone." She cursed. "I just knew the moment he skipped town that he'd set you back."

"I am *not* damaged goods."

"We all are, Kel. That's what happens when you have screwed up parents."

"Everyone has baggage," I said. "But that doesn't mean you have to let it define you."

"Good words. Except for the fact that you aren't living them. You're letting your circumstances define every moment of your future."

I ground my teeth together, trying to find the strength to not lash out at her. She was concerned. I got that. I was just really tired of every freaking person in my life thinking they knew what was best for me.

"Thank you for your opinion," I said, and was proud of the cool calmness in my tone.

"Ah," Melissa said, condescension in the sound. "And now here comes the icy politeness. Get mad, Kel. Fight for something. Fight for what you want, don't just let it slide by."

"Well, thanks for that, Dr. Phil. I'm going now, but since you are so interested in my life, I'll tell you this: I never felt an iota for Rex of what I feel for Justin. And if that's *stupid* then I'm inclined not to care."

I hung up and promptly turned off my phone.

Which was the precise moment I noticed the booted feet in my periphery.

Perfect. Just freaking perfect.

CHAPTER TWENTY-TWO

I closed my eyes. "How much did you hear?"

Silence greeted me.

"Awesome."

I turned my head and stared into the flames. Orange on top, blue near the grate. Hot and hotter.

Just like me. Or at least my situation.

"Henry asked you to marry him?"

"You heard that much of the conversation and *that's* what you want to ask?"

"What was your answer?"

Bad to worse.

I shoved myself to sitting, ignoring the bite of pain as I did so. "No. Of course it was *no*."

"Thank God."

"Wh-what?"

But Justin's hands made the answer to that startled question seem very unimportant. He gripped my legs, spreading them as he crawled right into my space.

His face was level with mine. His eyes blazed with liquid intensity.

"I don't understand you," I whispered.

"Fuck if I understand myself."

His lips took mine. They weren't gentle or exploratory. This wasn't a teasing kiss. This was want. *Need.*

Somehow I was flat on my back with Justin above me, our hips aligned exactly right, putting pressure just where I needed it.

And friction.

Let me tell you a thing about friction.

Too much equals bad.

Justin knew how to do it *just* right.

He'd propped himself up on one arm, presumably in deference to my ribs. But I wasn't feeling my ribs. I was feeling his body against mine, hard muscles under my palms, his erection grinding into me and sending my arousal into astronomical levels.

Never had I wanted a man to take advantage of me more.

Except even as I had that thought, Justin pulled back. He knelt between my spread legs, expression molten, chest rising and falling like a horse after a long, hard gallop.

Come have a ride with me, I wanted to say. Desperately.

The words stayed firmly lodged in my throat. But definitely not my mind.

Some of the mental statement must have run across my eyes because Justin cursed and flopped over to his back. "Don't look at me like that. I'm trying to not be an insensitive asshole, here."

I didn't reply. I *couldn't* reply.

Insensitive or not, complicated or not, I wanted Justin more than I'd wanted anyone in my life, Rex included.

"I know all about distance."

I snorted. "*Now* we're going to talk?"

He propped himself up on one elbow and bent to take my lips in a sizzling kiss that had my head spinning. When he pulled back, I had to actually unclench my fingers from his hair so I didn't rip it from his scalp.

"Yes, talk," he said, nuzzling my neck. He hadn't shaved, and the bristles from his stubble rubbed against my throat. If only he'd rub it somewhere else. Lower. "Because if we don't *talk* then I'm going to forget that you were kicked in the ribs by a horse barely more than twenty-four hours ago. I'm going to forget you slept with my brother and you're carrying his baby."

He slid his fingers into my hair, tilted my head back, and kissed me again. "All of the reasons to leave you be are going to disappear, and you'll be naked and beneath me."

My heart was pounding, my skin stretched taut with arousal. I could see his erection straining the denim of his jeans. "I wouldn't mind."

Justin groaned, lying back and flinging an arm over his eyes. "You're not helping."

I shifted onto my side and stared at him. It was hard to believe that he was anything like Rex, not when he was staring at me with that mix of fire and kindness. "Why didn't you drive me home last night?"

One hand clenched into a fist at his side before slowly relaxing. He released a slow breath. "Truth? Or the we-hardly-know-each-other answer?"

I didn't hesitate. "It always has to be the truth."

He thrust a hand through his hair. "Because I knew if you weren't here, weren't safe in my bed, I wouldn't have been able to sleep. I would have gone to your house and bullied my way in like the last time, stayed until I knew you were safe." A beat. "I don't know what kind of witchcraft you practice but you've got me under some sort of spell, sweetheart."

From any other guy I would have chalked the words up to a cheesy line, but with Justin, they came alongside sincerity so clear I couldn't ignore them.

Especially when he asked, "Why did you stay? You could have demanded that I take you home this morning."

I laughed, awkwardly. It was all well and good to put him on the spot. But when the tables were turned . . . "Why would I want to go home when I could be surrounded by luxury?" I smiled and it was ridiculously false.

Justin just watched me, his expression quiescent but somehow arresting at the same time.

Slowly, he raised one brow.

I caved. Like a house of cards.

"Fine. Okay. I wanted to stay." He'd already heard my conversation with Melissa, what the hell did it matter now, anyway? "You know I feel something too. It's beyond stupid, but it's there."

Justin tilted his head, one corner of his mouth curved. I wanted to kiss the little "c" that appeared.

I was also in ridiculously over my head.

"So what you're saying is that I'm irresistible?"

With a groan, I collapsed back.

He was on me in a second, lifting the hem of my shirt, calloused fingers running over my injury. "What is it? Your ribs? The X-rays were clear, but it's possible they missed a sliver of bone and—"

I grabbed his head and pulled his mouth down to mine.

When we came up for air a long time later, I rested my head against Justin's chest and admitted, albeit less begrudgingly than I would have a few minutes prior, "You're irresistible."

———

"WE SHOULD CHECK ON THE HORSES," I said awhile later, my front pleasantly warm from the fire, my back securely tucked against Justin's chest.

He'd grabbed a blanket from the sofa and a couple of pillows, tucking them around me with a practiced hand. They had eased the strain on my ribs and reduced me to a state of blissful relaxation.

"I already did," he murmured, the soft words rumbling against my spine. "They're the same as yesterday, nervous, but not overly freaked out. It's still a muddy mess getting over to them, but the water is flowing away from the stables and they're warm and dry."

"And fed?" I asked. "Theodore's wound?"

"And fed." He laughed. "The vet was able to make it out before this last storm hit, and she checked up on our favorite Appalachian. Theo's cut is almost healed." His breath was hot against the exposed skin of my neck. "All the horses have even had their daily slice of apple."

I mock gasped, turned my head, and narrowed my eyes at him. "You're trying to steal them from me. They only love me for my apples."

Justin pressed a kiss to my lips. "They love you for a hell of a lot more than your apples."

There was an undertone to his words that hinted at something deeper than horses between us, and I had to admit it freaked me the hell out.

Maybe all the more so because I might just like it.

"Good," I said and burrowed into the pillow, desperate to change the subject "Because I'm too comfortable to move."

"How's the morning sickness?"

"Better." It had been. The key for me was making sure my stomach was never too empty. "You know what you're talking about, Dr. Roosevelt."

One arm tightened around my waist and his hips pressed into me from behind. "God, I like that too much."

"What?" I smirked up at him. "Doctor?" I played the syllable over my tongue. "Isn't that the typical male fantasy?"

"It's *my* fantasy. I don't know about other dudes, but I'd sure as hell like to play doctor-patient with you."

I laughed . . . then harder, one hand coming up to hold my injured ribs in support, when he affected a wounded expression.

"You'd laugh at a man's pain?"

"Yup." I wiped a tear from the corner of my eye. "Especially when I've already offered to do something about said pain."

The atmosphere between us shifted and, abruptly, my amusement cut off.

Justin was watching me, some unfathomable emotion in his eyes. "You're beautiful when you laugh."

"I-I *am*?"

When had *that* word ever been put into a sentence about me?

I could confidently say never.

"You're frowning." He smoothed his fingers between my brows, physically brushing away the creases there. "And yes, even now, you're beautiful. I've thought so from the first moment I saw you."

This was too much. I couldn't have wooing and sweet words right alongside with heat.

I was going to end up broken. Damaged beyond repair.

Mentally, I took a step back. "Was that before or after I puked on your shoes?"

Justin's lips tipped up into a smile but it wasn't a true one. I knew that distinctly, even though we'd met hardly a month before.

"And that's precisely why I'm not doing anything about the *pain*." He slipped his arm from me, slid carefully free. "I think you're right. I'd better check on the horses."

He was gone, through the door before I could form a protest and call him back.

All things considered, it was better that way.

CHAPTER TWENTY-THREE

The rest of the day was a quiet affair. Justin returned from checking on the horses less than an hour after he'd gone.

But he hadn't come back to the library.

Which, I was trying to convince myself, was a good thing.

Rain continued to fall, transforming the formerly well-kept gravel drive and paths into giant muddy puddles. The skies were dark gray and foreboding, except that I'd always liked the rain. Being cocooned inside, listening to the drops patter against the glass of the windows, snuggling up with a fire was pretty darned perfect.

Even if it would be a bear to get home in the morning.

And I knew I needed to get home.

Back to reality. Back to relying on myself. Back to keeping my heart safe.

Of course, it didn't help that my body kept saying that safe was over-rated. I was tempted to chalk it up to YOLO-ing and jump Justin in the hall.

Pregnancy hormones were not to be messed with.

But, and this was also the especially unfortunate part, I had the notion that my reaction to Justin had nothing to do with the pregnancy and everything to do with the fact that he was kind and sweet, strong and sexy, and that he looked at me with enough heat to melt even the most determined block of ice.

"Pathetic," I murmured, closing the book I'd been reading and pushing myself carefully to my feet. I was loathe to leave the warmth of the fire, but I was hungry.

I detoured to Justin's room for a sweatshirt or a pair of sweats and was bending over—hey, moving was getting easier—one of the drawers when the door to the bathroom swung open.

With a gasp, I whipped around.

Holy H-E double hockey sticks.

Justin stood on the threshold of the *en suite*, steam billowing around him like a bad special effect from a Hollywood movie, but that wasn't what made my mouth water.

His body made me stupid. It was as simple as that.

Flat abs deviated into six precise squares of muscle, pecs I wanted to reach up and squeeze, and those little indents at his hips that I *needed* to drop to my knees to lick.

My eyes dropped. Widened.

He reacted to my presence in his room remarkably quick, bending to grab a towel and covering himself.

"You okay?"

I shook my head.

"Kel?" Justin's eyes were filled with concern.

"I—"

Screw it.

In one smooth movement that had my ribs protesting—not that I cared —I pulled off the sweatshirt and top I was wearing.

"What are you—?"

I pushed down the boxer briefs.

Never had I *ever* stood before a man as naked and exposed as I was in that moment.

And yet, I wasn't self-conscious.

It didn't matter that my hips weren't as narrow as they'd been a few months before, that my thighs were thicker, my stomach not as flat. Because there wasn't judgment in Justin's eyes.

Not an ounce.

Instead, there was only fire.

Then he turned his back on me and slammed the door.

My heart sank and all those feelings that I hadn't been feeling— shame, insecurity, embarrassment—flooded forward.

Eyes burning, I grabbed for the clothes, but before my fingers had touched the cotton, the bathroom door crashed open and Justin stormed out.

"You," he growled, stopping just inches from me, "are going to be the death of me."

He was still naked, and I couldn't really focus on anything except for the fact that mere centimeters separated our bodies.

I straightened and could feel the heat radiating off him, see the sinewy strength of his muscles, the faded white line of a scar across his right pectoral.

My mind hazed and I leaned forward, traced my tongue there, soothing that old hurt. Justin sucked in a breath then hissed out a curse.

One hand came up and I traced the ridges of his abdomen.

He was breathing heavily now, a slight sheen of sweat breaking out over his body as he held himself in rigid control. Except, he'd come out of the bathroom.

Except . . . he was naked and standing in front of me.

My fingers moved lower.

And the leash snapped.

Justin's mouth crashed down on mine, his tongue neatly separating my lips and slipping inside to tangle with mine. He swept me up into his arms and strode toward the bed.

I expected him to drop me to the mattress, considering how furiously he was kissing me, but instead he lowered me slowly.

"Are you sure?" he asked, pulling back to stare in my eyes.

My hands were trembling, actually trembling with desire as I reached up to tuck a strand of his hair back in place. Then because I wanted to and, hell, I was already naked in bed with the man, and I figured that gave me the right to touch pretty much anywhere I wanted to, I ran my fingers through the slightly-longer-than-military-grade locks.

Justin groaned, bent his head so I'd have better access. "God, that feels good."

He was like a giant house cat, chest rumbling with pleasure as he pushed against my palm. I smiled inwardly and continued to stroke him.

"I can't remember the last time someone has touched me like that." He shuddered.

"Touched you how?"

"Like you like it, too."

I frowned and his eyes opened, pupils dilated with pleasure.

He gave me that half smile, the one that effectively turned my insides to mush. "Not clinically, not for a drill or a procedure. Not because you have to. Because you want to."

God, did I want to.

Not until he chuckled did I realize I had said the words aloud.

My cheeks went hot and I dropped my gaze to somewhere in proximity of his chin.

"Kel."

I shook my head. Maybe I could be like one of those superheroes and manifest a power under duress.

Like to turn off all the lights.

Like to go back ten seconds.

But no powers appeared, and Justin didn't let me avoid his stare, not for long anyway.

He pressed a kiss to my forehead, my nose, my jaw . . . and sucked my nipple into his mouth.

I about came off the bed.

"There," he said, releasing my breast. "That's better." And promptly took my other nipple into his mouth.

He was gentle, which I was thankful for, given they were extremely sensitive, but it was also pretty much the best sensation I'd ever felt. His mouth was hot and wet and beyond skilled.

I wound tighter and tighter as he alternated between breasts. Every nerve in my body focused on that one part of me. Goose bumps prickled my skin, sweat broke out behind my knees, on the back of my arms. My spine stiffened, and I bucked.

Justin pressed my hip into the mattress, his big hand hot and dangerously close to the space between my thighs as he held me still for his ministrations.

His teeth grazed my skin and that was it for me.

I exploded, wave after wave of pleasure caressing me from the inside out, leaving my limbs lax and limp.

"Well," I said, when I could breathe again. "That was new."

A smile flickered across his mouth. "Yeah?"

"You mean pulling a Quick Draw McGraw?" I laughed at myself, unable to be embarrassed, not when the orgasm had very nearly been soul shattering. "Yeah. No. It usually takes me a bit longer."

Like a lot longer. Like sometimes never.

Somehow, I doubted that would be an issue with Justin.

Who was looking like he'd conquered space, proctored world peace, and cured every disease on Earth in the last five minutes.

And given the way I was feeling, his masculine pride wasn't undeserved.

Didn't mean I was going to let him have the upper hand. Not for long, anyway.

I reached down and curled my fingers around the length of his erection. "Now, let's see what we can do about *this*, shall we?"

CHAPTER TWENTY-FOUR

KELLY WAS GOING to be the death of him.

There was absolutely no way of avoiding that.

Her fingers on him were everything. And by everything, Justin meant every *freaking* thing.

Firm and sure, a little smile curving her lips as she stroked him, quickly made every intention of pleasuring her, and not himself, fly out the window.

She deserved better. More. Someone who didn't feel broken inside.

Except with Kelly, he didn't feel broken.

With Kelly, he felt like, maybe, he could be the man he was destined to be.

Her grip tightened, and his eyes rolled back.

Sensation ripped down his spine and he knew he was two seconds away from losing it all over her.

The thought of exploding across her chest, her nipples pouty and red from his mouth, her ivory skin silky smooth and tinged with the salt of her sweat, didn't help his situation in the least.

He tried to pull back, but she tightened her hold on him . . . and suddenly he wasn't trying very hard anyway.

Hard.

He was that. Harder than he'd been in his life. And about to blow his load like a teenager.

"Kelly," he began, intending to tell her to stop. But the words came out more like a plea.

Then she slid down the bed beneath him and took him in her mouth.

That was it for him.

Her mouth was hot, wet . . . and it had been nearly a year. He wasn't like some of the other guys. He didn't slake his lust with the women on base.

Their almost predatory following of the soldiers had been off-putting.

At the moment, he almost wished he had.

If only so he didn't lose it in thirty seconds.

Hell. Who was he kidding? It took barely ten. *If* he was rounding up.

Tearing free of her mouth, he exploded.

The world might have ended, and he wouldn't have given a damn. That was how good it was. The freaking world could have blown up, and he wouldn't have cared.

Kelly slid up the bed, and he flopped to the side, tugging her against his chest. He inhaled in the scent of her hair under his nose—softly floral with a dash of horse. "Are you smirking?"

She snuggled in, ass pressing against his hips, and his body flared to life. Like he was going through puberty again.

God, it was hot when she did that.

"Yes," she said, turning her head to press a kiss to his wrist when it rested beneath her neck. "I think you"—she shifted again—"liked it."

"I haven't been this horny since I was sixteen and saw Jessica Larsen changing in her car."

Kelly snorted.

Justin feigned outrage. "I was sixteen and she had a really nice rac—"

"Shh." She rolled over, kissed him. "I don't want to hear about other girls, even ones from more than a decade ago."

"How about—"

She kissed him again, and he broke away, laughing. When was the last time he'd been teased? When *he'd* teased someone?

His life had been way too freaking serious for that.

Well, it felt *good* to laugh.

It felt good to be with Kelly.

He pressed his mouth softly to hers, kissed her with all the tenderness he possessed, could practically feel the walls around his reserve cracking under the strain.

This was a woman he could lose himself to.

The thought sobered him, and he pulled back. Her eyes were closed, her lashes half-moons of silky black against her skin. She had freckles on her nose, an adorable smattering that made him want to spend hours with her, just memorizing their location. Her lips were swollen and wet, and a flush still colored the tops of her cheeks.

She was, in a word, beautiful.

He wanted her to be his.

But this situation was so beyond screwed up that he didn't know where to begin.

No.

He wasn't in the habit of lying to himself. Justin couldn't really say he didn't know where to begin. He knew where he wanted to start, to go, but he'd also witnessed the result of his father going there with his mother.

And witnessed the devastation in its wake.

How could he go there?

How could he *not?*

Shit. *He* wasn't used to being the total flip-flopping screw-up. That was Rex. But he couldn't logic his way out of this one, not with his heart so twisted up.

Justin was well on his way to a full-blown panic when Kelly's eyes slid open, filled to the brim with sleepy relaxation. She studied him for a long moment then smiled and touched his cheek.

"I'm hungry," she said and pushed up onto her elbows. "Let's go eat."

Justin was already walking down the hall before he realized she'd soothed him without even saying a word.

CHAPTER TWENTY-FIVE

"Mmm," I mumbled, shoving a cracker topped with cheese into my mouth. "I'm so hungry I could eat a horse."

Justin smiled, the slightly haunted expression almost completely vanquished from his face.

He was so quiet and steady that his emotions were hard to read, but I was starting to understand him. Though he was stoic at times, that didn't mean he didn't feel; the turmoil was just buried a little deeper than most folks.

But I knew all about burying.

"You'd never eat a horse."

"True." I grabbed another cracker. "It really is a horrible saying."

"You're so hungry you could eat an elephant?"

I shuddered. "No way. They're so intelligent. Did you know they cry if their family members die?"

Justin cut a few more slices of cheese and tossed some grapes on a plate then shoved it and the entire box of crackers at me. "I didn't know that."

He turned to the freezer, opened the door, and stared at the contents. "Italian?"

Yum. More cheese. "Yes, please."

"Okay, so lasagna or pizza?"

I hesitated, torn between what seemed all of a sudden like a very diffi-cult decision.

And he laughed, a rich sound that made me smile sheepishly in response. "It's a tough call," I said. "I mean they're both carbs and cheese, but how can anyone decide between them?"

"Impossible."

I would have smacked him for mocking me, when the little jelly bean inside me was basically siphoning off all my nutrients and making me cranky, but I liked the lightness in his tone and amusement in his eyes too much to risk losing it. Instead, I glared and pointed down at my stomach. "Baby growing here. Bring on the carbs."

Justin pulled a pizza out of the freezer then a pan of lasagna out of the fridge and set them both on the counter. "Oh, carbs will be brought."

How he could make the words sound so freaking sexy were beyond me. It wasn't just the hormones, though they weren't making it easy on me. I wanted to lick the man like he was my very own personal popsicle.

Our little orgasm exchange in the bedroom earlier hadn't done nearly enough to extinguish the need inside of me.

But he'd taken a mental step back for some reason, and since I was well-familiar with cerebral retreats, I'd let him.

Didn't stop me from wanting to jump right back into his bed and carry on from where we'd left off.

"Okay," he said. "How about I'm so hungry I could eat an anaconda?"

I snorted, eyes shooting to his. They were innocent. Too innocent. Yup, the innuendo was definitely intended. "You're being sixteen again."

He winked—winked!—and my heart did a little tap dance. "You bring out the best in me."

Ignoring the way that did absolutely nothing to settle my racing pulse, I said, "I'm so hungry I could eat an entire pizza. How about that?"

"Too cliché."

I popped a grape into my mouth. "I'm so hungry I could eat an antelope?"

Justin pondered this as he put the casserole dish in the oven then opened the box of frozen pizza. "You don't have any sentimental feelings toward antelope?"

"Nope. Not especially."

"Not even baby antelope?"

"I'm not talking about eating baby antelope!"

He raised his hands in mock surrender. "Just considering all the possibilities."

"You're a monster," I deadpanned, before narrowing my eyes and waving a cracker at him. He laughed. "And stop considering possibilities. It's annoying. Just take my words as what they are."

The air went tight, all amusement over antelope and anacondas forgotten.

"I'm not used to taking anyone at face value," he said quietly.

"Well, how about you take a chance on me?"

The words were unusual.

I didn't put myself out there. Not ever. Or not before Justin. He'd marked me, changed me in less time than it took most people to plan a weekend away.

Which was a frightening thought. Especially since I had the feeling that everything in my life was going to be measured in terms of B.J.—Before Justin—and A.J.—After Justin.

B.J.

Oh God, he was corrupting me. I felt my lips begin to curve and laughter bubbled up in my throat.

He raised a brow.

Was I really going to lead with the fact that I'd made a mental blow job joke? "I'm sorry. It's just that . . ." I pushed the grapes around the plate, making two eyes, a nose, a smile.

It was just that the man made me smile. And, for once in my life, I wanted to leap from the cliff and really *go* for it.

Rolling my eyes and resisting the urge to dish on my dirty mind, I began to work in earnest on the crackers and cheese.

I felt rather than heard Justin move. He crouched next to me. Then his fingers were tilting my chin up and those green irises were boring into mine. "Just what?"

"So pushy." But it was impossible to hold back my shiver. I might not like being ordered about, but when his voice went all stern like that, a hint of growl on the edges . . . I liked it.

Very much so.

His thumb pressed gently on the center of my lips, parting them and making me suck in a breath.

Not missing a beat, he slanted his mouth across mine. Which was basically what I'd been wanting since we'd left the bedroom, and I didn't bother to play coy. My arms came up, tugging him close and almost making him lose his balance in the process. But he caught himself on the edges of my chair, caging me in.

The kiss was sweet and sensual, building heat with the promise of more.

Except Justin was in careful control. I felt it in the tenseness of his frame, the rigidity of the shoulders I gripped.

It was pleasure contained.

Which pissed me off.

I didn't feel contained. I was torn wide open and vulnerable and—

His mouth moved along my jaw, nibbling until he reached the spot just behind my ear. When his tongue darted out to caress the skin there, I lost my mad and simply grabbed onto sensation.

Such a small, unobtrusive place and yet he might as well have melted my spine from the inside out.

I moaned, fingers slipping down to grip his nape and hold him to me. Justin obliged. Until he didn't. "What were you thinking about?"

"Huh?" He bit down. "Oh!"

"What made you laugh before?" he demanded.

Another swipe of his tongue, another brush of his mouth. The slight sting of teeth.

I would never make it as a spy with Justin around.

"Blow jobs." He grinned, a wicked smirk that loosened my lips and made the rest of the truth pour out. "And maybe, how in the short time we've known each other, you've changed my life."

To which his response was something I would have never predicted.

He all but flew backward with a curse. Of course since I was still basically attached to him barnacle-style, I nearly toppled out of the chair.

His hands steadied me, but I could tell it was an instinctive gesture. His mind had gone somewhere.

Somewhere unpleasant.

Justin strode to the sink and braced himself on the counter, head hanging as though a heavy burden was atop his shoulders.

And maybe it was.

I rose carefully from the chair and walked over to him. The closer I got, the stiffer the set of his backbone, until he was so fiercely rigid that he might as well have been a statue.

Slipping past him, I opened the oven and checked on the lasagna. It was hot, but the cheese needed melting, so I uncovered it then set about readying the pizza.

Well, tearing the box apart and setting the frozen dough on a cookie sheet.

I set the tray inside the oven then looked around the kitchen, trying to puzzle out the man within.

The room was standard Roosevelt Ranch with clean lines and modern finishes. Stainless appliances, an old farmhouse sink, all artfully arranged in distressingly expensive country chic elegance.

"I was hungry," I blurted.

Justin glanced up, looking perplexed instead of haunted.

"For a lot of my childhood, I was hungry." Leaning back against the counter, I let my eyes drift away. It was too easy to remember a different kitchen—smaller and dirtier and . . . emptier.

"My mom was always flighty. She spent money on ridiculous things and couldn't hold a job. Then my dad left . . ." I concentrated on the bite of the edge of the countertop into my back. It grounded me, held me in the present instead of the past. "Things deteriorated from there. Melissa was only five years older than me. She did her best and things did get better as time went on."

But those years until Melissa had been able to get a solid job had been tough.

"She was fourteen when she got a job at Henry's dad's restaurant. He'd give us meals, box up untouched leftovers to bring home. It was the only food aside from beans and ramen we could afford." I shook my head. "I guess that's why—" I shrugged.

Justin finally spoke. "Why you panicked when I threw the leftovers away earlier."

My sigh was equally long as it was loud. "Yeah. I make enough money to afford what I need now. It's stupid, but old habits are hard to break, I guess."

"Yes," he said quietly. "They are." A pause. "And not stupid. Not at all. Old habits are the only things that protect us sometimes."

And with that enigmatic statement, he pulled open the oven and extracted the lasagna.

Five minutes later, I was sitting down to a heaping plate of noodles and sauce and cheese.

I didn't enjoy it nearly as much as I thought I would have.

CHAPTER TWENTY-SIX

As was often the case with the weather in my particular corner of Utah, things changed rapidly and without much warning. The rain that had been characteristic of much of the day transformed to full on monsoon-style as thunder and lightning made a reappearance and gallons of water seemed to pour from the sky.

Justin and I were back in the library, sitting on opposite ends of the large leather couch. I was perched sideways with a book in my hands as he watched some TV show on his laptop.

It felt decidedly domestic. It also felt exactly right.

Because I'd decided that I was going to put my fears aside. That I was going to see where things with Justin went.

Cart before the horse, I reminded myself. He hadn't made any promises, and it wasn't like I had a track record with men wanting to stick around—Henry aside.

Speaking of Henry, I turned on my phone and sent him a text, asking if he needed me to come in. I'd sent one the previous day, and had received a near immediate response telling me not to be ridiculous.

Today was no different.

I told you not to worry about anything until you were fully recovered.

Aw. I really loved my friend.

I'm okay. I don't want to leave you in a lurch.

His reply made me snort.

You're fired if you come in before Monday.

I <3 you too.

After exiting to the home screen, and dutifully ignoring the texts and voicemails from my sister, I opened the weather app and frowned.

"Hope you like rain," I told Justin.

He glanced up from the laptop. "More coming our way?"

I nodded, attempting to ignore how much I liked the word *our* when referenced to the two of us. It was too soon.

And cautioning my heart was hopeless. I was already in too deep.

"Rain for as many hours as this tracks," I said, turning the screen so he could see it.

"Yeah. That doesn't look good."

My phone buzzed with a flash flood advisory and then a few seconds later, another text from Melissa.

Road's washed out. Stay at the ranch.

I warred between irritation that she was giving me orders and relief that she was still talking to me, after my outburst earlier. I stifled the teenager in me that wanted to reply with a snarky retort and embraced the adult side that would soon be a mother.

I will. You and the fam stay safe.

A pause. Then she replied.

You're my family too.

My eyes went a little misty.

I know. I love you.

And Justin, too. If it happens to go that way.

It's not like that.

Then what's it like?

Shit. What *was* it like?

Complicated.

Always is.

I snorted as I watched the "…" blink as she continued to type.

Be careful. Be safe. We'll talk this out when you're back in town.

And that right there was why I loved my sister.

Deal. I <3 you.

<3s all up in here.

Stop trying to be cool.

It's not trying when you already are.

I laughed aloud, felt Justin's eyes on me.

The lights flickered as I said goodbye then set my phone on the table. "Think the power will go out?"

"Supposedly Rex ordered generators," Justin said, rolling his eyes. "So the power going out is a distinct possibility." He closed his laptop. "You and your sister make up?"

"We always do."

"Wish it was that easy with me and Rex."

His tone made the subject seem decidedly off limits. Except that he'd brought it up in the first place.

"What happened with you two? Why aren't you close?"

Justin was silent for a long time, long enough for me to think that he wouldn't answer, that it was just a slip.

"Our childhood was . . . complicated."

"Yeah? How?"

He put a hand on his neck and tilted his head back, stretching, rolling the tension from his shoulders. "Grief does funny things to people." A sigh. "I actually think we would have both been okay if my dad had been able to get it together. As it was, we both have different baggage, just from the same scenario."

"I know *all* about baggage," I said lightly.

"Yeah."

I waited to see if he wanted to say more. The similarities between our upbringings were acute, money and luxury aside.

"You're still not close to your father?"

"No." And the wealth of pain in those two letters was immense.

It was a reminder that hurt didn't abide by societal rules. It hit all ranks, tore down even the wealthiest families. Food during my youth had been scarce at times. I'd worn hand-me-down clothes, lived in a pathetically small house, missed out on fancy toys.

I'd had to work hard, *very hard* for everything in my life.

In some ways, Justin had it easier. He'd been given every opportunity.

Except that I'd had Melissa and Justin had . . . no one.

I picked up my book. Then put it back down again, rubbing at my ribs.

Justin's brows came down, and he practically teleported to my side. "What is it?"

I dropped my hand. "Nothing. Just stiff from being in this position."

"Let me see." He lifted my shirt before I could respond and, *damn girl,* I could get used to him doing that. Though I'd rather it was because he wanted to strip me bare and kiss every inch of me than because he was concerned about my injury.

I batted his hands away. "I'm fine."

"Who's the doctor here?" He reached for me again. "Let me see."

His fingers were stroking my skin gently, raising ley lines of warmth in their wake. It felt good to have him touch me, so why protest? I leaned back.

"The bruising hasn't gotten worse. Can you still lift your arms?"

I did so, folding them over the back of the couch and liking the way it made my shirt ride up further. Or rather, liking the way Justin's jaw tightened when he glanced at it riding up. My boobs were a little extra lush—thank you, baby—and since I was braless, the undersides peeked out beneath the hem.

In fact, I was dangerously close to a wardrobe malfunction.

Justin appeared to appreciate the fact. Though, he was demonstrating his superb self-control once again.

"Maybe you need a better look?" I asked innocently and raised my shirt the last half an inch. I was rewarded when he cursed the air blue. This man. He did something to me, made me into a different person— more confident, more assured. Perhaps it was because I'd never seen disdain in his eyes when he looked at me.

Or maybe it was because he'd spent the better part of his life taking care of others.

Or because I knew he wasn't indifferent to me.

"Kel," he warned, fingers tightening on my waist.

Higher. I wanted them higher.

"God, I love it when you growl my name like that."

He glanced heavenward, as though for patience. Except his hands didn't release me, and I could see the proof of his arousal through the denim of his jeans.

"Sweetheart . . ."

"I want you. I don't care about the consequences or complications. We're here now, together, and I—"

"I don't want to hurt . . . you." Justin's pause made me hesitate. It also made me finally recognize *exactly* what his problem was.

He was running scared.

I tugged my shirt down, shoved myself up, and snatched my book. My body was on edge with need, my tone sharp. "I get that it sucks to lose people, to be the one left behind struggling to put the pieces together."

He thrust a hand through his hair. "You don't understand what it was like."

Like hell I didn't, was my immediate reaction.

Thankfully, I was rational enough to realize that just because we'd gone through similar things growing up, Justin's experiences had surely been different from my own.

I may finally be ready to take the risk of us and he may want to as well . . . or at least, he wanted me to trust him, to believe that he was going to be consistent and honest, that he wouldn't run at the first sign of trouble.

But Justin still wasn't ready for an *us*.

He had walls up I couldn't break down and he needed to be willing to take that last step himself, to put himself out there, to put his heart in peril.

Just like I was.

"Then tell me," I said, earnest now. "Talk to me. *Help* me." I smacked the book against my thigh. "We haven't known each other for long, I get that. But I'm trusting you to not be like your brother—"

"I'm not Rex."

I forced a breath. "A fact I think we've well established. But *I'm* also not your mother or father or Rex. I'm like you, Justin. I don't just give up when things get hard. If I say I'm going to stick, I stick."

His jaw clenched at the mention of his family and I felt a blip of alarm before pressing on. Might as well lay the cards on the table.

"I like you, Justin, probably more than any other person I've ever spent time with." Biting then releasing my lip, I said, "You know what's between us is special. You said as much yourself, so why are you pulling back now?"

Why, when I'd finally decided to make the leap, was he pushing me away?

Silence fell, tense, and protracted. My nails bit into my palms as I waited.

And waited.

"Or not," I murmured, clutching the book to my chest and rising from the couch. Justin sat back, giving me space, letting me slide off without a word.

The book I was reading was a romance novel, one of my favorites. I'd left it at the ranch at some point, and had been happy to find it on the library shelf earlier in the day. But in that moment all it gave me was the distinctly painful reminder that real life didn't often resolve itself the happily-ever-after way fiction did.

Goody me. Perfect timing as always. Thanks, world.

I paused to study him for just a second longer. "I'll drive home in the morning." Then I turned and strode for the hall.

He let me go.

The man let me walk away with nary a protest.

Yup. Real life blew sometimes.

Especially when I realized that I'd left after promising to stay.

CHAPTER TWENTY-SEVEN

"CRAP," I muttered and whirled around. I couldn't leave. If I did I would be doing the same damn thing I'd just accused Justin of.

Running when things got hard. Taking the easy way out.

Protecting myself instead of fighting for what I wanted. For once, I was willing to fight for a relationship, and I couldn't give up so easily.

I started back for the library.

I didn't get very far.

Justin stood in the doorway, less than five feet away. Even that distance felt like too much.

"I'm so—"

No.

I didn't let him finish his apology. It was unnecessary, and I figured we'd shared enough words over the last day.

I dropped the book.

It took three steps to close the space between us and, in a move that might as well have been choreographed in a rom-com, I found myself in Justin's arms. He tugged me close, plastered me against his chest. Our mouths smashed together, all raging desire and no finesse.

And still, it was the best kiss ever.

"Hold tight." It was all the warning I had before Justin swung me up into his arms. He kissed me again, and I hardly noticed that we were moving.

The next thing I was aware of—besides calloused fingers, demanding lips, and hard, *hard* . . . muscles—was the cool cotton of sheets beneath my back.

I glanced up and saw we were in his bedroom, one bedside lamp on, red numbers of the alarm clock declaring it was 10:52 p.m.

As I watched, lightning flashed outside the windows, a pale white glint filling the room for a brief second. Then everything went out. The lamp. The clock.

The room was pitched into darkness.

And yet Justin didn't stop kissing me, caressing me, *loving* me.

It was somehow more sensual without the light. More perfect with our fingers occasionally fumbling over articles of clothing as we tried to get each other naked as rapidly as possible.

Gradually, my eyes began to adjust and shapeless shadows became darkened shoulders, narrow hips, flat abs.

He slipped free of his sweats, tore off his shirt then mine. I was clad only in his boxer briefs until he slid those down too.

When he disappeared off the side of the bed, I strained to see. Had he begun to have second—*twentieth?*—thoughts?

"Just—"

His head popped up whack-a-mole style on the left side of the mattress, teeth flashing white in the blackness. "I was looking for a condom before I realized—"

The reminder should have made me embarrassed. It didn't. I was in the red zone, at the get-inside-me-before-I-murder-you level, and I didn't care about paltry things like birth control.

Stupid, but then again I *was* already pregnant.

"I'm clean," he said, probably reading my silence as disapproval rather than desire I was attempting to wrestle under control. "But I can still—"

"It's not that." I blew out a breath. My voice was husky, the need blatantly displayed. "I'm just"—another sigh—"horny as hell."

His amusement was palpable, even amongst the shadows.

"Oh," I said. "And I'm clean, too."

I'd been tested at my first appointment with Dr. Clark, had felt thankful that amongst the things Rex had given me, an STD wasn't one of them.

Hot breath on my ankle snapped my focus back to the man in front of me.

Or should I say, *below* me.

Lips on my calf. A dart of his tongue behind my knee. Then his mouth was climbing higher until it stopped in my . . . well, pretty much the place that needed him most.

He nipped and kissed, sucked on me harder than a jawbreaker. The orgasm ripped through me, a fire blazing through a tinderbox of a forest.

Then he was slipping inside me, transforming the pace from frenzied to sweet. Justin was gentle, so gentle, gliding in and out, fanning the flames of my desire until I writhed beneath him.

But as though we were of one mind, Justin knew exactly where to stroke, where I needed pressure or calming, and I was soon flying through another peak as Justin chased his own.

I'd never felt more complete than when he found his pleasure, never felt more satiated than when he tugged me against him and held tight as we watched the storm rage outside the windows.

"Guess Rex didn't get the generators," I said into the dark quiet.

He laughed, the puff of air moving my hair and tickling my temples. "Guess not."

"I don't think I care," I mumbled drowsily as he pushed the strands back.

Justin kissed my forehead. "I definitely don't care."

And warm in my own little slice of heaven, I let sleep take me under.

———

A FEW HOURS LATER, the power hadn't come back on, and I sat on the kitchen counter trying to save the important things from the rapidly defrosting freezer.

Namely the ice cream.

I'd woken ravenous and horny.

Justin had easily taken care of problem two. Problem one was slightly more complicated in that I'd had to get dressed and force myself from the warmth of his embrace.

But the little parasite—and I said that with the kindest of intentions—was demanding sustenance.

I'd slipped on a T-shirt and fresh boxer briefs then, trying not to wake Justin, had tiptoed from the room, a flashlight he'd found somewhere grasped in my hand.

Not that my efforts had been worth anything.

His drowsy voice drifted into the hall after I'd flicked on the flashlight. "You okay?"

"Yup. Just hungry."

"I'll come with." There was rustling before the sound of feet padding across the floor.

"No. It's okay—"

He entered the hall, looking all rumpled and deliciously sleepy. His hair stuck up in multiple directions, and he was shirtless, a pair of basketball shorts riding low on his hips.

My fingers were itchy with the need to touch. Especially with the peek-a-boo of those handle things just above his pelvis . . . or stupid-makers, as I'd mentally dubbed them.

As in, they made *me* stupid.

It was his fault for having them, not mine that I wanted to grab on to them and—

"Whatcha thinking about?"

I blinked and came back to the present, my cheeks flaming when I caught the knowing expression in Justin's eyes.

"Ice cream." I held the container against my chest when he came over and peered inside. "No. Mine. Haven't you ever heard to not come between a pregnant girl and her dessert?"

"Mmm." He leaned down, all that bare skin way too close. His nipple was half an inch from my mouth for Christ's sake. A. Half. Inch. "I've suddenly got a hankering for mint chocolate chip."

My lips twitched and I glanced up. "Hankering?"

He nodded. "I was going for southern charm."

"Well don't. And also"—I drew an "x" in the air—"hands off."

"No sharing?"

"I only share when I'm not guilted into it."

"Hmm."

"What do you mean *hmm*?"

In a move faster than I could track, and certainly faster than I could block, Justin swiped down and scooped up a dollop of ice cream.

I made a sound of outrage but before any words could follow, his finger was tracing my lips, slipping into my mouth.

It should have been ridiculous, an idiotic move that made me uncomfortable.

It wasn't.

Instinctively, I sucked the ice cream from Justin's finger and was rewarded with a groan. It rumbled through his chest and across to mine.

When had he taken the container and put it aside? When had he gotten so *close?*

There was no processing because his mouth descended to mine and then he was kissing me. The mix of hot and cold, of sweet and slightly tart made my head spin.

He stumbled backward with me plastered against him and sat in a chair or on a stool or hell, maybe it was the floor. All I knew was that my hands were sliding down to free him.

A flex of his hips, a shift of mine, and he was inside.

"Oh, my God," I said, rocking back. "That is really freaking good."

"Yes." He wove a hand through my hair and kissed me. "But it'll be better if you move. Promise."

I laughed. When had I ever laughed while having sex?

Never. That was when. Which meant this wasn't just sex. I mean, I'd known that before, but now I *really* knew.

O.M.G. I was descending into insanity. I sounded like a confused college coed.

Really, *really?* Ugh. It was horrible.

"Kel?"

My eyes flew down, a chagrined smile pulling up my lips. "Sorry. Having an argument with myself."

There were lines around his mouth, a sheen of sweat on his forehead. But his tone was light. "As amusing as that would be to hear aloud, any chance you might move any time soon?"

"Oh!" I flexed my inner muscles in the way I'd discovered he really liked during round two.

He groaned and it was pained. "You're a menace."

I smirked. "I try."

But even as I was reveling in my sheer feminine power, Justin's hands came to my hips and yanked me flush against him.

My breath caught, then transformed into a moan as he started moving in me.

I grabbed his shoulders and held on. There wasn't anything sweet or particularly gentle about this round. The legs of the chair—it was a chair, after all—scraped loudly against the floor as the force of his movements drove us backward. There weren't soft words, tender caresses.

This was fast. Hard.

My ribs gave a miniscule protest to the action, but the rest of my body didn't give a damn, and the mix of slight pain and pleasure sent my desire skyrocketing.

Later I might look back on the decibels my moans reached with mortification. In that moment, nothing mattered except sprinting for that peak, scrabbling over the edge, and enjoying the plummet back to Earth.

We were both still panting when the kitchen came back into focus.

I turned my head and rested it against Justin's sweat-slicked chest. His heart absolutely thundered beneath my ear.

"My ice cream!" I cried out.

It was probably all melted.

The man beneath me burst into laughter, so hard that the chair creaked ominously.

In one smooth movement, he was on his feet with me in his arms.

He tossed his head in the direction of the wooden chair. It sat awkwardly on the floor, one leg not quite right.

I winced. "They don't make furniture like they used to?" It was an attempt at remorse even though I didn't feel particularly guilty. I found that it was impossible for me to feel bad about spending time with Justin.

A chuckle as he carried me from the room. "I'll always look back on it with fondness."

We were halfway down the hall before I realized. "Wait!"

"What?" He stopped. "You need more food?"

"No." I wasn't hungry any longer. Funny how that worked. "It's just. The mess . . . I really should—"

He handed me a dishtowel he'd grabbed from who knew where. "I think this will cover things until we can shower."

My cheeks flared hot. "Not *that*. The kitchen. The ice cream!"

Justin laughed. "Don't worry. I got it."

I wasn't used to people pulling my share of the weight. "You don't have—"

"When a man says he's got it, *he's got it*." A pause, and I knew he was thinking of Rex. "Or this man, anyway."

Abruptly, my protest seemed less important than making him forget the past for a little bit longer.

"*This*"—I tapped my finger against his chest—"man has gone three rounds in six hours. I think that's the surest sign of *having it* I've ever experienced."

He was quiet for a beat and I thought maybe he wouldn't play along. Then he chuckled and the knot in my chest loosened. "Who would think I'd be turning thirty-three in a few weeks. Not when I have the stamina of a teenager."

"But better lasting power."

Justin laughed and bent to kiss me. "I like you, Kelly Hamilton," he said once he'd set me on the bed. "Flashlight is on the nightstand. Holler if you need me."

If you need me.

I found that I wanted to need him. A whole hell of a lot.

CHAPTER TWENTY-EIGHT

Morning light trickled through the window. It seemed very bright after so many hours of dark.

The storm was over.

What else was?

A heavy arm was wrapped around my waist, the masculine body behind me prone. But I knew Justin wasn't asleep.

No. He was too still.

"Hey," I said softly.

To Justin's credit, he didn't pretend he hadn't been awake. He rolled so his body was over mine and stared down at me. "You okay?"

All that naked male above me took my breath away. As thus, I couldn't do anything except nod.

Plus, morning breath. 'Nuff said.

"Sure?" One side of his mouth turned up. "I'm liking the way you're looking at me, sweetheart, but I kind of need the words."

I tugged the blanket up, a barrier between my stinky dragon breath and Justin. "I'm sure. Last night was . . . incredible."

Except it sounded like *snedible*.

"A ringing endorsement, I'm sure." He reached for the blanket, and I cringed back, clutching it to me like I had the mint chocolate chip ice cream a few hours before. "What's wrong with you?"

In a movement so fast I had no chance of stopping it, Justin reached up and yanked the blanket away from me.

His eyes trailed down then drifted back to meet mine. There was appreciation in his gaze and need, somehow more need.

"Okay," he said, hand sliding along my side and up to cup my breast. I hissed out an oath and arched into his palm.

Him touching me was pretty much the best thing ever.

"So it's not embarrassment." A brush of his fingers across my nipple.

"Uh-uh."

He bent, as though to take my breast in his mouth but froze, the aching bud an inch from the motherland.

I wanted more.

Now.

"Then what?" His tongue flicked out and my chest shot up, trying to physically shove myself home.

Justin turned his head, the straight-up, yellow-bellied stink. "Tell me."

"My breath, okay? It's bad." I gasped out. "Now please—"

"Is that all?"

My groan of displeasure was loud when he straightened, moving away from my breast.

I might just kill—

The thought didn't even have a chance to finish manifesting in my mind before he was kissing me, shoving his tongue past my lips and basically taking my mouth in a way that showed very clearly he did *not* give a damn about my breath, morning or otherwise.

"Now," he said once he'd finally pulled away. "Let's try this again. Are you okay?"

I could barely string two words together, that's how okay I was. But I nodded, wove my fingers into his hair, and tugged him back down. "Yes." Then. "More."

Justin gave me more.

———

THE POWER FLICKERED BACK to life just as the sun fully emerged from behind the hills in the distance, prompting Justin to coax me into the shower and *assist* in my washing of all those hard to reach spots.

He left me with a comb and a fresh set of clothes that smelled deliciously of him to go and rustle up something for breakfast.

I dreaded to see what the kitchen would look like when I went down.

It was pretty much as bad as I expected. Little piles of flour dotted the counter, four—*four!*—bowls perched precariously about the space.

And a pan was smoking.

Smoking.

I must have made a sound because Justin glanced up from the almost fire and gave me a chagrined shrug as if to say, "I tried."

"Shoo." I turned off the burner and slid the pan back off the heat before turning on the griddle portion of the very expensive stove to preheat. Then I stared down into the bowel of batter he'd managed to splatter over the counter.

"How were you in the military? Aren't they supposed to be really clean and organized?"

His brows pulled down. "I am."

I swiped a streak of batter from his cheek. "Case in point."

"Okay, so cooking cleanly isn't my strong suit. I didn't cook much when I was serving."

"And I bet Rosa cleaned up after you when you were a little boy." I cupped his chin and adopted a sickly sweet voice. "Those innocent green eyes. *No, dear, you don't have to do the dishes.*"

Justin pulled free and if I wasn't mistaken, his cheeks were a little pink.

"Oh, my God, it's true, isn't it? You pulled sad face on Rosa and had her wrapped around your finger."

He slanted me a look. It very nearly made me take my words back and apologize.

Then I saw his mouth . . . which was trying very hard to not smile.

"Oh, you're *good.*" After snagging the bowl from his hands—it looked like pretty darned perfect pancake batter, so clearly that portion of the cooking event wasn't the issue—I ladled spoonfuls onto the griddle.

The circles sizzled and began to bubble.

"You'll want to wait until the entire back bubbles and they all burst."

Turning, I raised a brow. Did I look stupid to him? I could make pancakes. It wasn't a gourmet three-course meal, for Pete's sake.

"Sit." I pointed the ladle at him.

He sat.

Not in *our* chair, I noticed, which was propped carefully against the far wall, but at the barstool opposite the marble counter that held the massive cooktop.

It was one of those units that must have cost more than my car: four burners, an indoor grill, and the griddle.

Which cooked pancakes that were seriously on point.

Or maybe that was Justin's batter.

The picture in my head sprang to full, vivid color. Justin and I on the ranch, cooking together, living together, laughing together. My belly getting bigger as Jelly Bean grew and him smiling down at me, the genuine one that made my heart flutter and hope sprinkle my soul like glitter.

Because who didn't like glitter?

With a deep breath, I tucked the image close and sent up a mental wish to God or Mother Nature or whatever forces were at work in the universe for it to come true.

Once in my life, I could have a dream come true, right?

"What are you thinking about?" Justin's question was soft, but enough to snap me out of my revelry.

"The baby." It was the truth. Kind of. Close enough.

"Are you worried?"

I flipped the pancakes. "Not in the way you think. My ribs are on the mend. I don't have any cramping or bleeding, so no physical symptoms." I rolled the handle of the spatula in my hands and sighed. "I'm sure it's what every person thinks when they find out they'll be responsible for a child. There's a lot of worrying and dreaming and *hoping* that I'm not the one who'll screw up."

"Except that you will."

My eyes flashed to him. "Geez, thanks."

He slid from the stool and walked over to me. "I didn't mean it like that. It's just something I learned in the military that was very different from medical school. When you're a doctor, you like things to proceed in an orderly fashion. There's a treatment plan, triage procedures. Of course, things often veer off track, because no case is ever exactly textbook, but there are always those protocols to fall back on."

"That makes sense." I'd watched *Grey's Anatomy*, I knew what happened in hospitals.

"I've seen that look before. The armchair quarterback who watches *House* or *Grey's Anatomy* or reruns of *E.R.*" He tapped my nose. "I did a lot of general practice stuff. Checkups, monitoring. I didn't diffuse bombs inside of people's chests."

"Oh."

He chuckled. "Try not to sound so disappointed. The emergency department can get busy and exciting, just not quite enough for a prime time drama."

Justin took the spatula from me and began scooping pancakes from the griddle, starting to set them on the counter before I tsked and held up a plate. After the dish was full of piping hot carb deliciousness, I set it aside and spooned another batch on to cook.

Once I'd put the bowl down, he tugged me into his arms and continued, "The military is different. You'd think they would be similar and, don't get me wrong, in many ways they are. Chain of command, lots of rules, and plenty of protocol." He paused. "The difference is that when things are exploding and bullets are flying, you don't have time to think. It's all instinct. They've trained that instinct into you, but it's still not flipping through the mental encyclopedia medical school ingrained in my mind. You act and act fast." His voice dropped. "And you hope like hell that you're doing the right thing."

"What happens if you don't? What happens if the thing you did wasn't the right one?" I caught a glimpse of his face and immediately regretted asking.

It was grave, his expression haunted, emerald eyes frosted over.

"You scramble. You MacGyver a solution. You pray." A pause. "And if none of that works, sometimes people die."

My eyes stung as I wrapped my arms tightly around him. Justin was stiff, his body practically carved from marble.

"So what you're saying is that I'm going to kill my baby."

"What?" He pulled back and bent so our faces were level. "I didn't —*oh*. Who's the good one again?"

I touched his heart. "Sorry. It was funnier in my head."

Truth was, I'd wanted to shock him out of the past and was happy it had worked.

Justin tugged my ponytail and said, "Flip those pancakes." He picked up an apple from the counter and washed it before cutting it into pieces. His eyes pointedly met mine as he dropped the slivers of the core in the trash.

"And they say men can't be trained."

He snorted as he grabbed a bunch of grapes and ran them under some water before slicing a basket of strawberries.

We worked in companionable silence for a bit, Justin cutting fruit as I flipped pancakes like a pro . . . at least until my mind latched on to a fact I hadn't clued into before.

"I just realized you're a doctor. That you've been a doctor for a while and you're thirty. How does *that* work?"

"I'm thirty-three." Justin lifted one shoulder. "And it works because I graduated high school at thirteen."

"So you're a freak." I deliberately widened my eyes. "Great. Not only am I dating someone better looking than me, but he's also freakishly smart."

"You think I'm good looking?" Justin dropped the knife next to the strawberries and crowded into me, all up in my space, his mouth curved into a deliciously sinful smile.

"Not even going to comment on the freak part?" Why was I breathless?

Oh yeah, because Justin was *Justin*.

"Nope."

"Come on." I gave him angry eyes, which meant of course he didn't budge. At all. "Fine," I snapped. "You know you're gorgeous. Not to mention way out of my league."

He grinned. "There was one drawback to being a freak."

"Yeah?"

"I was so young the girls didn't look twice at me."

My lips twitched. "So what you're saying is that in order for me to get a guy like you, I've got to find one who's been scorned by women his whole life?"

"Exactly."

I snorted and plunked my head onto his chest. "You're ridiculous."

"And we're dating."

My heart gave an excited little scream. "Yes, we are."

CHAPTER TWENTY-NINE

Justin had put syrup in the shape of smiley faces on my pancakes. Two dollops for eyes, a tiny "u" for the mouth on each of them.

"What?" he asked as I stared at my plate, not eating. "Oh." My gaze flashed up and he winced. "Yeah, about that—"

His cheeks had gone an adorable shade of pink.

"Hey," he protested, reaching for my plate. I batted his hands away. "So I like my food to look happy. What's wrong with that?"

"Smiley—" I choked back a laugh.

He was just too stinkin' cute.

"Fine. Okay? Rosa always did that for me. I thought—"

Aw.

I plunked myself in his lap and wrapped my arms around his neck. "Thank you."

His brows pulled down.

"I'm not teasing you." I smothered my smile. "Okay, not much, anyway."

Justin gave a little growl that made my insides go all tingly.

I held my fingers up, separated by the smallest amount of air. "Only this much."

A snort, but he reached around me and folded the pancake in half before holding it up to my mouth.

"Uh—"

"Eat." He shoved it past my lips, forcing me to take a bite.

I chewed. Swallowed. Opened my mouth to speak—

He repeated his trickery, obliging me to take another bite.

Fool me twice and all that, I held up my hand, blocking him. "You're cute, but I can feed myself, thank you very much."

Opposable thumbs would do that to a girl.

Justin swiped his finger through the syrup on my plate and painted it across my bottom lip.

"What are—?"

"Getting my taste." He kissed me.

As things were often the case with Justin, the simple touch quickly spiraled out of control.

Which was why his hand was under my shirt, cupping my breast as I attempted at swallowing his tongue when the front door opened.

Apparently, we had a thing for chairs.

A distant part of me heard the heavy wood panel close, acknowledged the steps on the floor, but before I could get my body to move away, dammit, those footfalls entered the kitchen.

"Well. I didn't see this coming."

I knew that droll tone, knew that voice.

With a gasp, I wrenched away from Justin, almost tossing myself from his lap.

And immediately clamped a hand over my mouth so I didn't *toss* my cookies. *Shit. Fuck.* Those two curses just circled in my mind, round and round, as I stood on shaky legs, and stared at Rex.

Who was leaning against the frame of the kitchen doorway, all brutal derision, and callous carelessness. A little behind him stood an older man with eyes as green as Justin's, but his expression was pure smirk, pure Rex. It was uncanny, really, that little half smile both men wore.

Part amused. Part disgusted. Part unsurprised.

The emotions connected with my insides, but somehow I wasn't wounded.

What I had with Justin wasn't something tawdry. I hadn't been going down my list of ever-revolving bed partners—not that it would matter even if I was, because *hello*, slut-shaming had no place in my life.

Justin and I had danced around each other for weeks. And we were dating.

Weren't we?

I glanced behind me, where he still sat in the chair, looking decidedly shell-shocked.

"No words, little brother?" Rex gave a laugh, but it was angry, brittle even. "I didn't think you had it in you, to be honest."

That got Justin moving. He stood up and tucked an arm around my waist.

My stomach settled. This was complicated, but it would all be okay if—

"You decided to take your turn with Rex's whore, did you now?" the older man said, the words as frost-laden as the ranch's streams come February.

If this was a movie, the scene would have gone deadly silent, all the characters in the script staring in shock. But it *wasn't* quiet. In fact, Rex gave a little laugh.

A laugh. Because I was *such* a whore.

I sucked in an outraged breath as Justin stiffened next to me. "Don't talk to her like that," he snapped out.

"Why? That was *your* word for her, if I remember correctly."

Justin's arm dropped from my waist.

I glanced up and saw the truth in his eyes. He *had* called me that. Pain took my breath away, cracked my heart open, and stomped any remaining hope within into so much dust.

Justin's father pushed Rex to the side and strode forward until he was less than a foot away. There was a folder in his hand that he slapped loudly down on the table. His eyes locked with mine. "Sign them."

He was big and aggressive, and wore an expensive three-piece suit. Tie, vest, jacket, leather shoes, all of it pristine, even though the roads and path leading up to the house had to be giant mud pits.

He was taller than Justin, and I had to tip my head back in order to stare into his eyes.

And then I wished I hadn't.

Cold. His gaze was so cold.

There wasn't fire like Justin when he studied me, nor cavalier interest, as though I were a not-so-funny joke, like Rex's. *This* man was iron, a statue for all that I got from him—unless you counted disdain, I guessed.

Because that was the single thing I could feel radiating in the space between us. Disgust. Absolute and complete disgust.

I'd never had another person look at me like that.

"Sign what?" I asked. The folder was unopened on the table, a manila snake next to plates of pancakes with happy faces on them.

Happy faces.

Fate had a cruel sense of humor.

"Your check is inside. Just agree to leave us be."

Justin made to grab the papers but I stayed his arm and picked it up myself.

My fingers shook, my heart was pounding so hard it was practically in the back of my throat.

But I wasn't a coward. I opened the damn thing.

I scanned the words, struggling with the legal mumbo jumbo, which was the only reason it took me so long to understand what was actually written there.

What they wanted me to sign.

"You want me to give away *my* baby?"

I flipped the last page—a contract saying I would forfeit my parental rights after delivery—and saw the aforementioned check. It was signed *Vincent Roosevelt* in bold scrawl, but that wasn't my biggest focus.

Never had I *ever* seen that many zeros.

Ten million dollars.

Ten million.

What in the ever-loving-pile-of-crazy was wrong with these people?

"Why does it have my due date on it?"

"Justin shared that particular detail with us," Vincent said. "You'll get your money, just not until my grandchild is safely in this world."

My eyes flashed up and over to the man in question. He'd gone still and his lips pressed into a flat line when I pulled the check from the paperclip, holding it up.

"You did this?" I asked. The paper was stiff, official. Cold.

"Yes." He backed up a pace.

It was the most painful step of my life and I hadn't even taken it.

"Why?"

A shrug, words that spoke of nothing we'd shared. Nothing I'd *thought* we'd shared. "It's what I do. I clean up messes."

Ah. His tone made it very clear that *I* was the mess in question.

Crinkle.

My hand had clenched tight, scrunching the check. My heart squeezed even tighter. But when I spoke, my voice was calm, cool even. No one would guess at the world of pain I was in.

Rex had hurt me. But Justin . . . he'd decimated my heart.

"You Roosevelts certainly know how to treat a girl," I said, carefully flattening the check out.

I slipped it under the paperclip and walked away. My purse and borrowed clothes from the hospital were in Justin's room.

"Where are you—?"

"Kelly." A hand on my arm.

Justin's.

His touch was more painful than when Theodore had kicked me. I wrenched away.

"You promised you wouldn't leave." His voice was quiet, but not quiet enough.

Rex and Vincent laughed. "Women don't stay. You know that, son. Unless it's for a bottom line. And your . . . *girl* there is definitely after a bottom line."

I ignored them and asked Justin, "Do you believe that? After everything?"

Vincent strolled over and inserted himself between us. "He believes it. Who do you think ordered the background check? Who demanded that Rex pay you off? Who—?"

Tuning out the rest of his words, I stared into Justin's eyes, willing him to deny it, to give that small slice of hope in my heart that wasn't completely destroyed something to wish for.

Except the truth was there.

Written in unforgiving green eyes.

All of a sudden, I was exhausted. "I might have shared my body with Rex, but I gave you so much more. I gave you pieces of myself I've never let anyone else see—"

Vincent snorted.

"As for you," I said, turning to Justin's father. "I feel sorry for you."

He rolled his eyes and held up the folder before shoving it into my hands. "You forgot your check."

This time when I walked out of the kitchen, no one stopped me.

CHAPTER THIRTY

I was home long enough to change clothes and pack a bag. The road to town was washed out, but I wasn't interested in town.

Escape.

After texting my sister to let her know I was fine—and what a joke *that* was—I got in my car and drove.

I loved the ranch, but sometimes a girl wanted the city.

Denver was a five-hour drive, and I needed the quiet of the empty road, the distance from my real life.

I took the turnoff for the Red Rock Amphitheater almost without thinking. Melissa and I had come here many times during our teenage years, watching the crazy people exercise by running up and down the hundreds of steps, occasionally catching a concert for a band we'd scrimped and saved up to see.

But today I was there for the view.

Gravel flicked against the undercarriage of my car as I drove up the winding road. I hadn't realized I'd been driving without the radio on, sitting in silence for so long.

It suddenly was *too* quiet. Too lonely. Too smothering.

I parked and rested my head on the steering wheel.

Tears wouldn't come, and I wanted them too. Why couldn't I cry? I wanted to let out all this raging pain inside me, the hurt shredding my insides. I wanted to purge it all so I could just be numb.

Numb wasn't in my future.

A *rat-a-tat-tat* on my window made my head jerk up.

"Thought that was you," Esther said, her words muffled through the window. "Come help an old lady up these steps."

I blinked. Blinked again. Nope, she was still there.

And sometimes when you wanted to forget all that was your life, it crept back in anyway.

"Are you drunk?" she all but shouted. "That isn't good for the baby, you know."

Hurriedly, I pulled the handle and opened the door. My legs were a little unsteady after all the time in the car.

"Esther? What are you doing here?"

She wove her arm through mine and inclined her head toward the car behind us. "Millie and I took a little adventure to Denver."

I glanced in the car and noticed Millie in the passenger seat. She was one of Esther's cronies, a widow who had an affinity for cat sweaters and fanny packs. When she waved, I waved back.

"Millie wanted to stay in the car."

"Why?" Why come all this way and not see the sights? "She doesn't look tired." Actually, Millie looked a little flushed and her smile was on the wrong side of big.

Esther chuckled, patted my arm. "She's high, dear."

I stumbled.

Esther steadied me. "Millie wanted to try one of those pot brownies. Then she wanted to try three more."

"Oh."

Millie was seventy-five if she was a day. She was also currently steaming up the window of Esther's car and drawing smiley faces in the condensation.

Smiley faces. A pulse of pain and I hurried to shove the memory with Justin down.

"Do you do that often?" I asked, instead of focusing on the mess that was my life. Edibles were a hell of a lot more interesting than reliving my many mistakes.

"Do you mean do we come to Colorado to get high?"

"Uh." A pause. "Yeah?"

"Then, no. Not often anyway," Esther added, then grinned at what must have been a shocked expression on my face. "Dear, we might be old, but that doesn't mean we're just sitting at home watching *Wheel of Fortune*. In fact, Millie and I were bingeing on *Game of Thrones* last week. I want to be like that Sansa, feeding her husband to his own dogs. Or maybe Arya . . ."

And note to the universe: this elderly woman was way more hip than I was.

Quotes from *Black Beauty*, I was all over it.

Game of Thrones, not so much. I always ended up cringing when the horses were hurt, no matter that it was fake.

Esther prattled on about *GoT* as we walked up the staircase leading to the top of the amphitheater, not pausing to do important things liking breathing, even though I was puffing like a locomotive.

Also noted: she was in better shape. Thanks for that, universe. I really needed *that*.

"This view," Esther said on a sigh when we'd reached the top.

I nodded and felt *it*. The settling, the shifting inside me. All a person needed to do was stand on a mountain and stare out at the valley. Rolling hills, the city in the distance, and the biggest sky around. Miles and miles of it.

Everything would be okay. My heart would heal eventually, but it was better this way, better that Justin had broken my heart before I'd gotten too attached.

The hand on my cheek startled me, as did the thumb wiping the tear away.

I hadn't realized I'd been crying.

I should have. My chest rose and fell rapidly and it wasn't from physical exertion, not this time.

Esther slipped her arm around me and leaned against my side. She let me cry it out, let me pour all of the hurt onto the mantle of red rock and open sky. And when I'd finished making a spectacle of myself, she rubbed my back and stared silently forward.

"Sorry," I snuffled and wiped my eyes on my shoulder.

"Don't be. You looked like you could use a good cry."

My lips pressed together. "Yeah."

"That Roosevelt boy?"

I nodded.

Her pale blue eyes were kind. "Come on." She snagged my hand and tugged me toward one of the aisles, which had about twelve thousand steps leading down.

Which meant we'd have to come back up.

I balked at the top and Esther rolled her eyes. "Saddle up and go for *this* ride, Kelly. You'll feel better at the end." She squeezed my hand. "Plus, exercise is good for the baby."

"You're going for the baby offense?"

A lift of one slender shoulder. "Whatever works. And *that* is life advice you can take straight to the bank."

We walked down the stairs.

"What did he do?"

"He wants to pay me off and take the baby." I released a shuddering breath when Esther looked at me aghast. "I know. His father apparently is very rich and connected and . . . I don't know."

All I knew was that the baby was mine and I wouldn't give him or her up.

Another step down. Another. Another.

"The bastard."

"Yeah. And a rich one." Who was willing to throw ten million dollars around like it was nothing. "I never wanted any of this. I told Justin because I felt that Rex deserved to know, not because I was looking for a handout."

"I know, sweetie. These Roosevelts sound like Class A assholes."

A rusty, brittle laugh snuck free. "Yes. They are," I said, thinking of Vincent's insinuation that Justin had called me a whore and his not denying it.

Of course, I *had* slept with brothers—*twins*—and hadn't felt guilty about it.

So riddle me that, Hamilton, I thought.

We were at the bottom before Esther spoke again, her voice subdued. "I'm sorry I encouraged you to go after him, I didn't know that—"

"God." I gripped her hands. "Nothing anyone said influenced my decision to sleep with Justin. It was all me, all me wanting to see the horses, to see Stella, and then not being able to resist all the chemistry between us. I just thought that—" I sighed because I thought that after all we'd shared, after we'd opened up and confided our pasts, our fears, our hurts . . .

"Things would be different."

CHAPTER THIRTY-ONE

Justin stared at the slip of paper on his nightstand and understood in an instant just how critical a mistake he'd made.

The check he'd thought Kelly had taken was voided, her name crossed out and "Not on your life" scrawled over the top in angry black letters.

He traced the words then sank down on the bed that still smelled of Kelly.

Nothing was missing from his room. Or destroyed, for that matter.

Even the sweatshirt he'd loaned her was folded neatly on a chair.

If he'd been the one judged so horribly, he would have been tempted to trash the place.

But not Kelly. *Never* Kelly.

"Fuck me." Justin punched a pillow. "Idiot." Stood and paced, tried to come up with a plan.

FUBAR.

His life was quite literally *fucked up beyond all recognition.* And *he'd* done it.

With a muttered curse, he stood, went to his dresser, and began pulling out clothes. He had to fix this. Even if Kelly didn't forgive him, she had to know that he didn't think she was a whore or a gold digger.

For a moment in that kitchen, he'd panicked. He'd seen that check in her hand and had remembered all the times he'd paid off Rex's women.

How they'd not cared about what Rex had done once they'd held a check for ten or twenty thousand in their hands.

How demands had disappeared. How the *women* had disappeared.

And Kelly had held a check worth a thousand times more than the others.

Which should have tipped him off immediately.

His father was the reigning king of the Roosevelt fortune, but he didn't throw that kind of money around.

It had been some kind of test. A sick one. A disgusting one.

One that was exactly like his father.

Shit. Forget clothes, he had to go after her *now*.

Justin shoved his feet into shoes and snatched up the check. Seconds later, he strode down the hall, past the kitchen, which was still riddled with the aftermath of the pancake fiasco, and into Rex's study.

His father was behind the desk and appeared to be going through the report Justin had been pulling together. It detailed all the little idiosyncrasies about the ranch. Rex was slumped in an armchair, legs spread, and he had a glass in his hand that was half-full with amber liquid even though it was barely ten in the morning.

"So you think this place can be profitable," Vincent said, without looking up.

It wasn't a question, and his father's voice was cool, professional.

Justin went from being pissed at himself to raging mad at the entirety of the male populace of the Roosevelt family.

"I think Kelly passed your test," he snapped, tossing the check at his father. It fluttered across the gleaming oak surface to land facedown.

Brows raised, Vincent flipped over the slip of paper. His eyes flicked to the words Kelly had written and one-half of his mouth curved.

But his father didn't deny that the whole thing *had* been a test and that knowledge made Justin's blood boil.

"What are you going to do?" Vincent asked, straightening before leaning back in the leather recliner, hands teepee'd over his chest in what Justin had always thought of as his father's classic businessman pose.

"I'm going to go after her."

A sigh. "It'll be a mistake."

Rex took that moment—precisely the wrong one as usual—to speak up. "I told you to offer her the horse instead."

Crack.

Justin had whirled, his fist connecting with Rex's jaw almost before he realized he was moving. And . . . *God*, it felt good. The decanter went flying out of Rex's hand, liquid spilling to the rug and coating the air with the bitter tang of whiskey.

"You're a fucking bastard."

"Tell me something I *don't* know," Rex said, cupping his face. "Do you think it's easy having a goddamned saint with a hero complex for a brother? Not only are you a fucking genius who goes to medical school at sixteen, but you join the military and risk your life? Then you've got to sweep in and *save the day* for me? Like I can't take care of my own shit?"

"You can't!"

"Because I've never been given the chance!" Rex shoved him. Hard.

Justin barely held his ground. "You've been given a dozen chances."

But his brother continued on, ranting and incapable of listening. It was trademark Rex. "Then you've got to poach on the one woman who I actually like—"

"You *fired* her! Just dismissed her from the job she loved. *After* you slept with her."

"I'm not the only one who dismissed her."

Which sapped Justin's anger in an instant. It was an uncomfortable feeling, knowing that Rex spoke the truth. He *had* dismissed Kelly, hadn't given her the benefit of the doubt, and had instead allowed old insecurities to well up.

"Are you both done?"

His teeth ground together at his father's condescending voice. He turned, opened his mouth—

"No."

Justin's head whipped around when Rex spoke. He saw the punch coming, but reacted too slowly.

Rex's fist collided with a crunching sound, the red haze of pain radiating out from his eye and all along his spine.

And it was on.

Justin launched himself at Rex.

"Boys! Stop!" Vince shouted.

Justin didn't stop, especially when Rex tried to knee him in a very sensitive location—it was just like his *dick* of a brother to go for the unsportsmanlike spot.

"You're a fucking joke," he spat and pinned his brother to the ground, a forearm to the throat. Blood dripped out of Rex's nose and one eye was already swelling.

Good. Because Justin's own eye hurt like a mother.

Rex choked and scrabbled at his arm, but Justin didn't release him. "You're a ridiculous man-child who wouldn't know a good thing if it hit him in the ass."

His brother didn't say anything, simply struggled against Justin's hold and when he couldn't get free, he pulled what Justin considered the trademark asshole move: Rex spat on him.

"Nothing more than a joke," he said and pressed his arm harder into Rex's throat, firmly enough so that Rex gagged before turning his head to wipe his face on his shoulder.

"That is—" Vincent began.

There was something off about his father's voice, a strange tenor that made Justin flick his eyes over . . .

. . . then leap to his feet when Vince wavered and grabbed at the corner of the desk, his hand on his chest.

Down his father went, tumbling like a pile of bricks.

Justin caught his head before it cracked against the leg of the desk, reached into his pocket, and pulled out his phone.

He tossed it to Rex. "Call 9-1-1."

CHAPTER THIRTY-TWO

"You look like hell," Henry said as I walked into his office Monday morning. He sat at his desk, going over the books or inventory or something similar that involved a lot of hair-pulling, if his mussed locks were any indication. My boss and friend was disheveled in the best way.

I just wished he had a woman in his life who appreciated it.

"I love you too." I tied my apron around my waist and stashed my purse in my locker. "How's your mom?"

He shrugged. "The same. Still too fiery for her own good. She wants you to come over for dinner."

"Okay. Tonight?"

"I'm supposed to hog-tie you, if need be."

"Not necessary." I smiled and it felt forced. "So long as she's making lasagna."

"Would she make anything else?"

"I think the question is . . . *can* she make anything else?"

"True." Henry stood and crossed over to me, dropping his hands on my shoulders. He stared into my eyes for a long moment then sighed.

When he tugged me into his arms, I didn't protest. His hugs were pretty damned good.

Warm. Comfortable.

Safe.

"Sure you still want to turn me down?" he asked, breath puffing against my hair.

It was tempting to jump at Henry's offer, and he must have sensed my desire, because he gripped my arms and held me away from him, bending slightly to meet my eyes.

"Kel?"

I shook my head.

"We could be good together."

I shored up my spine and stepped out of his embrace. Henry deserved better. That was the bottom line. No matter what I was going through—broken hearts, pish—*he* deserved more.

More than friendship. More than affection. More than sisterly love.

"You'll be a good uncle."

Henry went still and I wasn't so self-absorbed that I didn't see the glimmer of relief cross his face. "Yeah?"

"Yeah."

"Also. This just in. I'm swearing off men for a bit."

And by a bit, I meant forever.

He chucked me under the chin. "You'll be okay."

"Of course I will."

Neither of us acknowledged the fact that my voice didn't sound very convincing.

———

TABLES WERE WAITED. I was appropriately chipper, and if customers were nicer to me than normal, it was probably because everyone in town already knew I'd had my heart broken by two Roosevelt brothers.

Skill, I had.

And, yay for me, every time the door opened, I was unable to squelch the hope that Justin would be standing there, flowers in hand, public apology on his lips.

Obviously, I was ridiculous. Stupid.

But sometimes there isn't a cure for stupid.

Sighing, I hoisted a tray and ignored the twinge of pain from my ribs protesting the movement. I was only five days out from the injury and though I was taking it easy, I wasn't healed enough to be free of all physical reminders of the accident.

Then there was the fact that I hadn't been to the ranch in two days.

I missed being there. My heart always a bit emptier without Stella and the other horses nearby.

But it wasn't *my* ranch. They weren't *my* horses.

And I wasn't glutton for punishment.

Besides, it wasn't like Justin had come crawling into town.

"Here."

Rob, Melissa's husband, came up behind me and snagged the tray from my hands. He was in full police uniform, duty belt loaded up, and it was easy to see what had attracted my sister to him. Charisma, confidence, and a uniform. It was a deadly trifecta to the female heart.

"Your sister is freaking out."

I raised a brow. "Is this a new development?"

Melissa wasn't exactly known for being even-keeled.

"She's worried she hurt your feelings."

I grabbed a stack of napkins and nodded toward the front of the restaurant. "For Esther," I said, pointing to the elderly woman's table. "And she didn't. I'm just . . . trying to cope, I guess."

Rob was quiet as we dropped the plate at Esther's table and I got everything set just as she liked it, which today included a wink and butt-pat for Rob being the "sexiest waiter I've ever had the pleasure of being served by."

He deftly stepped out of the way before it became more than a pat. "Thank you, ma'am."

"See you Wednesday!" she called as he started to follow me into the kitchen.

Rob stopped, sighed. "You promised me you wouldn't call the department any longer unless it was an emergency."

"It will be," Esther replied, eyes sliding down then back up. Slowly. Her gaze drifted to me and she grinned before mouthing, "Man candy" or at least that's what I thought she'd said.

Which basically sealed the deal. She was way cooler than me.

And also . . . kind of predatory.

"She do that a lot?" I murmured.

"Wednesday, police. Friday, fire department," he gritted out, setting the tray on the stack we had in the kitchen.

I snorted. There was no other reasonable reaction. Esther was awesome, and I hoped I would be as ballsy as her when I grew up.

"It gives you something to do, I guess."

He rolled his eyes. "Trust me, I've got plenty to do without being called to Esther's house to fix her leaking sink, or retrieve her hearing aids from beneath her couch, or to see if there was a burglar in her crawl space—"

I couldn't help but notice that all the tasks involved Rob bending over.

"She's probably lonely. I bet Melissa would invite her to dinner." I couldn't help adding, "And maybe seeing you without the uniform would help."

"Doubt it." He smiled. "But yes, that's a good idea. Now stop trying to distract me." He fixed me with a stare that made my inner rule follower want to sit down, shut up, and spill my guts.

"Put that away," I said, waving my hands at him.

"*What* away?"

I swept my hands up and down. "All of it." The uniform, the magnetism, the—

Rob crossed his arms.

Ugh. "I said put it away, not add to it. Enough of the cop-ness, you're too good at it."

That got his mouth curling upward. "Yes, I am. Now spill."

I sighed and leaned back against the counter. "I'm not mad at Melissa. Today is literally the first day I made it into town. The roads, you know."

"I do know about the roads, since I removed the barricades this morning." A pause. "But that wasn't my question, and you know it."

Unfortunately, that was true.

"I'm not mad. I'm not!" I added when he snorted. "This has nothing to do with Melissa. I've answered her calls, texted her back. I'll go and see her today. It's just—"

My voice cracked.

It was just . . . that I was heartsick.

"Aw, crap, Kel. I'm sorry. I shouldn't have pushed." Rob put an arm around me.

I pulled free, took a deep breath. "Don't. My hormones are bad enough right now. It's not your fault, but if you start being comforting I'll be blubbering all over your pretty uniform."

A shrug, a small smile. "Why do you think it's black? Hides the stains better." He tugged me in for a hug.

That was it for me. The tears broke the dam, and I sobbed all over Rob's shirt.

I wished I could blame it on hormones.

But Rob had been with Melissa long enough to know that sometimes a girl just needed to cry it out. He gave me that and a little privacy to go with it, tugging me down the hall into Henry's office when the other waitress on shift that day came into the kitchen to get her plates.

"M-m-my t-tables," I said when he'd closed the door.

"Henry's got ya."

And so I cried, wishing the whole time that it were in a different set of arms.

Wishing that things were different.

Knowing they couldn't be.

Rob held on until I pushed back. I'd barely sucked in a breath before he was handing me a tissue, a bottle of water, and a cold pack.

The last startled a laugh out of me.

"What can I say? I'm prepared."

"You are." A deep breath. "Thanks."

He waved that away. "Just go and see your sister, okay?" he said and tugged on the end of my ponytail. "For yourself just as much as her."

I nodded. "Okay."

"I've met Justin a few times," he said, pausing in the door. "And for what it's worth, I think he's a good guy."

He was. Unfortunately. I think it might hurt less if I could have chalked it all up to him being like Rex.

"He hurt me."

Rob grimaced. "Which makes me want to tase him in the balls. But, Kel, sometimes we men are scared too. Even when we seem tough on the outside." Rob put his hands up. "That is *not* an excuse for his behavior, since I'm sure he was a dick and doesn't deserve you. Only insight. In case there might be something there."

"I—" My words caught in my throat. "I don't know if I can do that again. Make myself so vulnerable. It was so new and yet I feel like my insides were shredded."

"I'm sorry, sweetheart."

"Me too." But also maybe a little glad that if it had to happen, it was early on.

Before I'd gotten even more attached.

Look at me finding a positive and making progress.

Woohoo. Go team.

"Be brave," Rob said and left, muttering something under his breath that sounded decidedly like, "I'm definitely tasing him in the balls."

CHAPTER THIRTY-THREE

I drove up to Melissa and Rob's house after work and had barely gotten out of my car before my sister was running out the front door.

She hugged me tight and sniffed hard.

"Okay, drama queen," I said. "Chill out and take me inside. I need something to eat."

It didn't matter that I'd already had my lunch break, that it was four o'clock and I was supposed to meet Henry for dinner at six.

Nothing saved my sister like cooking or cleaning. Give her a task to channel all that excess energy, and she was better off.

Kind of like training a horse. Or a dog.

Now *that* was an analogy that she definitely wouldn't like.

"Okay I'll make you a salad, all those leafy greens are good for the baby's brain," she said, tugging me into the house before leaving me to raid the fridge.

I wrinkled my nose at the bag of romaine lettuce and steeled myself to eat whatever she made. It would be good, I knew that, but when I'd asked her to feed me, I'd been thinking more of chocolate chip cookies and less about amino acids.

"I haven't forgotten dessert," Melissa said. "You just have to eat your veggies first."

"And we've gone back fifteen years," I quipped.

She huffed out a laugh as she retrieved a mason jar from the cupboard and added olive oil, vinegar, salt, and pepper. Then she put the lid on and shook it.

"Did you just really make your own salad dressing in a mason jar?"

A smirking smile. "It's not that hard."

"You're ridiculous . . ." Her shoulders stiffened. "And also ridiculously impressive. I love you, sissy."

The closest I got to making my own dressing was buying a bottle of ranch from the grocery store.

Melissa turned and her eyes were wet. "You haven't called me that in years."

Because I'd been so wrapped up in all I'd lost that I hadn't thought about anyone else. Well, that was going to change.

I hugged her tight. "Thank you for being awesome."

She sniffed and pulled free. "It's a skill." Her hands were moving again, placing the lettuce on a cutting board and slicing it rapidly into perfect pieces.

"I could teach you."

It was a tentative statement. My sister already expected me to turn her down.

"Okay," I said instead, surprising both myself and Melissa.

Normally, I'd poo-poo the idea out of hand. I didn't have time for mason jars and Pinterest successes—okay, *fails*.

I was *busy*.

But it wasn't all about me. Not any longer.

I was also going to be a mom, and moms needed to know how to make things. I couldn't just call on Melissa every time Jelly Bean was hungry.

Yeah, I got that the little grapefruit inside me was a long ways away from eating a salad, but shouldn't I be able to do these things?

Even if it introduced mason jars to my life?

Cooking. Making a Halloween costume.

Turning a cold, impersonal house into a home.

That was on me.

"Really?"

I nodded. "Yeah, really."

A tear slid down her cheek and I groaned.

"But only if you're not blubbering around. You sure you're not the pregnant one, sissy?"

She choked out a laugh. "Believe me, that ship has sailed. I'm just so happy."

"That you get to teach me how to use mason jars to store something other than horse tack?" I smirked. "Or because you've perfected your Miss America impersonation?"

"Shut up, you." But Melissa wiped her cheeks. "Grab a jar and let's get to work."

She showed me how to make the dressing, how to properly hold a knife, even the easiest way to chop up the head of lettuce.

My sister was clear, informative, and concise. And impressive. I couldn't forget impressive.

"Why have I never let you teach me how to cook before?" I asked as we sat at the kitchen table, jars in hand.

"Same reason I never asked you to teach me how to ride a horse before, I guess." Melissa shrugged. "I kind of felt that if I showed interest, it was taking something away from you. Like I'd never be as good as you, so what was the point?"

I froze, fork stabbed into the salad. Because—holy cape, Batman—that was exactly how I'd felt. "We are seriously screwed up."

"Agreed." A beat before Melissa's eyes took on a mischievous glint. "I blame Mom."

I snorted. "I like this strategy."

"You heard about hubby number ninety-seven?"

"Yeah. He's the *one*," I said, imitating my mother's voice.

Melissa speared a mouthful of salad. "Apparently."

I took a tentative bite and discovered jarred food wasn't all bad. "Good?"

"Yeah," I said. "You really should have a blog."

She glanced down at her lap. "I started one."

"What? That's so cool." I pulled out my phone. "Let me see."

My sister opened her blog's website and Facebook page and after ooing and ahhing over the videos, recipes, and pictures, we demolished a plate of brownies she'd had hidden away somewhere.

"Where did these come from?" I asked.

"Every woman has to have secrets."

I laughed before sighing. "Oh, sissy, what am I going to do?"

Melissa popped a cherry tomato into her mouth and chewed. "Just the same as you always do. Put one foot in front of the other."

"What if my legs can't hold me up?"

"Then you crawl."

———

IT SEEMED that all I was doing that day was eating. I sat on the back porch of Henry's mother's house with a plate of lasagna and garlic bread on my lap.

The air had a slight bite of cold, telling me that fall was just around the corner, and I was finally feeling like myself.

Well not like myself, exactly.

Changed.

But perhaps not for the worse.

Henry sat next to me as his mom, Catherine, bustled about her kitchen. She was a whirlwind, a friend, another person I'd kept at a distance when I'd been forced to leave college and return home.

Early twenty-somethings could be really stupid, and I wasn't an exception.

"How's the restaurant—"

"Can you grab the big pot down from the cupboard?" Catherine called from inside the house.

Henry pushed to his feet with a sigh. "This is why I need to move out."

"Besides the fact that she cooks and cleans and folds your tighty-whities?"

"They're black, and I definitely wash them myself."

I laughed. "I know and"—I inclined my head toward the house—"she seems to be feeling well enough for you to find your own place."

"Yeah. Except then she'd be alone."

"I don't mind being alone," Catherine said, pushing through the screen door. "Sometimes I just wish I were a little taller." She shot her son a pointed look. "Henry, that pot?"

I bit back a smile. The unreachable—and nonexistent—pot in the back of the tall cupboard had always been Catherine's tactic at getting the men to leave us alone for *girl* talk.

"I am so going to reorganize this kitchen so it makes sense," he grumbled.

"My house. My kitchen. My cupboards," she all but sang as Henry went inside.

"Never fails," I murmured.

Her mouth curved. "What are the kids saying nowadays? Hashtag truth?"

I grimaced, scraped up the last bite of lasagna from the plate. It was seriously delicious . . . and also the one thing Catherine could cook. "Something like that."

There was a bang and a crash from inside the house, and Catherine smothered a giggle.

"How is it that they never catch on?" I asked, amused myself.

Henry's mom's eyes went a little sad. "Like father, like son."

"I'm sorry." I touched her hand. "How are you doing with everything?"

"Better." She shook her head. "No, scratch that. I've finally pulled my head out of my you-know-what. Enough to know that you turned Henry down when he asked you to marry him."

Crap. I winced.

"It's just that—"

"No. You misunderstand me, honey." Catherine patted my knee. "Thank you for saying no."

The plate almost toppled from my lap. "Uhh . . ."

"Henry loves you. You both have been inseparable since your sandbox days, but—no offense—he doesn't *love* you."

"I know." Because I felt the same about him. I'd do just about anything for my best friend, except take away his chance to find the right woman to love him the *right* way.

No matter how scared he was of another broken heart.

"You've always been a strong girl," Catherine said. "When your mother sold your horse and spent your student loan money, I saw you bend, bend so far that you were almost on the ground. But you didn't break, honey. And I'm proud of you for that."

I swallowed hard, the memory of the betrayal painful despite how much time had passed. The worst of it was that my mother still didn't think she'd done anything wrong.

My scholarship would have paid for tuition, but I'd taken out the loans for housing and books and to board and feed Lexy—the horse I'd saved and scrimped and mowed lawns and delivered newspapers and worked on the ranch to pay for.

I'd made the critical mistake of having my mother co-sign the agreement when they'd required someone over the age of eighteen . . . and I'd paid dearly for it.

She sold Lexy and drained my bank account because her husband at the time had wanted to go on a vacation to Bermuda.

Bermuda.

And without Lexy, without *money*, how was I supposed to go on? It took years to bond with a horse—to truly become "one" enough to compete effectively—and I couldn't afford to take out more loans.

"There wasn't anything to be done about it," I said. "Lexy was gone, and I couldn't afford to buy her back. The money was spent."

Catherine gave me a sad smile. "I never wished to be rich more than that day."

"You and me both," I said with a rueful laugh. "Even Melissa and Rob offered to borrow against their retirement." I hadn't let them, of course. Not as a young family just starting out, not with my nephew on the way.

"They're good people."

"Yes, they are." I met her eyes. "And so are you."

Catherine looked away, but I hoped she would take what I said to heart. She and Brad, her husband, and Henry had kept me sane during my school years. They had no blame in any of this.

Eventually, I'd struck a deal to work on the ranch for the previous owner and to put all my wages toward the purchase of Stella.

I'd almost been there too.

But then old Mr. Johnson had died, and though Rex had promised to follow through on the agreement when he'd purchased the ranch, that was clearly going to be out of the picture now.

"I'm sorry I wasn't there for you, Kelly." Catherine sighed, rubbed a hand across her forehead. "I made so many mistakes when Brad died, not the least of which was allowing Henry to move home."

"You were devastated. It's understandable."

"It's not understandable to ruin my son's life."

"But it's not your fault your husband had a heart attack—"

Catherine took my empty plate and set it on the table. "I know that. Trouble was, that wasn't the only thing I have to feel guilty about. I should have sold the restaurant, shouldn't have let Henry move home. He had opportunities in New York he'll never get back."

"He'll make new opportunities. He wanted to be here for you—"

Catherine placed a hand on my belly. "I think you already understand that a mother has to be the one to make sacrifices for her child, not the other way around."

I blinked as emotion swelled within me, and I suddenly understood her pain and regret with crystal clarity.

"What do you want for this little one in life?" she asked softly.

Now that was a question and a half and as such, I tried to make a joke of it.

"For my child to enjoy your lasagna as much as I do."

"Kelly." It was a chastisement, a familiar, motherly one at that.

I dropped my head to her shoulder. "You know what my childhood was like. I felt like we were always struggling, always having to be strong and brave and never let on how bad things were at home. *And* I had Melissa looking out for me."

My sister had dealt with it all on her own even while taking care of me.

Catherine brushed back a strand of my hair. "I wish we'd stepped in sooner, sweetheart. Brad and I talked about it. Hell, everyone knew your mama wasn't fit to be a parent. But we worried if we reported her then we'd lose you both . . . and we loved you girls so much."

"I know. *We knew,*" I said. "This town takes care of its own."

I remembered food appearing in the freezer, grocery bags left on the porch. Free hot lunches at school. Catherine taking me out to buy clothes.

It had taken me awhile to understand that it was charity and not much longer than that to feel ashamed because we needed it, but looking through Catherine's lens of understanding—as an adult, a mother, a citizen who felt helpless—I finally understood.

She'd seen two girls struggling and hadn't ignored us. She'd done *something*. That something seemed inconsequential to her, but it had been critical for Melissa and me.

I can't imagine how we would have survived without it.

"My mother was never dangerous," I said, wanting to reassure her. "Just detached."

"Yes," Catherine said. "She was. Or rather *is*."

I was quiet for a moment, listening to Henry's mutterings in the kitchen as he continued his search for the nonexistent pan.

"I want my child to never be hungry," I said, so quietly I could barely hear my own words.

I felt her nod. "To not want for anything."

"No, I didn't say that." I lifted my head and glanced up at Henry's mom, earnest now. "Wanting isn't bad. They can *want* for a new PlayStation or designer jeans. I don't want her to *need* for anything. I want her to have so much love that she doesn't know life without it. I want her to have mint chocolate chip ice cream and bananas and whipped cream. I want her to have everything she needs but to still want. To strive. To—"

I broke off, my heart pounding.

Catherine tucked a strand of my hair behind my ear. "To what?"

"I want her to *want* enough so that she never gives up on her dreams like I did. So that she fights for them tooth and nail, if necessary."

"I have the feeling that you'll fight tooth and nail for *her*."

I had that feeling too.

Henry burst out the kitchen door. "I've taken the whole frickin' cabinet apart and can't find it anywhere. Are you sure the pan was in there?"

"No," Catherine said. Henry glared and I burst into giggles. After a beat, they both joined in.

And for that moment, sitting under the stars on a cool evening with friends—no, with *family*—and surrounded by laugher, everything seemed right in the world.

CHAPTER THIRTY-FOUR

Justin was functioning on about three hours of sleep . . . spread out over about three days, which meant he was seriously hurting.

And that wasn't even including the aches in his jaw and side from the fight with his brother.

Not that Rex was around. He'd disappeared the moment his father had been wheeled into the hospital and they'd hardly seen hide nor hare of him over the last seventy-two hours.

Knowing Rex, he was probably screwing some young nurse in a supply closet, à la *Grey's Anatomy*.

The good news was that Vince would live. The bad news was that his father needed triple bypass surgery and had apparently needed it for months.

But he'd been too busy for a *pesky* surgery.

Too busy to take care of himself.

"Mom would've been pissed," Justin murmured as his father slept on the bed, wires and tubing wrapped around his limbs like garland around a banister.

Lines were practically etched into the pale skin around his father's mouth and across his forehead. His hair was uncharacteristically mussed. He'd lost weight.

Vincent Roosevelt had never looked less like Justin's father than in that moment.

His father was a patient. A frightened, hurting patient whose future was uncertain.

One corner of his father's mouth turned up and his lids fluttered. After a moment, sharp emerald eyes met Justin's. "Yes, your mother would have been furious at me."

Justin's breath caught. He could literally count on one hand the amount of times his father had mentioned his mother in conversation since she'd passed.

"How's the pain?" he asked instead of latching on to the topic like he wanted to. His father was sick and didn't need the extra stress of reminiscing about his beloved wife.

Vince's eyes narrowed to slits, his lips pursed as though he'd sucked on a lemon. "Fine."

"Dad, you need to seriously consider doing the surgery—"

Rex strode through the door, a glimmer in his eyes that only came from taking advantage of unsuspecting females.

Justin had to give it to his brother, he had the stamina of a teenager.

"Dad! Heard you were awake from the nurse." He gave a wink as he crossed the room and sank into an empty chair, plunking his feet on the end of their father's bed. Vince winced but didn't verbally complain. "When are you springing this joint?"

"Later today."

Justin sat up. He thought they'd already nipped this nonsense in the bud. Vince needed surgery. Or he could die. *Literally* die. "Dad—"

"Great! Because I have this idea for an investment . . ."

Vince closed his eyes as Rex expounded on his latest get-rich-quick scheme. Justin watched as his brother heaped on the bullshit and found he literally couldn't listen to it for another second.

Shoving to his feet, he said, "I'll be back." And he didn't give a shit that he'd interrupted Rex.

"What?" his brother asked, rising also before crossing the room to get in Justin's face. "You too good to even be in my presence now?"

They'd existed in taut peace ever since their father's collapse and subsequent rush to the hospital. It had been successful mostly because Rex had been too shocked to talk much that first day and then he hadn't returned until the minute before.

Justin gripped the doorframe. "Fuck off, Rex. I'm too tired to even hear your voice."

Rex puffed up like a pissed off hen. "You're such an arrogant prick."

Justin rolled his eyes, but was conscious of the *beep-beep* of their dad's heart monitor speeding and kept his voice soft. Deadly, but soft. "You realize you're killing our father, don't you?"

Rex shoved his face into Justin's. "You realize you fucked my girl!"

What in the ever-loving hell?

"Is that what this is about?" Justin hissed. "Your *pride*?"

"It's about *betrayal*. It's about trying to take what's mine."

After counting mentally to ten, Justin—quite calmly, he was proud to say—said, "You dumped Kelly."

Rex threw his hands up. "That's not the point. I'm your brother and you went behind my back—"

The words triggered . . . understanding? Justin finally saw *everything* a hell of a lot clearer.

"You're right."

His brother sputtered. "Wh-what?"

"I get it now." Justin stared at a face that was as familiar as his own, eyes that held the pain of losing their mother in a car accident at too young an age.

Loss changed people in dramatically different ways.

"I broke the code." He shook his head, leaned back against the doorframe. "The way you left . . . I thought you didn't care about Kelly. But I was wrong, wasn't I?"

Rex stilled. "No." His jaw went tight. "She's nothing."

"She's *everything*."

The room went still, and Justin's eyes flicked over to where his father was watching them wearily.

"Mom was everything too. The glue that held us together, the piece that's left us all searching." He touched his chest. "School and the military." Pointed at Vince. "Money. Work." Rex. "Women. Success."

Pushing off the door, Justin began to pace. "I never understood before. I never looked at myself. Without Mom, we just fell apart."

Rex took a step back. "It's not about Mom."

"It *is*." Justin stopped. "Don't you see? We keep trying to fill our lives with what was missing and it's been here the whole time."

"*No*." Rex's face was pale. "This has nothing to do with Mom. She's gone and—"

"Kelly started to mean too much to you. That's why you ran."

His brother shook his head. "No. You want her, you have her. She doesn't mean anything to me."

"You're scared. I get that." Justin released a slow breath. He felt jittery, as though he'd just completed a mission and adrenaline was flooding his body.

Everything finally made sense.

"I'm freaked out too," he said. "Kelly is special. I've never felt this way about a woman before. It's like the sun is shrouded by clouds when she's not nearby. I know I should offer to big the bigger man, to step back and let you have her, but I can't. She's too important."

Rex's jaw tightened. "You realize that she's carrying my baby, right?"

"Which makes things complicated, but not impossible. You're my brother, my twin. I could never shut you out, but Rex, I also can't let Kelly go without a fight. I love her."

"Love." Rex sniffed. "We Roosevelts know nothing about love."

"We Roosevelts know *everything* about love," Justin said. "We love with our entire beings, with all of our soul."

"I care about Kelly—"

"But you don't love her," Justin said. "Not like I do. Not like she deserves."

When Rex didn't reply, Justin put a hand on his brother's shoulder. "Do you really want to put a child through a relationship that's not based on love? Can you really do that to your baby?"

Their parents had been devoted to one another. So much so that Vince had been devastated after their mother's death, had thrown himself into his businesses.

They'd lost him alongside their mom.

But when their mother had lived . . . their childhood had been filled with so much love and laughter and hugs it had nearly overflowed.

To say their lives had been idyllic was an understatement.

Which is why it had hurt them both so much to lose it, to lose her, to lose him.

"I know the baby isn't mine, but that doesn't stop me from already loving her with every piece of my heart."

"H-her?"

Justin dropped his arm, stepped back. "We haven't found out the gender yet, but I can't stop myself from picturing a girl with Kelly's eyes, her nose, that little dimple at the corner of her mouth."

"You really love her, don't you?"

"I do."

Rex took a long time to reply. "I think I could have loved her." A pause. "If I'd had the chance."

"She's special."

"Yes," he said and his eyes were distant, his mind somewhere else. "She is."

"I'll have the surgery."

Both brothers' eyes shot toward the hospital bed at the sound of Vince's voice. Justin, for one, had completely forgotten they were still in their father's hospital room.

Vince fixed Justin with a look. "I'll have the damn surgery, now get your ass out of here and get your woman. The good ones don't come around more than once in a lifetime."

Justin didn't argue. Without a look back, he walked out of the hospital.

———

EXCEPT KELLY WAS REMARKABLY difficult to track down.

She wasn't at home. Or work. Or the stables. He finally managed to get her sister's address and showed up at Melissa's home . . . only to be told by her police officer husband that he was trespassing.

Her phone was turned off. He'd even stalked her on Facebook and he hadn't been on that in well over a decade.

Justin was ready to risk the cop husband and chain himself to her sister's front porch when a little old lady showed up at the ranch.

She was maybe five feet with several inches of poofy white hair and a cat sweatshirt. Gemstone necklaces lined her throat, white sneakers shone almost as bright as the jewels.

A bony finger poked him in the chest with surprising strength. "Tomorrow. Five p.m. on the dot. I'll keep Kelly at my table. But don't be late." Another poke. "And if my sandwich is cold, you're buying me a new one."

Justin blinked, his mind reeling. "I love her."

"I know. And she loves you too." The woman's eyes softened slightly. "Hence my interference."

"If you can get me a chance to just talk to her," he said, "I'll buy you a sandwich every day for the rest of your life."

The old lady sniffed. "An easy thing to fulfill, since I'm already eighty-six and probably won't live much longer. Still, I'll take your statement in the spirit it was intended."

She turned and walked down the driveway, pausing at the door of a large beige sedan. "I shouldn't need to say it, but what the hell. Hurt her again and the last thing you see"—her foot tapped the front tire—"is a pair of these pinning your dying body to the road."

As she tore off down the driveway, Justin realized he'd just had his life threatened by an eighty-six year old woman in a cat sweater and didn't even know her name.

Instead of feeling violated, he grinned. He was starting to love small towns.

CHAPTER THIRTY-FIVE

I HEFTED the tray of Esther's food, balancing it before gathering the requisite extra napkins, two slices of lemon, and four-tonged fork because she didn't like the three-tonged version Henry now used at the restaurant.

The older woman knew what she liked, but I didn't mind. It was nice to think about inanities instead of the fact that my heart felt like it had been grinded against a cheese grater.

"You're off the clock, Kel!" Henry called from the kitchen.

I glanced up and saw that it was a minute after five in the evening. "I know. I'll finish up Esther and then head on out."

He nodded, hands working furiously as he sautéed something or other on the stove. "Don't clock out until you do."

Rolling my eyes—he was determined I make as much money as possible before the baby came—I pushed out the swinging door and walked into the restaurant.

Then immediately wanted to run right back into the kitchen and hide.

Like I'd been doing ever since I'd heard that Justin was looking for me.

He sat at Esther's table, the two of them deep in conversation that halted when they noticed me.

I should be a grownup and walk over there. Be polite and impersonal.

Screw that.

I should run. Fast and far.

Especially since just seeing Justin made me . . . hope.

Dammit. *He* made me hope and long and *yearn* for a second chance with him even though he'd been the one to throw me aside.

I took a step forward and—nope—I wasn't going to do it.

Swiveling, I started for the kitchen only to find Henry standing arms crossed in front of the door.

Really?

"Talk to him at least," he said softly. "You know you're miserable without him."

For God's sake. I released a breath. "Fine," I snapped and stomped to the table. But I didn't put the tray down.

Justin rose from the booth before I could get my good glare on, snagging the platter from my hands. "You shouldn't be carrying that. Not so soon after the accident."

"I-I—*fine*." I tossed my hair, slammed the lemon, fork, and napkins onto the table. "You can serve the food."

I started to turn away but didn't even get halfway around before the tray crashed to the floor. Esther's sandwich hit my toe and bounced off my shoes, splattering the laces with mayonnaise. A piece of lettuce fluttered down to land on my ankle, and her spare glass of water splashed against my socks.

Arms akimbo, jaw certainly dropped open, I stood there.

Finally, I found my voice. "What. The. Hell. Was. That?"

"It's not quite the impression you made the first time we met," Justin said, "but I think it got your attention."

"You're crazy."

"Maybe. But I'm also crazy in love with you."

Then he dropped to one knee. *One freaking knee.*

"Marry me, Kelly."

A girl could go twenty-six years without a marriage proposal then be practically inundated with them.

"Stand up," I hissed, conscious of the restaurant having gone silent, every eye avidly watching.

Justin didn't move, so I grabbed his arm and yanked hard. I was well aware that he was letting me move him, that if he'd wanted to stay in place he could have easily outmuscled me.

And somehow that slight act of bending, of giving into my wishes made a crack start to form in my armor.

Hell, who was I kidding?

I had no armor when it came to Justin.

Henry was still blocking the door to the kitchen when we approached and he didn't glance at me, only gave Justin a fierce look and said, "You and I are having words when Kelly is done with you."

Justin nodded. "Understood."

I made a noise of disgust—*men, seriously!*—and shoved Henry out of the way. "I can fight my own battles—"

"But you shouldn't have to," they said simultaneously.

Which is when I realized precisely how much trouble I was in.

"You're buying me another sandwich," Esther said or rather shouted from her table.

Justin smiled and pulled out a wad of bills from his wallet. "Whatever she wants, as often as she wants."

Henry pocketed the cash, his expression approving. "You can use my office," he said and went back into the kitchen, presumably to fix Esther another sandwich.

"You make that boy court you," Esther called.

I released a shaky breath, forced my voice to be light. "I'm not even sure I'm going to let him get that close."

"If I had a man chasing me with a butt like that, I'd let him get as close as he wanted."

Justin snorted and even I had to chuckle when a chorus of feminine voices chimed in with their agreement.

I shook my head. "This town . . ."

"Is incredible."

There was no point in arguing. It *was* incredible and I loved living here.

What I didn't love was the entire populace speculating about every facet of my life.

But that was the trade off, wasn't it?

"Come on," Justin said and took my arm.

"Afraid I'm going to escape?" I quipped, ignoring how even the touch of his fingers against my bare skin felt incredible.

A shrug. "If you ran, I'd just come after you."

"Like you did before?" I shook off his arm and pushed through Henry's office door, critically aware of the fact that I hadn't seen Justin in days.

He stopped, shut the door, and leaned against it. "I was coming after you. At least until my dad had a heart attack."

I gasped. "I'm so sorry."

"He's okay. Or will be with surgery."

Guilt reared its ugly head and, dammit, I didn't want to feel guilty. I wasn't the one in the wrong here, I hadn't betrayed anyone and—

My hand flew to my belly. There was something . . . a fluttering . . . a twitch. Not pain, exactly but—

"What is it?" Justin asked, pushing off the door and dropping to his knees in front of me. This time it didn't unnerve me. It felt right.

"I-uh. I—" There is was again, a pulse, the lightest quivering. "I think it's the baby! Oh my God. The baby is moving."

Justin's hand covered mine, pressing my palm lightly into the rounded space just beneath my belly button. The feeling intensified and instinctively I knew.

It wasn't gas or cramps. It was my baby.

My eyes flicked down to Justin's, saw his were glassy with tears.

Our baby.

He might not be the biological father, but somehow through the craziness of the last weeks, he'd become something more.

He cared.

"Do you really love me?" I asked.

"Yes."

Not a beat of hesitation. A statement, unerring and unapologetic.

"I think I love you too."

Justin released a breath. "That's a good thing."

"You hurt me."

"I was scared . . . and beyond stupid. I would have been here sooner if my dad hadn't—"

I put my palm up, stopping his words. It was more important than ever for me to be in control.

Part of it was that I wanted to protect myself, that I couldn't just forget everything that had happened between Vince, Rex, Justin, and myself.

"If we're going to do this, I'll need time to trust you again."

"I understand."

I needed to retain some control because I'd grown. I wasn't the same person, the same girl who folded and accommodated and gave in.

A fighter.

I would fight for the baby growing inside my womb. I would fight for myself.

I would fight . . . for the things I wanted.

Which happened to include Justin.

"Does that mean you'll marry me?"

"No."

He blinked, stood. "No?"

"No." I lifted one shoulder, my mouth curving. "Well, okay. Probably I will. Eventually."

Justin bent, leaning over me, crowding me back against the desk. His emerald eyes were intense. "Eventually?"

His lips were a hairsbreadth away from mine.

I nodded. "Eventually."

A kiss that stole my breath, that seared my soul. His hands wove into my hair, knocking my ponytail askew as he pressed his body to mine.

I'd missed every hard, masculine, glorious inch.

When he released me, I made a noise of protest, a shameless murmur that I coupled with wrapping my arms around him to try to drag him back down.

He resisted. "Marry me."

"No." A beat. "Yes, but not any time soon."

We locked stares. His was frustrated, and I wondered what shone in mine. I wanted to get lost in the moment, to throw caution to the wind, but I'd done that already.

And been burned.

So if Justin and I were meant to be, we would take our time and truly discover that.

"I love you," I murmured.

His face softened. "I have more groveling to do."

A nod.

He laughed softly. "Noted." Calloused fingers tucked a strand of hair behind my ear. "But note that we Roosevelt men love hard and love for life. You're it for me, Kelly, and I'm not going anywhere."

I smiled, my heart swelling with hope. I hadn't any chance of keeping Justin out anyway and his words, his tone, his sincerity . . . well, he might as well have stitched himself directly to the organ.

I stretched up on tiptoe and kissed him.

No surprise that I quickly forgot about the fact that I was in Henry's office, that the entire restaurant was probably crowded in the hallway, listening in.

I opened my mouth and let him in, opened my soul to his. I forgot about hurt, forgot about the past.

It was time to think about the future.

Eventually my body needed oxygen, and I pulled away, my chest heaving, my legs practically jelly.

Justin cupped my cheek, his breathing not any steadier than mine. "So where do we go from here, sweetheart?"

I smiled and covered his hand with my own. "Now you're going to give me some of that courting that Esther demanded."

"Damn right I am." With a chuckle, he lowered his head again, and I couldn't help but think that our future had just been sealed with a kiss.

With laughter and a kiss.

Not a bad way to begin.

CHAPTER THIRTY-SIX

Justin drove the car carefully up the gravel road, acutely aware of Kelly and the baby—*their* baby—in the backseat.

Abigail Violet Roosevelt had been born on her exact due date, after a remarkably uneventful final five months of pregnancy, and a short, albeit not pain-free, labor.

Five months of happiness. Five months of the past slipping further away to where it should be . . . the past.

Sometimes he still missed his mom, would feel a pang that she wasn't there, that she couldn't meet Kelly or her grandchild, but overall he was content.

And madly in love.

If the guys he'd been in the military with could see him now, there'd be no shortage of teasing, and he didn't even care.

Not when Kelly had given him another chance.

Of course, she hadn't married him yet, but she *had* given Abby the Roosevelt name and moved in the month before, so Justin figured he was getting close to convincing her.

Either that or he was going to bring a minister to the house and guilt her into it.

Smiling, he parked, turned off the car, and carefully opened Kel's door.

"You've never been more beautiful," he said and kissed her before helping her out.

He lifted Abby's infant seat free of the car, amazed all over again at how small she was.

Tiny. Innocent. Beautiful like her mama.

Justin had never really understood the appeal of kids before he'd met Kelly. Oh, he'd imagined himself having them someday, but from the moment he'd seen Kelly, from the second he'd discovered she was pregnant, he'd felt a pull from the life growing within her.

That tug had only grown as the pregnancy progressed and now that Abby was safely delivered into the world, Justin's heart was full.

Kelly unlocked the door to the house and he carried Abby inside, setting the seat on the floor and carefully undoing the straps because he had to hold her.

"Justin?"

The tone of Kelly's voice made every nerve in his body stand on alert. "What is it?"

He turned and saw a manila envelope and his heart sank. *Shit.* What had Rex and his father done now?

Vince had been staying at the house, recuperating until a few weeks before when he'd flown out to give Justin and Kelly some *space* as he'd called it. Rex had been his usual self, popping in for a few days before disappearing just as quickly.

All had seemed well, but then again . . . manila envelopes didn't exactly have a great track record in his family.

Cradling Abby, he crossed to Kelly and glanced down at the papers.

For a moment, his eyes wouldn't process the words on them.

He blinked. Read again. And his heart threatened to burst.

Rex. *Rex* had done perhaps the first unselfish thing in his life.

"These are relinquishing his parental rights," Kelly said, shocked. "I-uh. I don't know what to say."

Justin flipped the top sheet aside. "And for me to adopt Abby."

She gasped. "You'd do that?"

"Are you kidding me? I've been *dying* to do that."

Her eyes welled and tears spilled down her cheeks. "I love you."

Keeping one hand behind Abby's head, Justin bent and kissed Kelly. "I love you too. But I have to say that Rex has once again stolen the show."

Her brows pulled together in the most adorable little frown that he wanted to smooth away. "Show? Stolen?"

Justin smiled. "Well, maybe not stole, but he definitely outdid me. Here. I wanted to give you this sooner but, considering everything, it seemed more appropriate after Abby was here."

He handed her an envelope—not manila.

"Justin?"

"Open it."

Inside were papers for ownership of Stella.

Kelly peeled back the flap and clapped a hand to her chest. "Is this real?"

Justin nodded. "It's *really* real."

The most beatific smile crossed Kelly's face and she gently slid her arms around his waist, conscious of not jostling Abby.

Then she said the best thing ever.

"Oh, I'm *so* marrying you."

HEARTBREAK AT
ROOSEVELT RANCH

CHAPTER ONE

I STRAIGHTENED from putting the last plate into the dishwasher and stretched for a towel to wipe my hands. I was exhausted after twenty-four straight hours with the kids, and Rob still wasn't home. Not to mention, I needed to make cupcakes for Max's school—and somehow do it without sugar.

So the ensuing crash upstairs was not welcome.

Dropping the towel, I whisper-sprinted up to the second floor—running on tiptoes while hopping, leaping, and skipping over every toy obstacle, creaky floorboard, and rogue crayon along the way.

The light was on in Max's room, and considering that I had made this trek a half dozen times in the last hour, I was out of patience.

"You need to go to sleep," I growled, throwing open the door, my fierce mom glare already in place.

Except the devil child *was* asleep.

He'd fallen out of bed, crashed onto an entire village of Legos—scattering them to hell and back—and was dead asleep.

My heart gave a little squeeze even as the logical part of me recognized the giant mess I'd be picking up tomorrow.

It was just that face.

A cupid's bow of bright pink lips, slightly parted, rosy cheeks, and mussed hair. The boy was cute, and it was hard to believe he was part of me, that he'd come from my body.

I clucked my tongue at myself, knowing I was being ridiculous and romantic and *Melissa-like* because I'd spent the day with Kelly and her toddler, Abby.

My baby sister had a baby. And a man. And was all grown up—

Oh God. There I went with the tears again.

Swiping a finger under each eye, I navigated the minefield of toys as I made my way over to Max. I gave an internal grunt as I lifted the little—or not so little, anymore—monkey and tucked him back into bed.

One hastily constructed barrier of pillows and blankets and stuffed Minecraft toys later, and I was heading back out of the room.

I flicked the light off, started to leave—

"Too dark, Mommy," he murmured.

A sigh. Back on it went. "Good night, sweetheart."

"Night."

This time I made it to the top of the stairs before a sound stopped me.

It wasn't the kids. No. This was more like . . . buzzing?

I cocked my head and listened, then made my way to my bedroom, a growing pile of toys in my arms as I went.

The door was open, and I walked inside, dumping the pile on the coverlet before stopping to pinpoint the sound.

I felt my pockets for my cell. Not even two days before, I'd scoured the house for my phone, it somehow having fallen out of my pocket, ending up under the dresser. It had taken darn near fifty calls and a search of the entire house before I'd found it.

Those locating apps were all well and good, but they couldn't tell a person which room in a house their phone was. Which meant the app, for my day-to-day exploits, was pretty much useless.

I hardly left home at all except for the kids' activities and school pickup or drop off.

Or if Rob needed something down at the station.

And that was fine. My place was at home. The kids needed me, Rob needed me. It was just that sometimes . . .

No. Don't get sidetracked.

My phone *was* in my pocket. The sound wasn't coming from beneath the dresser.

It was coming from the bed.

I peered under, saw nothing, and I was reaching for Rob's flashlight in his nightstand when I realized where exactly the noise was originating from.

My hand slid between the mattress and box spring, jumping a little when the object buzzed against my fingers.

"What—?" I pulled it out, saw it was an older-looking iPhone. Why was there—

Then I saw the texts. An entire screen worth of them.

And my heart froze solid.

I'm heading to the hotel.

Where are you?

Don't keep me waiting, honey.

I need you.

The question wasn't why Rob had hidden a phone under his side of the mattress. It was why someone named Celeste was calling him honey and telling *my* husband that she needed him.

Downstairs, I heard the garage door rumble open and close, the clink of Rob's keys on the kitchen counter. "Miss?" he called softly up the stairs.

My voice was gone, my throat tight. My eyes burned, and still, I held the phone. It wasn't until I heard him walking down the hall to the bedroom that I sprang into motion.

I shoved the phone back under the mattress and scooped up the toys.

Rob stopped short in the doorway. "Oh." He smiled. "I called you."

"Sorry, I was cleaning."

He touched my cheek, slid past me. "You don't have to do that."

"It's my job," I said brightly, and if it was too bright then what did it matter anyway?

My husband was moving toward the bathroom, already unbuttoning his shirt. "Is there a plate for me?"

I turned, saw he'd paused, and forced a smile. "Yup. I'll heat it up for you."

"Thanks, love."

"Of course." I walked out of the bedroom but didn't go downstairs.

Instead, I hesitated in the hall, silent and waiting.

And my gut tied itself into knots when I heard Rob's footfalls across the carpet, the slide of his hand beneath the mattress as he pulled out the phone.

CHAPTER TWO

"MOOOOOOOOOM!"

The camera in my hands jumped, and that perfect angle, the *perfect* highlight of the sun's rays coming through my kitchen window and traipsing across my gorgeous display of a salad—if I did say so myself—disappeared in a flash.

No pun intended.

Footsteps pounded across the floor overhead. *Eight* feet. From two kids and one dog. The trio was streaking across the hallway, preparing to hurtle themselves down the stairs.

Which meant I had approximately twelve seconds to get the shot before chaos descended.

Back up on my tiptoes, extending my arm precariously over the plate as I leaned—read: contorted—myself in such a way as to obtain that perfect angle without marring the photograph with something as egregious as my shadow.

Bang. Bang. Bang.

"Ow!" Allie. She'd just turned five and was a terror on two legs. "I'm telling Mom!"

"Almost there," I puffed.

"It was *your* fault." Max. My sweet boy. Now eight and not so little.

"Ruff!" The dog. The terror on *four* legs. Rocco was seven months old and sixty pounds of exuberant energy, potty accidents, and counter surfing.

But Rob loved the fluffball.

Rob.

My eyes burned.

The trio slid around the corner into the kitchen, Rocco colliding with the far wall.

His brakes weren't great yet.

With the group's appearance, the noise level in the room rose to deafening.

Click.

I checked the shot and breathed out a sigh of relief. Perfect.

Stepping down from the stool I'd been perched on, I stashed my camera carefully out of reach of canine and human troublemakers then stowed the plate in the fridge. Another taste test wouldn't hurt, just to perfect the recipe.

And really, I wasn't going to waste one crumb of that goat cheese. Not when it was so expensive and difficult to find in Nowhere, Utah.

Or rather, Darlington, Utah.

"Mom."

Max stood with his arms crossed. He was tall for his age with dark hair and eyes and the spitting image of Rob, a fact that made my bruised heart ache all the more.

Allie was like me: slender, tall, and blond with pale brown eyes and skin that never failed to burn in the sun.

We needed to invest in sunscreen stock. God knew we bought enough of the stuff.

Both kids were talking over each other, furious frowns pulling their brows down as they tried to prove their point . . . or, rather, ruin my eardrums by being the loudest.

Even Rocco chimed in with several well-timed barks.

I did what I always did in these situations.

I stood silently. And waited.

It never took long, I'd found. If I tried to raise my voice over theirs, tried to shout my way for quiet, like Rob did, nothing. He used his magical cop skills to reign tough over the kids—and dog, I thought, as Rocco eyed the countertop like it held a king's trove of treasure.

My voice didn't do that.

My glare did, however.

Rocco paused mid-leap and plunked his front paws back on the tile floor.

Max was the first human to stop contributing to the noise. Older and wiser, he was.

Allie went on for a few more beats before her eyes widened and her mouth clamped closed.

"Max, explain your side first."

"I was playing with my Legos, and Allie barged in and broke my set—"

"I did *not!*" Allie protested.

"It's not your turn to speak," I told her.

She huffed and crossed her arms.

"She broke my house, and I'll never be able to find all of the pieces, and I-I—" Tears welled in his brown eyes, and I had to steel my heart against those glistening orbs. He might be cute, but he was also smart.

Too smart for *my* good.

"Okay," I said. "Allie, your side."

"He took *my* Lego set, and I wanted to get the pieces back. It was my house, and he can't keep it."

"You let me borrow it!" Max said, indignant.

"I *want* it back."

"I—"

"You—"

I waited.

The second round took less time.

"What happens when you fight over toys?" I asked.

Two sets of eyes went wide. Rocco whined and lay down on the floor, burying his nose in his paws.

Max glanced at Allie. "How about you use my Legos and build your own house?"

Allie considered this. "And then when we're done we can switch back!"

Max nodded. "Okay."

They ran off, Rocco trailing their progress, leaving with as much noise as they'd entered the room.

"Ten minutes until bath time!" I called, but they were already out of earshot.

With a rueful smile, I pulled my plate from the fridge and a fork out of the drawer.

"You're sexy when you pull that stern glare out."

I shivered at the voice in my ear, the chest very close to my spine. My body knew my husband's on an intrinsic level, and so I didn't jump in surprise or shriek in fear.

Instead, I melted into his warmth, soaked up his scent.

"Hi, baby," he said with a soft kiss to the side of my neck.

"Hi, yourself." I turned, slipping carefully out of his embrace. Because even though I loved this man with every fiber of my being, he might not feel the same.

Text messages from another woman.

A hidden cell phone.

Sudden long hours away from his family.

Cheating.

There was a strong possibility that the man I loved was cheating on me.

CHAPTER THREE

The snoring was killing me.

Absolutely killing me.

I rolled to my side, plunked my pillow over my head, and . . . it did absolutely nothing to muffle the sound of chainsaws erupting from my husband's nose and mouth.

"Rob," I said and poked him. "Roll over."

"Sorry," he muttered as he turned to the other side and promptly fell right back asleep. The snoring stopped, but the breathing didn't.

The heavy and very *loud* breathing.

I blew out a sigh and stared at the darkened ceiling. I don't know why I bothered. It was the same thing every time. He snored; I woke up. He stopped and went back to sleep. I stayed awake.

It was mom brain. The moment I was even partially awake, my mind raced and I started listing all of the things I needed to do for the next day.

I forgot to pack a snack for Max tomorrow.

Allie needs to wear orange, not the purple shirt I'd set out for her.

Rocco needs to go to the vet for his last set of shots.

A new blog post had to be created, new recipes tested, photos taken. All while the kids were in school. And to complicate things, Allie was in kindergarten, which was only half a day, so I got to add two trips—there and back—to school because neither of their pickup or drop off schedules aligned. So my four free hours were really only three, and now we had a dog who needed to be walked as well.

I closed my eyes, my chest tightening, my respirations shallow.

I'd spent so much of the last few months feeling overwhelmed. And for a girl like me—a tightly strung perfectionist who struggled to cut loose—that was almost the kiss of death.

Unstrapped from a roller coaster that raced along the tracks, barely hanging on by my fingertips.

My eyes flashed open. There was no way I was going back to sleep now.

Carefully, I slid from beneath the comforter and slipped from the bed. Rocco wagged his tail in his crate, a little rap that had me shushing him as I navigated the shadows. I closed the bathroom door behind me. Only then did I flip on the light.

Which wasn't kind. Thank you, fluorescents.

The woman I saw in the mirror wasn't quite a stranger, but she didn't look like me.

Not exactly anyway.

She was older. Plainer. *Grayer*.

Gross.

Look. I got it, I know we're all supposed to be kind to ourselves, to love our wrinkles and gray hairs, but dammit, four o'clock allowed for some self-pity.

Okay?

I released a sigh. Not okay.

The problem with being a perfectionist is that it carried over to all parts of my life. My skin didn't glow enough, my stomach wasn't as flat as it had once been, my ass wasn't high and tight, my thighs jiggled—

And now *that* was enough self-hate for this time of day.

I glared at my pale brown eyes in the mirror, warning the inner haters to shut it before splashing water on my face and pulling a brush through my hair. I scrubbed my teeth, slapped on some deodorant, and then made my way into the closet.

My favorite stretchy skinny jeans were fresh out of the wash, and I wrestled my way into them, pairing the dark denim with a blue floral blouse and a stack of necklaces.

I snagged a pair of flats but wouldn't put them on until I was well away from the Sleeping Beauties. A swipe of mascara and a quick application of blush were the final touches I added before I turned off the bathroom light and waited for my eyes to readjust to the dark.

Rob was back to snoring when I crept through the bedroom. I shook my head and closed the door behind me, heading for the top of the stairs.

That was when I heard the first noise.

A moan. The rustling of bedclothes. I dropped my shoes and bolted for Allie's bedroom.

She began crying.

"Mom!"

I skirted the mess of toys on the floor, picking my way across with all the finesse of an American Ninja Warrior.

"What's wrong, honey?" I asked.

"I don't—"

I was already reaching for her when she exploded.

Okay, not exploded exactly. More like Poltergeist-vomited, all over me. It dripped down my hair, soaked into my blouse, my jeans, the carpet, and bedding.

Perfect. Just perfect.

Allie began crying in earnest, and I soothed her as I swept her into my arms. We made it to the bathroom in record time.

I set her down in front of the toilet, holding her hair back when she gagged again and again. "I'm sorry, honey," I said when she stopped. Then I wet a towel and wiped her face and neck. "Let's get you out of these clothes."

She was shaking, tears sliding down her cheeks. "I'm sorry, Mommy."

"Shh. Not your fault." I wrapped her in a towel and cuddled her close until she stopped shivering. "Let's get you a quick bath, and then I'll set you up on the couch, okay?"

"O-okay."

Fifteen minutes later she was in clean pajamas, wrapped in blankets, and tucked into the couch, a bucket within arm's reach.

I went back upstairs to strip the sheets and clean the carpet. Then I carried all of the dirty linens back down to the laundry room and tossed them in the washer. By now the vomit had mostly dried on my clothes and hair, and I was in desperate need of a shower.

Time would tell if this was the stomach bug plague or if Allie had just eaten something that didn't agree with her.

Would one fall? Or would they all?

I snorted quietly as I slipped back into the bedroom, only to be bowled over by Rocco, wagging tail and wriggly butt. Rob must have let him out. He sniffed the carpet, did a one-eighty.

Uh-oh, potty time.

"Come on," I said, opening the door.

He pushed past me and sprinted down the stairs. I hustled after him, not wanting him to wake up Allie, who'd finally fallen back asleep.

But I needn't have worried. He bypassed the living room completely and went straight to the back door. "Good boy," I told him and opened it just wide enough for him to slip out. The icy morning breeze shot through the gap, having the dual effect of kicking up the smell of puke on my person and cutting directly through my still-damp clothes.

I shivered. "Hurry up, dog."

Rocco took a few more minutes. It was too cold to leave him outside, young as he was. Of course, *he* was the one with the thick fur.

Finally, he was done and sprinted for the opening into the house.

Or rather, crashed into the door, since those brakes were still under training.

"Come on, goofy," I told him as I snagged his collar and corralled him past the sleeping Allie on the sofa.

I'd already lost count of the trips up and down the stairs and it wasn't even six yet. Who said my butt wasn't high and tight? At this rate, I'd be a Kardashian in no time. Rocco wriggled his way alongside me, not fighting when I stuck him back in his kennel. Though that was probably because I promised him breakfast after I'd showered.

The bathroom light shone through the crack in the bottom of the door, and the bed was empty.

That plus the absence of chainsaw sounds told me Rob was in the bathroom.

Who was the detective now? I thought with a smirk.

I crossed to the bathroom and opened the door.

Or tried to.

It was locked.

I frowned.

Tried again.

"Rob?" I knocked, tilted my head when I heard . . . was he talking to someone? "Rob?" I asked louder.

The sounds inside the bathroom cut off. After a pause, he called, "Miss?"

"The door is locked."

Another pause. Then footsteps. The locked *clicked* before the door swung open. Rob was wrapped in a towel, his chest bare and glittering with drops of water. Normally, I'd have been distracted by those little beads of liquid. Today I barely noticed because there was a mark on his neck.

A suspicious bruise on the base of his throat—

Where someone might have kissed him.

And that someone had not been me.

Rob smiled, but it looked strained. "Sorry, hon. Force of habit." He turned and walked into the closet, closing the door behind him.

I was still on the threshold, blinking after him, when the door popped back open and he stuck his head out. "You look cute, by the way."

Before I could stammer out a thanks, the door shut again.

Had he not noticed the puke? Or was he trying to be nice because it looked like I'd been put through the wringer?

Or perhaps most important of all, had I imagined the mark?

CHAPTER FOUR

As with most moms, my shower was short and cold.

Between Allie's bath, the laundry, and Rob's shower, all the hot water was gone. Again.

Which didn't normally bother me, except I was coated in dried puke, had to wash my hair, and it was approximately minus eight thousand degrees outside.

Okay, fine. I exaggerated.

But still.

I rushed the shower, hissing as the cold water streamed from my hair and down my back.

Rob came out of the closet just as I stepped out, shivering more violently than Allie had been an hour earlier. He wore a button-down shirt, tie, and slacks.

"You look nice," I said, unable to ignore the fact that the shirt covered his neck. Should I pull it down and confront him?

"Meeting with the chief today."

Darlington was too small for its own police force. Rob worked at the county sheriff's office. The bigger force meant more resources for our little group of towns and better coverage.

"What about?" I asked as I wrapped a towel around my head.

"A case I've been working on."

"What case?" I ran the towel up one leg, then the other. Rob's eyes followed the movement.

"Can't talk about it yet," he said. I frowned, but before I could press his answer—we always discussed his cases, if not in specifics then at least in generals—he went on, "When was the last time you had something besides a salad?"

I straightened, pulling the towel around my breasts. "What do you mean?"

"You're too thin, Miss."

"What?"

He crossed over to me, pulling the towel open and splaying one hand over my side.

My heart skipped a beat. Calloused fingers. Rough skin against smooth. I forgot about the bruise on his neck, about the phone and suspicions. I wanted his hand to move.

Up or down. I almost didn't care.

I *needed* him to touch me.

His head dropped next to mine, hot breath on my neck, my ear. "You need to eat more."

It took a second for the words to process. I stiffened, leaned back.

Not that it mattered since Rob had already stepped away.

"This isn't like college," I said. "I am eating."

He studied me for a long moment, dark eyes piercing, black hair slightly damp and hanging over his forehead.

I wanted to push the strands back, like I used to.

Instead, my throat tightened when he tugged the sides of my towel together, tucking the cotton sheet under each arm.

"Keep it that way," he said.

"I like salads." My tone was defensive, but then again so was his.

"Add some protein to them."

Eyes burning, I turned away. "Check on Allie before you leave, she woke up puking but is back asleep on the couch. I'll be down in a bit."

I walked into the closet and closed the door, leaned back against it.

We used to leave doors open, no barriers between us.

And now . . .

I was glad the wood was there.

———

THE HOUSE WAS quiet when I made my way downstairs, hair in a ponytail, jeans and blouse swapped for sweats and a T-shirt.

If Max was next on the plague patrol, I wanted to be prepared.

Rocco's crate had been empty when I'd gotten out of the bathroom, so I hustled to the back door, in case Rob had taken him outside to go potty and forgotten to let him back in.

I flicked on the floodlights and saw the yard was empty.

Hmm.

The pup was usually great about staying nearby and out of trouble.

He didn't go to the bathroom in the house—at least not too often anymore—and there wasn't any food out for him to snag off the counter. He also didn't chew anything except shoes, and we'd taken to keeping those in our closets so—

My flats. I'd left them at the top of the stairs when I'd gone to Allie. I ran up the steps and groaned.

One was missing.

It was always the left shoe.

I snagged the right one and ran back to the kitchen. No Rocco. He wasn't in the laundry or dining rooms either.

Which meant.

I walked into the living room and saw him, curled up like the cute demon he was, right at Allie's feet. Gnawing. On. My. Shoe.

When there were a half dozen chew toys scattered across the carpet.

I dropped my head back to look at the ceiling, counted to five, and snagged a rubber bone from the floor. His ears dropped when I approached, the sad, poor little puppy dog eyes in full force.

"I'm not letting you keep it," I muttered. "I don't care if it's ruined."

He whined and dropped his head to what had once been half of my favorite pair of flats. Brushed gray suede with turquoise bows.

"This," I said, and swapped it for the bone, "is your chew toy. Not my shoes."

Rocco whined again and gave me a pathetic look.

"I still love you."

His tailed tapped against the couch.

"A little."

He grumbled but buried his nose into the blankets and closed his eyes.

Shaking my head, I went into the kitchen and tossed the shoes in the trash. Then I called the sick line for school, leaving a message saying Allie would be out that day.

I moved the laundry around, pulled out my notebook of recipes, and had just opened my laptop when I heard a noise that made my gut churn.

Retching.

I ran into the living room, but Allie was still asleep.

Another trip up the stairs—*this* is why I was thin, freaking two-story houses—and found Max bent over the toilet.

I rubbed his back, gave him a cool cloth, and sat next to him.

He glanced up at me with bloodshot eyes. "I didn't make it, Mom," he said. "I'm sorry."

"In bed?"

A nod. "And the carpet."

I closed my eyes. Not even six-thirty and I was exhausted.

"I'm sorry," he said and his chin wobbled.

"Not your fault, buddy," I told him. "I'm sorry you're not feeling well." I handed him a cup of water to swish his mouth. Luckily he hadn't gotten puke on his clothes, since there wasn't any hot water. "Can you wait for a bath?"

He nodded.

"Okay. Let's get you settled downstairs."

"Can you carry me?"

This is why I was thin, Rob, I thought as I carried sixty pounds of kid down to the living room, before running back up to fetch blankets and a pillow. *Then* repeating the trip to bring the dirties to the laundry room and switch everything around.

I'd barely managed to get Max's carpet cleaned when I felt the swirling in my gut.

Oh God. I'd known I would fall eventually. I'd just hoped—

For what exactly? To be spared? For a miracle?

Those didn't happen to me. Not any longer, at any rate.

Moisture pooled in my mouth, my stomach rumbled. Dropping the cloth I was holding, I sprinted to the bathroom and barely made it to the toilet before I heaved.

The plague was upon me.

CHAPTER FIVE

Rob shrugged off his suit jacket the moment he walked into his office. His promotion to detective had been a great opportunity, something that he'd wanted for years.

Unfortunately, it came with the suit requirement.

He loosened his tie, undid the top button of his shirt, and logged into his computer.

Just after seven in the morning, the precinct was fairly quiet.

Which was just the way he liked it.

Fewer people, fewer distractions, a smaller risk of getting caught.

"Fuck," he muttered, grabbing the mouse and pulling up his email. He was waiting to hear back on a set of prints that had been discovered at a meth lab in Campbell, the next town over from Darlington.

Campbell, Darlington, and Douglasville formed the Tri-Hills community. Separate they were too small to each house decent fire and police departments. Together meant they had more resources and could afford better equipment and staffing.

But that also meant that he was dealing with crimes that Darlington itself didn't often experience.

Drugs were nearly nonexistent in his hometown. However, Campbell was more isolated and closer to the border of Colorado—which had legalized marijuana.

Consequently there was some spillover into their small Utah community.

Not that meth and pot were on the same level, but they had seen a rise in seemingly drug-related crimes—burglary, muggings, home invasions— in recent months.

Which meant there was a new player in town.

His job was to figure out how to take that person, or people, down.

Simple, that, he thought with a sigh. *If only it were easier than clearing his inbox.*

Rob had one hundred and sixty unread emails, all sent overnight, but none of them was the one he'd logged in to see.

He wanted answers, dammit. Especially since he'd seen those finger-prints with his own eyes . . . or the bruises created by their owner, anyway.

Angry purple marks marring the skin of a young girl who'd stared sightlessly up at the ceiling. Her skirt hiked up, her shirt torn, blood trick-ling from the corner of her mouth.

But it had been her bracelet that made him remember her. That made the case personal.

Strings of yarn woven together, knots sloppily tied.

He didn't know if a younger sibling had made it for her or a babysit-ting charge or if it was something totally different.

The trouble was that he couldn't get his own kids out of his mind.

He pictured Max, tongue poking out as he concentrated, carefully knotting yarn together. He imagined Allie picking colors—pink, pink, and more pink—to make a bracelet for Callie, their babysitter.

And then his mind swapped Callie for the girl in the house.

Rob blew out a breath and shoved up from his desk, his chair teetering then colliding against the wall with a *bang.*

"Hey."

The voice was soft, feminine, and sexy as hell.

Which meant he knew exactly who it was before he even glanced up from straightening the chair.

"Celeste," he murmured.

A flash of white teeth framed in lush fire engine red. Curves for days encased in the department's blues. Blond hair pulled into a perky ponytail.

Breasts. Ass. Hips. Waist.

This woman had it all.

Just not for him. He preferred his women thin and lithe, like his wife.

She closed the door, thrust out her breasts as she leaned back against it. "I need you."

"I'm busy," he said.

"Too busy for me?" Celeste pursed her lips in a pout.

"Yes."

She laughed.

Because apparently she liked a challenge.

Or wouldn't take no for an answer.

She strode forward like a model traversing a catwalk, all smoldering eyes and swaying hips.

Shit. Here they went. Again.

The chair slipped from his grip and bumped into his desk. The little frame standing next to his monitor rattled, fell forward.

His family's smiling faces disappeared.

Celeste crossed around his desk, drew his hands to her waist, and . . . rose on tiptoe.

He fended off her octopus arms then pushed her backward until the ass that the rest of the department drooled over was firmly seated in the chair in front of his desk.

"Spill it, Celeste."

She smiled and it was wide and predatory. "Want to hear about the case we're working together?"

Fuck. His. Life.

CHAPTER SIX

"I'm dying," I told Kelly into the phone.

"I'll come over," my sister said immediately. "Abby and I will distract the kids so you can get a break."

"No," I said. "We're on quarantine. Stomach bug. I don't want Abby to get sick."

"Oh no!" Kel said. "The kids picked up something from school?"

"Yup," I said. "And then me."

My sister groaned. "That sucks." A pause. "Anything I can do? I can pick stuff up from the store and leave it on the porch, prison style."

I shook my head but promptly stopped when it made a wave of dizziness blur my vision. "How is that prison style?" I asked, flopping back onto the couch cushions.

"I don't know—" A cry echoed through the airwaves. "Oh, that's Abby."

"Mom," Allie whined, suddenly appearing like whack-a-mole next to the couch arm. "I'm hungry."

I put one finger up, indicating that Allie needed to wait. "I think both of our kids are saying the same thing, albeit in different ways," I told my sister. "Thanks for the offer. I'll see you soon."

"Call me if you need anything—" Another angry cry interrupted her. "Love you. Bye!"

I hung up and closed my eyes for a moment, trying to summon the energy to move. The problem with being the last to get sick was that the first person to fall was usually recovered by then, and if patient zero was a kid . . .

Recovery time was seriously limited.

"Mooom!" Allie said. "I'm so, so, so, so, *so* hungry."

My lips twitched, and I opened my eyes. "Let's see what I can do about that, okay?"

We walked into the kitchen together, and I pulled a bottled sports drink out of the fridge, then some saltines from the pantry. I poured her a small glass and put a handful of crackers on a napkin.

"Start with this. You hold it down, and I'll make you something else, okay?"

"Okay," she said, spraying the table with a fine mist of cracker crumbs and spit, since she'd already gobbled down several of the bland squares.

I sank down in the chair opposite her, the sleeve of crackers in my hand. My stomach was not ready for anything, not even the cardboard-like snack.

Allie didn't seem to mind the taste, however. She pounded down the little meal and asked for more.

"Let's watch one episode of *Bubble Guppies*, and if you don't throw up then I'll make you dinner, okay?"

Brown eyes fixed me in place. "Mac and cheese," she said. "From the blue box."

I shuddered. It was a favorite of kids everywhere. Pasta and fake, powdery cheese that tasted like socks.

It was also probably the single meal that I had enough energy to make at that point in time.

"Deal," I said.

"Woohoo!" Allie streaked from the kitchen and launched herself onto the couch. "*Bubble Guppies* and mac and cheese!"

Max glanced up from his iPad—yes, they both had an iPad and don't judge, I'd bought them on sale last Black Friday. But they had literally paid for themselves that afternoon alone. "*Bubble Guppies* is stupid."

"Is not!"

"Is too."

Distraction was key when a parent was sick and alone.

"Max, pick a new app to download," I interrupted. "Allie, what episode?"

And with Rob working long hours—

"Really?" Max said. "I can?"

"I want the parade one," Allie said and danced around. "I love *Bubble Guppies*!"

"Pick one from your wish list," I told him, not wanting him to spend the entire episode deciding. "Allie, it's starting," I said after deftly scrolling through the On Demand program and choosing the correct episode.

"How about this one?"

I glanced at the price—$4.99—and grimaced. I hated paying for apps, let alone that much. Still, I really wanted twenty-three minutes of peace and quiet.

And so I caved.

Ten seconds later, it was downloading and I was closing my eyes on the couch.

"Mom! It's over!"

My eyes flew open. Why were my kids always shouting?

"Want to watch another one?" I asked, voice gravelly as I struggled to sit up.

"No," she said. "I'm hungry!"

My sigh was pathetic. I knew it was. It still didn't have any effect on my kids.

"I'm hungry too," Max announced.

"You still have to pass the puke test." I shoved myself up from the couch.

He giggled. "You said puke."

"Yup." I smiled and smacked a kiss on top of his head. "We've had a lot of puke all over the place today."

Wiry arms wrapped around my middle. "I love you, Mommy."

And my heart melted. "Come on," I said, hugging him back. "Let's go cook up some cardboard."

———

THE BED DIPPED, and I rolled over to see Rob sitting on the side of the bed.

"Is there anything for dinner?" he asked.

"Not today," I said. "We were all sick."

His dark brows pulled down. "You were? Why didn't you call me?"

"I texted you three times."

"You did? I didn't get them." He pulled out his cell and unlocked it. The little green box had a red bubble with a three in the upper right corner. He tapped it and, lo and behold, my messages were there.

Any chance you can come home early? The stomach plague has hit.

I'm feeling really lousy, could use some help.

So much puke. I need backup.

"Shit," he muttered.

I reached over him, tapped the lower case "i" on the right side of the screen, and swiped off the mute function.

"Maybe don't put your wife on Do Not Disturb?"

"Oh, I didn't realize—"

I sighed and flopped over to my side, facing away from him. My heart felt fragile, ready to shatter into a million pieces. I kept telling myself that *I* was crazy, that things were fine and we were going through a rough patch.

But . . .

This didn't feel like a rough patch. It felt like—

I bit my lip hard, stopping the thought before it could completely materialize.

We'd worked through tough times before. Every couple had ups and downs. What made us different was that we could talk to each other about anything.

Or we used to, anyway.

I turned my head so I could see him over my shoulder. "Not realizing things seems to be the theme with you lately, Rob. Can we talk about what's going on? It's not like you to be so detached."

Silence.

He sat six inches away from me, eyes on his phone, and he didn't even look at me.

He. Didn't. Look. At. Me.

In that moment, I felt ten years old again. Begging my mom to see me. To want me. To value me.

And in that moment, I hated my husband for making me feel that way.

I wasn't that little girl any longer. I knew my own worth. I—

Didn't beg for love. That came internally. I loved myself.

Because Rob had given me the strength to learn how.

His touch made me jump.

It was a gentle caress, one soft brush of his thumb beneath my eye to collect a drop of moisture I hadn't realized was there.

"Miss, I—"

His phone rang. He glanced down at it, and I held my breath, waiting for him, *wishing* he would decline it.

He didn't.

His finger swiped across the screen.

"Hello?" Rob said and walked from the room.

CHAPTER SEVEN

"Bye, Mom!" Max yelled the next day as he jumped out of the car and headed for his classroom.

"Love you!" I called through the open window.

"Love you, too!" he called back.

I smiled and pulled out of the drop-off line, soaking up the sentiment even as I recognized that the little boy I was raising wasn't so little anymore.

"You're next, Allie."

"Okay, Mom," she said, then went right back to humming the ABCs.

"Feeling all better?"

"Mmmhmm." A pause. "I miss Daddy."

"I know, honey," I said, even as my heart squeezed tightly. I missed her dad as well. "But he's working hard to keep everyone safe."

"From the bad guys?"

"Yup." I nodded, and when we stopped at a signal—one of five in the entire town—I met her eyes in the rearview mirror. "Daddy has an important job, but he loves us very much. Did you know he snuck in after you were asleep last night and tucked you in?"

She smiled, brown eyes widening. "He tucked Mr. Tails under my arm."

Mr. Tails was the rainbow stuffed cat Allie carried with her everywhere. She'd had it since she was a baby and though it was definitely tattered, she loved it.

Mr. Tails was also currently buckled into the seat next to Allie.

Safety first, in our family.

"He sure did, and he always puts your blankets just right, doesn't he?"

"Yup."

The light turned, and I pulled forward. "Should we sing a song before your school?"

"The Silly Pizza Song!"

I groaned. "Again?"

"Again!"

I laughed, but since this was our routine, the song was already cued up on my phone. I pressed play, and the song blared through the car's speakers.

We sang about crackers and candy and banana-topped pizza until it was time to drop Allie at school.

Back at home, I finished throwing the kids' sheets and blankets that remained from the previous day's Operation Plague into the washer before sitting down with my laptop and a cup of coffee in the kitchen. I pulled up my blog, replied to comments, checked that the next several posts were cued up to publish automatically, and wrote a quick check-in about the drama of the previous day.

At least being sick had the benefit of providing me blog material.

I shared my latest recipe video to Facebook, then a pretty and stylized shot of the finished product to Instagram.

When the business part was done, I finally got to do my favorite thing. Cook.

In honor of yesterday, I made soup.

Not standard-issue, bland chicken noodle soup, but hearty, filling, and a little-bit-spicy-sweet potato with rice, carrots, and kale chicken soup.

It was delicious, and I found myself sampling, then breaking down and heating up a loaf of homemade sourdough to go with it. I scooped up a large helping, buttered several slices of bread, and ate my first peaceful meal in what felt like an eternity.

Each bite brought something slightly different to my palate. The creaminess of the cooked sweet potatoes, a little explosion of brightness when parsley landed on my tongue. Salty, tangy, savory, the crunch of the sourdough's crust when I dipped it in the soup, and just a hint of sweetness when I got a bite with everything all at once.

I ate the entire bowl. Plus, half the loaf of sourdough.

My phone chimed as I was styling a bowl for photographs.

"Hello?" I answered, distracted as I sprinkled an artistic arrangement of crumbs next to the spoon. I'd taken a bite from one last slice—someone had to do the hard work—and placed it on a pretty blue plate next to the bowl of soup. That way I could link both recipes on my website.

"Miss!" My sister's panicked voice exploded through the airwaves.

My stomach clenched, mind reeling at what could have happened. Was Abby okay? "What is it?"

"I burned dinner!"

I laughed, relief coursing through me.

"It's not funny."

"Kel, you *always* burn dinner."

"Well, I have no backup plan and Rosa is on vacation."

"It's only one o'clock," I said, adjusting the angle of the bowl and spoon before snapping a few photos. "You've got hours. Order a pizza. Or defrost something from the freezer. I know Rosa stocked it for you."

Rosa was Kelly's husband's housekeeper. She'd been with the Roosevelt family since Justin was a child and was an awesome cook. She was also getting very close to retiring, which meant that those days were coming to an end.

"I can't," Kel said.

"Why not? Or have Justin bring something home."

Kel sighed. "He offered, and I got all mad."

I snorted. "Kel . . ."

"I know. I *know* I can't cook, but then he got all superior about having someone cater this, and I just lost it."

My phone between my ear and shoulder, I took a few more shots then put my camera down. "Cater what?"

"Justin has work people coming over tonight, and I—"

"Wanted to impress him?"

Kel huffed. "Yes."

"You know you already married him, right?"

I felt her eyes roll through the phone. "Doesn't mean I don't want to impress him."

Yeah. I knew the feeling.

"Okay, I have to grab the kids, but as long as you don't mind the monsters coming with me, I'll bring by some ingredients and we can cook together."

"Are they recovered?"

"We're more than twenty-four hours in the clear, but if you'd rather not risk Abby getting sick, I can just drop by some stuff for you to heat up."

And hopefully not burn.

"Hmm." Kel was quiet for a moment. "No, I'd probably ruin that too. If the kids were well enough to go to school, I'm sure they're good to come."

"Sure?" I asked.

"New mom jitters," Kelly said. "I'm sure."

"Okay." I did a little jig in the kitchen. I was going to cook for new people, and that made me happy. "How many and any allergies?"

"Six people including Justin and me, and, um . . ."

"You don't know about allergies?" I asked, filling in the pause.

"I didn't ask."

"Okay, *ask*. And then text me. I'll stop by the store on the way over."

We hung up, and I bustled around the kitchen, packing up the soup, downloading my photographs from the memory card and onto my laptop. I'd bring my camera with me, knowing this too would give me good material for a blog post.

How often did I cater events?

Never.

Not that cooking dinner for six people really counted, but I was excited for the chance to try out some new things.

I portioned the soup into containers and put them in the freezer before running out the door to pick Allie up from school.

"Did you have a nice day?" I asked while we meandered back to the car. We had thirty minutes before I had to get Max. Enough time to do . . . basically nothing.

"Uh-huh." A pause. "I'm hungry."

My lips twitched at the familiar exchange. She wouldn't dish on the details of school until she had a little food in her belly. "I've got a snack for you in the car."

"Yay!"

Hunger forgotten, or perhaps more acute, Allie picked up the pace and sprinted for the car.

Minivan.

It was a minivan.

I'd gotten to the point in my life where I drove a minivan.

Rolling my eyes at myself, I pushed a few buttons on the key fob to remotely start it and then opened the side door.

Minivan or not, those perks were good.

Allie found the thermal pack I'd put on the floor in front of her car seat and quickly unzipped it.

"Swatermfelon!" she shouted before shoving a piece into her mouth. "I rofe swatermfelon!"

Of course I had to translate that—"I love watermelon!"—since her mouth was full, but I knew my baby girl.

And she loved all fruit, most especially watermelon.

"We'll get Max, stop at the grocery store, then head for Aunt Kelly's, okay?"

Allie paused in her inhalation of the melon. "Did she burn something again?"

I laughed as I buckled her in. "What do you think?"

"Definitely."

CHAPTER EIGHT

"So what are we making again?" Kelly asked, her eyes wide as she surveyed the mass of bags on her kitchen counter.

"It's basically chicken, rice, and veggies," I said as I unpacked ingredients and began lining everything up.

"Oh."

"It's *fancy* chicken, rice, and veggies, okay?"

Kel sighed in relief. "Okay."

I peeked out the kitchen window, watching the kiddos play with Henry, who was Kel's best friend from high school. He was also a very good chef in his own right and worked at the local restaurant his family owned.

"You sure Henry doesn't mind watching Max and Allie?"

"Nope. He wanted some time away from the diner, and the kids are a good distraction."

I raised a brow at that very nondescript explanation. Kel put her hands up. "Not my story to tell."

"Hmm." I gathered the canvas shopping bags, folding them up and setting them on the counter. "And why didn't you hit him up to cook?"

"I did," Kelly said. "He wouldn't bail me out."

I bumped her shoulder, nodding at the sink so she could wash up. "I see how it is, I'm second best?"

"That's not—"

"Second best," I sing-songed, walking over to where Abby was stacking blocks in a playpen in the corner of the kitchen. It was shoved between the wall and a wood table and chairs, one of which looked a little lopsided. "Just like this chair," I said as I pushed it out of the way and smacked a kiss on Abby's head.

"Your eyes"—emerald green just like her daddy's—"are gorgeous."

The water turned off, and Kelly came over, drying her hands with a towel. "They are. I thought she might look like Rex, and then . . ."

"Justin is her dad, Kel. Not Rex." I put an arm around her shoulders. "You have the papers to prove it."

"I wish I hadn't—"

"You made a mistake, but you got something precious and valuable from it, yeah?"

Kel nodded, and I went for levity.

"Plus, it's good you chose to make a mistake with twins because it makes explanations a lot easier."

Kel had previously been in a relationship with Justin's twin, Rex, and had ended up pregnant and alone . . . at least until Justin had showed up in Darlington.

They'd hit a few bumps but had eventually figured it out. Or I'd thought so anyway.

"Are you unhappy?" I asked, taking in her pale face and the lines around her mouth. "You don't have to stay with—"

"I'm not unhappy," Kel said. "I'm freaked out."

Abby had been thoroughly entertained with her wooden blocks, but at the sound of her mom's worried voice extended her arms. "Up, mama."

"Why?" I asked as Kelly swept her from the playpen.

"I'm pregnant again."

I shrieked. "What?"

"I know." Kelly hugged Abby tightly before the little girl squirmed to be put down.

"But—but how?" I shook my head. "Okay, don't answer that." I crossed back to the kitchen island and began washing vegetables.

Kel giggled. "No details?"

I wrinkled my nose as I began chopping onions. "No, thanks."

My sister corralled Abby in the kitchen as I moved on to chopping carrots and lettuce. I peeled some potatoes, trimmed some asparagus, and then set all the veggies to the side. "So are we celebrating?"

"Justin doesn't know yet," she said, biting her lip. "I—uh . . . we moved so quickly with Abby and the wedding and now . . ."

I put the knife down. "That's not what has you worried." I fixed her with a glare. "Spill."

"What if he loves her less?" Kel asked. The question was quiet and almost drowned out by Abby's babbling of "Ma! Ma! Ma!"

"Oh, Kel." I crossed around the island and sat down on the floor in front of Abby. The sweet little girl crawled into my lap and tugged at my hair. "How could anyone not love her?"

"She's not his. Or not entirely anyway."

"Bullshit."

Kelly and Abby both stared up at me with wide eyes. I sent up a silent prayer that the little parrot wouldn't pick that moment to begin mimicking me.

Her first curse word courtesy of Aunt Melissa. Yeah, that would be awesome.

"Justin loves her. He loves you."

"But what if he thinks it's too soon."

"He won't."

Kel sighed and sat back onto her heels. "How do you know?"

I smiled. "I know."

"But *how*?"

I took my sister's face in my hands and turned it to the doorway, where Justin stood. His face was a little pale, his eyes a little wide, but he was grinning.

"Is it true?" he asked.

Kel bit her lip and nodded shyly.

Justin was across the room in a few short strides, scooping Abby up, and then pulling Kelly into his arms. "How are you feeling?" he asked fiercely.

"Fine. Not sick at all," Kelly said. "Or not yet anyway."

He smiled and hugged them tightly as I backed slowly away. I'd give them a few minutes before I went back and finished cooking dinner.

Justin's voice trailed after me as I slipped out onto the front porch. "I'm not going to call you an idiot, but what were you thinking? I love you both so, so much."

And, *ding*, that was the correct answer. Good job, Justin.

Henry and the kids were running like maniacs over the front lawn, tagging each other and then sprinting away, giggling and falling all over the place. Adorable little monkeys.

I slipped back inside, found the kitchen empty, and got back to work. The thought of another baby made me smile. I loved babies. They were so squishy and fluffy and smelled yummy.

Okay, I knew I was weird.

I didn't want another one for myself, but I did like the idea of being an auntie again.

Most of the perks but less of the work.

Smiling to myself, I got back to my own work. From what Kelly had told me, the clients were coming over at five thirty. I threw together a quick appetizer of brie, cranberries, and candied walnuts then sliced up and toasted another loaf of my sourdough bread, deciding that my sister owed me big time for parting with my favorite snack.

Maybe I'd put her on babysitting duty for the monsters. Rob and I hadn't had a date night since—

I couldn't remember.

Frowning, I sliced herbs and mixed them with butter, then pounded the chicken breasts until they were very thin. I spread the herb butter over the surface before rolling up each piece and searing it in a pan. It would give the chicken a little color—anemic-looking food did not taste yummy—and some nice texture.

And though I snapped pictures each step of the way, my mind was on autopilot. When *was* the last time I'd spent some time alone with my husband that wasn't a half hour on the couch before I fell asleep?

Years.

It had literally been years since I'd been on a date with Rob.

A knot loosened in my chest. Well, that was clearly the issue. We'd grown apart. But I could fix that. I could eliminate the distance between us, and we could go back . . . find ourselves again.

It was so simple.

We needed a date night.

I rolled my eyes. We needed more than a date night, but spending some time alone together would be the first step across that bridge. I would call Callie and set up a time in the next couple of weeks.

"Okay," I murmured, sliding the pan with the chicken into the oven to finish cooking. "I can do this."

We could get back on track. We *had* to. I glanced out the window at the little monsters now collapsed on the grass, pointing up at the clouds in the sky. I could picture their voices calling out the shapes, knew that I would do literally anything for them.

I could fix my marriage.

For them.

For me.

CHAPTER NINE

I'D JUST SAT down to my laptop after dropping the kiddos at school the next morning when my phone rang.

"Hello?" I answered without looking.

"You're a goddess."

My lips twitched at my sister's voice. "Tell me more."

Kelly laughed, but her voice was sincere. "Thank you, Miss. For bailing me out."

"And for writing a full page of instructions that even you couldn't mess up." I'd finished up the food, leaving it all to warm in the oven, before gathering the kiddos and scooting home.

"Hmpf," my sister said, then sighed. "Okay fine, it's true. And the MacAlisters loved your food. I was going to take credit for it all, but then I knew I'd have to attempt to replicate it and—" Abby shrieked in the background. "Hold on."

I listened to Kel gather up Abby, sounds muffled as she attempted to hold toddler and phone alike. When she came back on, she was panting.

"I—ouch. That's Mommy's hair, Abby-girl. I just want to—*ow*—tell your auntie something."

"Want to call me back later?" I asked as I went through some photographs from the previous night. "Oh, did you happen to take any pictures of the prepared plates? I forgot to take some."

A pause. "It wasn't on the instruction sheet."

I grinned, tapped a few keys on my laptop. "So that's a no. It's okay, I guess my mind was somewhere else."

"You could always make it again," my sister said, way too innocent.

"It'd be a real struggle, but I could be employed to make sure it didn't go to waste."

"Nice try," I said and glanced at the clock. I needed to get off the phone in the next couple of minutes. I was volunteering in Max's class in addition to my normal work stuff, and time was already tight. "What did you want to tell me?"

"Oh! So Tammy MacAlister is the wife of Justin's work colleague. I guess their fathers invested in the same tech start-up or something, and now the boys are trying to figure out if they want to put more capital into the business."

I struggled to prevent my eyes from glossing over. "Okay."

"But that's not the exciting thing," Kel said.

"What is the *exciting thing*?"

"Tammy works for that food channel. You know the one on TV with all the celebrity chefs, and she loved your food. Like, *loved* it. Raved about it." Kelly was talking fast, and my heart was pounding, blood swooshing past my ears as I tried to process what my sister was telling me. "And then I showed her your blog and Instagram—which damn, I didn't realize you had ten thousand followers, Miss! That's amazing."

I held my breath.

"Melissa?"

I released it, strived for a calm voice. "I'm here."

"She wants to meet you. She wants to run a camera test and see some more of your food and—"

"Holy arancini."

"I know—what?"

I collapsed back against my chair. "They're fried balls of rice. Italian. Super delicious." I waved my hand through the air. "Never mind that. How? *When*? I—"

"I told Tammy I would pass along your information to her if it was something you were interested in."

That gave me pause.

Okay, not really. Because *this*—a cooking show! Eek! It was something I'd always fantasized about, but had never believed was remotely possible.

"Yes, please," I said calmly.

"Can we squee now?" my sister asked.

"Oh my God," I said. "I hope so."

And then we squeed.

———

AFTER KELLY and I completed our squeal-fest and hung up, I fired off a quick text to Rob.

Call me when you can. I need to tell you something!

I settled in for the long haul, editing pictures, finding the perfect descriptive words for my soup recipe from yesterday. Of course, I shared a few more details of our recovery from the Plague—not too much, because it was a food blog, after all—but I did think my readers liked it when I let them in to my own life a little.

And the sick kids, dog eating my shoe, it was too real not to share. I purposely didn't say funny, either. It was too soon after the plague to be funny—

My poor shoes.

But I fully expected to be able to laugh about it all in approximately . . . eight and a half decades.

Snorting, I scheduled the post then moved on to selecting which photograph would look best on Instagram when my phone rang.

I lurched for it, thinking it could be Tammy and all my cooking show dreams, but it was Rob.

Which was almost as good.

"Hi!" I said. "I've got the best—"

Wind wove through the speaker, rattling against my eardrums. "Are the kids okay?"

I stiffened at the shortness in his voice. "They're fine. Why?"

"You said to call."

"I need to tell you something. I have really awesome news—"

A voice intruded on their conversation. "Sorry. You'll have to tell me later," Rob said. "I need to go."

"But—"

"I'm at work, Miss."

"Yeah." I paused, throat tightening, eyes tearing up.

"Bye."

Before I'd opened my mouth to reply in kind, he'd hung up.

My heart twisted, aching as though it had been stabbed. I tried to tell myself that his job was dangerous. Important. That my text had been ambiguous so he'd called right away.

Because he'd been worried. He cared.

But he hadn't asked about me.

And the voice on the other end of the phone, the one that had barely reached my ears over the wind and noise, was female.

CHAPTER TEN

Rob hung up the phone and glanced over at Celeste as he slipped back into the car. "Good?" he asked.

She clucked her tongue. "Wife calling when you're at work. So cliché."

No, he thought. What was cliché was his wife calling when he was with his *girlfriend*.

Fake girlfriend, but cliché nonetheless.

"Okay, so what do we know about this building?"

Celeste straightened, all traces of femininity vanishing from her voice as she began listing what the surveillance of the last few weeks had discovered.

Which, unfortunately, wasn't much.

"So we've been watching this place for weeks and haven't seen a single shipment come in or out? Haven't witnessed a deal?" He shook his head. "Why are we wasting our time here?"

She tapped a finger—complete with bright-red polish—to her lips. Melissa would never wear something so flashy. His wife wasn't about upkeep. She liked things simple and underdone.

Skirts with flowers. Lacy shirts. Jeans and flats mixed with the occasional pair of sweats.

No heels. Nothing ostentatious.

Not like Celeste.

Even in the department-required button-down and slacks, she oozed sex.

"They're doing something here," Celeste said. "I can feel it. I just don't know if they've moved operations because we're keeping an eye on things or if we haven't figured out all the moving parts yet."

"And our source says he got the drugs here?"

"Not exactly. He said that all his dealers dried up. Refused to sell to him again until he got clearance from the boss."

"And the boss was here."

Celeste nodded.

Rob sighed and stared out the windshield at the nondescript warehouse on the outskirts of Darlington.

He didn't want this shit within a thousand miles of his family, let alone the twenty between this building and downtown Darlington.

Tri-Hills was supposed to be a family-friendly community, a place that was safe for kids to wander, for the elderly to not have to worry about being mugged or assaulted or their homes being broken into.

He worried that times were changing, that the town he'd grown up in wouldn't be the same for his kids.

Which was life, he supposed, but not what he wanted for *his* family.

"All right," he said. "Let's keep up the surveillance. But we'll run your idea by the chief."

Celeste squealed then leaned up as though to kiss him on his cheek. "You're the best, Robbie!"

He dodged, turning on the car before reversing out of the alley and heading back for the station.

Celeste chattered on about her plan to take down the dealer, expanding on some good trains of thought and doing a very thorough job of brainstorming by herself since he wouldn't be able to get a word in edgewise with her current mood.

Not that he wanted to.

He was more focused on the smear of red lipstick on his collar.

CHAPTER ELEVEN

I was in a mood.

A bad one.

And for no other reason than my blueberry pie recipe was off.

The kids were in bed, close enough to sleep that they wouldn't be coming out because they needed another cup of water or their light wasn't bright enough, or one of the multitude of other reasons their creative little minds came up with.

Rob was asleep on the couch, the TV a soft murmur that barely reached the kitchen.

And my pie was off.

It wasn't the crust. *That* was tender, salty, and slightly sweet. Perfect. It was something in the filling, something that tasted off.

I popped an unused blueberry from the bowl into my mouth. Tangy but not bad. The butter was fresh, as was the cream. I'd picked them up from the store that morning.

Maybe it was the eggs?

"Hey."

I whirled around and saw Rob leaning against the doorway of the kitchen.

"Hey," I said, setting down the carton I'd picked up to check the expiration date.

"You're up late."

He didn't move from his position. Once he might have come over, taken me in his arms, teased me about my obsession over the pie, then kissed me until I forgot all about recipes and blueberries and fresh eggs.

"I don't have the plague any longer," I blurted.

He raised a brow. "What?"

"Never mind." Why had I said that? Why was I scared as hell to tell him that I might have a chance at a cooking show? That *I*, a small-town girl who'd married young and not amounted to much might have a chance to realize my dream? Why couldn't I tell him, ask him to hold me close and tell me everything would be all right?

Why couldn't I find a way to breach the wall that had been erected between us?

"Meliss—"

"How's work going?" I asked.

Three words that closed him up tighter than a vault. His face flattened out—no emotion, no twinkle in his eyes. "Fine."

"I—uh. Okay." I turned back to the eggs, blinking rapidly, but I managed to get a look at the expiration date. Which was several weeks in the future.

So not the eggs, the milk, or butter. What the hell was wrong with my pie?

"You should go to bed."

I shrugged, surveying the counter. The answer must be a simple one. The pie wasn't inedible, just not quite right. "I've got to fix this."

The pie.

My marriage.

"Why?" Rustling came from the doorway, and I turned, heart skipping a beat as he walked toward me. "It's just a pie."

Perhaps it was.

But it wasn't *just* a recipe gone wrong. Somehow this had become about everything that had gone wrong with our relationship over the last few months. The slow rot, trailed by the rapid disintegration of our communication. Maybe we'd been lazy, too comfortable in our ways. Relationships took work, and we'd sat back on our laurels too much, assumed that everything would always be good. That when it wasn't, we would still find a way through.

But I was at a loss now.

I kept bumping into that brick wall, unable to find my way over, under, through, or around.

And, frankly, I was almost tired of trying.

"It's not just a pie," I snapped. "This matters to me, and I know that you've been wrapped up in whatever has been happening at the department lately, but this"—I waved my hand at the kitchen—"is important to me."

My chest heaved as I waited for him to respond.

Except, he didn't.

Silence stretched as we stood three feet apart, a visually perfect slice of blueberry pie on a plate, ready to be photographed.

The distance between us may have been the Grand Canyon for all that I was able to cross it. He didn't know about the cooking show, or rather, the possibility of one. I hadn't wanted to tell him in front of the kids, in case things didn't pan out. We'd eaten dinner together, and he'd taken the kids up for a bath and books while I'd done the dishes.

It was all very routine. When he was home, he did bedtime then relaxed with a show while I cooked.

Sometimes I propped my iPad up in the kitchen to catch up on the latest Netflix craze or Rob sat with me while I worked, acting the part of official taste-tester.

But more often than not of late, he hadn't been home to play that role.

He sighed. "I get that it's important to you, but the pie isn't life or death."

"Of course not." My eyes dropped to the floor, one that Rob and I had laid together. It wasn't perfect but it did the job.

I almost snorted. If that wasn't an analogy for our current circumstances . . .

Silence.

"I'm not happy," is what I wanted to say.

I didn't get the chance.

Rob turned and walked away. "Try not to stay up too late with your *pie*."

———

"WHAT AM I GOING TO DO?" I said into the phone two days later. Or shrilled, more precisely. If shrilled was a verb, which I hoped it was, since that was all my brain could come up with.

"What, Miss?" Kelly asked, distracted.

I could hear Justin's voice in the background—murmurs punctuated by soft laughter—and had an idea why she was distracted.

Normally I'd hang up, because gross. Today I was freaking out.

"She's going to be here in ten minutes, and I'm not ready!"

The kids were at school. Tammy, the wife of Justin's colleague and the food channel producer, was due any moment. And I hadn't done—

"Switch to FaceTime."

"What?"

Kel sighed, and my phone began trilling with that distinctive chirp. Automatically, I swiped, accepting the call. My sister's smiling face appeared on the screen. Justin was behind her, resting his head on one of her shoulders.

"You look beautiful," she said and Justin nodded in agreement. "That is the perfect Melissa outfit."

I glanced down at my jeans and blouse and my second favorite pair of flats. "You think? It's not too casual?"

"No. Perfect," Kel said firmly. "Where's the dog?"

"At puppy daycare."

"Good." She nodded. "Contain the little monster. Okay, show it to me."

"Show you what?"

"The spread."

I bit my lip and turned the camera around, moving the phone to give her a glimpse of the entire kitchen table filled with food. Including another blueberry pie that was perfect this time. Turned out I'd forgotten lemon juice last time around and it wasn't until after midnight when I'd spotted the yellow fruit perched next to the bowl, that I'd realized.

Kelly gasped. "Holy hell, Melissa. That's incredible."

I shrugged. "It's nothing—"

"You're crazy, now stop. Tammy will love you—" The doorbell rang.

"Oh God," I hissed. "She's here."

"Then let her in," Kel said. "I love you. You're awesome." I was just hanging up when she blurted, "Bring the leftovers later!"

Snorting, I hit the red button, pocketed my phone, and rushed to the front door.

CHAPTER TWELVE

TAMMY MACALISTER WAS a perky redhead with bright blue eyes. Her smile was warm.

"Come on in," I told her. "Can I get you a drink?"

"Water is fine," she said and followed me into the kitchen. "Oh my."

I winced, facing her. "I got a little carried away."

"This is beautiful." She crossed to the table. "Soup. Sandwiches. Pasta salad. Blueberry pie. If it tastes as good as it looks, I'll be a thousand pounds before I leave."

I laughed, my nerves starting to relax. "No guarantees," I told her as I grabbed a glass and filled it with a pitcher of my infused—strawberry, orange, and mint—water. "Please have a seat."

"There never are." But Tammy smiled and sat. "That's the problem with really good food."

I handed her the glass before taking the opposite chair. "I'm nervous," I blurted.

She grinned. "Me too. It's not often that I pick up my clients via my husband. But that chicken!"

"Good?" I asked, biting my lip.

"Delicious."

I blew out a breath. "I'm glad you enjoyed it. That recipe is one of my favorites and way too easy for as pretty as it looks."

"I did like the appearance the fresh herbs gave it," Tammy said. "Parsley and sage?"

I nodded. "Plus a little rosemary. Too much gives the chicken almost a soapy taste. A little hint brings out those savory notes without overpowering the flavor of everything else."

She nodded, and I wondered if I'd gone on one of my tangents. Sometimes I waxed poetic about food, to the eternal boredom of Rob and Kelly. But Tammy didn't seem bored. In fact, her eyes were warm when she said, "Tell me about your blog."

"How about we eat while I tell you?" I asked. "That way the soup doesn't get cold."

Tammy winked. "I like the way you think."

I grabbed a bowl and scooped up some chicken soup for her then filled a plate with a little bit of everything—a finger sandwich, pasta salad, petite fours, pie. It was way too much food, but at least she could take a bite of all that I had to offer.

As she ate and I served up a plate for myself, I told her how I'd started the blog because I'd been slowly going insane when Max was an infant and wouldn't sleep during the night.

He'd only sleep upright and strapped to my chest. Which wasn't exactly conducive for *my* sleep.

So instead of wallowing, I'd taken to cooking.

At least when I was a zombie the following evening from lack of sleep, dinner had already been made. By the time both of my kids were sleeping through the night, I'd had a stack of recipes but my body was used to being up half the night.

I'd played around with plating and taking pictures and had finally taken the social media plunge.

The rest was history.

"I remember those days," Tammy said. "Being so tired that you could hardly think straight."

"Being a mom is hard," I agreed. "Easier on the sleep part now, but harder in different ways."

Tammy tilted her head in question.

"They fight. All the time."

She smiled. "I only have the one, so I didn't get to experience that particular joy of motherhood."

"You're not missing out," I said. "Trust me."

We laughed, and then a quiet descended. I tried to give off some semblance of a calm, put together TV personality, but inside my nerves began to roil again. I'd given the background, she'd tasted my food. Next would come judgment.

"Your kitchen is beautiful."

I blinked then smiled. "My husband and I redid it ourselves."

"Really?"

I glanced at the cabinets that Rob had refinished a bright white, the tile backsplash and floor we'd installed.

"Really. With the exception of the countertops, we did it all." I shrugged. "Luckily it was all cosmetic—electricity and plumbing I draw the line at."

"I would too." Her laughter was bright and contagious, and I finally *finally* chilled.

This is going to be what it is, Miss, I thought, my pulse steadying. *You can't control everything.*

"Okay," Tammy said. "Ready to hear how these things normally work?"

I nodded. "Yes, please."

Tammy smiled as she pulled out her phone, snapping a few pictures of the spread. "I discuss you with my bosses, show them your blog, go on and on about how good your food is, and then we fly you to New York for a screen test."

My eyes were wide. "New York?"

Broadway. High rises. The subway. And *food.* So. Much. Food.

"Yup." She touched my hand and stood. "I'll be in touch once I talk to my bosses, and then we'll figure out a few days that work with your schedule to get you to New York. Sound good?"

I bobbed my head, pushing to my own feet. "That sounds fabulous."

We walked to the front door, and Tammy gave me a hug before she left. "It was such a pleasure to meet you."

"You as well. Safe travels."

Once she'd gotten into her car, I retreated to the kitchen and leaned back against the counter.

A screen test? New York? How was this real life?

I stayed there for a few minutes, frozen in shocked delight. And then I called my sister and we squealed.

After that very appropriate display of glee—occasionally we were allowed to act like teenagers, right?—I began packing up the leftover food. I'd take it to Kelly and Justin's house before I grabbed the kids from school.

Payment for services rendered. Or for being an awesome sister.

Twenty minutes later, I was loading up her fridge when my phone rang.

It was a local number, but one I didn't recognize.

"Hello?"

I could barely hear anything—it was all static and wind and voices.

"Hello?" I said again.

"I can't tell my wife . . ."

My heart twisted at the sound of Rob's voice.

"I've got two kids. This is about them . . ."

Knees trembling, I leaned back against the counter when the call suddenly went crystal clear, wind and static gone. Rob's voice came through with perfect clarity.

"No. She's nothing."

Click.

The call ended, and I glanced down at my phone.

Nothing.

Nothing.

My eyes slid closed, my legs trembled.

Nothing.

I jumped when my phone rang again, and I swiped to answer, putting it up to my ear without looking at the ID.

"Ms. Mitchell?"

My voice wavered as I spoke. "Yes, this is her."

"Hi, this is Sandy from Bow Wow Patrol, and I, um, don't know how to tell you this . . ."

My eyes flashed open, and my stomach dropped. Oh God, what had Rocco done?

"Rocco escaped the outside enclosure, and we can't find him anywhere."

My knees gave out, and I sank to the floor, head dropping back to lean against the cabinets of Kel's kitchen.

"How long has he been missing?" I asked, shoving Rob to the back of my mind.

"Just about an hour."

I nodded though Sandy couldn't hear me, glancing at the clock and mentally making a plan. "I'm just outside of town. I'll stop by my house to double check he didn't somehow make his way home and then be there."

That would give me about forty-five minutes of search time before I had to pick up Allie from school.

Hopefully, it would be enough.

CHAPTER THIRTEEN

It wasn't enough time.

Kelly was at a doctor's appointment—her first visit, and I didn't want to ruin what should be a happy moment—so I rushed across town and grabbed Allie from school. We drove to Bow Wow Patrol. Sandy met us outside, breathless and covered in leaves.

"We found him!" she said. "But he's—" Her eyes trailed over my shoulder to where Allie stood and the words cut off. "H-U-R-T."

My stomach clenched. Hard.

"Bad?"

A nod.

"What's bad, Mommy?" Allie asked.

I crouched in front of her and rested my hands on her shoulders. "Rocco got a little boo-boo, but he'll be okay," I said, hoping it would be true.

Standing, I turned to Sandy. "Where is he?"

"In the back."

I nodded before handing my phone to Allie. "Why don't you have a seat in the lobby and watch some videos?"

"Okay!" She snagged it and scampered for the automatic sliding door leading into the doggy daycare, Sandy and I trailing after her, talking quietly.

"How bad?" I asked.

"I think his leg is broken, and he has some cuts that need cleaning." She paused, glancing over at Allie, who was now perched in a chair and thoroughly engrossed in the phone. "I found him at the bottom of a ravine."

"Wait here, honey, okay?" I said when Sandy pulled open the door to the back.

The receptionist gave me a sympathetic smile and nodded at Allie. "I'll keep an eye on her."

"Thanks," I murmured before following Sandy back.

And my heart broke.

"Oh, poor baby," I crooned, dropping to my knees inside the room where Rocco was. He was wrapped in a blanket, and the parts of him that I could see were covered in scratches and abrasions.

He shifted, trying to stand, and cried out in pain.

"I'm sorry, sweetheart. I'm so sorry," I said softly, continuing to talk to him as I pulled the blanket back and examined his leg.

My throat went tight at the angle—the *wrong* angle—of the bones. I needed to get him to the vet right away. I reached for my phone before realizing it was currently occupied by Allie. "Can I borrow your phone?" I asked Sandy.

"I called Dr. Johnson a few minutes ago. They'll be ready for you as soon as you get there." She sighed. "I don't know how he got out. We've pulled all the dogs inside and are inspecting the fence. I'm so sorry."

I pushed to my feet. "Thank you for finding him. It would have been —" My voice cracked and I blinked rapidly. "Thank you."

Sandy nodded before helping me carry Rocco out to my car. We got him settled then I returned to the lobby for Allie. "Thank you for being so patient, sweetheart," I said as we walked outside. "Rocco needs to see the vet, so we're going there next."

Allie's light brown eyes went wide. "Will he be okay?"

"Of course." I stroke her baby soft cheek. "He's got a couple of big boo-boos, but the vet will fix him right up." I got her buckled into her car seat, sent a silent prayer that my words would be true, and drove to the vet's office.

The moment my car pulled into the lot, Dr. Johnson came through the doors, scooping Rocco up and carrying him inside.

Allie and I spoke to Jane, the receptionist, before picking Max up from school. Luckily, Kelly was home from her appointment by the time we were heading back to our house, and she zipped over to hang with the kids.

It was only when I was back over to the vet's office that I realized I hadn't called Rob.

Nothing.

The word, said with a dismissive tone I'd never heard in my husband's voice before, blared through my mind.

And he loved Rocco. How would he react to his dog being hurt on my watch? Because of something that *I'd* wanted to do. I'd shoved Rocco into daycare and hadn't bothered to keep him safe.

I slid my phone back into my pocket.

Jane smiled when I came through the doors. "I was just going to call you."

A smile was good, right? It meant Rocco would be okay?

The dog destroyed my shoes and wreaked havoc with the best of them, but I still loved him.

"How is he?"

"Pretty banged up, but Dr. Johnson has the specifics for you. He's waiting in exam room three."

At her nod, I slipped past the desk and walked down the hall, knocking before pushing into the room with a three posted outside the door. Rocco was curled on a pile of blankets, looking very drowsy but a lot more comfortable than when I'd dropped him off.

He sported a cast on his back right leg and a myriad of bald spots where they must have shaved him to clean out his cuts. A blue compression bandage was wrapped around one front leg, white gauze peeking out from beneath it.

"Oh, poor Rocco," I said, and crouched down next to him.

"It looks worse than it is," Dr. Johnson said, appearing like a ninja in the doorway that led to the restricted back area for staff and patients only.

He was holding a file but set it aside to crouch next to us, giving Rocco a little scratch under his chin.

"Rocco's a lucky boy. He had a few spots that needed stitches, mainly on his legs and head, as his fur protected him elsewhere." Rocco's eyebrows perked up at his name before he settled his head more firmly on his paws with a sigh. "There was a small fracture in the tibia of his right hind leg, but that should heal without issue."

"Okay," I said, the twisting in my gut settling slightly. "So he's okay?"

He nodded, a small smile curving his mouth up. "My only concern at this time is internal bleeding. From what Sandy told me, it seems like he had a pretty big fall."

"What?"

She'd told me they'd found him at the bottom of a ravine, but I hadn't put two and two together. My heart twisted further as I imagined him falling, scrambling to stay upright, crashing into rocks and sticks, hurting, scared—

I swallowed hard and closed my eyes for a long moment.

"He's okay," Dr. Johnson said.

I nodded, blinked to clear the tears.

"I'd like to keep him overnight for observation. His X-rays and ultrasound are clear, but just in case."

I nodded again. "Okay."

He stood up and grabbed the folder. "Stay with Rocco as long as you want. Just check in with Jane when you leave."

Rocco shifted, resting his head on my thigh, and Dr. Johnson slipped into the back, closing the door behind him.

I scratched Rocco's ears gently, allowing my eyes to commit every visible inch of his body—and his many injuries—to memory. I tucked those into my brain, to the section that was extremely good at holding on to guilt.

Those I'd rehash later, punishing myself until I felt I'd suffered enough to make up for his injuries.

Selfish. I'd acted like my mother, pawning my responsibility off onto someone else just so I could have my fun.

I'd had my fun.

And Rocco had gotten hurt.

And . . . it was my fault.

A tear trickled down my cheek, but I brushed it away. I didn't deserve to purge the emotions, didn't get to excise the guilt. I had promised myself that I wouldn't be like my mother. Not ever.

But look what had happened. I'd turned into exactly the kind of selfish bitch she was, and so I had to experience this guilt over and over and over again.

Until I learned. Until I was better. Until I had made up for it.

CHAPTER FOURTEEN

I HEATED up a meal from the freezer but I don't remember what it was that I actually ate. The kids didn't complain though so it must have been taco casserole, mac and cheese, or something with chicken tenders.

"He's going to be okay." Kelly squeezed my arm. She'd stayed for dinner but Justin was waiting for her, so she and Abby were heading out. She hugged me. Tight. "Just remember that."

Words wouldn't come to form a response, not when my imagination was reliving what poor Rocco had gone through, so I just nodded. He was only a dog. It shouldn't be bothering me so much. But Rocco was innocent, and he'd been at doggie daycare so I could have my meeting.

And Rob loved him.

I sighed. I loved the furball too.

Dammit.

I blinked hard.

"You know—" Kel winced and broke off when Abby yanked at a lock of her hair. She untangled little fingers and said, "I know you're really good at it, but sooner or later you have to shed that martyr cape and let the rest of the world help."

All the air left my lungs in a rush. "You don't know what you're talking about."

My sister—my *younger* sister's face was full of pity "Oh sweetie. I love you, but you're wrong."

"I'm—"

"No one is perfect," she said. "Or expects *you* to be." Abby let out a screech and Kelly smiled down at her daughter. "Time for bed, huh?"

She called out a goodbye and headed for her car.

"I know I'm not perfect," I muttered, closing the door and slumping forward to rest my forehead against the plank of wood.

"How about perfect for me?"

Rob's voice made me straighten and my eyes immediately fill with tears. I turned, regret pouring through me when the smile he'd been wearing slipped from his face.

My news would further cement that.

He was in uniform, his duty belt still around his waist. I'd always loved him in blues. He was the female fantasy come to life.

"What's wrong, babe?"

The question, filled with obvious concern and actual emotion for the first time in what felt like forever, coupled with him extending his arms, made me forget everything. The woman's voice in the background of the call, the way he'd said I was nothing, his distance, how he'd been so oblivious and missed so much.

I wanted those arms around me. I wanted that comfort.

I wanted my husband back.

With a sigh of relief, I stepped into his embrace. Tears slipped down my cheeks, dripping off my chin and pooling onto the collar of my shirt. With Rob, it had always been different. All the walls that existed to keep me safely distant weren't there with him.

But lately they'd crept in with my husband, and I didn't know how to stop building them.

Not when he kept hurting me.

Not when I allowed myself to *be* hurt without talking to him.

Yet in that moment, none of it mattered. I had my husband, my best friend, and he was there for me.

"Shh," he said, stroking the hair back from my face. "Whatever it is, it'll be okay."

"Why's Mommy crying?" Allie asked.

I sniffed, trying to quiet my sobs. I didn't want to upset her or Max.

"Mom?" Max asked, grabbing me around the leg.

"I-I'm okay," I said, my voice only slightly shaky. "Just a little upset."

"Why don't you guys go pick out your books, and I'll read to you tonight?" Rob said.

"Okay!" Allie started to run off before making a skidding turn and throwing her arms around me. "Love you!"

"Love you too, baby."

Max touched my arm, and I glanced down at him. He studied me for a long moment before nodding and pressing a kiss to my hand. "Love you, Mom."

"Love you too, buddy."

He ran upstairs.

Rob waited until the pounding footsteps had faded before he took my hand and led me toward the kitchen. "Okay, spill," he said, pushing me down in a chair then crouching in front of me.

"It's Rocco. He got out today and fell down a ravine. H-he broke his leg, and Dr. Johnson wants to keep him overnight in case of internal bleeding." I took a deep breath because my voice was getting shrill and my eyes were filling with tears again.

"How did he get out?"

It was a reasonable question. And also one I didn't want to answer.

"Sandy isn't sure," I hedged.

Rob raised a brow and sat back on his haunches. "Why would Sandy be unsure?" His tone was harder now, laced with no-nonsense cop.

"Because Rocco was at Bow Wow Patrol when he got out."

"Why?"

I hesitated.

"*Melissa.*"

"This isn't how I wanted to tell you." My eyes went to a spot over his right shoulder, mentally dissecting the kitchen clutter. I needed to sort the mail, finish the dishes—

"Melissa"—my gaze flashed back to his face, angry and dark—"you need to tell me what the fuck is going on."

I burst to my feet. "I wanted to tell you. I tried to tell you, but you blew me off."

"We talked last night."

"Gah! I hate it when you do that." I paced the floor we'd laid together and wasn't that memory a nice little slap in the face at a moment like this? "Nitpicking my words, tacking on little disclaimers so that you don't have to be wrong. *Yes*, we talked last night. *No*, you didn't give me enough of your precious time so that I could tell you what's been going on in my life."

He opened his mouth, closed it. Then he sighed and said, "I thought it was *our* life."

"It hasn't been *our* life for a long time." When he didn't reply, I said, "You might have been home with me and the kids in body, but your mind wasn't here, your heart wasn't and *hasn't* been here for months."

Silence.

"You pulled back, Rob, and I miss you."

For a second, I thought my husband might actually make an appearance. His eyes softened as he stood and crossed to me, lightly brushing his knuckles down my cheek when he got near.

Then his face closed down. "What haven't you told me?"

He might as well have slapped me. The words were cold, his expression tight and frigid.

I recited the facts in monotone. "I cooked for Justin's work colleague a few days ago. His wife is an executive at a cooking channel. She loved my food, checked out my blog and recipes, and asked to set up a meeting with me today. They want me to come to New York for a screen test."

"No."

I blinked, startled from my recitation. "What?"

"No. You can't go to New York for a screen test."

I stepped back.

Rob stepped forward.

I lifted my chin. "Why not?"

"Your place is here. The kids." He shook his head, turned away. "Rocco already got hurt because of this stupid idea—"

"Rocco getting hurt was an accident."

"Because of this woman and her meeting," he said, taking his own turn at pacing the floor. "He would have been at home if not for that."

"It's not Tammy's fault Rocco was injured."

"Fine," he snapped and thrust a hand through his hair. "It was *your* fault."

My stomach twisted, that wonderfully painful guilt flooding in. I held it close, let it batter me even as I pretended my husband's words hadn't cut me deep. "You're being unreasonable."

"You're being irresponsible."

I laughed. Laughed until my stomach hurt and tears threatened. I'd been called a lot of things in my life—by my mother, by jerky kids at school growing up, even by Kelly in her teenage years when I'd been more mom than sister.

But never by my husband.

"Irresponsible." A shake of my head. "That's bullshit, and you know it."

"I—"

The pounding of footsteps radiated through the floor above our heads and was punctuated by a resounding, "MOM!"

It also gave me the out that was needed. My insides felt like they'd been sliced by knives. I was exhausted. I was hurt and emotional and . . .

"Go read to our kids," I murmured.

For once, I didn't head to the fridge, didn't pull out ingredients and start cooking my pain away.

Instead, I grabbed a bottle of wine from the counter, a glass from the cupboard, and headed out the back door.

Some things just called for wine.

I didn't look back as I went through the door and settled myself into a chair on the deck. I didn't need to. This house and family were my everything, and I could track every movement without a wasted glance.

I heard Rob climb the stairs—not bothering to avoid the creaking one. I listened to the kids' muffled but clearly excited voices as they talked about their days. I watched the glow disappear from the deck as their lights were flicked off. I heard quiet footfalls descending . . . and that damned squeaky step again.

I heard Rob's car start up.

And drive away.

I finished the bottle of wine.

CHAPTER FIFTEEN

I woke up with a pounding headache and a violent urge for bacon, eggs, and hash browns.

Food would have to wait for aspirin to kick in though.

With a groan, I rolled to the side and saw the time.

Of course.

The kids were going to be late for school.

But that seemed slightly less important when I noticed that Rob's side of the bed was untouched. For all the years we'd been married, the only times he hadn't slept by my side were when he'd been on a night shift.

I guess that wasn't the case any longer.

Forcing my eyes from the neatly made half of the bed, from the pillow that was undented, I hustled into the closet.

No time for emotions and regrets.

My kids needed to get to school.

I brushed my teeth, threw my hair into a ponytail, and grabbed the first set of clothes my hands touched.

Three minutes for me being somewhat presentable to the rest of humanity might be a record.

I poked my head into the kids' bedrooms and, finding them empty, rushed down the stairs, hopping over the creaking step, and skidding to a halt in the kitchen.

My sister was there, helping Allie into her backpack. Max was sitting on the floor, already wearing his, and playing with Abby.

Kelly glanced up and smiled. "After yesterday, I figured you might need relief this morning." She straightened the pack on Allie's shoulders. "Now you just turn around and go enjoy a nice long shower. I'm taking the kids to school. Dr. Johnson called your cell earlier and said Rocco would be ready to come home around noon."

My eyes flashed to the counter, and I saw my phone there. I guess I'd been so out of it the night before I hadn't brought it upstairs.

"Rocco!" Max yelled, making Abby laugh.

I smiled.

"I've got these guys today," my sister said. "You take care of getting the fluffball settled."

The tension in my gut eased. "You're a goddess."

Kel bowed. "I know. Go get in the car, munchkins," she said to the kids, raising her key fob and pressing a button. We watched through the kitchen window as the two doors to her minivan slid open. "Never thought I'd say it, but minivans rock." A grin. "Now, go spend an inordinate time on personal grooming while you have the chance."

"Breakfast?" I asked as she scooped up Abby.

"Done," Kel said as Max and Allie sprinted out the front door without a look back.

"Boosters?"

She nodded. "Justin installed them last night."

I let out a relieved sigh. "Thanks, sissy."

"Anytime." She hugged me and went outside.

I waved after she'd settled Abby into her seat, smiling when she pushed a button and the doors closed.

Minivans *did* rock.

Then I saw Rob's note propped next to the coffee pot, and my smile slipped away.

Will be at Henry's if you need me.

I CRUMPLED the paper and jammed it into the overflowing trashcan.

What the hell did that mean?

I grabbed a coffee cup and filled it. Was Rob hanging out for the morning? Is that where he'd spent last night?

Had he left and was staying there permanently?

No. We hadn't gotten to that point. Right?

Right?

Dammit. I hated this, I thought, bustling around the kitchen as irritation and fear and concern washed through me. I grabbed a package of blackberries and some homemade vanilla yogurt, layering it and the berries into a bowl before topping with a few scoops of granola.

I sat down at the table, spoon in hand but stomach no longer hungry.

There was so much between Rob and I—baggage, barriers, resentment

—but we'd always been able to talk things out in the past. Except . . . maybe we'd never really dealt with it all.

I knew I'd done my fair share of ignoring the small stuff that I hadn't wanted to battle over, and God knew, I was good at boxing up emotions I didn't want to deal with.

Was this how marriages imploded? Too much compartmentalizing, too much ignoring of the problems and pretending that everything was okay?

No.

That wasn't us. This was just a rough patch. We'd get through. We always did.

I stood up, setting my bowl in the sink, and turned to head upstairs for a shower. But there was that trash again. The lid sat askew, papers spewing out onto the floor. Reminding me of everything that wasn't right in my life.

Ugh.

I shoved the garbage down angrily, slammed the top closed. "Couldn't he have at least taken the flipping trash out before he left?"

Left me.

Left us.

Then tears were in my eyes and dripping down my cheeks. I pretended they didn't exist as I climbed the stairs. I ignored them as they mingled with the warm water of the shower.

And, fancy that, my eyes were dry by the time my body was.

My heart, on the other hand, was bruised and aching.

———

"SO HE'LL NEED the cast for a few weeks, then we'll take another X-ray, and if all is good, Rocco will be a free man." Dr. Johnson smiled as he patted Rocco on the head. "Or dog, rather."

"In the meantime, I've got to keep him calm?" I glanced at Rocco's tail, already tapping against the floor like a propeller spinning a million miles per hour.

The vet snorted, a lock of his dark brown hair falling forward over his eyes. "Do your best. Most dogs don't start to perk up for a few days." He gave a pointed look at the propeller tail and Rocco's bright eyes. "But I think this one will prove me wrong."

"He's got energy," I agreed.

Dr. Johnson touched my arm. "Speaking of energy, are you okay? You look a little"—he hesitated like he realized he was hovering in dangerous territory—"overwhelmed."

"I'm fine."

"Rocco will make a full recovery."

I nodded. "I know."

"Any other questions or concerns?"

Silence descended, and I struggled to hold everything inside. I wasn't the vent-to-strangers type, but there was something about the white coat and doctor's office setting that made me want to spill my guts.

In the end, old patterns persisted and my guts stayed firmly *not* spilled.

I thanked the vet, bent to lift Rocco up—

"It's not your fault," Dr. Johnson said.

My laugh was brittle. "That's what everyone keeps saying."

He raised a brow. "Then it's probably true."

"You're probably right."

A smile and a flirtatious wink. It would have been overkill on a less attractive man. On Dr. Johnson—young and muscular and sweet—it only added to the general appeal.

When had I started to notice the general appeal of other men?

Right around the time that my husband might have been unfaithful.

Any amusement I felt dried up at that thought. Dr. Johnson must have noticed it because he snagged my keys from the exam table, scooped up Rocco, and headed for the door.

"I'll get him settled in your car if you want to head to the checkout desk."

"Thanks," I said, but he was already out the door.

Well, what was seeing one more male's back? They were familiar territory these days.

Sighing, I grabbed my purse and left the exam room.

I paid, careful to save the receipt because Bow Wow Patrol was going to reimburse me, and walked outside to my car. Then stopped dead. Rob was standing next to Dr. Johnson, the pair in an intense conversation.

A conversation that abruptly ended when I came over to them.

Rob gave Dr. Johnson a hard look as he patted Rocco on the head. That look transformed into a fierce glare when the vet stopped in front of me and squeezed my hand.

"Hang in there, okay?" Dr. Johnson waited until I tore my eyes from my husband and met his. "And you need anything, don't hesitate to call." He handed me a card. "Cell's on the back."

"Thank you," I whispered as he walked away.

My gaze hit the pavement, tracing the cracks as I took a deep breath and prepared to navigate the glacial ice storm that was my husband.

Peace. All I wanted was peace.

I shored up my spine. "Hi."

"Hey."

"I—I'm sorry about Rocco. It was a horrible accident, but Dr. Johnson says he'll make a full recovery."

I paused. Waited.

Nothing.

I bit my lip, pressed on. "So, anyway. I need to get him home so he can rest." I hesitated a beat, thinking my husband would respond to me. When he didn't, I went on rambling, "Then I have to pick up Allie and take her to Kelly's for her riding lessons, and for some reason I agreed to ride with them. Then Max has a playdate with Caleb after school then I'll pick him up from soccer and . . ."

I ran out of steam.

And got silence back.

Awesome.

Seriously, why did I bother?

I pushed past my husband. A man who, just months before, I would have said that I knew better than myself.

This cold person in front of me was a stranger.

"I'm tired of being shut out," I muttered, tearing open the passenger door and tossing my purse inside. "I'm tired of feeling like a pathetic puppy that keeps getting kicked. I'm"—I sighed as fatigue flooded through me—"just tired."

Rob was still standing by the open trunk of my van, but now he was scratching Rocco under the chin.

"You shouldn't leave him unsupervised with the trunk open," Rob said. "He already got hurt once on your watch. You need to be more careful."

"You mean be more careful and supervise when you're *right* there?" I asked, slamming the door and walking toward the trunk. "Because by my count you've got two eyes and hands, and you're fully capable of supervising."

Rob's stare snapped to mine, but he didn't apologize.

He didn't say anything further either. Which, really, at that point, I considered a win.

I shoved between him and the car, checking that Rocco was safely away from the trunk so I could close it.

"What's this?" Rob asked, fingers plucking into my back pocket.

"What's what?" I asked, after the lift-gate clicked closed.

"This."

I turned, saw that he was holding the card Dr. Johnson had handed me. "It's the vet's card." I shrugged. "He's been very kind and helpful about Rocco."

Rob snorted. "I bet he has."

Are. You. Fucking. Kidding. Me?

Now, I don't get mad often. I really don't. Sure, little things annoy me and pester my thoughts. But I'm the stewing type, not the blow-my-top-like-a-volcano type.

Until I hit the Point.

I'm guessing anyone in the universe could see that I'd hit *that* Point.

Everyone except my husband.

Because he had the flipping audacity to take a step toward me, pin me between the van and his hard body, and glare down at me.

"What's between you and the vet?"

I lost it.

"What's between you and the girl on your phone?" I hissed and shoved at his chest, knocking him back a step. "What's with you and the lipstick on your collar? What's with you and not coming home last night?"

I yelled the last at the top of my lungs.

Pulling air through my nose, I tried to drop the volume of my voice. "I don't know what's going on with you or work or us, but I do know that the last freaking thing you should be spending any energy on is wondering whether or not there is anything between Dr. Johnson and myself. I don't even know the man's first name."

Rob stared at me for a long moment before throwing the card in my face. "It's Sam, and it's right there next to his cell number."

"Great." I crumpled the card in my palm and turned away. The door handle was cool beneath my fingers as I yanked it open.

I threw myself into the seat, tossed the card into the cup holder with a plethora of other trash, and tried to close the door. Unfortunately, it wouldn't go anywhere when I tried to slam it.

"Where are you going?" Rob snapped, his hand holding it open.

"I think I told you that already." I pulled on the door again. It didn't budge. Damn strong fingers.

"I'm not done discussing this," he said.

Ignoring his words and the open door for the time being, I jammed my keys into the ignition and turned on the van. It was a cool day outside, but the interior was getting warm already, so I directed cold air back toward Rocco.

Then I plunked my head on the steering wheel and counted to ten.

When I was done, I lifted my eyes to Rob's. "Why do you have an extra cell phone with someone named Celeste texting you all the time?"

His jaw tightened, but he didn't respond.

"No words now?" I asked. "Or no explanation as to why I'm getting butt dials and overhearing you say I don't matter? That only our kids do?"

"Melissa, it's—"

Hope bubbled up inside me.

"Is this something with work?" I asked desperately when he hesitated. "Something you can't discuss? Something that isn't about us?"

Please let that be the case.

"You don't have to confirm or deny it," I said, knowing that my words were rushing together as I grasped at any explanation for why my marriage was exploding. "Just wink or something. Or—I've got it! A code word. Marshmallow. Or banana. How about banana?"

Rob shook his head. "It's not work."

Those pretty little bubbles of positivity disintegrated. A giant boulder dropped straight onto my gut.

I was going to be sick.

"It's not work?" I repeated dumbly.

"No."

Breathe. In. Out. *Don't lose it.* "I need to get Allie from school."

"Okay." He dropped his hand from the door, turned away from me.

"Rob?"

He stopped, turned back.

"Don't come home tonight."

CHAPTER SIXTEEN

I WANTED to do something reckless.

Dumb and stupid and reckless.

But that wasn't me. So I was here.

Here being on top of a horse under the watchful eye of my sister and staring down at the ground that suddenly seemed like a lot farther than six feet away.

Allie sat on a pony—I was trying not to make a stink that it was several feet shorter than my own horse because she was my daughter, after all—next to me. She was grinning and wriggling in the saddle, beyond excited that I was riding with her.

Kelly was the horse whisperer, not me. I could barely keep my seat and was petrified the entire time.

My daughter, on the other hand, had inherited the horse gene and had quickly moved from corral rides to long, traipsing gallops through the fields of Kel and Justin's ranch.

Roosevelt Ranch was rapidly becoming known as one of the premier horse breeders in the country, and it was all because of my sister. She'd worked with the previous owner of the ranch for years, had even been given a college scholarship because she'd been such a talented equestrian. But when Justin's brother—one Rex Roosevelt and once a serious scumbag—had bought the ranch and nearly driven it into the ground, Justin and Kelly had taken over.

Now it was awesome, and the stables were busy. Which was just the way Kel preferred.

Breeding, boarding, teaching kids—and sometimes adults, in my case —to ride, was what my sister had always dreamed about.

That and a big family.

I smiled as she brought her horse up next to Allie's and adjusted her helmet, tightening the buckle so that it didn't slip from her head. Justin held Abby in his arms and was carrying her through the stables as they checked out the horses.

I had the feeling that Abby would be riding better than me in no time.

"Ready?" Kel asked, coming alongside my horse.

"Did you have to give me the biggest one?" I moaned.

"Yup." A quick smile. "Plus, he's the sweetest one. Theodore—"

"Theodore?" I squawked, ready to launch myself from the saddle. Theodore was known in the stables as the most rambunctious and troublesome of the horses.

"Kidding," Kel said, grabbing my shoulder to steady me. "This is Sweetheart. She's gentle and as sweet as her name. It's where Allie started. We use her for the five-year-olds."

I gripped the reigns tightly. "I hear the amusement in your voice, and I don't like it."

"You'll be fine."

"How'd your doctor's appointment go?" With all of the craziness of the day before, I hadn't thought to ask.

Kel glanced over and whispered out of the side of her mouth. "Twins."

My eyes went wide.

She laughed. "I know. I guess it's not a surprise considering that Justin and Rex are twins, but holy sh"—she cut the word off when Allie glanced over—"horses hooves, three under four. How are we going to survive?"

I forgot that I was on top of an animal-powered death machine for a second and squeezed Kelly's hand. "You'll survive. You're an amazing mom. And Rob—"

The words stalled. I'd been about to say that Rob and I would be there for her.

But would he?

"We'll be there for you guys," I finished, feigning a look down as though Sweetheart had been responsible for the bump in my words. Never mind that she was acting the perfect *sweetheart* and had hardly moved.

Kel, at least, didn't seem to register the blip as anything major. She laughed, repositioned my hands on the reins, and nodded at the rolling hills. "Let's get you moving before you chicken out."

I mock-frowned, shoved the turmoil far, far down. This was my time with Allie and Kelly, and I wasn't going to ruin that.

———

"THAT WAS SO FUN, MOMMY!" Allie yelled as we got back into the car and headed to the field where Max's soccer practice was being held.

We were both dusty and I, for one, was going to be sore in the morning. I'd also agreed for some reason to take more lessons from my sister.

Kelly was convinced that I was going to become an expert horsewoman.

I had my doubts about that.

But it *had* been fun, and so I was coming back in two days for another ride on Sweetheart.

Now that statement sounded both extremely odd and strangely dirty.

"It *was* fun," I told Allie. "Thank you for letting me come with you."

"I love Bruce," she said of her pony. "He's funny."

I grinned back at her in the rearview. "You mean that he poops a lot."

She giggled. "You said poop."

"It's true."

Her laugh warmed me from the inside out. "I love you, Mommy."

"I love you too, Allie-girl."

She broke into a story about a ball, the playground, and two mean girls. Then transitioned into one about the book they'd read at circle time, before discussing the proper piece placement for the doll puzzle at school.

By the time we reached the field, her school stories had run out and she'd moved onto horse ones.

Max ran up to the car, bag hanging on his shoulder. I waved at Caleb's mom, rolling down the window to confirm that I had the boys for the same routine but at our house the following week, then drove home.

Then it was dinner and homework, baths and bedtime reading. By the time I sat down to work on my next blog post it was after ten. *I* hadn't gotten a bath yet, but I had work to do, lunches to make, and dinner to think about for the following night, since Allie had a late swimming class.

Deciding to combine two tasks into one, I started making the kids' lunches and documented the process for the blog.

Sandwiches and fruit weren't the most exciting blog material, but they were something, and my white cheddar with apricot jelly and sliced green apples on thick crusty pieces of sourdough were to die for.

The combination was one of my favorite snacks, and as thus, I'd just sat down to one on the couch—midnight snacks were the best—when my cell phone buzzed.

"Hello?" I said hesitantly into it when I didn't recognize the number.

"Melissa? It's Tammy."

I somehow both tensed and relaxed at the same time. Tensed because Tammy held my dreams in the palm of her hand and relaxed because I liked her. A lot.

"H-hi, Tammy. How are you?"

"It's not too late to call, is it?" she asked. "I'd normally never phone this late, but then I got confirmation from the network and got excited, and . . . well, here we are."

I waited until she paused then said, "No. I'm normally up pretty late."

"Oh good. Okay, here's what's going to happen. I've got a flight in two days for you to New York. You'll come out and film a segment in the studio and we'll go from there." I could almost picture her ticking items off on her fingers. "I need two recipes from you by tomorrow so I can have the food purchased."

"Oh, wow. Okay."

"Any recipe you want," Tammy said. "Oh! And I know you need to be home with your kiddos, so I've scheduled you to fly in on a red-eye, film in the morning, and then fly home that same evening." Her voice lowered conspiratorially. "And my hope is that if everything goes well, we can film in your kitchen or your backyard. Ooh! Or maybe we can convince your sister and her yummy of a husband to let us film on the ranch. That would be a gorgeous location. Rolling hills, sweeping sunsets." She sighed. "That kitchen."

I set my plate on the coffee table and sat forward on the couch, my mind spinning.

"Sound good?"

I blinked. "Uh . . ." I hesitated, but only for a split second before I got my stuff together. "Yes. It sounds great."

Already my brain was working on our schedule. Mentally calculating the kids' after-school activities and sorting out the coverage I needed. I had enough food in the freezer for dinner, and I could make breakfast and lunch ahead of time. I'd need to get them to and from school—

"Perfect! I'll email you the details and see you in two days!" Tammy paused. "Don't forget those recipes!"

With a *click*, she hung up, and I stayed put on the couch for a couple of seconds, stunned motionless by the whirlwind that was Tammy.

Then I jumped into motion.

I practically dove into the kitchen, gathering my two favorite recipes: chicken and dumplings and a cabbage-apple slaw.

They were simple, delicious, and easy to make with cheap ingredients.

They were me. They were my blog.

I could stretch several elements to last many meals. And I'd had to on multiple occasions when my mother had gotten drunk and gambled all our money away.

Food had been my demon growing up. Never enough of it, constantly slipping more to Kelly since she was younger, and it was my job to take care of her, to make sure her belly didn't rumble with hunger.

It had gotten so bad that I'd felt guilty for eating, for taking one bite out of her mouth. I'd gotten really skinny. *Too* skinny. Not quite anorexic. At least, I don't think so. But I hadn't been in a healthy mental space.

Rob had saved me from that. And the town.

Darlington was good people. We'd had anonymous deliveries of meals and groceries, from those who knew my mother wasn't a good person. Not that our father was innocent or much better—as an absentee dad, he was just as negligent.

We'd never had any authority intervene on our behalf because I had hidden our problems. Because I hadn't asked for help. Because I'd been scared we would be split up if someone reported us to child protection services.

So when I'd finally gotten a job and could support myself and Kel, I'd pinched every penny and bought cookbooks, studied up with Henry's dad at his restaurant in between waitressing shifts, practiced and experimented and *ate*.

Now food was my therapy.

And I was ready to share it with the world.

I slipped on an apron, pulled out the ingredients. I would run through the recipes, make sure they were perfect.

My phone buzzed, and I extracted it from my pocket. A text from Rob was on the screen.

Go to sleep. It's late.

I gasped, and my eyes flew to the window. Headlights flashed in the driveway before a car backed out and drove away.

I'm going to New York.

Silence then another buzz.

I wish you wouldn't.

I didn't reply. Instead, I rolled out the dough for the dumplings and whipped up the two recipes.

The little balls of dough turned out perfect. Delicious, well-seasoned, and melt-in-your-mouth. The apple slaw was the perfect complement. It was light and tart and contrasted with the creamy sauce nicely.

I stuffed my face, froze the leftovers, only wishing a little bit that Rob was there to sample with me.

I didn't understand what was happening with us, what I'd done wrong.

But I did know that I wasn't giving up on my dream, whether or not my husband wanted me to.

CHAPTER SEVENTEEN

"And I don't know if Rob will be working or not," I said, gathering up my purse and prepping the lie I'd already thought up ahead of time. "He's pretty busy with a big case."

Kelly studied my face for a long moment before nodding and reaching across the console to give me a hug. "Well, Justin and I will be there with Abby so either way. It'll be a big sleepover."

I winked. "I don't think you'll be getting a lot of sleep."

Justin was with the kids, and they'd been running around the backyard like maniacs when Kel and I had driven away two hours before.

"I'm considering this training for what's to come," she said.

I cupped her cheeks in my palms. "I love you."

"That's because I'm awesome." She nudged me in the direction of the terminal. "Now, go. I'll try not to burn dinner tomorrow."

"How about you try not to burn *anything*?" I laughed, shook my head at her extended middle finger, and got out of the car. My suitcase was in the trunk so I retrieved it and with a wave to my sister, threw my purse over my shoulder, and headed inside.

I was flying out of the Salt Lake City airport, and it felt strange to be by myself. Strange in that it was *easy*.

I walked to the counter, waited in line, and checked my suitcase without once having to referee a fight or tell someone to keep their voice down. It was so quiet.

And honestly, I was torn between really liking it and feeling a little lonely.

My kids were awesome. I loved them to Jupiter and back.

Yes, they could drive me up a wall. Yes, it was nice to have quiet. But I also missed hanging out with them.

Not having them next to me made me realize just how isolating my life had become over the last few years.

I needed to make an effort to get out more, to reconnect with old friends. I'd been trailing in the wake of my life for so long, just trying to get through, just barely surviving the homework and after-school activities, Rob's constantly changing hours, and the blog.

And what was the result?

I was lonely.

I had my kids. I had my sister and her family. But my life felt a little empty.

Well, that was going to change.

I was going to change.

———

I WOKE, eyes crusty and mind groggy at a voice blaring through speakers.

". . . the plane is preparing for descent, please place your tray tables and seat backs in the upright position."

Blinking, I shifted, stretching my sore neck and thinking it had been a lot easier to sleep on a plane when I'd been younger.

Though I'd only flown two times before—to my honeymoon with Rob and back.

Those times I'd had a warm chest to cuddle into, strong arms to keep me upright.

A flash of memory sparked to life in my mind. Crystal blue water and white sand. Hot, sticky air. Jerk chicken. Plantains. More spice than I'd ever experienced in my life.

And Rob.

Rob smiling down at me. Rob holding me close on the ocean's edge, the bright orange sun fading into the horizon. Rob with eyes that softened as he looked at me.

The jar of the plane bumping against the tarmac pulled me out of my reverie.

Then came the taxiing to the gate, the long wait as the doors were opened and people filed off. I shuffled my way up the aisle like the rest of the cattle.

The airport air was stale. I wrinkled my nose as I made my way through the terminal and toward baggage claim.

Please let my knives have arrived in one piece.

I was wrinkled, my clothes rumpled and my hair no doubt sticking up in multiple directions. I needed a shower, a good bed, and about two days straight of sleep.

But since that wasn't on the docket, I slipped into a bathroom, pulled out my makeup bag, and made the best of it. I brushed teeth and hair, fixed smudged eyeliner, and added lip gloss.

Taking a big breath, I focused on my reflection in the mirror, encouraging the fierceness in my pale brown eyes. I nodded once in approval, shoved my makeup bag into my purse, and marched toward baggage claim.

I had this.

I SO DID NOT HAVE this.

I was ridiculously incompetent: fumbling with my knives, calling ingredients by the wrong names, and forgetting to wash my hands after handling raw chicken.

So freaking stupid.

I could do these recipes with my eyes closed, but I couldn't apparently do them with the black, unfeeling eye of the camera fixed on me.

"I'm sorry," I said as Tammy came over. "I'm nervous. I know I need to get it together."

She smiled, but her gaze held concern. "Don't worry. Nerves are totally normal."

What was not normal, I was sure, was the amount of bungling I was accomplishing.

Stupid. So stupid. I was going to ruin my marriage and this opportunity in one shot.

"Why don't you step outside and take a quick break? Call home, zone out for ten minutes. I'm going to have the studio cleaned up, and we'll start again for a few more takes."

I nodded and wiped my—now clean—hands on a towel. "Okay. Thanks."

The studio I was in was on the third floor of a building somewhere in New York City. I said somewhere because I literally had no clue where I was, other than surrounded by skyscrapers, traffic, and chilled air tinged with the stink of too many cars and people.

New York was some people's mojo, but it definitely wasn't mine.

A car had picked me up from the airport and driven me straight to the studios, where I'd met several executives. *That* part had gone well. They were friendly and we'd had a good rapport.

Then had come the camera.

Staring at me.

I shuddered and pulled out my phone to call Kel.

At the last moment, I changed and called Rob.

I don't know if it was because I was alone and he'd always been my rock. I don't know if I was glutton for punishment. I don't know if I just missed my husband and wanted any piece of him that he was willing to give.

Ring.

Ring.

Ring.

Ring.

My heart clenched hard. I needed him and he wasn't there. Again—

"Hello?"

My words caught in my throat, stifling my response.

"Miss? You there?"

For some idiotic reason, I nodded, though he couldn't see me, and the lack of my answer made frustration radiate through the airwaves.

He sighed, and I heard a rustle, knew he was about to hang up.

"Rob," I whispered, thinking it was too late, that it was too quiet, that he was already gone.

"Melissa."

It was just my name in his voice, but it meant so much more. "Hey," I said. "I just—"

"Needed me."

My nerves slipped, the sadness slid away. Irritation flooded in instead. "I don't—"

"Melissa. I talked with Justin when I came home last night and Kelly was driving you to the airport." His voice went a little harder. "Thanks for letting me know about the trip, by the way."

"I told you I was going. Plus when were we supposed to chat?" I interjected. "You haven't exactly—"

He ignored me. "I'm assuming you've arrived in New York and you're second-guessing yourself. Every time that you do something out of your comfort zone you do this."

"I—"

"You're good enough, Miss. Trust that."

I paused, letting the words wash over me, holding them close.

"If that's it, then I need to go."

I pursed my lips together. Throwing me a tiny bone, then right back to normal.

At least I knew where I stood.

"Thanks for the pep talk. It was—" I shook my head. "You did your duty. I won't bug you again."

"Melis—"

Pressing that red circle felt good.

I turned my phone to silent when it rang again and stared at the lock screen as I rejected the call. Allie and Max had their arms around each other and were giggling like fools.

This is why I was here. So they could see me as enough. Not just their mom, not just a robot to clean up after them, a short order cook to make their meals.

I had value and—I closed my eyes, took a long inhale, and let it out slowly—I wanted them to see it.

I wanted Rob to see it.

I—

"Ready?"

Tammy smiled at me from the open doorway.

Slipping my phone into my pocket, I smiled back. "I'm ready."

CHAPTER EIGHTEEN

"THAT WAS FANTASTIC," Tammy said, clapping her hands together.

I breathed a mental sigh of relief and set down the plate I was holding. "Once I got over the camera."

"That's the hardest part," she agreed and came forward, hugging me tight as she whispered in my ear, "Nothing's set in stone, of course. But this is going to knock everyone's socks off."

I pulled back slightly, taking in her kind blue eyes, porcelain skin, and curly red hair. She was beautiful in an Irish nymph sort of way. "You think?"

A nod. "I know."

My knees felt a little weak, but it was from joy and relief, rather than fear for a change.

"Well, phew."

She laughed and slipped her arm around my waist. "Now come on, we have time for an early dinner before I have to get you back to the airport."

"That sounds perfect," I said.

New York wasn't so bad, I thought an hour later, eyeing the gorgeous plate in front of me and not wanting to ruin its beauty by sticking my fork in it.

"Pork belly with caramelized walnuts, a cranberry vinaigrette, and micro greens," the server said.

"Aka very tasty bacon," Tammy said with a wink.

"This looks incredible." The pork belly was a gorgeous brown, and when topped with the crimson-colored dressing and edible flowers, the whole effect was stunning.

"If you keep looking at it, it'll just get cold," Tammy whispered.

"True," I said with a grin and dug in.

Then promptly moaned.

So, *so* good.

"Okay," I said once I'd finished the entire portion, stopping just short of licking the plate. "New York may not have the wide open skies and fresh air of Utah, but it's not the worst."

"If you love food, there's no better place," Tammy said.

At that moment, as a plate with a gorgeous chocolate tart was being set down in front of me, I found I couldn't disagree.

———

"MOM!" Justin and I walked through the door to find the kids sitting at the round table. Kel was perched on the countertop, eyeing the coffee pot like it was a pile of gold and she was a marauding pirate.

"Have a cup," I told her as the kids jumped up from the table and hugged me tightly. Their little arms could squeeze hard when they were motivated. I squeezed back. "Missed you little munchkins."

"I already had one," my sister said with a pouty lip.

Justin scooped up Abby and wrapped his free arm around Kel's waist. "Decaf?" he offered.

My sister frowned. "What's the point?"

"The taste?" Justin said.

"If there's no caffeine, there's no point," Kelly declared. "I'd rather have my calories in chocolate. Or—oh!" Her eyes found mine as I stood and the kids ran back to the table to finish their breakfast. "Can you make that blueberry pie again? With the fresh whipped cream? And the crumbly crust?"

I laughed. "Sure. Let me get the kids off to school, and I'll whip one up."

"Oh," Kel's eyes flicked over my shoulder. "I thought Rob was taking them."

"Rob's at work—" I turned, words stopping when I saw my husband standing in the doorway behind me.

"Can Daddy drive us, Mom?" Max asked.

Traitor.

But I smiled and nodded, not looking at Rob as I crossed to the fridge and pulled open the door. "Of course."

I didn't miss the look Kel and Justin exchanged as an awkward silence fell over the kitchen. A silence that was broken when Allie spilled her glass of milk all over the table and floor.

Perfect. A distraction was just what I needed.

I snatched up a towel and a bottle of cleaner, reassuring Allie when she would have started crying that it was just an accident and not a big deal. I bustled around, mopping up the milk, pouring another glass for Allie, grabbing a pack of cinnamon rolls out of the freezer and shoving them in Kel's hands as I all but pushed her, Justin, and, consequently, Abby out the door.

My sister gave me squinty eyes over her shoulder and I knew a hard conversation was coming soon.

Ugh.

But Rob was behind me, still in the doorway, still quiet and staring. I called goodbye to my sister, Justin, and Abby then whipped up two lunches for the kids and crammed them into their backpacks, which I plunked onto their shoulders.

"Hurry now," I said, "or you'll be late for school."

Hugs and kisses to the kids, swirling around, avoiding my husband, being a busy bee pretending all is perfect.

"You forgot to kiss Dad, Mom," Max said. "You always kiss Dad."

I froze, eyes locking with Rob's.

He leaned in. I bent forward, closed my eyes, and waited.

His lips hit my . . . cheek.

"All right, buddy," Rob said. "Let's hit it before we're late."

I thought I was a strong person, but in that moment I felt very weak.

The kids were out the door. The house was quiet. I was alone and holding a carton of blueberries.

What the hell was I doing with my life?

CHAPTER NINETEEN

"Hey," a feminine voice said two days later. The greeting was accompanied by red nails scratching lightly down his spine.

Rob shivered, slung an arm around Celeste's waist to tug her tightly against him. She slid closer still, and plunked her ass into his lap. He shifted, adjusting those hourglass curves sideways over his legs.

"Is that a banana in your pocket . . ." she began, lips curved up and one perfectly shaped eyebrow raised.

"No," he muttered, jutting his chin up and flicking his eyes over her shoulder when she glanced back at him.

Her bottom lip slipped out for a moment before she sighed and looked forward.

They were in deep, four towns over where Celeste had stumbled upon a lead for who was dealing in the Tri-Hills. And by deep, Rob meant that he didn't know the next time he would be home. He hadn't been able to tell Melissa or his co-workers about the case.

It had all happened fast. He'd pitched Celeste's plan to his chief and they'd fine-tuned the cover—Rob was out on parole for an arms deal gone bad. Celeste was his girlfriend who liked the white powder too much.

Celeste's source had then secured them a meet . . . or rather an invitation to a party filled with addicts and criminals.

The rest was up to them. They were to infiltrate the group and find the supplier.

And because there was some suspicion that the dealer was being assisted by dirty cops, he and Celeste were strictly reporting to their chief, who was working with the police chief of *this* town on a one-on-one basis.

It was a shit show. A twisted mess and a plan that screamed half-cocked. Alone and one wrong move could mean their lives.

But Rob just had to think about the murdered girl to get his head on straight.

If he didn't solve this, if he didn't manage to remove this poison from the Tri-Hills, Allie could end up the same.

Damaged. Broken. Scared.

Dead.

So for now, they partied. The house was gross, stinking, and disgusting. There was booze, piles of drugs around—lines of coke literally dotted every flat surface in sight—and what he assumed were illegal guns.

He was fucking miserable.

When he'd been promoted to detective, his thoughts had drifted toward stolen pies from the bakery and teenagers releasing goats in high school hallways.

Not drugs and weapons and murdered girls in nondescript warehouses.

Not a woman who wasn't his wife sitting in his lap while he was deep undercover.

Not a wife who seemed intent on frosting him out and choosing her precious recipes over him.

Or a family who didn't seem to miss him when he was gone. He'd left a note because it was early. Had expected a text or call in response before he'd had to lock his personal cell phone away.

Instead, he'd gotten nothing.

Maybe he'd been working too long of hours for too many years. Maybe he'd put other people before his family. Maybe he'd pushed everyone away.

But he couldn't get that young face out of his mind, nameless, lifeless, and so pale. Her body stained with blood and bruises. Her skirt shoved up, fear fixed in the position of her limbs, in the scratches and marks on her arms.

She'd fought.

And he was throwing everything he had into fighting for her too.

Celeste laughed—a shrill, annoying sound that grated on his nerves. But the man sitting across from them seemed to like it. He crooked a finger at her, and Celeste clambered out of his lap, flashing him her red lace thong in the process.

He used to think that ass was gorgeous, but now it just seemed like she was trying too hard.

She dropped herself in the man's lap—tall, expensive suit, clear eyes unlike the rest of the druggies in the room—ran her hand down his chest, and leaned up to whisper in his ear.

The man glanced down at Celeste, studied her for a long minute, then smiled as he trailed fingers up her thigh.

Rob stood, ready to stop the man from assaulting his partner, cover be damned.

Celeste stopped him.

By grabbing the man's hand and tugging it higher.

CHAPTER TWENTY

"WHAT DO you think about my nails, Auntie Kelly?" Allie lifted her hand and showed off the alternating pattern of purple and bright pink. "Mommy says she's going to put sparkles on too."

I smiled and glanced over at Max and Justin, who were watching some animated show about teenaged superheroes. "Should we do Aunt Kelly's next?" I asked, smiling teasingly at my sister, who was about as far from sparkles and hot pink as a woman can get.

Allie giggled, which made Abby laugh, and Kel raised her hands in surrender.

"Not for me, silly girl. Nail polish doesn't hold up too long in the stables."

Justin glanced over, winked. "But I was looking forward to seeing you sparkle."

I sent him a mock-glare. "You're supposed to say that your wife always sparkles."

"I wasn't sparkling much when I was losing my guts this morning."

I glanced back at my sister. "Oh no. Has it started already?"

She nodded. "Worse than last time." A shrug. "I guess that's to be expected with two of them this time."

Allie cocked her head. "Two of what?"

We all froze before Justin came up with the best distraction for my horse-crazy Allie.

"Horses. Two new ones in the stables."

Allie shrieked. Which made Abby shriek. Which made Max glare and cover his ears.

"Actually, we have three new horses boarding this week." Kel's eyes caught Justin's, and I had difficulty holding back my jealousy at the shared look of understanding that passed between them. Rob and I used—

No.

"One is only two years old," Kel continued. "With the cutest heart-shaped marking just between his eyes."

"Really?" Allie clapped her hands together, probably mussing the polish I'd just painstakingly applied. "Can I come tomorrow and see him? Please? *Please?*"

Kelly laughed. "You know you're welcome any time, but," she added when Allie began spinning in circles and jumping up and down, "you need to check with your mom first."

I glanced down at my phone, frowning when I saw the calendar jam-packed with after-school activities. "Tomorrow isn't going to work, sweetheart."

The bottom lip came out.

God, she was cute. It wasn't going to work, but she was still cute.

"Max has soccer, and we're driving carpool, and you have Girl Scouts right after school." I shook my head. "We just won't have time to get out to the ranch."

"But—"

"We still have our riding lesson the day after, so we'll go over then, okay?"

The bottom lip didn't move.

Then it did, transforming into a brilliant smile.

"Daddy can drive me."

Her dad, whom I'd texted and hadn't gotten any response from. Who'd simply left a note saying:

On a case, not sure when I'll be home.
-R

Was that days? Hours? Weeks? *Months?* For how long?

Her dad. Who'd already been gone for two days, and I was still no closer to answering any of those questions.

"Dad will probably be working," I said. "We can't—"

I cut the words off before I could say "count on him." Because our kids didn't need to hear their father wasn't reliable.

"Dad is never home," Max grumbled.

I didn't affirm that I had been thinking the same thing for a while. Instead I said, "Dad does a very important job. He's helping to keep everyone safe."

My sister made a noise, but when I looked over at her, she wouldn't make eye contact with me.

I frowned.

Max sighed. "I know," he said, his voice wavering the slightest bit. "I just wish that he could make some of my games. I've been working really hard."

Max *had* been practicing hard. He'd been practically living and breathing soccer for weeks.

"Dad will be so impressed at the next game he comes to, buddy," I said. "You've improved so much."

"Yeah."

Max reached for the remote, turned off the TV, and stood. "I'm tired. I'm going to bed." He said goodbye to Justin and Kelly and goodnight to his sister before heading up the stairs.

"I'm tired" were words I'd never heard him utter before.

He was a fighter of sleep, not an acceptor. Always had been.

Which meant he was upset. Certainly about his dad, but what if it was something else as well?

"I—"

"Go," Kelly said. "We need to head home anyway." She scooped up Allie and pulled her in for a hug. "Go brush away those sugar bugs on your teeth, and I'll see if I can pick you up from Girl Scouts tomorrow, deal?"

"Yes!" Allie fist-pumped then sprinted upstairs to her bathroom.

"You don't have—"

"Don't you dare finish that sentence," my sister said. "I've got auntie privileges, and indoctrinating Allie to horses is one of them." Her voice dropped. "But I have sister privileges too, which means we need to talk about what's going on with Rob. Things aren't right between you two."

I sighed and dropped my head forward, staring at the one nice pair of flats that Rocco hadn't managed to destroy—probably since he was still uncomfortable and moving quite slow with the cast and cone of shame.

But staring at the blue leather didn't make the truth any less obvious.

"They're not right," I said. "We're not in a good place."

"Have you . . . well, tried to talk about it?"

My eyes flew up, locked with hers. "All I've done is try to get through to him, but there's nothing there in return. No understanding, no support! He didn't want me to go to New York. He hates the blog. He hates that I've found something to spend time on that's not devoted solely to him." My chest heaved. "It's—I just don't know what to do. I probably won't even get the show, but how could he begrudge me the chance? This is the one thing I've always wanted . . ."

"I know, Miss."

"Culinary school was too expensive when I had the chance." I leaned back against the wall, rattling the framed pictures of Rob and me and the kids—happy, cuddling, giggling—that lined the hallway. "Then I had to drop out of college to work and pay to put Rob through the academy." My hands were fists, and I smacked one against my thigh. "I did it because I loved him, because I wanted the chance for him to do what he loved. So, after everything we've been through, how could he begrudge me that?"

Abby squawked in Kelly's arms, and I jumped, having completely forgotten that she and Justin were still in the room.

This is why I bottled things up. This is why I didn't vent about the really big stuff to other people and *especially* not to Kel. Once the statements were out there, I couldn't take them back. They were always there, tainting future interactions, influencing how they would relate to Rob.

I didn't want to ruin their relationship with him.

I didn't want to badmouth him to them.

I just . . . wanted my husband back.

Justin's expression was fierce. "I'll pay for you to go to culinary school if you don't get the job." He reached over and pulled me into a hug. "And if you do get the job, you can film at the ranch. I'll get a babysitter to help with the kids." He leaned back. "God knows, we're going to need all hands on deck as it is."

"You don't have to—"

Justin snagged Abby from Kel's arms. "We're here for you, Melissa. We're family, and that means we have your back, Rob be damned." He glanced at Kelly. "I'll get her settled. Come out when you're ready."

He slipped out the front door, closing it quickly behind him and limiting the rush of cold autumn air into the warm house.

Abby's jacket was on the bench by the front door, as well as the diaper bag. I scooped up both and handed them to Kel.

She was looking at me sadly. "Is it really that bad?"

I nodded.

"Damn."

Silence. Then, "I know."

"I thought you guys had it all figured out."

My laugh was brittle. "Believe me, I did too."

She played with the zipper on Abby's purple coat. Pulling it up, down, up, down. "What happened?"

"I wish I could say I knew exactly what." My hands found the hem of my shirt, and I ran my fingers over the threads forming the seam. "He was promoted to detective six months ago, you know, and he's just been different."

"Different how?"

"Distant? I try to talk to him, and he seems unavailable. Longer hours."

"Do you think the job is getting to him?"

"That and—" Oh God, was I seriously going to confide in my sister about this? It was so . . . embarrassing, I guess, that my husband might be cheating on me.

What kind of woman did that make me? What kind of wife?

Kel's hands froze. "What?"

"I think he's having an affair."

CHAPTER TWENTY-ONE

My sister's eyes met mine, and there was a shadow in them.

A shadow that made my stomach drop.

"You know something," I said and, yes, there was accusation in my tone, but she was my sister. And if she knew something but hadn't said—

"I don't know anything." Kelly winced. "Okay, there was a rumor, but that was it. I heard it once and never again." She shrugged, bit her lip. "I just assumed it was small-town gossip at its best."

Damn.

I slumped back against the console table in the hall, the one that Rocco always managed to knock over. Probably because two of the legs were wobbly, I remembered . . . right before I almost went ass over teakettle two feet from the front door.

"Easy," Kel said, in that calming voice of hers. The one that made even the most rambunctious of horses settle. "Everything is—"

"It's not small-town life. Not—" I broke off. "Not after everything I've heard and seen."

Red lipstick on his collar.

She's not important.

My kids are.

"What did you hear? What have you seen?" Steel in that tone now, and while I appreciated the layer of I'm-gonna-cut-a-bitch, there I was again, sharing too much information. Unfairly influencing.

"Anyway," I said. "He hasn't come out explicitly and confirmed anything, but he's not here. He says he's on a case, but he doesn't respond to my messages, doesn't pick up when I call." I sighed, deciding to just let it all come out. The damage was already done. "He has another phone with text messages from a woman named Celeste. Add in bright red lipstick on his collar . . ."

A bright red that didn't match my skin tone, but that wasn't exactly the point now, was it?

"Celeste McDermot?"

My eyes flashed up. "I don't know," I said. "Why?"

"Because last I heard there was a Celeste at the station. A transfer from Denver who was looking to get her teeth into some real case work."

I frowned. "What kind of case work is there in Darlington? Stolen cows? A run-over mailbox?"

Kel shrugged. "I haven't heard anything else. Maybe she was on desk duty or something in Denver and wanted to actually patrol, or something."

"Well, I don't think patrolling involves calling my husband baby, do you?"

"No," Kel said. "It doesn't."

We fell silent.

I opened my mouth, to say what, I really had no idea. I'd felt this way since I saw the first text, as though the foundation of my life had been shaken off its piers.

And I guess that wasn't surprising.

My life and Rob's had been intertwined forever . . . or, well, since grade school.

He'd been there through my mother's various abandonments—when she would take our money and disappear to gamble it away. I'd gotten smarter as time went on, trying to hide the cash I'd earned from odd jobs, from my shifts at the diner in little caches throughout the house.

But she'd always found them.

And when nineteen-year-old Rob had let me hide it at his apartment, tucked in a shoebox under his bed, my mother had cleaned out Kelly's bank account.

Classy, she was.

It had been a while now, thankfully, since I had seen or heard from her. My mother may be dead, for all I knew.

How horrible of a person did that make me for not caring what had happened to her?

I should have compassion for a troubled woman, abandoned by a deadbeat husband, two mouths to feed, and no money.

Except, I remembered.

I remembered her turning the donations away, not caring to accept food for us and only wanting cash. I remembered coming home to find the house torn to shreds because she'd been searching for more money.

I remembered my stomach growling and trying to stretch food so that Kel wouldn't be hungry.

I remembered having to figure out how to pay bills, taking cash directly to the power company and the city offices just so we'd have electricity and water.

I remembered mowing every lawn in our neighborhood, delivering the paper, babysitting, working at the diner.

I remembered it all.

But most of all, the hardest, most piercing memory of that time is me trying every single damned thing I could do to make her love us.

It hadn't worked.

And now, I guess, I had a husband who felt the same way.

Kel hugged me tight. "I love you, you know that, right?"

I sniffed, nodded. "Yup." I forced a laugh. "And you're not so bad yourself."

She pulled back, cupped my cheek. "I need to get out there."

"Go," I said and opened the door. "Take care of them. Don't worry about me."

Kel squeezed my hand as she passed. "Someone has to."

CHAPTER TWENTY-TWO

"Just you and me, kid," I told Rocco a few days later.

His tail thumped in response, bouncing against the couch cushion. I'd had a "no pets on the furniture" policy when we'd first gotten him.

I snorted. Yeah, which had lasted all of a couple of hours.

But on this night, cool air creeping into the house and the heater not making headway on the chill in my bones, I was happy to have the little fluffball of energy next to me.

Even if I'd had to lift him onto the couch.

His leg was healing, but his injuries had definitely taken their toll. He moved a little slower, a little more painfully.

Yay, another thing to feel guilty about.

Dr. Johnson said that he would be stiff and sore for a while, but by the time six weeks rolled around, it would be a challenge to keep him calm. I'd even seen glimpses of that deadly propeller tail and pair of mischievous eyes in the exam room.

But two weeks in, another X-ray to make sure the bones were setting properly, and a fresh, smaller cast, and there was still no sign of his former puppy exuberance. He was more careful, more guarded, and less of an innocent goof.

"So rom-com or action?" I asked, picking up the remote and scanning through the movies available for free.

Allie and Max were having a sleepover at Kelly and Justin's. They were watching the latest kids' flick, not even out in theaters yet, since Justin apparently knew someone in Hollywood who was a big-time producer.

Food TV and Hollywood. Kel had jumped a few degrees in social circles when she'd married Justin.

Not that anyone would know if they ever met him outside of the office. He wore T-shirts and cargo pants.

Cargo pants.

With like a hundred and seventy pockets.

As a former military medic, he said he needed to be prepared, but I rather thought that his affinity for cargo pants was like women with dresses that had pockets.

I love your dress.

Thanks! It has pockets!

Snorting, I made my selection. "Romance," I announced to Rocco.

His tail thumped again.

"Glad you agree."

He sighed.

"Always a critic," I muttered. And now I was having a conversation with a dog. Great.

Still, I scratched his head, settled back with some sea salt and garlic butter popcorn, and lost myself in the movie.

The boy and girl met, fell in love before the girl messed up, causing the boy to leave, and they'd just about gotten back together before my eyes got too heavy and I drifted off.

I woke sometime later, the house dark and cold, Rocco snoring next to me.

I couldn't tell what had woken me. A creak? A buzz? I glanced at my phone and the screen was blank of notifications. All I saw was the picture of the four of us—Rob, Allie, Max, and me—acting crazy and covered in white after a flour fight while making some pie. Kel had taken the picture, and I'd always loved how happy and carefree we'd been in that moment.

But the picture wasn't why I was awake.

Creak.

That wasn't the house settling, that was the loose board in the hallway.

Rocco was suddenly awake, his hackles coming up, a deep growl resonating out of his chest before he burst from the couch and took off down the hall.

His reaction finally made me move. I unlocked my phone, dialed 9-1-1, and found the nearest weapon.

Never more had I wished for a gun in the house, but aside from Rob's service weapon, I didn't normally like having any firearms at home.

Rocco's nails scratched against the floor, his cast making a scraping noise as he turned the corner. I heard a male grunt and a crash before Rocco made a high-pitched squeal of pain.

My heart dropped, and I clutched the lamp tighter as dispatch picked up.

I rattled off my address. "Someone has broken into my house. They're still here—" Rocco gave a ferocious bark before crying out again. Shit. Shit. "Hurry!"

Then I did what was probably—no, was *certainly*—a really stupid thing. I hung up the phone and took off into the hallway, lamp raised.

But all I saw was the front door slamming closed.

I flicked on the lights, swiveled around behind me, afraid someone was going to sneak behind me, like in the movies.

The house was still. Quiet.

Rocco whined.

"Oh, honey," I said, tears stinging my eyes. "You did so good, buddy." I crouched and set the lamp down, seeing his crumpled form and the pain shading his black eyes. "I'm so sorry."

I needed to move him. I was scared to hurt him more than the man had already done, but he was right in the path of the door and shards of glass were all around. Wincing when one bit into the bottom of my bare foot, I carefully slid my arms under his body and lifted.

He whined.

"It's okay, honey. It's okay." I moved as gently as I could, hardly noticing the pain in my feet as more glass sliced through my skin.

I was just setting him on the couch when I heard the sirens and screeching tires as the—two, by the sound of it—cruisers pulled into my driveway.

"Police!" they shouted through the front door.

Rocco growled.

"It's okay," I told him. "I'm here!" I yelled. "In the family room."

The front door banged open, and footsteps pounded down the hall.

One of the officers—McMann, I thought his name was—came into the room, while several of the others fanned out to presumably search the house.

"I think he's gone," I said.

McMann nodded. "We'll check anyway."

"Okay," I said.

We waited in silence for a few minutes. Finally footsteps came down the stairs, and a gruff voice declared. "All clear."

I glanced away from Rocco and saw McMann, two officers I didn't know by name, and Hayden, one of Rob's close friends and a regular visitor to our house.

Or used to be. Before he'd gotten married and found a wife who was able to keep the self-professed worst-chef-in-Darlington in edible food.

"Melissa, are you okay?" he asked, crouching down in front of me.

"I'm fine," I said. "I know you have to question me, but can I please call Dr. Johnson first? I'm worried about Rocco and—"

My voice broke, but I took a breath and forced it to steady out.

"I want him to be seen as soon as possible."

"Of course," Hayden said. "Where are the kids?"

"Kel's," I said.

He released a sigh of relief. "Good night for it."

I nodded and stood. Then nearly collapsed back down with the first step.

Now that I'd noticed it, my feet burned horribly. I glanced down and saw blood staining the carpet.

"You're hurt," Hayden said, reaching to steady me.

"Just a few cuts from the glass," I said, limping toward the kitchen. "I'd forgotten."

"Wait—"

I didn't. I knew Dr. Johnson's card was somewhere, and he'd written his cell on it. I'd taken it from the car and put it with a stack of papers that I needed to sort through but never seemed to find the time. The vet office would be closed, so I needed his cell number.

"Miss, stop," Hayden began. "You're getting blood all over—"

"Doesn't matter," I said, rifling through the stack and sighing with relief when I saw the card near the top.

"Find what you're looking for?"

I nodded, held up the card.

"Good." Hayden swept me off my feet, nodded at McMann. "Call an ambulance." I started to protest the last, but he cut me off as he set me gently on the couch. "Your feet are sliced to ribbons," he gritted out. "Now sit and don't move. I'll grab your cell."

Rocco eyed Hayden a little warily but didn't growl again. He seemed to realize that the officers were the good guys, there to help.

Or maybe he recognized their uniforms because Rob used to wear one so often.

Hayden handed me the phone then crossed back over to McMann and the others. They began to discuss perimeters, patrols, and paperwork as I dialed Dr. Johnson's number.

It rang a few times before a groggy voice answered. "Hello?"

"Hi, uh, Dr. Johnson. This is Melissa, Rocco's—" My voice caught.

I heard rustling on the other end. "What's wrong?"

"Someone broke in, Rocco tried to protect me. He's hurt really bad, can I bring him in?"

"Are you safe?" His voice was fierce.

"The police are here," I said. "I'm good."

"I'm coming over."

"I can—"

"I'll see you in five minutes."

"Okay, the address is—"

"This is Darlington, Melissa. I know where you live." And he hung up.

When I set the phone down, Hayden glanced up from his conversation with McMann and came over. "There's a delay in the ambulance. They're stuck on a couple of calls in Campbell. Apparently tonight's a busy night. We'll drive you to the hospital."

"Dr. Johnson will be here in a few minutes. Rocco—"

He nodded. "We'll wait, and in the meantime, Davis and Cranz are going to go grab some plywood to board up your front door. They broke the sidelight to get in."

Ah. That's why there had been so much glass. Our front door only had one small window, but next to it was one of those long, skinny panes of glass. It had always been convenient to see who was at the door—read, avoid solicitors. Although, I supposed the pane also made it easy to see *inside* . . . and created a boatload of glass shards when someone decided to break in.

"I need to sweep up—"

"McMann is on it."

My bottom lip trembled, and so I bit it. Hard.

"None of that," Hayden said, but his voice was gentle. "You're one of us. We look after our own."

CHAPTER TWENTY-THREE

I winced as the nurse sprayed something cold and antiseptic into the cuts on my feet.

"Sorry," she said.

"I'm fine." But tears burned, and I bit my bottom lip to keep from crying out.

"Just a bit more glass," the nurse said and probed, probably gently but it felt like the fires of hell. "Almost done."

"Uh-huh," I said through gritted teeth.

"You know that my sister's daughter is in Allie's class. Ashley is my niece." She stopped, glanced up at me.

"Ashley's great," I felt obliged to reply. She *was* great, but while the nurse was clearly trying to distract me, I couldn't help but think this was really not the time for small talk.

She glanced back down. "My name is Haley, and my sister is—"

"Maggie," I said.

"Right." Another squirt of burning cold. How a liquid could set my skin on fire with sensation and yet still feel icy was beyond me. "She gave me a piece of that banana cream pie you made when she had Luke, and it was seriously the best thing I've ever eaten."

Food.

Now *that* was something that could take my mind off things.

"I love that recipe." I sighed. "The whipped cream. The fresh banana flavor." Haley switched feet, but I barely noticed. "There's nothing medicinal about it. And it's so rich. Perfect for a mom who needs a little indulgence after a baby."

"Plus, she said it freezes well," Haley added.

"It does," I said, excited now. "And you can add chocolate chips and a ganache and it's extra decadent."

"What else do you like to cook?"

I laughed. "What *don't* I like to cook, I think is a better question." Haley smiled up at me. "I like recipes that are simple and fresh for the most part, but I don't mind getting lost in something that occasionally needs careful balancing of a bunch of items in my pantry. It's like an extra difficult Sudoku or something."

Haley snorted. "Well, I admire you. I can't cook a thing to save my life."

"Come over," I offered spontaneously before frowning. "When I have a front door again, that is. I'll show you a few things."

"Really?" She set the tweezers on the tray and picked up the dreaded squirt bottle again.

"Really," I said through gritted teeth.

"Cool." A pause. "Last time, I promise."

I nodded as she let loose a stream from the bottle, mentally cursing up a storm even as I tried to distract myself from the pain by recounting substitutes for sugar in my favorite cake recipes.

"Done," she said. "The doctor will probably glue some of the smaller wounds, but a few will need stitches."

I wrinkled my nose.

"I know." She stood and started rummaging through cupboards, setting out various supplies as a familiar face walked into the exam room.

"Dr. Johnson," I said, surprised.

He smiled. "I won't stay long, but I just wanted to come and tell you in person that Rocco is fine. A little banged and bruised, but no internal injuries and his leg is still healing correctly."

I swallowed hard. "Thank you."

His hand found mine and gripped tight. He leaned close. "Where's your husband?"

I shrugged. "Working."

But I think the uncertainty must have shown in my tone because his eyes held mine for a long moment.

I didn't blink, *couldn't* blink. There was an intensity in Dr. Johnson's gaze that made my pulse speed up. It reminded me of the way Rob had looked at me. The way he *used* to look at me.

I wanted that. So badly.

Unfortunately, I didn't want it from this man.

"Dr. Johnson," I began.

"Sam."

"Sam," I repeated. "I can't—"

His lips quirked into a rueful smile. "I know."

The doctor—the people one, rather than the animal one—popped into the room and began peppering me and Haley with questions.

We both answered with alacrity until he sat on a rolling stool and started demanding supplies while engaging Dr. Johnson—*Sam*—in conversation about his practice.

Haley glanced up at me and rolled her eyes.

I rolled them back, at least until the shot came.

If I'd thought the irrigation that Haley had done had hurt, the shot numbing the bottom of each foot was way worse.

"It's better if you don't look," Sam said, turning my face toward his. He dropped his voice to a whisper. "Also, that guy is an arrogant jerk, but he's the best plastic surgeon for miles."

"How do you know that?"

"Because Justin called in a few favors to get him here," he murmured, warm breath hitting my ear.

It was a strangely intimate place to be, wrapped in a pair of arms that weren't my husband's.

"Which I know," he continued, "because I called Justin myself."

I stiffened, and this time not from the shot. My feet were numb, the only sensation I could feel now a distant tugging.

Which was unnerving, but also not the point.

I pulled back, glared.

"Your sister needed to know."

"I know," I said. "But not until morning. She's—she needs her rest."

Sam raised a brow. "I *know*," he replied, saying he knew clearly why my sister needed rest. There really were no secrets in Darlington. "Which is why I called Justin instead. He needed to be aware in case . . ."

"In case what?" I frowned.

"In case whoever went to your house, went to Kelly's next."

I gasped. The doctor paused, asked if I was okay. "Sorry." I waved him on. To Sam, I said. "Why would they—"

He shrugged. "Wouldn't be the first time an officer's family was targeted."

"Oh." I sat back, stunned.

"I'm not saying that it's anything besides an attempted robbery, but sometimes it doesn't hurt to be careful."

"Careful," I murmured.

I wondered if Rob was doing just that.

CHAPTER TWENTY-FOUR

Rob stumbled into the chief's office a little after midnight, bleary-eyed and unshaven. It had been five days since he'd been home.

Five days of sleeping on a disgusting motel floor.

Five days of attending drug riddled parties.

Five days of not getting any closer to solving the case.

Who was bringing the drugs in?

Fuck if he knew at this point.

All he wanted was a bed, a shower, and to sleep for twelve hours.

Chief glanced up from the stack of paperwork. It was their scheduled meet, once a week at midnight, when the station was closed and prying eyes were safely tucked away. "What are you doing here?"

Rob stopped. "It's—"

Chief put up a hand. "I know it's our time. But why aren't you at the hospital?"

Life was funny sometimes. He was literally dragging ass, had barely been able to shake the car tailing him and safely make the drive from Campbell to Darlington. His mind was foggy.

But the moment the word hospital left the Chief's mouth, he was suddenly, abruptly awake.

"What happened?"

"Melissa—"

His gut managed to both unfurl and clench at the same time. Thank God it wasn't the kids, but Melissa. Sweet Melissa with her honey hair, her light brown eyes, her soft smile—

"—house was broken in to. She's hurt."

And that unfurling disappeared completely, his gut twisting itself back into knots, a cold sweat dripping down his spine.

Fuck.

Fuck. Fuck. *Fuck.*

"I gotta go," he said and walked straight out of the office to his car. His personal vehicle was parked at the back of the station lot, hidden in an unused corner with little to no lighting.

It was the perfect place to hide.

Something he'd been doing too damned much of lately, he thought as he got in and cranked the engine.

Music was playing in the background and it was a mindfuck.

Because it was their wedding song.

He was instantly transported back to that day, to promising to love and cherish, to respect and honor—

He'd been doing a fuck-all job of that lately, working on a case, not home, leaving his wife to be injured when he wasn't there to protect her.

Rob tore out of the lot and drove to the hospital.

It only took ten minutes, but they were the longest of his life.

The nurse at the reception desk knew him on sight. If there was one good thing about being a cop, it was that he tended to know the right people in an emergency. "She's in ten."

He nodded and pushed through the door after she'd buzzed him in. His boots clipped against the tile floor as he strode quickly down the hall.

Seven, eight, nine . . . ten.

One inhalation to calm himself before pushing through the door.

His wife was laughing.

His wife was in another man's arms, laughing. She was pale, but appeared otherwise uninjured.

And she was in another man's arms.

Rob saw red. He stood there like a fucking idiot as a swathe of crimson literally passed over his vision.

Melissa's eyes drifted up from the man—*from the fucking veterinarian*—and finally noticed him standing in the doorway.

"R-Rob?"

"Out," he ordered.

"No."

It wasn't the vet that replied, but another man. This time the one kneeling at Melissa's feet.

He snorted. How fitting.

Then he actually noticed her feet.

And his throat went tight.

They were sliced up like chunks of meat that the doctor was slowly trying to piece back together.

He threaded the needle through the skin, pulling the two sides together.

Melissa winced, bit her lip.

The nurse, a blond in her twenties that Rob didn't recognize, noticed. "Stop," she said. "Feeling's returning."

"Damn." The doctor put down the needle. "I'm sorry we'll have to numb you again. Sometimes it just doesn't work as well in certain patients."

Melissa nodded. "It's okay." She closed her eyes, stiffening and letting out the slightest whimper when the doctor picked up a syringe and pressed it into the sole of her foot.

"Tell me about the time Allie decided to cut open her beanbag," the vet said, clearly trying to distract her, and making Rob feel lower than the dirt on the bottom of his boot.

Melissa's lips twitched. "It was the biggest mess. Looked"—she hissed—"like it had snowed, ah, inside the house."

Rob took a step forward, tired of standing there like a useless idiot.

"I had a dog once that decided to chew mine up," the vet said, gripping her hand and deliberately turning his back on Rob. "Took me three vacuum bags to get it all up." He rubbed her arm. "I still find those little balls in the house sometimes."

Melissa chuckled as she sank back against the bed, the doctor having finished with the syringe. "Me too."

"Why didn't you put her completely under for this?" Rob asked.

The doctor glared. "Because we don't generally need full anesthesia for stitches. Now, keep your comments to yourself, or get out. I want to finish this."

"Maybe you should just step outside until we're done," the nurse said.

"I'm her husband," Rob countered.

The nurse shot him a look that said, "So what?"

He opened his mouth to reply, but Melissa's voice stopped him. "Rob."

A warning. Just like with the kids.

And just like with the kids, it worked.

He dropped into a chair in the corner, sighed heavily, and bit his fucking tongue until it bled.

Then he watched his wife hold the hand of another man.

Watched as she looked to him for comfort.

It was excruciating.

"Shit," Melissa hissed, jerking back.

"Damn," the doctor muttered, reaching for another syringe. "And we were almost done."

"Don't bother with the shot," Melissa said. "That's worse than the stitches."

"You're sure?" the doctor asked.

"Just do it."

"Miss—" Rob began.

She shook her head at him. "Go," she said to the doctor, who nodded and went back to stitching.

Sweat broke out on his wife's forehead, and her normally bright-red lips went ashy gray. The vet didn't try to talk to her then, just held tight to her hand.

The room went silent except for the sound of Melissa's labored breathing, and Rob found himself leaning forward in his seat, gripping his knees in an effort to not jump up and throw the doctor halfway across the hospital for hurting his wife.

He hadn't felt this fucking useless since watching Melissa giving birth to the kids. But at least he'd been the one getting ice chips and holding hands and wiping the tears away.

This was fucking agony.

Then finally it was over.

The doctor stood and pulled off his gloves. "I'll leave discharge instructions with the nurse."

"Haley," the blond nurse said. "Just like I've told you a dozen times."

"Haley," the doctor repeated, either ignoring her sarcasm or exceptionally dense. "Good. Go over the instructions with her."

"Planning on it," Haley muttered as he breezed from the room, white coat flapping behind him and expensive shoes clicking on the tile floor. She began gathering supplies, tossing them, and moving to a computer in the corner.

"He's an asshole."

Melissa's tone sounded almost normal, except for the little waver at the end. And the sheen of tears in her eyes, the paleness of her skin.

"He's very good at what he does." Haley attempted neutrality. Then she rolled her eyes and shrugged. "But he *is* a giant asshole."

Melissa laughed.

It was a real one.

And as that tinkling sound washed over him, warming him from the inside out, Rob realized this is what he'd been missing out on.

CHAPTER TWENTY-FIVE

I squeezed Sam's hand. "You'd better go," I said softly. "Thanks . . . for everything. You didn't have to come." I gave him what I knew was a very watery smile. "To the house for Rocco. Here. You didn't have to stay."

For the first time since I'd met Sam, he looked uncomfortable. "It was nothing."

"It was something to me," I said sincerely and reached up to give him a hug. "Now go back to sleep."

"Unlikely," he said with a short laugh, arms wrapping gently around me. He pulled away. "Rocco's at the hospital, stable and comfortable, but we'll sort out what else he needs in the morning."

"It is morning," I said, glancing up at the clock on the wall.

One side of his mouth curved up. "How about at a more reasonable hour of the morning?"

"Deal," I agreed and waved as Sam left the room, not missing the fact that he and Rob shared a long cold stare before he walked through the door.

Haley wiped her hands on her scrubs. "Well." She sucked a breath through her teeth. "I'm going to get those discharge papers and supplies together."

Traitor.

But she missed my narrow-eyed glare because she was gone.

I glance at Rob, and blurted, "You look terrible."

He rolled his eyes. "Thanks. Good to see you too."

My husband had at least three days of beard growth, and the man could not grow a beard, so his face was covered in uneven patches of prickly-looking hair. Black circles darkened the skin beneath his eyes, which were bloodshot. He'd lost weight and clearly hadn't been eating or drinking properly.

If I didn't know better, I'd think he had a drug problem.

But I did know him. Or, at least I thought I did.

And drugs weren't on the plate of things Rob could tolerate.

"It is good to see you," I said softly. "Hasn't been much of that lately."

He paused, opened his mouth then closed it. His eyes flicked to mine, "What happened?"

That wasn't what he'd been about to say. I'd have bet my last casserole on it. But what was I supposed to do? We were in the middle of a busy hospital, this wasn't exactly the best time to have a discussion about the future of our marriage.

"Someone tried to break into the house."

His face darkened. "Where are the kids?"

"Spending the night as Kel's."

"Do they know what happened?"

"Justin does because Sam called him." His eyes narrowed at my use of Dr. Johnson's first name. "We decided to let Kelly sleep, with the babies and all—"

Rob stood and pushed his hands through his hair. "What babies?"

"I—" My voice faltered. He hadn't been MIA for long, but *God* he'd missed so much. "Kel is pregnant with twins."

"Holy shit," he muttered, pacing the room. "That's—"

"Yeah," I said. "That was my reaction as well. Three kids under four."

"Gross."

I snorted and lay back on the bed, suddenly exhausted. My feet were throbbing more by the second. I wanted painkillers—oral ones this time, because fuck needles—and to sleep for about a decade.

I wanted to wake up and have my life back to normal.

I wanted to wake up and have Rob back.

Talk about gross, I thought, mentally kicking myself in the ass. *Get it together, woman.*

Gentle fingers on my forehead, pushing back locks of hair, stroking the skin behind my ear softly. God, I loved that. "What's wrong?"

"You're not seriously asking me that question, are you?"

Dammit, now tears were leaking out of the corners of my eyes. I'd been strong. I'd held it together, but one flipping touch from Rob, and I was sobbing like a toddler denied an ice cream cone.

I needed his touch, craved his affection, and yet it had nearly destroyed me.

"No," he said. "I wouldn't be stupid enough to do that. Of course not." Dry humor laced his tone, but I wasn't feeling very amused.

When he slipped his arm under my shoulders, preparing to pull me into a hug, I squirmed away. "Not here," I murmured. "I can't. Just not right now."

"But you'll let *Sam* comfort you?" he snapped.

My eyes shot to his, angry and hot. I needed him away from me. I needed him not so close. If he were sweet and kind, if he brushed my tears from my cheeks and held me like he used to, I'd forgive him for everything. I'd forget about these last few months. I'd force the doubts and fury and hurt into the back of my mind, lock the door, and throw away the key. I'd move on and never deal with the issues destroying our relationship from the inside out.

And eventually we'd be right back to where we started.

So I said something to get that distance. Even though it nearly killed me to do so. "Sam's comfort doesn't come with strings."

"You're fucking kidding me, right?" Rob burst out. He turned away, shoulders stiff. "You're fucking kidding me." His hands came up, gripped the back of his head. "How is this my life?"

Haley tentatively walked into the room, discharge papers in hand. "Ready to go home?"

"I don't know," I said softly. "I really don't know."

But I wasn't talking to her. I was talking to Rob.

And he knew it.

CHAPTER TWENTY-SIX

"I NEED A SHOWER," I said, taking one hobbling step toward the house.

"Wait." Rob closed the door behind me, scooping up the plastic bag with my purse and other belongings inside it. "I'll—"

"I've got it."

Another step. Fuck monkeys, it hurt.

"Let me—"

"*I've got it*," I snapped. "I'm not weak."

"I never said you were." But Rob didn't argue further, just walked past me and into the house.

I took one more step, nearly crying with the pain, and wondering why in the heck I was insisting on playing the martyr. Not that it mattered, I thought. Rob was gone again. I leaned against the hood of the car, tentatively placed my right foot forward. Red-hot pain sliced through me. "Son of a—"

Maybe crawling would be better.

The door leading into the house was wrenched open, a stool holding the plank of wood back.

Rob marched out, fury in his eyes. His cheeks flushed, his hair a mess. He had the look of a man who'd been pushed too far.

I'd pushed him too far.

My lips parted. A tendril of heat tightened in my stomach. My fingers curled, seeking purchase on the smooth metal of the car.

What the hell, body? This was *not* the time.

He didn't say anything. Not a single word. Not one sound came from his throat.

Instead, he closed the space between us in a matter of heartbeats. His mouth was very close to mine, hot breath puffed on my cheek, my lips. It smelled of the cinnamon gum Rob liked, glazing my tongue, making me yearn for more of the spice against my mouth.

I remembered the first time Rob kissed me. We were all fumbling hands, heat, and teenage desire.

And he had chewed that cinnamon gum.

I'd inhaled the scent, let it soak deep inside me.

Then, just like now, that piece of wholly, intrinsically Rob centered me.

"I . . ."

"Not. One. More. Word." One arm snaked behind my shoulders, the other slipped behind my knees.

He lifted.

One second I was using the car as a crutch, the next I was in his arms, cuddled close to his chest.

Rob had the *best* chest for cuddling, firm and muscular but not too hard. I didn't want to snuggle with granite. I wanted give. I wanted a mix of soft and rigid . . .

Well, at least on his chest I did. Elsewhere I preferred hard all the way.

The absurd thought made me laugh.

I clamped a hand over my mouth when Rob glared down at me.

"What is it?" he gritted out.

"Nothing," I said, but in his arms I felt as though I were floating through a fluffy cloud.

Or maybe being carried on the back of a swan. Flap. Flap. Flap. We went up the stairs.

"I want a shower," I said when he set me on the bed.

"It's already warming up."

"Mmm," I said and grabbed for the hem of my shirt, yanking it up and over my head. Rob had seen it all anyway. My sweats were next. I shoved them down, only slowing when I inched them over my feet so as to not disturb the bandages wrapped around them. My underwear and bra were the last to hit the floor.

I frowned down at my feet. "I'm not supposed to get them wet, am I?"

He cleared his throat, eyes drifting down my body in a way that I might have thought was desire, if he wasn't seemingly interested in a woman like Celeste. A woman who was supposedly all curves and sex appeal and red lipstick and—

"No," he said. "The doctor recommended forty-eight hours. I'll grab a bag. We can wrap your feet in it and top it with a towel. Should be good enough for a quick rinse."

I laid back on the bed, hardly noticing when Rob left. It was hard to concentrate on anything when I was so comfortable. The bed felt like clouds.

More clouds.

I frowned.

I don't think I'd ever compared a surface to clouds and now I'd done it twice in as many minutes.

"Got some," Rob said, coming back into the room with two zip-top bags and a handful of rubber bands.

"Mmm," I said and spread my arms on the duvet. "This is like silk. No." I giggled. "Like clouds."

Rob shook his head. "You'd make a terrible drug addict. They gave you a half tablet of oxycodone and you're high."

"I'm not high," I said, brows pulling down. "This really is as soft as clouds."

"How many times have you thought about clouds in the last five minutes?"

I frowned, and he laughed.

"I guarantee it's been at least five." He circled my ankle and tugged me toward the end of the bed. "You always fixate on one word when you're drunk—though it's not usually clouds, *that* must be a perk of the good drugs."

"I don't fixate on words—"

"Awesome-sauce? Spectacular? Ginormous?" He raised a brow. "Any of those strike up a memory in that pretty mind of yours?"

I crossed my arms. "No."

"Oh, Miss, you're unbelievable." He wrapped the bags and rubber bands around my feet then lifted me from the bed. "You're also the most beautiful thing I have ever seen."

My breath caught. Clouds were pushed from my mind.

"What did you say?" I asked, hesitant. Surely I'd heard wrong. He hadn't—

Rob didn't use words like beautiful. Not to describe me.

"Feet out," he said instead of answering, setting me on the shower floor and adjusting the spray so that warm water splashed down my back. My feet remained outside the door. "Here." Gentle hands tucked a towel around my legs. "I know it isn't the warmest shower, but it's better than nothing, yeah?"

"Yeah," I said softly, knowing in my heart of hearts I wasn't talking about the shower.

"Hair?"

I nodded.

He reached up for the bottles of shampoo and conditioner then helped me wet my hair and wash it. Surreal was the only way to describe this scenario. My head felt full of clouds, and that wasn't the drugs talking. Any side effect of the oxycodone had disappeared at Rob's words.

His hands massaged my hair and shielded my eyes from the suds as he rinsed it clean.

I'd never felt so taken care of. I'd never felt so cherished.

How was that possible when everything was so broken?

He helped me from the shower and to the stool at my vanity. I hated going to bed with my hair wet, and apparently Rob remembered that since he grabbed my blow dryer and comb from the cabinet.

Gentle strokes unknotted the tangles before he stood and gestured to the blow dryer. "I'm helpless with that thing, but I'll grab you some pajamas."

"Rob?" I asked as he moved to the closet.

He turned back. "Do you really think I'm beautiful?"

Silence. Nothing except his eyes on mine, fathomless, his expression incomprehensible.

After a long minute, my eyes dropped to the blow dryer, and I flipped the switch, filling the room with the whooshing noise of air.

But I could have sworn Rob said something, and it sounded an awful lot like, "Yes, Miss. I really do."

CHAPTER TWENTY-SEVEN

I DIDN'T DO anything fancy with my hair, just blasted the strands until most of the moisture was gone, and when I switched the blow dryer off Rob was back at my side. A long-sleeved shirt and pajama pants in hand.

It was my favorite set, both silky soft and very warm, and very welcome because I was feeling chilled after the whole open-door-shower-situation.

"Ready?" he asked after he'd helped me dress.

I nodded. "Thanks."

Arms around me, a warm chest next to my ear. The bed beneath me, cool sheets, a hot husband . . . who pulled back and tucked the covers around me.

He was leaving.

"Don't," I said before I could stop the word and reached out to grab Rob's arm. I guessed those drugs hadn't completely worn off because normally I wouldn't have asked. I *never* wanted to come across as needy and, dammit, I knew it was important to rely on yourself, first and foremost.

But, the truth was, I didn't want Rob to go.

I wanted my husband next to me. Even if it was all just pretend.

"Please," I murmured.

Someone had broken into the house, Rocco was hurt a second time because of me, my feet were beginning to sting again, and . . . I was so damned lonely.

He pulled away. Slipped from my grip as easily as if it were nothing.

My throat tightened, tears filled my eyes, and I slammed them shut, not wanting them to slip free, not wanting him to see.

It didn't matter.

They slid through my defenses, wet my cheeks, dripping down to soak the cotton of my pillowcase.

Then the bed dipped.

I sucked in a breath. "I—"

"Not tonight," Rob said, wrapping me in his embrace, turning me gently so that my face was pressed against his chest. "Just let me hold you tonight."

My only answer was to scoot closer.

———

I SHOT to waking a few hours later. Early morning light trickled through the window of my bedroom, and the house was still.

But something had woken me.

I pressed my hand to my chest, trying to calm the racing organ as I sat up and listened.

Then I heard it.

Rob's voice.

It was hushed, barely a masculine rumble.

I glanced at the door, saw it wasn't quite closed. I could just make out the silhouette of one arm raised to his ear. He was on the phone.

My eyes flicked to his nightstand, to his cell on the polished wooden surface.

He was talking on *that* phone.

And we were right back to reality.

"*Celeste.*" Rob's pleading voice raised enough for me to hear it clearly. "Please don't do this."

Pain knifed through me.

And dammit I was tired of this man hurting me. I was on a perpetual merry-go-round of pain and really freaking sick of it.

"Celeste— *Stop*. Listen. You mean too much to me to—"

Fuck. This. Shit.

I threw the covers back and stood.

Then promptly collapsed to the floor in a pile of silk and throbbing limbs. I was an idiot for many things, least of all was forgetting about the fact that my feet were stitched together like Frankenstein's face.

"Moron," I muttered through clenched teeth, flipping over to my hands and knees and crawling my way into the bathroom.

"Please think this through," Rob said just as I reached the end of the carpet and the beginning of the bathroom's freezing cold tile. I'd loved the pale gray shade until I was actually pulling myself across the glossy surface. Nose distance from it, I thought it was really quite ugly.

Or maybe that was my heart talking.

"Don't do anything rash," my husband said to *another* woman just as I closed and locked the bathroom door.

I wriggled my way to my robe and wrestled it on before sitting on the step leading up into our bathtub.

Clean lines, gray and sky blue, double sinks, separate bath and shower, walk-in closet. Cozy white bath mats. A vanity with a gorgeous stool. Fluffy bath sheets . . . and not those tiny towels that hardly covered anything.

The bathroom was a representation of everything I'd ever wanted.

Right?

Rob and I had done nearly all of the work ourselves.

I remembered how proud I'd felt of the space.

We'd done it.

We.

That *we* was gone now.

Plink. A tear dripped down my cheek, dropped to the marble step. Followed by another. And another. And—

"Ugh," I growled, so beyond tired of crying. I was just done.

Done with it all.

There was a knock at the door. "Miss?"

I ignored Rob, instead turning on both bath taps to high, letting the sound of the rushing water drown him out.

"Melissa!" I heard him shout.

"I'm fine!" I shouted back.

"Why's the door locked?"

I didn't respond, rotating back to the tub and feeling the water. A bath suddenly sounded like a fabulous idea. I adjusted the temperature, flicked the lever to engage the plug, and began wrestling off my robe and pajamas.

The doorknob rattled. "Let me in."

I snorted. Unlikely.

"Melissa."

"I. Can't. Hear. You," I said lifting myself to the top of the tub before executing some kind of fabulous swing-my-leg-over-with-a-triceps-dip. "Thank you Pilates videos," I murmured.

Thunk.

The door shook in its frame.

"What?" My eyes swiveled toward the pane of wood. Was he really trying—?

Thunk.

Another impact. Another shudder.

"I'm *fine!*" I yelled, not wanting to be down another door.

Rob was either taking his turn to ignore me, or he hadn't heard me because his only answer was another jar against the door. Except this one was followed by a crash as the wood splintered and the lock gave way.

My husband stood, chest heaving, in the doorway. He stepped over the threshold, crunching splinters of wood beneath bare feet as he walked toward me. He wore a pair of old jeans that were as soft as butter, but his eyes were hard and angry.

"What the hell were you doing with the door locked?" he snapped. "You could have hurt yourself, and I wouldn't have been able to help."

I forced my eyes away, studying my toes as I leaned back in the tub. I could almost pretend he wasn't there with the noise of the water drowning out his footsteps.

Unfortunately, it didn't drown out his anger.

That was a pulsing cloud filling the room, weighing down on my chest, my heart.

I was hurting, I was worn down, I was . . . done.

Rob wrenched the taps off, reached across the tub to get right in my face.

"What were you thinking?"

His hair was mussed, twin tracks present from him running his hands through it. His face was slightly flushed, with just the hint of pink on his cheekbones. Hot breath, tinted with cinnamon teased my lips.

It did nothing for me.

It did absolutely . . . everything.

But I couldn't do *this* anymore.

"I want a divorce."

Rob stared at me for a heartbeat.

Just a heartbeat with those scorching black eyes before his mouth was on mine.

CHAPTER TWENTY-EIGHT

Rob wanted to strangle all of the women in his life.

Least of which his wife.

What was she thinking, walking on her feet? Trying to lift herself into the tub. She could have slipped and cracked her fucking head open, and then where would they be?

"I want a divorce."

His fingers dug fiercely into the granite surrounding the bath, so tightly that he was surprised the stone didn't crack under his grip. What the hell was wrong with her?

A divorce? Really?

He was never going to let that happen.

Rob leaned down, intending to get in her face, to remind her that they weren't this couple, that they made decisions together, that—

Her lips.

God, he'd always loved her lips.

Berry red and plump, they'd always reminded him of raspberries. Or maybe strawberries. She'd been wearing strawberry Chapstick the first time he'd kissed her.

Sweet. Succulent. And way too tempting.

Back then *and* now.

He closed the distance between their mouths. The kiss he gave her wasn't like the ones he typically gave her, not pecks or quick hellos and goodbyes, goodnights, cursory touches to prove that they still loved each other.

This kiss was heat.

It was frustration and anger. It was passion and fury. It was desire and tongue and lips and—

"Fuck!" he shouted, pulling back and bringing one hand up to the corner of his mouth as he sat back on the edge of the tub.

It was teeth.

Melissa's teeth.

Blood was on his fingertips when he pulled them away from his lip. "What the hell, Miss?"

She didn't look at him, instead staring at her toes, which were perched above the water and resting on the edge of granite. Her breathing was hitched and she reached forward to push the lever to drain the tub.

Rob shouldn't stare, but his wife was in front of him naked, and his eyes drifted down her body, noticing every curve, every freckle, every stretch of silky skin. He'd kissed each inch of Melissa a hundred times over.

Just not recently.

Which he suspected was a big part of the problem.

The water drained slowly down her skin, pooling at her breasts then her stomach, then her thighs, then it was gone and she was fully exposed in front of him.

Except for her face.

That was turned away.

He ran a finger down her arm and she jumped, turning farther away from him, her shoulders and hips twisting until she was practically a pretzel in an effort to escape his touch . . . his presence.

"You're—"

"I'm not too skinny, dammit," she screamed, scaring the shit out of him.

He jumped, almost falling from his perch. But then he really looked at his wife, saw what she was doing.

And it nearly broke his heart.

Stiff shoulders. Tense muscles. This wasn't frustration. It wasn't a spat that he could smooth over with a few words.

There was a fucking cavern between them.

How the hell had that happened?

How the hell hadn't he realized it *was* happening?

His voice was quiet. "I was going to say you're beautiful."

Melissa didn't reply, didn't move, didn't look at him.

Rob felt panic crawl into his gut and twist hard. His wife was a live and let live kind of woman. Not much got to her, and even if it did, she was able to compartmentalize it away. To put on a good show and move forward.

She didn't shut down.

Except, a voice niggled, with her mother.

Her mother had hurt Melissa so many times that eventually there hadn't been anything else.

No feelings. No more emotions spent. No energy.

Nothing.

Their relationship had become such an empty shell that when Sonya Harrison had finally left for good, Melissa hadn't cried.

Just as she wasn't crying now.

His gut twisted tighter.

"Melissa," he said and rested his palm on her shoulder.

She stiffened, somehow her delicate little body went even tighter until he could see the striations of her muscles through her skin, until the flesh under his palm felt like the granite around the tub.

He pulled back. Stood.

Would have left if he hadn't seen the relief creep into her frame.

She wasn't as locked down as she would like to portray.

Rob grabbed a towel. One that he remembered fighting with her over in the home goods store. They had been sixty-eight dollars apiece, and he'd abjectly refused to pay that much for a piece of cotton.

Melissa had threatened to never make her chicken and dumplings again.

He'd caved like a cheap suitcase.

They'd bought four of the expensive towels—because she'd needed two, one for her hair and one for her body, and of course they couldn't buy an uneven number of towels—and . . . he loved using them.

They were like silk, cozy and cuddly, and if a man of his profession ever got caught saying, hell just *thinking*, those words, he'd have been razzed out of the department.

He spread the towel over her, hating that she jumped at the contact, then reached into the tub and pulled her into his arms.

She started to squirm, but Rob merely tightened his grip, cognizant of her feet as he maneuvered her from the bathroom, across the carpet, and into their bed.

When he reached for the covers, Melissa tried to scramble from the mattress, but hell if he was going to let her escape now before they hashed this out. There was time, dammit. Even if it meant explaining everything.

"Stop," he muttered, pulling the quilt up and over them both, trapping her legs by throwing one of his over the top.

"Let. Me. Go," she said through gritted teeth as she bucked against him.

Then she cried out in pain and he felt like the biggest jackass on the planet.

"Melissa," he said, pinning her shoulders down and sitting back on her legs to prevent her from getting free. "Stop."

Not that she made it easy on him. She was wilier that Old Man Jacob, and that fucking octogenarian had tried to knee Rob in the balls after getting caught red-handed stealing Betty Jenkins' mailbox.

The entire mailbox.

Rob didn't understand people.

But he understood his wife.

Or he thought he had.

Because he barely recognized the woman beneath him. The coolness in her gaze, the underlying hurt, the stiff body below his.

"Talk, Miss."

She lifted her chin, turned her eyes to the side.

"I'm serious. Either talk or we stay here all day."

He wasn't bluffing.

And she knew it.

CHAPTER TWENTY-NINE

I STARED up at Rob and wanted to smack him.

Of course, to do that I'd actually have to be able to reach him.

Either talk or we're staying here all day.

Ugh. Freaking idiot men.

Did he think he could control me? Did he think he could bend me to his will? Did—

Hell yes, he did.

And why wouldn't he?

I *had* bent. Too many times. Bent and bent and *bent* until I'd felt as though I would break.

No more.

I lifted my chin, made my voice fierce. "If they offer me a contract, I'm taking it."

Rob's brows drew down, forming a little divot I used to love smoothing away. Then again there were a lot of things I used to love doing.

Including my husband.

Who was hot and hard on top of me.

Who knew that restraining me while I was naked would turn me on? Apparently my body was seriously into kink.

Gross.

Except, not gross. Because Rob's stomach was flat, his jeans were unbuttoned and—my eyes flicked down—he wasn't wearing underwear.

I felt like banging my head against the headboard. I probably *would* have if I could have reached it.

He. Is. Screwing. Another. Woman.

I can't be attracted to a man who'd do that to me. I just can't.

But I was.

And Rob knew it.

His eyes darkened. His hips dropped a little heavier against mine, letting me feel the weight of his arousal.

He liked restraining me too.

After all these years, I never would have expected to find something new that pushed both of our buttons.

Rob had always been gentle with me—soft and sweet and tender. I'd liked it, been satisfied . . . when we'd been able to make time to *have* sex with two small kids and a husband who worked insane hours.

But maybe I'd like something more too.

Which was a thought that had never crossed my mind. Not until recently anyway.

I was supposed to be grateful and thankful and whatever else that the universe decreed. My family was safe and healthy. We had food and security and—

Sometimes I wanted more.

Did that make me a bad person?

Maybe. I sighed. *Maybe, it did.*

"I hope you take the contract."

My eyes flew up, collided with Rob's. His were molten, dark and bottomless, inviting me to swim in their depths if only I could find the courage to dive deep into the blackness.

"W-what?"

"If you get an opportunity to do what you love, I want you to take it."

My voice caught in my throat, and then I shook my head.

He lifted one hand from my shoulder, rested it on my cheek. "I'm serious, Melissa."

I pulled away. "I'm serious too. I'm taking it, and it doesn't matter if—"

He bent, slanted his mouth across mine.

This time I didn't bite him. I wanted to. At least for a second. But then his hand slid from my cheek to my chin and held my head in place as he plundered my mouth.

Literally plundered. Like a rake or rogue or pirate.

Or at least that was how I pictured one of those types of men from the historical novels I loved. They took charge in their heroine's bed, making the poor girl—or in this case, my poor *brain cells* fizzle to almost nothing.

Rob's tongue pushed into my mouth, sliding along mine, coaxing, no cajoling, no *demanding* that it tangle with his. He pressed me into the mattress, laying the full weight of his body against mine as his other hand moved from my shoulder to my hip. His fingers were there . . . *almost there.*

I gasped, and he kissed me harder, pressed me firmer, tugged me closer until I didn't know where I ended and he began, until I was kissing him back just as fiercely and wildly.

I yanked at his pants, ripping at the waistband and shoving them down as far as I could reach.

Then he was naked.

"Oh God," I said when he finally released my mouth.

"Yes," he quipped, running his tongue down my stomach, delving it into my belly button.

For once, I didn't feel an ounce self-conscious. This wasn't about stretch marks or saggy boobs or lumps and curves where they shouldn't be. *This* was about heat and feeling and passion and desire.

This was needing my husband's tongue on me, *in* me more than my next breath. This—

"Oh fuuuck." I bucked when Rob pressed his mouth to me and gripped his hair like it was a steering wheel as I ground against his face.

I don't think I'd ever been this aroused, or at least not this quickly. Of course, it had been months since I'd had a good orgasm.

It wouldn't take months to have this one.

His tongue pressed, his fingers slid home, and I was gone. Flames licked up from my center to explode throughout my body. I glanced down, half expecting to find I'd turned to ash, but ash couldn't feel.

Not the emotions. Not the torment and need and *want.*

Everything with Rob was twisted up, knotted, and so fucking sick.

And I was worse.

Because I wanted him still. I wanted more. I wanted him inside me.

He lifted his head, grabbing the corner of the sheet as he sat up to wipe his face. My eyes slid away from the glistening on his chin, ashamed and turned on at the same time.

"Miss—"

I couldn't.

Not when his voice was that soft. Fuck. Tears burned. My chest rose and fell in rapid movements and not because my husband had just taken me on the fastest, strongest, biggest roller coaster of an orgasm of my life.

I didn't want to feel any of it.

Not the betrayal and agony, not the hope. I wanted to forget it all.

"Sweetheart." A swipe of Rob's thumb along my cheek. "Don't cry—"

I shook off the tendrils of emotion creeping in, the forgiveness for my husband, the urge to forget all and carry on like nothing was wrong.

I would probably hate myself for this, but I didn't want tender. I didn't want my heart involved.

I wanted a rough, raw fuck. I wanted to get lost in sensation and feel nothing but pleasure.

So I brushed his hand from my cheek and reached down between us. He was hot, hard as steel.

His breath hissed between his teeth and he went to pull my fingers away.

I stroked faster, held on tighter.

"Babe—"

"Mmm," I said, need coiling between my legs. I accepted the flames of desire because it cauterized the painful edges of my emotions.

It was all reduced down to rough. To smooth, warm. Wet.

I tugged Rob closer, biting at his neck, scratching his back with my free hand, pulling him tight, accepting him inside.

"Melissa," he groaned.

"Harder," I panted, arching up. Pain bit through my consciousness, my feet not quite ready for the exertion, but my body was. And that slice of hurt put me on the razor's edge. "Rob. Rob. *Rob.*"

"Fuck," he said, pounding into me. "Melissa, please say that you're with me. Please—"

The sheets abraded my back, the pillow bunched under my neck, the blankets tangled at my feet, and I didn't care one bit. Not when the pleasure was twisting, spinning tighter and tighter. "P-lea-se d-don't s-stop." I gasped out, his strokes breaking the words into multiple syllables.

He gripped my hips and stroked harder, deeper than before. His eyes were on mine, burning, excruciating as he took in every detail of my response. I ignored the plea, his need for connection, and focused on his body instead.

The way the cords of his neck strained, his skin shiny with perspiration, the ripple of his abs as he moved in and out, in and out.

And then I didn't have to worry about avoidance.

My eyes slid closed as my orgasm bubbled over and swept through me.

I was barely aware of Rob pounding into me one more time before he cursed and exploded.

I held onto that shield of pleasure as long as possible, gripping tight to the sensation, never wanting to come down.

But I did.

I eventually became aware of Rob on top of me, of my husband stroking my hair and holding me close.

His smell, his body, his touch. Initially, it was only that. Physical. But then my mind cleared, and it all came pouring back in.

Anger. Hurt. Betrayal.
And the worst . . . disgust.
With myself.

CHAPTER THIRTY

I shoved at Rob's shoulders, wanting him off me, out of me, away. Far, *far* away.

"Miss—" he began.

I shook my head, squirming harder, shoving more fiercely. "Off," I gasped. "Off now."

"Am I hurting—?"

"Get off me!" I screamed.

Rob's face hardened, but he sat back. I scrambled up, sliding to the side of the bed and swinging my legs to hang off the mattress.

It was only the pull of my stitches that stopped me from standing and running away.

I dropped my head into my hands, hot tears leaking from the corners of my eyes. What had I just done?

A warm palm landed on my shoulder, making me tense up.

"Why are you running?" he asked, as though genuinely perplexed why I might be pulling back from my cheating husband. One whom I'd known was cheating and *still* slept with.

Real freaking smart, Melissa.

"You're kidding right?" I snapped and yanked at the comforter, wrapping it tightly around my body. "Why would I be disgusted for fucking you? *Why?*"

"Disgust—" He snorted in disbelief, shoved to his feet. "That's a really shitty thing to say."

I laughed coldly. "No. A really shitty thing to do was to fuck your coworker and then disappear from our lives. To throw me and our kids away like we didn't fucking matter. *That* was the shitty thing to do."

Rob began pacing, his footsteps pounding even through the thick carpeting. "I've been on a case and couldn't contact you much, but I sent texts for you and the kids every morning and night. You were the one who never responded back."

I wasn't proud of what I did next, but I was a woman at her wit's end.

My fingers wrapped around the heavy protective case surrounding my phone, and I chucked it at my husband's head.

"Then where—" I watched the phone fly and collide with Rob's chest after which it plunked to the carpet. I know, I know, my aim sucked. "Where the fuck are they? Because I never saw a single one."

He bent and scooped the phone up, unlocking the screen before presumably scrolling through my texts.

Then he crossed to his nightstand where there were two phones. He snatched the non-cheater one that we'd picked out at the store together, leaving the other on the polished wood.

He pulled something up on the screen and shoved the phone in my face. "Look."

My eyes flicked down.

I read.

And my stomach twisted into knots.

I still don't know why you're not responding to these, but the case is almost closed. I'll be home soon, and we can talk. I love you and the kids.

I scrolled up, read another text.

I'm sorry about being away so much. I miss you. Tell Max good luck at his game.

I miss you and the kids so much. Being away for work sucks, and I would give anything for some of that blueberry cobbler you were perfecting a few weeks ago.

"It was pie," I murmured before shaking my head at myself.

Not the point.

My finger swiped as my eyes rapidly devoured the texts, seeing the words and not understanding. He'd sent them every day, every single day and night. But I'd never received them. Not one.

I love you, Miss. I wish I were home instead of here.

"I don't understand," I said when I'd gotten to the top of the list. "I didn't get any of these."

Rob was scrolling through my phone, reading the texts I'd sent him over the last few weeks. Texts I hadn't received responses to.

"I didn't get any of these either," he said gruffly.

We glanced at each other. What the hell was going on?

Suddenly, he cursed and came around to sit on my side of the bed, snatching the phone from my fingers.

"What—?"

"I just remembered something." He tapped several times on his phone screen, cursed, then tapped a few more times. "Fuck," he said. "Fuck me. She did it. She did it to *me*."

"Who did what?" I asked softly. My heart was starting to pound, hope an unstoppable bubble in my chest. Could it be a misunderstanding? Was it all just technology gone wrong or—

"Celeste fucked with my phone," Rob growled. "She put you on the blocked caller's list and then changed your contact information. Look."

My eyes flicked down, and I frowned at seeing my cell under the blocked numbers list. It was there, sure as my kids never managed to turn off the lights in their bedrooms. Or bathrooms, or pretty much any room in the house.

But who was to say Rob hadn't put it there?

He sighed at the expression on my face. "I didn't block you, Miss."

"Okay." I nodded even though I didn't feel one hundred percent confident. He'd been so distant these last few months, and this was almost too easy an explanation.

"Want proof?"

I shrugged.

He tapped at the screen again, pulling up the contacts section and scrolling down. When he stopped at W my heart caught.

Because there were two listings for wife.

One was "Wife." The other was "wife."

"Capital Wife" was the blocked listing. Rob flicked backed to the messages screen and sure enough "lowercase wife" was the number he was texting. It should have been my number, but when he clicked on the little circle near the top of the message chain, I saw that it didn't match my cell phone.

"I know this number," he said pointing at the screen, "because it's Celeste's work cell."

"And you just know Celeste's work number?"

Rob raised a brow. "We've worked closely together these last few months."

I snorted. "Yeah. I know."

"What's that supposed to mean?"

"Only that it's obvious to everyone in this town that you've mixed duty with a slice of on-the-job-pleasure and that Celeste was your favorite version of it."

"That's bullshit."

I stopped and glared at him. "Oh, so you haven't kissed her? Had your hands on her and her hands on you? You haven't touched or fantasized or *fucked* her?"

"What?" Rob jumped to his feet. "Of course I haven't."

"Rob." I sighed and stared up at him. "Aside from the lipstick on your collar that you came home to *me* with, you were seen."

His shoulders hunched up, protective and defensive at once, and that churning disgust made a comeback, twisting my gut, raising my blood pressure.

"I haven't slept with her," he muttered. "And any touching or kissing was strictly for the case."

"That according to you? How does she feel about it?" He froze and so did my heart. "Yeah," I murmured. "That's what I thought."

"Celeste can be a little persistent, but she knew I was married. That everything had to be on the level. We only pretended to be a couple when it was necessary to further the case."

The case. The God damned case.

My fingers clenched on the comforter. "Was the case so important that it was worth ruining us?"

Rob sank onto the bed next to me and took my hand. "It didn't ruin us. We're in a rough patch is all."

"My husband has been accusing me of cheating on him with our vet, when he's been pretending to sleep around with his beautiful coworker. Further, he—*you*—" I glared fiercely at him. "You deprioritized me and our kids until we had to either stop missing you or learn to live without you. And none of that goes into the lack of clarity you have about what the kids and I have been going through or addresses the jealousy or justifies the fact that you tried to stifle my dream." I flopped back and stared up at the ceiling. "What am I supposed to say, Rob? Oh, there was a cell phone snafu, everything's fine now?"

"I—"

"Because none of it is fine." I plunked my hands over my face. "It all sucks. I'm lonely and hurt and disgusted that I still want you. The kids miss you. They miss their dad who used to come to sporting events and school plays. I miss the man who didn't freeze me out and shut me down at every turn."

"I had to," Rob said. "I couldn't risk bringing our family into the case."

I propped my elbows beneath me. "Why not?"

His face closed down, and I knew that I would never get the answer that I might hope for, never get the explanation or understand if it was all truly worth it.

"Never mind," I said. "I get it. I'll never be worthy enough to confide in. I understand that I'm not part of"—I made air quotes—"the sheriff club and couldn't possibly understand all the idiosyncrasies of police work, but I was here, waiting and willing to be by your side." My voice broke. "If only you hadn't thrown me away."

"I didn't—"

"I don't understand why you're still here." I spread my legs and pointed between them. "Are you that desperate for another lay? Have another itch for me to scratch since Celeste isn't here?"

"Miss. I haven't—"

"Fuck off, Rob. Just fuck the hell off."

I interrupted him because it was easier to do that than allow his slick, charm-filled lies to fill my heart. It was easier to pull back and have distance rather than face the truth.

My family was imploding.

CHAPTER THIRTY-ONE

HE NEEDED TO COME CLEAN.

About everything.

If Rob wanted to keep his wife, he needed to tell her everything.

The investigation, the drugs, the kisses, and touches. He had to lay it all on the table and not leave out a single detail.

Because if she found out later that he'd glossed something over, any trust he'd earned back would be gone.

"Miss," he said, talking louder and faster when she would have probably interrupted to tell him to fuck off again—and rightly so, he had to admit. "Three months ago there were a series of robberies in Darlington, do you remember?"

She paused and he held his breath.

"Yes," she replied after a long moment.

"They were connected to a crime ring that was interwoven throughout the entire Tri-Hills area." Her brows pulled down and he added, "Darlington is still relatively safe. The burglaries were on the outskirts of town, if you recall?" She nodded. "But things are getting bad in Campbell and Douglasville and that's spilling over here at home."

"Has anyone been hurt?"

His heart squeezed. God he loved his wife. "Yes. A nineteen-year-old girl was murdered. She was blond with light brown eyes and a sweet face."

Her exhale was shaky, and he took a chance.

Careful to keep the blanket wrapped around her, he slid over and pressed his shoulder against hers. "Yes, she reminded me of you. Before Max and Allie. Before this house. A blameless girl who'd been hurt, and I vowed that no more innocents would be caught in the crossfire. But that's not everything, because she also reminded me of Allie and Callie and loads of others. I just couldn't get that girl out of my head." He placed his hand over Melissa's. "So when Celeste came to me with a plan that bordered on risky, I took it to the chief."

"Why was it risky?"

"No badge, no weapon, no backup. Chief was convinced that someone on the inside was easing the dealer's way. So it was just Celeste and me to watch each other's backs as we tried to infiltrate the gang. Problem was what we initially thought was just a couple of backwoods meth labs turned out to be a huge ring of cocaine dealers." Her hand twitched. "Yes," he said softly. "Big money, big crime, and big time over our heads. Which is why I was coming in tonight to tell the chief that we needed to pull out and involve the FBI. But—"

"Celeste wasn't happy."

Rob risked linking his fingers with hers. Melissa didn't pull away. "No, she wasn't. But the break-in here couldn't have been a coincidence." He swallowed hard, his voice gruff. "Now I'm worried I might have brought something huge down onto our heads."

"The kids—"

"They're safe at the ranch," he assured her. "I spoke to Justin before Celeste, and he's aware of what's happening. Between the extra patrols from the department and the private security he called in, that place is locked down tighter than Fort Knox."

"But—"

"They're fine, and you will be too once I get you there."

She nodded but didn't say anything for a long time. And when she did eventually speak it wasn't what he expected.

"Can you grab me some clothes?"

"I—"

Pale brown eyes flashed up to his, slender fingers scrunched the floral pattern on their bedspread. "I'm aware there is more we need to talk about," she said, her tone bordering on ice. "But this isn't exactly a conversation I want to have while I'm naked."

"I like you naked," he said.

Her eyes warmed for a second before her face closed down. "Yeah."

Rob bent to catch her gaze with his own. "Miss?"

She shook her head. "Now isn't the time for that conversation. There are more important things we need to talk about."

"Maybe." He caught her chin when she tried to look away. "But why did that hurt you?"

Tears made her eyes glassy. "It doesn't matter." A shrug. "It's an old hurt anyway."

"This conversation is going to take all night if I keep having to tear the information out of you."

That startled her into a laugh. "I guess so, huh?" She sighed. "It's just that I don't think you've said that you liked my body the way it is in a long, long time. I'm always too thin or I need to eat more, or you won't let me forget the one time I let anxiety get the best of me, and I stopped eating."

"What?" He sat back on the bed, genuinely surprised. "I love your body. I say you're beautiful all the time."

Melissa bit her lip. "I don't want to be a jerk here, but think for a second and tell me honestly if you can remember a time when either of us talked about anything other than the kids or their school or getting them to some extracurricular activity." She gripped the blanket tighter, and Rob got up to grab her a tank top and a pair of pajama pants. He'd been hurting his wife for a very long while. The least he could do was get her some clothes.

"And I'm not innocent either," she said, her words coming fast as he walked back to the bed, clothes in hand. She always did that when she struck a blow in an argument. Tried to make everything else a little softer, tried to shoulder extra blame so that he would somehow feel less culpable.

But her words were the truth.

When was the last time he'd looked at Melissa as his wife first and not the mother of his kids?

Those two facts were inexorably tied together, and so that made them impossible to separate. Except . . . when was the last time that he'd just thought of her as the woman he loved?

Years.

"We've been drifting apart, and I haven't been good at bringing us together," she said. "I let the blog and TV show come between us."

He helped Melissa slip the tank top over her head then carefully guided her pajamas up and over her feet.

"I'm not jealous of the blog." He guided the pants past her hips. "And I meant it when I said that I want you to do the show. I do. I was worried about the exposure, that someone might connect something, and it would put you and the kids at risk." He laughed bitterly. "Turned out that I was able to do that all on my own, no media presence necessary."

He tucked the comforter around her, the weight of all the ways he'd hurt her bearing down on him.

Damn, he'd really fucked this whole thing up.

"Miss?"

She cocked her head to the side, probably because the nickname was so rasped out that it was barely recognizable.

"Yeah?"

"Maybe you should divorce me."

Good God, he couldn't even get that out correctly. Couldn't even man up and say what he was thinking. She should dump his ass and move on with her life, find someone to take care of her—almost any jackass would do a better job of it. Melissa needed to find someone to appreciate the gorgeous, loving, selfless, amazing woman she was.

That someone hadn't been him, and yet he hoped, *hoped* that she might forgive him.

So her next words gutted him.

"I probably should."

CHAPTER THIRTY-TWO

My feet ached, my stitches burned, and my heart felt as though it had been shattered then pieced agonizingly back together.

Bruised. Tender. And somehow whole again.

"Rob," I said when he nodded and stood, obviously not understanding my previous words, not hearing the "should" as I had.

I should, but I couldn't. Not when the whole situation was twisted but unintended, agony without malice.

He froze at the sound of his name on my lips, looking back at me with dark eyes devoid of hope.

And that hurt perhaps more than anything else.

Rob was my husband, but he was also a man who couldn't abide failure—his, not others.

Other people's failures he understood.

His? Those were unforgivable.

I knew he'd be much, much slower to forgive himself than I would.

Maybe it was my childhood. Maybe it was the fact that I'd been hurt over and over and *over* again by my mother. Maybe I was just beyond screwed up and incurably distant.

But . . . I could compartmentalize the hurt away. Tuck it deep down until it wasn't festering and instead was only a throb and then a pulse. Shove it away until it was nothing and then continue on living my life.

God, I was so screwed up.

"No, you're not," Rob said, and I blinked, realizing that I'd spoken aloud.

"Yes, I am." I put my hands on the bed, ready to push up to standing only to remember . . . my feet. *Argh.*

"This is so annoying!" I smacked my palms against the mattress, the sharp noise extremely satisfying when nothing else in my life seemed to be. Okay, well not *nothing* else. Fifteen minutes ago had been pretty freaking satisfying. It's just that I wanted to stand up. I wanted to *move*.

Toward Rob.

But I didn't know exactly how to do that. Could we really put the last couple of months behind us?

Logically, I understood.

Internally, my heart still throbbed.

I couldn't quite justify or comprehend how exactly we'd allowed ourselves to be pushed apart. What if the whole sick pattern repeated itself during his next case?

"What's annoying, baby?" he asked.

"I want—"

"Shh." His hand came up, covering my mouth. Which was pretty damn rude, thank you very much. I started to pull it off when I noticed his body. His jaw was clenched, his shoulders up and taut, and every muscle from his brows down to his toes was locked and loaded, ready to spring.

"Fuck," he hissed, eyes on the door, on me, on the bedroom. "I'm going to take my hand off, quiet okay?"

I nodded.

The hand was gone in an instant, and he was at the door in the next, closing it, engaging the lock with a click, and flicking off the light.

I wanted to ask what the hell was happening, but Rob was in cop mode and I'd promised him quiet.

And I'd never seen him like this, aggressive, catlike, silent but carefully coiled and ready to strike.

"Closet," he mouthed, scooping me up around the waist and carrying me through the bathroom.

I cursed my feet again even as I felt one hundred percent secure in his arms.

It's just that I wanted to be helpful. I didn't want to be one of those idiot fictional women who turned to the male lead and said, "What do we do now?"

Even though I was barely stifling the urge to do so.

At least until I heard the noises. Glass breaking. Footsteps pounding.

"Text dispatch," Rob said, setting me down in the closet and closing that door. Which didn't have a lock.

He slid our dresser in front of it, pressed four quick buttons on the safe on the wall—the one that held his service weapon, which I'd insisted on because of the kids—and pulled out his gun.

The *click* of the safety being removed sent a shiver down my spine.

"Miss."

I looked up into black eyes. The closet was dark, his face barely visible, but I could picture his eyes in my brain. They'd be kind but intense. Telling me to move my ass . . . but in a nice way, if that was even possible.

"Text them. Now." He listed a series of numbers and our address, which I dutifully typed into the phone and hit send. "Good," he said, and hunkered down in front of me, carefully sliding us into the deepest corner of the closet. Back behind our winter parkas and ski pants, behind our summer clothes—many months from rotation again—back until my spine hit the wall.

The smell was slightly musty, and as patently ridiculous as it was, I actually made a mental note to pick up an air freshener for the space.

Bad guys were invading our house, and I was making a shopping list.

That was some kind of screwed up.

But before my mental list got longer, I heard it.

Or rather *them*. On the stairs.

Rob seemed to get impossibly tenser, his body shielding mine as we heard the footsteps pound closer. They weren't bothering to be quiet. Instead they clumped through the hall, slamming doors, breaking things.

I mentally followed the footfalls through the second floor. Into Max's room. Then Allie's. And once again, I was beyond grateful for my sister.

Thank God my kids were not here.

Eventually the sound made it to our room.

I heard male voices and felt the house vibrate as they crashed against the door.

"That'll make three ruined doors in one day," I muttered.

Rob huffed out a laugh, shifting slightly in front of me as the crash reverberated through the walls.

"Stay behind me," he whispered. "No matter what."

My heart clenched. I nodded.

"Promise."

"Promise," I whispered.

And then the closet door shuddered.

CHAPTER THIRTY-THREE

I WATCHED the silver handles of the dresser rattle as the door was inched irrevocably forward. They rose and fell to the wood surface making a tinkle that was way too delicate for the current situation.

Then I heard them.

Quite possibly the best sound on the planet.

Sirens.

Quietly at first then louder.

The gap was wide enough now for the barrel of a gun to peak through into the closet. That black metal tube might have been the most frightening thing I'd ever experienced.

I worried it would gain enough purchase to turn and point at Rob. Then aim and pull the trigger and—

A curse rent the space, and the gun suddenly disappeared.

Footsteps pounded away from the closet, down the stairs, out across the back deck.

Blowing out a relieved breath, I started to rise to my knees.

Rob shook his head, placed a hand on my shoulder to steady me.

That was when I heard them.

Softer footfalls out of the bathroom, hitting the creaking step on the flight of stairs, slipping out the back door.

A chill slid down my spine, and my teeth chattered.

There was something immensely terrifying about the casual pace of the last intruder, as though they didn't care about the police sirens bearing down on the house, that froze my blood.

I didn't like it.

Didn't like the feeling it gave me.

But I didn't have a lot of time to process that emotion because there was a whole other series of crashing and banging and pounding footsteps.

"Police!" The dresser rattled again.

"Identify yourself!" Rob shouted.

"Rob?"

Rob sighed and stood. "Hayden," he said to me. "Yup," he called. "I'm going to move the dresser so we can come out."

Sticking his gun into the waistband of his jeans, he shifted the set of drawers back and out of the way. Then he flicked on the light, waited a moment, seemingly to allow his eyes to adjust to the sudden brightness, and cracked the door.

I was still blinking against the spots of white in my vision when Hayden stuck his head into the closet.

"Everyone okay?" His gun was still drawn, but resting at his side.

"We're fine," Rob said. "I need to get Melissa out to the ranch and talk to Celeste."

Hayden's eyes cooled, flicked to me crawling my way out of the corner. "I think that—"

I ignored them both, trying to pretend the flicker of pain at the mention of her name didn't actually hurt. I had clarity now, and while everything in our marriage wasn't magically fixed or perfect or hell, even average at this point, I understood the situation better.

I was just storing all the information aside until later when I could decompress and process. When I wasn't bra-less in a house filled with police officers who'd just managed to unwittingly scare away some men who wanted to seriously hurt us.

Or that was what I presumed, anyhow.

For now, I wanted to get the hell out of this house, get to Kelly's and hug my kids tight.

I wanted to pretend that there wasn't a drug ring the next town over. That my husband hadn't disappeared on me, only to reappear and try to play shining knight.

I wanted to concentrate on the fact that I might have a shot at my dream and that Max might score a goal in his next soccer game, and that I was totally going to let Allie enter that equestrian tournament she'd been begging me about.

I was going to pretend my house wasn't full of three broken doors, who knew how much shattered glass and ransacked drawers.

I was going to go and hug my kids.

Reaching up, I snagged my rattiest, coziest sweatshirt, yanked it from its hanger, and slipped it over my head.

"Let's go," I said, hobbling over to Rob.

"Miss." He frowned, glancing down at my feet. "You shouldn't—"

"We're going," I gritted out. "Now."

I was a woman on the edge. I'd been pushed too far.

Terrorized in my own home. Twice. A husband who withheld information to *protect me*.

Yes, there were mental air quotes on that.

"Melissa—"

"Now, Rob, God dammit!"

I smiled sweetly at Hayden, even as I shoved past him rudely. I'd probably be embarrassed by my actions later.

But I'd. Had. Enough.

"Bye, Hayden."

"Bye, Miss."

Ouch. Ouch. Each step was ridiculously painful. I was probably due a pain pill, but I didn't want to take the time. So I moved on my heels like some sort of deranged mummy and used every handhold and surface I could reach to help disperse my weight.

And I made it as far as the bathroom sink before I found myself slung up and over Rob's shoulder.

I grunted as all the air whooshed out of my lungs. "What are you doing—?"

"I miss my sweet wife," he muttered, navigating us to the bedroom and then down the stairs. "Where did she go?"

"You—" I fought his grip, nearly sending us both down the remaining steps.

Rob cursed, clamped me tighter against him, and finished the descent. "She used to be so easygoing, so caring. Now all I get is a fight." Louder, he said, "McMann, I'm taking her to Kelly's then I'll come back to give a statement."

"Roger that," McMann responded, and I could hear the amusement in his tone.

Asshole.

Out the front door, down the porch steps, and Rob continued talking. "A nice wife. A family. All I ever wanted. All I ever needed. Instead I get this—"

He popped me on the ass.

The *crack* didn't hurt, but it did make me see red.

And it made me do something I never thought I'd do.

I socked him.

Hard and right in the kidney.

"Oof."

All of a sudden I was right side up, having made a not so gentle landing in the passenger seat of my minivan.

Rob rubbed his back, and though I felt guilty, I couldn't bring myself to apologize.

After a moment, he crouched in front of me. His hands were on my knees, his eyes level with mine. "All I ever wanted was you, Miss."

I turned my head away.

"I like it when you punch me."

Shocked, my gaze whipped back to his.

"What—"

"I like it when you get angry." His palm came up to cup my cheek. "I like it when you're pissed off. I love it when you lecture me on the finer arts of baking powder versus baking soda."

I sniffed, opened my mouth to retort—

His lips brushed mine, softly, gently, a barely-there caress that was gone almost before my brain processed it had happened.

"I like it when you're angry because it means you care."

CHAPTER THIRTY-FOUR

I BRUSHED back Max's hair and pressed a kiss to his forehead. He was hot, that special kind of inferno that kids always seemed to radiate when they're sleeping.

He sighed, rolled to his side, wriggling deeper underneath the covers.

"Love you, snuggle bug."

Had he been awake, I would have received an eye roll in return, but since he was dead to the world and I'd just been through a potentially life-threatening situation, I figured I had Mom Cred.

In that, I was allowed to use whatever cheesy nicknames for my kids I wanted.

"Mom?"

I jumped when Max's eyes flew open and he stared up at me.

"Yeah, bud," I murmured. "I just got here so I thought I'd come in and say good night."

"M'kay." His lids drooped.

"Love you." I pressed another kiss, shoved up to my heels and shuffled through the Jack and Jill bathroom to Allie's room.

I wondered briefly if they'd have to give the bedrooms up when the twins were born, before internally chuckling. There were at least another six unused bedrooms at the ranch. Kel and Justin would have to make a lot more babies before my kiddos had to give up the privilege of their own room at Auntie Kel's house.

Also, this just in: thinking of my sister procreating was gross.

I rolled my eyes, gripped the doorframe, and made my way over to Allie's bed. I found that walking on my heels wasn't so bad.

She was sleeping on her back, arms and legs spread eagle, little body taking up as much of the mattress space as physically possible. She'd kicked the blankets off, so I pulled them up and tucked them tightly around her.

No doubt they'd be in a pile at the foot of the bed in no time, but I couldn't just let her stay uncovered.

She might get cold.

I leaned close, brushed a finger down one soft cheek, and pushed a strand of hair off her forehead. Her breaths were long and even, laced with the scent of her bubblegum mouthwash.

"Night, sweet pea," I whispered and tucked Mr. Tails, her ratty stuffed cat, under the blankets with her before stepping back.

Allie didn't reply, her sleep unhindered by my fussing. I limped my way out of the room and closed the door behind me.

Then nearly screamed when I saw the man in the hallway.

"Sorry, I didn't mean to startle you," he said softly. "I'm Danny with the security company. I wanted to introduce myself. I'll be on patrol inside all night."

My heart was thundering, and I placed my hand on my chest to steady it. "I'm Melissa," I said, happy my voice sounded relatively even. I mean the man was a giant. Several inches taller than Rob, and with arms that resembled tree trunks. Add in the tattoos and—I forced my eyes away— was that a bullet wound on his neck?

Or a freshly healed over one, anyway.

Holy soufflé. Just what kind of people did Justin know?

"Nice to meet you," I said into the silence that had fallen. What did one say to a man who looked like he could crunch you into a million pieces? He was going to petrify the kids.

But then Danny smiled, and I saw a kindness in his eyes that instantly put me at ease.

Okay, maybe he wouldn't frighten the kids so long as he kept that grin at the ready.

Danny extended an arm and handed me a cell phone.

It wasn't mine.

"Uhh," I said eloquently, even as I took the phone. It was the latest model of i-whatever and way nicer than my cracked screen, super old and slow version.

"A clean line." He shrugged. "Just in case. Your contacts are prepro- grammed. And if you need anything, security is speed dial under one."

"Okay." I stared at the blank home screen, half-expecting to see my picture of the kids and Rob and somehow disappointed when I didn't.

"Or you can text."

I nodded. Of course they wouldn't load family pictures on the phone.

But why then did it feel so wrong that they weren't there?

Ignoring the niggling, I thanked Danny and slipped past him.

Since I wasn't usually invited for sleepovers at my sister's house, I didn't have my own room. But Justin had said I could sleep in the empty bedroom directly across the hall from the kids. And no surprise, it was gorgeous, filled with expensive furniture I could never dream of owning and linens that probably cost more than my car.

Not that expensive furnishings and sheets were Justin's thing any more than they were Kel's, but Justin's family was old money, and that meant they came with things like a live-in housekeeper and thousand-thread count towels.

My sister had definitely moved up several spheres in the social echelon since Justin had come around.

But silky sheets and a luxurious mattress weren't necessary tonight. I was beyond exhausted from the events of the last day, and I would surely have fallen asleep no matter where my head landed.

After hobbling to the bedside, I pulled back the comforter and swayed a little. Given the swirling sensation in my head, the pain pill that Justin had forced on me must be starting to work.

But only just, I supposed, since I didn't have the urge yet to talk about clouds.

I wrinkled my nose, flipped off the bedside light, and flopped onto the pillows, tugging the blankets up and carefully slipping my feet beneath them.

Not even one day as an invalid, and I was already sick of it.

How was I supposed to parent if I could barely walk?

And it wasn't even like I had a broken limb and could manage on the other leg. Nope, I'd managed to mangle the bottoms of both feet.

Brilliant. Excellent work, Miss.

Sighing, I closed my eyes and waited for sleep to overtake me.

Son of a beignet, mother fillet of tilapia, and whatever other culinary curse words I could come up with—I really needed to curb my current penchant for the f-bomb if I didn't want to risk the kids picking it up. That thought was mute at the moment though, because my brain had decided that despite two break-ins in less than twelve hours, one ER visit complete with stitches, glue, and irrigation, and then some seriously way too adult and contentious conversations with my husband, it was not going to let me sleep.

No. It wanted to pour over every detail of the intrusions, of the words exchanged with Rob.

It wanted to focus on the sex. Which had been—

I bit my lip.

Really, really good.

My mind deconstructing each detail of the night was probably the only reason I heard Rob slip into my room.

I knew instantly it was him, in the way that a person's body knows another body as well as their own. Sudden awareness, a flash of heat, of comfort, and still, unfortunately, a small slice of hurt.

He was almost silent because Justin's house didn't have squeaky floors or unoiled hinges, but despite the darkness, I could track his movements. The careful closing of the door, the soft footsteps across the carpet, the careful descent . . . into the chair near the foot of the bed.

"No," I said and felt him freeze. "Here." I lifted one side of the comforter.

After a second, I heard him push to his feet. Then he was fully clothed in bed next to me.

But it was okay because he pulled me into his arms, held me tight to his chest.

It was okay because he was Rob, because he was my husband, because he smelled good, and his chest was the same soft-hard combination of man that had given me comfort so many times over.

"You were wrong to do what you did," I said.

His lungs expanded and compressed beneath my ear. "Yes, I was."

And then I fell headlong into sleep.

CHAPTER THIRTY-FIVE

"But Mom!"

I crossed my arms and glared down at my daughter. "Absolutely not."

It was Saturday evening, one day after the events from hell, and I'd just woken up. Which was totally going to mess my brain up for the week, but sleep schedules aside, my mom duties didn't end.

"Your Aunt Kelly isn't feeling well," I reminded her. We'd taken that route rather than explain it was because of a security risk that we couldn't allow Allie to go for a ride.

"Uncle Justin can—"

"Your Uncle is taking care of Abby and—"

"Allie."

Rob's voice warmed a trail down my spine. I glanced over my shoulder. He'd been gone when I'd woken up, but had reappeared like magic to carry me downstairs and settle me on the couch.

When I'd protested my feet were feeling better after the full day's rest, he'd simply rolled his eyes and lifted me up into his arms.

Then he'd tucked a pillow behind my back, settled a blanket over my middle, and handed me my dose of antibiotic along with a glass of water.

"Your mother said no." Rob crossed his arms. "So it's no."

I saw the explosion brewing before Rob did.

Cheeks going red, lips pressing tightly together before her chest filled with air.

"It's *not* fair."

"Sweetheart," I said. "We've talked about this. Sometimes things don't go to plan, and we have to make changes on the fly."

I purposely used an idiom I didn't think she'd understand, hoping the confusion and her typically incessant need for questions would diminish some of her anger.

Maybe it wouldn't always work, but it did this time.

"Why are you talking about a fly?" Her skin was still flushed but not nearly as much as before, and instead of tears in her eyes, she had questions.

"*On* the fly, honey," I said, grabbing her hand and pulling her close so I could cuddle her against my chest. Sometimes there was nothing better than the smell and feel of your kid. Soft and fragile and so, *so* precious.

Last night had reminded me of that. For a moment, I thought I'd never get to see her again, never get to hold her.

Even if she was going right back to driving me crazy less than twenty-four hours later.

"It means that sometimes things change without reason, and we can't control them. It means that we can't get upset about it." I held her pale brown eyes with my own. "We can be disappointed, but it also means we can't throw a temper tantrum because we understand that stuff sometimes happens."

Her brows pulled together, and I waited as she processed my words.

"You mean like when I spilled the milk?"

My lips twitched. "Which time?"

She giggled. "When you were going to make Max's birthday cake."

I nodded. "Yup. Just like that. Did it bother me at all?"

Her head bobbed like a marionette. "Oh yeah."

"But did I get mad about it? Did I yell at you?"

"No." She frowned. "You helped me clean it up, and . . ." I watched her mind work, smiling at the little v that formed between her eyebrows as she concentrated. "We went and bought more milk."

"Exactly." I stroked her hair back. "There was an issue, and we made the best of it. Max got his birthday cake a little late, and you helped me make the decorations a little extra special, right?"

"Right." Allie nodded firmly. "So Aunt Kelly and Uncle Justin can't go with me. But I can go by myself!"

She started to push off me.

I snagged her arm and sighed.

Sometimes when you thought you had it all figured out as a parent, your kid decided to throw you a curveball.

———

"AND SHE COULDN'T DECIDE if she wanted to be a land narwhal or a sea unicorn . . ." I read to Allie a few hours later.

"Look!" She pointed at the picture. "Rainbows come out of her horn."

"That's cool," I said and read on about the little unicorn that couldn't decide where she belonged, but discovered in the end that sometimes the place you end up belonging might be the place you least expect.

Damn. Sometimes kids' books were deep.

My lips twitched, and I glanced over at Rob who was sitting on the floor next to the bed and reading emails on his cell phone.

Not *that* cell phone, thankfully. Though my stomach still clenched at the thought of Celeste and the case and what Rob had actually done with her in the name of "case work."

He must have felt my gaze on him, because he put the phone down and met my eyes. His were earnest, the typically unfathomable black depths, strangely clear, and I knew it was his attempt at a truce, at putting the past behind us.

See, they seemed to be saying. I'm not a mystery. I have nothing to hide.

I wanted to believe that. For sure, I did. It would be simpler for me to shove it all away and just move forward, but I couldn't help but feel as though something between us was irrevocably changed.

And based on the way his eyes flitted from mine, focusing on the plush area rug near Allie's bed, he seemed to think the same.

Sighing, I closed the book and fussed with Allie's blankets, tucking her and the ragged Mr. Tails under her arm and pressing a kiss to her forehead.

"Night, sweetie," I said and carefully found my feet.

Rob stood, no doubt to continue carrying me around the house like I was his personal parcel, but I waved him away. Justin had brought me the crutches we'd forgotten at the hospital, and I could maneuver fairly easily between them and walking on my heels.

Much easier than the previous night, that was for sure.

I bent, snagged them up, and slid them under my arms. "I'm going to say goodnight to Max."

Carefully, I maneuvered through the shared bathroom and into Max's bedroom. He was lying on his floor, reading a graphic novel about underwear and a superhero. I rolled my eyes, wondered how many times he'd reread that one, and said, "Time for bed, little dude."

"Aw, Mom!" he groaned.

"Nope," I said, crutching closer. "No whining. It's late and it's lights out."

He wrinkled his nose, but set the book aside and crawled into bed.

I put the crutches on the floor and perched next to him. This was usually our time for a chat about the day or whatever random topic he decided he wanted to quiz me on. I'd already discussed the three branches of government, global warming, and the qualities of diamonds versus gold—and that was just this week.

Thank God for our local library, or I would have never survived the inquiries. Me not knowing the answer to his plethora of questions made for a great excuse to visit.

But today he didn't ask me about executive privilege or when the national parks were first established. Today, he asked me something much harder.

"Are you and Dad going to be okay?"

My throat tightened. Especially when he stared up at me, his eyes so similar to Rob's.

He was a mini-me of my husband, a portal to the past, to how Rob and I had been twenty years earlier.

And it was that history that made the question both the easiest and the hardest of my life to answer.

I tucked the blankets up to his chin, reached to pull the bottom up, exposing his feet to the fresh air.

Another thing that was just like his dad.

I smiled down at Max, knew in my heart my words were the truth. "Yes, buddy. We'll be okay."

CHAPTER THIRTY-SIX

I'D JUST WOBBLED my way into the kitchen when Kelly walked in through the back door. She was trailed by two men from the security company Justin had hired.

"Hey," she said as I plunked myself into one of her wooden chairs and set my crutches within arm's reach. "You're awake."

"I am."

She grabbed a bowl of watermelon from the fridge and came over to sit at the table with me. Her eyes flicked to Rob, who was standing guard behind my right shoulder and didn't seem to plan on sitting any time soon.

"How are your feet?"

A shrug. "Better than expected. Can you tell Justin thanks for the crutches?"

She nodded, squeezed my hand, and dug into the melon.

I smiled. "Can I risk snagging a piece? Or will you gnaw off my fingers?"

"Funny," she said, a dribble of juice running down her chin. "These babies, they just make me so hungry all the time." She paused, her hand coming to her stomach. "Either that or nauseous. *Ugh*." She pushed the bowl away, wiped her mouth, and leaned her head back to glance at the ceiling.

"Rob," I said and all but shoved the bowl at him. "Take that away and grab the saltines from the pantry. They're on the top shelf."

"I haven't had time to go to the store," she said.

I carefully patted Kel's knee. "I hid an extra box in there last time I was over." I smiled when her relieved eyes met mine. "For emergencies just like this."

Rob was back before I finished speaking, a sleeve of the cardboard-like crackers in hand.

I swear, there was nothing better for any stomach ailment than saltines.

I opened the package, thrust a few crackers at Kel, and turned to ask Rob for a glass of water, but he was already there, cup in hand.

Without a word, he set it within Kel's reach.

My eyes shot to his, and I felt the band around my heart, my lungs— the one that had been making it impossible for me to breathe, to feel anything deeply . . . I finally felt that band snap.

I had to look down, to take a couple of deep inhalations as I studied the grain pattern on the table and willed the tears away.

Was it relief I felt? Or fear?

Fear that I'd opened myself up to Rob again, that I couldn't continue to hold myself separate and safe.

That I'd go back to being the Melissa of the last few months.

Shut down. Distant. Weak.

Rob cupped my jaw in his palm. He shook his head, just once, as though he knew what I was thinking . . . as though to say, "Never again."

And then he kissed me.

It could have been our first kiss all over again. His lips were so gentle, so softly coaxing against mine. As if he were scared I'd pull away. As if he had to convince me to stay and give him a chance.

But here was the thing.

This was Rob. This was me. This was *us*.

I tilted my head to deepen the contact, to shatter all those walls I'd erected against him. I pressed closer, wrapped my arms around his neck.

There could never be anyone else.

Only Rob.

We broke apart, maybe a minute, maybe an hour later. I'd lost all track of time in his arms.

He panted slightly as he rested his forehead against mine.

"Miss, I'm sorry."

"I know," I said. "I'm sorry too."

We stayed like that for a minute, huddled together in our perfect slice of the world.

But all things had to come to an end.

And this one, the first good one between Rob and I in what seemed like an eternity, was shattered by a text message.

How fitting.

CHAPTER THIRTY-SEVEN

Rob put down the phone and turned back to his wife, but he couldn't bear it. His eyes flicked away, around the kitchen that had mysteriously emptied when he'd started sucking his wife's face.

Fuck. He stood, thrust a hand through his hair, knew he was making it stand on end but not able to give a damn.

Not about his wife. He fucking loved having her in his arms. There was nothing better.

But he didn't usually do it in public.

He glanced back at her, ignoring the slice of hurt in her eyes, ignoring the cell phone on the table.

It wasn't the secret one. No, he'd given that one to the FBI when they'd showed up earlier that morning and told him they'd taken over the case. That they were the right big shots for the job, and all would be wrapped up in a nice little package soon. He just needed to sit at home and twiddle his thumbs like a good boy.

Never mind that *his* wife had been hurt. That she'd been targeted twice. Never mind that his blood was boiling and he wanted to cut the fuckers into little pieces for daring to harm a hair on her head.

He bit his tongue and forced his inner Neanderthal to stop raging and his brain to start working.

Rob had been a cop a long time. He understood the chain of command.

He knew this case was out of his league. The department didn't have the right resources, and clearly his cover had been blown.

But . . . Celeste was still in.

And she'd just texted begging for his help.

"Rob," Miss said, and he turned back to his wife. The beautiful woman he'd just finally started rebuilding bridges with, their peace tenuous at best.

"You have to go," she said.

His knees wobbled. Actually felt like Jell-O until he got his shit together and manned up.

"Miss, it's not—"

She pushed to her feet and took a step toward him, stopping with a wince and an annoyed breath. "Come here."

He closed the distance between them, pulling her off her feet, and sat in the chair, trapping her in his lap so she couldn't get away.

Not that she'd get far with her feet—

And damn, didn't that guilt feel great?

What had he gotten his family into?

"Hey," she said softly, touching his jaw and forcing his stare to hers. "I'm the one who's supposed to be good at guilt trips, not you."

He snorted. "Hilarious, Miss."

"I understand now, honey." She dropped her head to his shoulder and sighed. "I still think the way you went about everything was wrong. That we should have talked it out, but I made lots of mistakes too." Lifting her chin, she met his eyes again. The hurt wasn't completely gone, but it was tempered with regret and . . . with hope.

God, he sounded pathetic.

"But this"—she touched the cell on the table—"*this* is what you are. If someone needs help, you go. You *have* to. I know it, and I think you know it too."

"I—" Except the words wouldn't come. How could he leave his wife again after everything had happened?

How could he leave her for Celeste?

"It was never about—"

"Her." She shrugged. "I know that. Now." Melissa gave him the softest, sweetest smile. "It was about us."

He nodded, started to shift her back to her own chair.

"But," she said, and her voice took on an underlayment of steel he rarely heard. "You're not running off half-cocked. I know you can't bring the department back into this, not after handing off the case. So you need to talk to Justin's security team. You need to have a plan." She glared at him. "You have to do this as safely as possible."

"I will," he promised and felt his lips twitch up. "Half-cocked?"

Melissa sighed. "Oh my God. You're impossible."

"You love me."

She touched his chest, where his heart beat a rhythm that only she could create. "I do. Heaven help me, I do."

CHAPTER THIRTY-EIGHT

I watched my husband's back as he left the house after several hours of planning with Justin's security team, and although the view was familiar as of late, it wasn't accompanied by all the angst and hurt of the past months.

This time I was nervous for him and praying that he would be safe.

But I wasn't hurting.

For once I wasn't hurting.

My heart that was. I grimaced, tucked my crutches under my arms, and hobbled back to my bedroom. My feet were screaming for another pain pill, and my brain wanted sleep.

I knew I probably wouldn't get it, not with Rob out there, facing who knew what, backed by Justin's former military comrade's security team. I knew the men were capable, that they trained for just these matters. And I understood that Justin would never put his family's safety—or mine for that matter—at risk. But that didn't mean I would be able to relax until I saw with my own eyes Rob was all right.

So I put some boring documentary on Netflix and tried to ignore how slowly time was passing.

The kids would be up before I knew it and then I'd be suitably distracted, I thought as I broke a pain pill in half and took a sip of water to swallow it.

For now, binge-watching.

I must have dozed off during the documentary on Nixon's impeachment in the seventies—riveting content I know—but then I was suddenly wide-awake.

I sat up in bed, pressing the button on my phone to see what time it was.

Blinking against the bright screen, I saw it was just after five in the morning. Barely two hours after Rob had left, and yet, I couldn't shake the feeling that there had to be a reason I was awake.

I grabbed my crutches and aided by the pain pill—which was only making me feel *slightly* high and squidgy . . . which I didn't even know for sure was a word and was probably a sign that I was high as a kite—I made my way to the bedroom door.

It wasn't the most graceful journey, but I got the job done.

Then I carefully made my way down the stairs. But since I was drugged and could practically hear Rob's growling voice in my ear, I did it by sitting down and scooting on my tush the entire way.

No headers down the stairs for me, thank you very much!

I made my way to the fridge and started pulling out ingredients for a breakfast casserole. I was awake and might as well make the most of it. But just as I'd set the milk on the counter and was reaching for the carton of eggs, my new phone rang.

Loudly.

"Dang," I muttered, realizing that I hadn't programmed the settings on the new cell Danny had given me. I lurched for it, swiping my finger across the screen. "Hello?" I huffed, leaving my crutches for a moment and using the wall to make my way out the kitchen door and on to the back porch.

"Melissa!"

"Tammy!" I said. "Hi!" My voice was too bright, and I knew it.

So, apparently, did Tammy. "What's wrong?" she asked. "Why are you out of breath? Oh, God. Did I interrupt something with that hubby of yours—"

"No!" I said quickly. "I hurt my feet is all."

"Your *feet*?" she said, incredulous. "As in both of them?"

"Yes." I waved a hand. "It's a long story. I'm fine. Anyway, I was trying to go outside so I could talk without waking the house."

I heard rustling, imagined her looking down at her phone to check the time. Then more rushing, and she was back. "Oh shoot, honey. I didn't realize it was so early out there. Sometimes I lose track of the time zone thing. I hope I didn't wake you."

I smiled. "It's okay. I was already awake."

"Cooking?" she asked.

"Of course."

"What recipe?"

I shrugged, silly that it was since she couldn't see it, then said, "I wasn't really going to follow a recipe. I was just going to make a breakfast casserole with bacon and potatoes and eggs."

She swallowed, and I could practically hear the drool through the airwaves. My talk of bacon and potatoes was making me hungry too. Especially when she asked, "Cheese?"

I chuckled. "Of course."

"Yum." Then her voice went stern. "I'll need pictures after you're done of course and"—she laughed—"maybe to come visit."

"You sound like Kelly now," I said.

"Aw. How is your sister?" Tammy asked.

"Pregnant," I said. "With twins."

"What?" Tammy shrieked a little. "Omg! Those babies are going to be adorable."

I sighed. "I know, right?"

"So right." She laughed again. "I feel like I'm jumping all over the place here, but we always seem to get off topic when we talk, like we're old friends just phoning for a chat."

"I feel the same," I told her.

"I'm glad. And doubly so because the network feels the same! They want to offer you a contract."

"What?" My voice was shrill. Happy. Shocked. But still shrill. "Are you serious?"

"Do croissants have butter?"

"Oh my God!" I slumped back against the wall. "I can't believe this. I —just—*oh*— This is amazing! Thank you, Tammy. Thank you so much."

"You did it on your own, honey. I'm just happy to be part of the process," she said. "I'll send the contract over. Take a look then have a lawyer review it. I'd still like to use the ranch to film if possible, but we can talk more logistics later. I'm sure you want to share the news with your family."

We said goodbye, and I leaned against the house for a moment, feeling almost numb.

Had that really happened?

Or was it the imagination of a drugged up brain?

I glanced down at my phone, saw that the incoming call was logged there, clear as the memory of the conversation with Tammy was imprinted in my mind.

The squee in my throat bubbled up, but I forced it down.

I was going to have a cooking show.

It was going to be amazing.

Already my brain was filled with recipes to try out, ingredients to drive into Denver for.

There was this awesome cheese store in the city, and I could make something with spinach and Gruyere or a dessert with green apples and white cheddar. Traditional, mid-west, but slightly more refined.

And Rob loved the Havarti from there. I could bake up some sourdough and then make fancy grilled cheese sandwiches with it. Bacon. Caramelized onion jam. Maybe some Swiss for tang.

I paused. I think I'd figured out what my drug-induced obsession word was this time around.

Cheese.

I was already thinking of the block of cheddar on the counter as I turned for the door.

But—

I rotated back around, trying to figure out what had pinged my brain, what had made my spine go ramrod stiff with alarm.

The sun was still behind the hills, the sky just the slightest hint of pink, readying for the day. The air was chilled, and the lawn appeared black.

So what was making the hairs on my nape stand on end?

And then I saw something that should be black and was decidedly not.

Light poured out of the open door to the barn.

CHAPTER THIRTY-NINE

I DIDN'T STOP to think. Just shoved my feet into a pair of my sister's boots that sat on a rack near the door, thankful that she wore a size larger than my own as my stitches protested the action.

But I pushed the pain aside because the barn door was wide open. The lights were blazing.

My sister had been raised better. She knew to close the door behind her, to flick off the lights.

My daughter, on the other hand, did not.

And Allie's words from the day before were suddenly blazing through my mind.

"I want to ride, Mom!"

"I can do it myself."

"I don't need Aunt Kelly."

Part of me hoped that I was wrong.

The rest of me knew I wasn't.

So I took off across the lawn, my commandeered boots hurting worse than a sugar burn and the hems of my pajamas getting soaked by the wet grass.

I wasn't entirely familiar with the horses and who should be in what stall. Hell, I didn't even know exactly how many Kel owned at the moment or how many were boarding.

I did know that there was a sign near the tack room with each horse's name and their stall number, and so I went there first.

Which is probably why I didn't notice the open stall doors at first.

At least not until I'd noted where Allie's favorite horse was supposed to be and then hustled down to number twelve.

"What the—" I muttered, seeing that the doors at four, six, eight, and ten were all pushed open. I checked twelve just to be sure. I could have read the board wrong. Maybe Kel had moved the horses somewhere else? Maybe—

Hell. Who was I kidding? My sister was never more thorough or organized than she was with her horses.

Still, I checked twelve.

Because that was where Allie had to be.

Twelve was empty.

My eyes slipped closed, and I took a breath. My stomach was crawling with panic that I was desperately trying to swallow down. I didn't even know if anything was wrong yet.

I spun around and felt the toe of Kel's boot catch on something.

I bent and a wave of frost shot down my spine.

Mr. Tails was on the floor of the stall.

I didn't have time to think of a cooking curse word substitute. I couldn't come up with anything except . . .

"Fuck me."

And my phone rang.

This time my fingers fumbled to answer it for a completely different reason than Tammy's call from just fifteen minutes earlier.

This time I knew if I answered it, everything was going to go to hell.

I just knew it.

Yet, what other choice did I have? I needed to pick up.

After swiping my finger across the screen, I lifted it to my ear. "Hello?"

"You're a bitch, you know that?"

My voice had disappeared. I blinked dumbly. Both because the insult had taken me by surprise and also because I felt faint prickles of familiarity at the voice. It was female. Cold. And filled with hate.

Had I heard it before?

"Answer me!" the woman screamed.

My throat unclenched. "I'm sorry?"

"Damn right you should be," she hissed. "Or you *will* be. If you don't do exactly what I tell you." A pause. "Say you fucking agree, you dumb slut."

I closed my eyes, forced my pulse to calm. It was pounding so loudly in my ears that I could barely hear the woman. "I'll do whatever you want."

"You'd better. If you want to see Rob again." Her laugh wasn't maniacal, but it was damn near close. "Or your precious Allie."

There it was.

The reason I'd run to the barn instead of staying inside the house. The reason my palms were sweaty and my hands shook.

Allie.

I clenched Mr. Tails in my fingers, feeling the material strain under my grip. But I couldn't loosen it because . . . Allie.

"If you want to see your daughter alive, you'll saddle a horse and ride straight out from the barn. You'll go over the hills and then follow the old cattle trail south. From there you'll receive another phone call."

"But there aren't any horses—"

This laugh was maniacal. "There is one horse left. And he's a mean sucker."

My gaze flashed down the corridor to the odd-numbered stalls, and I saw one door was indeed closed.

Three. I frowned, trying to remember which horse would be there—which, I got was a really stupid thing to consider when the animal was the means to my daughter's safety, but my brain was my brain, and it was rapidly trying to digest everything that had happened in the last twenty or so minutes.

And that was a dream coming true followed by a hell of a lot of fucked up.

So I probably shouldn't have been surprised when Theodore popped his head over the door.

"Oh. There he is now," the voice in my ear said. I'd nearly forgotten about the phone, but now I whipped around, half expecting to find the woman in the barn with me.

How else had she known that Theodore had appeared?

"Look up," the woman said.

I did.

"Now wave to the cameras," she sing-songed. "And know that if you do anything except saddle that horse and ride out, your daughter will pay the price. No phone calls. No texts. No running into the house for some more of those security guards." Her voice went chiding. "Rookie mistake, by the way, letting Rob pull off the exterior guards for his rescue mission. The company should have known better and sent more men to cover the holes."

"They're—" I bit off the rest of my words, mentally kicking myself for almost telling her what Rob had planned for the security.

More guards were coming. Actually, they would probably be there soon. Justin had said they would be at the ranch near daybreak.

She laughed and I realized I *really* didn't like the way she did that. It sounded like shards of icicles were piercing my eardrums, even through the call's airwaves. I didn't like how cold it felt, how unhinged and frenetic.

And my daughter was with this madwoman.

"Who are you?" I asked, despite myself.

Another cackle. "You'll find out soon enough. Now you'd better move. Your fifteen-minute timer begins now."

CHAPTER FORTY

Since I didn't have any pockets, I shoved the phone into Kel's boot then ran down the hall to the tack room.

I had only the smallest clue what I needed, having been in the room with my sister a time or two. I scoured my brain, desperately trying to remember what she'd put on Sweetheart for our trail ride with her and Allie.

Thank God everything was labeled.

There was a section that said Theodore and in it sat a saddle, a blanket, and one of those things with reins that fit between a horse's teeth. I started to pick up everything I could then froze, glancing up and searching the corners of the room.

Were there cameras in here? Could I risk a call?

No. The cameras out in the barn might have microphones. And if that woman heard me not following her instructions . . .

A text! I could—

But dammit, what if they were tracking my phone somehow? They'd gotten past the security team once. Who was to say they hadn't hacked the cell?

Shit. I had to do something. My eyes scoured the room, searching for a brilliant idea. I was running out of time, so I grabbed the only thing I thought was safe.

Snatching up a marker, I wrote on the whiteboard posted near Theodore's gear:

Hills. South on cattle road. Phone call. Woman. Has Allie.

Please let someone see it.

Then I picked up the equipment and sprinted out of the room.

Theodore was staring at me, and I wondered if he'd kill me when I tried to saddle him. This was the horse that had kicked Kelly in the stomach when she'd been pregnant with Abby.

My sister said it had been a freak accident. That he'd spooked during a lightning storm, that he'd been hurt himself and hadn't meant to hurt her. She said he was actually a misunderstood sweetheart.

I hoped she was right.

I shoved open the door and slipped inside the stall.

"Fuck," I muttered. I really hated horses, and I especially hated how big Theodore was.

I dropped everything to the stall floor, jumping when Theodore snorted and pawed the straw with his hoof, but forced myself to calmly pick up the blanket and reach to put it over his back.

He shied away, snorting again and bobbing his head in a way that I knew was not happy.

Allie was out there. I needed to hurry. I *had* to do this.

Dammit. *How* was I going to do this?

I needed to channel Kelly. WWKD. What would Kel do?

"Hey, sweetheart," I said, speaking in the same tone I'd heard my sister use before. "Did some people come in here and scare you?"

He huffed.

"I'm sorry. They're scaring me too. And I think they scared Allie—" My voice caught, and I swallowed, reaching with the blanket again. This time Theodore allowed me to drape it over his back. "I don't know where they've taken her, but they say I need to ride you out over the hills. Can you help me do that?"

He turned his head slightly, eyeing me as I lifted the saddle and set it atop the blanket. Luckily I was fairly tall for a woman; otherwise, I never would have reached.

"I'm not sure that I'm even putting this on correctly," I murmured. "You'll let me know if I hurt you, right? I don't want to hurt you, Theo."

He moved so fast that I didn't have time to react. All of a sudden his head was next to mine, and I stumbled, trying to move back. I knew he'd bitten Justin before. But he didn't try to bite me.

Instead he rested his head on my shoulder for the briefest of moments and blew air in my ear.

And I felt my eyes fill with tears.

"Thank you," I said, arms coming up to pat his neck. "Thank you, Theo."

I buckled the strap around his middle and reached for the reins. Theo let me slip them up and over his head. I didn't think I knotted them correctly, but it was a joke to think I had a chance in hell of controlling Theo anyway.

The saddle was on. There were reins.

Now I just needed to figure out how to get onto his back.

Kel or Justin had always given me a boost in the past, and I had no clue where the mounting block that Allie usually used was.

And I was running out of time.

I opened the stall door and started to lead Theo out of the barn.

He froze and my heart sank.

"Please, boy. I need to find—" The words stoppered up in my throat when he knelt, seeming to invite me to climb onto his back. I scrambled up, felt the saddle sway slightly as he straightened and barely managed to hold my seat.

But it would do. It *had* to.

"When we get out of this," I said, lightly tapping his sides with my heels. "I'm buying you a whole truckload of apples."

———

I BUMPED AGAINST THE SADDLE, squinting in the dim light as Theo trotted or cantered, or whatever speed wasn't quite a full gallop for the hills.

"You can go a little faster," I said. "I'll hold on tight."

He made a horsey noise that was either agreement or disbelief but picked up the pace.

The wind whipped in my face, yanking my hair around. It stung as it slapped against my cheeks and the corners of my eyes.

This was just not for me, I thought as a bug flew into my mouth.

Up and over the hill we went, and I tugged gently on the reins, slowing Theo as I looked for the trail. "South," I said, mentally going through the old adage Never Eat Shredded Wheat, "is to the right. There!"

I guided Theo to the start of the trail, and he began to walk down the path.

My phone rang in my boot, startling both me and Theo.

"I'm sorry," I said, trying to retrieve it without losing my seat. "Hello?" I answered once I'd finagled the cell free.

"That was sixteen minutes," she said.

My heart squeezed. "I'm sorry. I went as fast as I could—"

Her voice sounded positively gleeful. "Do you *want* me to hurt your daughter?"

"No!" I practically screamed. "Please. No. Don't. I'll do anything you want."

"I *wanted* you to be where you are one minute ago."

"I'm so sorry," I said. "How can I make it up to you?"

"You can shut the fuck up," she snapped then sighed, not saying anything for a long minute. I wanted to go on begging, pleading, but I didn't think it would be wise when she'd told me to can it, so I waited, heart pounding, throat tight.

"Ride on this path until I call you again." She hung up.

I blew out a breath. "You heard her, right Theo?"

He snorted, tossed his head, and trotted down the trail.

CHAPTER FORTY-ONE

The gunshot should have made Theodore spook.

It certainly made me almost lose my grip on the saddle, but Theo seemed to feel my weight shifting and moved, helping me regain my balance.

"Good horse," I said, stroking his neck as I kept my eyes on the person who'd stepped onto the trail in front of us.

By my guess, we'd been riding for close to an hour. The sun was just peeking over the horizon and though the world was still filled with shadows, they were growing less ominous and more like the real-life objects they were—trees, bushes, tall grass.

But the person—the *woman*—who'd stopped us on the path didn't look less frightening in the gaining light.

The gun in her hand certainly didn't set my heart at ease.

"Get down," she said, and hers was the voice on the phone.

"Why are you doing this?"

Click.

I knew that sound. It was the faint metal-against-metal noise of a gun's safety being removed.

"I said *get down*." She pointed the pistol at Theodore. "Unless you want me to shoot your perch first."

I lifted my leg from the stirrup and practically dropped from the saddle. It wasn't graceful, and my feet weren't prepared for the sudden weight. I ended up on my ass in the dirt with throbbing soles, but I'd gotten down.

The woman bent at her waist and laughed.

It was just as disturbing in real life as it was over the phone.

Ignoring her, I pushed to my feet and carefully stood in front of Theo, blocking him as I purposely let go of the reins and tried to shove him back in the direction of the barn.

He wouldn't budge.

"Go," I said, shoving his shoulder. At least I could save him. Or maybe someone would see him and realize—

"Freeze."

"Where's my daughter?" I blurted because the woman suddenly looked very scary.

She ran up to me and pressed the gun to the center of my forehead. "You don't speak unless I tell you to. You don't move a fucking muscle until I tell you to. Do you understand, you stupid, *stupid* bitch?"

I nodded.

Theo's head popped over my shoulder, and he bared his teeth.

The woman shoved his head away. "Shut up, you dumb beast."

Theo's teeth flashed, and he moved with the quick serpent-like speed he'd displayed at the barn.

He gripped the woman's arm and bit down. Hard.

She screamed, dropping the gun, and blood gushed everywhere. It was bright red, a crimson color that made me gasp and glance up at her mouth.

Because that was crimson too.

The same fire engine red I'd found on Rob's collar.

And I knew. Suddenly, I knew.

"Celeste," I whispered. Her eyes flashed to mine as she staggered to her feet.

I stumbled back against the pure hatred in her gaze, tripping over something in the dirt. Glancing down, I saw the gun had fallen between us.

I didn't think. I just dove for it.

The metal was warm against my fingertips, so much warmer than Celeste's icy hands as she grappled with my wrist.

For a second, she almost managed to rip it from my grasp, but I had a sudden burst of strength because I knew that if she took the gun from me that I was going to die.

It was the only bargaining chip I had, and I needed to keep it.

I tucked my feet between us and kicked her hard in the stomach. She grunted and held tight, both hands gripping and twisting my wrist. I felt something snap underneath my skin, cried out as a burst of white-hot pain shot up my arm.

But I didn't let go.

Instead I shifted the gun to my uninjured hand, tore my throbbing wrist free of her grip, and dug my fingers into the bite on her forearm.

She screamed, lurched away.

And I didn't let go. I moved with her, climbing on top of her and screaming at the top of my lungs, "Where the fuck is my daughter?"

"Funny, I was wondering exactly the same thing," came a cool voice.

I didn't have a chance to turn around and confirm my suspicion. The words had barely processed and my brain started pinging with alarm as it tried to comprehend—

Crack.

There was a flash of pain as something collided with my skull and then everything went black.

CHAPTER FORTY-TWO

S_ONYA_ H_ARRISON_. In the flesh.

Sonya Harrison. My mother.

Sonya Harrison, who I hadn't seen in so many years that she was almost a stranger.

Almost because even though her face had more lines and her hair was more gray, even though her skin had that thin papery quality that only came with age, her eyes were still the same.

They were my eyes.

"Mom?" I asked. Questions pounded the inside of my skull. Or maybe that was the headache from whatever I'd been hit with.

I tried to push to my feet but found I couldn't. My hands were bound behind my back, my ankles tied together. What the hell was going on?

"Where's Allie?" I asked, head spinning as I tried to search for my daughter. I was no longer on the trail. Instead I was inside a dark room, just able to see the outline of several windows and a door from the cracks of light shining in through their perimeters.

Brighter sunshine. So it was later than when I'd been on the trail. But how much later? How long had I been gone?

Someone snorted, and a light flicked on.

I blinked against the brightness, and when my eyes settled, I decided that I liked the room better dark.

"Where's my daughter?"

"As I said earlier," my mother replied drolly, "that was my question. Though I guess I should have said I was wondering where my *daughters* were." Her gaze slid to Celeste's and went disapproving. "You know Cal doesn't like to be kept waiting."

Celeste's face clouded. "I don't give a fuck what Cal wants." She turned to me, and I think I would have been terrified by the malice in her expression if I weren't still processing the *daughters* comment.

Did she have Kelly? What about the babies? If they hurt her—

Celeste lifted the gun, and I cringed back.

My movement didn't matter. She aimed. Shot.

I screamed as the bullet tore through the skin and muscle above my knee.

Sweat broke out on my forehead, tears streamed down my cheeks. My wrist and feet, which had both been throbbing before barely registered a peep as a burning pain consumed me.

"You idiot," my mother screamed. "We need her! If she dies, we won't have a way to get the money."

"Kelly," I murmured.

"That's right," Sonya said. "We need Kelly." Firm hands pressed on my thigh, and I screamed again as something was wrapped around my leg and yanked tight. "Hush now. Cal will be annoyed enough without you carrying on."

"Take this." A slap across my cheek had me opening my eyes to a glaring Celeste. She held a little baggie of white powder in front of my face.

I shook my head. Drugs were a no and besides that, how was I supposed to take it? My wrists were still bound.

"Take it!" she screamed, hands grabbing for my mouth, no doubt to force it down my throat.

I'd heard of drugs being laced with fentanyl, knew that it had killed people. Aside from the fact that I'd never taken an illegal substance before, I definitely wasn't going to willingly consume whatever white powder was in that bag.

I could barely handle a half of oxycodone. Who knew what a bag of drugs would do to me?

"Stop."

The voice this time was different. And male. And—

I struggled to not empty the contents of my stomach on the floor as my mother squealed, launched herself into the man's arms, and latched onto his mouth.

This must be my mom's new flavor of the month.

The man, Cal I assumed, tolerated my mother's attention for all of ten seconds before he roughly shoved her away.

He was tall, probably several inches over six feet and built. His skin was tanned, almost weathered, as though he'd seen many days on the back of a horse. He reminded me of the ranch hands Kel hired to help out with the horses.

"Enough," he said and wiped his sleeve across his mouth. "You can blow me later. We've got things to do."

"You can always just do *me*, Cally-bear," my mother said, blinking coquettishly up at him.

I threw up a little in my mouth. Really, it was all so gross.

"Stop with the nickname," he ground out. "It's Cal. And we need to move with this." His eyes flicked to mine. "This her?"

My mother nodded. "My oldest." A snicker. "Though not the prettiest." She glanced across the room, and my stare frantically followed hers. Had I missed something? Was Kel here?

But Sonya's eyes didn't stop on my sister.

Or at least not on one I recognized. They came to a rest on Celeste.

Daughters.

Kelly wasn't here.

Daughters.

"Holy shit," I muttered.

Celeste smirked. "She's kind of slow isn't she?"

"Not the prettiest. Not the smartest," my mother confirmed.

I studied Celeste, tried to find some similarity, because could it really be? And if it was true, *how* could it be?

But as I looked more closely, mentally erased the full face of makeup, the crimson lips and smoky eyes, I saw that there was indeed a resemblance between her and my mother.

She had Sonya's mouth, the angle of her jaw. Celeste had Kelly's cheekbones, the same color of hair.

Son of a sinking soufflé, *she* was my sister.

"This isn't really happening," I said. "This can't be happening. This—this isn't—I can't. I've—" My voice gave out, the words stifling. My heart was pounding, my skin was clammy, and whether from the shock of the news or the gunshot wound, I very nearly passed out.

"Hey." A gentle hand touched my cheek. Cal was staring at me. "Your other sister isn't here. Neither is your daughter. This was a ploy to get you, you understand?"

His face had somehow softened despite the hard lines etched into the skin around his eyes and mouth. This was a dangerous man. An evil man. I could feel with every fiber of my being that he wouldn't hesitate to kill me.

And yet his caress on my face was tender. His voice soft.

It was absolutely terrifying.

"Do you understand me?"

Allie was safe. Kelly was safe. That was all that really mattered.

I nodded.

"Good," he said. "Let's go." He swung me up into his arms.

———

I DECIDED I didn't like the trunks of cars.

I also decided that if I didn't get out of *this* trunk, I was probably going to die.

It was cramped, dark, and disgusting. Something was sticky against my cheek and I didn't want to think about what kind of bodily fluids were currently inches from my mouth.

But I'd discovered that I could almost get my hands below my feet and around to the front. The trouble was they kept catching on the heels of Kel's boots. So I was trying to wriggle the boots off and get my hands around, but the cable tie around my ankles and the *flipping* gunshot wound in my leg meant that it was a lesson in agony by inches.

Finally, I felt one of the boots begin to slide free. Slowly, *slowly* it slipped off and I was able to pull my foot loose and use it to toe off the other. Without the boots on, the cable tie was loose and I—

"Come on," I muttered through gritted teeth as I tried to yank my unhurt leg free. "Yes! *Finally.*"

Now I just needed to get my arms around to the front.

Carefully, I bent my knees to my chest, my injured leg screaming at the movement. I had contorted myself into a pretzel many times over for a yoga class. This wasn't any different.

Plus, my pain in this moment didn't matter.

Not if I wanted to live.

I had just inched my bound wrists past my butt when the car hit a bump. I cried out in pain as I was bounced around the unpadded space, but the jarring movement did what I probably wouldn't have been able to do on my own.

It freed my arms.

Well, they were still tied together, but they were in front of my body, and that meant I could finally do something.

I crammed them into my boot and pulled out my phone.

It had been buzzing against my leg consistently for the last ten minutes, and I hoped to God that meant that somebody knew I was missing.

My bound hands were too wide to reach my cell, so I turned the boot upside down then spent a good thirty seconds chasing the phone around the trunk when the car took a sharp turn and it slid away from me.

But then it was in my hands, and I pressed the button to light up the home screen.

There were over one hundred missed calls and more texts than I could scroll through.

I ignored them all and called Rob.

"Miss?" he answered before the call completed its first ring.

"It's me," I said.

"Thank God." He sighed. "Are you okay? Where are you? The barn. The sign—"

I slid across the trunk as the car made another sharp turn, whimpering when I banged my leg against something sharp.

It was a screwdriver and I quickly stuffed it into the waistband of my underwear.

"Miss? What is it?"

The car started to slow, and I knew I was running out of time.

"Listen, okay?" I said. "Don't interrupt." I paused and when he didn't speak, I hurried to get out as much information as possible. "My mom is behind everything. Her new boyfriend is named Cal. I don't know if he's a drug dealer or what, but he's dangerous. And there were drugs in the room and Celeste is here. She's my—" The air caught in my lungs. "Well, you won't believe it, but she's my sister, and she said she had Allie. I went to the barn, saw Mr. Tails. I thought they had her." I dropped my chin to my chest, my voice broke. "It was stupid. I know that now because they have me, and they're probably going to—"

They were probably going to kill me. I was going to fight like hell to prevent that. But I didn't hold any false hope.

There weren't too many scenarios where I got out of this.

"Melissa," Rob said. "I'm going to find you."

"Of course you are." My words were filled with a confidence I didn't feel as the car pulled to a stop. "I love you," I said and hung up the phone.

Because I was afraid.

Because I wanted the last thing my husband heard me say not to be a scream of terror or pain, but a declaration.

Of love.

CHAPTER FORTY-THREE

ROB HEARD the phone click and lost his fucking mind.

"Fuck!" He whirled and put his fist through the wall of the chief's office. It made a satisfying crunch as it pierced through the sheetrock. "Fuck!" He yelled again and probably would have made another hole if not for his phone ringing a second time.

"Melissa?" he answered, not looking at the caller ID.

"No," came a male voice. "This is Dr. Johnson. Sam. The vet."

Rob was blinking slowly, trying to settle his heart rate and listen to the fucking man who'd flirted with his wife.

He assumed there was a reason the jerkwad was calling and it had better be good.

It was.

"Is there a reason I just saw your wife get pulled out of the trunk of a car on the old McKinney property?"

Rob's heart skipped a beat. "What are you saying?"

"I'm at the Sinclair Ranch checking on some injured cattle. I just saw your wife being pulled from the trunk of a car on McKinney land. There's an old barn just off route seventeen. It's maybe two miles beyond the last marker."

For a second, Rob couldn't say anything. Then he got his shit together. He glanced at the chief who hadn't said a word about him punching holes in the office wall but nodded at him now.

"Whatever you need," he said.

Rob nodded back. "Okay. Can you call Justin and have his security team meet us at the Sinclair Ranch? We'll proceed to the McKinney property on foot from there."

"Done," Sam said and hung up.

Everything that Melissa had told him in her rapid-fire recitation flashed through his mind. Celeste was her sister. Sonya involved. Drugs. And—

"Wasn't the lead FBI investigator who took over the case named Cal?" he asked the chief.

———

ROB PARKED his police car behind the Sinclair barn as the chief, Hayden, and McMann—the only officers, *friends* he'd trust with his wife's life— tore into spaces beside him, kicking up dust and rocks. Danny and the security team had beaten them to the location and were working on a plan to infiltrate the McKinney property where Melissa was being held.

Danny came over as Rob got out of the car. "I'm sorry," he said, shaking Rob's hand. "We should have waited until the new team came in before we left."

"They were watching. They knew they had to pull us out to get to her. And if Celeste is in this like I think she might be . . ." Rob shook his head and took the camouflage jacket and hat Danny handed him, along with an earpiece.

They'd rolled up to where Celeste had supposedly been held, the location she'd texted earlier in supposed panic, only to find the warehouse had been abandoned for some time. They'd known immediately something was wrong, but it had been too late, and by the time they'd gotten ahold of the security at the house, Melissa had been long gone.

She'd been smart, though, and thanks to her sign in the tack room they'd trailed her to an old outbuilding on the property. But aside from a large amount of blood on the floor, there had been no sign of his wife.

"It's beyond inexcusable—"

Rob cut him off. There would be plenty of time for the blame game later. "They would have waited for any moment she was unprotected."

He and Danny both ignored the way Rob's voice wobbled on the last word.

Because the last damn thing a man wanted to do was leave his woman unprotected, and he'd done just exactly that.

"We've got eyes on her. She's alive, and we're ready to move in an instant." Danny pointed at the cell Rob held in his hand. "Have they made contact yet?"

Rob tried not to notice how Danny had seemed to deliberately avoid the *and well* portion of *alive and well*. "No contact yet."

But the words had barely emerged from his mouth when his phone rang.

And not the one in his hand.

It was the other one.

Celeste's phone. Which had been returned to the chief by the FBI's lead investigator.

Who was named Cal.

This whole thing stank more than a barrel of week-old fish.

"Hold on," Danny said when Rob pulled the cell from his pocket and went to answer it. He gestured quickly to one of the men who handed him a device that he plugged into Rob's phone. "Location set?" he asked.

The man—Rob thought his name was Anthony—nodded. "Set to Justin's place."

"Go ahead," Danny said to Rob. "But you're not here. You're at Justin's. Quiet everyone!" he shouted.

"Got it." Rob swiped and put the phone on speaker. "Hello?"

"Robbie!" Celeste chirped. "Have you seen your wife? Because I have when I put a bullet in her."

Rob opened his mouth, ready to threaten her within an inch of her life, but Danny squeezed his shoulder, giving him a hand signal to calm down.

"Where are you?" he asked instead.

She laughed. "That is classified information." A tsk, and Rob heard typing in the background. "Ah good. You're where you're supposed to be. And you'll stay at your brother-in-law's ranch until I give you some directions." Her voice went hard. "No investigating on your own, that's how you got your wife into trouble in the first place."

A boulder settled in his gut. "What do you want?"

"You." Celeste cackled. "Just kidding. I want some of your brother in law's money. Five million. Cash."

Cold slid down his spine. "Celeste. I can't—"

"Oh, you will, Robbie," Celeste said cheerfully. "You will. Twenties and untraceable. I'm assuming you can do that by . . . oh, let's say midnight." She sighed, the air crackling through the phone's speakers. "Or perhaps sooner if you don't want Melissa to lose too much blood."

"Celeste—"

But she'd already hung up.

CHAPTER FORTY-FOUR

I was cold and getting more chilled by the second. We were in another room—only this one was actually a retrofitted barn and had been brazenly lit from the moment we walked in. Part of the reason it was so bright was because of the sun pouring in through skylights overhead.

The other reason was the heat lamps.

One full wall was filled with marijuana plants using said heat lamps. Two others held shelves with blocks of paper-wrapped packages. I didn't know if they held drugs or money, but I suspected there were both.

Near the door was a rack of guns. Illegal ones, by the looks of them. Or at the very least they vastly overpowered Rob's small police-issued handgun.

I was on the floor in the corner, trying to appear insignificant and attempting to stay out of sight.

I'd had enough time to slip my phone into my underwear—on the opposite side of the screwdriver . . . hopefully they wouldn't both fall out and give me away—and cram part of my foot into the cable tie around my ankle before the trunk had flown open. I hadn't been able to get my hands behind me, but no one had seemed to notice that particular detail.

So, I sat in the corner and watched the sun go down beyond the skylights.

"Here."

I glanced up and saw Cal had extended a bag of pretzels in my direction. I took them in my lap. "Thanks," I murmured, but I didn't eat anything from the open bag, only reached my hands in until he turned away, and then stashed the bag behind me.

I wasn't eating or drinking anything from this place.

Leaning my head against the wall, I stared back up at the skylights. I was in a strange sort of euphoria. Nothing hurt any longer, and while I was cold, I couldn't seem to muster up the energy to care about it.

I wondered if I was going into shock and if Rob somehow managed to find me—maybe track my phone—if I was going to die anyway.

The tourniquet on my thigh meant that I wasn't gushing blood, but I did have a steady drip that kept the cotton of my pajama pants wet and sticky. Add in my feet and my wrist—now purple and swollen—and I hardly felt human.

Which was probably why I didn't scream when I saw the shadow peer through the window.

Some angel of death had come to take me away.

Or not, I thought and blinked up at a man I'd only seen once.

Danny. From the security company.

I squinted and leaned forward, but Danny shook his head, raised a finger to his lips, and disappeared from sight.

That cold lethargy disappeared, and despite half my brain deciding that I had imagined the whole thing, the rest of me got ready.

I was down a leg, one arm, and the bottoms of both feet. But my ankles weren't bound, and I had the screwdriver down my pants.

By the way, that was a terrible euphemism that nearly made me snort aloud.

Not that the room at large would have heard it because the moment I thought it, the front doors blew open. My mother screamed, Celeste grabbed a gun off the rack and began firing through the wall. Cal picked up a pistol and crouched in front of me, eyes moving between the disturbance at the front and the back doors.

What neither of them saw or heard were the windows shattering and the men rappelling in through the ceiling.

I'd not have believed something could be so efficient or rapid if I hadn't witnessed it with my own eyes, but I did see it, and it was amazing.

One tackled Celeste from behind, ripping the gun out of her hands and using his size advantage to pin and then handcuff her wrists and ankles.

Not so nice, was it bi-otch? I thought before my attention was pulled to Cal and the two men who were working to subdue him.

Blows were exchanged nearly faster than I could track, and he seemed to just be getting the advantage of one of the men when Danny grabbed him from behind in a choke hold and took him to his knees.

Thirty seconds later, he matched Celeste and was cuffed hand and foot.

Danny turned to me. "Are you—?"

"Where is she?" Rob thundered, sprinting through the debris at the front of the house. Hayden trailed him, the police chief two steps behind.

I opened my mouth. "I'm—"

The arm around my throat and the gun pressed to my temple cut off my greeting.

"Stop right there," my mother said, and I felt the *click* against my skull as she turned off the gun's safety.

"Sonya," Rob began.

"Where's the fucking money?" my mother screamed, and when I jumped she pushed the barrel even harder against my skin. "Shut up," she hissed and asked again, "Where is the money?"

"Sonya," Rob said, taking a step toward us.

"Don't move a muscle, Robert," she spat. "You were always an interfering little shit, and this is no different. You couldn't take Celeste's warning with that dumb dog of yours. No, you *had* to keep pushing and because of you Cal missed his chance at a drop." The gun came off my head, pointed at Rob. "You cost us fifty million, you son of a bitch." The barrel returned to my temple, dug in violently. "And just when we'd had you set up to take the fall, you had to go to the FBI."

"Where your husband works," Rob said softly.

I hadn't even known my mother was married again. I'd lost track of the number of husbands, in all reality. But it would have been really helpful to know she'd had an FBI spouse named Cal before Rob and the chief had gone to seek the government's help.

"You should have gone to ATF," I muttered. Or any other organization besides the FBI.

Rob's mouth quirked at the corner. "I agree."

"Shut up!" my mother screamed and yanked me to my feet.

I cried out in pain and collapsed to the floor.

"Stop being such a baby. The drugs on those pretzels should have you flying by now."

Except I hadn't eaten the pretzels.

Except the screwdriver and my phone had fallen from my underwear.

"Get up!" She yanked at my hair, and I barely had time to grip the screwdriver in both hands and get my good leg under me before the gun was back at my temple.

"The money's not coming," I said, shifting my weight slightly as I rearranged the screwdriver.

"Miss," Rob warned

I shook my head, twisting my shoulders to look up at my mother.

"You're always looking for that easy payday," I told her. "But I can tell you this time that it's not coming."

"Hate to contradict you, Melissa," Danny said. He tossed a duffle bag on the ground. "But the payday is here."

"Open it," my mother ordered as I slowly shifted my head from the gun. She still had a handful of my hair, but there was nothing to be done about it.

Especially when I saw Danny hesitate and knew the bag was only a distraction.

One deep breath and I moved.

Using a technique Rob had taught me long ago, I rotated under my mother's arm and brought the screwdriver up hard.

My hair ripped and my scalp was on fire. The tip of the tool met resistance . . . then that resistance was gone.

The screwdriver slid home.

I screamed and let go, falling to the floor as the men ran forward and grabbed my mother.

But I knew before I saw the empty, unseeing eyes.

I knew she was gone. Forever.

CHAPTER FORTY-FIVE

"Here we meet again, huh?" Haley, the nurse who'd cared for me on my previous hospital visit said.

I made a face. "Not that I don't like you, but . . ."

She grinned. "I think you're just trying to get out of that cooking class you promised."

I laughed. "Get out of and cooking are words that I've never uttered."

It had been three days since the incident at the old McKinney barn, just over seventy-two hours since—

I closed my eyes against the bile that seemed to rise every time I remembered the incident, and since I seemed to be remembering the events every minute of every day . . .

"How's the pain?" Haley asked.

I peeled back my lids, watching her as she probed the bandage just above my knee and checked those on the soles of my feet. "It's fine," I said. "Nothing is hurting too badly."

She touched the splint covering my right wrist, glanced up at my face until my gaze locked with hers. "I didn't mean the physical pain."

"Oh." My eyes filled. "I'm okay. I just—"

"Am reliving it every second of every day?" she asked.

"Well . . ." I tore my eyes away, stared up at the ceiling. "Yeah."

"Don't let it fester, okay?" she said. "Promise me you'll talk to someone about it."

I tilted my head so I could look at her again. "You sound like you speak from experience on that."

Pink lips pressed together, and her pale skin went a shade lighter, making the freckles on her nose and cheeks stand out in sharp relief. But she didn't shy away from the eye contact. Instead, she straightened her shoulders and nodded. "You'd be right." She fussed with her ponytail. "It was a long time ago, but time doesn't always make everything go away."

"I—" But my words were cut off by a knock on the door.

"Hey," Rob said, and my heart fluttered. Like it used to, like it was filled with butterflies.

"Hi," I said and couldn't find the words to say anything else. I just stupidly stared at him.

"I'll see you soon." Haley squeezed my shoulder. "Don't forget what I said."

"I won't."

Rob came into the room, plunking himself in the chair at my bedside. The chair he'd refused to leave from the moment I'd come out of surgery, until I'd forced him out of it that morning in order to go home and shower.

"How are the kids?" I asked.

"Anxious to see you again." They'd come yesterday when I finally felt like I wouldn't scare them.

I swallowed hard. After I'd stabbed my mother—*no, Sonya,* because she was no mother to me—the tourniquet around my leg had given way, and I'd lost a lot of blood really fast.

It had apparently been touch and go there for a while, Justin working on me in the back of a police car as Rob had rushed me to the hospital.

In some ways, I felt lucky that I'd passed out and hadn't been awake during those frantic moments.

I had enough nightmares to last me.

"Will you bring them after school?" I asked.

He smiled. "Only way I could get them to agree to go in the first place."

"They love school."

"They love you more."

I sniffed, felt my eyes well. "No fair. I'm supposed to be keeping fluids in, not losing more."

Rob's face sobered, and he went very, *very* still.

"What?" I asked.

His gaze dropped to the bed, and he picked up my uninjured hand, laced his fingers through it.

"I thought I'd lost you," he said softly.

"Justin wouldn't have let that happen," I said.

"Not then."

The serious tone of the words made my breath catch. "We almost lost each other, Rob."

He shook his head. "I—"

There was another knock at the door, interrupting his words, though I almost felt it was timely.

Because I had the feeling this conversation was one that Rob and I were going to need to have many times over.

"I'm sorry to interrupt," came a male voice.

"Sam!" I exclaimed.

The vet walked into the room, glanced at Rob and my interlaced hands, and smiled. "I heard that you're going to be discharged tomorrow and wanted to talk to you about Rocco."

My stomach clenched. "Is he okay?"

Sam put a hand up. "Totally fine. He's been staying at my house because I wanted to make sure you guys were ready for him. Do you want me to keep him a few more days? Or to bring him over tomorrow?"

"Tomorrow," both Rob and I said.

Sam nodded. "Okay then. I'll just head back to the clinic—"

"A word?" Rob said.

"I don't—" I began, but Sam said, "Sure."

Rob stood, pressed a kiss to my lips. "I'll be right back. Outside," he said to Sam once he got closer.

"I—"

But they were gone, through the door, and I couldn't follow them.

"Ugh," I muttered and stared up at the television screen. It was on Tammy's food channel, a celebrity chef whipping up a meal for her closest friends. The sight of the lovely cranberry, apple, and brie-laced bread was almost enough for me to forget about the fact that my husband may be coming to blows in the hallway with our vet.

I tried to convince myself it would be fine. Though Rob had been stiff and quiet, he hadn't been angry.

Or at least I hadn't been able to feel his rage as though it was a tangible thing, like the last couple of times they'd interacted.

I forced my gaze to the TV, tried to think of how I'd modify the recipe, and just was really beginning to worry when Rob stepped back into the room.

"Is everything—?"

"Everything is fine, Miss," he said. "Sam and I just needed to come to terms with a few things."

I narrowed my eyes at him. "What things?"

One half of Rob's mouth curved. "He was the one who spotted you being pulled from the trunk of the car on McKinney land."

"What?" All thoughts of bread disappeared. "*How?*"

"Luck," he said. "Sam was seeing to some injured calves on the Sinclair Ranch. It wasn't a place anyone would normally be." His voice gentled. "But we're lucky he was."

I nodded and knew that someone had been looking out for me that day. Normally, I wasn't religious or spiritual or whatever, but I couldn't explain away the feeling that I'd been slightly more than lucky.

Sometimes things just worked out.

"So I was thanking him. For that. For Rocco." He sighed. "For looking out for you when I didn't."

"Rob—"

"Hey, speaking of lucky," he said, obviously changing the subject. I think Rob and I *both* needed to talk with someone. Apart and, perhaps, together. "I think you've got a friend in Theodore."

"What?" I said, suitably distracted and then promptly guilty because I hadn't given the horse a second thought. "Oh my God. How could I have forgotten him? Is he okay?"

Rob grinned. "Temperamental as ever. I guess he showed up back at the barn as Justin and the hands were rounding up the loose horses and created all sorts of trouble."

"What trouble?"

"Would only let Justin get him and then when he was back in his stall, kicking and ramming the door until Justin let him out. When he still wouldn't settle, Justin finally re-saddled him and decided to give Theo free reign." Rob chuckled. "It's crazy, really, Justin came up to the McKinney barn like an avenging cowboy, dust cloud, pounding hooves and all."

I held my breath, imagining the scene, and glad, really glad that Theo was okay. The fuzz bucket was growing on me.

"Justin said that once Theo heard the shots, he started galloping and wouldn't stop. It's like he knew something was wrong and that Justin was needed there."

"A bushel of apples," I said, feeling suddenly exhausted.

"What?" Rob asked.

"I owe him a whole lot of apples."

Rob squeezed my hand. "I think you made a new friend."

I closed my eyes. "He's not so bad."

"No," Rob said. "He's not."

CHAPTER FORTY-SIX

Six Weeks Later

"AND STIR THAT IN." I grinned at the camera when Haley shrieked. "Slowly, sweetie. *Slowly.*"

Haley sighed and grimaced when she glanced down at her splattered apron. "Great," she muttered. "And now I've embarrassed myself on national television."

Kel put her hand to her belly, her twin-sized baby bump now beyond obvious. "At least you didn't attempt to dip yourself into the pancake batter."

We were making brunch on a live stream, a new addition I'd added to the blog. It had actually been Tammy's idea, to get me more comfortable with the camera before we began filming in a couple of weeks.

And it was great, actually. All of my social media sites had jumped in traffic, and I even had my own YouTube channel.

A big part of that was the recipes.

The other portion, I figured, was the national news coverage that had come from Rob taking down an FBI drug ring and my kidnapping. Celeste and Cal were currently in federal custody awaiting trial, and while I still didn't understand why my sister seemed to hate me so much or had decided that she needed to take some sort of vengeance on Rob and me, I was coming to terms with the fact that I might never know.

"I hear pancake batter is good for the skin," I said.

"Who says that?" Kel groused, wiping at her shirt with a towel. "Stupid belly getting in the way," she muttered.

"*I* say that." I grabbed Haley's arm to show her the proper motion for whipping the cream.

Yes, I did it by hand. Yes, it gave me nicely toned arms.

The cameraman snorted and I snagged the small camera from his hands. "Okay, Rob," I said, grinning into the camera before turning it onto my husband. "Since you seem to have something to say, you can do it on film."

Justin laughed, and I rotated to face him. "Do I need to commandeer you too?" He was sitting behind a laptop, reading comments and questions to us that were posted during the stream.

"Nope." He raised his hands. "Unless it involves taste-testing bacon."

We all laughed, and I returned the camera to Rob who gave me a once over and raised a brow.

I sighed. I knew what that brow meant.

It was the signal we'd come up with over the last weeks. His sign to me that he thought I was overtired and needed to wrap things up.

I smiled and nodded and where I once would have ignored the gesture, I'd learned to appreciate the thoughtfulness.

He was trying to help me. He was worried.

And my leg *was* aching.

So I sped into action, finishing the pancakes, plating them up for the five of us alongside the whipped cream, bacon, and egg casserole that had been resting in the oven.

Rob didn't intervene, though I knew it was hard for him. Especially when I stumbled as I turned and my knee nearly gave out.

Now *that* would have been embarrassing.

The TV cook upending multiple plates on camera.

But I righted everything in time, got everyone sitting down and eating, and we ended the live stream.

After five weeks of therapy—I'd taken Haley's recommendation straight away—and three weeks of rehabbing my leg, Rob trusted me to know my own limits.

Things weren't perfect, but we were finding our way.

He set the camera to the side, swept me up in his arms, and deposited me on the couch in the next room. Thirty seconds later, he'd returned with two plates and fed us both.

He might trust me to know my limits, but he also wanted to take care of me.

And I was learning how to let him.

Haley sighed when Rob brought the two plates to the kitchen then lifted me in his arms again and carried me back to join the others, plunking me onto his lap in one of the wooden chairs around the old oak table. "I need a man."

I smiled up at my husband. "Yes," I said. "They're not so bad."

COLLISION AT ROOSEVELT RANCH

CHAPTER ONE

Haley

"JUST PLAY ALREADY," Haley muttered, fumbling with her phone as she pulled to a stop at an intersection on her way home from the hospital. It was late and she was tired and . . . she just wanted some boy band love, okay?

Exhaustion tugged at her brain and she sighed, eyes burning, shoulders aching. She was very close to tears.

She'd lost a patient that night.

It hadn't been her fault. It hadn't been *anyone's* fault. Sometimes those things just happened—accidents, everyone working frantically to pull someone back from the brink, a body failing—but that didn't make a patient dying on her watch any easier.

Her job was to save them.

Life was fragile. As a nurse, Haley knew that firsthand. But she'd also left her job at the busy county hospital in California and returned home to Darlington, Utah because she was tired of seeing people die every day.

She was damned good at compartmentalizing, but some things weren't so easy to shove down.

Sometimes those fuckers—e.g. *memories*—kept popping back up.

And sometimes the cases hit too close to home—

A horn beeped behind her and she jumped. "Shit." Her phone was still not cooperating, the poppy upbeat notes of her favorite boy bands remaining silently trapped inside the technological device that never seemed to work correctly.

Even though it was brand spanking new.

Even though she'd gotten a complete tutorial from her brother-in-law, who had gone through all of the troubleshooting with her.

Even though the freaking tech from the phone store had personally tested the Bluetooth by coming out to her car and showing her how it worked.

Technology. She repelled it.

Or rather, she was technology's kryptonite.

Two minutes around her, and she destroyed even the most powerful device.

"Yay me," she murmured, dropping the phone to her passenger's seat. Haley shouldn't be fussing with it anyway, not while she was driving, but —*sigh*—she'd really wanted to escape for the rest of her drive.

Apparently, that was not to be.

Checking for traffic, she pulled carefully through the intersection. Darlington was a small town, and signals were few and far between, but the roads at this time of the night were dark . . . and she'd had a deer jump right in front of her car once before.

The car that had honked at her turned to follow her down the bumpy lane, headlights very bright in her rearview mirror, the front bumper just inside that bubble all drivers had.

This one triggered her slightly-too-close alert but not the this-fucker-better-back-off alarm.

Her lips curved.

So, she might have gotten used to the more aggressive drivers of Northern California.

The thought of her first months in San Francisco, of the busy roads, the huge buildings, the patient care that both challenged and devastated her, brought a smile to her face. For all the reasons she'd come home, Haley was still happy she'd left Utah for a time.

Small town life was . . . well, small.

Or it had seemed that way before she'd left.

Now she saw how much her world had expanded by being . . . well, herself. Having *found* herself, as cliché as that sounded.

She'd left a little girl, never feeling like she could measure up, and had returned—

Still feeling like she would never live up to her expectations.

Ha. Well, that was life for a girl. But Haley *had* come back with the understanding that she was the one setting impossible standards. Progress, yes? As in, *she* was a work in progress.

Step one was realizing that not everything she did had to be perfect and exacting.

Which was all well and good for her Pinterest attempts—*cough*—fails.

It didn't work as well for her patients.

Hence the mental punch fest happening in her brain alongside the compelling need for cheesy pop music to provide her with some escapism.

Had she done everything right? What had she missed? What could she have done differently? Would any of it have made any difference?

No.

No, it wouldn't have.

Tears stung her eyes, and she blinked them away.

If Haley hadn't blinked at that moment, things might not have turned out as they did.

But she *did* blink, right as two other things happened simultaneously.

Music exploded through her speakers—the Backstreet Boys singing about the way they wanted it—and a deer jumped into the road.

By the time her lids had flashed back open, the jar of pop-tastic noise accelerating the process to near inhuman speed, the freaking deer was directly in front of her bumper and *definitely* within her bubble.

Frankly, it was firmly in the she-was-gonna-plow-it-down-and-make-a-deer-pancake zone.

"Fuck!" She slammed on her brakes.

Tires screeched. She braced for impact and then . . .

The deer executed a leap that was fitting of a figure skater and jumped clear of her car.

Haley sighed in relief. For a single heartbeat.

Because that relief disappeared before the next.

Her body was propelled forward as the driver who had been—and here came that damned bubble analogy again—following her too closely before, plowed into her from behind.

And she didn't even have time to snort about the dirtiness of that particular innuendo before the seat belt yanked tightly across her chest. Pain shot up her leg as her foot compressed more firmly on the brake pedal, but before she could focus too much on the sensation, her head smacked against the top of the steering wheel a moment before the airbag deployed and punched her in the face.

"Fucking bubbles," she slurred as everything went black.

CHAPTER TWO

Sam

SAM WAS EXHAUSTED.

He'd been in surgery for hours, trying to extract every last piece of shredded plastic from the belly of a six-month-old Yellow Lab named Dexter, and it hadn't been an easy procedure. The pup was severely dehydrated and had probably been at most a day from dying.

Dexter was lucky Sam had the ability to perform an emergency surgery in his clinic and hadn't needed to be driven all the way to Salt Lake City, an almost three-hour jaunt.

It had likely saved the dog's life that evening.

But it was also why Sam was bone-weary and driving along the dark road late at night.

He'd gotten through the surgery then helped his overnight staff make sure Dexter was stable, which meant he was hours past his normal shift length.

And considering he'd gone out to Roosevelt Ranch early that morning to check on a pregnant mare, Sam was lucky to still be coherent.

He was also in a hurry to get home and crawl into bed.

"Come on," he muttered, beeping his horn at the car in front of him. It wasn't familiar, a sleek black sedan with California plates he didn't recognize, and considering Darlington was a small town, that in itself was unusual.

Though being unfamiliar was also probably why the other driver was glancing at their phone. It was easy to get turned around out in the sticks. One wrong turn on a pitch-black lane and a car could enter a veritable Bermuda Triangle of farms, twisting roads, and hidden driveways.

Part of him felt he should offer help, but the rest was relieved when the other driver put down their phone and headed decisively to the right.

Of course, that was the direction he was going as well, though he wasn't going to complain, not when they were moving along at a good clip and his house was less than a mile ahead.

Sam could summon up some patience, at least for another few minutes.

Unfortunately for him, his phone buzzed, and as quickly as it took for his eyes to flick down to check the Caller ID then flick back up to the road, everything went to hell.

Brake lights flared bright red in front of him, casting the dark street in ghoulish repose, and the careful distance he'd been keeping between his car and the one in front of him simply . . . evaporated.

In one instant, he was way too close.

Cursing, he slammed on the brakes and swerved to the right.

He almost missed the little sedan.

What was the saying? *Almost* only counts in horseshoes and hand grenades?

Yeah. That was it. And the noise his SUV made crashing into the car in front of him was what he imagined a grenade going off sounded like.

The crunching of fiberglass meeting his metal bumper.

Glass shattering. Metal screeching.

Add in the squealing of his tires and the hissing of his engine after he'd come to a full stop, and he half expected to look out his cracked windshield and find that a war zone had materialized in the few heartbeats that had passed during the collision.

No war zone.

But there wasn't any sign of movement from the other car.

"Fuck," he muttered and shoved open his door. It took a hell of a lot of effort, which probably meant that with his luck, the frame was bent and his SUV would be totaled.

But none of that mattered.

He ran over to the sedan and glanced through the window.

The airbag had deployed, and the driver was slumped against the steering wheel and the rapidly deflating white nylon.

A long blond ponytail trailed down the woman's back, bisecting a medical scrub top that was patterned with galosh-wearing pigs.

His heart dropped, and he yanked open the door.

Because . . . Haley.

Horrible music blared through the speakers, and he winced as he checked Haley's pulse. It was strong, if a little elevated. Of course, then there was the fact that she was unconscious.

"Damn," he muttered, seeing the blood on the steering wheel. Guilt had already been flowing pretty free and loose through him, but now Sam felt even worse.

He'd hurt Haley.

"Fuck."

He whipped out his phone and called the emergency line at the police department, otherwise known as Rob Cooper, lead detective at the Darlington Sheriff's office.

"Rob speaking," he answered, voice clear despite the late hour.

"It's Sam. There's—"

"You up past bedtime karaoke-ing boy bands again?"

Sam snorted. "Hilarious. Now shut it. There's been an accident on Old Creek Rd. I rear-ended Haley Donovan, and she's unconscious." He sucked in a breath, checked for the mile marker and relayed that as well. "Can you send an ambulance?"

To Rob's credit, the man could switch gears with the best of them. He was also calm in a crisis. Then again, he'd had plenty of experience in dealing with them. Plus, Sam knew he'd be able to get an ambulance out faster than just him calling 9-1-1 on his own. Rob was unruffled, had good connections, and could directly coordinate with dispatch.

Haley groaned and started to push up.

"I'm getting off the line now," he told Rob. "She's coming around."

"Ambulance is on its way," Rob said then, "Don't move her unless you have to."

"Roger that." Sam hung up and pocketed his cell just as Haley flopped back in her seat. "Careful," he told her. "You—"

Fuck.

He'd seen the blood but not the large gash marring her forehead. Not to mention the fact that her face was going to bruise to hell and back over the next few days.

"Hold still," he ordered, shrugging out of his shirt and folding it quickly to make a compress. "You're bleeding."

"What's the matter?" Her hands came up to bat his away when he pressed it to the cut above her eye. "*Stop.* That hurts."

"Haley. Hold. Still," he ordered again and kept the pad firmly in place. Of course, the damned woman did not *hold still*, but at least she stopped trying to knock his hands off. "You were in an accident—"

She shook her head, as though trying to clear it. "Sam?" Her eyes finally focused on his. "I was in an accident? What happened? Did I lose consciousness?"

"Yes. I rear-ended your car when you slammed on the brakes. And yes," he gritted, "you were out for a couple of minutes. Now stop fighting me and hold this"—he brought her hands up to the compress—"so I can shut off the damned music."

"I'm not fighting you," she said, but because she finally did freeze, Sam didn't bother arguing further with her. Instead, he just reached over her and pressed the power button on her stereo.

The music kept playing.

"It never cooperates," she muttered. "Scared the crap out of me—"

"That's why you slammed on the brakes?" Sam asked, pressing the nob again.

The music played on. Another band crooning about how it better be them.

"Well, that, plus the fucking deer teleporting in front of my car," she grumbled. "How long was I out?"

He tried turning down the volume knob. Nothing. "A couple of minutes at most."

"My head wound?"

"You'll need stitches and a CT." She started shaking her head, and Sam leaned back, glaring at her. "You nauseous?"

Her lips pressed flat.

"Head wound. Loss of consciousness. Nausea? Dizziness? A killer headache?" Those lips stayed firmly flattened. "I'm guessing I'm right, and so as a nurse, if you had a patient with these symptoms, what would you tell them?"

Silence.

"Exactly."

She huffed. "My phone is on the floor." She pointed to the passenger's side. "You might be able to turn it off that way."

"Stay." Another order as he made his way around the car and opened the passenger door. Sure enough, her cell was on the floor and was miraculously undamaged. He pressed the button on its side, swiped up and turned off the Bluetooth.

Blessed silence rang out around them.

Which was promptly punctuated by sirens.

Haley sighed and glared over at him. "I'm guessing that's my ride?"

CHAPTER THREE

Haley

SO AS FAR AS embarrassments went, being wheeled into the hospital on a gurney, when she could damn well walk—okay, so maybe it was more like limp. Anyway, walking ability or not, being brought into her place of work on a squeaking stretcher, was pretty much right up there with her most cringe-worthy moments.

Especially since the small town Emergency Department was quiet and everyone blatantly watched as she was pushed in.

Roxy, the nurse who'd relieved her barely an hour before, grinned as she was pushed by. "Couldn't stay away?"

Dr. Hamilton was in charge that evening. He clapped his hands together, pretending to send a prayer up to the heavens. "Finally, something to do."

What was that about ER staff and dark senses of humor?

Oh yeah.

They all had it.

And in that exact moment their peculiar sense of comedy was *hil-ar-i-ous*.

Yes, she got it. She knew that while the hospital just outside Darlington had its rare moments of busy—though that was certainly still relative when compared to the county hospital in San Francisco that she'd left—it was more often quiet than slammed. She also knew that it had been exceptionally quiet that evening by the time she'd left.

So much so that had Haley been working, she would have looked at any arriving patient with the same amount of benefaction.

"Not much to do," she told them. "Stitches and maybe a sprained ankle."

Both of which meant that she probably wouldn't be able to work the next day.

Dammit.

That meant she'd be required to put in an appearance at Sunday dinner.

Fuck. Her. Life.

"It's something," Dr. Hamilton—*Julian*—said. "I need to practice my sutures."

Haley shuddered at the thought of being his guinea pig. "Dude. You're supposed to perfect them in medical school."

Lips twitched. "Maybe I'm out of practice."

Considering that although Julian was young and fresh out of his residency, he was one of the smartest and well-rounded doctors she'd ever met, Haley had no doubt his stitches would be more precise than a fashion designer's.

"Not likely," she said, pushing up to sit as the gurney was situated next to a bed and sliding herself over before the paramedics, Dean and Kristin, could help her. She was a nurse, dammit. She could move two feet, but even Haley had to admit that those two feet were really fucking painful. "Thanks, guys," she told the paramedics, waving as they left and hiding her wince, pretending her ankle wasn't a throbbing mess that was making her head spin.

Or maybe that was the head wound.

"Ten bucks there's a fracture in that ankle."

Sam's voice made her gaze fly to the open door. She hadn't expected him to come to the hospital. He'd been dealing with the police as she'd been packed into the back of the ambulance, all while declaring that she didn't need the transport, that she wasn't that bad off and could drive herself into the hospital.

Kristin hadn't even argued with her. She'd just nodded at Dean and the two of them had bundled her onto the gurney and off to the ER on the red-and-white express.

Thankfully they hadn't used the siren.

Small victories. Haley was all about them.

"It's just a sprain," she said with a glare, already thinking about how big the hospital bills were going to be. First, Sam crashed into her car, *then* he called 9-1-1—

Okay, so maybe if she hadn't slammed on the brakes . . .

Details. Details.

One of Sam's dark brown brows rose as if to say, "We'll see."

Yeah, they *would* see, wouldn't they?

Meanwhile, Julian and Roxy bustled around her—Julian putting in orders for X-rays and medications, while Roxy started a line and then hung a bag of antibiotics and fluid . . . and a little something for pain relief.

Sam stood unobtrusively in the corner.

Though he'd never been unobtrusive to her.

Haley's childhood crush hadn't changed. In fact, he was prettier than ever, more muscular and filled out and just . . . completely yummy and male.

He'd owned her heart the first time he'd helped her with her history homework, way back when she'd been in seventh grade and he'd been in eleventh. Sam had been gorgeous then, all long, lean lines and possessing a smile that made her stomach fill with butterflies.

Of course, he'd also been dating her sister Maggie, so that had been a problem.

Especially since he'd practically lived at her house for years because they'd dated all the way through high school and college. His constancy in her life meant that her crush had *years* to develop into something so painful and awkward and soul-crushing that she'd been determined to leave town when he and Maggie got married.

Only he and Maggie *hadn't* gotten married.

He'd left for vet school, and her sister had stayed.

No wedding. No more Sam.

Except, he'd returned to Darlington . . . and now so had she.

"Fuck," she murmured and forced her mind from the past.

"Sorry," Julian said gentling his touch on her forehead.

She didn't have the strength to tell him that his touch wasn't what was hurting her. Hell, by now she was floating on some good drugs and hadn't even felt Roxy cleaning the wound.

Her ankle still throbbed though.

Ugh.

Because that probably meant Sam was right.

Instead of going further down that particular train of thought, Haley shut her mouth and held very still as Julian closed up her forehead.

As predicted his stitches were perfectly straight.

"I told you," she said as she snuck a quick glance with her phone. Sam had returned it after managing to make turning off her playlist look as simple as pressing a button.

Technology. It hated her.

"Told me what?" Julian asked.

"That your sutures are perfect." She grinned at him. "In fact, they're fashion-designer worthy."

"I hear the mummy look is in right now," Roxy chimed in, holding up a roll of gauze before bandaging Haley's wound.

Haley rolled her eyes, and the motion meant she caught another glimpse of Sam in the corner.

Dammit, why was the man so fucking hot?

Even in the fluorescent lighting, his skin was a gorgeous tawny brown and his eyes resembled melted dark chocolate, while she knew hers bore a strong resemblance to mud.

Gross, sticky mud filled with horse manure.

Okay, so she was being dramatic.

But, really, the man was supermodel beautiful and despite having broken her sister's heart once upon a time, he'd grown into a seriously nice guy. The type to stop and pull over if he saw an old lady struggling to load her groceries in her car or to shovel his neighbor's driveway just because he happened to be outside digging out his own.

He was sweet. Kind. Sexy and—

It didn't matter.

Even if he did see her as a woman and not the awkward, gangly sister of an old flame, he was in the no-touch zone.

Fuck. Between bubbles and zones, she was losing her mind.

But there was a sister code and that meant no dating exes. Not ever. Even if it had been close to a decade since their broken engagement. Even though her sister was happily married to someone else.

Nope. No way.

She couldn't muddy the waters.

Not that Sam wanted to muddy them with her.

"Men," she muttered and Roxy, who'd been clearing off the rolling table, snorted before patting her shoulder. "I feel ya, girl." Her eyes flicked to Sam then back to Haley. "I'll come back when X-Ray is ready for you."

Haley nodded then gave Julian a thumbs up when he told her he'd check on her after the results were in and hurried from the room.

He'd just been notified that another patient was en route.

Which meant that the occupancy of the ER was about to double.

Sam pushed off the wall and moved toward her, drawing her gaze as easily as a bar of Godiva at a Chocolaholics Anonymous meeting.

Oh, look there she went again being ridiculous.

But shoving her mind down a track that had nothing to do with Sam and everything to do with ridiculous analogies had been her survival technique for years.

Yes, she could compartmentalize. No problem. Sam Johnson wasn't even in the room as far as she was concerned. It was all milk versus dark chocolate and—

Dammit, now Sam's *dark chocolate* eyes were on hers, his slightly roughened fingertips brushing across the back of her hand.

"I'm sorry you got hurt because of me."

The sheer amount of remorse in his voice pulled her out of her whirling mind. He felt bad? *She'd* slammed on the brakes.

"You do realize that it's the deer we both should be pissed at, right?"

His brows drew down. "I should have been paying closer attention." With a sigh, he straightened and turned, pacing away. "I should have given you more space, and I should have made sure I was more alert—"

"When the Backstreet Boys blared to roaring life on my speakers at the same time that a deer decided to try and commit death by front bumper?" She fixed him with a glare. "You should have known at that exact moment to slow down *and* be more awake?" Shoving her elbows under herself, she went to sit up, only to make it halfway before collapsing back down with a moan.

Sam whipped around. "Are you all right?"

"Fine," she said, keeping her eyes closed and waiting for the room to stop spinning.

He touched her shoulder "I think you probably have a concussion."

"So does Julian," she said, eyes still closed. "He wrote it in my chart."

"Hmm," Sam said.

Her lids pulled back. "What?"

"*Julian?*" he asked, so smirky and all-knowing.

She rolled her eyes. "He's too young for me."

Sam huffed. "Haley, you're all of—"

"Twenty-seven."

His jaw dropped open. "No, you're not."

Really? She narrowed her eyes, talking slowly to break it down for the infuriating man. "You, thirty-two. Me, twenty-seven. That's how math works."

"How did that—" He broke off.

"Happen?" she said. "Life, Sam. Life."

"Damn." He blew out a breath. "Still, life or not, I really *am* sorry I crashed into you.

Haley rolled her eyes. "Can we agree to just blame the deer?" Silence met her question, and she stifled a sigh. "And I didn't mean that Julian is too young age-wise for me. I just meant that he's too young . . . I don't know, soul-wise? Personality-wise? Does that even make sense?"

"No."

She opened her mouth to snap at him then saw the corners of his lips twitching. "God, you're just the same."

"No," he said, and his tone took on a hint of darkness that had her frowning as she tried to interpret it. Of course, that frown was followed quickly by a wince as her stitches pulled, distracting her from the topic at hand. And she was further veered from the blip of pain from Sam's past when he said, "But I do understand not shitting where you eat."

"Barf," she quipped before shrugging. "Not the most pleasant saying, but it is apt, especially in this case. I don't date people from the hospital. It's too complicated." Not to mention the dating pool was pretty small and also that she had sworn off men at the moment. After Brian—

Yeah.

Nope.

Not going there.

"I think Julian is technically a few years older than me in years," she said. "But much younger in life experience. At least outside of a hospital setting. Does that make more sense?"

Sam stared at her. And cue more silence, this time of the growing-more-awkward-by-the-second variety.

So, when exactly would it be rude for her to ask him to leave?

It wasn't that she wanted to be alone necessarily, but between the past and the awkward present and then adding in the dark circles beneath his eyes, it was probably better if they just parted ways and returned to being casual acquaintances.

Sam was as tired as she was. He needed rest. Not to pass a couple of uncomfortable hours in a hospital with a girl he knew from the past.

He might be a good guy, but he wasn't hers.

And it was critical that she remembered that.

"You should go," she murmured.

"I'm not—"

Roxy bustled back in at that moment, cutting off what would no doubt be a protest. Sam was a good guy and wouldn't dare to leave a damsel in distress. "X-Ray is ready for you."

"Great," she said as Roxy unlocked the gurney. "You really should go," she added as her friend started to wheel her out.

His eyes flashed. "You need—"

"Go, Sam." She made a shooing motion. "I'm fine here." When he looked like he would argue further, Haley fixed him with a glare. "Seriously. I'm. Fine."

"It'll be a little while before the on-call ortho can read the X-Rays anyway," Roxy added, and Haley could have kissed her.

"Fine." Sam threw up his hands. "I'll go. Call me if you need—"

"I'll be fine," she said.

He shook his head, following the gurney out. But where Roxy and

Haley turned right to head to X-Ray, Sam turned left and headed for the exit.

The blip of regret she felt, the little aching slice as he disappeared from sight, was familiar.

She was used to Sam Johnson walking away from her.

Though, this time Haley knew it was because she'd pushed him.

It was better for everyone that way.

CHAPTER FOUR

Sam

HE WALKED AROUND THE CORNER, paused and waited for the nurse to wheel Haley through the opposite doors.

Then he rotated around and strode back toward her room.

The doctor—*Julian*, he thought with a huff—came out of another patient's room. "Everything all right?"

Sam gave the other man a commiserating look. "Haley doesn't want to inconvenience me by having me stay." Okay, only a half-truth. She'd ordered him to leave, but he wasn't about to abandon her while she was concussed and sporting stitches, as well as a broken ankle.

And he'd seen enough broken bones to know that ankle was definitely fractured.

Julian nodded. "She's stubborn, that one. A hell of a nurse, though."

Sam didn't doubt that. Even as kids she'd been smart as hell, strong, quick-thinking, and possessed a streak of empathy that fit very well with her current occupation.

"But," Julian went on, "at the same time, she doesn't want you here—"

"I'll stay out of the way and keep quiet," Sam said. He appreciated that the doctor was willing to go to bat for Haley, but—"I just want to make sure she gets home safely."

Julian studied him for a beat. "I'm leaving it up to her," he said after a long moment. "If she wants you gone, I'll make sure you're gone."

There was steel in the other man's tone that Sam respected. Though it seemed at odds with the youthful naiveté Haley had described. Maybe there was more to Julian than she'd grasped.

Not that Sam would be railroaded into leaving. It was his fault that Haley was hurt, so he'd make certain she was safe and secure at home and then he'd crash—

Er, get some shut-eye.

But instead of saying any of that, he nodded—Julian could interpret that however he wanted—and continued back down the hall to Haley's room. Once inside, he plunked down into a chair and pulled out his phone.

Typically, he kept to a light schedule on Sundays. Some office visits for the clients who couldn't make it in during normal hours, a few home visits for horses or cattle on the surrounding ranches. But he saw with no little amount of relief that his schedule was completely clear.

Probably because Jane had known how late he'd worked that evening.

Sam glanced at the clock on his phone's screen and saw that it was nearly the *previous* evening at that point.

He knew Haley worked days and wondered why she'd been leaving work so late, especially based on the quiet Emergency Department surrounding him.

Maybe it had been busy earlier.

So, aside from checking in on Dexter, making sure the pup was still looking good after surgery, all he needed to do the next day was make sure that Haley was okay.

He could do that.

As long as he didn't hit her with his car again.

Snorting, he passed the time waiting for Haley by checking some sports scores on his cell. He'd gone to veterinary school in Minnesota and had become a bit of a hockey fan, though his fandom didn't actually extend to the state's teams.

His love of hockey had begun during the league's most recent expansion and as thus, he'd been following the San Francisco Gold since their very first season.

They'd begun shakily but were damned good now.

Of course, they were also currently helmed by the league's only engaged couple, Brit Plantain and Stefan Barie.

Sam was a sucker for their story—the first female player in the NHL and the captain of the team they both played for falling in love.

So, he was a romantic.

Haters were gonna hate.

Rolling his eyes at himself, Sam saw the Gold had won that evening and noted their position in the West. Playoff hopes were high, though it was still too early in the season for them to know for sure.

He hoped they did well, because he really wanted Brit to win a Cup.

Feminist *and* romantic. See? He was owning his Millennial status.

Throw in some avocado toast, and he was there.

He'd just pocketed his phone when he heard Haley's voice echo down the hall. Bracing himself for her reaction, Sam stood.

The same nurse wheeled the gurney in, and he knew the exact moment Haley saw him. Her words cut off, her eyes flashed, and red painted itself across her cheekbones.

"I thought I told you to leave."

The nurse sucked in a breath. "Harsh, girl."

"Shut it, Roxy," Haley snapped, though it held little heat, and the words were slightly slurred. "This one is trouble."

Sam helped Roxy position the bed and lock the wheels in place. "I did leave," Sam said. "I just came back."

Roxy—a women with shining black hair, curves for days, and a smile that seemed to light up the room—smirked at Haley. "You've got a live one with this one."

"Tell me about it," Haley muttered. "He was hot as hell then and even better looking full-grown."

Roxy's brows raised. "Full-grown?"

"Big. Bigger." She lifted a hand loosely gesturing somewhere in the direction of Sam's crotch.

Though he was inclined to believe she was referring to his height.

"*And* he broke my sister's heart."

Fuck. He and Maggie had been over for a decade. They'd—

"Holy drugs, Batman," Roxy said.

"Told you I was a lightweight." Her eyes slid closed.

"That you did." Roxy fiddled with the computer for a moment. "I'll drop your dosage." When Haley's eyes stayed shut and her breathing evened out, the nurse turned to face Sam. "Her ankle's broken."

Nailed it, he thought like an eight-year-old, but instead of saying that aloud he just nodded.

"It's not bad," Roxy added. "The tech will be in soon to cast it. Then you can get her home since she's clearly in no shape to drive."

"Works for me." He'd managed to drive his car to the hospital, but he'd definitely need to get a mechanic to look at the door . . . not to mention to find out if the unpleasant grinding sound it had made when in motion was indeed a bent frame or something less serious.

Roxy pressed a few more buttons on the keyboard then started to walk from the room. At the threshold of the doorway, she paused and glanced back at him. "Did you really break her sister's heart?"

Sam clenched his teeth tightly together. "I think it was more of a mutual shattering."

She studied him for a long moment but only said, "Hmm."

Then Roxy walked out, leaving him alone with a drugged-out Haley and just one thought running on repeat through his brain.

Haley thought he'd gotten even better looking.

Hmm, was right.

CHAPTER FIVE

Haley

"I DON'T NEED—"

Her protest was cut off as Roxy shut the door of Sam's SUV right in her face.

"Help," she finished, rather unnecessarily since she was talking to herself in the empty car.

Sam rounded the hood, heading for the driver's side, and she sighed for what felt like the hundredth time that day. The truth was Haley was exhausted and wanted nothing more than to collapse into bed, fall headlong into sleep, and pretend this day hadn't happened.

The driver's door stuck for a few seconds, Sam playing tug-of-war with it until it popped open, the overhead lights of the cab seeming to spotlight the cast on her right leg.

Yup. Broken.

Just as Sam had said.

Wonderful.

How the hell was she going to get to work? Hell, how in the *hell* was she going to leave her house to get groceries or toilet paper? She lived miles from the center of town and—

She was going to have to call her *mother*.

Why did Fate hate her so much?

"You okay?" Sam asked softly as he turned on the car and carefully backed out of the stall.

"Great," she said cheerily.

Just freaking out about being isolated and her cupboards being bare, since she'd planned to go shopping tomorrow . . . or rather later today.

Just cringing at the dressing down her mom was going to give her upon finding out that she'd been in an accident and hadn't—gasp of all the *freaking* gasps—called her.

Just feeling rubbed raw inside, not only from her injuries but because she'd lost a patient only hours before and then been in an accident.

The SUV came to a stop, and fingers brushed over her forehead. "Your leg is hurting you."

No.

Yes.

"It's fine," she eventually answered.

Haley was a bundle of tangled emotions and sensations—part adrenaline letdown, part throbbing pain from her ankle and head, part discomfort from the past rearing its fucking head, and all . . . regret.

She'd lost someone under her care, that was the worst of it.

But also weighing on her was the fact that it had been a decade, and she was right back where she'd started. Still mooning after her sister's ex, her body irrevocably drawn to his, her heart softening despite everything that had happened with the previous men in her life.

"It's a quick drive," he said and turned his eyes back to the road.

Not one flicker of mutual attraction, not one word about her drug-induced declaration of his sexiness.

Sam was gorgeous as ever, and he still thought of her as an asexual little tagalong.

One that slammed on the brakes to avoid a deer.

One that couldn't work technology and succumbed to the blaring soundwaves of the Backstreet Boys by braking even harder.

Le. Sigh.

They turned right onto Old Creek Road.

Sam flicked his gaze toward hers. "You're at the Robertson's—"

Her eyes caught a flicker of—

"Watch out!" she shrieked, pointing through the windshield.

He slammed on the brakes, and the SUV came to a shuddering stop inches from a deer.

That had jumped into the middle of the road.

Again.

Did all the ungulates in this area have a fucking death wish?

She and Sam looked at each other.

"Can we blame the deer now?"

His lips twitched. "Yes, I guess we can."

The buck loped away, disappearing into the brush along the side of the road. After a moment, Sam cautiously accelerated and continued with his question, though this time he kept his eyes firmly on the road. "You're at the Robertson's old place, right?"

She nodded, heart still pounding, and because she didn't want to risk another Deer-gate, she also said aloud, "Yup. The second driveway past yours."

"Got it." A beat of quiet then, "Backstreet Boys are still your favorite band?"

Her groan made him chuckle. "No, for the record, my musical taste has miraculously expanded beyond boy bands," she said. "I even like a few female pop stars now."

Now it was his turn to groan. "What about the classics?"

"You mean those eighties hair bands you used to be obsessed with?" she teased, falling into their old, yet very familiar pattern—arguing about her horrible taste in music as compared to his completely different, albeit still horrible, preference. "Give me a fun, upbeat song on the radio any day of the week. It doesn't have to be deep or soul-wrenching. I just need a slice of escapism."

He drove past his driveway, slowing down as he neared the one that led to her little ranch. She only had a couple of acres, the Robertson's having sold off most of their acreage to a neighbor when they had retired, but the tiny bunkhouse had been the perfect size for her.

Weekend DIY projects for the win.

"And why did you need the escapism today?" he asked.

Her heart squeezed. "I didn't say I needed—"

"You were listening to "I Want it That Way" at full volume. Fifteen years ago, that meant your boyfriend had dumped you." He flicked on the signal and cautiously executed the turn onto her driveway, as though half expecting another deer to jump out at any point during the maneuver.

Frankly, after their last two experiences, that wasn't a criticism.

Her own eyes were darting around, ready to reveal any deer kamikazes.

"I wasn't dumped."

"So, you and Brian are still together?"

Her jaw dropped open. "How do you know about Brian?"

"Maggie and I catch up every now and then." A shrug. "Apparently, your parents really like him."

"Yeah, well, they *really* like any man who might potentially marry me and knock me up." She sighed, reaching to unlatch her seat belt when Sam pulled to a stop in front of her house. "And not even in that order, as my mom stressed to me the last time I went over for dinner." Haley affected her mother's slightly shrill and very demanding tone. "I need more grandbabies, and it's your turn to have them. I don't even care if you have them without a husband."

Thanks, Mom.

Sam winced.

"Exactly," she muttered, popping her door.

"Hang on." He hurried out of his side then reached into the back for her crutches. Moving around the front of the car, he opened her door and helped her out, steadying her as she got her crutches under her.

He also had a knee scooter in his trunk, but considering her driveway was gravel, it wouldn't be much help except inside her house.

The crutches dug into her armpits, but she ignored the pain and took one faltering step in the direction of her front door. Between the uneven surface of the gravel and the leftover lightheadedness from the quote-unquote *good drugs* Roxy had given her, the wobble factor was legit.

"Don't hate me," Sam said, after she'd managed one more shaky movement. He swept her up into his arms, letting the crutches fall to the ground. "I'll come back for them."

Less than ten seconds later, she was at her front door and Sam was retrieving her keys from her purse, then she was inside her house and directing him toward her bedroom.

Directing Sam Johnson to *her* bedroom.

Yeah, get a laugh out of that one, universe.

Gently, he set her on her mattress then straightened. "Want me to grab you some pajamas?"

"God, yes," she said and pointed to her dresser. "Top drawer."

She blamed the drugs for not remembering that was also her underwear drawer. As in, it was filled with loads of very skimpy thongs and lacy bras she'd bought in anticipation of the wedding night and honeymoon she'd been going to have with Brian.

Sam pulled open the drawer and froze.

Haley knew her cheeks were fire-engine red. "Just the shorts and tank top on the right."

He coughed. "Right," he repeated, and a moment later he slid the dresser closed with a *thunk* before turning to face her. "Uh . . . should I call Brian?"

Fuck. How many more times was he going to mention Brian?

"Brian and I aren't together, okay?" she snapped. "He fucked around with one of my good friends, and I broke things off."

Sam's eyes narrowed. "He did what?"

She made a disgusted noise. "It doesn't matter. The only thing that does is that he's not in my life, and I'm sure as shit not going to call him."

"Your mom?"

The look she shot Sam should have eviscerated him.

"Okay, so not your mom." He crossed over to her. "Do you want me to call Maggie?"

"Sam," she said. "It's nearly one in the morning, and my sister has three young kids. I'm not waking her up for a few stitches and a barely broken bone."

"You shattered your ankle."

She huffed. "Two bones. And they're hardly shattered," she grumbled. "The orthopedist didn't even recommend surgery."

"You *want* surgery?"

Her eyes rolled heavenward. "Of course not! My point is, I'm fine. It's not serious. Telling them can wait until everyone has had a full night's sleep."

"You were transported by ambulance."

"And whose fault is that?" she said, gesturing him to turn around. He did so, though not quickly enough for her to miss the remorseful expression on his face and then feel guilty in exchange. "I didn't mean *that*," she said, carefully working her scrub top up and over the bandage on her head. "The accident was just that: an accident. I was referring to the ambulance ride and how unnecessary it was."

"You were unconscious."

Her day got loads better because she unhooked her bra and tossed it to the side before slipping on her tank top. "Yeah. I get *why* you called." A sigh. "I'm just not looking forward to paying the bill."

He started to face her again.

"Stop," she ordered, having already worked her pants down over the cast. "I'm half-naked over here."

Sam froze, face still pointed toward the wall. "Do you need money?" he asked after a moment."

"No," Haley answered truthfully. "It's not the money." She slipped off her underwear then tugged on the shorts. "It's just . . . embarrassing, I guess, my coworkers seeing me like that."

He considered her words for a long moment then said, "You still think you need to be invincible, don't you?"

Fuck.

How did he always know?

How was he *always* able to see straight into the heart of her and understand?

"I'm decent," she said, instead of answering him. "I'll call Maggie in the morning. Would you mind leaving the crutches at the foot of the bed along with the scooter?"

He rotated around. "I'll sleep on the couch," he said, moving over to help her adjust her blankets over her. "Just in case you need anything."

Now that sounded like an extra circle of hell, specially designed for her.

"No, Sam." She firmed her voice. "You've done enough already. Just leave the crutches and scooter then go home and crash. I'll be fine."

He raised a brow as he bent over and leveled serious eyes on her. "So, what you're saying is that you want me to go home and worry about you being here all alone? Worry so much that I'll toss and turn and—"

"You're laying it on thick." Exhaustion was creeping at the edges of her vision, and the one thing she *really* wanted to do at that moment was sleep, not argue with Sam.

He held up his phone.

"Either I stay on the couch or I call Maggie and wake her up."

Eyes drooping, Haley rolled her head to the side on the pillow and glared up at him. "Blackmail is how we're playing this thing?"

"Less blackmail and more making you see sense."

"Po-tay-to. Po-tah-to," she muttered. "Fine. You're on the couch, but only for tonight and because if you risked driving down to your house again, you'd have to navigate the deer gauntlet." Her lids blinked closed, and she had to force herself to focus. "Extra pillows and"—a wide yawn —"blankets are in my closet."

"Sleep now, Haley Bear," he said, brushing a kiss to her cheek. "I'll find them."

A decade ago, the kiss would have filled her with equal parts joy and liquid hot embarrassment. Such a painful crush she'd had.

But tonight, she was too tired to do anything aside from snuggling into her pillow and murmuring, "That nickname is seriously the worst."

Sam's chuckles chased her mind as sleep sucked her under.

CHAPTER SIX

Sam

SAM WOKE with an aching back and cramped legs.

Groaning, he stretched and rolled over then shot to rapid alertness as he nearly toppled off Haley's couch. He'd forgotten where he was.

And that was on Haley's ridiculously small love seat.

He pushed up to sitting and extended his arms over his head, tilting his head from side to side to work out the kinks.

Damn, he was getting too old to sleep in places that were not his bed.

Light streamed in through the windows, indicating it was well past his normal wake-up time of dawn. He stared out the clear pane of glass, enjoying the unobstructed view of undulating hills all colored dark green. The snow had melted, and spring was just around the corner.

Soon, he'd be spending almost as much time on the ranches helping with cattle as he did at the vet's office.

Luckily, he'd managed to hire another vet. Although Michelle would only be working part-time after coming back from maternity leave, Sam felt lucky to have wooed her over from the clinic in Campbell, a neighboring town.

Even though he loved seeing his human and domestic animal clients on a daily basis, his heart was truly with the larger livestock. There was something about the cattle and horses and, in rare cases, the bison, that drew him in.

Because they were generally less understood? Or just a bigger puzzle to solve? Or maybe even because their cases challenged his brain more?

Yes, to all.

But also, it got him out of the office and into the fields. He could feel the wind in his hair, the sun on his skin, and smell the various, though not always pleasant, scents.

Sam stood and picked up his phone. No missed calls overnight, that was good. He'd been so exhausted by the time he'd finally settled on the couch, that he worried he might sleep through an emergency.

Thankfully, no emergencies were to be had.

He sent a quick text to the night staff to check on Dexter then made his way into Haley's kitchen to rustle up some breakfast.

The rustling itself ran into a hiccup approximately two seconds after opening the fridge. As in, it was almost empty—a bottle of ketchup and a jar of pickles the only occupants. Swinging the door closed, Sam pulled out his phone and started making a list of the groceries Haley would need.

Milk. Bread. Cheese. Fruit. He wondered if she still liked bananas. When he'd been with Maggie, Haley had eaten them in near inhuman quantities. He drifted around the kitchen, pulling open cupboards in search of cereal or rice or some type of food that could sustain her.

Aside from a few packets of oatmeal, the space was bare.

Either she didn't cook at home, or she was in desperate need of a grocery run.

Sam sighed. That grocery run was going to be a lot harder now that he'd broken her leg.

He added a few more things to his list then turned to head down the hall. He'd peek in and see if she wanted him to grab anything else. But just as he'd walked through the doorway, his feet skidded to a stop. A bulletin board that he'd missed the first time hung near the door and conveniently at eye level was a notepad titled "Groceries."

Tearing off the top sheet, Sam grinned when he saw the first item on the list was bananas, written all in caps and underlined twice. So, she still liked them . . . and also there were so many juvenile jokes his mind wanted to make over her love of the yellow, phallic fruit.

But he was mature and shit, so he stifled his inner twelve-year-old and made his way on quiet feet to Haley's bedroom.

Sam was extra glad for his stealth when he poked his head in and saw that she was sound asleep, her eyes closed, her lips forming an O as her breaths came slow and steady.

God. She was beautiful.

All lean curves and porcelain skin, peaches teasing the creamy color. Her hair had lightened as she'd aged and was now more platinum than golden yellow, and her eyes . . . well, when they were actually open they were a shade that always reminded him of puffs of clouds trailing across the clear sky. Not just a flat shade of blue, but with little zigzags of gray and navy and . . . he'd never seen any like them.

Somehow, without him noticing, Haley had transformed into a goddess.

Who would have thought the tiny spitfire who'd trailed him and Maggie around would have grown into . . . *her*?

And maybe that wasn't fair, maybe he'd always shoved Haley into the little sister category because it was safer. They were not quite five years apart, and he couldn't think of her as gorgeous or sexy, not as a teenager. She'd still been in middle school, and he'd been readying to leave for college.

Not to mention the small fact that he'd been dating her sister.

But he and Maggie *weren't* together anymore, and further, they'd sorted out their differences. Now Haley was grown . . . and single.

And so was he.

Maybe—

Nope. Definitely not going there.

Groceries and then breakfast. *Those* were the things he should be thinking about.

He slipped from Haley's bedroom and quietly made his way to his car. His driver's side door took some serious coaxing—and cursing—to open, but he finally managed to get in and start the engine.

Along the way, he dialed Rob, the detective at the Sheriff's office with whom he'd spoken the night before. They'd had a tenuous relationship the previous year—Sam having stepped in to offer some help to Rob's wife, Melissa, when their dog had been injured and Rob had been busy on a case.

Rob hadn't liked that, and Sam had to admit he would have been pissed if another man had stepped in to take care of *his* woman.

But both Rocco and Melissa had been hurt. That in and of itself had trumped any rules of etiquette or Bro Code or whatever.

Sam had done what he'd *had* to do.

Thankfully, Rob had eventually seen reason.

He'd managed to solve the case that had been threatening the town as well as his family, and he and Melissa had patched things up. She'd even discussed some of their marriage hurdles in her last book.

Yes, he'd read it.

Yes, that probably meant he had way too much free time on his hands.

Or that his life was pathetically empty.

Yay for pleasant Sunday morning thoughts.

"Johnson," Rob said by way of greeting after the phone had rung a few times.

"Hey," Sam replied. "Thanks for the assist last night."

Rob scoffed. "It's my job."

"Not sure that coordinating ambulance dispatch on a Saturday night really is your job," he said. "But I appreciate it anyway."

"It got me out of the hundredth round of UNO," Rob said. "I should be thanking you." A pause then, "So you've moved on from rescuing married women to rear-ending defenseless ones?"

Sam turned onto the road that led to the center of town. "First, your wife pretty much rescued herself. And second, I blame the deer."

Rob snorted.

"Seriously," he said. "It's a problem. Another one jumped out right in front of my car when I was driving Haley home last night."

"Are you sure it was a different deer?" Rob was grinning, Sam could tell. The bastard. "Or maybe that one just really likes you."

"Third," he continued with his list, despite Rob's smartassedness, "That's gross and against the law. Not to mention, deer carry all sorts of disease-transmitting pests. Also, *fourth,* it's like the fucking deer gauntlet out here."

Rob burst out laughing. "Deer gauntlet," he repeated, almost hysterical.

"Hilarious," Sam muttered, but he was smiling. "Deer-mageddon better?"

"Hmm." Rob considered that. "Maybe Deer-pocalypse."

They both cracked up.

Eventually, Rob sobered. "But if it really is becoming a problem, I'll get someone from the city to trim back the brush along the road. Last time I was out there, it was pretty overgrown."

"Thanks, man. That should help." Sam signaled and turned into the lot for the grocery store. "We might also have to bring in Fish and Game if it continues."

"I think we might have a hotshot vet who could recommend that as necessary."

Sam smirked and agreed, and they talked a few minutes more about the logistics of that. He told Rob he'd pass along the name of his contact from the wildlife department so they could start moving Deer-gate after he got back to his house.

Ah. Small town life.

Though, Sam was much happier the Sheriff's Office was dealing with deer instead of drugs this time around.

He had the feeling they were, too.

Darlington was supposed to be a safe place to raise families and somewhere kids didn't have to worry about their moms getting kidnapped.

Melissa had been put through the wringer, that was for sure.

After saying goodbye, Sam hung up, pocketed his phone, and wrestled his door open before heading into the store. This early in the morning it was almost empty, and he breezed through Haley's list quickly, adding in a few treats—banana ice cream, banana bread, banana cake—as well as a bouquet of flowers.

Yes, he was still feeling really guilty about the accident.

Yes, he might have also been wanting to prove to her that despite what had happened between her and her fiancé and between him and her sister, there were still good guys out there.

Also—newsflash—yes, he might have wanted to show her that *he* was one of those good guys.

This was going to become a problem. He could already sense that.

But ignoring the shitshow that was no doubt barreling toward him, Sam simply added a cheeky little teddy bear to the cart and went to the register to pay.

Haley deserved to feel good.

Five minutes later, he was heading to his SUV to load up his car, leaving the cashier, who had been studying him with unhidden curiosity, behind. Five more minutes, he guessed. That was how long it would take for the question of who he'd bought the flowers and bear for to circulate around town.

Gossip had begun to move at near light speed since Esther, eighty years old if she was a day, had started a Snapchat three months before and then put out the call for any and all rumors.

She particularly liked using the detective filter, one that put her in a police hat and aviator sunglasses, while she discussed the merits of a particular theory about who was dating who or which teenager had gotten caught doing something naughty.

And because the snaps expired within a day, the whole town jumped on them the moment Esther posted.

How did he know about this?

Because he followed her.

Sam, meet sad, empty life.

Rolling his eyes at himself, he loaded the groceries into his trunk and then forced open his car door. He needed to get the SUV looked at, but for the moment it was running, and so that could wait until tomorrow.

For now, he needed to ply Haley with banana treats and flowers and try to tease a smile out of her.

Unfortunately, when he pulled up to her house and saw the scene that was unfolding there, he knew that smiles were going to be a long time coming.

CHAPTER SEVEN

Haley

HOW MANY YEARS would she spend in prison if she murdered her mother?

Would a judge understand that she'd been driven to the absolute brink and give her a lighter sentence because *her mother was driving her absolutely crazy?*

She'd woken up stiff and sore but relatively rested, all things considered. Sam had left her medicine and a glass of water within easy reach, along with her little knee scooter, which had been really considerate of him.

Of course, he hadn't locked her front door when he'd left. Which, one —this was Darlington so that was normally fine, and two—she'd probably been sleeping when he'd needed to leave and he hadn't wanted to wake her, so also fine.

What was decidedly *not* fine was the fact that the unlocked door had meant that her mother had let herself in.

Loudly and with all the drama her mother was so apt at providing.

The screech had nearly toppled Haley from her scooter as she'd made her way from the bathroom, after having cobbled together a sponge bath and wrestled her way into some sweats and a fresh T-shirt.

Forget the bra. Ain't nobody got time for that shit in that moment.

"Haley," her mother shrieked. "Your face! Oh my God, you look horrible."

"Good to see you too, Mom," Haley muttered then hissed out a pained breath when her mother pulled her into a tight hug. Her neck and shoulders were tender, and having her aching head plastered against her mom's generous bosom didn't feel all that great either. "Easy," she said, extracting herself. "I'm fine. It was so late last night, I was going to call you this morning."

"Except you didn't call!" her mom wailed. "I waited and waited, and you didn't call."

"I woke up ten minutes ago," Haley told her.

The hysterics cut out. Just like that. "Oh."

Yeah. Oh.

"Go sit down, Mom." She started to wheel herself forward. "I'll tell you everything that happened."

Her mom's blond curls bounced as she whipped her head to narrow her eyes at Haley. "*Everything?*"

"Every. Unexciting. Thing."

"Fine."

She flounced down the hall and flopped down into the armchair. Which left Haley the couch. That Sam had slept on. *Oh God.* Had he cleaned up the blankets? Did it look like a man had slept on her couch? Was there about to be another shrill rejoinder to join the first?

The wheels of her scooter squeaked as she made her way into the family room. Three. *Squeak.* Two. *Squeak.* One. *Squeak.* Blast—

Off?

Except not, because her couch looked exactly as it had when she'd left for work the previous day, down to the throw pillows in their proper position and her fuzzy sheep-covered blanket tossed over an arm.

She carefully maneuvered herself onto the couch—with no help from her mother. But wasn't that typical? Her mom swept in to look like she was saving the day, while at the same time stealing all the focus for herself.

And leaving drama and devastation in her wake.

Yeah, there was that.

Haley slipped her phone from her pocket, saw that it was barely nine. Was it too early to go back to bed?

Yes? No?

"It's rude to be on your phone in the middle of a conversation."

She opened her mouth, about to explain that she'd only been checking the time, before realizing that was a futile response. Her mom wouldn't listen. Ignoring anything that didn't fit with her particular viewpoint or argument was her mother's superpower.

So instead, Haley pocketed the phone and sat back on the couch. "How have you been?"

"Oh, terrible," her mom said, and she was off, lamenting about how difficult her life was, how challenging it was now that her father was required to travel more than ever for work, how lonely and quiet the house was.

Haley *could* have suggested that her mom travel with her dad. As empty nesters, there wasn't any reason for her mother to stay behind in Darlington, and they could easily afford it.

But her mom wasn't interested in solving her problems.

She just enjoyed complaining about them.

So, Haley shifted slightly, propping her foot up on a pillow and letting her back sink into the couch. Immediately, her nose was surrounded with spice and male and . . . *Sam.*

Her stomach clenched, memories flooding her. Of sitting next to him on a different couch while watching a superhero movie with him and Maggie. Of a quick hug when she'd failed a really important math test. Of him wrapping his arms around her and holding her tight as she'd shed tears over a jerky boy that had never been able to compete with him in the first place.

After all these years, he still wore the same aftershave or deodorant. Or maybe, he still just always smelled like Sam.

Like home—

"Are you even listening to me?"

Fuck. Haley had missed a rare moment requiring her to comment during one of her mom's diatribes.

They were like unicorns.

All sweet and rare and shit, but never missing a chance to gore a fucker.

"I'm—"

"All I do is love you!"

Haley closed her eyes and let her head flop back against the cushions.

"I spent two full days in labor, and you just—"

Where were the Backstreet Boys now? She could use them blaring to life on her phone and drowning out the verbal lambasting right at that moment.

"Hi, Mrs. Donovan."

The sound of Sam's voice made Haley's eyes flash open. He pushed through the front door, arms laden with grocery bags, and crossed to the kitchen island to set them down.

Then he turned to face her, pity in his gaze. "Hey." A pause before a soft question. "How are you feeling?"

She started to raise one brow and winced. "Fine. Though movement of any type is excluded from that sentiment."

His mouth quirked. "Good to know. I brought you—"

"Samuel Johnson," her mother interrupted. "As I live and breathe." She pushed to her feet, and all of the shrillness she'd been using with Haley disappeared. Yup, that sharp, cajoling tone was a gift reserved solely for her daughters.

She was a real giver, her mother.

Her arms went around Sam's waist, and he got the bosom treatment. His cheeks were flushed when her mom let him up for air. "It's good to see you, Mrs. Donovan—"

"Jenny, please." She tittered. "Mrs. Donovan makes me feel old."

"Jenny," Sam said. "It's been a long time. How are you?"

Haley winced, and that time it wasn't because of her injuries. Both she and Sam had been out of the game too long if they were making a rookie mistake like asking her mom that question.

As predicted, that question continued the rant, but instead of plunking himself onto the couch and listening in abject horror as the tirade continued, Sam made his way into the kitchen and began putting away groceries. Her mother trailed him like a puppy, talking a mile a minute as he began rustling through bags.

"And then Haley didn't even call me to tell me she was okay." Another wail.

Good God, but how was her father still married to her mother?

Probably because he traveled most of the year.

Snorting, she maneuvered herself back onto her scooter and wheeled her way into the kitchen. Her mother's voice was nails on the chalkboard, but Sam didn't seem to mind as he puttered around.

"And I didn't sleep a wink," her mom said. "I'm so exhausted I can barely keep my eyes open."

One second Sam had been putting the milk away in the fridge, the next he was a flurry of movement and words. "Oh, I'm so sorry to hear that," he said, hustling over to lace his arm with her mother's. "You should go home *right now* and get some rest." He tugged her toward the front door and then out on to the porch.

"Oh no, I couldn't leave her—"

"I insist, Jenny," Sam said, and their voices faded until Haley heard her mom's car engine start and gravel kick up.

She leaned her head to the side, peering through the window as her mother's car disappeared down the road.

Sam walked back into the house, one last bag slung over his arm. "I bought these before I realized I'd unleashed your mother," he said, crossing over to her and pulling out a colorful bouquet of daffodils, sunflowers, and tulips. He set it on the counter in front of her before extracting a palm-sized teddy bear from the bag.

It was purple—her favorite color—and sporting a mournful expression as it clutched a tiny pillow embroidered with "I'm sorry."

"I would have bought you the giant one," he said, plunking it into her palm, "if I'd known that I'd unleashed the famous Mrs. Donovan tirade on you."

Haley glared at him.

She could not be bought with some weeds and a sad-looking stuffed toy. "Apology not accepted."

His lips twitched, totally unaffected by her show of temper. "You always could hold a grudge."

A huff as she crossed her arms. "Well, considering *you* hit *me* and thus unleashed the wrath of Jenny Donovan, I think this particular grudge is warranted."

"Maybe." He tugged on the end of her ponytail. "But one could also say that *technically* you're not supposed to slam on the brakes to avoid hitting an animal."

"Yeah," she muttered. "*You* tell that to Bambi."

Sam burst into laughter. "God, you could always make me laugh." His fingers came up to brush her cheek. "I really am—"

"Not allowed to apologize again."

His eyes warmed even as his laughter faded. It took every bit of her restraint to not lean into his touch, to not stretch up on her tiptoes—*tiptoe*, rather—and press her mouth to his.

She wanted to feel that warmth inside her, to wrap herself in him, not just physically, but in all the emotions he evoked in her.

She wanted . . . him.

God. A decade had passed, and she still felt the same damn way.

She was pathetic.

"Haley."

One terse word, but *oh* how she loved the sound of her name sliding across his tongue.

She forced her gaze from his lips, from the mouth she'd imagined slanting across hers so many times before. His eyes, an intoxicating mix of brown and green and gold, locked with hers, but this time there was something different in their depths.

Not pity or derision, which she half-expected, given that she *had* spent the last ten years mooning over him.

Nor was it confusion.

"Haley," he said again. Lower. Huskier.

Could it . . . *might* it be heat?

That notion didn't compute in her brain.

Sam had never looked at her like *that* before—with awareness, with desire. His palm slid across her cheek, tangling in the hair on her nape.

"Haley."
A benediction? A prayer for . . . forgiveness?
His head lowered and—
Was this really fucking happening?
Sam kissed her.

CHAPTER EIGHT

Sam

HE WAS LOSING HIS MIND.

He could not be kissing Haley.

Could. Not.

Except he was.

And it was fucking incredible.

She was broken and stitched up and probably concussed, and Haley's kiss was still the best of his life.

He tore his lips from hers. "I'm—"

She clamped a hand over his mouth, and considering it still held the teddy bear he'd bought her, Sam basically ate fur.

But her words had him forgetting that fact.

"You are not allowed to fucking apologize," she growled.

His fingers rose to extract the bear from Haley's grip—and his mouth. He set it on the counter, then removed a few stray hairs from the corners of his lips. The fuzzy stuffed toy might have been cute, but it definitely wasn't edible.

"Not *allowed?*" he asked.

"No," she said. "I've been dreaming about kissing you for—"

Horror crept into her expression, and this time she clamped a hand over her own mouth rather than his.

He bent slightly, locked his gaze onto hers. "For what?"

"No," she said. "I'm not doing this." Haley pushed herself backward, the wheels of the scooter skittering against the hardwood floor as she rounded the corner of the kitchen island and attempted to escape back down the hall.

Nope. No way. No how.

But though she had wheels, he was faster . . . and had two working legs.

He slipped in front of her.

"Not a word, Sam," she snapped. "I took a pain pill, and I'm a lightweight, and that means I'm going to start blabbering about how I've dreamed about kissing you since I was thirteen, and that it was even better in real life than in my dreams."

Silence. His. Of the stunned variety. As in, he had been stunned into muteness because . . . she'd liked him for more than a decade?

"Haley," he began.

She'd pressed her hands over her mouth again, cheeks bright pink, tears flooding those beautiful blue eyes, but in response to her name, she just shook her head.

"Sweetheart," he said, gentler.

Her lids slid closed.

"A decade?"

Another shake.

"Since Maggie?"

She swallowed hard.

He took a step toward her, reaching for her, wanting to haul her close and hold her until she realized that she had nothing to be embarrassed about, that childhood crushes weren't a big deal. But the moment his fingers brushed her shoulder, Sam watched her eyes flash open, saw them fill with agony.

Because he was there. Because he was pushing this.

Hadn't he already done enough to her?

So, he stopped himself, forced his hands to drop back down to his sides. "I'll finish with the groceries," he said and turned back toward the kitchen, leaving Haley alone in the hall.

It was the absolute last thing he wanted to do.

But Sam did it anyway.

Forcing himself to walk away instead of fighting for what he wanted . . . well, that had become his specialty over the years.

Really, in the grand scheme of things, what was one more time?

———

SAM DIDN'T KNOW why he was still in Haley's kitchen.

He'd stashed the groceries, wiped the counters, straightened the bookcase, even alphabetized her now-antique DVD collection.

And she'd stayed in her bedroom.

All signs pointed for him to get the fuck out and yet . . . he couldn't.

She'd tasted like mint toothpaste, smelled like roses, felt like the softest silk . . . but sensations aside, he couldn't stop thinking about her revelation. Haley had liked him for years.

How? *Why?*

Perhaps more importantly, how hadn't he known?

Sure, they'd hung out a fair amount during his time with Maggie, but he'd never glimpsed one iota of a schoolgirl's crush from Haley. She'd been confident, self-assured and very busy with her own life.

To say his mind was blown would be the mother of all understatements.

Then he wondered if Maggie had known.

Hmm.

And why would it matter if she did? If Maggie *had* mentioned Haley's feelings to him, it wouldn't have changed anything, only served to make things uncomfortable for both him *and* Haley.

Maggie didn't like to make anyone feel uncomfortable.

Which had ultimately led to the demise of their relationship.

Sighing, he strode to the notepad in the kitchen, intending to leave Haley a note. He would go and check on her car, make sure it had been towed to the body shop as promised the previous night, maybe they could have a look at his door, and—

Crash.

Sam took off running before he'd even fully processed the noise.

He raced down the hall, into the bedroom, and found it empty. Spinning, he pushed open the door to the bathroom.

Haley was sprawled across the tile, and she was—

He averted his eyes.

Because she was naked.

She shrieked when she saw he'd come in. "Don't—*Sam!*" He'd dropped his eyes, just to confirm that she was, indeed, naked. And she *was.* So gloriously, sexily, *beautifully* naked that his cock twitched. Swallowing, he forced himself to focus, reaching for a towel and covering up the pertinent bits, even though he'd really been enjoying his view.

"What happened?"

Haley dropped her chin to her chest. "What do you think happened?"

"I *think* you were freaking out about something you didn't need to, and so you decided to do something you weren't ready for." He used one finger to tip her chin back up, enough that those pretty blue eyes met his. "Didn't you just tell me you were a lightweight with the pain pills? As a nurse, what kind of symptoms do patients have when taking these kinds of medications?"

She crossed her arms, tucking the towel more firmly across herself.

"I can tell you that my four- and two-legged friends often experience lethargy and dizziness." He raised a brow. "Sound familiar?"

Haley sighed. "I'm fine. I literally fell from like six inches. I bent over to look for a bag in the cabinet and got lightheaded."

He gave a quick once-over of the parts he could see and, deciding that she'd told him the truth, reached behind her to turn on the taps. "You couldn't ask for help?"

Her bottom lip poked out. "I just wanted a bath, okay?" Another sigh. "Plus, I thought you'd gone."

"Why would you think that?" He tested the temperature then plugged the tub.

A roll of her eyes. "Because I freaked out on you? Because I basically told you I've been mooning over you since middle school?"

Surprised that she'd just lay it out there after her earlier horror, he asked, "So, are we over the embarrassment now?"

"God, no," she scoffed. "But the cat's out of the bag now. I might as well own it."

He tried to hold back his smile, but Haley caught it anyway. "You're enjoying this, aren't you?"

"A man does like to be appreciated." He winked.

"Oh, my God."

Sam pulled open the cabinet door and surveyed the contents before holding up a plastic trash bag. "This should work." He slipped it over the cast and used the drawstring to secure it in place.

Haley gave him a grudging nod. "Thanks."

He stood, extended a hand. "Towel."

"What?" Her cheeks flared. "*No.*"

"I'm not going to look. I'm just going to help you into the tub. The towel will be in the way."

Narrowed lids. "So, this isn't an excuse to see me naked?"

"I *already* saw you naked, remember? It's definitely—" He'd started to waggle his brows like a dirty old man but stopped when Haley sucked in a breath. Her face paled, and her eyes shimmered . . . with tears? "An excuse to see you naked," he finished lamely.

Um, what the hell was that?

"Oh," she replied softly. Her throat worked, and her lips pressed flat. "That's not what I thought—" Her gaze flicked to the tub. "Can you help me into the bath now?"

"Sure." Sam kept his stare firmly on her face as she shifted the towel aside, trying to puzzle out what the hell was going through that brain of hers.

Had he said something—?

No. Brian. It had to be.

Fucking asshole.

"Sam?" she asked.

He blinked. "Right." Carefully, he slid his arms underneath her, attempting to ignore the silkiness of her skin, the curves pressed against him. "You're beautiful," he told her as he maneuvered her into the water, thoroughly soaking himself in the process.

"Sam."

His arms were still under her, his chest rubbing against hers, his sodden T-shirt the only thing separating their naked skin.

"I don't know what that prick said to you," he said. "But you're gorgeous, sweetheart."

She shook her head and whether it was in response to him calling her gorgeous or a denial of the prick's statements, Sam didn't know.

Life was odd sometimes.

A person could go thirty-odd years ignoring or, maybe not noticing was a more accurate description, someone, and then boom, one moment —one collision, one *fucking* deer—and everything shifted.

Everything changed and morphed and rotated until the person that had always been categorized in a certain way, changed.

Until that one person who'd been on the periphery became firmly planted front and center.

He'd known Haley.

He'd respected her, thought she was funny and sweet and a really cool person.

But he hadn't wanted her, hadn't noticed her eyes, her lips, her body.

Then *wham*, the pieces had come together, and he was left wondering how he could have missed her all along.

Sam tilted his head, lifting his mouth so he could whisper in her ear. "You're the most beautiful woman I've ever seen." When she opened her mouth, no doubt to deny his words, he leaned back and snapped. "*No.*"

Her eyes went wide.

"I know the timing was wrong before—we were teenagers and I was with Maggie. But I was an idiot to not notice how much you'd changed when you came back into town last year. Yes, your body is hot, sweetheart, but it's what's in here"—he tapped the spot above his heart—"that is truly beautiful."

"I've seen you at the hospital with patients. I've seen you with your nieces and nephews and your friends." He cupped her cheek. "On the inside, where it *really* matters, you're a good person."

She bit her lip, making him want to kiss her all over again.
But it wasn't the right time.
"Brian was a fucking idiot to betray you."
She blinked rapidly.
"But I think . . ." He trailed off.
"You think?" she asked softly.
"I think his loss might be my gain."

CHAPTER NINE

Haley

UH. What?

Another brush of Sam's fingers across her jaw before he straightened and turned to leave the bathroom. "No more shenanigans," he said, pausing on the threshold. "Holler for me when you're done."

And he walked out, shutting the door behind him.

"I—" She shook her head, looking around the room, half expecting the tile walls to provide her with an answer.

Sam thought she was beautiful. Inside and out.

What in the what?

It wasn't like she thought she was an ugly or even a bad person, but she could freely admit that her confidence had taken a hit after Brian. But then again what person was cheated on and *didn't* internalize the other person's actions? What person didn't take them as a blow to their self-worth?

Well, if she ever met another person who continued on with their life all fine and dandy and untouched by such a betrayal, then she'd be sure to ask them their secret.

Because Brian had screwed with her head.

Yes, he'd cheated, and that was bad enough.

But he'd also managed to drill down into her deep, vulnerable underbelly even before she'd discovered the affair. First, it was little comments here or there—stating how she needed to pick up another workout so she could be *healthy* for the wedding. Later, it became adopting a diet because her clothes didn't fit as well as they used to. Then it was dyeing her hair because she had gray showing. Or expensive wrinkle cream because she had fine lines developing on her forehead and around her eyes.

If he'd led with wrinkle cream, she would have told him to fuck off, but Brian hadn't. Instead, he'd slowly and persistently undermined her sense of self.

He managed to pinpoint all her insecurities—yes, she'd been twenty-five and getting gray, yes, she had laugh lines, yes, she'd put on a few pounds—and then just amplified each one by a thousand.

Add that in with the stress of working in a very busy emergency department in a very busy hospital and suddenly, she'd become a ball of nerves.

Doubting herself. Doubting her abilities.

"Ugh," she muttered, sliding down into the tub so her shoulders were under the warm water. Her cast clanged against the cast iron, but firmly encased in her post-pain-pill glory, Haley felt no pain.

The bathroom door cracked. "Please, tell me that wasn't your head," Sam said.

Despite herself, she grinned. "Not my head."

"Good." The wood panel started to close.

"Wait."

It paused.

"Thanks for helping me," she said into the little black line. "For staying."

"I'm here, Haley." The door started moving again, sliding against the frame but just before the latch clicked shut, she heard: "However long you need me."

Her eyes closed, and she leaned her head back against the lip. "But for how long though?" she whispered. Because sooner or later this bubble surrounding them would burst. Sam would go back to work at his clinic, she to the hospital. She'd be the little sister again, the amusing sibling of the girl he'd once almost married.

He'd go back to his world, and she'd go back to hers . . . only this time she would know exactly what it felt like to kiss him.

———

SAM POKED his head back into the bathroom just as Haley was dozing off.

Probably a good thing because she really didn't need to add a near-drowning to her concussion and broken leg.

Though, her head was starting to clear up.

Or maybe that was just the pain medication wearing off since her ankle had decided it needed to play an orchestra of aches and throbs and zings in concert up her leg.

"You're hurting," Sam said, holding up a towel and keeping his eyes locked on hers.

Not on her body. He was behaving all gentleman-like.

It was just too bad that she didn't want him to be a gentleman.

"I'm fine," she said, rubbing her pulsing temple.

He pulled the plug on the tub. "You're not fine," he said. "Besides your head, what's hurting?"

"Is this what you do?" she muttered. "Corner naked women in bathtubs until they reveal all of their secrets?"

"Is it working?"

She took the towel when he extended it in her direction, holding it above her torso until the water drained enough for her to drape it over herself. "No."

"Damn."

A twitch of lips that reminded her exactly how they'd felt *twitching* against hers.

The man was a menace.

Also. Concussion. *That* was why she was losing her mind. It was the only explanation for why her body had decided that despite the stitches and broken bones, she wanted him.

"What just went through your head?" he asked.

Yeah, no. Nice try. That was a fun fact she definitely *wasn't* sharing.

Snorting, Haley let him help her up to sitting. "Wouldn't you like to know?"

"I would," he replied, wrapping the towel more securely around her upper body. "Hence, the reason I asked."

He bent close and slid his arms around her and—*fuck*—but she liked that.

Except . . . she *couldn't* like that.

"So?" he asked, pausing there, somehow both too close and not close enough.

"So what?" She played dumb.

He snorted, brushed a lock of hair off her cheek. "What went through your brain?"

A sigh. "Nothing," she muttered, closing her eyes. Exhaustion pulled at her, making her mind fuzzy, her thoughts spinning around her brain like snow flurries.

Sam pressed his lips to her forehead, making her lids fly open.

His eyes were on hers, his mouth *oh so close.* She wanted it against hers again, she wanted to see if the second touch of his lips could top the first.

But why had he stayed? Was it guilt because she'd been hurt, or could it maybe be . . . attraction?

Ha. His sweet sentiments aside, that wasn't even in the realm of possibilities.

And so, she doubled down. "Nothing went through my head."

"Lie," he said. "But I'm not going to pressure a concussed woman any further."

Despite the kiss—because clearly, that was due to adrenaline at having successfully avoided a patented Mrs. Donovan tirade or guilt or hell, maybe *he* was mildly concussed—because she *knew* that Sam couldn't be attracted to her.

First, he was way out of her league.

Second, she'd admitted to a long-held crush, which was pretty much a ten-out-of-ten on the How Pathetic and/or Crazy Is She scale?

Third, and probably most important, he'd broken Maggie's heart.

Her sister was the one person in her life who'd always been there for her, and Sam had hurt her. It didn't matter that things between them seemed okay now. The end of their relationship had destroyed Maggie, and even putting aside the fact that Sam could just as easily do the same to her, Haley knew she could never be with someone who'd so thoroughly wounded her sister.

Nope. Not going to happen.

Even if he was an excellent kisser.

Really, that was *not* the point.

Sam wrapped his arms tighter around her and tugged her against his chest. Her heart fluttered, and she started to protest. "I can—"

"Shush," he said, cradling her close and standing. "I've got you."

Haley would have loved to blame her lack of further objection on her spinning head, or her aching leg, or the sudden, overwhelming fatigue enveloping her, but the truth was that being held so carefully, assured so confidently, felt . . . incredible.

He had her.

Yet, it all meant nothing, she reminded herself. It was a random kiss, the comforting words of an old friend, a gentle embrace for someone who was hurting.

That was it.

But as he helped her slip fresh pajamas on and tucked her into bed then brought her a bowl filled with banana ice cream, she wondered.

Was it *really* nothing?

Or could it possibly be the start of something more?

Nothing, she thought determinedly, after he'd taken the bowl back to the kitchen and she couldn't keep her eyes open any longer. *Definitely nothing.*

CHAPTER TEN

Sam

ANOTHER NIGHT. Another couch.

Or rather, another night, the *same* couch.

Sam had run home for a change of clothes while Haley was sleeping then had thrown together a simple meal of pasta and salad for dinner once he'd returned to Haley's house. He'd gone to wake her for the meal, but she'd been sleeping so deeply that he had decided to leave her be.

Her body needed the rest.

So, he had wrapped up a plate and left it in her fridge and then debated whether to go home or to stay.

Ultimately, he decided to stay again in case she needed him.

Didn't he mean, in case she got dizzy from the medication again?

No. He meant, in case she needed *him*.

Probably going to be a problem, but not one he was actively avoiding, especially when his phone pinged and he saw a text from Maggie.

It was just after dinnertime, and he knew that meant Sunday Donovan dinner had likely just finished. He *also* knew the meal had probably included a discussion of his appearance at Haley's house that morning.

Bracing himself, he opened the message.

Samwise. I don't know if I should hunt you down and slice you into tiny little pieces because you hurt my sister or thank you because you saved her from our mother.

God, that fucking nickname. Just because a guy had liked *Lord of the Rings* once upon a time. *But* he'd known Maggie for plenty long enough, and two could play that game.

Maggie-baggie. I expected you to show up and save the day.

A pause. Then:

One, I'd almost blocked that horrible nickname from memory. Two, that's why I'm texting. Is Haley doing okay? Lane is sick and Tim is out of town, so my mom decided to bring dinner to me. I couldn't get away until now, and Haley isn't replying to my texts.

Sam considered the question then figured he might as well answer it truthfully. Haley was beautiful and funny, and he wanted to get to know her as . . . well, an adult. Which made him sound like a total creep, but he'd been friends with the girl. The woman was a completely different mystery that he wanted to solve.

Did he want to be her friend? Yes, definitely.

But he also wanted more. He wanted to know her as a man knows a woman he cares about. Not platonically.

"Fuck," he muttered. Why was he beating around the bush? He was attracted to Haley. He liked her. He *wanted* her.

Big fucking deal.

Except—his phone buzzed again, reminding him that things weren't that simple. That he and Haley had history.

Sighing, he saw the follow-up question mark Maggie had sent. Then girded his loins and replied.

That nickname is a classic (and remember I have more before you pull out Samwise again). But nicknames aside, Haley's fine. I just checked on her a few minutes ago and she's sleeping. I stocked her fridge, am parked on her couch, and can keep an eye on her tonight. But tomorrow I have a full day and she could use some supervision. The pain medication makes her dizzy.

The " . . . " signaling the start of Maggie's reply began almost immediately. Then stopped. Then started again.

And one more stop.

Finally, Sam put Maggie out of her misery and just called her.

"Sam Johnson, you're sleeping with my sister?" she hissed.

He sighed. "Stop and rethink that statement," he told her. "Because that sounded like a Jenny Donovan special. I'm staying on your sister's couch because she's alone and aside from the broken leg, stitches, and concussion, her medication makes her dizzy."

"Oh."

He leaned back against the cushions. "Yeah, *oh*."

"I wonder why Brian didn't fly out."

Sam sucked in a breath. He wasn't touching that with a ten-foot pole.

"What the hell does that mean?" Maggie demanded.

Shit. He'd been with this woman for six years. She *knew* him, and she definitely knew when he was lying. Still, Sam tried to play it cool. "Me breathing?"

"No, not you breathing, you idiot," Maggie snapped. "What do you know about Brian and Haley?"

"Nothing," he said, thinking the idiot comment was probably well-earned. For as much as she knew him, he also knew her. And when Maggie got something in her head, she was a dog to a bone.

In these cases, it was best to divert and avoid.

"Sam."

He closed his eyes. "Maggie." A beat. "I'm hanging up now."

"Sam—"

"Goodbye, Maggie," he said. "I've got to be out at Roosevelt Ranch early in the morning. Make sure you check on your sister."

"Don't you—"

He hung up and sighed loudly.

Which is probably why he missed the sound of Haley's little scooter. "I didn't know you were on chatting terms with my sister."

Sam's eyes flew open.

His gaze traveled over her face. Her color was closer to normal, and there were no signs of strain around her mouth and eyes. "You're feeling better."

She was beautiful, even with the bandage marring her forehead, curls of black and purple creeping from beneath it and spreading across her forehead.

One half of her mouth curved up. "How do you always know?"

He shrugged and pushed up off the couch. "My patients can't talk to me." Pointing to the couch, he said, "Means I have to be observant. Now, sit. I'll heat up your plate."

"Plate?" Haley started to frown but paused midway and winced. Shaking her head, she shifted herself onto the couch. "You didn't have to cook for me, Sam. Hell, you shouldn't even be here. You've got your own job and your own life, and just because you're feeling guilty"—she pointed a finger at him—"and you *shouldn't* even be feeling guilty at all because I was the one who slammed on my brakes, remember? But just because you are doesn't mean that you should put everything that's happening in your own life on hold."

He had been waiting for a pause in her speech. "You done?"

Her gaze narrowed. "You going to be a pain in my ass?"

"Probably." He grinned. "But it's not going to stop me. For one, my life is boring. I have work and . . . work. My friends are all married with kids, and my parents aren't even in town right now." When her brows drew down, he said, "They winter in Florida, like a pair of migrating birds."

Her mouth curved. "I'd forgotten they wanted to do that. Did they ever get the RV they wanted?"

Sam chuckled. "It's nicer than my house. They spend most of their time traveling around the States and will occasionally grace me with their presence by parking on my driveway for a week or two."

He tucked a pillow under Haley's foot. "Living the dream," she said.

"They have their own Instagram account." He tugged a blanket from the back of the couch and draped it over her. "Last week, I saw my mom had used the hashtag YOLO."

She snorted. "Cooler than me."

"Ditto that." He straightened and headed for the kitchen. "I just made some pasta and salad, you hungry?"

Considering her response was her stomach growling nearly loud enough to shake the foundation of her little cottage, Sam hustled to the fridge and pulled out her plate.

Just as he was popping it into the microwave, she said, loudly enough he couldn't ignore it, not with the open floorplan of her kitchen and living room, "So, Maggie?" she asked.

Sam stifled a sigh. He'd never discussed with Haley—hell, he'd never really discussed with anyone—why he'd broken off his engagement with Haley's sister. That was between him and Maggie, and they'd made their peace when he'd moved back to Darlington to take over the veterinary practice three years before.

"Maggie and I talk on occasion." She was married with kids and happy. That was all that mattered to him now.

Sam pulled out the bowl of salad and brought it and a fork over to Haley.

"Really?" she asked as he handed it to her. "That's all you're going to say?"

"Would you like me to press you for more details of what happened with Brian? Especially since your sister apparently doesn't know you two broke up."

Haley speared a forkful of spinach. "No one knows we broke up except him and me, and well, *you*. Though I guess Susie knows, too." She jammed the spinach into her mouth.

"Susie your friend?" he asked.

"Uh-huh," she said around the bite before swallowing. "Though *former* friend is a better description. And I didn't deliberately not tell anyone we'd broken up. I just didn't go out of my way to . . . *tell* them."

"You've been back how long exactly?"

A cough trailed by a mumbled answer.

"Sorry?" He put his hand to his ear. "What was that?"

She made a face. "Thirteen months."

"Ah. That's what my Haley translator missed. Thirteen months is a long time to keep up the charade of a relationship."

"It's not a charade," she protested and shoved another bite into her mouth.

"Then what is it?" he pressed.

She chewed. Swallowed. "It's a—"

The microwave dinged.

He laughed. "Look at that. The universe is giving you time to come up with an answer." He started to walk back into the kitchen, but she stopped him with a hand on his arm.

"I don't need time," she said.

"I'm teasing you." Sam bent so that his eyes were in line with hers. "You don't owe me an answer."

Her expression warmed. "I know. But I think I might owe myself one."

CHAPTER ELEVEN

Haley

WHY WAS SHE PUSHING THIS?

Sam had given her the perfect out. An easy way to find some distance again and to avoid—

Well, she'd done entirely too much of *that* in her twenty-seven years.

"I didn't correct my mom or Maggie about Brian because"—she sucked in a breath—"I didn't want to deal with it. No." She shook her head. "That's not what I mean. I . . . just with me having a fiancé, things were easier, simpler. My mom didn't hassle me, Maggie backed off about trying to set me up with all of the single guys in town—"

She broke off.

Because that was what she'd been telling herself.

But what she'd been telling herself, the story she'd grasped on to tightly with both hands like when her niece, Ashley, had refused to let go of her blankie when she'd been a toddler, was absolutely and utterly an excuse.

She'd held on to Brian because—

"I didn't want to be pathetic."

He faced hardened. "You're *not*. That's ridic—"

"Don't say it's ridiculous," she said. "You're not in here"—she tapped her temple—"you're not in my brain. You don't know what it's like."

Sam froze. "So, what's it like?" He knelt in front of the couch, taking the bowl from her hands and setting it on the coffee table. "Tell me what's going on"—he gently touched one finger to her forehead—"in here."

She forced a laugh. "It's not a pretty sight."

"In the last twenty-four hours, we've done bruises, blood, and broken bones . . . I don't think we should be worried about things being pretty, do you?"

Her lips twitched. "Well, for starters, if you'd said that to me a year ago, I would have automatically assumed that you were saying *I* wasn't pretty."

"I—"

She waved a hand. "Yes, I know you didn't mean it that way at all. I just—I don't know, I guess I always have to fight the urge to immediately look for some hidden insult in someone else's words." Her chin wobbled. "It's stupid. Logically, I know that, but I still can't stop myself from digging for some buried slight. And I was like that *before* Brian."

He brushed his fingers over her cheek. "And after?"

"Being with him"—a long slow breath—"amplified every insecurity I've battled my whole life. Not thin and beautiful like Maggie. Not smart enough. Not perfect." Her voice dropped. "Unloveable."

Ugh. Haley blinked back tears and released another shuddering exhale.

Because, yes, she felt that way—or rather, she *had* felt that way.

But she'd grown since then. She understood herself better, knew she didn't have to be perfect, that she had value even if she was five pounds overweight or didn't automatically know the solution to a problem big or small.

Of course, that also didn't mean the echoes of those doubts were completely gone.

They framed every interaction, were a constant struggle to shrug off, to not internalize—

"That is such fucking bullshit."

Her jaw dropped open at his tone, but she didn't have a chance to respond because then his mouth was on hers. His lips were hard at first, almost angry because of what she'd admitted, but then they softened. His mouth gently coaxed hers, his tongue slipping between her lips, brushing against hers, tender and sweet and—

He pulled back. "I'm sorry. I didn't mean what *you* were saying was bullshit. Just that I hate you felt that way because you're gorgeous and smart and totally, utterly love—"

This time *she* kissed *him*.

There was no hesitation in his response. One second, he was mid-sentence, the next his mouth was firmly against hers and though he held her gently, Sam still managed to give her the hottest kiss of her life.

He nipped at her bottom lip and when she gasped, he slipped his tongue inside her mouth to tangle with hers. Calloused fingers slid over her nape, curled into her hair, angling her head so he could deepen the kiss.

Hot, a little rough, and so *fucking* good.

Haley pressed herself up, even as she yanked him down. She needed him closer, on top of her, *inside* of her. She—

A bolt of pain had her gasping . . . this time not in a good way.

Sam realized immediately, and he launched himself off her. She'd managed to pull him partway onto the couch, and while that was what her vagina wanted—or rather it wanted more, starting with the rigid length of him that was nudging her thigh sliding home—the rest of her body was intrinsically aware that she'd been in an accident the night before.

Sam was big. *Ha.* Okay, he was heavy. There. *That* was a better descriptor, one that didn't bring her inner teenage boy roaring to life.

"I'm sorry, baby," he said. "I forgot—"

She smiled up at him, heart pounding, head spinning—in pleasure rather than because of the concussion—her lips tender and swollen. "I forgot, too," she said.

He cupped her cheek. "I meant what I said. You have worth, sweetheart. And that doesn't come because your outside is pretty—though it *is* gorgeous—but because you're a good person and so damned brilliant and . . ."

Keeping all the negative things inside her brain had meant she'd been giving them power. But somehow, the moment she'd verbalized those deep dark thoughts, the moment she'd admitted aloud how much the burden carrying all of that had been weighing on her, it was almost as if their power over her disappeared.

Haley could take Sam's words at face value instead of sifting through them for a backhanded compliment.

She could imagine a world, imagine herself in a world where a man like Sam actually believed the things he was saying.

She could be pretty and brilliant and *imperfect*.

And that was okay.

Shock weaved through her, chased rapidly by awe. She didn't *have* to be perfect. She could be herself and still be worthy.

Huh.

Fancy that.

CHAPTER TWELVE

Sam

HE WAS knee-deep in horse manure and loving every minute of it.

Ankle-deep might have been a more accurate description. Though his arm was in what most would consider a much worse place as he examined Kelly Hamilton's horse, Stella.

Kelly and her husband, Justin, owned Roosevelt Ranch, which was quickly becoming one of the premier breeding operations in the States. Kelly was also Rob's sister-in-law.

See? Darlington was a small town. They didn't even need six degrees of separation.

Still, despite Kel managing a breeding program, Sam had the notion *this* particular pregnancy wasn't planned.

"Is she okay?" Kelly asked nervously.

He nodded. "Yup."

Kelly blew out a relieved sigh as he finished his exam then took a few minutes to discard the glove and scrub his hands with soap and water in the nearby sink.

"So, do you have any idea why she's been so moody?"

"I'm guessing because she's about three months pregnant." He could have confirmed that more accurately if he'd brought his portable ultrasound, but apparently Kel had been adamant that Stella was not pregnant when she'd scheduled the appointment with Jane. "So, I'm guessing this isn't planned?"

Melissa, Kelly's sister and Rob's wife, chose that moment to walk through the door, two thermoses of coffee in her hands. She'd obviously overheard him because she grinned and teased, "Like mother, like daughter?"

Kel shot her a sisterly glare. "Things happen sometimes, okay?"

Melissa bumped her with her shoulder. "I'm teasing because, yes, sometimes things do happen . . . for the better."

Kelly's face softened and she snagged a thermos from her sister. "Thanks for the coffee."

"You're welcome." Melissa turned to Sam and extended the second thermos.

"Oh, no," he said, despite the mouth-watering smell of the freshly brewed drink wafting to his nose. "That's yours. I couldn't—"

"I already had mine. I made this for you when Kel told me you were coming to the ranch." She shoved the cup at him and since he wasn't about to let good coffee go to waste, Sam took it.

As he drank his first sip, she asked, "How are you? I heard you had an . . . eventful weekend."

He made a face that had Melissa tipping up the bottom of the thermos and dumping another sip into his mouth. "Drink," she said. "Everything is better with coffee."

Sam obeyed then nearly groaned in relief as the caffeine headed straight from his mouth to his brain.

Yup. That was just what he'd needed.

"Better?"

A nod.

"Now, you'll tell us what happened?"

"You probably know as much as I do," he said. "But Haley is pretty banged up. She has a broken ankle along with a concussion and stitches." As he listed her injuries, the guilt peppered him anew. If only he hadn't—

"More coffee," Melissa said.

"Go easy on the full Missy offensive," Kel interjected, sipping her own coffee and leaning back next to him against the closed door of Stella's stall. "The poor man has had a time of it."

"I hope you're not feeling guilty," Melissa said. "Rob told me that a deer jumped in front of Haley's car. It was just an—"

"Accident?" He met her eyes. "And how would *you* feel if someone was hurt because you hit their car?"

Melissa wrinkled her nose.

"Yeah," he said. "That."

"Okay, *I* may have a problem with guilt but . . ."

"Don't finish that sentence, Sissy," Kel warned. "Because it's all aboard the pot-meet-kettle train." She grinned when Melissa smacked her. "Let's talk about Stella instead."

Melissa's expression filled with glee. "Yes, let me tease you about your horse's unplanned pregnancy some more."

"You're so sweet to me." Kel pushed up and wrapped an arm around Melissa's shoulders. Or maybe it was her neck, he realized with a grin. "So supportive—"

"Your horse is a hussy."

A mock gasp. "How *dare* you . . ."

Sam couldn't hold back his chuckle, even as their squabbling made him jealous.

As an only child with parents constantly on the road, he'd had more than his fair share of loneliness over the last few years. Yes, he'd dated some, but no one had stuck, and so he'd developed a pattern of working long hours and then going home to his meal for one at the end of the night.

Which might be a little pathetic, but instead of going down that particular line of thinking, Sam was just going to pretend it was totally completely normal for a grown man to be alone and . . .

It wasn't like he was *all* alone.

He saw his clients—people like Melissa and Kelly and, even Snapchat Esther, who'd gotten a new kitten. He traveled to the nearby ranches, which he supposed could fall under the client section of his life. But he went into town a lot, grocery shopping or eating at Henry's diner when he needed to be around people.

Might be a teensy bit pathetic, that train of thought.

But pathetic or not, Sam couldn't smother the feeling that he'd been waiting.

For what, he wasn't sure.

At least, he *hadn't* been sure until he'd crashed into Haley. Because after the collision, after the time at her house, after the *kiss* . . . he wondered if he hadn't been waiting all along for Haley.

"So, if Stella is such a virginal being," Melissa said, tugging Kel's arm from around her neck, "then how is she knocked up?"

"Immaculate horse-ception?" Sam deadpanned, earning him a smack from Kelly.

"Shut it you." Kel tapped her finger to her mouth. "But yours is a good question, sissy."

"What's a good question?" They all turned to see Justin striding into the barn, his and Kelly's daughter, Abigail, riding on his shoulders.

"Stella's pregnant," Kelly said.

"What?" Justin asked, sliding closer to Stella's stall when Abigail said, "Swella!" and leaned forward, nearly toppling herself from his hold.

"I've got you, sweetie pie," Kelly said, swooping in and hugging Abigail to her chest. "Do you want to see Stella?"

The little girl smiled. "Yes."

Kelly lifted her up so she could pet the front of Stella's head. "The twins?" she asked.

"Still sleeping," he said and held up a baby monitor. "Just this one"—he smacked a kiss to the top of Abigail's head—"that decided she was raring to start her Monday."

"Don't know where she gets the energy," Kelly said.

Justin waggled his brows. "I know."

"Barf," Melissa said, her eyes dancing.

Kel's lips twitched. "Why do I feel like you've been waiting years to say that?"

Melissa grinned. "Because considering the number of times you've said it about me and my husband, I definitely have been waiting to turn the tables."

"Terrible."

Melissa blew her a kiss. "You love me." She pulled out her phone, glanced at its screen. "Well, I just wanted to drop by and make sure everything was good with your first baby," she told Kel. "But it looks like Rob is sending out the S.O.S. to get the kiddos ready for school."

"Stella's not my first baby," Kel said then frowned. "Okay, fine, she basically is, but knowing you with your *own* babies, you've got the schedule down to the second and everything already laid out. Rob just needs to follow the plan."

A shrug. "Of course, I do." She grinned as her phone buzzed again. "It's just that plans tend to go out the window when Allie decides she doesn't want to wear any pants."

It was Justin's turn to frown as he voiced the same question Sam was thinking. "Can't she just wear a dress?"

Melissa smirked, patting him on the cheek. "Oh, you poor, poor dear. Just wait until that one"—she pointed at Abigail—"gets bigger. My daughter has decided that pants, shorts, sweats, skirts, dresses, *and* underwear are all too restrictive. She wants to be completely bottomless all the time."

Sam made a strangled noise.

Melissa's eyes flicked to his. "Case in point, Rob's reaction." She held up the phone so they could all see the screen and the GIF Rob had sent of an actor running around a room screaming.

They all shared a laugh as she hugged each of them in turn and then said goodbye.

Sam figured it was time for him to make an exit as well.

If he hurried, he might have a chance to check on Haley before he headed into the clinic.

"I'll swing by next week with my ultrasound and we'll see if we can find out exactly how far along she is," he said, gathering up his supplies and tucking them back into his kit.

"What I still don't understand is how she's pregnant in the first place," Kelly said, having set down Abigail and moved to the table to cut up an apple. She helped her daughter feed a slice to each of the horses one by one. "We've been so careful to keep the horses separate while they're in season and—"

Sam caught Justin's wince at the same time Kelly did.

"Justin Roosevelt," she began, thunder in her tone. "What *did* you do?"

He winced and held up the baby monitor. "Oh look, the twins—"

"That isn't even on," Kelly snapped, yanking it from his hand and twisting the volume dial. A picture filled the screen, showing two sleeping babies, each in their own crib.

"I should go—"

They didn't acknowledge him, so Sam began to make his escape.

He was at the barn door when he heard Justin confess, "So, like a month ago, remember you and Melissa took the girls to Disney on Ice? The twins were, well, *the twins*, and I may have forgotten Stella was in heat when I turned her and Theo out to pasture together."

Kelly gasped. "You forgot?"

Sam started to close the door behind him, figuring to give them some privacy for their argument, but when he turned to do so, he saw Justin had tugged Kelly close.

He should look away. He really should.

But instead, Sam found himself riveted.

"Admit it," he said. "You're not really mad."

She huffed, turned her head away, but not before Sam saw that she was smiling. "I get to keep the baby?"

Justin kissed her forehead, glancing over to check on Abigail who was practicing her saddling skills on a kid-sized stuffed horse. "As if we could ever give a Stello baby up."

"Stello?" Abby asked.

"Theo and Stella," Justin said as if it were obvious. "I've been coming up with combo names ever since I saw Theo mounting Stella and giving her his—"

Kel gave an outraged gasp. "Don't talk about her that way—"

Justin cut off the rest of her protest by kissing her.

Sam figured *that* was definitely his cue and tugged the barn door closed.

A few minutes later, he drove to Haley's house and couldn't stop the longing from swarming over him. He wanted what Jordan and Kelly had, what Melissa and Rob also had—easy, comfortable, teasing, even a little irritated . . .

But love.

All of it was love.

Sam wanted that.

And he thought he might want it with Haley.

CHAPTER THIRTEEN

Haley

IT HAD BEEN FIVE DAYS, and Haley was losing her fucking mind.

No work. No car—hers was in the shop with a wish and a prayer the mechanic could make it drivable again, not that she could drive anyway, considering her right ankle was the one she'd broken. She'd binged as many reality TV shows and documentaries as she could handle and had far exceeded her e-book budget for the month. She had even progressed beyond just talking to herself.

Now she was arguing with herself.

"No, you can't," she muttered as she considered crutching her butt out into her backyard for some fresh air and change of location. "Yes, I can." She hadn't needed any pain pills that day, so there was no risk of being too dizzy and cracking her head open.

But, she probably shouldn't.

The skies had opened up that morning, dumping buckets of rain onto Darlington and turning her yard into a giant mud pit.

"Fuck it," she said. "I'm going."

She tucked her crutches under her armpits and thumped herself to the back door. Her scooter was useless on the steps and just as much so on the uneven path weaving its way through her garden. Mother Nature might have wreaked havoc in her yard, but Haley couldn't deal with being sedentary any longer. She was used to moving, to being on her feet and running around the hospital for twelve hours at a time, not propping herself in front of her TV and her only exercise being when she wheeled herself down the hall to the toilet.

She needed to find a way to get back to work, even if it was just for charting or to answer phones.

Being here, alone, except for her sister's daily visit, meant she was going crazy.

Her sister had visited. Not Sam.

"So, he missed one day," she reminded herself. "He was probably busy with work and—"

He'd forgotten about her.

Haley wrinkled her nose. He *hadn't* forgotten about her. Sam had been by every morning and every evening. He hadn't stayed on her couch again, though she considered that a good sign, as in she had recovered enough from her injuries that she didn't need a babysitter.

Her concussion symptoms—mild to begin with—had all but faded. Her ankle still ached, and she was weeks away from being able to bear weight on it, let alone driving.

And Sam hadn't come that morning.

Or that night.

The sun was setting, and Haley had reheated the pasta he'd made for them the previous night for dinner. The man could cook—though to be fair to chefs everywhere, it *was* limited to one solid meal. As she'd waited for him to appear, she'd considered calling him to say thanks for the yummy leftovers, but one, she didn't have Sam's number and two, she wasn't sure she had the right to call him even if she did.

And . . . he hadn't come.

Which meant she was slowly, incrementally going insane.

Should she call Maggie for his number? Obviously, her sister and Sam talked regularly. But what would Maggie think or assume or pinpoint with laser-like accuracy?

That Haley liked Sam? That she missed him? That her sister was trying to horn in on her ex?

Sighing, she crutched a few steps farther down the path before carefully lowering herself to a dry spot, or rather, a space that was damp but not thoroughly soaked.

The evening air had a bite to it, just enough to make the end of her nose and the tops of her cheeks tingle. Rain aside, it really had been a beautiful spring week. Warm, but not the scorching heat of summer. No snow, no ice.

And she was hobbled by her broken ankle.

"Lame," she muttered, leaning back against a rock and staring up at the sky. The sun had technically already set, the evening entering its twilight state as its shadows began to swallow the sunlight, dark bleaching the colorful flowers of her yard to different shades of gray.

Yet, the moon was bright and full and beautiful, and a few stars were beginning to appear on the darkening curve of the sky, royal to navy to black. She reclined against the rock and just watched as day turned fully to night.

The moon, shining brightly and yet so alone was lovely in its own way, but its isolation did nothing to dispel the loneliness within her.

Sam owed her nothing . . . and he'd somehow still become an addiction.

Five days, apparently, was all it took.

She snorted. Because she knew it hadn't been five days, not this boy she'd crushed on for so long. *But* in those five days, Haley had grown to really like the man, and she wanted to know him further.

A dangerous thought considering what had happened with Maggie.

Also, one she hadn't been able to get out of her mind, despite the past, despite her misgivings, despite her sister.

"Ugh," she said, knowing she was twisting herself into knots for no reason.

Sam hadn't expressed any interest—

Cough. The kisses?

See what she meant about arguing with herself?

Yes, he'd kissed her.

Twice. *No,* three times.

Yes, it had been three times. But that had been on Sunday and it was Friday now, and he had been over eight times since the kiss—*kisses*—and . . . he hadn't tried to kiss her again.

In fact, he hadn't been anything aside from friendly.

No flirting. No searing eye contact. No gentle caresses and . . . no kisses.

She'd been friend-zoned.

Hence the late-night garden brooding.

Haley sighed, thus confirming said brooding. Sam had said all the right things, made her feel better, made sure she was healing and settled.

He'd done *everything* right.

But for a second there, she'd thought that maybe, just maybe she might have a chance at getting her mess of a love life straightened out. Because Sam was sweet and kind and hot and sexy and—

He wasn't for her.

"Yeah," she said, adding another broody sigh, just for good measure. "I need to remember that."

"Remember what?"

Sam's voice made her gasp.

But before she could scramble to come up with a response, the clouds she'd noticed but hadn't particularly processed as dark or storm-wielding, opened up and rain poured down across her backyard for the second time that day.

"Shit," she cried, reaching for her crutches and fumbling to get herself up onto her feet.

"Let me." Sam scooped her up into his arms. He stood, running to the back porch and depositing her beneath the cover, before returning for her crutches. After tucking them inside her back door, he swept back over to her, gathering her against his chest again and carrying her inside.

They were both soaked to the skin. Rivulets of icy water pooled in her hair, dripping down her nape, her face. Despite the cold, Sam was somehow still hot, his body heat almost scorching her through the layers of their wet clothes.

"Wait here," he said, setting her on the kitchen counter and hustling down the hall.

A heartbeat later he was back, setting a towel around her shoulders then wrapping one above her cast to catch the water.

Smart man. Brilliant man. Sweet man.

"Sam—"

He glanced up, and her breath caught at the heat in his eyes. "You okay?" he asked.

Where had all the reasons to give this man a wide berth disappeared to?

Because in *that* moment, his brown hair darkened to black, water dripping down his forehead, his cheeks, his mouth, his wet clothes sticking to a muscled chest, to thighs she wanted pressing against hers . . . *fuck*, she wanted nothing more than to reach up and slant her mouth across his.

He was staring at her as though he wanted her.

For a moment, she could actually believe it.

Sam cleared his throat, the heat disappeared. "Let me get you some dry clothes."

Haley lifted her hand, placed it on his shoulder when he would have turned away. "Wait."

"You—?"

She kissed him.

If he'd had a heartbeat of hesitation or resistance or any type of shock that her twisted mind might have interpreted as not wanting the kiss—not wanting *her*—Haley might have shut down.

But there wasn't any hesitation in Sam's reaction.

The moment her lips pressed to his, he was a flurry of motion. One hand came up to weave into her hair, his tongue slid through the seam of her mouth, slipping inside to tangle with hers. The other arm wrapped tightly around her middle, crushing her against all the long, lean muscle she'd been admiring only seconds before.

And it felt . . . right.

Also incredible, of course. He was hot as hell, and he was kissing her with so much intensity that her mind spun.

But it wasn't just heat, definitely wasn't solely desire.

This man kissed her, and the rest of the world fell away.

His fingers slipped under the hem of her T-shirt, sliding up her rib cage, leaving a trail of goose bumps in their wake.

She moaned, wrapped her uninjured leg around his hips. "Fuck." A gasp as she felt the hard length of him against her pussy. She wanted both of their pants off. Now. Then his fingers teased the underside of her breasts and she arched, wanting it all, wanting him inside, wanting his hand to move higher, to slip under her bra. "*Sam,*" she pleaded.

He nipped her jaw, soothed the slight hurt with his tongue. "You sure, sweetheart?" A brush of one fingertip across her nipple. "We should probably discuss—"

Haley yanked his mouth to hers and kissed him until they had to break apart for air. "Fuck discussions," she said and slipped her hand between them, pushing it into the front of his jeans and stroking the silken head of his cock that was peeking over the waistband of his underwear.

He groaned, hips thrusting forward.

She felt herself grow wetter, knew that she needed this man inside her or she would die.

Literally, it felt as though she would die if he didn't fuck her that second.

"Talk later," she panted, flicking the button of his jeans open, desperate to get both hands on him. "Fuck now."

His lips curved into a wicked grin. "That I can do." He yanked her T-shirt up and over her head, her bra followed a second later. He'd just cupped her breast and bent to take her nipple in his mouth when she heard a *crash,* then a shriek, then a "What the fuck?!"

CHAPTER FOURTEEN

Sam

WELL, this was awkward.

Maggie stood just inside the front door, a bowl of food overturned at her feet and fury in every line of her expression. She stepped over the pile of what looked to be noodles and strode toward them, eyes flashing.

Sam moved to stand in front of Haley, blocking her from view.

Her T-shirt had managed to hang itself on one of her barstools, so he snagged it then passed it to her.

"What in the fuck is going on?" Maggie snapped.

Sighing, Sam crossed his arms. "Maggie."

"Don't *Maggie* me—"

"This isn't what it looks like."

Sam's mouth clamped closed, and he spun around to face Haley. Um. What the hell was she talking about? *This* was exactly what it looked like. For fuck's sake, she'd been topless with her hand down his pants.

"Explain." Maggie.

"There's nothing to explain," he said. "This is between me and Haley."

Haley didn't look at him. "Mags. I'm sorry. I shouldn't have. I . . ."

Maggie, the woman he'd once thought would be his wife, didn't acknowledge Haley. Instead, she kept her brown eyes fixed on Sam. "How could you do this to my sister? You knew she had a crush on you." A shove to his chest. "What? Is this some sort of check mark on your bucket list, to sleep with sisters?"

"That's not fair—"

"You knew?" Haley shrieked, her cheeks going pink. "You knew, and you didn't say anything?"

Maggie shook her head, voice softening, the slightest note of pity lacing its way into her tone. "Oh kiddo, of course I knew. It was so obvious."

Sam had a lot of love for the girl who'd been his childhood sweetheart, but in that moment, he could have strangled her. It was a painful thing to witness, Haley wilting under her sister's tone and superior expression.

He tried to rescue the situation. "I didn't know. I swear, Haley. I mean I hardly noticed you until you came back into town, and I probably never would have even talked—"

Oh, fuck.

That wasn't rescuing. That was dive-bombing. Dropping a nuke on the situation and blowing it to fucking shreds.

Haley's face paled and hurt swam in her eyes.

"That's not what I meant—"

"Regardless," Maggie said, chiming in with perfectly terrible timing. "This is bad, Hays. You're vulnerable, and Sam isn't right for you."

"Vulnerable—" Haley began.

"Yes, you're hurt, and he's taking advantage."

Since that particular sentiment hit too close to home, it took a second for Sam to gather his wits.

"He absolutely isn't taking advantage," Haley said. "I mean, I know it was wrong to get involved with him—"

Wrong? Sam blinked. They were two adults and—

"*Of course*, he's taking advantage. Or rather, he's trying to assuage his guilt by being with—by making you feel good." She pointed at Sam. "This is what he does, Hays. He feels guilty and sticks around, and you have to be the one to stand strong and let him go."

"What the hell are you talking about?" Sam gritted out.

Maggie blinked, her face going carefully blank as she slipped out of her preaching attitude. It had always been hard to get her to shut up when she was going off on a tangent, but this absolutely took the cake. But finally, she did shut up, taking in what was no doubt a furious expression on his face because she bit her lip and flicked her gaze away.

Then Haley spoke, and his rage went to a whole new level.

"Look, I know he broke your heart and that you were really hurt and—"

Sam saw red. Literally, his skin went too tight, his teeth ground together so fiercely that he was surprised he didn't crack a fucking tooth, and a red haze tinted his vision.

Obviously, Maggie had never told Haley what had happened between them, what truly had ended their relationship. Sam had never said anything, never *would* have gone there because he was a fucking gentleman, but that Maggie had painted him like that to her sister . . .

His hands tightened into fists. Because fuck her.

Stand strong? Let him go? *Ha.* If anyone had broken hearts, it had been Maggie.

"Are we seriously going to go here?" he asked her.

Maggie paled, turned her gaze deliberately to Haley. "Maybe he's not taking advantage, but he's too—"

"Too what?" he asked, cold fury in those two syllables.

"I know what you mean," Haley said. Her eye flicked to the ground then back up to his. "You should go, Sam. This"—a cough—"let's face facts. This wasn't ever going to work out."

"What the hell are you talking about?" He reached for her, stopping when she cringed back. "We didn't even have a chance to—"

"Sam." She sighed. "You're *you* and I'm . . . *I'm* me. Let's face facts. We would have never gone anywhere anyway."

He frowned. "Haley, I'm not saying that I've fallen madly in love with you or that you're my soul mate or— We've just started getting to know each other again, but I like you—" He sucked in a breath. "I was hoping that we might—"

"What? Date? *Fuck?*" Haley let out an exasperated sigh. "Let's just leave it here, Sam. Let's just stop before someone gets hurt."

Yeah. Like him.

Again.

"That's the right decision," Maggie said.

Sam ignored her. "Is that what you want?"

Haley lifted her chin. "It's what I need, Sam. Brian broke me. I—I can't risk you doing to me what you did to Maggie."

"What did Brian—" Maggie began.

Sam had kept his eyes fixed on Haley's, looking for some sign of uncertainty or remorse.

He found neither.

Just perfect.

The Donovan sisters sure knew how to fuck with a guy's mind.

"Just go, Sam," Haley murmured.

He shook his head and strode for the door, stepping over the pile of noodles on the threshold. There, he paused and glared at Maggie. "I know we dated for six years, and both of us made plenty of mistakes during that time, but maybe you should share with your sister what actually happened between us." He pushed through the door. "Maybe then she wouldn't be using the past as an excuse to torpedo her future."

Silence before the door slammed behind him.

CHAPTER FIFTEEN

Haley

HALEY WATCHED Sam's SUV disappear down her driveway and couldn't stop the pang of remorse from coursing through her.

Had she just made the biggest mistake of her life, not hopping aboard the Sam train?

No. She'd jumped in headfirst once before, and look where that had gotten her.

"Well, good," Maggie said, brushing her hands down the front of her shirt. "That's a near miss." She bustled over to the spilled bowl and pasta, using her hands to scoop it up.

Yuck.

Carefully, Haley slid herself to the end of the counter and executed a perfect dismount onto her good leg. *Thank you, seven years of gymnastics.* From there, she maneuvered herself onto her scooter, grabbed a roll of paper towels and wheeled over to her sister.

"Here," she said. "I would offer to help—"

"But I wouldn't let you anyway," Maggie said, finishing their old joke.

As much as they ragged on their mom for never compromising, for always having to do it *her* way, Maggie was almost as bad. She was very particular and exacting and, frankly, that was exhausting sometimes.

But Haley had never really come up against it, or maybe she'd never pushed . . . same way as she dealt with her mom. It was easier to capitulate than fight over controlling every single detail, especially when she knew with one-hundred percent certainty that Maggie had her best interest in mind.

Except—

Except for the first time ever, Haley really wondered if Maggie really did have her best interest in mind. When it came to Sam, was her sister blind?

Was it old hurt? Protective sisterly love?

Or was there something else happening beneath the surface? Something that had happened between Maggie and Sam that Haley didn't understand.

"Mags?" she asked.

"What?"

"I—"

Her sister gathered up the bowl, dumping the contents in the trash and setting it into the sink.

"What—"

Maggie gathered up the dirty towels, rushing down the hall to throw them in the wash. When she came back into the room, she was carrying Haley's mop. "What a mess! I'd better get this cleaned up before you slip and break the other leg."

Her laughter was forced, and Haley debated what she should do. Obviously, Maggie didn't want to talk about what had gone down with her and Sam. She'd never been able to force her sister to do anything. *She* was the one to give in, to cave. Haley had absolutely zero skills in her social toolbox to help her deal with Maggie when she was like this. So, needless to say, she certainly couldn't force her sister to dish all. Not unless—

She dished first.

Fuck. She didn't want to talk about Brian, about her old job, about the myriad reasons she'd come home.

The past was the past, and they should leave it in the—

Ha. Now, *that* was a load of bull if she'd ever heard one. Haley had left the past in the past about as well as her mother let go of old grudges.

Which was not at all.

Could she talk about Brian? She'd already told some of it to Sam. Unwillingly to begin with, but she *had* felt better in the end.

Maybe this would just expand on that?

Maybe she could make herself *and* Maggie feel better.

Probably a pipe dream.

But it was worth a shot, right?

Right. She nodded and opened her mouth and just blurted, "Brian and I broke up."

Maggie froze in her mopping for a moment before resuming her left-right-front-back movement. Yes, her sister was particular enough about her day-to-day life that she even had a preferred technique for mopping.

Was it more pathetic that Haley knew her sister's chosen mopping pattern or that Maggie had a blueprint for everything, right down to the best way to soak up water from the floor, in the first place?

Either. Both.

She sighed, opened her mouth to expound.

"I surmised as much, considering you had your hand down Sam's pants when I first walked in." Maggie mopped faster. "I don't understand you, Haley. Are you desperate enough to take my seconds?"

Hurt sliced through her. "That's not fair."

"Or what?" Maggie was moving at warp speed now, the mop swooshing over the floor almost as quickly as her words shot like bullets into Haley's chest. "You never grew out of that pathetic crush. I mean, I swear it was so embarrassing to watch you mooning over him like a pitiful schoolgirl."

Tears stung Haley's eyes and she might have kicked her sister out of her house altogether, screamed and shouted and *hurt* her back, but this wasn't like Maggie at all.

Normally, her sister was nice, boarding on almost too nice.

She was particular but didn't lose her temper. Not ever. Hell, if someone didn't do tasks the way she preferred them, she was much more likely to thank the person before sneaking behind them to quietly redo it than yelling at them. Haley had rarely seen her sister raise her voice and she had never *ever* witnessed Maggie acting like this.

Mean. Horrible. Cruel.

Luckily, the shock of such a reversal in her sister's behavior meant that though Haley's feelings were hurt, she at least managed to hold on to a thin thread of rationality.

One that allowed her to say, "This isn't like you, Mags. Why are you acting like this?"

Maggie swallowed hard. "I'm not acting like anything. I'm trying to protect my sister is all." She lifted the mop and hurried back down the hall. Of course, her return to the kitchen was much slower.

Haley decided she'd had about enough. She positioned her scooter in front of the hall, blocking Maggie's path to escape.

Because she was smart enough to know that would probably be her sister's next move. Avoidance unless absolutely cornered. After which, she'd lash out and run. And the degree of lashing out she'd just experienced told Haley that the thing Maggie was hoping to avoid discussing was huge.

So, she blocked the hall and waited.

"Don't you want to know why Brian and I broke up?" she asked after her sister had stashed the mop and then turned back to the front of the house.

"Of course, I do," Maggie said, starting to inch around her. "I just—Tim texted and—"

Yeah. Nice try, Sis. Haley could see Maggie's phone sitting on the counter.

"Can you help me?" she asked, trying a different tack. "My leg's hurting, and I don't think I can get onto the couch."

Maggie sighed but stopped inching toward the front door and instead walked next to Haley as she wheeled herself to the sofa. "Do you need a pain pill?"

"No," Haley said. "Just a hand."

Maggie didn't argue, just slid a hand under Haley's arm and helped her transition, but when her sis would have pulled back, Haley grabbed her wrist.

"Mags." A plea. "Brian cheated on me. He—" She shook her head. "It was a good thing, ultimately, because I was in a bad place with him for a long time—"

"Did he hurt you?"

Finally, Haley saw a glimpse of her sister instead of the mean, avoidance monster.

"Not in the way you're thinking," she said. "But he was an asshole and managed to do a number on my confidence. For a long time, I thought . . . well, I *still* struggle with not measuring up, with not being smart or pretty enough to—" She broke off.

"To what?" Maggie asked.

"To—" Haley's eyes pricked. "I just—I know I can never measure up to you."

Maggie had been squatting next to her, knees floating above the ground as she got settled, but at Haley's words, her sister's legs gave way, her knees hitting the carpet with a *thump.*

"If you knew—" A tear leaked from the corner of Maggie's eye. "If you knew what I did, then you'd understand that I'm the one who needs to live up to you, Hays. I—" She sniffed.

"I don't understand."

"I can't—" Maggie jumped to her feet. "I need to go."

"Mags—"

The sound of her front door slamming, for a second time that evening, echoed through her house.

CHAPTER SIXTEEN

Sam

SAM SIGHED as he plunked his ass into a booth in Henry's Place.

Named after a Darlington local, Henry, and started by Henry's dad, Brad, the diner was a Darlington staple with home-cooked food and killer recipes that had been in the Miller family for generations.

Not to say that Henry hadn't improved on the menu, because he most definitely had. He'd gone to culinary school and then had cooked under several famous chefs in New York City.

It was only after his dad had gotten sick that Henry came home.

He'd stayed when Brad passed on, cooking at the diner, tweaking a few much-loved menu items for the better, and watching out for his mom.

But for some reason, he'd never left.

Rumor had it that he'd left someone in New York, though no one had ever been able to get the information out of Henry himself.

Sam picked up a menu and glanced at it, though he knew it by heart. It also helped that he usually ordered the same thing. Hamburger—medium—sweet potato fries, and water, because he liked to pretend to be a little healthy before he finished off his meal with a giant slice of Henry's chocolate cream pie.

Seriously the best.

Maybe he could become one of those people who medicated his feelings with food. He'd seen a study recently that said chocolate cured depression. He could totally do with an extra slice of pie.

He would also *totally* gain a spare tire.

Because he had a feeling that his emotions wouldn't be tempered in the least with chocolate or alcohol or—

"Your usual?" Tilly asked, coming over. A petite blonde in her early twenties, she often wore a smile that was as bright as her hazel eyes. She was also sweet, kind, and efficient.

"Yes. Thanks."

Sam often came in late after working, too exhausted to go home and cook, not when the diner was only a few blocks from his clinic.

Plus, it was a place with people. A place he could sit and listen and . . . feel like he belonged for a half a second.

Sigh.

He was being so fucking dramatic.

But Haley hadn't called or texted. She hadn't shown up and—

She couldn't show up anywhere, dickweed, he thought angrily. *Her ankle is broken.*

"Why the long face, Dr. Johnson?"

Sam's eyes flashed up at the same moment a stone dropped in his gut.

Esther.

AKA trouble.

"Hi, Esther. How's the kitten?"

She waved a hand. "Don't try to distract me by talking about Snuggles." But she pulled out her phone and extended it in his direction. "Adorable, as you can see." He barely had time to nod before she continued, "Anyway, I was just over there and saw you were by yourself. I thought Haley—*ah . . .*"

He'd made a rookie mistake.

He'd reacted.

And Esther was maybe more of an intensive investigator than Rob and all of the sheriff's office combined. Nothing slipped past her, especially nothing so obvious as a wince.

"Oh, so there is trouble in paradise?" She pulled up the note function on her phone. "Tell me all the details, I'll make it better."

"I didn't—"

Tilly set his plate down, took one look at Esther and her phone and all but ran off.

Traitor.

Esther tapped his hand. "How'd you screw up, Sam?"

He raised one brow. "So, it's *Sam* now?"

She smiled beatifically. "My little Sam, always so smart and trusting"—he snorted—"you know I can fix things for you. I love the idea of you and Haley together."

"Tell that to Haley," he muttered, shoving a fry into his mouth. "Or Maggie."

Esther stole the pickle from his plate. She knew all that happened in Darlington and that included the fact that he couldn't stand the bastardized version of cucumbers.

Either that or she really didn't give a shit and just did what she wanted.

Really, it could go either way.

"Well," she said, chomping on the pickle. "You did break Maggie's heart—"

That was enough. He shoved his plate away and stormed down the hall, stopping just shy of the bathroom to turn and drop his forehead against the wall. Esther would probably eat all his fries, and his burger would get cold just sitting there. Not that it mattered. The food, normally so filling and delicious, had tasted like sawdust.

So much for medicating with food.

He couldn't even do *that* right.

But Esther thought *he'd* been the one to end things with Maggie, that he'd been the bad guy, when in reality—

A cough.

Sam turned enough to see Henry himself standing behind him.

"Since you're not trying to dine and dash"—Henry jerked his head in the direction of an open door—"why don't you come into my office and not give Esther anything else to talk about?"

Sam glanced down the hall, saw Esther, fries sticking out of her mouth like sewing pins used to stick out of his mom's when she'd been working on a new quilting project. Esther's phone was pointed in his direction, probably cataloging his pathetic display for the whole town to see.

How had he once thought her social media channels entertaining?

Fine. It *was* supremely entertaining when he wasn't the sole focus.

He turned and followed Henry into his office.

"Hang tight," Henry said, after indicating the chair in front of his desk. He disappeared out of the door before Sam could respond then reappeared before he could really worry, two plates in his hands. "Chocolate, right?"

Sam nodded and accepted the plate as well as a fork Henry pulled from his apron pocket.

"So, you and Haley?" Henry asked around a bite of what looked to be lemon cream.

Sam sighed. "I'd thought—" He shook his head. "It wasn't to be."

"Like it wasn't to be with you and Maggie?"

"Fuck off." Sam dropped the plate on the desk and stood.

Henry was nonplussed and took another bite of his pie. "I'm guessing you didn't do the dumping, like all of Darlington assumes."

Sam had been on the threshold of the door when Henry spoke again and at the words, he froze, chin dropping to his chest.

"That's a no," Henry said. "So, why'd she dump you?"

He whirled around, glaring at Henry. "None of your business."

"Great," Henry replied, shoving another bite home, his next words slightly garbled. "I hate gossip. Shut up, sit down, and eat your pie."

Sam rolled his eyes, but he shut up, sat down, and started eating, glad when the pie started finally tasting like its usual deliciousness rather than cardboard.

"Haley's loyal to Maggie," Henry said when their slices were almost gone.

Sam grunted.

"She'd be hard-pressed to do anything that might hurt her sister."

"Yeah," he snapped. "Well, what about what Maggie *and* Haley did to hurt me?"

Henry set his fork down. "Now you sound like a pathetic whiner. Just talk to Haley, explain what happened. I'm sure once she understands—"

"I'm not going to spread all of Maggie's and my gossip over town." Sam set his own fork down. "We were finished years ago, anyway. It doesn't matter now."

A *plunk* as Henry dropped his boots onto his desk. "Except it obviously does."

Sam sighed. Because Henry was right. It *did* matter and—

"Why am I talking about this with you?"

The other man was several years younger than him and while they knew each other and were on friendly terms because of the diner and Sam's veterinary skills, it wasn't like they were besties hanging out every weekend.

Besties?

Now he was really losing it.

"You're discussing this with me because I'm infinitely wise and smart about all things with regards to the opposite sex."

"Yeah?" Sam grumbled. "If that's true, then why are you single?"

A shadow crossed Henry's face. "Let's just say that I'm infinitely wise at letting problems and miscommunications fester so much that they ruin a relationship from the inside out." He picked up both plates. "Don't let that be your fate, Sam. Not when you have a chance to work things out."

He left the office, but not before calling over his shoulder, "Food's on the house tonight. Word of advice, though, sneak out the back door before Esther loses patience and starts trying to find material for her next post."

Sam beat it out the back door, trying to ignore Henry's words.

He wasn't a glutton for punishment. He was done being hurt.

Sam was absolutely finished with the Donovan sisters.

CHAPTER SEVENTEEN

Haley

HALEY KNEW the knock at the door wouldn't be Sam, but her heart raced like it was anyway.

It had been a week since he'd left that night.

She missed him more than she'd thought possible.

But he hadn't returned the messages she'd left at the clinic checking up on him, hadn't stopped by . . . and it was probably for the best.

They—her with a man like *him*—would never have worked out anyway.

Plus, her brain was probably overestimating Sam's appeal, because she'd been cooped up with no one for company besides the occasional visit from her mom, sister, and Melissa, but even those were few and far between because the women close to her had their own lives which did not revolve around catering to her every whim.

Or extreme boredom.

Okay, so there was that too.

The knock came again, and Haley called, "Coming!" as she wheeled her way to the front door.

The knob hadn't rattled, a sure sign of her mother on the other side trying to let herself in, so Haley hurried over, eager to see who was visiting.

She wasn't prepared to unlock the door and see her sister's tear-streaked face.

"Mags," she said. "What's—"

"Have you seen *this?*" her sister shrieked, shoving her phone into Haley's line of sight.

"Uh . . ." She tried to read the headline in . . . apparently there was a Facebook group for Darlington? It was called—rather unoriginally, she thought, Darlington Drama. "What—?" She snatched the phone from Maggie's grip, saw its administrator was Esther.

Of course, it was Esther.

Lord of the Banana Cream Pies, please give her strength.

Because the lead story was, Haley Bear Breaks Hearts Home and Abroad, the tale of her broken engagement and "Our Own Dr. Johnson's Freshly Broken Heart."

Thankfully, Esther didn't really have any details about her broken engagement with Brian, but she did have a picture of Sam looking . . . well, heartbroken.

Maggie stormed by her, opening the cabinet door beneath the sink and pulling out some cleaning supplies. In seconds she was scrubbing the crap out of Haley's kitchen counter.

Sighing, Haley shut and locked the door then turned back to her sister. "I'm sure it's—"

"Don't say it's not nothing!" Maggie wailed.

Haley rolled her eyes, called on the Lord of Banana Cream again—at least the terrible innuendo tempered her irritation—and wheeled herself to the kitchen. "Mags," she ordered, grabbing her sister's wrist and all but wrestling the squirt bottle out of her hand. "*Stop.*"

Maggie froze, chest heaving.

"What the *hell* is going on?"

Her sister hung her head. "You're going to hate me."

"I couldn't hate you." Haley bumped her shoulder. "Then I'd have to like mom and we both know I can't do that."

Maggie snorted, but tears leaked out of the corners of her eyes. "I was horrible," she said. "I deserve to be hated." A shaking exhale. "I deserve for Sam to hate *me.*"

Haley's heart skipped a beat. "What happened, Mags?"

Her sister sucked in another breath then released it. "It was my fault. All of it. I just—" She wiped her face. "I respected what you were doing. *So much.* I hope you know that. Moving to California, going after your dream, doing something you loved, and damn all the consequences." She blew out a breath. "I couldn't even leave Salt Lake. Sam wanted me to go, but I couldn't—"

"Why?"

She sniffed. "Because I'd found someone else."

"You—" Haley sat up. "*What?*"

"I was young and stupid and so mad that Sam wasn't around." She shook her head. "He was studying and working, for God's sake, and I—"

"You cheated on him."

Maggie nodded.

Haley sucked in a breath. *Shit.* She'd . . . well, she'd really, *seriously* fucked up. Sam was—

Damn. Her chin dropped to her chest.

She needed to apologize, needed to hobble her ass down the street on her crutches and beg for Sam's forgiveness. She'd put all the blame for the breakup on his shoulders and he'd been the one wronged. But . . . right at that moment, her sister needed Haley to listen more than Sam needed his apology.

"I didn't tell him," Maggie said softly. "I just got swept away with the whole thing, and I didn't tell Sam that things weren't working out. He was studying and picking up extra shifts so we could live together in Minnesota, and I was"—her voice cracked—"I was hiding my engagement ring so that I could fuck around with Bradley."

Haley couldn't lie that she was relieved to hear that Tim wasn't the man Maggie had cheated on Sam with.

That would have made Sunday dinners awkward.

"So, what happened?" she asked, guiding them back into the living room. She sank onto one half of the couch.

Maggie stayed standing but her eyes slid closed. "Affairs have a shelf life. Someone slips up or gets tired of—" She pressed her lips together. "Bradley found out I was engaged and told Sam."

Haley touched Maggie's cheek. "And you lost both of them."

A nod. "Yeah." A long slow exhale and she opened her eyes, regret swimming in the coffee depths. "Rightfully so, of course."

"That's why you were so devastated when you moved home," Haley said. "Why didn't you tell me?"

"It's the worst thing I've ever done in my life," she said. "I didn't want you to think I was a horrible person, even if I was." Maggie sighed. "It was easier in a lot of ways to just let Sam take the fall, especially since he was hundreds of miles away." She sat next to Haley on the couch. "But enough about me and my screwed-up ways, why didn't you tell me about Brian? I'm assuming the cheating isn't a new development."

"No," Haley murmured. "It wasn't. But it *is* a big part of the reason I needed to come home. The memories in California were just too painful." She shook her head. "No. That's not completely it either. Yes, it *was* painful, but I also didn't want to admit I failed, I guess. Your life seemed so perfect that I guess I needed to compete somehow." She tugged Maggie's wrist, pulling her in for a hug. "I'm sorry I assumed that you were always infallible, it wasn't exactly fair to shove you into a box like that."

Maggie sniffed. "I liked being infallible."

"You like things carefully arranged and black and white." Haley chuckled. "We all make mistakes, Mags. We all mess up sometimes."

"It wasn't just a mistake." Her sister's chest shuddered. "I—"

"Hush." Haley gripped Maggie by the shoulders and shook her gently. "It was a shitty thing to do, we both know that." A nod. "But I still am so sorry it happened. To both of you."

She *was* sorry. That Maggie had been so miserable, she'd done something incredibly hurtful to the person she'd loved. That she'd been young and stupid and immature.

That she hadn't felt like she could talk to Haley about it.

And also she began to wonder if perhaps Brian's reasons for cheating had been less about her and more about whatever had been going on in his own messed-up mind.

Maybe he'd been miserable and hadn't been able to—

Or maybe he was just an asshole.

Either. Both. Because while Sam might be mature enough to forgive Maggie, Haley thought that forgiving her ex and former friend were going to take a bit longer.

Work in progress, remember?

Her sister's laugh was brittle as she pulled back. "*I'm* sorry I was such an idiot that I let one of the best men I've ever known go. That I wounded him so deeply he's still alone. That he somehow managed to forgive me when I can't seem to forgive myself."

"Do you—" Haley cut herself off, uncertain she had the right to ask the question bouncing around her brain.

"No, ask," Maggie said. "We've spent far too much of our lives not asking the hard questions, leaving things alone because we didn't want to rock the boat." She dropped her head to Haley's shoulder. "I love you. So much. And, God, I'm so sorry I said those things. I didn't mean them . . . I just—"

"Wanted to be an ostrich for a little while longer?"

She shuddered. "You know how I feel about ostriches."

Haley did. Which was the reason she'd brought it up. Her sis had an unreasonable fear of the large, flightless bird. Probably because Haley had watched a ton of nature documentaries as a kid and both of them had nightmares about the one that had included a scene of an ostrich disemboweling a hyena that had been trying to steal its egg.

"You know what I really want to understand?" Haley asked.

Maggie flinched but raised her chin. "What do you want to know?"

"Why in the hell didn't our parents monitor our TV time?"

Maggie snorted and then they were laughing or crying, or maybe both. Either way, it was long minutes before they got it together.

"I'm so, so sorry, Hays. I don't know how you or Sam could possibly forgive me." She covered her face with her hands. "You guys should date, keep exploring things"—a sniff—"Great. Now I sound like I'm trying to play the martyr, but seriously, I think you'd be great for each other, and just because I let all of my regret from the past bubble up and—" Her shoulders dropped. "I hurt you and I hurt Sam. Again. I'm seriously the worst."

Haley lightly punched her arm. "Honestly, it's kind of refreshing to see that you're not perfect."

Maggie made an outraged noise.

"It's a breath of fresh air to see that you're a normal human being that makes mistakes. *Ow.*" Her sister swatted her back, but harder. "See? You even beat up innocent injured women."

"You're the worst," Maggie muttered.

"I love you." Haley rested her head on her sister's shoulder.

"I love you, too." A bump of Haley's head. "Now, ask your question from before."

"It's a doozy," Haley warned.

Maggie straightened, mimed putting on armor. "I'm ready."

A deep, bolstering breath. "I was going to ask if you wish that you hadn't cheated . . . that you were still with Sam."

Maggie stilled for a long moment, considering.

"No," she finally said. "It led me to Tim, and the life I have with him is more than I could have ever imagined." A pause. "But I do regret that I hurt Sam. It's like this huge cauldron of shame that never fully goes away. I did something horribly wrong, and it's probably a fitting punishment that I'm not sure I'll be able to get over it."

Equal parts of relief and empathy filled Haley.

Because . . . while this conversation had made her see that she obviously owed Sam a giant apology, she also knew she'd been using that trademark Donovan avoidance with him even before she'd hurt him.

Yes, she'd kissed him. Yes, she thought to hop on the ride for however long he would accept her. But at no point had she considered that Sam might well and truly like her, that he might see her as a desirable woman he wanted to date. She'd just assumed—

No. She'd *distanced* herself because that kept her heart safe.

She deserved better. They *both* deserved better.

He should be in a relationship with someone who thought he deserved all the happiness the world, who was willing to be open and to put themselves out there. Who was firmly *in* with both of her feet.

Broken ankle aside, she hadn't been in.

But revelations aside, Maggie was still waiting for a response, and Haley knew they'd shared about as much emotion as they could stand. So, she lightened her tone and said, "Shit, Sis, you need help."

A snort followed by a side hug. "Now, that's probably the most truthful thing you've said all day."

"Great." Haley picked up the TV remote. "I'm brilliant and truthful *and* funny—"

"I didn't say *that*," Maggie teased.

"Ignoring you," Haley sang. "I'm brilliant because I'm ordering us a pizza and you're going to call Tim and say you need some sister time so we can binge our night away on nature documentaries."

Maggie smiled. "Make it the new season of *Queer Eye* and I'm in."

Haley pretended to consider that and Mags smacked her. "Abuse," she said. "Jeez! Okay, fine, grab the ice cream from the freezer so we can have dessert first, and you're on."

———

"GO," Haley mouthed, waving her sister off the following evening, after having staked out Sam's house with binoculars.

Yes, binoculars.

But it turned out she could see Sam's driveway from her living room window by watching from just the right angle and using . . . binoculars.

Stalker one-oh-one, sign her up.

But Haley's use of the magnifying device aside, she'd been able to see Sam drive up and settle in for the evening. She'd called Maggie and begged her for a ride several driveways down, since she didn't trust herself to make it that far on crutches and her scooter would only be bogged down in the gravel.

After another of Haley's shooing gestures, Maggie finally lifted her hand in resignation and reversed out of the driveway.

Like her own, this one was gravel.

So, the car and even her crutches made a lot of noise.

And the fact that the door remained shut did not speak well of her plan.

She might be crutching the distance between Sam's house and her own anyway.

Up the couple of steps to Sam's porch, a moment of balancing before she was able to ring the doorbell.

No response.

Haley bit her lip. Rang again.

Still nothing.

"Shit," she muttered, trying to convince herself he just hadn't heard, that maybe his bell was broken. So, she carefully shifted her weight and knocked on the door.

No answer.

Okay, so clearly this had been a stupid idea.

She turned, started to make her way down the steps. Sam wouldn't talk to her, wouldn't forgive her. And why should he? She'd made assumptions without letting him explain his side. She'd thrown away the new, fragile thing they'd just started building.

This was her own doing.

"Dammit." She took one hand off a crutch to wipe her face–sweat, not tears . . . which was a lie, but she only had so much dignity left, okay?

The door swung open and she whirled around then immediately lost her balance.

"*Ah!*"

Sam caught her.

Before she came close to colliding with the steps or the gravel or even the rough planks of the porch, he caught her.

Dammit, *why* had he caught her?

She deserved—

He cradled her against his chest, eyes studying her closely, but just when his expression seemed to soften, Sam's face turned to granite.

His hands were gentle though.

He deposited her carefully onto the steps, propped her crutches so they were next to her.

"Stay," he growled.

And it was then she noticed that he was only wearing a towel and his hair was wet.

So he hadn't been avoiding her.

He'd been in the shower.

Genius observation. But it wasn't entirely her fault that her brain was malfunctioning, not when there was so much tan skin and so many hard muscles on display. His chest glistened and that towel was . . . so *precarious.* Her fingers itched to knock it askew, to encourage it to drop to the porch, but one look at his face stalled the notion.

"Stay," he repeated and waited for her to nod. But when she opened her mouth to apologize, he turned and swept into the house, shutting the door firmly behind him.

She was getting *really* tired of doors being slammed in her face.

Haley had just stood up, ready to barge into the house and demand he hear her apology, when the door whipped open again. Sadly for her, he'd gotten dressed.

He took one look at Haley on her feet and sighed before sweeping by her and unlocking the doors of his SUV with a *beep.* A tug of the handle to open the passenger's side before he was heading back in her direction.

"Sam—"

He lifted her up into his arms again, swiftly deposited her into the passenger's seat. "Buckle in."

"I'm—"

A sigh as he reached over to secure her seat belt.

"Sor—"

The door slammed.

Again.

For the love of—

He yanked open the driver's door and dropped himself into the seat. "Sam—" He turned the key. "I'm really—" Blared the music. "Sorry—" Revved the engine as he reversed.

Haley sighed and switched off the radio.

He switched it back on.

Good gravy, how childish was he going to be?

She pressed the dial, turned it back off.

Less than her, apparently, because he left the music off.

"I'm sorry," she said into the silence.

Sam's only response was to maneuver into her driveway, turn off the engine, and then shove his way out of his side of the car. He came around and swung her up into his arms.

She cupped his cheek. "Maggie told me."

He shuddered and deposited her on her porch steps before returning back for her purse and crutches.

"I shouldn't have—"

He dug into her purse, extracted her keys to unlock her front door. "I can't do this."

"What?"

He scooped her up again, carrying her inside as she stared at him dumbly. *That was it?* He was just going to give up at the first sign of trouble? Except wasn't that what she'd done.

But she was trying to *undo* it. Trying to give them a chance at something that might mean everything.

"We need to talk—"

Sam deposited her on the couch, wheeled her scooter over to her, and plunked her purse on the table, setting her keys next to it. Her crutches went by the door, which he started to close behind himself.

"*Sam.*"

His only response was a shake of his head.

This time when the door shut, it didn't slam.

But it hurt all the same.

"No," she said. She wasn't going to let him do this, let him throw their chance at something good and meaningful all away because she'd been an idiot. Haley grabbed her purse from the table, rummaging around inside until she found her cell. It only took her a few seconds to dial a number she knew by heart.

"I need help," she said when the call was picked up.

CHAPTER EIGHTEEN

Sam

SATURDAY MORNING BROUGHT with it more clouds, rain, and biting wind. Sam had planned on being in the clinic all day, and so he hadn't bothered with more than a cursory check of the weather.

But best-laid plans and all that.

He'd gotten the call just after five in the morning from Hank, a local cattle rancher. Hank had been out on his normal A.M. rounds and had discovered a calf stuck in the mud and near-death. Pouring rain had made the conditions even worse.

By the time Sam had made it to the ranch, Hank had pulled the calf free, wrapped it in a blanket, and met him at the barn. They'd gone inside, trying to keep the calf warm as he'd worked on the young animal.

Ultimately, it hadn't mattered because Sam had been forced to euthanize the calf.

Hank had cried, Sam had felt like shit, and Saturday had continued on in Friday's fucked up track. He'd rushed back to his house for a shower in rain-soaked clothes for the second time in a week, wind and water seeping through the damaged driver's side door, and had been ten minutes late for his first appointment.

Saturdays were busy and on that particular day they were absolutely slammed, so it was just perfect that Michelle had needed to leave midway through the morning.

Not her fault, he knew, that she'd spiked a fever. Anyone looking at her could tell she was feeling miserable, and he couldn't exactly have one of his employees being patient zero of the town's latest flu epidemic.

So, he'd put his head down and slogged through the long list of appointments.

He'd barely even had time to miss Haley.

Haley.

Aw shit.

He didn't want to think about Haley or Maggie or the fact that he'd been burned twice in his life by the Donovan sisters. He needed to finish his final two appointments of the day and then go home and crack open a beer.

Or ten.

Jane knocked on the back door and popped her head into the hallway that spanned the space behind the patient rooms. "We've had a call from Melissa Cooper. Rocco's gotten into something and cut his paw. She thinks he might need stitches. Should I refer her over to the emergency clinic?"

Sam sighed. "No, tell her to bring him in."

He wasn't going to send his friend on a three-hour drive for something he could handle in half that.

Jane nodded and closed the door. He picked up the chart for his next patient—a ten-year-old and very temperamental Maltipoo named Precious—and girded his loins. Two—no, three—more patients, and then he'd been done with this horrible day.

Thankfully, Precious took pity on him that day, and the exam, shots, and nail trim went relatively easily, and the bearded dragon he saw for his last official appointment of the day was a fun and interesting case.

Turned out the little guy wasn't a fan of calcium worms and needed crickets added to his diet.

A quick trip to the coffee pot for a shot of caffeine before he gathered suture supplies and pushed through the door of exam room three. Immediately, he realized Jane had duped him and vowed to pay her back with multiple boxes of filing at his earliest opportunity, because seriously, the last thing he wanted to be dealing with at the end of his long and shitty day was this.

Haley.

With regret in her gaze and an apology on her lips.

He whirled and pushed back out the door, walking down the hall and shoving the supplies back into their proper spots as he went. He needed to get the fuck out of here, get his head on straight so that—

"Sam." Haley followed him, the wheels of her scooter squeaking against the industrial tiles. "I need to apol—"

"No apology needed," he said, dropping the last of the supplies into a drawer.

He kept walking, moving to his computer at the end of the counter and closing out what he absolutely had to. The rest of it could wait until Monday.

A touch on his arm. "Sam."

He moved away. "It's fine. I get it—"

"So, Maggie cheated," she said, all conversational-like.

Fuck. She'd said her sister had told her. But he'd hoped . . .

What?

That she'd never discovered how pathetic he was?

Shit.

"And you know it's not your fault, right?"

He shrugged, turning to meet Haley's eyes. And there was pity in her gaze. Awesome, so Maggie had definitely confessed all. He'd basically pressed her to, but Haley looking at him like that, like he was some poor wounded creature . . . well, it really didn't feel great.

Fine. Because frankly, it felt like shit and the perfect addendum to his day.

"Sam?"

He grunted, shrugged off his lab coat and hung it on the proper hook.

More squeaking wheels, but even if Haley hadn't had the equivalent of a cat's bell on its collar in her scooter, he still would have known when she moved closer. Her scent—roses—drifted forward, inundating his senses, and his nape prickled, instinctively knowing that she was only inches away.

This time he couldn't force himself away from her touch, not when she wrapped her arms around him and pressed her breasts against his spine.

Fuck. He wanted her so badly.

"I'm just saying that I know it takes time to accept it as truth, but what Maggie did was on her. Not you. Not in any way. As for us"—she sucked in a breath—"I was scared. I seized an opportunity to run because I'm fucked up and I was feeling unworthy and unlovable, and I like you. A lot." She squeezed him tighter. "I'm still recovering in the confidence department because I couldn't imagine how you might possibly be able to like *me.*"

He dropped his chin to his chest.

Haley didn't say anything further, just held him, and the anger he'd been stoking for close to a week disappeared.

"Dammit, sweetheart," he finally muttered and carefully disentangled himself so he could turn around and see her. "I like you. A whole hell of a lot, but I can't keep doing this." Her face fell, and he cupped her cheek. "I can't keep reassuring you that I like you, that I want to get to know you better. I want to take you out, see if the chemistry we have can develop into something more, but . . ."

"But what?"

"I need you to be all in, too," he said. "I need you not to have one foot out the door, expecting me to leave, to all of a sudden turn on you like that asshole did."

Her lips parted and she sucked in a breath. "I—"

"You deserve better for yourself, sweetheart. You're fun and kind and incredibly smart, not to mention beautiful"—she shook her head and he shook his in response—"That, right there. You don't see yourself clearly."

"I'm not—"

He rested his hand just above her heart. "You are the most beautiful woman I've ever seen. Not just the outside"—he tapped lightly—"but here, too. You're generous and sweet and—"

Her lips twitched. "Now I feel like I'm fishing for compliments."

Sam cupped her cheek. "No need for fishing. You deserve all those."

"And more?"

He chuckled and pressed a kiss to her forehead. "See? Funny *and* sweet. You deserve everything you want, baby."

"And what if what I want is you?"

"Then I'm yours."

CHAPTER NINETEEN

Haley

SAM DROVE Haley home in silence, but it wasn't like the taut quiet from her days with Brian. This was comfortable, neither of them needing to fill the air with words, their hands laced and resting on his thigh.

It was the biggest leap she'd ever taken, moving to California aside, and certainly the biggest gamble she'd taken with the opposite sex.

Haley had put herself out there, and Sam . . . well, he'd accepted her.

But he'd demanded that she be all in, too.

Could she possibly—?

Fuck yes, she could. For Sam, for a chance at something that meant more than any of her past relationships, she could not be scared for once. She could dive in and learn every little idiosyncrasy that made Sam . . . Sam. And she could damn well let him in enough to understand all the strange pieces that made her Haley Donovan.

It was funny, because even yesterday she would have said she'd given Brian *everything*, but the past week had taught her that was a lie.

She was really good at distance and it had existed even when she'd been at her most vulnerable with Brian.

She'd always held part of herself back. Always.

And he'd known.

Yes, he was an asshole, a terrible person who'd preyed on all her insecurities, who'd wounded her deeply by betraying her, but, truthfully, Haley had never been all in with the relationship.

Hence, her being less upset about losing him and more upset over the fact that she couldn't keep a man but Maggie could—

God. She was seriously screwed up.

"What just went through your mind?" Sam asked.

And so, Test One of their dating relationship was upon them. Did she prevaricate, avoid the issue? Or did she—

Haley told the truth.

Sam listened patiently as she worked it out—basically verbally vomiting all the thoughts swirling around her brain. When she was done, he squeezed her hand and lifted it to his mouth, pressing a soft kiss to the back of it.

"Thank you," he said. "I think that was the part that hurt me the most with Maggie. I shouldered all of this responsibility, thought it was my fault that she'd jumped into bed with someone else when ultimately, it wasn't really about me at all."

"Right." She leaned her head on his shoulder. "She was the one who was missing something. Same as Brian. And no matter how hard we tried, that *something* they were missing wasn't going to be able to come from me. Or you."

Sam nodded, kissed the top of her head. "Insightful."

She turned so her lips could smack against his shoulder. "Way too patient."

The half of his mouth that she could see curved up.

Haley felt her own lips curl into a smile. Her heart was buoyant, anticipation and hope in her blood. This—Sam—was the start of something really, *really* good.

She just knew it.

―――

"COME ON, HOP-A-LONG," Sam teased her as she crutched her way to his SUV the next evening.

He'd driven her home the previous night, depositing her onto her porch with a, "Go to dinner with me tomorrow?"

As if she could say no to that.

But she had demanded one thing before she'd agreed.

"Only if you give me your number."

He'd tilted his head, tapped a finger to his chin. "Hmm. I'm not sure—"

"Sam!"

He'd tugged her into his arms and stolen a laughing kiss, and pretty soon she was laughing, too, especially when they broke apart and he held up a hand with a magician-like flourish, her cell resting in his palm.

A few taps later, and he'd input his number.

"M'lady," he quipped, presenting it to her with another flourish, albeit a knightly one this time.

She'd taken it, carefully stashed it into her pocket. "You're a dork."

He'd bowed, pressed another smiling kiss to her mouth. "I'll double check my appointments tomorrow, but seven maybe?"

She'd nodded, and he'd clumped down the steps, yanked open his SUV's dented driver's side door but not getting in until she'd pushed through her own door and had shut it. Only then did he buckle up and drive away.

Haley knew. She'd watched.

It had been pretty much her best front door goodbye ever . . . okay, it was her best good night, no qualifier, just her and Sam being dorks, giggling and smiling and—

A hand cupped her cheek. "Are you feeling okay?" Sam asked. "We don't have to go anywhere, I can cook—"

This man.

She placed her hand over his, and because she was on crutches and he was so much taller than her and she only had one good foot to stand on tiptoe, she said, "Get down here and kiss me."

Sam didn't hesitate, just bent and slanted his mouth across hers. And as things seemed to happen with this particular man, their kiss quickly escalated from sweet and soft to scorching and intense. Her crutches fell to the ground, but Sam had her, hitching his arm around her waist and lifting her so she was sitting on the hood of the SUV and he was standing between her spread thighs.

Now *that* was something she could get behind.

"You're so fucking beautiful," he said.

"I—"

He kissed her again, slipping his tongue into her mouth to tangle with hers, angling her head so their mouths fit together just right. It was . . . fucking incredible.

So much so that when they finally pulled back gasping for air—or rather when she ripped her lips away, puffing like a locomotive while Sam trailed his mouth along the line of her jaw to nip at her earlobe then kissed the spot just beneath it that never failed to make her shiver—she said, "Maybe we should forget dinner and—"

A wicked smile curved Sam's lips and he kissed her again, scooped her into his arms.

Thank God, because if the man didn't get inside her in the next five seconds, she was—

Going to find herself in the passenger seat of Sam's SUV.

"Uh—"

Another press of his lips. A *click* as he snapped her seat belt in place. Then his lips were on hers again, moving in a rhythm that had her arching up against him, desperate now to have him close.

This time he pulled back with a curse. "You're dangerous to my health, woman." A glare, but a teasing one that quickly became laced with tenderness, his hazel eyes warming. "I like you, sweetheart. A lot. And I think you kinda, sorta like me"—she snorted—"so, let's do this right."

CHAPTER TWENTY

Sam

SAM HELD the door open to the diner as Haley wheeled herself through. He'd stashed her scooter in the back of his car because he knew just crutching down her gravel driveway was already tough enough. She might as well use the scooter whenever the opportunity presented itself.

The diner was busy, a half-dozen groups waiting in the lobby for tables. But such was Saturday night in Darlington. Henry's Place was the place to go for the best food in town and also hub central for town gossip.

So, him bringing Haley to the diner was sending a message to every person in Darlington.

She was important to him. They were serious.

Yes, it was too early for that particular train of thought, but he was having it anyway.

He wanted Haley and not just to see how things went or to investigate the possibility of what might be. She was . . . home. Or at least, Sam never felt more himself than when he was with her.

Hence, dinner at Henry's Place.

Sam waved at the hostess, Kara, who in turn lifted both hands to indicate they'd be waiting about ten minutes. He shot her a thumbs up then turned back to Haley.

"Stitches still coming out tomorrow?" He gently untangled a strand of her ponytail that had tucked itself under the bandage on her forehead.

She smiled up at him. "You tired of the Frankenstein look?"

A gentle kiss to the corner of the bandage. "You make stitches hot."

"Bitches got stitches?" She snorted. "Is that the new fashion trend?"

"I must have missed that in my latest issue of *Cosmopolitan*."

Haley wheeled herself a little closer, her breasts brushing against his chest. Sam bent, eyes on her mouth, suddenly wishing they were back in her driveway and he hadn't insisted on this date.

Why had he insisted on this date?

She licked her lips.

He leaned down and—

Click.

Sam blinked, glanced away from the dangerous distraction that was Haley, and saw that Esther had her phone pointed in their direction.

"Dammit," she muttered. "I could have sworn I'd turned that camera sound off." Her eyes shot to his, and she held up a very expensive, top of the line cell. "New phone," she said, flashing him a smile that was less chagrined and more satisfied.

"Esther!" Haley said, glancing between the older woman and Sam. "You were *not* taking pictures of us."

"Haley, girl," Esther said. "I'm glad to see you and Sam worked things out. How are you feeling?"

Haley crossed her arms. "Nice try, missy. That had better not be going on your Facebook page," Haley said.

"Of course not." Sam's shoulders relaxed. "It's going on my Instagram. Facebook is for old people." His eyes met Haley's, the obvious comment on the tip of his tongue. Esther *was* old, almost ancient.

She shook her head, lifted her lips to his ear. "She may be a million years old, but she's also way cooler than us."

"I heard that!" Esther said. "I—"

"Can't hear me saying that in your hurry to document these two, you forgot your to-go box?" Henry walked into the waiting area and handed Esther a container. "No?" he said, mouth twitching when she didn't respond. "Hmm. Funny how that works."

Esther narrowed her eyes. "Just because you make a good sandwich doesn't mean that you can be smart with me, young man."

"I love you, too, Esther," Henry said, kissing her cheek and pointing to an unoccupied table for two in the corner of the diner. "Kelly's booth"— Kel and Henry had been best friends since grade school and one of the perks of that was a permanent table with her name on it in the restaurant —"is open, jump on in there."

Sam thanked him and indicated for Haley to go ahead of him, but before they could move too far they heard Esther ask, "Are *you* dating anyone right now, Henry?"

Henry choked.

Haley snorted.

Sam grinned.

Because they all knew what was coming next.

"I know just the perfect girl . . ."

"Run," Haley whispered out of the corner of her mouth. "Before Esther turns her evil genius attention back to us."

Sam mimed a heroic push of Haley's scooter. "Save yourself!" he hissed and followed her as she giggled her way to the table.

"Henry's going to kill us," she said once they'd sat down.

Sam glanced over his shoulder, saw that Henry was still cornered by Esther, who was now showing him something on her phone. Probably pictures of that perfect girl she had for him.

"Meh," he said, shrugging. "It's about time he had a turn. Henry needs a girl."

"Or a guy," Haley added.

"Or a guy," Sam agreed. "And we both know that Esther will find him that right person."

"Agreed." She unfolded her napkin, plunked it into her lap. "If I didn't know better, I'd think she'd coerced those deer into jumping in front of our cars." A pause. "Oh! I've been meaning to ask you, what about *your* car? When are you going to get that door fixed?"

The waitress, Tilly, came over with glasses of water, setting them on the table in front of them. "I'll be back in just a second to get your orders," she said and hurried off to another booth.

He winced when Haley looked at him expectantly.

She wouldn't like what he was about to tell her, and she'd definitely feel guilty about it.

"I'm actually thinking about dealing with it. I'm due for a new car anyway."

"What?" she asked. "Your SUV is practically brand new."

It was. He'd splurged for a new one, complete with heated seats and remote start because those early mornings driving out to the ranches were cold as fuck and because he worked hard for his money, dammit, so he could have one nice, frivolous thing.

A shrug.

"Sam—"

Tilly popped back over, and they spent the next few minutes ordering food. Once she'd gone again, Haley fixed him with a look. "Spill."

"Don't feel bad," he began, "because I believe we've already established that I was the one at fault—"

"Oh Lord. Do *not* tell me that my inept blasting of Backstreet Boys totaled your car."

"Okay," he said. "I won't tell you that." He took a sip of water.

"Sam!"

"It was the deer's fault, remember?"

Haley wrinkled her nose. "Oh my God. I—shit. I'm *so* sorry—"

She was so fucking gorgeous and sweet and . . . he really wanted to kiss her.

So, he did.

He leaned right across the table and cut off her stammering with his lips. It was only supposed to be a moment of brief contact, a brush of two mouths, but then Haley wrapped a hand around his nape and pulled him back down.

The diner faded, the other patrons, the table's edge that was digging into his stomach disappeared.

It was just him and Haley and—

A *whoop* made them both jump.

Cheeks flushing, she retreated, groaning and putting her hands over her face. "I didn't mean to—"

"Get it, girl!"

Esther.

They both looked at each other and shook their heads.

But they were smiling.

And before they'd eaten their meal, all of Darlington knew that Sam Johnson and Haley Donovan were back to being an item.

Small town life at its finest.

CHAPTER TWENTY-ONE

Haley

"SO, do you think that purple or pink goes best with my cast?" Haley asked Melissa.

"You can't wear a T-shirt on a date," Melissa said.

"Why not?"

Slender arms crossed. "Do you or do you not want to sleep with this man as soon as possible?"

"Uh, that's a definite yes."

"Good," Melissa said. "Then no T-shirts." She began to rifle through Haley's closet.

"Sam *likes* my T-shirts," Haley argued.

"Yes. I'm sure he likes whatever you wear. The man is absolutely crazy about you." Melissa pulled out a dress, considered it, then tucked it back away. "The point is that you've got a stubborn man who's trying to be honorable, and he thinks that means giving you more time to get used to the idea of you two dating."

"I don't want more time," Haley muttered.

Melissa pointed her finger toward the ceiling. "Exactly."

Haley wasn't exactly sure what that *exactly* meant, but her friend had thrown her a bone in the best possible way by bringing her both food and a break from the boredom that was surrounding her.

Three weeks since the accident.

One more before the hospital would allow her back for desk duty.

Three more till the fucking cast came off.

Ugh.

Okay, so maybe that ugh was less from missing work and more from missing Sam.

She'd only seen him three times in the last week. Once during their date the previous Sunday—after which he'd dropped her on her porch with a scorching kiss that had fueled more than satisfied—then briefly on Monday when they'd devoured the pizza he'd brought them for dinner before he'd been called to an emergency at the clinic. Tuesday, Wednesday, and Thursday, he'd been a few towns over, assisting a neighboring vet with vaccinations and deworming for cattle on a slew of ranches. Friday and Saturday, the other vet had returned the favor for the Darlington ranches.

He'd come by the previous evening, but after a single glance, Haley had sent him home.

Exhaustion had pulled at the contours of his face, his skin was pale and waxy, and the dark circles under his eyes were no joke.

So, home to sleep.

And she'd spent another evening on the couch entertaining herself.

Which sounded dirty, but unfortunately for her wasn't. On a side note, and why she'd begged for Melissa's expertise that evening, was that Haley was definitely ready for dirty.

Desperate for it really.

Sam had texted earlier, asking her to dinner again—not that she'd ever tell the man no. She loved spending time with him and also she had a plan.

And that plan did *not* involve Henry's Place on a busy Sunday night.

That plan involved getting *busy* on a Sunday night.

Wow.

She shook her head at herself.

Clearly, she'd been alone too much because those puns were *bad*.

"What are you grinning about? Wait, I don't think I want to know. What about this?" Melissa held up a black dress from the back of Haley's closet.

Haley could have kissed her. "*That's* perfect! Miss, you're awesome."

"Yeah, *that* I know," Melissa said and searched through the huge duffle bag she'd brought with her. In no time at all, she had Haley stylized to perfection. "Your feet are bigger than mine. But these"—she pulled out a pair of clunky heels from the closet—"will work perfectly. Or the left one will anyway," she teased.

"Hilarious," Haley said, but she hugged Melissa anyway. "Thank you."

"Aw, young love," Melissa crooned.

"Ha. As if you and Rob have room to talk," she accused. "The two of you are so lovely-dovey it's almost puke-worthy."

Melissa sat down on the edge of the bed. "That took a lot of work, Haley Bear."

She lifted her brows. "Really?"

"It's a cute nickname."

"It's—" Haley shrugged. "Okay, it could be worse. But . . . things really are okay with you and Rob, right?"

Melissa flopped back onto Haley's bed, careful to not jostle the outfit she'd painstakingly put together. "I can honestly say that the last year has been the most difficult of our marriage. I felt betrayed by Rob—and not just because of the rumors, but also because he didn't trust me enough to tell me what was going on in his head." She sighed. "But I also took on and then internalized *so* much. I was resentful, lonely, sad, and it wasn't all from our marriage, my childhood played a big role as well. Of course, I didn't think I needed to tell him that I was struggling. I thought he should just *know*." She huffed out a laugh. "Which is why we clearly needed therapy."

"But it helped," Haley said, lying down next to her.

"*Ohh* yeah. If only to just get us back on track. My tendencies are to pull inward and distance everyone around me—" She broke off. "Look at me going on and on. We're fine. Yes, we're a work in progress, but I can honestly say I'm happier now with Rob than I ever have been."

Haley leaned her head on Melissa's shoulder. "I'm so happy for you guys." She hesitated then decided that since Melissa had shared so much, she could bare her heart a little bit, too. "Also, I hear you. About the distancing stuff, I mean. Sometimes it's safer to be in my own head and heart and to not let anyone else in."

Miss rolled over and leaned up on one elbow. "But Sam is different."

"*So* different. God, I was so painfully awkward with him when I was younger, but now it's like so . . . so *easy* almost. He gets me, and for the first time ever, I'm seriously ready to jump and he wants to take it slow." Haley groaned. "And I know that's the responsible adult thing to do, but . . ."

"You don't care."

"I don't care." Haley *thunked* her head back. "Also, I'm horny."

Melissa tugged at a strand of Haley's hair. "Having dated a particularly stubborn and protective man myself, I can say that you've got the right plan in mind. Corner him, blow his socks off with those sexy legs. Oh, and skip the underwear, bend over, and flash a little—"

"Miss!"

Melissa cackled. "But I'm only half-kidding. The man wants you, half the town witnessed just how much in that kiss last week. He just needs a push."

"In the form of no underwear under my dress."

A shrug. "What can I say? It works." She grinned. "Just promise me you won't heat up the dinner I brought for you guys until *after* he's seen the peep show."

Haley smacked her shoulder. "You're terrible."

"Maybe," Miss teased. "But I'm also getting lots of orgasms, so I think you want a piece of this pie." At her words, they both froze. Melissa grimaced. "Okay, so not the best word choice. I'm going to stop talking." She pushed off the bed, extended a hand to help Haley up, then pretended to knight her with one of the heels she'd pulled from the closet. "Go forth and jump Sam's bones."

CHAPTER TWENTY-TWO

Sam

SAM DIDN'T THINK he'd ever slept that late . . . or definitely not since his teenage years. He'd shuffled through his front door the previous evening at a quarter past nine, dropped his jacket by the front door, stepped out of his boots, then stumbled into bed and hadn't moved until almost noon.

The benefit of approximately fourteen hours of sleep was that he had more energy than usual.

And he wanted to use that energy in a very specific way.

But he'd promised himself and Haley that they would take it slow, and in his mind that meant he was going to wait until her cast was off before they explored the physical stuff.

Physical stuff?

Fuck, he needed to get it together.

He wanted Haley. Badly. But she'd been through a lot with Brian, and that meant he needed to tread carefully. She needed to understand that—

He had fucking blue balls?

Yeah. That was a certainty.

But not the whole story because Haley had to know that she was beautiful and worthwhile and he wanted her so much that he'd been tempted to stroke himself to orgasm in the shower that afternoon.

Okay, no. She didn't need to know *that* part.

Just that—

Why was he waiting the full six weeks again?

"Respect, douche canoe," he muttered to himself in the mirror as he fixed his hair and slapped on some deodorant. "Haley deserves some fucking respect, not a meaningless one-night stand."

Except, it wouldn't be for one night, would it?

Because Haley was—

Fuck. He had the feeling that Haley was *everything*.

Hence, him not wanting to screw it all up. Sighing, Sam left the bathroom and headed to the kitchen for the flowers and the banana cream pie he'd begged Melissa to make.

He set the pie and flowers on the passenger's seat then rounded his SUV and forced his way into the driver's seat. His insurance had finally gotten back to him, and though he'd take a hit on the length of the loan, his new SUV would be delivered on Wednesday.

At least he wouldn't be in a wrestling match with his door multiple times a day.

Okay. Focus.

He'd pick Haley up and take her out to the diner or maybe for pizza, because it would have to be away from Haley's house and the temptation of stripping her naked and continuing where they'd left off in her kitchen the other day. But maybe afterward, he could trust himself enough to go inside for a drink and a slice of pie and not get her naked.

Not likely.

So, maybe the plan needed to be to get *her* naked but to keep himself clothed.

Yeah, *that* he thought he could do.

"Go team," he muttered, knowing he was way overthinking this, but not able to stop.

Not when Haley meant so much.

He kept his eyes peeled for deer as he navigated the short distance from his house to hers. Rob had been true to his word and the brush had been cut back, so Sam hadn't seen any kamikaze Bambis lately, but he wasn't exactly at the trust stage yet.

A few minutes later, he'd parked in Haley's driveway and was bounding up the stairs as she opened the door. He saw a glimpse of one bare knee resting on the scooter and . . .

He couldn't process the rest.

Because Haley was wearing a tight, short dress that highlighted every single curve.

"Hi," she said, her eyes warm, her smile satisfied, her breasts all but spilling out of the low V. "Is that Melissa's banana cream pie?"

A completely nonsexual question, but she bent over as she strained to see the container in his hand. Her breasts, fuck, but her breasts. She flicked her gaze back up to his. "Oh, Sam," she moaned. "I can't wait—"

And that was it for him.

He barely had the presence of mind to set the flowers and pie on the little bench that sat just inside her front door before he was reaching for her and sweeping her up into his arms.

Sam kicked the scooter aside then slammed—and locked this time—the door.

A heartbeat later his mouth was on hers.

He turned, pinning her back against the wood panel as he kissed her with every bit of pent-up lust from the last weeks. Her breasts were soft against his chest, her thighs around his hips the best feeling in the fucking world. He slipped his tongue into her mouth, stroking it along hers until she finally pushed at his shoulders.

"Air," she gasped.

He kissed her again, long and deep and slow before nipping at the corner of her lips and then trailing his mouth down her neck and between her breasts.

Her fingernails bit into his shoulders as he nibbled and licked all of the exposed skin. "Sam," she groaned, encouraging him down while arching her breasts up. Her cast hit him in the back of the knee, and he sucked in a breath, shoring up his patience.

Fuck six weeks.

Tonight, he was going to make Haley come until she couldn't see straight.

"Please," she said, thighs clenching around his waist. "Please, don't stop."

"Shit," he gritted out, knowing that he wouldn't be able to reach everywhere he wanted to, knowing that she needed slow and steady and —she undulated against him, making stars flash behind his eyes, nearly destroying the hairsbreadth of patience he'd managed to steal—Haley needed a bed so her leg—

"Sam." Her mouth found his, and this time she took the lead, driving his desire to a fever pitch. His blood roiled beneath his skin, his cock was hard and aching and—

Forget the bed.

Couch. That worked.

He strode over, setting her down so her leg with the cast was stretched out along the cushions and the other was on the floor. The sight of her legs slightly spread, of her uninjured foot in a strappy black sandal—

"Fuck, you're beautiful," he said, his voice sounding like he'd swallowed sandpaper, and he dove between her thighs, hitching her dress up and finding . . . *holy, fucking shit.* "Why aren't you wearing any underwear?"

Her teeth found her bottom lip, but there was heat in her gaze. "Because I knew I didn't need it."

His mind hazed over.

He couldn't think up a pithy one-liner, couldn't summon sweet words. Instead, he could only focus on how desperately he needed her to come on his tongue. So, he spread her thighs farther, bent, and pressed his mouth to her pussy. His cock twitched at the first taste of her, sweeter than the banana pie he'd brought, but then her hands were in his hair, tugging him closer, and Sam focused solely on Haley, on what made her groan and rub more firmly against him, on what made her breath catch, on what had her crying out.

He flicked his tongue against her clit and was rewarded by a moan. A finger inside and curling upward had her hips undulating, but she really liked it when he spread her wide and just licked her.

"Sam—mmm." Her head fell back to the cushions, her hips jerked forward. "*Fuck*. Mmm. I—"

He slipped his fingers under her ass and yanked her closer, flicking his tongue, licking her faster and faster until her hands tightened almost painfully in his hair.

And then he nipped.

Haley screamed as she came.

Fuck, but was that the best noise ever.

Her dress was shoved up around her hips, her pussy bare and glistening, her eyes were closed, a blush dusting the tops of her cheeks. She was the most beautiful woman he'd ever seen.

Ever. Hands down.

His heart pulsed.

Because he loved her.

Of course, he loved her.

What wasn't there to love?

For all the attraction, for all the lust raging inside him, Sam wanted Haley because she was as beautiful inside as she was on the outside.

Her eyes flicked open.

"Hi, sweetheart," he murmured.

"Hi, yourself," she said lazily, dropping her hands, which had still been in his hair, to his shoulders. "Come here."

He leaned up and kissed her.

"Nice surprise?" she asked when they broke apart.

"Nice surprise," he agreed and slid his hand up her bare thigh. "Very nice surprise."

"Good. *Sam*—" She sat up when his fingers teased the wet heat of her, nearly knocking her head against his.

"Shh," he said, shifting so he could gather her into his arms. "Now that I know what you like"—he stood—"I need to perfect my technique."

Haley groaned. "Good God that was terrible."

Sam suckled her bottom lip. "So, that's a no?"

"Fuck no, it's not a no," she said. "Your mouth on my pussy was perfect. It's your pickup lines that need work."

This woman. He had a boner that was aching and desperate, his every muscle tense, his mind hazed with desire, and still she made him laugh.

"I love you," he blurted.

Her face—*fuck,* but her face fell.

So, he kissed her.

Before she could really hear the words and panic, so she didn't pull back before he could prove himself. She met his tongue stroke for stroke, held him tightly as he walked them down the hall to her bedroom. But she tore her lips from his when he set her on the mattress. "Sam—"

He kissed her again.

Because he was the one panicking now. All his plans had been ruined with one blurted sentence. She would—

Haley turned her face from his, placed her hand over his mouth when he would have pressed it to hers again. "I—" He slid his hand back up her thigh, slipped fingers between. *In.*

"Sam—"

He knocked her hand aside and kissed her with every single one of the feelings that were roiling within him. If only he could convince her that—

"No!"

Sam froze, saw her face and jumped off her.

"Shit. Haley." He turned away, thrusting a hand through his hair. "Fuck. I'm sorry. I'll—"

"Will you shut the fuck up and listen to me?" she snapped, and cold tore through his every cell. He'd been here before. He put himself out there, and women didn't feel the same, and now he'd fucked up with Haley, and—

"Sam. Look at me."

He always took it like a man.

This time wouldn't be any different.

No matter that Haley made him feel more than all the other women combined.

He straightened his shoulders, spun around. He wouldn't make a scene. He'd go and leave her to her life and—

"I love you, too."

Her words were a gut punch, but the best kind.

"Oh."

Not the most eloquent response, but fuck, Haley loved him, too? How? Fuck. It was—

"Hey." She snapped her fingers. "Did I kill you?"

He shook his head, opened his mouth.

"Good," she interrupted. "Now, get back down here and don't renege on your promise of more oral sex."

Sam started to reply, started to ask if she was all right, to double check she was with him, but then Haley spread her legs and slid her fingers down between her thighs.

Fuck it all.

Talking could wait.

CHAPTER TWENTY-THREE

Haley

SAM DEFINITELY DIDN'T RENEGE on the oral sex front. He parked himself between her thighs and licked her until she absolutely lost her mind.

And then exploded into orgasm.

Twice.

But when he went to press his mouth to her after her third orgasm, she halted him with her hands on his shoulders. "Not on your life, mister."

"Mmm." He licked his lips. "I think I can convince you otherwise."

Haley shuddered. "My clit can't take it."

A brush of his fingers made her groan. "I think it can."

She let him stroke her once, okay three, okay maybe ten times more. But just as she was really starting to lose her mind, she reached into her nightstand and pulled out a condom.

"No, it can't. Here." She tore the packet open with her teeth and shoved it at him. "Inside me. Now."

Hesitation was rampant in his expression. "Maybe we should wait—"

Yeah, that wasn't happening.

She snaked her hand down and flicked open the button on his jeans. "Hal—*oh, fuck—*"

Oh, fuck was right because he was hot and hard and velvety.

"Yes." She slid herself down, executing a move that was quite acrobatic considering her bum foot, thank her very much.

"What—" His protest cut off as Haley sucked him into her mouth.

"Fuck." He groaned. "Baby, I—"

She gripped him with both hands and stroked.

Sam dropped his forehead to the bed above her shoulder, hips thrusting. But he only let her caress him for all of two heartbeats before he was tugging her hand away, tossing her back up onto the pillows. The condom was on a second later, and . . . he paused.

"You sure—"

Nope. No more talking. No way. No how.

Haley wrapped her good leg around his hip, lifted herself up, and—*oh . . . God . . . yes*—slid him inside of her.

He shuddered, locked his eyes onto hers. "Haley."

Just her name, but somehow a thousand emotions sewn into those five letters.

And she felt every single one of them, too, in her soul, her mind, her heart.

"I know," she murmured, reaching up to cup his face. "I know."

Because this was so much more than just an act. This meant something.

It meant *everything.*

"Kiss me," she said. "Show me."

And he did.

Sam pressed his lips to hers and began to move.

———

"ABOUT TIME you got your ass back in here!" Roxy said, rounding the high counter of the nurse's station to hug Haley on Friday the following week. "I've missed you. How's the leg?"

Haley gestured to her cast-covered ankle. "Still broken, but I've only got a few more weeks to go."

Roxy leaned against her desk, smoothed the long black tail of her hair over one shoulder. "Well, I hear that convalescence agrees with you."

Haley picked up a file, pretended to be firmly engrossed in the patient report she'd already read once. "I have absolutely no idea what you're talking about."

"Lies." Roxy plunked into the empty chair. "But I'm not going to pressure you, not when I can just get the gossip from Esther."

"Oh lord." Haley dropped the file.

The little old lady was trouble of epic proportions, and Haley and Sam's budding relationship was her preferred brand of trouble at the moment. She'd livestreamed their return to the diner—her words, not Haley's—then had featured their subsequent movie date, evening shopping trip, dinner at Melissa and Rob's, and even their visit to Roosevelt

Ranch so Sam could perform an ultrasound on Kelly's horse on the town's Facebook group.

Stella was ten weeks along, fitting in with the timeline of Justin's horse menses faux pas.

Which was a statement Haley would have never thought she'd hear, let alone think.

Still, Kelly was thrilled, albeit very much a nervous horse mom. That in and of itself was hilarious, considering her job was running the breeding program. But Haley understood that some things couldn't be kept at a distance. She had a hard time seeing patients as simply patients sometimes—case in point, Melissa, who'd been her patient before she'd become her friend.

Because of that, Haley wasn't going to tease Kelly . . . not too much anyway.

Besides, she'd really enjoyed seeing Sam in action, loved how confident and capable he was when handling both Kelly *and* Stella, soothing both anxious females, human and horse, with equal aplomb. So, she was going to keep her mouth closed and try not to get banned from future veterinary house calls.

She'd also wondered why he didn't have pets of his own, considering how good he was with them. He'd always had a menagerie of cats, dogs, miniature pigs, and even geckos during high school and college.

Sam had shrugged when she asked. "I had to put my last dog down a few years ago, and I just decided that I'd wait until I had more spare time before I got another one. Plus, and this will sound bad, but after taking care of everyone else's animals all day, sometimes I just want to go home and not worry about anything but myself."

"That makes total sense," she'd told him. "Sometimes I just want to leave someone choking when I see them in a restaurant because I want to not worry about anything."

He'd almost swerved the truck off the road, so quickly his gaze had snapped to hers.

"I joke," she'd said, palms facing out.

Sam had scowled. "Not funny." A pause before his lips twitched. "Is this part of that dark ER humor?"

"Probably." She'd winced. "No, definitely."

"Noted," he said, but had rubbed the dashboard of his new SUV lovingly. "You are also now banned from joking while driving."

A nod. "No JWD. Got it."

And in one of those perfect moments, he'd laced his fingers through hers and glanced down at her, hazel eyes a warm mix of brown and gold and green. "I love you."

Her breath had caught, her heart fluttered, and she'd said, "I love you, too."

Simple moments and yet they meant so much. He was just—

"Earth to Haley Bear!" Roxy called, bumping Haley's chair with her own. "Shake off the Sam fog and get to work."

Since she was technically off the clock and waiting for Sam to come pick her up, Haley wasn't exactly worried about her productivity. What concerned her more was the fact that the nickname *Haley Bear* had apparently caught on.

Next time she saw Esther, she was going to take her phone away.

That woman had absolutely no shame.

"Foxy Roxy," Haley said.

Roxy might be younger than her, but they'd both grown up in Darlington and were still close enough in age that Haley knew own Roxy's embarrassing nickname. Thus, one mention of *Foxy Roxy* was all it took to get the other woman to behave.

That and: "Just remember, my list of embarrassing details about you doesn't end with nicknames."

Roxy nodded rapidly. "No Haley Bear." Another nod. "Got it."

Haley lifted her fingers, pointing them at her own eyes then in Roxy's direction. "Make sure you don't forget it. Otherwise I might have to let Esther know who spray-painted Old-Man McDavid's cow in high school."

"You *wouldn't*."

Haley only raised a brow in response.

"You would. Damn. You're mean, Haley Donovan."

She nodded. "And don't you forget it."

"I won't." Roxy's department phone rang, calling an end to her short break, and she pushed to her feet. They were surprisingly busy as they moved into the evening shift, but at least that would make the time go by fast. "Anyway," Roxy said. "This is my Friday, so I won't see you until next week." She waved and started hurrying down the hall, pausing only to call over her shoulder, "Make sure you share all your good Sam time with Esther. I need to live vicariously."

"Hilarious," Haley muttered, glancing down at her phone screen. Sam was supposed to have been there twenty minutes ago, and he hadn't responded to her text saying she had finished up and was ready to go whenever.

He'd probably had to deal with an emergency himself or a late patient. That normally wouldn't have been an issue with her, medicine—whether for people or animals—didn't always run on a perfect schedule. But he'd also insisted on dropping her off that morning since she couldn't drive yet, and now she was stuck.

Maybe Maggie or Melissa could come pick her up. She could catch up with Sam later.

She pulled out her phone, texted her sister first, and received a response barely thirty seconds later.

In Salt Lake for Ashley's dance tournament. I'm sorry. I'd order Tim to come get you, but he's in New York for a work trip.

Damn. After telling her sister not to worry about it, she tried Melissa next. Melissa's producer texted back a few minutes later.

Melissa will be done filming in two hours.

Shit. She'd forgotten her friend was back at Roosevelt Ranch filming the latest season of her cooking show. Melissa was a hell of a cook, hence the reason she'd been so excited when Sam had brought over her signature banana cream pie the other day. After sending a quick apology for interrupting, Haley sat back in her chair and considered what to do.

"Hey." Haley glanced up at the sound of Julian's voice. He'd been relieved by the night shift doctor and had his lab coat over one arm and his keys in his other hand. "Your shift ended a half hour ago. Everything okay?"

"Fine. I'm just waiting for Sam." She held up her phone. "He's running behind."

"Oh, well I'm heading out. Did you want a ride?"

"Do you mind?"

Julian rolled his eyes. "I wouldn't have offered if I minded." He tilted his head toward the doors. "Come on, Mario Kart."

"That nickname better not stick," she grumbled and hopped onto her scooter to follow him out to his car.

"You're welcome," he deadpanned, but held open his car door for her as she slowly and ungracefully maneuvered herself into the passenger's seat. A tug on the end of her ponytail had her glancing up and glaring when she saw him bite back a smile. "Not going to bring any suicidal deer down on me, are you?"

She buckled her seat belt. "You're lucky you're a good doctor."

He rounded the car, sat in his own seat, and strapped in. "Everyone's lucky I'm a great doctor."

"And modest, too."

Julian snorted. "Damn right."

"Just drive, Jeeves. You're not funny."

He backed out of the parking spot. "Except I am."

Haley sighed. She had the feeling this was going to be a long ride home.

CHAPTER TWENTY-FOUR

Sam

HIS GAZE WAS TRACKING the seconds on the clock in the back of the clinic. Two more appointments and then he and Haley could have the rest of the night together. Well, actually the whole weekend. He'd blocked his Friday and Saturday, Michelle having offered to give him a break, and the clinic was closed on Sunday.

After the business of the last week, Sam was definitely ready for some alone time with Haley.

He'd dropped her at work that morning and was anxious to know how things had gone. Was she going stir crazy on her first day back, not being able to do more than glorified filing and the odd consult? Or was she just satisfied being out of the house?

Well, he wouldn't be able to discover the answer to either of those questions until he got his shit done.

Shit, quite literally . . . in one of the cases anyway.

They'd had a golden retriever with an intestinal blockage the previous day. The pup had required surgery and follow up, and they were now waiting for him to move his bowels before he could go home.

Sam's job was so glamorous.

Snorting, he poked his head in on the vet tech who was walking Buddy. She shook her head.

Damn. So, another night in the hospital with monitoring for Buddy, and then Michelle could check on him in the morning.

His last appointment of the day was a simple one in some ways and extremely complicated in others. He only needed to give a few routine vaccines. The complication came in the form of a litter of six eight-week-old kittens.

He spent the last hour of his day, quite literally, herding cats.

By the time he escaped the room of kittens, he'd been scratched, bitten, and licked. Definitely the combination he *wanted*, unfortunately it wasn't with the species—or person—he wanted.

Sam spent a few minutes washing up and checking in with his overnight staff before he got into his SUV and headed for the hospital.

Halfway there, he remembered the present he'd left at his house for Haley. His eyes flicked to the clock, saw he still had a half hour until he had to pick her up from her shift.

Plenty of time.

Plus, she would be exhausted and starving after her first day back.

He had to think that banana cream pie would be a welcome addition. Okay, so he knew it would be, even if the slice he had wasn't Melissa's recipe. Rather it was something Henry was introducing at the diner. He'd given Sam a piece earlier that day after he'd gone to the diner for lunch.

"Should have brought it to work with me," he muttered as he drove down the narrow two-lane road. Then he would have been able to give Haley her treat without having to make this drive.

Oh well. He hadn't exactly been thinking straight, not after Haley had sent him a few very suggestive texts that had all but melted his brain.

Sam turned onto Old Creek Road, his mind full of those sensual promises.

She was going to stay at his house for the first time that night, and he had all sorts of plans for the various services in his house. The kitchen counter, the shower, the hot tub, the washing machine, the shoe rack—

Well, his mind might be a little overstimulated, but at least it had creativity.

With a snort, he took one hand from the wheel and pressed the knob to turn on the radio. Nothing happened.

"What?" His gaze scanned the screen for a second before focusing back on the road. Nothing had changed with the stereo, despite the new SUV, so it wasn't operator error.

He pressed the knob again.

And silence.

"Hmm." He twisted the dial up—nothing—and down—nothing. He turned the other dial, pressed other buttons.

Still, the cab of his vehicle was silent.

Whatever, he didn't need music anyway. He was almost to his house and would fiddle with the system there. If nothing worked, he'd get the dealer to fix it.

See? Look at him. The man with the plan.

Hopefully, Haley would appreciate all his plans. Though—he couldn't hold back his smirk—there had been no *hopefully* with regards to his scheming the previous night. She'd loved them, especially the part where he'd managed to get them both naked.

Naked time was seriously the best time.

If Haley had heard any bit of his last thoughts, Sam knew he'd never live it down, but she *wasn't* there and so that meant he had carte blanche to imagine all the ways he wanted to bring her to orgasm.

And there were many.

With his mouth—her standing with one leg over his shoulder, him kneeling between her thighs. With his fingers—her in that dress again, no panties of course, him sliding his hand up her bare thigh and teasing her to a slow and intense orgasm. With his cock—

"Fuck!"

Two things happened at once.

One, the kamikaze deer had returned, and two, his radio blared to life, static blasting through the speakers and making him jerk the wheel.

He'd been so busy imaging all the ways he'd like to have Haley in his bed that he'd missed Suicidal Bambi on the side of the road. That combined with the jar of sound meant that—

He was fucked.

Sam tried to jerk the wheel back to center, but it was too late. His brand-new SUV was heading straight for the ditch on the side of Old Creek Road.

He slammed on the brakes.

The deer jumped clear of his bumper at the same moment his tires shuddered and tried to find purchase on the shoulder.

Purchase wasn't to be found.

The front wheels plowed into the ditch, slamming him forward against the steering wheel.

Everything went black.

CHAPTER TWENTY-FIVE

Haley

SHE GLANCED down at her phone screen in worry. She'd texted Sam for the second time and had yet to receive a response.

That in and of itself was unusual.

What was also unusual? The churning in her gut.

Perhaps in the past she might have thought that Sam was ignoring her, punishing her for some perceived slight like Brian used to. But Sam wasn't like that, and . . . she was worried.

"Why don't you call the vet clinic if you think something is wrong?" Julian asked as they got off the highway and drove through downtown Darlington. "That way, if he did get caught up with a patient, you'll know and can relax."

Haley gaped over at him. "How'd you get so smart?" she blurted before realizing the sentiment would make him even more arrogant.

He grinned. "I was born this way."

Rolling her eyes, she dialed the number to Sam's office. His receptionist Jane picked up. "Darlington Veterinary, how can I help you?"

"Hi, Jane," she said. "It's Haley. Is Sam still there?"

There was a pause. "Umm no, Haley. Sam left to get you"—there was a pause as though Jane were leaning over to check the clock—"over an hour ago."

The worry, the churning in her stomach, intensified.

Because something was wrong.

Very, very wrong.

She barely processed thanking Jane, just hung up and dialed Sam's number. It rang once and went straight to voice mail.

"Nothing?" Julian asked.

Haley shook her head. "Nothing." A beat as she dialed again. Got voice mail again. "He's probably fine. Just—"

"Let's keep going to your house," Julian said. "We can start our search from there."

"*Our* search?" Her gaze found his.

Julian nodded. "I'm not going to leave my best nurse to handle things on her own."

"Your best nurse?" She attempted to play along, even as she dialed Sam's number for a third time, got his voice mail for a third time.

Fuck.

Something was seriously wrong. She knew it.

Julian touched her shoulder. "He's fine. I'm sure this is just a misunderstanding.

But he didn't sound sure. Not at all.

Julian paused at the stop sign then turned right onto Old Creek Road. "Sometimes cell coverage is bad out here—"

His words cut off as they came around a corner and saw an SUV—*Sam's* SUV, plowed into the ditch on the side of the road. Smoke rose from beneath the hood, glass glittered across the roadway, and . . . there was no sign of Sam.

Julian skidded the car to a stop, threw on the hazards. "Stay here."

Then he was out of the car and sprinting for the SUV.

Haley opened her door and hopped out, reaching into the back seat to grab the med kit she knew Julian stored there. Throwing it over her shoulder, she kept as much of her weight as possible off her ankle as she ran after Julian. Which wasn't a lot, given the shooting pain up her leg.

She ignored it.

Because the whole area smelled like gas.

Julian had opened the driver's door by the time she reached him and was feeling for Sam's pulse.

Please, God, let there be a pulse.

"Unconscious," he said, and she relaxed, dropping the kit and extracting a collar. They'd need to immobilize him before they moved him. Sam took the collar and secured it. "Back up. I need to move him in case the gas catches."

Haley hopped away, extracting her phone and dialing 9-1-1, as Julian lifted Sam from the SUV and carried him a safe distance away. Dispatch picked up her call, and she gave them the rundown of injuries as Julian called them out to her.

It was a good thing Julian moved Sam because the moment they heard sirens in the background, flames burst from beneath the SUV's hood.

Haley had knelt next to Sam, helping Julian by putting pressure on a cut on Sam's shoulder, so she saw the first moment Sam's eyes opened.

"Fucking deer," he groaned and started to sit up.

They kept him in place, but not before he saw the flaming ball of fire that was his new SUV. Sam's eyes flashed wide. "That's not—" Heat radiated in the space around. "Oh, fuck me, it *is*."

Haley thought he was referring to the brand-new SUV going up in flames, but then she saw where his gaze was focused.

"Holy—"

Julian's jaw dropped open.

Because a family of deer stood directly in the middle of the road, staring at them, their beady eyes almost menacing.

"Deer," Julian muttered. "Fucking deer."

The sirens grew louder, and the deer held their ground for one long moment before jumping the barrier and hopping off into the nearby field.

A fire truck roared to a stop beside them, and after checking to make sure Sam was good, that Julian and Haley had it under control until the ambulance arrived, they immediately went to work on the fire.

"Deer trying to kill me," Sam muttered, eyes fluttering closed, limbs going limp.

"He's fine," Julian reassured her. "But I swear, he might actually be right. Those deer might seriously be trying to murder him."

CHAPTER TWENTY-SIX

Sam

IT WAS NEARLY a week later before Sam was able to sort out in his mind exactly what had happened. One minute he'd been heading to pick up Haley's pie, and the next he was waking up in the hospital with a concussion.

He didn't remember the roadside rescue or the apparent attempted killing by the murderous deer.

He remembered pie, a soft hand in his, and kind blue eyes staring down at him while he lay in a hospital bed.

Lucky for him, his bodily injuries were minimal. Concussion aside, he didn't have any broken bones or cuts requiring sutures. He just had his slightly addled brain and nightmares about deer lying in wait on the side of the room.

Thankfully, his buddy Dan at Fish and Game had come down to investigate the issue. It turned out that a fawn was trapped behind the fence of the ranch next to his house. The deer were hanging around close to the road because the mother deer wouldn't leave her baby.

"That's so sweet," Haley said, sitting next to him on the couch as Dan explained the problem and how they were going to make it safer for them to drive.

"Tell that to my SUV," he muttered. Or his head.

"Shh," Haley said. "Don't ruin it."

Dan shook their hands then stood, and Haley tried to follow suit. Sam pressed her back into the couch with narrowed eyes. "Don't you dare. That ankle needs rest."

She'd set herself back a week of recovery after her hop-a-long road escapades, but luckily none of the bones in her leg had been reinjured significantly.

"Samwise," she began.

"Haley Bear," he warned, cutting her off. "Don't start with me."

She crossed her arms, but her lips had curved. "You're sexy when you're bossy." Dan snorted, and she waggled her fingers at him. "Bye now! Thanks for saving us from the homicidal deer."

"A good woman," Dan said as Sam walked him out.

"Yes." He paused, opened the front door. "She's also mine."

"The concussion turned him into a caveman, Dan," Haley called. "Don't mind him!"

Dan chuckled and hesitated on the threshold. "Still yours?" he asked. "Despite the smart mouth?"

Sam couldn't hold back his smile. "Still mine. Always and forever."

Haley chimed in. "Also, he loves my smart mouth."

Dan grinned and said, "He ever screws up, sweetheart, and I'm next in line. I like my women with smart mouths and a little fire under the surface."

"Go away," Sam said and slammed the door.

Haley gasped, probably because that had been rude as fuck, but Sam found he didn't give a damn, not when after days of doctors and visitors and gossipmongers—hello, Esther—he finally had his woman alone.

"Hi," she said when he crossed back over to her. "Gonna kick me out now, too?"

He rolled his eyes, gathered her into his arms. "Didn't you hear what I said?"

"You mean the 'mine and always and forever' stuff?" She shrugged. "I thought that was just a ploy to get Dan to leave."

For a moment, she seemed so uncertain and sad that Sam almost rushed to reassure her. But then he saw the twinkle in her blue eyes, the twitching of her lips.

"Not funny."

"Too much?" she asked.

"Never," he told her. "You'll never be too much for me." He paused. "But also, yes, I want you for forever, and no, it's not a joke or a ploy. I love you, sweetheart and . . ."

She yawned, snuggled close. "And insert romantic words here?"

"Yes, *exactly* that," he teased and kissed the top of her head. "Pretend I just recited *all* the best romantic lines and that you fell madly in love with me."

"Too late," she said with another yawn. "I was already madly in love with you. Also—"

She curled into his side when he lay down on the couch, and when she didn't add anything further he asked, "You also what?"

"I want the always and forever."

He grinned.

"With Henry," she added with a smirk. "Because his banana cream pie might be even better than Melissa's."

Sam growled, and she burst into chuckles, and he couldn't resist following suit, not when he loved the sound of her laughter and her smile and even her terrible—truly *terrible*—attempts at humor.

He brushed a lock of her hair off her forehead and said, "You'll always keep me on my toes, won't you?"

Her laughter cut off, serious blue eyes meeting his. "Why do you say that like it's a good thing?"

"Because it is, sweetheart."

"Even though I'm a pain in the ass?"

He kissed her. "But you're *my* pain in the ass."

Haley grinned. "Such romance."

"You're my *beautiful* pain in the ass?"

"Better," she said, laughter in her words.

"I'll keep working on it," he quipped.

She cupped his cheeks. "I love you, Sam Johnson. Don't ever change."

And he knew the one thing that would never change was how much he loved this woman.

"Now"—she tried to affect a stern expression and failed miserably—"go get me that banana pie from the fridge."

He kissed that laughing mouth . . . and got up to get the pie.

REGRET AT ROOSEVELT

PROLOGUE

Henry

HENRY WIPED down the final table. He was beyond ready to go home and crash after a busy Sunday evening cooking at the diner.

He'd already flicked off the neon "Open" sign and dimmed the lights. The kitchen had been scrubbed and reset for the next morning's breakfast rush, and he'd sent Tilly off about an hour earlier—she'd had a date, and Henry didn't mind sweeping up or stocking the tables with all the necessities for the next day.

Paper napkins, ketchup, salt and pepper, sugar. They weren't what had been on the tables in the Michelin-starred restaurant he'd cooked at while living in New York five years before, but they were his childhood.

His way of feeling close to his dad.

God, he missed his dad.

The bell hanging on the front door rang, and he mentally cursed at having forgotten to lock it.

Beginner mistake.

He'd worked half his childhood in the diner, had closed it down more times than he could count.

And somehow, he'd forgotten to lock the front door.

Hopeless.

"I'm sorry, we're closed," he said, deliberately not looking as he reached to straighten a salt shaker that was slightly askew.

"So, this is your place, is it?" The softly accented voice made him freeze.

Italy. Warm Tuscan sunlight, softly rolling hills through wine country. Cheese and pasta and pizza and . . . *her*.

He accidentally knocked the shaker to the floor. It didn't break because this was a family place and they'd learned long ago that plastic was safer with the kiddos, but Henry watched in slow horror as the lid popped off and salt spread out on the tile floor.

Though his horror didn't come from the spilled salt.

No. It came from the fact that she was there.

He turned. Saw for sure he hadn't been mistaken.

She was there.

Isabella Mariano was in Darlington, Utah. Inside his restaurant.

"*Buona notte*, Henry."

He'd last seen her as she'd gotten on a plane heading the opposite direction of where he'd needed her, flying away when he'd asked her to stay, bolting while his heart had been left to shatter.

"Isabella," he said coldly.

If she noticed his tone, she didn't comment on it.

Then again, she was good at that.

"What are you doing here?" he prompted when she didn't say anything further.

She swept over to him, heels clicking on the tile floor, more beautiful than ever. Her brown hair fell in perfect waves, her killer body was clad in sleek designer clothes, and a diamond ring on her left ring finger sparkled in the dim light.

Diamond ring.

On her left hand.

He processed that, but her words still hit him like a two-by-four to the temple.

"I want you to cater my wedding."

CHAPTER ONE

Henry

HENRY WAS MAKING A MOTHERFUCKING Cobb salad.

Fuck it.

He was already in Hell. He might as well embrace it.

He slammed the metal bowl onto the counter, grabbed a head of romaine lettuce from the walk-in—and only romaine, because fuck the tasteless, useless iceberg variety—then walked back over to the stainless steel table that had served as the prep area for the last three decades Henry's had been open.

His dad's favorite meal.

The first quaintly American—Isabella's wording, not his, because Henry would have called it old-fashioned and boring—thing that he'd cooked for the woman who he'd once hoped to marry.

The woman who'd abandoned him before he could ask, who'd left him when he'd had to go home and take care of his dying father.

The woman who'd supposedly loved him.

His eggs had five more minutes on the stove—because if he was replicating his dad's favorite recipe, Henry figured he might as well also use the tricks his father had taught him as well. Thus, he'd boiled the eggs for three minutes then turned off the heat and covered them for another eighteen. He'd get perfectly yellow yokes without any unseemly green outer layer.

Worked. Every time.

"Fuck," he muttered.

The only difference between his version and his dad's was the quality of the produce. Fresh tomatoes from his garden, organic eggs and chicken from a local farmer, ridiculously expensive but delicious bacon.

Sighing, he washed the lettuce and shredded the chicken breast then chopped and fried up the bacon so it was in mouthwateringly, some might say *heavenly*, crispy bites. After setting it aside to drain, he spun and grabbed the eggs from the burner, peeling them with a practiced efficiency that only came from working close to twenty years in this very kitchen.

The white tore, exposing the perfect yellow yoke inside.

Rookie move.

"Dammit." Henry dropped his chin to his chest and sighed. He wanted to throw the egg in the trash, but he had too much damned respect for the food that came into his kitchen to do such a thing. Instead, he set it aside to turn into egg salad later. Then he peeled the next egg.

No torn white on this one.

He grabbed his favorite knife and a heartbeat later perfectly even portions of egg lay on his cutting board. Next came the avocado.

"What are you doing?"

The voice made him jump and his knife slipped, slicing through his fingertip as easily as it had the egg earlier. He held back his f-bomb only because the voice that had startled him hadn't belonged to an adult.

He gritted his teeth, wrapped his hand in a towel, and turned to face Allie.

Her mom, and his long-time friend Melissa, stood behind her daughter, eyes trailing from his hand to the ingredients on his board.

Kelly would have been better.

Melissa's sister and his best friend was hopeless when it came to food. *She* wouldn't be able to tell the difference between some lettuce and fixings in a bowl and the component parts of a Cobb salad.

Melissa, on the other hand?

She was a celebrity chef, complete with her own cooking show and cookbooks and an absolutely huge social media following. She definitely knew the ingredients of a Cobb salad.

"Who ordered the Cobb?" she asked, walking over to the metal strip that held any outstanding tickets. "The town knows that you don't like making it. Someone have it in for you?"

He snorted.

Someone had it in for him, all right.

Her gaze trailed over the open tickets, no doubt seeing that no one had actually ordered the salad. He opened his mouth to come up with an excuse for why he was making it—aside from punishing himself that was.

Melissa raised her brows.

Henry just shrugged.

What *could* he say?

Bella had swept back into his life and driven him insane again?

Accurate, but more information than he was willing to share.

Luckily, Melissa didn't know *why* the thought of making this particular dish always struck a chord with him.

She didn't understand that it was the combination of past and present, of Isabella and his father, of pain and heartbreak and a really, *really* dark time. She also didn't know that he had finally been moving on with his life, finally dating again and thinking about the future when who had waltzed into the restaurant less than twelve hours before?

The source of that pain and heartbreak and really dark time.

Or, *one* of the sources anyway. Because he couldn't put his father's death all on Isabella. She didn't cause his dad's heart attack or the triple bypass surgery or the subsequent complications after the surgery.

But she hadn't been there.

Henry had asked, and Isabella hadn't come.

And now she wanted him to cater her fucking wedding?

Yeah, that would happen as soon as Hell got its first snowy day.

Allie grabbed his wrist and gently peeled back the towel. Normally, Henry would have reacted faster, stopped her from seeing. But Isabella had rotted his brain, and he definitely was *not* operating on all cylinders. Allie's eyes filled with tears. "Uncle Henry, I'm sorry. I—"

He finally got his shit together.

Squatting down in front of her, he brought his hand behind his back. "Not your fault," he said and wiped away one of the glistening drops that slid free from her eyes to drip down her cheeks. "All this for a little scratch?"

"Th-that's more than a scratch—"

It was.

But he wasn't going to tell a first-grader that.

"Nope," he said. "I've had way worse. This is nothing. Your mommy will slap a Band-Aid on for me, and I'll be good as new."

"Band-Aids make everything better." She nodded sagely.

He chucked her under her chin and walked over to the kit that he kept on hand for just this reason. Not that he usually needed to use it. Typically, it was his part-time chef who'd been wounded. Not Henry.

Cuts. Catering weddings. So many new things.

Lucky him.

Stifling a sigh, Henry pulled out the kit then began washing the cut. "What are we learning how to cook today?"

He and Allie had been having weekly cooking lessons every Monday afternoon after she got out of school. It had started when Melissa had needed a spare set of adult eyes to keep track of Allie while she'd been filming and all other available adults had been busy working.

Desperate, she'd called him, and Henry . . . well, the kitchen had seen plenty of kiddos over the years. It wasn't a big deal. He'd pulled out his old metal stool, positioned it next to him at the counter, and put Allie to work tearing basil leaves.

He'd taught Allie what a Caprese salad was that day.

She'd surprised him by being all-in to make homemade mozzarella cheese.

And he'd started living again.

So, Allie came by on Mondays.

Henry *knew* that. Which meant he shouldn't have been surprised by her appearance, shouldn't have allowed himself to be so caught up in the tangled fucking bullshit from his past that he hadn't heard her coming.

First-graders *weren't* quiet.

Case in point, Allie, tears now forgotten, pounding over to the hook that held her hot pink apron, yanking it off, and tying it on before walking quickly—because one of the first rules he'd had to be strict with her about was absolutely no running in the kitchen—over to where her stool stood along one wall and dragging it in place.

He and Melissa winced at a particularly loud screech.

"You don't have to keep doing this, you know," Melissa murmured, grabbing his hand from beneath the water and putting her Mom Skills to work.

"I like doing *this*," he said. "Plus, give that babysitter of yours a break every once in a while."

"You mean me? Or Rob? Because you certainly can't mean Kelly." Her lips twitched. "She's got her hands more than full with the twins and Abby."

Henry nudged her shoulder. "Why do you seem gleeful about that?"

"Only because she gave me the biggest runaround in middle and high school."

"Good of you to admit it." He flexed his fingers when Melissa finished with the bandage, testing his grip, and then slipped on a rubber glove so he could finish his shift and still be sanitary.

"I want to make a Brad Recipe!" Allie said, or rather yelled.

Because first-graders—or at least *this* one—were not quiet.

And though Henry wished he could say his flinch was volume-related, it wasn't.

Because Brad was *his* dad. And a Brad Recipe was one that came straight from his father's box of handwritten index cards. Allie had stumbled onto them a few months back, and it had been fine. The five years that had passed since he'd lost his dad hadn't made the pain go away, but they did make the memories more palatable.

Henry could actually remember the good things.

Not succumb to regret and that huge yawning cavern that was in the place where his dad should be.

He swallowed hard, but forced out an "Okay."

Which was all the encouragement Allie needed. She sprinted over to the shelf and pulled down the little plastic box then proceeded to search through it with all the relish of a girl after his own heart.

Food. Learning new techniques and recipes.

He dug chicks who were into food.

Like Isabella.

Fuck, he'd fallen for her hook, line, and sinker.

Melissa touched his shoulder. "You sure you're"—her eyes trailed to the ingredient-laden board from his ill-advised Cobb salad—"up for this today?"

"Go." He pushed her in the direction of the door. "Do fancy TV things. I've got this."

She paused, turned back. "It's just dubs, and I'll reimburse you for the ingred—"

"Shh." Another nudge since this was the same argument they had week after week. He didn't need to be reimbursed for hanging with Allie. He loved the kid, just as much as he loved Kelly and Melissa and all their respective kiddos. They were family, and you didn't charge family. Nope. No way. No how. "Go on now with you. Enjoy being a big-time chef."

Her lips twitched, but she nodded and left, pressing a kiss to the top of Allie's head as she did so.

Henry crossed over to his partner in crime. "So, what are we making?"

"This one!"

He glanced at the card she held up. "Black Forest Icebox Cake," he read. "One of my favorites." He dropped his voice to a whisper. "We can also swap out the cherries and dark chocolate and make a cookies and cream version."

Her eyes went wide. "Really?"

"Really really."

She jumped up from the stool. "I'll grab the cookies!"

"No samples on the way," he called.

Allie's shoulders dropped slightly in disappointment—Henry knew all her tricks by now—but she didn't stop moving until she'd returned with the cookies and the rest of the ingredients he called out to her.

Once everything was set out and measured, she pushed up her sleeves and clapped her hands once. "Let's get to work."

Henry grinned as he handed her the cream to whip up in the mixer. "Yes, let's."

Work was exactly what he should be focusing on.

CHAPTER TWO

Isabella

SUNLIGHT STREAMED through the window of Darlington's only bed and breakfast, hitting her straight in her jet-lagged, emotionally exhausted brain.

Wincing, she rolled over and jammed a pillow over her head, desperate for a few more hours of sleep. She'd gone to bed too early then had been up most of the night before falling back asleep just as the first rays of sunshine had begun peeking over the hills in the distance.

The sun was well into the sky now, illuminating the tiny town that Henry called home.

In some ways, it reminded her of *her* small town, barely a blip on the surrounding geography, only a few streets to its name, and only a couple of thousand residents.

But where her home had been cold, this place was warm.

And she didn't mean temperature either.

There was life to Darlington, warmth and softness, and . . . she was letting herself get lost in fantasy. She'd grown up in Italy for God's sake. That was the definition of warm, especially in the summer months.

Maybe it was the people.

Or rather, the absence of *some* people.

Shaking her head at herself, she braved the bright light and sat up. Isabella reached for her cell on the nightstand and groaned. Thankfully, she'd set it to *do not disturb*, because otherwise the sheer multitude of calls, texts, and voicemails would have turned her minimal sleep into no sleep.

"Fuck," she muttered and dropped it to the bed.

It had been stupid to run, she knew that. But it had been even stupider to come back here and think that she could repair what she'd shattered before.

Especially when she led with, *"I want you to cater my wedding."*

She wasn't getting married.

Or, not any longer anyway.

That she'd thought she could go through with the whole thing had been a . . . mistake.

Huge understatement.

Snorting, she slid from the bed and walked into the bathroom then twisted the taps inside the shower until hot water poured out and began filling the room with steam.

Her father was a persuasive man and the thought of being persuaded down that particular avenue—read: lifelong commitment and *marriage*—had finally snapped her back to reality.

He had already prompted her to make the biggest mistake of her life.

She didn't need him coaxing or cajoling, or whatever synonym that wasn't popping into her head at the moment, her into Huge Life Mistake Version Two. Isabella had been weak for the past five years. That was long enough. It was time she got her head out of her ass, act like the grown woman she was, and live her fucking life.

And she wanted to live that life with Henry.

Which she'd pretty much screwed up since her first words to him were about catering a wedding she'd run away from.

But, dammit, it was the first thing that had popped into her head when she'd seen him there, looking as gorgeous as ever. Her throat had tightened, her pulse spiked, and she'd felt like she was going to faint. All she could think was *this is right.*

Henry was right.

She'd been meeting with wedding planners and florists and cake decorators and caterers and—

She'd. Just. Blurted.

The first thing to come to her mind.

Which had pretty much been the worst thing. Henry had been on the defensive, closed down and eyes cold before she'd verbal diarrhead that nonsense. After? Well, his expression had been telling those ice caps in the Himalayas they were too warm.

So she'd fled.

Whirling around and hightailing out of the diner and back across the street to the bed and breakfast. Once safely ensconced in her room, she realized she was starving, but everything in town was closed and no room service was to be found. Isabella had not so successfully filled her empty stomach with stale crackers and tap water.

Such a gourmet meal for a professional chef.

Not that she'd been doing much "chefing" as of late. That had been a moment of rebellion, according to her father.

Heaven forbid she find something she was passionate about and dive in.

Heaven forbid . . . she have a fucking spine.

Isabella sighed as she stripped and stepped into the shower, letting the hot water flow down her head, her hair, her nape. She rested her head against the tile wall and tried to center herself, to find the cool and calm woman she'd been since she'd walked away from Henry.

But that woman was in hiding, camouflaged like a son of a bitch, and currently unreachable.

Henry was mad. Hurt. Cold.

Of course he was.

Because he didn't know.

And instead of telling him, she'd waltzed in and tried to hire him. Which was *so* something her father would do. Throw money at a problem until it resolved itself one way or another.

"Ugh." She sighed again, letting the water stream over her until her stomach rumbled, protesting her last meal of crackers and the long stretch of airline and airport food before that. Her flight had been via first class, but try as they might, plane food was still just that . . . and *that* wasn't great.

She needed fuel and to shore up her mind.

But she especially needed to stop sighing like a love-struck teenager.

It was time for Isabella to woman-up and get her man back.

Even if she had to hire him to cater a wedding that was never going to happen.

CHAPTER THREE

Henry

HE WAVED as Allie jumped out of the car and then headed up to the front door of the main house at Roosevelt Ranch.

Yup, he'd said main house.

His best friend growing up had done well when she'd married Justin Roosevelt. While the former army medic might come across as unassuming and normal, his family definitely was *not*.

The Roosevelts were richer than Croesus and way above the typical Darlington pay grade, but Justin didn't care about his family's money. In fact, he'd only recently stepped in to help his father with some of the business after discharging from the military.

His focus was his family and supporting Kelly as she lived her dream of running *the* premier horse breeding operation in the States.

Roosevelt Ranch was the perfect place for that.

Kel had practically grown up on the ranch—before it had gained its current namesake. She'd always been horse crazy and had worked her way into free lessons.

Now she had a set of stables that were so impressive and luxurious they nearly rivaled the main house.

The huge front door opened, and his friend patted Allie's head as she bustled inside, but when he waved and would have driven away, Kel shook her head, taking a step toward him. And considering she had a twin in each arm, Henry knew he was trapped. He'd wait—*no* he'd get out of the car and go to Kelly before she tripped and injured herself or one of the kiddoes on the gravel drive. He'd do it because he was a soft-hearted sucker who often got caught in women's webs and—

Fuck.

He turned off the ignition, popped his door, and got out of his car.

"Hey," he said, slamming it and walking over to her. He slid Jessie from her arms, cuddling the little girl close. Her vibrant green eyes were sleepy. "Did you just wake up from a nap?" he murmured, and she cuddled closer.

"Rocket ship," she said.

Kel laughed.

And speaking of getting caught in a female's webs.

Jessie had him wrapped up tightly in hers. Not that her brother, Jax, didn't have him just as snared.

Henry liked kids.

Always had. Always would.

And since he didn't and probably never would have any of his own, he had no problem being the fun uncle.

"Rocket ship!" Jax said, raising his head up from his mom's shoulder.

"Not so sleepy anymore, are you?" Kelly said with a laugh.

"Rocket ship!" Jessie said again, much more enthusiastically and thus, confirming her mom's statement.

Kel glanced at Henry. He shrugged.

"Okay, two rocket ships each and then you need to go find daddy and bug him for letting you fall asleep." She shook her head. "Goodness knows what this late nap is going to do to your bedtime."

"It's summer," Henry said with a shrug.

"Yes, it is," Kel agreed. "But that doesn't mean bedtime doesn't need to happen."

"Ah, to be a parent."

She smacked him, and he stepped back to prepare Jessie for her first rocket ship.

"Don't hit, Mama," Jax said.

Henry's lips twitched. "Yeah. Don't hit."

She glared, but he ignored it as he dangled Jessie's feet just off the ground, shaking her gently like a rocket ship engine's flaring to life. They counted down together. "Five . . . four . . . three . . . two . . . one!" And she blasted off.

Or rather, he tossed her high into the air, caught her, and then flew the Jessie rocket ship back and forth over the path before landing her safely in front of Jax and Kel.

Jax immediately wiggled his way out of Kel's arms. "My turn!"

Henry obliged and was sweating by the time he finished the four rounds. He waved as the kids ran off to find Justin, heart swelling when they stopped mid-sprint then turned around and threw their little arms around his waist.

"Wuv you!" Jessie said and ran off.

"Wuv you!" Jax parroted, following her.

This was why he'd never moved back to New York. He'd gone for an adventure, to be someone important and famous in the restaurant world, and to make a boatload of money. He'd done it, too, made the money, had begun to be *somebody* in certain high circles, and then . . . his dad had gotten sick.

And he'd discovered that being a part of this circle was so much more valuable.

"So," Kel said. "Cobb salad?"

Or not.

He turned. "I've got to get back to the restaurant."

Kel caught his arm. "Is this about the beautiful brunette with the Italian accent?"

"How do you know about Isabella?" He'd rotated back to face her before realizing his mistake. She'd called his bluff, and he'd caved.

Kel's smile was beatific. She swept a hand around them. "This is Darlington, remember? Plus, she's staying at the B&B, and certain key people saw her walk into your restaurant the other day." He groaned, but she ignored him. "And then this morning, you're making a Cobb salad that no one ordered. Melissa checked and told me, and we put two and two together. So *she's* the reason Cobb salads are anathema? Why? Did you know her back in New York?"

He sighed, somehow following all of that and knowing that if he didn't give her some details she'd hound him until the dogs came home, no pun intended. "Yes."

There. That ought to be enough.

"Yes?" She raised a brow. "Just *yes?* Seriously?"

"Bye, Kel." This time when he turned for his car, he got his ass in gear and didn't stop, not even when she huffed and he heard her footsteps on the gravel behind him.

"Henry," she began, hand on his arm.

He brushed it off. "Leave it, Kel. Please."

"I—"

He was saved by a loud crash, followed by crying from inside the house. He stopped, gestured inside. "Go."

Kel glared, but she was already hustling toward the noise. "This isn't over," she called as she reached the front door.

Yeah, that was exactly what he was afraid of.

CHAPTER FOUR

Isabella

SHE CLOSED her laptop with a disgusted sigh. Her bank account was pathetic . . . as in pathetically empty.

Her father had acknowledged her disobedience by cutting her off. Which she'd known would happen, of course. No one crossed Roberto Mariano, most especially not some helpless female creature.

Isabella groaned then pushed herself to her feet and forced herself to take stock. Her bank account had just over a thousand dollars in it, and while her father considered the amount a pittance, she knew how to make it stretch.

She'd done it before in New York.

She'd make it work this time around as well.

Her first step was to get out of the bed and breakfast because who knew how long her credit card would work—

Isabella's stomach growled with a vengeance.

Okay, so her *first* order of business was to get some food into her belly. Then to get out of the bed and breakfast and into something cheaper . . . and hopefully more permanent.

Because she wasn't leaving without Henry.

Feeling slightly less depressed, she picked up her purse and left the room.

That mild buoyant feeling lasted the three minutes it took for her to descend one flight of stairs, cross the quaint two-lane road, and push through the diner's doors on the other side.

More than a dozen eyes turned in her direction, narrowed, and then flicked away, the small town's version of a cold shoulder.

Isabella didn't have to be a rocket scientist—and she most definitely wasn't smart enough to delve into aeronautics—to know that.

Less than twenty-four hours and word had gotten around.

She remembered Henry talking about the town gossip train, explaining that something would happen in the morning and by the after-noon, every person in Darlington would be able to recite the details verbatim. But she had thought he exaggerated. Isabella was from a small town herself and aside from a few interfering grannies, most people kept to themselves.

She decided she rather preferred *that* option. Especially when faced with the onslaught of narrowed lids and subsequent dismissal.

Click.

The noise made her jump, her gaze darting from left to right before finally catching a flash of movement in front of her.

An elderly woman wearing a purple sweatshirt with a pair of kittens on its front stood in front of her, the latest model i-whatever in her hand. When Isabella's eyes met hers, she lowered the phone and smiled up at her.

It was unnerving, that smile.

As though the little old lady with tufts of curly white hair could see straight into her soul.

This would be the point that Isabella's grandmother would cross herself and pray to the Holy Ghost for protection, but Isabella herself had never been much for religion or the old ways or—

And now she was sad.

A hand slid into hers, making her jump for the second time in as many minutes.

"Come with me, dear," the woman said, tugging her in the direction of a booth. "I'm Esther."

"I'm Isabella," she said and started to dig in her heels. Based on Henry's reaction when she'd walked in before and that of the current patrons dining, she'd made a mistake coming here. She should leave before she caused a scene.

And what was that about fighting for Henry? her conscience reminded her.

Well, she wasn't exactly anticipating it being so . . . public.

She knew she had a mountain to climb and so many things to explain, but—

Fine. She was a fucking coward.

"I should go," she began.

Esther gave a surprisingly strong tug for a woman her size. "You need to eat something, girlie. You're practically skin and bones."

Her father saying the same thing would have hurt Isabella's feelings. Then again, his words were always a critique, definitely not said with the same sort of exasperated tone as Esther's—as though she were a naughty child rather than solely a source of disappointment.

Plus, the diner smelled wonderful.

Sweet laced with savory, the remnants of breakfast trailing into lunch and even an early dinner. The heavy note of fried food mixed with something that made her mouth water. Tangy, spicy . . . sultry.

Henry's food.

Her stomach rumbled just as Esther pushed her down into a booth.

"See?" she said. "You're hungry and need to eat."

Isabella nodded and relinquished the battle she was losing anyway. Plus, Esther was the one person who didn't seem to hate her, so she'd be wise to not alienate a potential ally. "Yes, you're right."

Esther nodded. "Of course, I am."

Isabella smiled and picked up the menu the woman shoved in her direction. "What do you like to order here?"

"Oh, I'm boring and always get the same thing." She waved a hand. "Can I call you Bella?"

Her heart skipped a beat. Only one other person in the world had called her Bella . . . and he was the person this restaurant was named after. "Um, sure," she said and picked up the menu that lay on the scarred tabletop. "What's the same thing?"

The strands of jeweled necklaces that hung around Esther's neck tinkled as she tilted her head. "What *same thing?*"

Isabella smiled. "What's the dish you always order?"

"A fried chicken sandwich with a side of Brussels sprouts."

Except the explanation hadn't come from Esther.

Isabella glanced up and saw a very annoyed Henry standing at the end of the table, a plate in one hand.

"Sounds delicious," she murmured.

Esther lifted a plastic glass of water to her mouth, two wedges of lemon bobbing in the cup, and took a long swallow. "It's the best thing on the menu."

"I'd better order one then," Isabella said.

"No," Henry snapped, his tone harsher than she'd ever heard before.

Isabella's shoulders came up, protecting herself against the onslaught that was certain to come.

She froze and waited.

Then waited some more because the verbal onslaught never actually came. So great, she was sitting there in a restaurant full of people who were pretending to ignore her, but in actuality were probably watching her like a hawk so they could talk about her later, with her shoulders up around her ears and her spine bowed like a pathetic ring-hoarding creature.

"I—" she began, forcing herself to straighten.

"Bella is hungry," Esther interrupted, patting her on the hand. "We'll share the sandwich until you can bring out another one." She preempted Isabella's argument by picking up her knife and cutting the sandwich in half. "Bring an extra plate, dear," she told Henry then speared a Brussels sprout on her fork and held it up. "Try this, Bella. You'll never have a tastier vegetable."

Isabella took the fork and bit into the green sphere.

In an instant, flavors burst to life on her tongue.

Salt and pepper. Oil and smoke. A light sweetness trailed by a depth of earthiness. Her eyes widened as she chewed, the slight crunch of the outer leaves giving way to a smooth center.

She swallowed, forcing herself to smile in Esther's direction and all too aware of Henry's heavy gaze on her.

After wiping her mouth with a napkin, she dared sneak a glance in his direction.

His eyes were unreadable, but she thought that she might detect hope in the pale blue depths. Or if not that, then perhaps they were empty of anger.

"It is the most delicious vegetable I've ever eaten," she said, sincerely feeling that.

For some reason, that seemed to make him furious. His eyes flashed, and he glared down at her for a moment before pushing the plate back an inch so it was closer to Esther. "Eat," he told her. "Before it gets cold. I'll make Isabella something."

And then he was gone, striding across the floor, pushing through the pair of swinging doors with circular windows.

Walking away from her when there was so much to say.

Well, if that wasn't a role reversal, then Isabella didn't know what was.

"What happened between you two?" Esther asked between bites of sandwich.

Isabella froze for a heartbeat before telling the truth. "I messed up."

"Well, that much is clear, dear, but I want to know all the juicy details for the town's Snapchat." She pulled out her phone. "Do you want sparkling sunglasses or a unicorn horn?"

"I—" Isabella shook her head, the words not computing. "Um . . ."

"Unicorn horn," Esther said with a nod. "Good choice."

And then, before Isabella could stop her, she found herself the object of Esther's cell phone's camera.

"Tell us, dear, how you broke our Henry's heart . . "

Which was the exact moment she decided that coming to the diner had been a huge mistake, no matter how tasty the Brussels sprouts.

CHAPTER FIVE

Henry

HE WAS GOING to kill Esther.

Or at the very least rip her cell phone from her old, wily hands and launch it straight into the trash can.

Isabella's cheeks were bright red, her shoulders curved up as though to form a shield, and Henry spared a thought for what had happened to the cheerful, confident woman she'd been back in New York.

Fearless. Never at a loss for words.

But she didn't look fearless now.

She looked mortified and panicked and, *fuck it all*, he couldn't stop himself from rescuing her.

Sucker that made him.

He set the bag of food he'd boxed up for her on the table, having intended to feed her as requested by Esther while getting her out of sight, as his heart demanded, and wrapped his hand around her elbow.

Then he snagged the cell from Esther, turned it off, and tugged Isabella from the booth.

"I need to borrow you."

"Hen—" Esther began, a complaint about him ruining her fun no doubt on the tip of her tongue.

"Meal's on the house today," he told her and snatched the bag of food before leading Isabella through the double doors and into the back of the diner. He bypassed the kitchen on the right, walked past the bathrooms and his office on the left, not stopping until he pushed out into the alley behind the restaurant.

An old wooden bench from his father's days sat along the brick wall.

He pushed her down onto it, shoved the bag of food into her lap, and turned to leave.

Her fingers on the back of his hand stopped him.

It could barely be called contact, the brush of skin to skin was so feather-light, but the force didn't matter. Not when it was Isabella. *Always*, it had been like this. Fire in his veins, lightning strikes contained in a human body, the barest touch and he half-expected to glance down and see himself turned to ash.

But that had been their problem, hadn't it?

They'd burned too hot, flared too quickly.

And in the end, he'd been left with nothing.

He stared into her eyes, a deep brown that had always reminded him of espresso, and she flinched back, eyes tearing away from his, dropping to the ground.

Fuck.

"I'm sorry I didn't come here with you. Back then," she added when he didn't reply. And how *could* he reply? That wound was a horrible, festering thing. It didn't heal.

It *never* healed.

Apologies didn't bring his father back.

And . . . that wasn't Isabella's fault.

She hadn't spent years smoking away her life on that very bench. She hadn't eaten poorly or disregarded doctor's orders.

She just . . . hadn't dropped everything to come home with him.

He'd vilified her for that because it was easier to be mad at her than angry with himself, easier to blame her for not coming when in reality, he felt horrible because *he* hadn't come back sooner.

"I didn't know what else to do," she whispered.

"Yeah," he said. "Me neither. I just knew I needed someone to be there for me."

Her chin dropped to her chest and she nodded.

"It wasn't fair for me to expect that person to be you."

Isabella's eyes shot to his, lips parted in surprise. "I—"

"We were new and hadn't been together long—" He shook his head, tried again. "While I clearly thought we were something more . . . permanent, it wasn't fair for me to expect you to feel the same—"

She pushed to her feet. "Henry—"

God, he loved when she said his name, a soft 'h,' a slightly rolled 'r'—

"It wasn't like that. I *loved* you. I just . . . had to go."

"Why?"

Why then? Why when he needed her? Why, when for the first time in his life he'd asked a woman to stay, had she gone?

She shook her head, clutched the bag of food to her chest. "I should have stayed. Should have told you—"

Breaking off with another shake of her head, she stepped closer to him.

Close enough for him to smell her, close enough for the breeze to flit her ponytail forward and for the soft tendrils to tease his cheek, close enough for him to remember exactly how good it had been between them.

"Tell me what?" he asked.

She bit her lip.

"Bella." He used his old nickname. He shouldn't have. It was too familiar, but, fuck it, he *was* familiar with Isabella. Henry knew how quickly she could chop an onion, knew she could make him really fucking delicious pasta with a recipe that was more touch than measurements. He knew the sound she made when he kissed her properly, could perfectly recall the feel of her beneath him.

He knew this woman in the depths of his soul.

"Henry," she murmured and stepped closer.

The back door flew open, would have cracked her in the head if Henry hadn't managed to catch it.

A man emerged, tall, dark, and movie star handsome. While Henry was confident enough in himself to recognize the other man as objectively attractive, he also immediately disliked him. His teeth were too white, his facial hair too groomed, his pale pink linen suit like he was trying too hard. And his knee jerk reaction was warranted, Henry thought, because the man immediately took Bella into his arms and kissed her long enough that he had to look away, a red haze filling his vision.

This wasn't his woman.

It didn't matter who kissed her.

"Isabella," the man said and while Henry had been expecting an Italian accent to match Bella's, his was strictly American. "I've come, my darling. Where's this ranch that you talked about for the wedding?" He turned to Henry, whose gaze had jumped to the couple at the mention of the ranch. "You must be the caterer? My Isa mentioned this place." He glanced down at the bag in Isabella's hands. "Oh, darling, did you get some samples to try? We should go back to the room and *sample* them."

Henry shuddered at the connotation imparted in that word and started to turn back for the diner.

He caught sight of Bella's face as he did so.

The man had taken the bag from her, was running his free hand through her ponytail.

And she looked absolutely miserable.

Not his problem.

"Isa, darling . . ."

She cringed, and he remembered how much she hated being called Isa.

"I've missed you."

Not. His. Problem.

She extracted herself. "Sergio."

The man's eyes had been focused on Bella's breasts. The sharp tone had his gaze flying up to meet hers.

"Yes, darling?"

"I need you . . ." Her stare flicked to Henry's then away. "I need to talk to you. Alone."

Inexplicably, a giant boulder dropped into Henry's gut, stealing his breath.

For a moment, he'd thought she was going to tell Sergio, *"I need you to go."*

Insane.

Delusional.

Some other adjective Henry wasn't going to search his brain for. Because it didn't matter. Clearly he'd lost his mind. She wasn't miserable. She was about to get married.

He turned, caught the door handle, and tugged it open.

Isabella's voice stopped him on the threshold. "Henry?"

"Yeah?" he asked, not turning to face her. His pulse sped while an unbidden, and decidedly unwanted, thread of hope wove into his heart. But still Henry didn't turn, unwilling to risk seeing a dismissal in her expression. Not again.

"Thanks for the food."

He was really glad he couldn't see her face.

"Sure," he said, tone somehow casual as he let the door close behind him.

And that panel slamming shut was the perfect end to the most painful chapter of his life.

Good riddance.

CHAPTER SIX

Isabella

Sergio grabbed her arm. "Let's go," he gritted out.

"No." She yanked free, stepped back when he would have grabbed her again. "I already told you. I'm *not* marrying you."

Black brows drew together. "That's not what your father—"

Fuck. They'd had this conversation so many times. Her father didn't get to decide every single detail of her life, and he sure as hell wasn't going to choose the man she was going to marry. She'd been weak when she had accepted Sergio's proposal in the first place, mostly because she'd thought Sergio actually loved her, that she would grow to love him in return.

Because what Isabella wanted most in the world was to be part of a family.

By blood wasn't even a requirement because she'd learned over the years that shared DNA didn't always mean love and respect were present. She'd adopt or have babies, make friends who liked her for herself. She'd have Sergio, whom she didn't love, but perhaps her affection for him might develop into that one day.

And then she would finally be happy.

Except things didn't work out that way.

"My father is not me," she said.

"He promised."

There.

There was the hard edge that Sergio had been so careful to hide from her at first. He'd been so perfect, pretending to really care about what she was saying and feeling, responding with all the right things. He'd charmed her father and that didn't often happen, but then again what her father wanted most in the world was a son.

One daughter. No sons.

His everlasting disappointment.

Things might have been better if she'd been interested in the family business, but investments and stocks made her eyes glaze over, the same as her waxing poetic about olive oil did to her father.

They'd agreed tacitly to not discuss their mutual interests.

Which had been for the best, and everything had been great for the two years she'd spent in New York.

Until her father decided that her playtime was up.

Until *she* decided that she wanted to be with Henry, not the man her father had picked for her.

That man hadn't been Sergio. No, Sergio was the last in a long line of *respectable* men her father had chosen—which meant they were good at business and would carry on the mantle of MR Investments respectably when her father passed and would give him reasonably attractive grandbabies.

What it *didn't* mean was that they were kind or loving or gave two shits about her.

Most had looked right through her or treated her with near disdain while sidling close to her father, but fortunately, they'd all also eventually pissed him off. Thus, the pressure to marry them had passed and they were discarded as easily as a used tissue. But there was always another man.

Another man to care more about her father and the business than her.

She was the enticing little bow on top.

Until Sergio.

He'd played the game right, had managed to not piss her father off while also manipulating her.

She had been such a fool.

"You're coming home," Sergio said through gritted teeth. "I didn't put in all this time to just let you go."

She snatched the bag of food from his hands. "*You* should go home," she said. "I'm done dancing to my father's tune. I don't love you. I never have. I'm not—"

One second, she was glaring up at him, the next she was pinned against the brick wall, his hand around her throat. "I don't give a fuck whether you love me or not. Your father will cut me out of the business unless you come home and marry me. So you're going to shut up and—"

Isabella didn't think, just reacted.

Her knee came up hard, hitting him squarely in the groin.

Sergio collapsed to the ground.

Unfortunately, the hand around her neck didn't release, and she found herself dragged down alongside him, unable to break her fall. Her side collided with the concrete first, and she felt the thin silk of her shirt tear, her skin beneath it burn. The next to hit was her hip and finally her head, which made her bite her tongue and her mouth fill with blood.

One hard tug and she managed to extricate herself, rolling gingerly to her feet and picking up the now-mangled bag of food from the ground.

"Go home, Sergio. Leave me to my life."

He only groaned in response. Relieved that he didn't seem to be in any shape to come after her again, Isabella hurried out of the alley. Luckily, there were a few napkins in the bag, and she grabbed one out as she hobbled around to the front of the diner.

She was ashamed to say tears were running down her cheeks. That, along with her entire body hurting and the sharp tang of iron in her mouth, and she wasn't the most together she'd ever been in her life.

Especially when Sergio shouted her name and staggered out from the alley.

"Isabella, I'm not—"

She limped on, wanting to make it across the street and into the bed and breakfast. She'd left her phone, but maybe the girl at the front desk could—

She waited for a car to pass before crossing the road, but when she glanced back Sergio seemed to have regained himself. He was hurrying after her with only the slightest hitch in his step and gaining on her quickly.

The car that had driven by her stopped, but Isabella barely heard it in her effort to put as much distance between herself and Sergio.

Instead, what she *did* hear were footsteps closing in and Sergio's annoyed grunts.

She couldn't let him catch her.

Instinctively, she knew that. He'd been irritated before she'd kneed him, and that had resulted in him tossing her against a wall and choking her.

If he caught her now?

Bella shuddered to think.

She moved faster.

The door to the bed and breakfast was just feet away, and Isabella lunged for it only to have her head jerked back roughly as Sergio caught her ponytail.

Which was the exact moment she heard something else.

A deep male voice.

"Let her go and step back." Her eyes darted to the right, and she had never been more relieved in her life to see a police officer. He wore a deep blue uniform and approached them slowly. "*I said* to let her go." Icy steel in his words.

Sergio released her hair, and she hurried to put some space between them.

"Someone want to tell me what the hell is going on?"

Bella found it almost impossible to push words past her now-aching throat, and before she managed, Sergio chimed in, sounding sickeningly nonchalant.

"My fiancée and I are just having a little disagreement."

"I'm not his fiancée," she managed.

"Then why are you wearing my ring, darling?" he asked sweetly.

She'd considered pawning it, that was why. However, in that moment she didn't give a damn about any money it might bring her. She yanked it off, flung it on the ground. "I'm not his fiancée anymore."

"And you like beating up women who *used* to be your fiancée?" the officer said just as a squad car roared up the street beside them, lights flashing.

"She merely had a bad fall."

One black brow went up. "She fell, and you caught her by yanking her hair out of her head?"

Sergio shrugged. "Her hair got caught on my watch."

"Hmm."

Sergio shifted like he was going to move toward her, and the officer caught his arm. "Have a seat over here," he ordered, tugging Sergio down onto the curb a good ten feet away from her.

Isabella blinked, wavering on her feet, but a strong hand caught her.

"Easy now," Esther said, steadying her.

The doors opened on the other squad car, and a female deputy got out. She was short with a tight blonde ponytail and kind eyes. "Rob?" she asked, glancing between Isabella and Sergio.

"Domestic disturbance," he replied. "Would you mind taking her statement?" He hesitated before adding, "Maybe somewhere she can sit down?"

The woman nodded.

"Thanks, Pam."

Another nod before the woman crossed over to Isabella. "Hi," she said. "I'm Officer Harting, but you can call me Pam."

"H-hi," Isabella said then lifted her chin and forced her voice to steady. "Did you want to go inside so we can talk?"

"That would be good."

Isabella nodded and patted Esther's hand. "Thank you. I'm fine now."

Esther glared up at her before extracting several tissues from her fanny pack, "You're bleeding all over that pretty shirt of yours." She pressed them to Bella's arm.

"Oh!" Bella's eyes shot to the spot, and she saw the blood dripping down her fingertips. Damn. She must be cut deeper than she realized.

Officer Harting held up a black rectangular-shaped bag. "I've got her covered, Esther."

"Good."

The older woman stayed where she was.

"This is not going on the town's Facebook page."

Esther rolled her eyes. "Clearly not," she said, and Officer Harting's formal stance relaxed slightly. At least until she said, "It's much more fitting for Snapchat."

Somehow, Bella felt her lips twitch.

And honestly, it was nice to feel something aside from terror or numbness.

She'd seen the sharp edge of Sergio's temper just once before . . . and had the scar to prove it.

It had been the final straw, the piece that had given her the courage to leave.

But somehow, she'd almost convinced herself that she'd imagined the entire thing. That he hadn't actually hit her that night after the benefit, that she *had* been a little too tipsy and tripped down the final few stairs. That he hadn't been furious with her moments before it happened for embarrassing him.

Because she'd had an opinion that didn't agree with his.

Because she was supposed to be seen and not heard.

Even though he'd convinced her that he was a nice guy and actually liked hearing her opinions.

Just not when they contradicted his. Or in public when she was playing the role of arm candy. Or, preferably, that she'd just shut the fuck up and do what he said.

Esther stomped her foot, making Bella jump. "Look at her. She's half stunned. She needs a hospital, not an interrogation."

Bella shook her head and winced when the movement made her head ache even more. "I'm fine," she said. "I just need to sit down for a few minutes and eat something. I slept through breakfast and got in too late for much of a dinner last night."

Esther tsked. "You're already too skinny as it is."

The admonishment made Isabella smile, but when she glanced up at Officer Harting, the other woman looked concerned. She held up her finger. "Can you follow this?" she asked, moving it side to side.

"I'm not concussed, I—" Except just tracking the digit made Bella's brain feel like it was going to burst out of her skull.

"See?" Esther said. "Not fine."

"I'll wrap her arm and drive her to the ED."

"Oh, no. I'm—" Bella started to shake her head again and stopped with another wince. She really needed to stop doing that.

"No arguments," Officer Harting said. "You need to be cleared medically before I can take your statement." She made short work of wrapping Bella's arm then led her over to the front seat of the squad car. "Take it slow now."

Considering the amount of pain coursing through her body at the moment, slow wasn't a problem.

Officer Harting reached over her and buckled Isabella's seat belt before she could reach for it then softly closed the door. Bella watched through the windshield as the female cop moved across the road and spoke to Rob—at least she'd thought she'd heard that was his name—for a few moments then got back into the car. Just as Officer Harting had started up the engine, another police cruiser drove up, but she just waved and clicked the transmission into drive.

"Thank you, Officer Harting," Isabella said.

"Just doing my job." A shrug as she tossed Bella a smile, pale green eyes twinkling in the late afternoon sunlight. "And call me Pam, please. All that Officer Harting stuff gets really tiring."

Bella's lips twitched. "Pam. Thank you."

"Does he have a history of violence toward you?" The question was quiet in volume, but deadly in tone.

"No," Isabella denied immediately and then was forced to qualify her statement nearly as quickly. "Only once before. I thought—I didn't think he'd follow me here."

Officer—*Pam*—nodded grimly.

"I'm not the kind of woman to stand by and let someone hurt me." Except, hadn't she done just that? *No, dammit.* She'd fought back. Both times she'd fought back.

"You don't strike me as such."

Bella lifted her chin. "I'm not."

Pam nodded. "I believe you." A beat before, "Why don't you close your eyes and relax? It's a twenty-minute drive to the hospital."

"I'm—" Her gaze caught on movement outside of the car.

Henry slammed through the diner's door, skidding to a stop when he saw her in the front seat of the police cruiser, jaw dropping open, hand extending toward her.

Bella closed her eyes, blinking against the burn of tears.

She couldn't face him.

Not now.

Maybe not ever.

CHAPTER SEVEN

Henry

TILLY CAME UP BESIDE HIM. "You should go."

"What?" Henry blinked, clearing away the image of the blood on Isabella's pale face. Bright red and so much of it that it had covered her from temple to jaw bone.

He never should have left her in that alley.

"You should go after her," Tilly said again. "Frank and I can handle the kitchen."

"I—" He shook his head, tried for a second time. "I should stay and—"

Tilly sighed, hazel eyes taking on the slightest bit of disappointment. "Henry," she said. "Like it or not, she's yours, and you know you'll never forgive yourself if you don't go after her."

He dropped his chin to his chest, knew she was right. Like it or not, some part of him would always belong to Isabella. "Will you show Rob the security footage? There's a camera in the alley." He handed her the key to his office, where the cameras' hard drives were stored.

Tilly nodded. "Of course."

With that, he hustled over to his car and drove to the hospital. By the time he pushed through the doors to the emergency department, Isabella had already been taken into the back, but he did manage to flag down Melissa's friend, Haley, who promised to come and get him when Bella was ready for visitors.

And then he waited.

A familiar feeling when it came to this woman, though this situation was totally unique.

Rob texted him around an hour in, telling him he'd reviewed the footage and would be taking the hard drive it was backed up on.

Henry thanked him then tried and failed to hold back his question.

What did it show?

Rob's reply came a second later.

You know I can't tell you that.

Henry sighed.

Yeah, I know.

His phone buzzed.

Just know that he's a bastard and your girl fought back.

There was that phrase again, the whole of Darlington assuming that Bella was his. It was presumptuous and patently untrue, but then he thought of that asshole Sergio kissing her and worse, of him hurting Bella, and Henry knew that he'd never be able to affect disinterest.

Isabella was inside of him, woven deep and knotted tightly, and he'd never had any chance in Hell of excising her.

Not then. Not now. Not ever.

Haley waved him over to the counter. "She'll need to be admitted overnight. She has a slight brain hemorrhage—"

"*What?*" His gut clenched. Fuck, why had he left her alone with that bastard?

Haley touched his hand. "She's going to be okay. It's minor, and they're treating it with medication. Dr. Hamilton doesn't think she'll need surgery."

Medication. Doesn't think. Surgery. Henry's mind spun.

"Look," she said. "Isabella will be fine. She's conscious and her pain is under control. She . . ." Haley bit her lip. "She also asked me to tell you to go home."

Henry glared at her. "How does she even know I'm here?"

"Don't take that tone with me, Henry Miller. Lest you forget, I hauled your ass home once after you tossed your cookies in Mrs. Davidson's class, or did you forget?" Crossed arms, a narrow-eyed glare. "Do you *want* me to remind the town that your nickname for a time was Henry the Spewer? Because I still have the pictures."

Jesus.

This woman was insane.

"I am *not* insane," Haley snapped, and Henry could have kicked himself for being so off his game he'd said that aloud. "I'm protecting my patient. She told me I could give you the very basic details because she knew that you were stubborn enough to not leave without a modicum of assurance. And that's it. Legally, I'm required to safeguard her privacy."

"Hay." He sighed. "I can't just leave it at that—"

She shook her head. "I'm *legally* bound to follow her wishes. You're not her husband or even her emergency contact. And we both know that you definitely don't have power of attorney—"

"Fuck," he muttered, turning away and thrusting his hand through his hair.

"But—" her voice gentled softly. "I *do* know that the door to the department is undergoing maintenance and that it's not currently locked." He whirled around, hope springing to life. "And that she's in exam room four, at least until she gets moved upstairs."

Henry crossed over to Haley, gripped her by the shoulders, and kissed her cheek. "Thank you."

She waved him off. "Just don't be an asshole and make me regret my moment of weakness."

He nodded, hurrying over to the door Haley had indicated and slipping through. Luckily the waiting room was empty aside from him, their small county hospital rarely busy, especially in the early evening on a weekday. He checked the signs, following them until he found room four, and knocked quietly on the closed door.

"Come in," came Bella's voice, and Henry's heart hurt all over again to hear it rasp through the wooden panel. He was going to kill the bastard.

What kind of fucking name was Sergio anyway?

A sexy Italian one that Isabella had apparently wanted to marry.

Fuck.

"Hello?" she called louder. "You can come in."

Henry sighed, tried to focus and calm emotions that had been roiling like a pot about to boil over since Bella had reappeared in town.

Twenty-four hours.

Was that all it had been? It felt like a lifetime, like too much had changed for it to have only been one day.

"Enough," he muttered, forcing himself to focus as he pushed through the door.

Then almost went right back outside so he could hunt Sergio down and tear him to shreds. The side of her face was scraped up, and bruises had already begun to form on her cheekbone and around her eye. Her arm was bandaged, and an ice pack was positioned on her right hip.

He'd let that happen.

Her gaze dropped to the bed, but not before he saw shame cross her expression.

And, didn't she see? She didn't have a single thing to feel ashamed about. It was all on the fucking scum of the earth that was Sergio. It was on *Henry* for not recognizing the bastard for what he was, for not protecting her, for leaving her and—

"Why are you here?"

The ice in her tone made him smile. Somehow, it made him smile.

Because it reminded him of the first time he'd laid eyes on her.

She was the assistant pastry chef in his friend's restaurant, and he'd come in to meet Brian for an early lunch and to compare their thoughts on a local farm that wanted to sell its produce in gourmet New York eateries.

He hadn't been impressed with the produce, but he *had* been mesmerized by Isabella Mariano.

Irritated by his interruption, beautiful eyes sparking fire at him when he'd dared asked for a taste of the gelato she'd just taken out of the ice cream machine. She'd tossed her ponytail over one shoulder, huffed as she scooped some of the concoction into a bowl and all but tossed it at him.

Lavender and honey and his taste buds—and quite frankly—his heart had never recovered

She'd been fire tempered by frost, and he'd fallen headfirst for her.

And he *still* couldn't remember a single word from that meeting with Brian.

But the texture of that gelato, the way the flavors had exploded on his tongue, *that* he could remember.

"Hi," he said, tucking the memory safely away and moving to take the chair at her bedside. He forced lightness into his tone. "You look like you tangled with a very aggressive stand mixer and barely lived to tell the tale."

Her glare had been epic, but the mention of the stand mixer saved him.

Or at least he pretended it did.

Because her lips curved into a small smile and she glanced up at him. "Remember the cooking class?"

"When the so-called expert didn't know how to secure the attachment and it flew through the kitchen?" He grinned. "How could I possibly forget?"

Bella touched her uninjured cheek, the faintest white line visible. "It was the first time I had to have my face glued together. I didn't even know that was a thing." Her smile faded, and she shifted uncomfortably on the bed. "Apparently, I'm making it a regular occurrence."

"Is your hip hurting you?" He reached for the ice pack, intending to adjust it.

"I'm fine."

He raised a brow. "Reminiscing about Super Glue aside, you're definitely not fine. I mean, look at you—"

The wrong words.

Henry realized that exactly a heartbeat too late.

As in, they'd already crossed his lips, and the damage had been done.

Bella's face fell, any trace of amusement in her espresso eyes disappearing.

"I didn't mean it like that."

"I know." She started to shrug, broke off with a wince.

And silence.

"Bella, sweetheart, I'm sorry."

Her gaze flew to his, shock loosening her words. "What could *you* possibly have to be sorry for?"

"I shouldn't have left you alone." He caught the ice pack when she gingerly shifted in his direction. "I could tell you were uncomfortable, and I was so wrapped up in my own feelings that I—"

"Henry." She rested her palm on top of his. He hadn't even realized he'd been gripping the railing of the bed. "I left you, remember? You have nothing to be sorry about."

There was something in her tone that prickled on the edge of his consciousness, but before he could tug at the thought, she let go of his hand.

The contact shouldn't have made a difference.

It was the barest touch of skin against skin.

And yet, its absence was almost painful.

"You should go," she said, turning her head away. "I think that nice nurse already told you that much."

"Haley did try to give me the brush off."

Bella pressed her lips tightly together then grumbled, "Didn't work, apparently."

"No," Henry said, biting back a smile. "It didn't."

She huffed, not looking at him.

"And I already called Anastasia at the bed and breakfast," he announced. "She packed up your stuff for you and dropped it by my house."

Bella stared at him, mouth open in surprise.

"Is there anything you really need? Medication? A phone charger?"

Her teeth clacked together. "No," she gritted out.

"Okay, great." Henry crossed one ankle over the other. "So, we can just hang out and catch up."

"Catch. Up?"

"Yeah," he said. "Isn't that why you came back in the first place? You wanted to reconnect?"

"I—"

"I know I've wondered what you've been up to these last five years."

"It's—" Her jaw worked for a long moment. "We're not old friends, Henry. We parted on . . . " Bella trailed off.

"Bad terms?" he asked, feeling way more casual than he actually felt. "You could say that."

"I'm—you didn't even want to talk to me yesterday."

He leaned back in his chair. "Things are different today."

"Because Sergio hurt me?"

"Yeah."

She scowled.

"But also because I've never stopped thinking about you, Isabella."

She froze, presumably in shock, and though his casual position didn't change, Henry definitely didn't feel anywhere *near* casual about the statement that had just crossed his lips.

Maybe he'd thought it and maybe deep down he'd known it was the truth, but Henry hadn't planned on exposing himself to Bella, not when her betrayal was still so raw. Five years hadn't made the sight of her walking away from him disappear from his mind. Five years didn't erase the painful memories of nursing a broken heart, a dying father, and a devastated mother.

Five years didn't make the past go away.

But five years without Bella had taught him things, too.

He didn't want more years without her. He wanted more time *with* her.

She'd just opened her mouth to reply when there was a knock and the door swung open.

Haley popped her head in. "They're all ready for you upstairs," she announced cheerfully before pausing and glancing between them. "Everything okay in here?"

"We're fine," Bella said before Henry could order Haley to go right back out that door and not come back until Bella had told him what she'd been about to say.

"Good," Haley said then ignored him completely as she crossed over to the gurney. She unlocked the wheels, pulled the bags attached to Bella's IV off the pole and set them on the bed next to her. "Let's get you upstairs then and settled. The doctor ordered another CT to see about the hemorrhage, so no food until that reads clear, I'm sorry to say."

Bella groaned. "I don't think I could ever be one of those girls who fasts or even goes on a diet. The hunger is worse than the headache and dizziness. Henry," she said, seeming to suddenly remember he was still there. "You should go home and sleep."

He ignored that, rising from the chair.

"My guess is that you'll be able to have breakfast in the morning," Haley said and started to push the gurney out into the hall. "Tonight you'll rest, and we'll make sure you're on your way to recovery." She paused, glanced back at Henry, her expression decidedly leaning toward *well, are you coming?*

Oh, Henry was definitely coming.

He wasn't leaving his woman alone.

Not ever again.

CHAPTER EIGHT

Isabella

THE NICE NURSE, Haley, had lied.

Her night wasn't restful, not in the least.

She was poked and prodded all night, as the nurses checked all the regular vital signs—blood pressure, temperature, oxygen levels—but also were constantly monitoring her brain.

Not exactly comforting knowing she'd somehow managed to hit her head in the exact right way to cause a hemorrhage.

A hemorrhage that barely warranted the name, according to the neurologist who'd come in to check on her around midnight. She was trying not to freak out about the fact that her brain was bleeding.

But her brain was bleeding!

Still, the doctor had studied her scan then had put her through a series of strange exercises before assuring her she would be fine. Of course, the words didn't comfort her so much as the fact that aside from the nagging headache and dizziness, she actually felt better, too.

Her mind wasn't so foggy, and the pain was more migraine level and less her skull was too small for her brain.

Fingers on her cheek startled her.

"How are you feeling?"

Her eyes met Henry's. He hadn't left her side the entire evening, had even followed her down to the CT suite, though the tech had made him wait outside the room.

They hadn't talked much throughout the night and though he'd stayed in the room when Officer Harting—*Pam* had returned to take Bella's statement, he hadn't commented on her side of things.

His expression *had* turned deadly though.

Eventually, Pam had left, but Henry still hadn't spoken much, just watched her through lidded eyes all while studying her with an intensity that made her skin prickle. When she'd finally succumbed to sleep, it had been a welcome relief.

"Hungry," she whispered when his fingers brushed her cheek again.

He smiled, dark circles underneath his eyes. "If your scan is clear, I think breakfast might be on the menu. Though, I'm not sure how good hospital food is."

"I don't care about quality at the moment. I need quantity."

His lips twitched. "*That* I can arrange."

"What time is it?" she asked. Her room overlooked a street light and so the same dimness had filtered through the closed blinds all night, giving her no clue to the time. Then there was the fact that her cell phone was with the rest of her stuff.

At Henry's house.

They needed to talk about that.

Oh boy, did they.

But maybe not right now.

Because she was really freaking hungry.

Henry seemed to read her mind because he pushed out of the chair he'd been camped in for most of the night and stretched with a quiet groan. "I'll go and see if I can find the nurse. Maybe I can at least rustle you up some Jell-O."

"Oh, my God. That sounds amazing." Her stomach rumbled loudly. "Lime, please. Or at least, any flavor aside from grape."

He chuckled. "Is that your fine palate speaking?"

She grinned, this teasing, smiling Henry she knew, and it made her heart happy. "Absolutely."

He slipped out of the room, returning a few moments later with the nurse who nixed the idea of any food, even Jell-O, until a final scan was complete and read by the neurologist. She did let Bella have a cup of ice, though, along with a tiny container of apple juice. And somehow the little bit of sugar hitting her tongue was the best thing ever.

"I'll get everything moving," the nurse, a pleasant older woman named Alice, told her. "Breakfast is on the horizon."

"I've heard that before," Bella grumbled good-naturedly.

This time the nurse was right. Isabella was scanned, the images read and she was declared to be on the mend by the neurologist, and even a breakfast tray had been delivered to her room, all within two hours.

Lukewarm eggs and floppy bacon had never tasted so good.

She downed the side of sourdough toast, after slapping an obscene amount of butter and jam on it, and it was pretty much the best thing ever. *Ever.*

She was so focused on eating, she even forgot that Henry was in the room.

At least until he wiped a dab of jam from the corner of her mouth. Her breath froze in her lungs, eyes flying up to meet his then trailing down to his lips. He sucked the drop of strawberry sweetness off his thumb, and she would swear to God that she felt that suction on her—

Bella blinked.

She had a brain injury for fuck's sake. Not to mention two stitches on her temple, glue above her eyebrow, and abrasions all down her arm. She was a wreck and . . . Henry was still Henry.

Her body knew his.

Her body remembered how good it had been between them.

She released a shaky breath and picked up another slice of toast, finally remembering her manners. "Do you want it?"

His expression warmed. "No, sweetheart. I might go grab something from the cafeteria and sneak home for a shower though."

Bella bit her lip, knowing she had absolutely no right to want him to stay with her. Hell, she'd told him to go a half dozen times. He had his own life and had already sacrificed more than enough by spending the night with her.

But that didn't change the fact that she'd always felt better when Henry was near.

Mentally, she rolled her eyes at herself.

What had happened to being strong and finding herself?

How was that supposed to be true if she crumpled like a weakling just because she was a little bruised up?

This is hardly a normal situation, her brain—now bleed-free—reminded her.

That didn't change anything.

And great, now she'd gone around in mental circles long enough that Henry was looking at her with concern on his face.

"Of course," she told him. "You should check on the restaurant. I'm sure they're missing you."

"Tuesday is my day off." He frowned. "Are you feeling dizzy again or confused?"

No more than normal.

He grinned as though he'd read the thought in her mind though she knew for a fact that she hadn't spoken aloud.

She *better not* have spoken aloud.

"Get out of here," she ordered. "Go enjoy your day off. Th-thanks for staying. I'll pick up my stuff from your place as soon as possible."

He crossed his arms over his chest. "I'm coming back, Bella. And your stuff can stay at my house however long you need. I only had Anastasia drop it by because she'd told me you intended to check out today, and I didn't want you to have to pay for a night you were in the hospital."

"I—"

Thunderstorms filled his eyes as he glared down at her. "You're not considering going back to that asshole, are you? Is that why you want me to leave?"

"What?" She pushed the table holding the tray of food away from her. "*No.*"

"You were engaged to him."

"*Were* is the key word there," she snapped.

"It didn't seem so key when you asked me to cater your wedding."

Yup.

There was that.

"Henry," she began.

"It's none of my business," he said, holding his hands up, palms facing out. "But if the bastard was willing to do that to you in a public place, I'm terrified to think of what he might do to you in private—"

The blood left her face in a rush, leaving her almost as dizzy as she'd been the night before.

"You already know that, don't you?"

She swallowed. "It's why I left. My father . . . well, he was persistent that I marry Sergio, and I—" She shook her head. "Sergio had me convinced that he loved me."

"What did he do?"

A careful question, and yet Bella easily felt its quiet deadliness. "He showed me he didn't."

Henry dropped his hand onto her thigh, squeezed gently. "That's not an answer."

"It's enough." She blew out a breath. "I left and didn't expect him to follow me. Hell, I'd half-convinced myself the whole thing was an accident. And then in the alley, I thought I'd explain that I didn't want to marry him and he'd leave—"

"I take it he wasn't happy."

"Apparently, my father is threatening to take away his role in the business if he didn't bring me to heel."

"I'm not going back," she added when he didn't say anything. "I won't. I—"

She broke off.

"You what?"

"I wanted to live my life for myself."

Truth.

But not all of it.

She'd left because of Sergio and her father and knowing that she finally needed to find her own way, but she'd come to Darlington, Utah of all places, for a very specific reason.

Henry.

He cupped her unbruised cheek. "You deserve that."

"Why aren't you angry with me anymore?" she blurted, covering his hand with her own when he would have stepped back. "I hurt you. You asked me to come, and I couldn't—"

"I realized that I'd been blaming you for my father's death."

Isabella's heart stopped.

How did he know? How could he possibly know? She'd—

"But I finally got my head out of my ass." Henry slipped his hand free and tugged lightly on a strand of her hair. "My dad had many chances to change his lifestyle. The experimental surgery was successful, and we were beyond lucky that the hospital had a fund for patients in his situation—those who couldn't afford the recommended treatment—because that meant my mom wasn't stuck paying off hundreds of thousands of dollars in medical bills."

Bella began breathing again. He didn't know. His father *had* gotten the treatment.

"But he didn't change after the surgery." Henry sighed. "I loved my dad, but he wasn't much for following orders, even from a medical professional. The second heart attack took him three months after he'd gotten out of rehab."

"I'm so sorry."

He shrugged. "Yeah, me, too. But I felt worse for my mom. She'd thought they'd come through it all and they'd have many more years together. Then boom, he was gone."

"But you lost him, too."

"Yeah," he said with a sigh. "I did."

"And I let you deal with that alone." Bella had gone because she hadn't seen another way, but she still wasn't sure it had been the right thing to do. In the end, it hadn't saved Henry's dad and it had cost her so, so much.

No.

It *had* been the right thing.

She would have known that she hadn't done everything in her power to save Henry's dad. Money meant nothing to her own father, and it had given Henry and his family a chance. She'd been the tradeable commodity in the deal.

So, she'd traded herself for experimental surgeons and fully-paid hospital bills.

In exchange, she'd been the perfect daughter for five years.

But she'd done her time. She wasn't going to marry Sergio, and her father could keep his money.

"I wasn't alone," he said softly.

She was glad for that, would rather it be her who'd been alone. Hurting, aching, desperate to call him and confess why she'd left. Bella felt that same urge in this moment, to tell him she'd left for noble reasons, but it didn't change the fact that she *had* gone.

She'd sold herself to her father.

Yes, Isabella had chosen it, thinking it was the only thing she could do when she'd discovered that Henry and his family couldn't pay for his father's surgery, but that didn't make it any less shameful.

Especially when it was all for naught.

He'd died anyway.

God, when she'd heard that Henry's dad, Brad, had died, she'd blamed herself. She hadn't chosen the right doctor, hadn't pushed her father for enough money.

But it hadn't been her fault.

And it still didn't change a fucking thing.

She'd left. Henry had lost his dad.

"I'm glad you weren't alone," she said softly.

"Yeah," he said. "Me, too."

They stared at each other for a long moment until a knock at the door forced their gazes apart. Alice popped her head in.

"Good news," she said. "It looks like you'll be discharged by this evening. The doctor will be in to discuss it with you soon."

Bella thanked her then glanced up at Henry and pretended to make a face, desperate to lighten the mood between them, to firmly stow the past back where it belonged. "I thought you said you were going to shower."

He smirked, sniffed under one armpit then the other. "I stink that bad, huh?"

"Worse than that time you burnt the entire batch of minestrone soup." She shook her head in mock-reproof. "It was an eight-quart pot. I don't know how you managed that."

He raised one brow. "I seem to remember one very specific distraction."

Bella's cheeks heated, remembering exactly how good that *distraction* had been. "Get out of here," she ordered.

"I'm going"—he kissed the top of her head—"but I'll be back in a little bit, okay?"

"I'm—"

"Don't say fine." He strode for the door. "I'll be back."

She huffed. "The least you could do is say that in your best Arnold impression."

"You still like the *Terminator* movies?" He paused on the threshold.

"Of course." She rolled her eyes. "They never get old."

"Good," he said. "You and me, *Terminator* marathon at my place tonight."

No, that wasn't going to happen. She was going back to the bed and breakfast and would find a place to stay in the next few days. There would be no crashing at Henry's house. She wasn't a weakling with no other plans or a place to stay.

Bella would find a way to make it work.

On her own.

"I'm—" she called.

The door shut behind him, cutting her off.

And Isabella flopped back in the bed, dizzy from the turn of events. Anger to acceptance. A dash of heat. Decisions that had wrecked everything but hadn't made one lick of difference.

But Henry didn't hate her.

She'd take that.

She still wasn't staying at his house though.

———

"STOP ARGUING," he growled. "Your brain was *bleeding* yesterday. You're not staying alone at the bed and breakfast."

"I wouldn't be alone," she snapped, batting his hands away when he tried to lift her from the wheelchair the hospital had insisted on pushing her out in. "Anastasia lives there."

He crossed his arms, jaw flexing as she maneuvered herself into his car.

Would it have been easier to let him help her?

Yes.

Less painful?

Probably.

Were those two facts going to change her mind about letting him help?

Hell no.

And . . . *there*. She made it into the seat without falling flat on her face, so that was a win. Bella had to take them where they came because she had the feeling she was going to lose the battle about staying at Henry's house.

He pushed the wheelchair back to the nurse waiting at the hospital's doors. She'd wisely chosen to step away from their argument.

"Your stuff is at my house," Henry said, plunking into the driver's seat and starting up the car. "It makes sense to stay there. At least for tonight."

"Fine."

He'd been shifting into drive, but her agreement had him freezing. "What?"

"It's a rational point," she said.

"I know it is," Henry replied. "Hence, me suggesting it. I just didn't expect you to be—"

"Rational?"

His hands rose in surrender. "You said it, not me."

She snorted.

"I was going to say something to the effect that our arguments never used to resolve themselves this easily."

Bella shrugged. "Maybe we've both matured."

A beat of quiet before they both started laughing.

"Not likely," he said, reaching over and lightly squeezing her hand. "I don't think stubbornness declines with age." He put the car into drive and pulled out of the parking lot.

"Henry?"

His eyes were on the road as he checked for oncoming traffic. "Hmm?"

"I like arguing with you."

He wasn't looking at her, but she still saw his cheek crease as he smiled. "I like arguing with you, too, sweetheart."

And then Bella shut up and let Henry drive her home.

CHAPTER NINE

Henry

HHE LIFTED A SLEEPING Isabella out of his car just over twenty minutes later, and Henry realized he could have saved himself an argument if he'd just agreed with Bella about taking her to the B&B and then just driven her around until she fell asleep.

Note to self for next time.

Stifling a chuckle, he carried her through the garage and into the house.

His phone buzzed as he set her on his bed, and he tugged the blanket up and around her before quietly leaving the room. Another vibration came just as he extracted his cell from his pocket.

Henry glanced at the screen and saw that it was a message from Rob. And Kelly.

"Shit," he muttered, knowing that word had gotten out and it was only a matter of time before his friends descended on his house to get a glimpse of Isabella.

Thus, he dealt with Rob first. It was easier, a request that Henry bring Bella to the station the following morning. He sent a reply, telling Rob that he'd text when she was up the next day.

Kelly was more problematic.

She didn't know anything that had happened in New York.

And if she found out that Bella had hurt him so deeply, his best friend's protectiveness would most definitely come out.

But then he read her text.

I already like her because you like her, just remember that before you try to push me away. I love you.

Well, didn't he feel like an asshole?

It's not that, Kel.

Lies.

I've known you since kindergarten. Don't try that B.S. with me.

Of course, she'd called him on it. He'd always had a fondness for strong women—Kelly, Bella, Melissa, his mother—and had been lucky enough to have plenty of them in his life. But in this moment, after battling with Bella, with Kel holding his feet to the fire, he thought he might see the appeal of a doormat.

He snorted, walking down the hall to the kitchen.

Okay, that was another lie.

There was something about a woman with fire inside her that was utterly entrancing. No, it didn't always make things easy nor did it make for smooth sailing, but he wouldn't trade Bella for a limp dish towel.

After grabbing a beer from the fridge, he crossed over to his couch and flicked on the TV, pondering what to say to Kel.

Eventually, he decided on the truth.

She's the one from NYC, Kel. I need time to figure it out.

A heartbeat later and she'd confirmed why she was his best friend.

I figured. Just know I'm here when you come out the other side. Or if you need a midnight vent session. God knows the twins get me up often enough ;)

He popped the top on his beer.

I love you.

His phone vibrated.

That's because I'm extremely loveable.

Henry shook his head, but he was smiling. He'd gotten lucky in kindergarten when he'd punched that little asshole who'd been tormenting Kelly. It was an auspicious start to a friendship, but one he couldn't regret.

Of course, he was also *really* lucky she'd turned him down when he'd proposed.

He picked up the remote and scrolled through the channels. There was a Gold Hockey game on—not the closest team, but one of the local kids had been drafted by them a few years back, and Henry always got a kick out of watching Blue on the ice.

The kid had moves.

During second intermission, the hairs on the back of his neck prickled. He glanced over his shoulder and saw Bella hobbling down the hall.

May the hockey gods give him patience because Henry was damn sure that the doctor who'd discharged her had made Bella promise to take it easy on that leg.

He pushed to his feet, ready to remind her of exactly that, when she stumbled.

Two quick steps and he was there, catching her arm and helping her over to the couch.

"Thanks," she murmured.

He grunted, grabbed her bottle of pain pills off the table and handed her one, along with a bottle of water he'd snagged from the kitchen.

Bella didn't argue with him, and that told Henry enough about her condition. She was hurting, and he needed to give her space, no matter the tempting picture she made sprawled out on his couch.

Her lips curved into a tremulous smile after she'd handed him back the bottle. "I didn't realize you had such a long hall."

He snorted, his own lips turning up. "Either that or you're stubborn to a fault?"

She shrugged—or attempted to anyway, aborting the motion mid-move with a wince. "We've established that fact already." Her nose wrinkled before he could confirm or deny that particular statement . . . which was probably a good thing. "I need to get out of these clothes."

Henry's gaze drifted down. She was wearing a pair of donated pale blue scrubs, since he hadn't thought to bring her a change of clothes. Not that he was complaining—the set was slightly too small, emphasizing the curve of her breasts and hips, dipping low on the front.

Yes, he knew she was convalescing.

No, he wasn't dead.

Isabella was beautiful, and sex had never been their problem. Since he'd begun acknowledging his own role in the events from five years before, his brain was having a hell of a time reminding his body that she'd given him absolutely no reason to think that she might still be attracted to him.

Also, this just in, he was an asshole to be popping a boner when she was injured.

What was he? Sixteen and hormone ridden?

Henry was a grown man, and he shouldn't be studying that exposed V of skin between her breasts like it was an oasis and he was a parched man in the desert.

But good intentions or not, he *had* noticed that sliver of skin.

And he couldn't *un*-notice it.

Not as she shifted to lie sideways on the couch so the cushions supported her hip. Not as he helped her. Not as the too-tight top slid up and his hand accidentally brushed the soft skin on her side.

He jerked it back, but it was too late. The shock of awareness had hit him like a ton of bricks.

Bella's breath hitched, eyes flashing wide.

"That—"

Henry straightened. "I'll go grab you some food. I'm sure you're still hungry."

White teeth nibbled on a pink bottom lip. He wanted it to be *his* teeth, *his* mouth.

Not the right time. Too soon. Too—

"Henry?"

He blinked, focused back on the woman in front of him, instead of the swirling mass of thoughts in his mind. "Yeah?"

"Will you touch me again?"

CHAPTER TEN

Bella

Damn.

She'd broken him.

Bella had asked him to touch her and in response, he was rooted in place, jaw clenched, shoulders stiff.

"Henry?" she prodded.

That got him moving . . . or at least blinking. And after a moment, he glanced over at her, eyes tracing down over her body and jaw tightening further.

Because he wanted to touch her? Or—worse—because he didn't?

"You're probably hungry," he said, angling his body away from hers.

Because he didn't want her.

Damn.

She couldn't lie. That hurt. Here she was drooling over the man, admiring the way he'd filled out over the last few years. He'd gotten harder, muscles more defined, thicker in all the right places, not to mention the scruff on his jaw he was sporting. She wanted that rubbing in *all* sorts of places.

Her throat, her breasts, between her thighs—

But he didn't want that. He'd forgiven her, and that alone was enough.

"Yeah," she agreed. "Food would be great."

So would an orgasm, but Bella was trying to be grateful for what she had. She was safe, Henry was there, and even though she'd woken to images of Sergio's hands were wrapped around her throat again—

"What is it?" A finger brushed the back of her hand, and she opened her eyes to see Henry had come close.

He was touching her, though not in the way she really wanted.

Greedy mofo, wasn't she?

She forced a smile. "I'm—"

One fingertip pressed to her lips, stalling the rest of her statement. "You finish that sentence, and I'll forget my intentions to leave you alone to heal."

"Why would I need to be left alone?" He didn't move his hand when she replied, and the sensation of that roughened finger skimming over her lips as they moved sent shivers down her spine.

"Because you're hurting."

"Not so much anymore."

He slid his hand lower, the back skimming along her throat, fluttering over one collarbone then the other. "Then why do your eyes look like that?"

Bella frowned. "Like what?"

"Shadowed."

Her lungs froze. "I'm just tired is all."

"Nope. That's not it."

Ugh. There were two reasons, dammit, that her eyes were quote-unquote *shadowed*, and she didn't want to share either of them with Henry. "Do you have anything you can heat up for me?" she asked, instead of divulging the truth. "I really am quite hungry."

One brown brow lifted.

Waiting for an answer.

In the end, she told him the lesser of two evils because she'd rather be viewed as horny than a pathetic coward who'd fled the bedroom at the first sign of a nightmare.

"Fine." She huffed. "I want you, okay? You're sexy and gorgeous and my pussy has been very lonely as of late—" She clamped one hand to her mouth, closed her eyes.

The damned pain pill was loosening her tongue because she had *not* just said that.

"You and Sergio didn't—"

The name made her flinch and quickly shake her head.

Bella reveled in the feeling for a moment, the swish-swish of her brain floating in her skull. She almost would have thought she was drunk, except no booze.

Just very strong pain pills apparently.

Well, note to future self, no more of those.

"No," she said. "Sergio and I did. At first. Just lately, I couldn't—"

This was wrong. Telling Henry about her bedroom life with Sergio.

"Couldn't what?"

She dropped her head back to the arm of the couch. "It doesn't matter."

He sank onto the cushion near her feet, plunking them into his lap and rubbing the arches. "It matters to me."

"He couldn't make me come, okay?" She sighed. "No one can, except for you and my vibrator"—her lips pursed—"and only one of those is always at the ready."

"First, know that I'll be circling back to the orgasm thing in a moment because I'm *always* ready when you're around." Henry shifted his hips, and her foot bumped against—*oh*, she liked *that* a whole hell of a lot. "But more importantly, why don't you think I want you?"

"Because I hurt you. Because you don't want to touch me and maybe things will never be the same between us again. Because you got all pretty and handsome, and *my* boobs are saggy, and I've got cellulite and—" She squealed when Henry reached for the hem of her top. "What are you doing?"

"Seeing what's sagged."

She slapped his hands away. "Not a chance, Henry Miller."

He chuckled. "There's my girl." A squeeze to her feet. "I'm going to say this once, so pay attention."

Bella raised one finger. "Just so you're aware, I think that pill has gone to my head." Her voice dropped to a whisper. "I think I'm high."

"Focus," Henry said, though he was smiling. "I guess I'll be open to saying it twice, in case my lightweight of a woman doesn't hear it the first time—"

"Hey."

"I gave you a quarter of a pill."

"So?"

"So *nothing*," he said before his eyes went serious enough that any more words stalled in her throat. "You're beautiful. End of story. I want you even though you're hurting and slightly high. I've wanted you from the moment that I first saw you in Brian's kitchen." He reached up to cup her cheek. "Wanting isn't the issue."

Her heart skipped a beat. "Then what is?"

"It's been five years."

Her brows pulled down. "Yeah, so?"

"You were just engaged to a bastard that hurt you."

"S-Sergio doesn't matter."

Henry sighed. "Except he does. Because he's the reason for the shadows. Maybe you *are* worried that things between us won't be the same if we try to see where things go." A shrug. "But that's not all of it. And you know what? I hope it's *not* the same between us. I hope we've grown up a little because I want things between us to end differently."

She sucked in a breath.

"In fact"—his eyes warmed—"I don't know that I want them to end at all."

"Henry—"

"I know." He sat up. "I know it's crazy and too soon, and while I definitely want to take things slow between us, I also know that I've never felt one iota for another woman what I feel for you. You've always meant *so* much, sweetheart, and I want to see where things go—"

"I'm high."

He smirked. "Yes, I know."

"No," she said. "I must be really, crazy high because you did not just say those things, Henry. You did *not* just give me hope. You *didn't*—"

"I'm right there with you, baby. Big feelings, big risk, big hope."

"But I hurt you," she whispered.

"You weren't ready, and I pushed." He shrugged. "I wish you hadn't left, that you'd stuck around and explained your feelings, but we can't go back now."

Oh, God. She had to tell him why she'd left. She understood now. It wasn't shameful. She'd sacrificed everything for the man she loved, and Henry had to know that.

He had to know he meant *that* much.

"I—"

"I want to forget about the past. I want you to stay, and we can see if we're as compatible now as we were back then."

"I want that, too, but—"

He kissed her.

She was dizzy from the pain pill, from her emotions, from the heavy weight of the past, but the feel of Henry's lips against hers made all of that disappear.

Heat was the first thing to take over. It began at her mouth, spreading down and outward, making the tips of her fingers tingle, her breasts swell and ache, her stomach flutter, and her thighs press tightly together, an ache of an altogether different kind filling the space in between.

She wanted him on top of her. Inside her—

Bella gasped when his tongue slid into her mouth, tangling with hers. He'd moved so he was alongside her, his back to the cushions and his deliciously hard chest against her side. Fingers wove into her hair, coaxing her head back, as he brought their mouths more firmly together.

Oh, God.

He kept his hands in her hair and though she wanted them to move lower, to tease and soothe all her various aches, she knew he was taking it slow.

Well, if a heart-shatteringly, hot as fuck kiss that had almost reduced her to ashes could be considered *slow*.

Regardless, aside from their bodies touching lengthwise, Henry's hands were decidedly less busy than his mouth. But that didn't mean *hers* had to be. She rested them on his chest, squeezing the yummy pair of pecs she found there for a moment before sliding lower.

Henry broke away, hot puffs of air teasing her lips.

Bella tilted her head, wanting his mouth again, but he carefully extracted himself and sat up.

"I think I promised you food."

She propped herself up on her elbows, trying desperately to clear her spinning mind as he slid from behind her and found his feet. "Henry—"

"Dangerous." He pressed a kiss to her forehead. "Beautiful woman." One more kiss before he turned and headed into the kitchen, the sound of pots and pans and cheerful whistling drifting into the living room.

When he returned a few minutes later, two plates in hand, and Bella saw what he'd made her, her heart swelled with hope all over again.

Maybe this time they would be different.

Because he'd made her a Cobb salad.

CHAPTER ELEVEN

Henry

HE WAS COOKING for the breakfast rush.

He definitely didn't want to be, but Frank had caught a cold, Michelle, his other full-timer, was working the evening shift, and Steven, the part-time chef he was training, was away on a trip with his girlfriend that they'd both been saving up for. Henry wasn't about to ruin that.

Bella had fallen asleep over salads, and so he'd carried her into the bedroom, tucking her safely under the blankets, knowing that her body needed all the rest it could get.

He'd slept in the spare bedroom and had woken to the smell of freshly brewed coffee.

Yeah, he could get used to that. Not the sleeping alone on the cramped twin bed part, but the waking up to find a beautiful woman in his house.

He especially could get used to the sight of Bella in his kitchen. She'd thrown together a crepe batter, sliced berries, and freshly whipped cream.

All before five in the morning.

The sun hadn't been up, the call to his cell had woken him for a shift that wasn't normally his, and so he could have still been sleeping—and he was old enough to really appreciate his sleep—but Henry hadn't been able to summon up one fuck to give.

Not when he was able to watch Bella cook crepes for a few minutes, her hips swaying slightly from side to side as she hummed a soft song.

Obviously, she felt better, and the delicious breakfast she'd made had been a nice by-product, but Henry hadn't been able to shake the rightness of the moment.

Bella was right.

And he could still taste her on his tongue, even though it had been hours since he'd dropped her off at the police station, even though he'd tasted a plethora of other dishes since eating her crepes—

He smirked as he imagined Kel chiming in with a comment along the lines of *"So that's what the kids are calling it nowadays?"*

So wrong.

And yet so right because he'd like to eat Bella's—

"Fuck." Henry hissed out a pained breath and whipped his hand back. He'd burnt himself because he was spending too much time focusing on Bella's *crepes* and not enough time on the growing pile of tickets in front of him. "Shit," he muttered, grabbing the pan off the heat and sticking his hand under a stream of cold water for a few precious seconds.

It was enough to take the edge off the pain and to reduce the burn to a dull throb.

Henry had burned himself often enough to know that the injury would kindly remind him of its presence throughout the day, but he didn't have any more time to waste.

The thing about breakfast was that it had to be made fast and served even faster. No one wanted to eat cold eggs or bacon or pancakes. Of course, that meant he had to have way too many pans working at the same time and that he definitely didn't have time to be slowed down by a burn.

He dried his hands on a towel and slid the pan back onto the burner, keeping his head down and his mind focused on cooking until he'd dug himself out of the hole he'd made, a good half hour later.

Sweat soaked through his T-shirt, and the front of his apron was splattered with grease and pancake batter and—

"You used to cook a lot more cleanly."

He'd be lying if he'd said his heart hadn't skipped a beat when he looked up and saw Bella leaning against the door, a smile teasing the corners of her mouth.

Her eyes were brighter today, her shoulders more relaxed.

Even the bruising and abrasions on her face were beginning to fade.

"I learned from the best," he said, stepping away from the stove and checking for any new tickets. Figuring that he had at least a couple minutes, Henry stripped off his apron and hung it on a peg then took Bella's hand and led her down the hall to his office.

She scoffed but followed him. "My workstation was always clean."

"Is that what you call being doused in flour?"

Her eyes narrowed. "That was one time, and you know it was because the bag had a tear in it."

"If you say so," he teased.

She growled, trying to extricate her hand from his, but they'd reached his office, so he just tugged her over the threshold, shut the door behind them, and lowered his head to hers.

Her hands came up to his shoulders and he half-expected her to push him away, but then they slid around the back of his neck and pulled him closer.

So. Fucking. Good.

Her tongue danced with his, darting in and out in a rhythm they'd perfected five years before and they stayed like that, kissing until his lungs screamed for air. Henry drew back, but he needed to keep touching her. He slid his hands up and down her sides, bent to nip at her jaw, her throat.

"Henry," she moaned and one leg wrapped around his waist.

He barely had a brain cell left to register the blip that came with his woman potentially hurting herself from the action, but then she tilted her pelvis, aligning it firmly against his cock and groaning in pleasure.

The single cell poofed away like so much smoke.

He lifted her, pressing her spine to the door and took her mouth in another head-spinning kiss.

It was glorious. It was absolute heaven.

Until the knock at the door.

"Henry?" came Rachelle's voice. She was one of the two waitresses on the schedule that morning.

He cleared his throat, cock aching, chest heaving. "Yeah?"

"We've got a bunch of tickets piling up."

Bella slid one leg to the floor then the other, and the loss of feeling her pressed so intimately against him was almost enough to make Henry cry.

"Just changing my shirt," he called. "Be out in two minutes."

"Roger that," Rachelle said. "Did Isabella find you?"

Yes, the whole town now knew Isabella by name, and their protectiveness for him had morphed into sympathy and protectiveness for her. All of that was thanks to Esther's social media prowess.

He wanted to be her when he grew up.

Though, maybe minus the ogling.

"Not yet," he lied.

"Hmm. I'll go look for her, tell her you were changing, and that you'll be back in the kitchen in a minute."

"Thanks," he said.

Bella giggled as they listened to the sound of Rachelle's footsteps moving back down the hall.

"Hush you," he said, making sure she was steady before whipping around to find a clean T-shirt. He tugged off his sweaty one and tossed it to the side, then turned in a rush when he heard her make a noise that sounded like choking. "You oka—"

"Oh, thank you, Jesus," she murmured, eyes on his chest, his stomach, lower.

"Bella, sweetheart, you can't look at me like that," he groaned.

She licked her lips.

And fuck, but his cock threatened to break in half.

"Put on the damn shirt," she hissed, slamming her eyes closed and turning to scrabble for the door handle.

Her actions weren't in the correct order, obviously, and so she was still fumbling around by the time Henry shrugged on the shirt and crossed back over to her. "It's safe to look now," he said, brushing her hands away and turning the knob. "Come on. You can keep me company in the kitchen."

Better than him stripping her naked in his office or burning the entire restaurant down, he realized with a sigh as they slipped back into the kitchen, because he'd forgotten to turn a burner off. Luckily, it was his practice to keep everything except for the actual food cooking away from the open flames, and them staying on for hours on end *wasn't* unusual. Since nothing was cooking at the moment, everything was good.

But still, he didn't typically leave the flames unattended.

He'd been too cautious to risk it after his father had started a grease fire.

The right practice, he'd decided long ago, was to shut everything off if it was going to be unattended, even for a few minutes.

Apparently, the cautious part of his brain had left the building when Bella had shown up in his kitchen.

Be smart, H-man. But don't forget to live.

Hearing his father's voice, even just in his mind, was like a punch directly to the gut. The words were one of his favorite sayings.

Don't forget to live.

Well, Henry certainly felt alive for the first time in years.

Bella tugged her hand from his then walked over and grabbed two clean aprons, dropping one over her head before handing him the other. She clapped her hands together. "All right, chef. Where do we start?"

"No, sweetheart." He pointed to the stool. "You should rest."

She rolled her eyes. "I'll just remind you before that pile of tickets gets any bigger that your orders don't work on me and that all arguments end in my favor."

"Not all—" he began then broke off with a sigh when she raised a brow.

Okay, fine, even if it wasn't *all* of them, Henry definitely didn't have time for an argument in *this* instance.

He thought fast, picking up tickets and scanning them, trying to find an item that wouldn't tax her too much.

"Can you do pancakes?" he asked.

Pancakes were a safe bet, especially with breakfast winding down and the batter already made.

She scoffed. "With one arm tied behind my back."

Henry scooped up a stool and placed it in front of the griddle. "How about with a chair under your bottom instead?"

Bella rolled her eyes, but she didn't argue about that, so Henry considered it a win.

"Ready?" he asked, going back to the tickets and picking up the first one.

"Yes, chef."

His lips twitched at her pert response before his amusement faded and he began calling out items.

The next couple of hours passed in a flash.

Breakfast turned to lunch and pancakes became grilled cheese and patty melts, and Henry couldn't remember a time he'd had as much fun in the kitchen as he was having that day. Bella was tart and endearing in equal terms, and she was scarily efficient, having familiarized herself with the kitchen in record time.

When he'd questioned her about it, she'd shrugged and said it was like the restaurants they'd worked at while in New York.

Henry supposed that was true.

He'd reorganized after his father died. Aside from everything needing a deep clean, Henry hadn't been able to work in the cluttered space. He hadn't had the brainpower or energy to come up with his own system, and so he'd transplanted one that he knew like the back of his hand.

The diner's kitchen was pristine. It was organized. And it was filled to the brim with Bella.

Henry decided he liked it that way.

She wiped her forehead on a towel after they finished the final lunch rush ticket, and he wanted to kiss her all over again.

But he didn't.

Because when he kissed this women, his mind went to mush, and Michelle was due in at any moment. But then Bella smiled up at him, a few strands of deep brown hair having slid free of her ponytail to curl around her face. She was incredible and . . . he forgot about being good.

He needed to live.

Henry pressed his mouth to hers the exact moment Michelle strode into the kitchen, bellowing, "The savior is here! Oh gross! Stop sucking face. That's not sanitary."

Bella jumped back from him, eyes widening.

"Get on tickets, Michelle," he told his employee. "All the prep is done for tonight."

"Wow, you can kiss *and* cook?" She raised a brow.

He glared. "You're fired."

Bella gasped, but Michelle just grinned. "He's kidding," she told Bella. "Henry fires me at least once a week."

"Unfortunately, she does *not* stay fired," he grumbled.

Bella's lips twitched. He slipped off his apron, helped her out of hers. "Call me if you need anything."

"I won't."

He sighed. "Humor me."

Michelle sighed. "Okay, I promise if I get into an existential food crisis, I will call you because I do *not* need help with dinner service." She pointed to the door. "Now go forth and kissy face. I've got the diner."

They exchanged goodbyes and waves before heading out into the hall.

"Now what?" Bella asked as they stopped long enough in his office for him to retrieve his wallet and car keys.

He thought about that for a long moment.

"Everything good at the station?"

She hesitated for the briefest moment before nodding. That short delay had Henry making a mental note to confirm things with Rob later. But for now, he wanted to spend some time with Bella outside of the kitchen.

"Want to see something cool?"

CHAPTER TWELVE

Bella

HER BREATH CAUGHT as she stepped out of Henry's car.

Rolling hills of green for as far as the eye could see. The wide-open space was dotted with the occasional tree, but the real show-stealer was the sky. It was absolutely beautiful in shades of orange and red and blue.

How did it seem larger than life here in Utah? It wasn't as if she'd never looked up at the sky before.

Was it Henry?

Or maybe it was the fact that she was finally making some decisions for herself.

She'd left. Her father wouldn't control her any longer.

And she had Henry . . . or at least a potential with him.

So, dammit, she was allowed to feel a little buoyant and hopeful and—

Fingers brushed the space between her eyebrows. "What's got you looking so fierce?"

She turned to him. "I was thinking that I've stared up at the sky my entire life and that I've never seen it look so beautiful. Also," she added before he could reply. "I was thinking how lucky I was to have a second chance with you and vowing not to screw it up."

He snorted. "*I'm* the lucky one."

"No, I'm—" Bella stopped, smirking up at him. "Is this our version of I-love-you more/No-I-love-*you*-more?"

"God, I hope not." He slipped an arm around her waist, pausing when she stiffened in surprise to ask, "This okay?"

She hurried to nod. "It's"—her teeth found her lip, bit down—"actually really nice."

"Actually nice?"

"Don't push it." She glared.

"Come on," he said with a chuckle. "This isn't what I wanted to show you. Or not all of it anyway." He led her over the crest of a hill, and she gaped at the huge boulder perched on the opposite side. "It's silly, but this has been my place since I was little."

Bella let him help her up on top of the giant rock. It was taller than her, but a series of foot and hand holds made it easy enough to scale. Her hip gave only the slightest protest as she pulled herself on top.

"Wow," she murmured.

The view was even prettier from there. A river snaked through a valley in the distance, spreading a deep emerald green along its length.

He pointed to the right. "That's Roosevelt Ranch over there."

Squinting, she could make out a few buildings tucked into the landscape. "Ah, the home of my aborted wedding," she said with a sigh. "It looks as gorgeous as the pictures made it seem. Is it true that the stables are as big as the house?"

"Since Kel enlarged them, yes." He tucked back a strand of hair that had come loose from her ponytail. "How did Sergio know about Roosevelt Ranch?"

"He caught me looking up Darlington." She wrinkled her nose. "I know I shouldn't say caught because it implies I was doing something wrong. The truth was that I kept tabs on you over the years. The diner's Yelp page is bookmarked on my laptop."

"What?"

"Pathetic, I know. I'd vowed I'd stop when I got married, but I'd wanted to make sure you were okay, and that meant I spent a lot of time searching for news articles about you or Darlington."

"Bella—"

"Talk about silly," she said with a laugh, words coming faster because the fact that she'd cyber-stalked her ex was critically embarrassing. "But I knew about Roosevelt Ranch because it came up in the news a lot for its breeding program." She shrugged. "I used to pretend that I was here instead of there"—and she was venturing into dangerous territory—"so this view living up to expectations is amazing."

"Sweetheart—"

"I also heard about murderous deer and a drug ring that involved a corrupt FBI agent, but that was more of a national story—"

His finger pressed to her lips, cutting off the flow of words.

One large hand plunked onto her thigh, squeezed gently. "There's a lot to unpack there. Hold tight," he added when she opened her mouth to reply. "Because I think what's most important is for me to know why you wanted to be here instead of there." He bent so his eyes were level with hers. "Sweetheart, if you wanted to come, why did you wait for years?"

That was the question of the hour.

Her gaze flitted to the hills. "It's complicated."

"I've got time for complicated."

Bella wavered for a moment more. If she told him the truth, would it make things better or worse? She didn't want him to feel bad that she'd done what she'd done, but at the same time, she needed him to know that she'd loved him enough to sacrifice for him.

And in the end, *that* was what decided it for her.

Henry mattered. He needed to know that.

"We met in New York."

He nodded. "Yeah, that's right."

"We fell in love there, we cooked and lived together and were building a future with each other."

"Yes." It was more cautious now.

"But I was lying to you then. Not about us," she rushed to say. "Just about my life back home. I made it seem like my family supported my decision to move away and go to culinary school." She shook her head. "The truth is that they were adamantly against it, and it was only because my mother left me a small trust fund after she passed that I was able to go.

"My father controlled *everything*. What my mother and I wore, what we ate, what I studied at university." Bella blew out a breath, remembering the misery of those years. Things had gotten slightly easier when her mother had fallen ill because they hadn't been trotted out to functions every night of the week like prized bulls. But then her mother had died, and things had gotten exponentially harder.

"I didn't know," he said.

Bella smiled, though she knew it was sad. "No one did. I was really good at pretending. But obviously, my mother knew what he was like, and she made sure the money she left me was in my name only."

On her death bed, she'd forced Isabella to promise her that she would go after her dream.

It was what had given her the courage to go to culinary school in the first place.

And pay for it all up front, in case her father found a way to wrest away control of that money.

She hadn't considered failing or not liking it, not for a moment.

That had been her chance to get out.

"My father thought it was just me sowing my wild oats, that I would run out of money and come home, but he underestimated me."

Henry smiled and cupped her cheek. "What did you do?"

"I graduated, got a job in New York. A shitty one at first and a shitty apartment to go with it. But it was mine, and I was finally *living*. It was fabulous."

"I used to love watching you in the restaurant," he murmured. "You'd take such joy in the process."

She sighed, resting her head on his shoulder. "I did love it."

"So then what happened?"

"I met you. We fell in love." She hesitated. "And your dad got sick."

He stiffened.

"It's not like you think," she whispered. "I remember all the phone calls, how upset you were when things weren't looking good. I-I overheard you and your mom talking about how you couldn't afford the surgery."

She straightened, studying his face, but Bella couldn't read anything in his expression. It was blank, his eyes guarded.

"I didn't have enough left," she murmured. "My money had gone to school, to living costs when I initially moved to New York. And my father had been pressuring me to come home for a long time. He wanted me to get married—"

Henry's eyes went dark. "To Sergio?"

"No," she said. "Not him, at first. He had someone else picked out."

His expression hardened, and her heart skipped a beat. Every cowardly inch of her was saying to stop here, that Henry didn't need to know everything. But . . .

He *did* need to know.

"I told him, no, obviously. I was with you, and I thought—well, I thought you and I would eventually get married," she said, watching as his lungs expanded as he took a deep breath. "But then your dad got worse, and you were leaving, and the surgery was his last hope . . ."

"No. *No.*" Henry shot to his feet, and the speed of it startled her, almost toppling her from the boulder. He steadied her then jumped down to the ground, thrusting a hand through his hair as he paced.

After a long minute, he turned back to her.

"Bella, sweetheart, tell me you *didn't*. Tell me you didn't leave so my dad—"

He broke off, pain in his eyes, his words.

She swallowed. "I had to."

"Fuck." He spun away. "*Fuck.* All this time I thought—" He turned, walking back toward her, head in his hands.

She shifted, wanting to get off the boulder, to go to him, but froze when he clambered back up the rock and stopped, his face only inches from hers. "Why, baby? Why would you do that?"

"It was the only way for your dad to have the surgery . . ."

His eyes closed and for a moment, Bella thought he'd stopped breathing, but then he was crushing her to him, his arms wrapping tightly around her, his breaths in shaky exhales.

"Y-you shouldn't have done that. You shouldn't have. You shouldn't—"

She hugged him back. "I had to."

"No."

"Yes."

He leaned back, eyes slightly reddened. "*No.*"

She crossed her arms. "Yes."

Henry sighed. "At the very least, you should have told me."

"And you would have let me do it?" She raised one brow.

"Of course not."

Bella huffed. "Well, that's exactly why I *had* to."

"You had to unilaterally decide the future of our relationship?"

Oh, he was mad.

Well, tough shit.

Because she was mad, too.

She popped to her feet—not a smart thing to do when perched atop a boulder. Henry caught her before she toppled down the hill, gripping the tops of her arms and looking as though he wanted to shake some sense into her.

Hmph.

She wanted to shake some sense into *him.*

"It was the only thing I could do," she snapped. "*I* had the opportunity to help your father get the surgery, and—"

"It didn't make one bit of difference in the end!" He clenched his jaw. "All it meant was that I lost him *and* you."

Her breath caught. "I know."

But she wasn't going to apologize for doing it. If she hadn't gone, if she hadn't gotten the money and figured out a way to get Henry's dad the surgery, she wouldn't have been able to live with herself knowing that she hadn't done everything in her power to help him.

She might not have ever met Henry's dad, but Henry was engrained in her heart and though she didn't want to hurt him, she would do it all again in the end, if it meant that his dad had been given every chance to live. Broken hearts could heal, or at least the *emotionally* shattered ones could. The physically malfunctioning ones needed outside help.

She'd done that and as much as she'd hated to be without him in her life for that many years, as painful and wrenching as it had been, it was what she'd *had* to do.

"I can see it in your face," he grumbled. "I can see that no matter what I say, it won't change your mind that you did the right thing."

"That's because I did."

He shook his head. "*Woman*," he warned.

"*Man*," she countered.

His lips curved, hers followed suit.

She touched his cheek. "You're not mad anymore?"

"I'm furious." He picked up her hand, pressed a kiss to her palm. "But I understand why you did it."

Bella let out a relieved breath.

He tugged them both back down to sitting, tucked her firmly against his side. "Why didn't you come back sooner?"

"I only just found out your dad died."

Clarity danced across his eyes. "The newspaper article about the diner."

"Yes." She'd been doing her weekly search of Darlington news, living vicariously in her mind, pretending that she was part of the mix—maybe she'd take horseback riding lessons at the ranch, open a little bakery downtown—when she'd spied the article about Henry honoring the five-year anniversary of his father's death by serving his favorite dishes for half off, with all proceeds going to a heart health charity.

She'd seen Henry's picture in the article. He'd been smiling down at Kelly Roosevelt as she'd held a tray filled with plates on her shoulder.

He'd looked so happy.

And she'd known that she couldn't marry Sergio.

Even if Henry never forgave her, even if they never had a future together, she couldn't tie herself to a man who didn't make her feel the same things that Henry did.

She hadn't even planned on coming to Utah in the first place. But after she'd slipped out of her father's estate and made it to the airport, she'd discovered that the first international flight had been to Salt Lake City.

Kismet.

That was the only explanation.

Now she was here, and Henry knew everything, but he was still staring down at her with affection in his eyes.

"You're so beautiful," he said.

Her heart skipped a beat. When he said those things like that, like he believed them, she felt so damned much. "I've missed you."

He tucked her head back onto his shoulder, kissed the top of her head. "I'm just glad you're here now."

"Me, too," she murmured.

They sat like that, watching the sun sink lower in the sky, the reds and oranges of earlier transforming into navy and black. Only when the stars had started to peek out at them did Henry slip from the boulder and help her down.

Her hip protested after sitting so long in one position, but it quickly loosened up as they hiked back up the hill then down the other side.

"So," he said, pulling open her door, "does this mean you're going to be my girlfriend?"

She smiled. "You've got to date me first."

"You're living in my house. I think that constitutes as dating."

"I won't be living there for long. Pam told me about an apartment above the bookstore downtown. She gave me the landlord's number today."

He was frowning down at her, so she tugged the door closed, cutting off whatever argument he was going to throw her way. "Why would you do that?" he asked, plopping down into his seat. "We lived together in New York. We—"

Bella dropped her hand to his thigh. "I need this time to work on me."

A snort. "That's a brush-off line if I ever heard one."

"I need to figure out who I am without Sergio, without my father pulling the strings."

He made a face.

"Also, I love you," she said. "I've never stopped, but that doesn't mean we shouldn't take things slow. For God's sake, I've only been in town three days and we're already playing house."

"I—" He shook his head. "You still love me?"

Bella patted his cheek. "Don't be stupid."

"I—"

"Am going to give me time."

Henry sighed. "I love you."

"You'll let me lease the apartment?"

One brow came up. "Considering I own it? Yes, you can stay in it for as long as you want."

She'd guessed as much when Pam had suggested it with a twinkle in her eyes and a smirk on her lips. "And you'll charge me rent?"

He shook his head. "If you'll be the diner's pastry chef?"

"Does a diner *need* a pastry chef?"

"*I* need you and believe me, the customers will kill for your food. Hell, most of the pies and cakes are your recipes anyway."

"Fine," she said. "I'll work for you until I save up enough money to open my bakery." A shrug. "God knows, I need the practice. Today was my first time in the kitchen in five years."

"What a waste." He touched her cheek. "A bakery?"

"Yeah. I've always wanted to own one."

He kissed her. One press of his lips and her head was spinning, desire swimming through her body, urging her to crawl over the console and into his lap. But before she could do that, he broke away, hot breath fanning over her lips.

Calloused fingers on her cheek, her throat. "I can't wait to see what you do." Another hot kiss that sent her temperature sky high. "I know it's going to be great."

And damn, if she didn't already love the man, those words would have done it.

"Come on," she said, wrapping her hand around his. "Let's go home."

"Will you promise to feed me?" He waggled his brows.

She laughed. "I thought *you* were the fancy chef?"

"Not anymore," he said, way too innocent as he turned on the ignition and maneuvered the car back down the road. "I'm just a small-town cook." A beat. "Who's really, really hungry."

This man. God, she loved him.

"You just want me to make pasta."

Guilty eyes flicked to hers then back to the road.

Bella stretched over the console to kiss him on the cheek. "How does fettuccini sound?"

"As perfect as you are."

She made a barfing sound, but secretly, Bella loved the sweet words.

CHAPTER THIRTEEN

Henry

HE STARED at the angry woman glaring at him through the window of his front door and sighed.

Really, it had only been a matter of time before this happened.

Bella had been in town for just over two weeks, and he'd spent nearly every waking minute with her. The town was in a whirlwind between her sudden appearance, the incident with Sergio—who'd been released on bail then had promptly skipped town like the bastard he was—and the fact that Henry had spent the last fourteen plus days walking around with a stupid ass grin on his face.

They were also in a frenzy over her baked goods.

He couldn't keep tiramisu in stock, her lemon cream pie had been chosen decisively over his, and her blueberry cobbler had sold out within the first hour.

Three different people had begged Bella to make pans for their birthdays.

And one of their birthdays wasn't for six months.

She'd blushed at the attention, thanking them and promising to make a fresh batch for the following day.

So, yeah, Henry didn't think that Bella's dream of a bakery was that far off.

But *Bella* wasn't the one staring angrily at him as he strode down the hall to his front door.

Nope. Unfortunately for him, that was his mother.

He paused, considering the wrath he'd face if he turned around now and pretended he hadn't seen her.

"Don't you dare!" Her voice was shrill enough to pierce right through the wood and glass.

Girding his loins, he opened the front door.

His mother swept inside, pausing briefly to kiss him on the cheek. "I have been hearing about this blueberry cobbler all week," she said, striding into his kitchen. "It's all the ladies at the Garden Center can talk about, but does my own son bring me any?" A long-suffering sigh. "No. I waited and waited—"

"Mom, you've been home all of one day," he interrupted, sliding past her to open up his fridge. He did, in fact, have a pan of blueberry cobbler hidden away. It had been Bella's *practice run* and though she'd proclaimed it unworthy for sale, he'd thought it was delicious and wouldn't let her throw it away. "Hold the tirade for a minute."

Now, he served up a scoop on a plate and popped it in the microwave.

Bella would have his hide for that later, for daring to put her masterpiece in something as terrible as a microwave, but she'd just have to deal. He needed to get cobbler into his mother's mouth as quickly as possible.

"Up," he told her, pointing to a barstool as the microwave dinged.

Turning, he grabbed a carton of vanilla ice cream from the freezer, spooned some on top, and then passed the plate over.

She all but snatched it from his hands.

Henry waited as she ate, well familiar with her tactics. His mom was sneaky— distract, avert, wait for her opponent's guard to drop . . . then *bam*, a shot directly to the head.

Or maybe, in this case, the heart.

Luckily for him and his budding relationship with Bella, his mother had left the morning Bella had arrived in town. She'd gone on a cruise with some of her girlfriends, returning just the day before.

Which was the only reason he hadn't gotten a visit along these lines before now.

"That is delicious," she said, scraping the side of her spoon across the plate to get every last drop.

"Yes, it is."

"And this Isabella made it?"

He nodded.

"This is the same woman who broke your heart in New York."

Henry took the plate and set it in the sink. "There was a misunderstanding."

"Hmm." She sat back, crossed her arms. "Has Kelly met her?"

"Not yet." He mirrored her position. "The kids are keeping her busy."

"And also because you told her to stay away."

He could almost hear the arrow swooshing through the air, the *thunk* as it struck a bull's-eye. Also, Kelly was a big, fat traitor for telling his mother that fact.

"She's worried about you."

Well, now that was a lie. Kel hadn't swooped in like his mom, but she *had* been texting him and the theme of those messages wasn't worry.

"No, Mom," he said. *"You're* worried, and you don't have to be. Bella is—"

She was everything.

Simple as that.

But also, she made things exceptionally complicated. It had been him and his mom for so long that he didn't know what she'd do without him. Hell, he still went over once a week and mowed her lawn, and the last time there'd been a power outage, she hadn't known where the breakers were.

"Fancy switches," she'd called them.

But it was more than that, more than the man-of-the-house stuff. His mom was alone, and if he was busy with his own life, then what would she do?

"Oh no," she said, glaring at him. "Wipe that look off your face right now. I'm a grown woman, and I don't need my son to look after me." She sighed and her expression softened. "I already allowed that to go on for too long. I took advantage of you, Henry, relied on you too much, stole you away and kept you home when I should have been pushing you to go back to New York."

"I *wanted* to stay."

"No. You felt like you *had* to stay." She slipped down from the stool, crossed over to him. "That was my fault. I—"

"Maybe at first I didn't want to be here," he admitted. "But I love this town, Mom. I couldn't imagine living anywhere else."

"And if this *Bella* decides that small-town life isn't for her?"

"That's not an issue."

"It could become one."

He shrugged. "If it does, then we'll figure it out. Together," he added when it seemed as though she'd protest.

"Your mom is right to worry," came a quiet voice.

Both of their gazes shot to the doorway. Bella stood in the hall, eyes warm but expression careful.

"It's a mother's job to worry about her baby."

Henry groaned.

Because that was probably the only thing Bella could have said to put his mother at ease.

It was, in fact, one of his mom's favorite statements.

Case in point, the beaming smile that spread across her face. "Exactly. Please come in, dear," she said. "I'm Catherine."

"Isabella," Bella replied as she walked into the room, arms laden with bags.

She'd been sweet-talking the local farmers for extra produce and it looked as though today she'd scored—he took the bags from her—apricots.

The sweet smell hit his nose and promptly made his mouth water.

She kissed him on the cheek, murmured a soft, "Thank you." Then, arms free, turned to his mother. "It's so lovely to finally meet you, Catherine. How was your cruise?" She smiled at his mom's surprised expression. "I hope you don't mind, but Henry showed me a few pictures of your travels. It looked absolutely beautiful."

"It was wonderful," his mother said. "And I've been hearing all about you and your wonderful desserts since I got back. I'm happy to say your blueberry cobbler far surpasses the hype."

Bella whirled around to face him. "You did *not* feed your mother my reject cobbler!"

Henry shrugged helplessly. He'd been between a rock and a hard place and plus, the *reject cobbler* was fucking delicious.

"Hush now." His mom wove her arm through Bella's, thus saving him from his woman's wrath. "Henry's father was just the same way, not liking anyone to taste until the recipe was just perfect." She started tugging Bella into the family room. "But I'll tell you what I used to tell him. Sometimes, the perfection is found in the mistakes."

Bella froze for a moment then smiled down at his mom. "You know what? You're absolutely right."

Approximately one minute later, they were giggling together on his couch.

He snapped a pic with his cell, sent it to Kel.

Traitor.

She replied within a few seconds.

I had to do something. Plus, it looks like they're thick as thieves already. Should I be jealous?

He rolled his eyes.

You turned me down, remember?

A beat.

Oh, I remember. So when can I meet her? Or better yet, when are you going to bring her to the ranch so I can get her on a horse? Theo's out because he's strictly Melissa's horse now. But I have others.

Henry stifled a chuckle.

Too many others, according to Justin.

His phone buzzed again.

Lies.

He smirked.

Maybe. Maybe not. How about Monday?

A heartbeat before her reply came through.

Monday is good. I promise not to cook.

Henry shook his head as he picked up the phone and called in an order for a pizza. Based on the amount of cackling, he anticipated their conversation was going to take a while.

His mom was sharing baby stories.

"And then he whipped off his undies and streaked off down the aisle, his little butt jiggling as he ran. He was so fast and more slippery than a greased hog. I just couldn't catch him—"

Bella burst out laughing, and his mom joined in.

For fuck's sake.

But Henry couldn't hold back his smile when he joined them on the couch.

He would endure any amount of embarrassment if it made the two most important women in his life laugh like that.

CHAPTER FOURTEEN

"So lovely to meet you again, my dear," Catherine murmured, pulling Bella down for a tight hug.

Henry's mom really was tiny . . . or maybe it was just that Bella was too tall?

Either way, she had to stoop down to receive the hug.

So worth it, though, she thought as Catherine gave her the perfect Mom Hug. Tight, but not too much so, long enough to show she cared, but not so prolonged that it drifted into the creepy sector.

Just . . . perfect.

God, she missed her own mom.

Shoving that thought away, she hugged Catherine back. "You don't have to go," she said for what must have been the fifth time in as many minutes. "I know you just got back from your trip and must want to see—"

"Pish." A wide smile as she stepped back. "I'll pester him tomorrow. For now, you two lovebirds enjoy your evening together."

The three of them had chatted for the better part of an hour before the doorbell had rung and the pizza Henry had ordered appeared. There was enough for the three of them to share, but Catherine had refused to stay.

"But you haven't eaten," Bella said, not wanting Henry's mom to feel like she was being run off.

Catherine patted her hips. "I've eaten more than enough over the last few weeks. Plus, I had your delicious cobbler." Her lips tipped up into a smile that was very much like Henry's. "Pretend I'm living vicariously and having dessert for dinner," she mock-whispered.

Bella giggled.

"Talk to you both soon," Catherine called, showing herself out the front door before Bella could force her to stay for pizza. She watched through the window as Henry's mom walked to her car, got in, and drove away.

Apparently, she wasn't the only one watching.

The moment his mom's car was out of sight, Henry's arms were around Bella's waist, and he was tugging her back against his chest.

"I missed you."

She scoffed, turned in his embrace to snuggle closer. "We were apart for all of two hours."

"Two hours too long." A roll of her eyes, but because his eyes were sparkling with humor, she didn't tease him. Especially when he pressed a kiss to her temple and asked, "Where'd you get the apricots?"

"You wouldn't believe it if I told you," she said and launched into the crazy story about the farmer and his runaway dog she'd corralled outside the apartment. "Thank God I got the new cell phone because he was just sitting there on my stoop, paws crossed and the saddest expression on his face. And when I opened the door, he just ran inside. Luckily for him, he had tags. I called and . . ."

Had ended up with four full bags of ripe and juicy apricots.

"I don't know how much pizza I can eat," she confessed. "I think I ate a half dozen apricots just on the walk over here."

Henry grinned, nuzzling the side of her throat and leaving goose bumps in his wake. "There's a dirty joke somewhere in there."

"Leave it hidden," she quipped, but the words weren't exactly steady.

He spun her to face him. "So you're not hungry?"

She shook her head.

"Does that mean I can kiss you now?"

Bella didn't justify that question with a response. Instead, she rose on tiptoe, wrapped her arms around his neck, and kissed him.

His reaction was instantaneous.

One second, she was in control, the next she found herself lifted onto the kitchen counter, his hard cock pressing against her and his tongue darting into her mouth in a rhythm that had her seeing stars.

God, they'd done so much kissing over the last two weeks, taking it slow, but also driving her insane by increments.

Her body remembered what it had been like between them.

Her heart wanted to be close to him like that again.

Even her brain said go for it.

But when she snaked her hand down, grappling with the button on his jeans, he caught it, pulled back from the kiss, and smiled down at her.

"Dangerous." One more smack of his lips against hers, before he started to reach for the pizza box. "We really should eat this before it gets cold."

Bella saw red. She pulled away from him and stomped her foot. "Are you kidding me?"

His lips twitched, and her anger swiveled into irritation.

Though, truthfully, it was nice to see the glimpse of the old Henry. The one who teased her and drove her crazy and didn't treat her like a piece of fragile glass. Because while, yes, they had spent the majority of the past weeks together, while they'd kissed and touched and held each other, there had been a careful distance between them.

As though Henry were waiting for something.

For her to leave again.

Or maybe . . . for her to prove she wouldn't.

He tucked a strand of hair behind her ear. "But, yes, I *am* kidding."

Bella shot him a mock-frown. "Not. Funny."

"From where I'm standing it is." He grinned when her mock-frown turned real. "Sure you don't want to just eat pizza and watch a movie?"

The same thing they'd done more often than not. Oh, they'd gone out and watched a movie in the local theater, in addition to sitting through a few more sunsets at his spot. They'd even played a game of miniature golf that she was absolutely terrible at. But most of the nights had involved food and just spending time together.

Now that the heavy topics had been dealt with, they'd been able to chat about all the fun stuff.

Fancy ingredients, jerky head chefs, favorite reality shows.

Places they wanted to visit.

Not Italy, for her part. Oh, she loved the country she'd grown up in, but it had felt like a prison so much over the years that the thought of going back did *not* appeal. Then there was the fact that it would bring her closer to her father.

Not preferred.

He'd remotely shut down her laptop and cell, canceled her credit cards, closed her checking account. Bella now had no funds, aside from what she earned at the diner, and one suitcase of clothes to her name. Thankfully, she wasn't on a visa—she was a dual citizen, since she'd been born in the States and her mother had been an American—because if Bella *had* been, her father certainly would have found a way to make her life miserable.

For the first time in her life, she was truly on her own.

Which was perfectly okay with her, if not for the fact that she kept waiting for the other shoe to fall.

For her father to find some string to pull.

But she wouldn't dance to his tune. Not this time. He had nothing to hold over her head and—

"I was kidding about eating the pizza."

The husky words startled her out of her thoughts.

She blinked. "Pardon?"

"Did I ruin the moment?"

"N-no," she stammered, trying to get her mind to clear. "Thinking about my father did that."

Henry made a face.

"Sorry. Sorry. I just—" Bella pursed her lips. "Ruined the moment."

He grabbed the box of pizza, picked up her hand again, and tugged her down the hall to his bedroom.

Figuring it was best to keep her mouth shut after she'd spent the last few minutes off in dreamland, before mentioning the libido-killing subject of her father, she just followed along.

He didn't stop until they'd reached the bed.

Once there, he tossed the pizza on it, turned back, and bent, pulling off his shoes. Hers went by the wayside next. Then Henry whipped off his shirt.

"Uh." Not that she was complaining.

"Shh," he said, unbuttoning his jeans and pushing them down.

That wasn't hard, considering the way her mouth had gone dry at the sight of all that naked skin. His chest was lickable, and her fingers actually tingled with the urge to touch his abs or maybe stroke down the muscles of his arms or maybe . . . *okay*, she wanted to touch him everywhere.

He slipped his fingers under the hem of her T-shirt and tugged it up and over her head then helped her shimmy out of her jeans.

And then he stopped and grabbed the TV remote.

Her brows yanked together, throat unsticking. Yes, the view of him bending over was yummy, but she'd rather him be bending for a reason that was not turning on a television.

Like bending so that his mouth was between her legs.

Yup, *that* she could get behind.

Before she could suggest that, he started streaming an old romantic comedy and set the remote down. *Okaay.* Five years had passed. Maybe he was into some weird, kinky stuff now?

Like old romcoms featuring fake orgasm scenes and heroines with beautifully curly hair.

Unbidden, Bella reached up to straighten her ponytail. *Her* hair didn't hold a curl. *It* would never look like that—

She squealed as Henry swept her up into his arms.

Her mind flickered, losing focus when all that hot naked skin pressed against hers.

"What are you—?"

"I'm getting you out of your head," he said, setting her down on the mattress, following her down so that full length of him was over the top of her. *Fuck, that was nice.* He nuzzled her neck. "We've got pizza. We're sort of watching a movie. So you can just relax and focus on you." His mouth tipped up. "Or rather, on *us.*"

She raised a brow. "Naked?"

"If that's what you want," he said, amusement curling through the words.

"You seem to have gotten us there with very little effort."

He stroked one hand along the outside of her thigh, up her hip, her rib cage, and stopped, fingertips teasing the sensitive skin just below her breast.

She shivered.

"You cold?"

A roll of her eyes. "You know that's not why I have goose bumps."

"Yeah?" He brushed his mouth along her jaw, down her throat.

"Y—" He nipped the spot just above her collarbone, and her hands wove into his hair, arching closer, needing— "Yes."

His tongue darted out, sliding down until it traced along the top edge of her bra . . . so damn close and yes, so freaking far from where she wanted him. "Then why?" He nudged the cotton out of the way, grazed the hardened bud of her nipple, and she jumped, heat pooling in her stomach, her thighs clenching together.

And that was enough.

She could hardly remember what they were talking about, could barely remember her name.

She wanted him.

She wanted Henry.

Now.

Enough teasing. Enough taking it slow. Just . . . enough. She wrapped her legs around his waist and yanked him down, so his lower half was firmly pressed against hers. Bella got one glimpse of his expression— proud and self-satisfied that he'd gotten her out of her own brain, no doubt—before she gripped his head and brought his mouth to hers.

She couldn't fault the man for his smugness.

His plan had worked after all.

But now it was *her* job to drive him slowly insane.

CHAPTER FIFTEEN

Henry

HE WAS LOSING his fucking mind.

Bella was beneath him, legs around his hips, his cock pressed against her pussy, and only two layers of thin material separating him from the motherland.

And she was wet.

So much so that he could feel it soaking through his boxer briefs.

This was supposed to be about driving *her* crazy, getting her so turned on that she didn't have the mental space to think about anything except the two of them and how good it felt for them to be together. He'd wanted to get her out of her brain and far away from the worries that had left shadows in her eyes.

Yes, Sergio was gone.

No, her father hadn't contacted her, aside from decisively cutting her off from him in every way he could, but luckily Henry's woman was smart and a hard-worker. She'd more than earned the wages at the diner, had insisted on paying him rent, refused to let him buy her a new cell phone. She—

Kissed him.

And then *his* mental space emptied.

No more thoughts of fathers or exes. Nothing except sensation and need and raging, all-encompassing desire. He slipped his tongue into her mouth, let his hips drop more firmly against hers, making them both groan.

She nipped his bottom lip, and he nipped back.

Then reached beneath her back to unhook her bra. Two seconds later, she'd slipped her arms free and tossed the garment aside before tugging his head down to her breasts.

Fuck, yes.

He probably should have eased into it, teased her slowly, but the sight of her hardened nipples was too much. He sucked one into his mouth, drawing deeply and loving the way her hands wove into his hair to hold him there.

His other hand slid up her ribs, wanting to tease her other nipple, to caress her breast, but he couldn't get the angle he wanted without crushing her.

One quick movement had their positions reversed, Bella's delicious breasts swaying in front of his mouth. Henry didn't hesitate, just ratcheted up, seized her breasts in his hands, and got to work, alternating between his lips and teeth and tongue, pinching and circling the stiff peaks, reveling in the way she cried and arched against him.

"*Oh God*," she groaned, undulating against him.

The two layers between them that had been so thin and tempting before now created an uncomfortable sort of friction. It was a nuisance that he wanted gone.

Skin to skin.

Sliding home.

Delving deep.

His cock went painfully hard.

Bella moved against him, pelvis rocking faster, the rhythm making stars flash behind his eyes, his mouth faltered on her breasts. He moved his hands to her ass, shifting her slightly, holding her tight, and her breath caught.

"H-Henry."

Desire had him hardened to a fever pitch, but he knew that tone, knew that she was close.

She started to slow her movements, probably wanting to wait for him.

Well, *fuck that*.

She was beautiful when she came.

And it had been five years too many since he'd seen it.

He pulled her more firmly against him, sped her movements so that her breath caught . . . then transformed into a moan.

"I—"

He leaned up, took her nipple into his mouth, and sucked deeply.

"*Oh*." Her lips parted, and she threw her head back. Fuck, it was the most beautiful thing he'd ever seen. Pink staining her cheeks, eyes slammed closed, lips parted on a moan as she moved faster and harder . . . until—

"Mmm. Oh my God. *Henry*."

She shattered, her orgasm having her stiffen for one long moment before she collapsed against him, hips still moving, her groan of pleasure the sexiest thing he'd ever heard.

"Fuck," she murmured, lips to his shoulder, body limp. "Just fuck."

He grinned, gave her exactly ten seconds to catch her breath, then flipped her over onto her back and dove between her thighs.

She shrieked, but by the time she'd recovered herself enough to protest, Henry had her underwear off, her legs spread, and his mouth on her clit. *Gently*, because she'd just come, but he circled the nub with his tongue, sucking lightly, stroking his fingers through her folds.

Soaking wet.

Hot, liquid heat.

So. Fucking. Gorgeous.

He stroked slowly at first, building her back up, enjoying the sweetness of her against his taste buds. He knew she liked firm pressure against her clit, so the moment she could take it, he flattened his tongue and circled the bundle of nerves, teasing her until she cursed at him and then, biting back a smirk, he gave her what she really wanted.

Hard and fast and demanding.

He slipped a finger inside, curling it up against her G-spot while sucking deeply on her clit.

Within seconds, she was writhing, hips jerking, moans coming in rapid succession, but he rode the wave with her, bringing her higher and higher until she screamed his name and tightened around his finger.

She flopped back on the mattress, chest heaving. It did all sorts of wonderful things to her breasts that he was having trouble ignoring, since his cock was still rock-hard, but he wasn't an asshole. He didn't expect anything from Bella in return. He sure as fuck hoped for it, but he didn't expect—

Her hand snaked down, gripping him through the damp fabric of his boxer briefs.

His groan was garbled, and his hips shot up, cock seeking more of her.

Hand. Mouth. Pussy.

He almost didn't care.

Except, who was he kidding.

Henry was desperate to be inside her again, but he also knew it was important for her to have control after spending so long without it.

Her fingers ran down the length of him. Back up.

Down. Up.

Driving him slowly insane.

"Henry?" she murmured.

He gritted his teeth. The heroine faking an orgasm on the TV behind him wasn't helping his control in the least. He just kept thinking about how much he liked the sound of Bella as she came. "Hmm?" he replied.

"Are you going to get inside me?" she asked. "Or are you just the ultimate tease?"

His eyes flew open. He hadn't even known he'd slammed them shut.

But Bella's question had them flashing wide then promptly stifling a curse as he tried not to embarrass himself. She was naked and spread out beneath him, her breasts on full display, and, while she'd dropped her hand from his cock, she'd wrapped her legs around his hips in its place.

One layer of fabric between them.

It was not enough.

It was too much.

She arched, bringing their pelvises into perfect alignment. "Are you going to make love to me, Henry?" she asked. "Or do I need to distract *your* mind?"

He could barely process her words he was so turned on. "I—" He broke off on a groan when she shimmied against him, and the devil woman had the nerve to smile sweetly up at him, mischief dancing in her eyes.

"Distracted enough?"

Another movement that had sweat breaking out along his spine.

"So. Fucking. Dangerous," he growled, having at least retained enough presence of mind to reach over her and pull out a condom from his nightstand drawer.

A heartbeat later, he'd torn it open with his teeth.

One more to strip off his boxer briefs. Another to roll it down his length.

He paused, lungs tight, heart pounding.

"Yes," she murmured.

And he couldn't have waited another second to be inside her.

Slowly, Henry slid home, jaw clenching at the perfectness of her. Wet and tight and hot, it was almost too much. But it had also been too long. He wanted to savor her, appreciate the way she felt, the way being like this with her made *him* feel. He wanted—

She tightened around him. "Move, Henry."

Savoring was suddenly the last thing on his mind.

He pulled out, pushed back in, tilting his hips so he rubbed against her clit while also hitting her G-spot. Yes, he was chasing an orgasm that was already prickling on the edges of his consciousness, but fuck if he was going to allow himself to fall over the precipice without Bella coming at least one more time.

Her fingers dug in his shoulders, a moan escaping her lips.

Yup. That was the spot she liked.

And he liked the motion, too. *Way* too fucking much.

Because his best intentions or not, his orgasm was coming

Too fast. Too fast.

He didn't realize he'd spoken the chant aloud until Bella cupped his cheek and said, "No, baby. More. *Faster.*"

The leash on his control snapped.

Henry *moved*. In and out, faster and faster, until her Bella was groaning and moving against him, coaxing him on and then . . . finally—*thank God because he was so fucking close*—she stiffened and cried out, tightening around him.

That was it for him.

One stroke. Two. And he exploded.

CHAPTER SIXTEEN

Bella

SHE WAS HUMMING as she worked in the kitchen, slicing the apricots she'd gotten from Jim and throwing them into a pot to cook down into a compote.

Bella was going to break her own rule by staying over at Henry's place.

He was getting dressed so he could drive her home.

Ridiculous man.

She'd rented the apartment for a reason. Before tonight she had made herself go back home, no matter how late her and Henry's time together went, because she'd thought it important to have some distance between them as they got to know each other again.

Tonight had shown her that was a joke.

Keeping him at arm's length when they worked side by side and spent every waking moment together was impossible.

And then there was the fact that she didn't *want* there to be space between them.

Maybe it wasn't the most prudent decision, maybe she'd end up with a broken heart in the end, but Bella also felt like she had wasted enough time. Who knew how long she had on this earth?

She wanted whatever time she had to be spent with Henry.

Plus, he insisted on driving her home every time, even though the distance between the house and apartment was only a few blocks.

Equal parts sweet and infuriating.

Sweet because he cared, because he kissed her so gently at her front door.

Infuriating because she'd left an abusive relationship, flown halfway around the world, and started a new life. She didn't *need* him to drive her home.

But, her brain countered, he didn't need *her* to cook for him.

Well, she cooked because she cared, because it was one way for her to show it.

Bella wrinkled her nose, knowing that Henry's driving her home was along the same vein. It was obvious, logical, but she didn't want her brain to be logical or mature.

She wanted to pout.

A hand snuck onto her cutting board, stole a sliver of apricot.

"I thought I was going to drive you home."

She turned, pointed the knife at him. "Not anymore. Get the blue cheese out of the fridge. I have homemade crackers in the oven."

He hesitated, eyes drifting down to the end of her knife.

Then he shrugged, but Bella saw his lips twitch before he turned and dug out the cheese. After he'd set it next to her, the oven dinged, and he glanced inside before she could ask him to check on the crackers.

"Another minute," he murmured, pressing a kiss to the side of her neck and snagging another apricot off her board.

She sighed but held up another piece.

He ate it, nipping at her fingertips and making the space between her thighs clench.

Three orgasms, she reminded her vagina. *Just chill already.*

But it didn't want to *chill*. It wanted Henry again.

Bella gave an internal snort. When had her vagina become autonomous? Because it wasn't just that she desired Henry or that she really loved it when he pounded into her, his cock hard and deep. Nope. *She* wanted him.

Every part of her.

Which was why she announced, "I'm staying."

He froze, tray hovering, crackers stalled mid-retrieval. After a moment, he blinked, extracted the sheet pan, and set it carefully on the counter.

"I don't mind driving—"

"I'm. Staying," she growled, grabbing a piece of apricot and shoving it into her mouth.

First, he complained about driving her home. Now he wanted her to go.

What the fuck?

"Fine," she snapped, slamming down her knife. "I'll go."

Hands on her waist, lifting her and plunking her down on the opposite counter, well away from the sharp blade and simmering pot on the stove. Henry nudged her thighs apart, stepped between them. At which point, her vagina decided it was time to party, or rather, that it wanted to party with Henry's cock, but Bella knew she needed to hold it together.

Why? her vagina cajoled. *You like it.*

Well, there was *that* argument. She did. She really—

"I don't want you to go."

Bella glanced up at him, eyes widening. "What?"

He smiled. "You heard me."

"But—"

"I've been pestering you to stay," he said. "You don't honestly think that because you'd surprised me with your proclamation that I don't want you to stay, do you?"

Her mouth opened. Closed.

"Or maybe you're worried that because we've had sex that something has changed?"

"Something *has* changed," she grumbled.

"Has it?" he asked. "Or are you just feeling vulnerable?"

Ugh. How did this man always know exactly what she was feeling? She didn't want to feel vulnerable. She *wanted* to feel like she did before. All happy and orgasm-drugged and—

"That's it, isn't it?" he teased. "My brave, tough, gorgeous Isabella is scared."

She pushed at his chest. "Shut up," she snapped, but even as the sharp words penetrated the air between them, Henry just continued to smile. The jerk actually kept smiling. "Back up," she said, shoving him again. "I need to get the crackers off the tray and check on the—"

He didn't budge.

She sighed, stared at his rather lovely kitchen. Pale gray cabinets, white countertops, a double oven, and a big eight-burner stove.

"Sweetheart." Henry cupped her cheek and waited until she finally brought her eyes back to his. "I love you."

Her breath caught.

Hearing those words never got old.

"I'll drive you home." A kiss to her forehead. "Or not." Another to her cheek. "You can stay." Her other cheek. "Or not." He brushed his mouth across hers. "Don't you see? I just want you, sweetheart. Wherever or whenever or in however much you're willing to give."

"I—"

She sniffed.

Henry sniffed.

They both reacted at once, darting over to the pan on the stove. He pulled it off the heat and shot her a sheepish grin.

"My compote!" Bella glared at him, but she couldn't stay mad, not when he looked at her like that. She sighed, lips turning down into a frown. "It's ruined."

He swiped a finger into the pan, licked off the burned fruit mixture, and winced.

"Yup. It's ruined."

She shook her head, exasperated, but feeling decidedly less flayed open. Because of Henry. Because he'd pestered and annoyed and cajoled her into realizing that he was vulnerable, too, that his emotions were as big and scary as her own.

That he wanted her to stay but supported her if she went.

Another piece of her heart was imprinted with Henry's name.

The man kept saying *she* was dangerous.

Well, *he* was the one who kept snatching parts of her soul, taking them and transforming them into something more, transforming *her* into a different person.

One she liked a whole hell of a lot.

One he loved, even with her grumbling and snapping and—

He spun her around, pressed a hard kiss to her mouth. "Plus, if you're going to stay, we can make another batch." A smile that stole her breath. "That's the thing about second chances. We have the opportunity to make them even better than the first time around."

Bella stayed.

And she made another batch of compote.

And, Henry was right.

It was even better.

CHAPTER SEVENTEEN

Henry

MONDAY NIGHT WAS BEAUTIFUL. One of those perfect summer nights where the air was warm, but a light breeze prevented anyone from getting too hot.

The kids were out in full force. Max and Allie, Rob and Melissa's kids, felt it was their duty as the older cousins to lead little Abigail astray. Or in this particular case, through an obstacle course of blocks, jump ropes, and chairs. Even the twins, who were toddling like crazy over the lawn to keep up with their cousins, tried desperately to get in on the action.

Bella watched the activity with a smile on her face.

She'd won over Kelly and Justin easily, coming prepared with a tray of apricot cobbler—Henry had talked to the farmer and now she was inundated with the small orange fruit—and a huge layered chocolate cake that the kids had gaped over.

Melissa had crossed her arms upon seeing the desserts, sending Bella a mock-glare whose intensity was tempered by the amusement in her pale brown eyes. "You'll have me out of my job in no time."

"Never," Bella had replied before her cheeks went pink. "I have to admit that I have all of your cookbooks."

And another one bit the dust.

Melissa had taken the tray from Henry then lead Bella into the huge kitchen of the main house. It was where her cooking show was filmed and where, in fact, the producer asked if he could have the cameraman, who was at the house to film some additional scenes that would be edited into shows later in the season, take some shots of the desserts.

Bella had agreed and then pretty soon she was talking about her cake on camera, bubbly and confident and charming everyone in sight.

First Esther. Then the town. Him. His mother. His best friend. Television producers.

When would it stop?

Henry smothered a grin. Probably not until she achieved world domination.

"It's really nice to see you so happy."

He turned and saw Kelly with Jessie on her hip. She reached for him, so he swung her up into his arms.

"Rocket ship!" she yelled.

He groaned.

Kel laughed.

And speaking of it being really nice to see someone happy. He was thrilled that his best friend had found someone like Justin. Unlike his twin brother, Rex, who was the biological father of Abigail and a royal asshole, Justin was a good guy.

Rex, on the other hand, had taken advantage of a lonely Kelly, knocked her up, then skipped town.

Of course, Kel had forgiven him. Especially after Rex had terminated his parental rights, thus allowing Justin to formally adopt Abigail.

Justin had been there for Abby and Kel almost from day one, and the little girl knew no other father. He was a good one, too. Engaged, funny, kind, and caring. And though he was quieter than Henry's own dad had been, there was something about Justin that reminded him of his dad.

Loyal. Always had his back.

He watched Justin swoop in and grab Jax before the little boy—who'd somehow managed to scale a fence post—fell to the ground.

A quick word, an even quicker squeeze, and the toddler was on his way again.

Case in point.

A tug on his ear brought his attention back to Jessie. She was frowning at him. "Rocket ship!" she repeated.

Henry did a quick round of math. Five kiddos. Two of which were getting too damned big for rocket ships, but who still would definitely want them. One back that wasn't getting any younger.

"Just two," he told her.

Tiny lips pursing as they considered his deal then a nod.

"Two," she agreed.

Kel smirked. "I'll help Miss bring the plates out. Maybe by then you'll have thrown your back out."

"Why are we friends again?" He huffed, lowering Jessie to the ground in preparation for takeoff.

"Because I'm awesome." She turned for the house. "And my kids love you."

"Thee. Two. One!" Jessie shouted, still working on her R's.

Henry knew what she meant anyway and rocketed her high into the sky. Which was all it took for four pairs of child-sized feet to pound his way. Their voices layered over one another, each demanding their own turn, until finally, Jessie declared firmly and loud enough to be heard over the cacophony, "Two each."

Surprisingly, the kids all agreed and sat down for their turn.

After the tenth and final takeoff, Henry collapsed on the grass. "Who's going to give *me* a rocket ship?"

There was a pause before Jax said, "Daddy!"

Henry laughed and gave Jax a fist bump. "I think you're right, bud. He's the only one strong enough to lift me."

The kids nodded in solemn agreement before Kel's voice rang out over the lawn, announcing dinner was ready and ordering them all to wash up. At the prospect of food in the near future, they took off, leaving him a limp pile of exhaustion in the grass.

"You're really good with them."

He'd known Bella was there, felt the prickle of awareness on his nape, the skip of his pulse.

She extended a hand, a silent offer to help him to his feet.

He placed his fingers in hers, tugged hard.

"Eck!" She squealed, plopping down on top of him. The elbow he received on her landing was probably well-deserved, but it was also why it took him a moment to catch his breath.

"Hey," he said, wrapping his arms around her, keeping her close when she tried to get up.

"We—"

He kissed her.

She stopped trying to push off him and kissed him back. It was affection mixed with exasperation, longing with a dash of tempered heat. Sweet and soft and almost soothing, but with just the slightest edge of desire that had his pulse pounding.

A shriek penetrated his brain, jarring him enough that he pulled back.

Bella's eyes were closed, her lips red and swollen.

"Do you want kids?"

Because he could picture a little girl with the same espresso eyes, identical brown hair.

Her eyes flashed open, mouth working for a few seconds before she actually got the words out. "Of course, I do," she said. "Someday in the future, for sure." She glanced over at the front door of the main house when another happy yell reached their ears. The door was wide open, the threshold empty, the kiddos having disappeared inside. And by the sound of it, they were having a great time washing up. "Henry, we should—"

"One more minute," he said and kissed her again.

She melted against him, one minute turning into more like five, or maybe ten.

The second time they pulled apart wasn't due to a kid, but rather because of Kel's mom voice. Turned out she had a really good one.

Or, at least knew the exact right threat to get Henry moving.

"Hey, love birds," Kel yelled from the front door. "You have exactly one minute before I'm setting the twins on you. They're hungry and impatient, and *you know* how they feel about Aunt Melissa's homemade mac and cheese."

Henry shuddered. The twins liked to eat.

They also redefined the word hangry. Hevil was more like it.

"Coming," he called, shifting Bella off him and shooting her a sheepish smile as he stood. Her hair was a disaster, the ponytail having come halfway loose, tendrils falling all over the place. He extended a hand down to her, tugged her to her feet, wondering if he should offer to get some of the grass out of her hair or off her clothes or her—

She sighed, brushing herself off before lifting the hem of her T-shirt away from her body and shaking it.

Little pieces of grass fluttered to the ground.

Accusatory eyebrows in his direction.

Note to self, rolling around on the lawn got a lot more complicated when he had roving hands.

Next was her ponytail, sliding the band free, shaking out her hair for a few quick seconds before sweeping it right back up into the holder's tight grip. He'd watched her do the same thing a hundred times when they'd been together in the past, but seeing her do it today reminded him how grateful he was to have this second chance.

To have her here with his friends. To have her in Darlington at the diner. To know his mom loved her as much as he did.

The only bittersweet part was that his dad wasn't there.

Henry knew that feeling would never completely go away, but after having discovered what Bella had gone through to help his father, without even knowing him. Finding out that she'd sacrificed everything to give him one final chance . . . she had to know that she absolutely owned Henry—heart, soul, fingers, toes.

Every piece of him belonged to her.

One quick tug to her ponytail and she turned back to him, coming close enough to rest her hands on his chest, rising on tiptoe to press a quick kiss to his cheek.

"Come on, my sweet, troublesome man."

Dropping to her heels, she snagged his hand.

And Henry knew that though this was the beginning, everything would be all right.

CHAPTER EIGHTEEN

Bella

A FEW DAYS LATER, she found herself alone in the diner.

She'd just turned off the lights, all the staff had finished their rounds of cleaning and sweeping and restocking tables, and Henry had zipped off to help Tilly, who'd gotten a flat a few miles out of town.

Bella had ordered him to go, knowing there was prep work to do for the following morning and also wanting to get a head start on some baking.

There was a real wedding at the Roosevelt Ranch this weekend.

She'd gotten to see the space at dinner the other evening. The new pavilion and gazebo had just received the finishing touches—twinkly lights everywhere, beds of brightly colored flowers, rows of coordinating gingham topped hay bales with thick pads carefully concealed so guests' bottoms wouldn't get poked. Mason jars and tea lights and horseshoes and cowboy boots.

They'd thought of everything.

And now completed, it was more gorgeous in person than the pictures she'd drooled over a couple of months ago on their website.

Probably more importantly, or at least more importantly to *her*, was the fact that Bella got to make the wedding cake. Initially, Melissa was going to do the honors and film the process for her show, but the bride had gotten camera shy on Monday morning, and so they were scrambling to draw up a new idea for the episode.

Melissa had still offered to make the cake, not wanting the couple to not have one, but then over bowls of delicious mac and cheese, Kelly had suggested that maybe Bella could make it.

"Could you really?" Melissa had asked, relief creeping into the edges of her expression. "I can do it, but I'm not a pastry chef. I've seen the things you've made"—she'd pointed at the chocolate cake that was sitting under a mesh dome in the center of the outdoor dining table—"case in point, that gorgeous confection. I could meet with you and the bride and—"

Bella had put her hand on the other woman's arm. "I'm happy to help, however you need."

And she meant it.

There was something different about this town, about the people in it. Not only did Darlington look after their own, but they freely offered up help without expecting anything in return.

Offers to help her carrying in groceries to her apartment, boxes into the diner. Rides to Henry's house if she was walking from downtown.

Frankly, it had been unnerving at first.

But she'd quickly learned that was the way Darlington worked.

She'd watched Esther scoop up a crying baby in the diner, bouncing him around the tables so his frazzled mom could eat. Henry had left to change a tire with nary a second thought. Melissa had offered her the chance—and the payment she'd been going to receive—to make a wedding cake.

The town was wonderful.

Oh, there was the occasional jerk or curmudgeon or stupid teenager. In fact, Rob, Melissa's husband, had her in hysterics at dinner on Monday as he'd described trying to figure out who had been stealing mailboxes from the neighborhood and putting them all on Mr. Watson's—one well-known Darlington curmudgeon—lawn.

So different from home when she'd been sequestered on the estate, lonely except for the internet and books.

So different from New York, which had been exciting and different and filled to the brim with noises and scents and people.

She really liked it here.

And while it had only been a few weeks, Bella couldn't imagine living anywhere else.

She hummed as she worked, dicing up peppers and onions and carefully stowing them in the walk-in. Next came shredding cheese, making sure there were enough eggs and flour and baking soda.

Breakfast service was always busy, and the town loved Henry's omelets and pancakes.

Speaking of which, she went ahead and mixed up some pancake batter. It wouldn't hurt to sit overnight, though it might require some thinning in the morning since the flour molecules tended to tighten up, thus thickening the mixture, over time. Still, it would save Frank a step.

Pulling out her phone, she sent him a picture, letting him know it was there for him in the fridge, then washed up.

The soft chime of her cell signaling Frank's reply had her frowning.

She hadn't remembered turning it off silent.

Shrugging, she wiped her hands on her apron and turned for the shelves holding the dried goods. Henry still wasn't back from fixing Tilly's tire, so she figured she might as well get a head start on the wedding cake.

The bride, Shelby, wanted four tiers, all with different flavors—chocolate-peanut butter, lemon-coconut, vanilla, and salted caramel—and Bella was beyond excited to get started. The actual design would be simple, no topsy-turvy stacking or thousands of gum paste flowers. Which was a good thing because the wedding was in two days, and though Henry and Frank had both offered to help, their strong suit wasn't in crafting edible flowers. Not to mention, the diner wasn't exactly designed for baking. Oh, there were commercial ovens, along with heat and humidity that would wreak havoc on fondant, gum paste, and chocolate.

Still, she had cake pans and all the necessary ingredients to at least get the cakes baked. Melissa had sent her the recipes the bride had taste-tested and chosen, so she didn't have to start from scratch.

But, she couldn't help herself from making a little tweak here or there.

Today, she was starting with the chocolate peanut butter.

Melissa's recipe called for peanut butter chips in the batter, Bella had a little trick to bypass that.

She ground her own peanuts into butter, added local, organic honey, and thinned the mixture with a little milk. Then she swirled it into the pan with the chocolate batter so the two flavors would be more evenly mixed.

Using a small pan at first, she prepared the two components, swirled them together, and slid it in the oven.

Then she set about making some buttercream frosting that she'd freeze and later thaw to cover the outside of the cake. By the time that was finished and stowed safely away, the cake smelled done.

A press to its middle, another long sniff, and she let it stay in for two more minutes as she stacked dirty dishes into the sink.

Her stomach rumbled when she pulled out the pan.

"Oh, yes," she murmured. "You're absolutely perfect, aren't you?"

"I used to say the same thing about you."

Bella whipped around, saw who was in the doorway, and dropped the pan.

The hot cake broke into pieces, burning her legs through her jeans, her feet through her shoes.

But she barely felt it, not with the terror gripping her so tightly.

Her eyes darted around, searching for an exit even though she knew she was trapped.

Still, she had to try to get away.

They stepped into the kitchen.

Heart pounding, she waved a hand to the stools Henry kept along one wall. "Why don't you sit down?"

And then, when their gazes slid to the line of chairs, Bella made a run for it.

CHAPTER NINETEEN

Henry

THE OLD IDIOM, no good deed went unpunished, was proving to be true.

Henry hadn't minded coming to help Tilly, not when it was dark and she had told him she hadn't been able to get a hold of Trent, who owned the only tow truck in town.

But that was an hour ago.

Before he knew the tire was a stubborn asshole that wasn't going to cooperate. First, the lug nut had jammed, then the jack hadn't wanted to work. Then just as he bent near the car to retighten the bolts, some jerkwad in a huge black SUV had sped down the dimly light road, nearly mowing him and Tilly over.

"Not local," he muttered, making sure to give a better look out for traffic as he knelt next to the car again.

"Probably from the wedding," Tilly said. "Out of towners always drive like crazy people."

"They don't know about the murderous deer," he quipped, making her laugh.

The thought made his lips twitch, remembering how the story of Haley and Sam's run-ins with the numerous deer on this road—two motor accidents that had resulted in two totaled cars and one broken ankle . . . and no injuries to the deer themselves—had reached Bella over in Italy.

He tightened the lug nuts, lowered and removed the jack, then stowed it away in Tilly's trunk.

She hugged him, pressed a kiss to his cheek. "You're the best, Henry.

Thank you."

"No problem." He squeezed back. "Now go. Enjoy your night."

Tilly waved as she sank into her driver's seat. "Enjoy your kissy time with Bella."

"Hush, you."

Laughing, she closed the door, started up her car, and drove away.

Henry pulled out his cell as he headed to his own car and sent Bella a text.

Finally done. Should I meet you at my place or the diner?

He waited a couple of moments, half-expecting her to text back, but also half-expecting her *not* to. She'd mentioned starting the wedding cakes, and when she was in baking mode, her awareness of her cell phone went by the wayside.

Figuring it would be faster to go to the diner and check if she was, in fact, baking, he started the ignition and headed back into town.

He'd check there first then go to his house.

The drive back into town took less than ten minutes, and one look at the diner through the large plate glass windows at the front of the restaurant told him Bella was still inside. Lights from the kitchen illuminated the round windows of the doors leading down the hall.

He parked on the street, turned off the car, then was moving around the keys on his ring to select the one to the diner's front door when he saw that it wasn't quite closed.

The hairs on the back of his neck prickled.

Pulling out his cell, he used his other hand to tug open the door, wincing when the bell above it twinkled.

Part of him hoped Bella would hear it and come out of the kitchen, and worry tightened his gut into knots when she didn't.

Ridiculous.

She was probably distracted by the cakes.

But the door was unlocked.

That didn't mean anything. Hadn't he just left it open when she'd shown up in town? Darlington was safe—

He reached the doors leading back into the hallway, pushed them open.

And that was the moment he knew his worry wasn't unfounded.

Because silence was the only thing that greeted him.

Not the sound of a mixer or pans rattling. Not Bella's humming as she maneuvered around the space or even the noise of the industrial dishwasher.

He unlocked his phone and dialed Rob as he ran into the kitchen, only realizing that as the call rang that he didn't know what he would tell him. But by the time Rob answered, he knew.

The kitchen was in utter disarray.

A cake pan was overturned on the floor, crumbs of chocolate scattered and squashed into the tiles. The stools lay on their sides, the oven doors open and filling the space with heated air.

"Henry? Are you there?"

The voice in his ear startled him.

His mind was racing, his heart in his throat. He'd almost forgotten he'd been calling Rob.

"This had better not be a booty call butt dial," he grumbled, the words fading, as though he'd brought the phone away from his ear.

"Rob!" Henry said loudly.

"Henry? You there?"

"Yes. I'm at the diner. Something—" His voice broke.

Instantly, Rob's tone went from a mixture of amused and annoyed to alert. "What is it? What happened?"

"Bella." He sucked in a breath. "Sh-she's gone."

————

RED and blue lights flashed through the front windows of the diner, flickering across the tabletop of the booth Henry sat in.

He dialed Bella's cell again, for the hundredth time in the last hour.

It went straight to voicemail.

Again.

And again.

Fuck. Why hadn't he insisted she come with him?

The officers were in the kitchen, taking pictures, fingerprinting the scene while Rob stood near the front door, talking on his cell in a hushed voice that sent Henry's temper prickling.

Why wasn't anyone doing anything?

Why were they all just standing around, twiddling their fucking thumbs when Bella was out there—

He clenched his jaw, forced himself to breathe.

It would do no one any good to run off without a plan.

Clearly, something had gone horribly wrong. Sergio had come back and—

Pam sat down in front of him, notepad open, green eyes holding a hint of sadness. "Are you—" She hesitated.

Henry put down his cell. "What?"

"Are you sure that she didn't just . . . leave—"

He burst to his feet, thrusting his hands into his hair and gripping tightly. *"Are you fucking kidding me?"* he hissed. "You've seen that mess in the kitchen. The overturned food and chairs and—" He swallowed hard, fury in every cell of his body. "And you think that she just up and walked out of here?"

There were fucking drag marks in the doorway, streaks of chocolate smeared into the floor, down the hall.

Pam—fuck that, *Officer Harting*—pushed out of the booth. "I *have* to ask these questions, Henry. We need to have all the information if we're going to find Bella."

"She did not just leave," he growled. "She was testing recipes for the wedding cake she promised to deliver on Saturday. We had plans later tonight to watch a movie. I-I—"

Words failed him.

A hand dropped onto his shoulder, squeezed firmly.

"Steady," Rob said. "We'll find her."

Henry nodded, even though his stomach was churning. "Any word on Sergio?"

He was the most obvious culprit at this point. Who else would want to take Bella? Who else had the most to lose?

No one.

That was who.

And if Henry had wanted to destroy the fucker before . . . well, *now* the need to eviscerate him was the crux on which his every emotion revolved.

Rob shook his head. "Last report had tracked him down to the private airport outside of Salt Lake. Flight plan had been filed for New York, but those can be changed in the air. No credit card records or pings on his passport. For all we know, he's back in New York."

"Or, he could be here."

Rob nodded. "Yes, he could be."

"Fuck."

"It'll be okay," Rob said. "Stay calm and clear-headed. We'll need that."

Henry nodded.

Rob's cell rang and he squeezed Henry's shoulder again before stepping away to answer it.

Pam closed her notebook, stashed it in the pocket of her uniform. "Keep trying her number," she said. "We'll find her."

Except two hours went by.

Then four.

Then eight.

Then twelve.

And there still wasn't a single sign of Bella.

CHAPTER TWENTY

Bella

SHE'D MADE A CRITICAL MISTAKE.

She'd assumed that Sergio had given up on her. That when he'd skipped town after posting bail, he'd realized she wasn't worth the strife and wouldn't come back. She'd thought he wouldn't want to risk getting picked up for the assault charges the District Attorney was planning on filing.

She'd thought she was safe.

What she *hadn't* figured on was her father.

On him showing up in Darlington with his bodyguards and Sergio in tow. She most definitely hadn't anticipated being bundled into the back seat of an SUV or hustled onto his private plane.

And now she was back in Italy.

Staring out at what most would consider a beautiful view—the bright blue waters of the Mediterranean, fishing boats in the distance, colorful buildings surrounding her.

But Bella saw beneath the pretty exterior.

She knew about the concrete wall, the cameras, the guard at her door.

She knew she was trapped.

Sinking down onto the plush chaise lounge, one of the gorgeous pieces of furniture in her expensively furnished prison, Bella stared out the window, trying to figure a way out of her father's house.

No money. No passport. No phone.

Fuck.

She was well and truly fucked.

Her eyes burned with tears, but she refused to let them fall. She hadn't gone back on her own, she'd been forced by a father who had somehow lost his mind. Someone in the house would help her. They *had* to.

But she just couldn't figure out why her father had done it.

Bella was a disappointment, and he never finished a conversation without letting her know that painful truth. He'd threatened to disown her more than once. So why, when she'd finally left for good, had he done this?

Why had he come after her?

She couldn't figure it out. It just—

"None of this makes any sense," she murmured.

A knock at the door had her jumping to her feet, hands braced in front of her. The thick wood panel opened silently, one of her father's bodyguards entering with a garment bag draped over one shoulder.

Bella stepped back, putting the chaise between them.

His name was Raul and he was the one who'd so effectively subdued her at the diner.

She'd barely made it two steps into the hall before he grabbed her, one hand in her hair, the other gripping her wrist and twisting her arm behind her back. He'd had her completely immobilized in under ten seconds.

In the back of the SUV in ten more.

And at the private airfield in less than an hour.

Now Raul dropped the bag onto the bed. "Get dressed."

She shook her head. "No."

His deep brown eyes narrowed. "Get dressed or I'll do it for you."

Part of her felt like she should continue refusing, just on principle. She didn't want to be here. She was desperate to find a way to get out and going along with any of his—and presumably, her father's—orders didn't help her cause.

But one look at his expression warned her that she really didn't want to refuse.

He'd get her in whatever was in that bag and it wouldn't be difficult for him, no matter how big of a fight she put up.

"All right," she said.

"Makeup. Hair. Thirty minutes." He spun around and left the room, and despite the seriousness of her situation, Bella had a hard time not sticking her tongue out at the clipped-out orders.

"Sit. Stay," she muttered, waiting for the door to shut completely before she crossed to the bed. She *would* have locked it behind him, but for obvious reasons, the lock had been removed.

Sighing, she unzipped the bag. A gorgeous navy dress with ruching on the bodice and a lace overlay on the skirt was inside.

No doubt it would be a perfect fit, but it was all Bella could do to not throw the garment out the freaking window. Just the thought of dressing up for her father, for Sergio, for playing the fucking doll all over again turned her stomach.

Or maybe it was the fact that she hadn't eaten for close to twenty-four hours.

She hadn't trusted the food on the plane—her father had kidnapped her already, why would he balk at a simple thing like drugging her into submission. So, she'd refused the food, readying herself to throw a tantrum at customs.

Except *that* opportunity never presented itself.

Her father had stepped off the plane, exchanged some words with an official—and no doubt some bills alongside them—and then they'd been allowed to disembark. Raul had been by her side, the grip on his arm a painful reminder of how easily he could subdue her, and Bella hadn't known whether to show her hand and fight or to go along and try to find a way to escape later.

She should have fought.

Because security at her father's compound had intensified since the last time she'd snuck out.

Before it had felt like protection, safeguards to make sure she wasn't at risk from someone who might try to get to her because of her father's business interests—not that anyone ever seemed to recognize her. She was the floor lamp positioned artistically in the corner of the room, pretty scenery that no one remembered.

But *now*, it was clear the security was in place to keep her there.

How naïve she'd been.

And now she worried she would never see Henry again.

The way Sergio had looked at her on the plane—

Bella shivered. He'd been furious, expression frosty and some dark emotion in his eyes that had her keeping a careful distance from him. She'd embarrassed him again. Not only that, she'd made him look like a deranged fool with a dangerous lack of control, *and* she'd dared to bring charges against him. Then there was the fact that she'd taken up with Henry.

If her father succeeded in marrying her off to him?

She was petrified to consider what he might do to her in retribution.

He'd pushed her down the stairs, had tried to choke her, had chased her, yanking her by the hair. And most of those had been in full view of the public.

Or at least somewhere that they could be easily discovered.

If she were in his home?

Well, Bella thought she wouldn't survive the year.

Because she would keep trying to get out. And keep trying. She would never stop trying to get back to Henry.

Never.

Her eyes drifted back down to the gown in front of her and her sigh was despondent.

Because, for now, she needed to get dressed.

———

HER HEELS PINCHED like a son of a bitch. The dress was way too tight.

Either she'd gained weight since moving to Darlington or Bella's father was trying to punish her.

She stifled a snort.

Because, one, *of course* he was trying to punish her and, two, she *had* probably gained weight.

All those late-night meals with Henry. All the taste-testing of new desserts she'd planned for the bakery she wanted to open. All the—

Her jaw dropped open as a group of men entered the room.

She'd been shuttled downstairs and into an empty parlor they'd often used for her father's business gatherings. As usual, all the chairs had been removed, replaced by several tall cocktail tables—the kind people stand up to eat at—the sideboard covered with a variety of her father's favorite dishes.

Also as usual, she'd been left standing alone in the space for close to an hour.

Well, alone except for Raul, who was standing near the room's only door.

But that wasn't what made her jaw drop.

"Justin?" she whispered, hope making her heart buoyant.

Aside from dinner at the ranch, she'd only met Kelly's husband a couple of times, but he *had* to recognize her. Or, her heart swelled with hope, maybe they'd found her.

Maybe he'd come to rescue her.

She knew enough about him to understand that his family business was powerful and well-respected.

He could—

But then his eyes connected with hers and her heart sank.

Because he wasn't looking at her with concern or even recognition. No, instead he gave her a faintly appraising once-over, starting at her face and ending at her toes, but other than that, he barely paid her any mind, turning to focus his attention back on whatever her father was saying.

Part of the act.

It had to be.

But . . . what if it wasn't?

What if Justin wanted her family's business more than he wanted to help her? What if—?

No.

Kelly wouldn't have married such a man.

She couldn't have.

But as Bella straightened her shoulders and crossed over to where the men were chatting, she couldn't stop the niggling in her brain that Justin would be able to get her out.

She'd barely reached them when her father shot a glare in her direction. "Wine, Isabella," he snapped. Her hesitation, her moment spent trying to meet Justin's eyes earned her a sharp pinch on her arm. She sucked in a breath, trying and failing to hold back her wince.

"*Now.*"

"I'll help you," Justin said.

Relief coursed through her. He was going to get her out.

He trailed her to the refreshment table, waving off her father's protests. "I'm a guest in your home, it's the least I can do."

Bella grabbed a bottle, positioned herself so her father couldn't see her face.

"Justin," she hissed. "I'm so glad to see you."

He froze, head jerking.

There was something about his eyes . . .

Blinking, she forced herself to focus, to go as slowly as possible as she positioned six glasses and began carefully pouring the red wine made from her father's favorite variety of grapes, Sangiovese.

"I'm . . ." He pressed his lips together, expression bland, as though he were carefully considering what to say. "I'm married."

Bella shook her head. "I know that. Kelly—"

Fingers gripped her wrist, and she nearly dropped the bottle of wine. "What the fuck do you know about Kelly Hamilton?"

Her breath caught and she steadied the bottle. "It's Kelly Roosevelt now," she whispered. "It's me, Justin. Bella. You know I know her and Abbie and the twins. You know *me.* You know I'm Henry's—"

"Isabella!" her father bellowed.

"Coming," she called, grabbing two glasses and hurrying over to give them to him and Sergio before rushing back over to the table and snagging two more.

Justin caught her arm. "Twins?" he asked, hoarsely.

And that was the moment she knew, the moment the pieces aligned in her head and her heart sank to her toes.

"You're not Justin, are you?"

He shook his head, left the sideboard with his glass in hand, rejoining the circle of men.

Bella dropped her gaze to the carpet, blinking back tears as she walked over to distribute the rest of the wine to her father's business associates. Then she strode back to the sideboard, leaning her back against the wall.

Sergio shifted, as though he were going to join her, but her father took him by the back of the neck and whispered something in his ear.

Something that made dark, angry eyes shift in Bella's direction.

Shit.

He listened for a long moment before nodding.

"Food, Isabella," her father ordered in Italian after he'd finished speaking to Sergio. "The others will be here soon, but they can serve themselves."

The men laughed, all except Justin—or the *not* Justin—who probably didn't speak enough Italian to understand the remark.

But *she* got the message loud and clear.

These men were the inner circle.

These men mattered.

And Bella was expected to serve them.

If she didn't—

She shuddered to consider it. Her father had always been demanding, but not like this, not ordering her around in front of the others like she was no better than a servant, and she understood that in her father's eyes, she was worth exactly that much. There was no more slack on her leash, no room for her to go live her own life.

She would do as he wanted, or she would pay the consequences.

He'd find her, no matter where she went, and he'd drag her back here.

She'd never get out.

She would never have the life she'd dreamed of with Henry.

Eyes burning, she began to prepare the six plates, hardly aware of what she was putting on the white porcelain.

"I'm Rex," the not-Justin said, having come back over to refill his glass of wine.

She nodded, moving past him to pile a few shrimp onto her father's plate.

"I'm Justin's twin."

Her breath caught. *Of course,* he was. "Did he—" Hope bubbled up, and she whispered. "Did he send you?"

Silence.

And fuck, hope fizzled like so much smoke.

"No," he finally said.

She nodded, picked up the plate and bringing it to her father, who promptly sent her back to remake it.

"The pastas are touching," he said, as though she were daft and a little marinara mixing with garlic cream sauce was the worst crime she could commit.

But she was reeling and upset, feet screaming, heart aching . . . and so, she remade the plate.

And then again when he said the shrimp were cold.

Never mind that they were *supposed* to be cold.

Finally, she produced a plate he didn't reject, and she worked her way through the others, who all had their various requests.

All except for Rex.

"Henry?" he asked, accepting the plate she thrust at him.

Her eyes shot up, and she nodded.

An eternity passed, several indiscernible emotions crossing his expression, before determination set in. "Trust me," he whispered, and that damn hope bubbled to life again.

But, really, Bella should have known better.

It had been *one* fucking evening and it already felt as though her heart had spent an eternity on a roller coaster. Maybe she had a chance. Maybe she didn't. No, of course she didn't. But maybe—

Rex's fingers brushed the back of her hand. "Just trust me."

Except, he didn't do anything to warrant that trust.

Instead, Rex ignored her the rest of the evening, demanding more plates of food and eating like a glutton as the rest of the men—the lower circle of her father's associates—joined the party. And that said nothing of how much he drank.

He kept refilling his glass. Over and over. Until Raul had to sling his arm around Rex's shoulders and escort him from the room.

Until Bella was alone, all over again.

Rex Roosevelt was just like the rest of them.

———

SHE'D JUST HUNG the dress back up in her closet when she heard a noise that sent the hairs on her nape prickling and her movements into high gear.

Someone was breaking in.

Or rather, someone had let themselves into her room since her door didn't have a lock.

She'd shoved a chair in front of it, for all the good that did her in this moment. The screech of its feet sliding against the tile floor was what Bella had heard.

Hurrying, she threw on the first clothes she could reach—sweats, a T-shirt, even bare feet into sneakers. Both because she didn't want to be in just her underwear if it was Sergio who'd come in and also because she wanted to have the chance to run if the opportunity presented itself.

Then she searched for a weapon.

The fancy suite she was being kept in had a designer wardrobe and makeup filled drawers, silk sheets, and plush rugs. A luxurious prison, to be sure, but not one exactly rife with weapons.

In the end, footsteps prompted her to grab the first thing she saw.

A curling iron.

She darted into the bathroom and snatched it up then hid behind the partially open door.

"Isabella?" came a hushed male voice. The footsteps drifted closer.

She clenched the plastic handle tightly, lifted it above her head.

A shadow crossed the threshold of the bathroom then a leg . . . a torso.

Bella closed her eyes and swung.

Thunk.

"Fuck!" the voice said, stepping fully into the bathroom and wincing as he rubbed the top of his head.

She froze. "But you're drunk." A whisper.

Rex's mouth curved. "Either that or I'm really good at pretending I am."

"I saw you drink those bottles of wine." Two of them. By himself.

"I drank a few glasses," he admitted. "But your father's fern drank more. I probably killed it"—a shrug—"though I don't think that'll bother you much."

Bella smiled. "Not at all actually."

"Good," Rex said. "So, you want to get out of here?"

She laughed at the casual tone he used, like they were getting ready to leave a restaurant or a boring party.

"Yes," she said. "I'd like to go home. But what about the guards?"

"I was busy while I was passed out drunk in my room. I called in some help and"—he held up a bag—"I found your passport."

Hope bubbled up in her. "But—"

He took her arm. "There's too much to explain now. We need to be in position in ten minutes. Can you trust me to get you out?"

She looked into his eyes, saw earnestness but also the barest hint of a shadow, as though he expected her to say no.

But, fuck, what choice to Bella have?

Stay and—

She shuddered to think of it.

Or trust Justin's brother and hope that he kept up his end of the bargain.

A nod. The decision not one that took long to ponder. She wanted to get home to Darlington, to Henry.

She'd do whatever it took.

"Get me out of here, Rex."

CHAPTER TWENTY-ONE

Henry

HE WAS SITTING in the kitchen of Roosevelt Ranch when Justin's phone rang.

Two days without a word from Bella, forty-eight hours with no sightings of her or Sergio, but still Henry's heart leaped at the vibration.

Maybe—

Justin shook his head slightly. "Just Rex."

Once Henry would have thought Rex to be pretty much the worst kind of scum out there, but now he knew differently. Rex was an asshole, but he was on a completely different scale than Sergio.

Justin rejected the call, slid it back into his pocket. "How are you—" He broke off with a sigh and pulled his cell back out. "Let me get this. Otherwise, he'll just keep calling." He swiped, put the phone up to his ear. "Listen, Rex. This isn't a good—*what?*"

Henry straightened at the shocked tone but then rolled his eyes.

The bastard had probably made another shitty business decision. Or knocked up—

"Okay," Justin said. "Okay, I'll—*we'll* be there in . . . *fuck*, I don't know. As soon as we can." He hung up. "Let's go. It's Bella. I'll explain on the way."

"I—" Shock had Henry in its grip for one long moment, but then Justin rushed for the front door and the action sprung Henry into motion.

They ran to the garage, bypassing the wedding, but spending precious minutes navigating around all the cars before they managed to make their way to the main road. All the while, Henry's head was spinning, wanting to demand information, but knowing he needed to wait until, at the very least, they maneuvered past the reveling guests.

The moment they were clear, Justin dialed Rob and put him on speakerphone.

"I just got a call from Rex," Justin said. "He's on the private plane and will be landing at the airfield in less than an hour." His eyes shot to Henry's, and he said the unbelievable words Henry had been hoping for since Justin had mentioned her name. Impossible, because how could Rex have anything to do with Bella, but still wishing for them all the same.

"Rex says Bella is with him. Apparently, he met her father in Italy, they were going to do business, but then Bella was there and—" Justin shook his head. "Well, that's all he would say. That she's fine and next to him, and they're landing at the airport in just under an hour."

To Rob's credit, he regained himself faster than Henry.

"Holy shit." Then a deep breath rattled through the airwaves. "Okay, I'll get on the horn and see who's closest so they can meet the plane and make sure she's safe. How long until you guys are there?"

"Depending on how fast I drive," Justin replied, "hour and a half?"

"Me, too," Rob said. "Drive fast. I'll clear your way."

He hung up, and Henry turned to Justin.

"Do you think Rex—" He cut off the question, not wanting to voice the possibility that Bella might not actually be on the plane.

"No," Justin said quietly. "She's there."

And then he floored it, making the drive in less time than Henry could have imagined, but it was still the longest hour and a half of his life.

Finally, *finally*, they pulled into the private airfield parking lot. A jet was parked there, the only large plane amongst the single engines. Its doors were open, the stairs extended.

Henry waited just long enough for Justin to put the car into park before popping his door and sprinting up the stairs.

He didn't breathe until he saw her.

Curled up on a leather couch, blanket pulled up to her chin.

"She's just sleeping. Couldn't hold out any longer."

Henry turned and saw Justin's twin standing near the cockpit. Officer Harting stood next to him. He hadn't registered them, hadn't seen anything aside from Bella.

"Is she—"

"She's okay. Just exhausted. We didn't have the easiest time getting out of Italy."

Henry nodded, figuring that was enough for now.

Later, they would have the whole story.

Right now, he was taking her home.

He crossed over to Bella, scooped her up into his arms, and carried her down the stairs. Justin was there, opening the back door, helping him maneuver her inside. A few minutes later, they were on the road again.

Rob flew past them in a cruiser, and a few seconds later Justin's phone rang.

He answered with the volume low, though Bella hadn't stirred.

"You got her?"

"Yes," Justin said. "I can't take her back to my house. Henry's?"

"Yup. I'll get a car there. I'm going to speak to Rex and then I'll head to Henry's place."

"Should I make some calls?"

Henry had managed to get a seat belt around Bella's waist and still hold her, cradling her against the bumps, but he was following the conversation, still understood what Justin was alluding to.

Kelly's husband had spent many years in the military, and he knew some very powerful folks in private security.

Henry was all-in for whatever they could do to ensure Bella's safety. He'd sell the diner, move out of state, change his name, find a way to finance bodyguards—

Anything, so long as she never had to go through this again.

Anything so he didn't have to spend another sleepless night petrified that she was hurting and scared . . . or worse.

Rob cleared his throat. "Will they stop that asshole from coming after her again?"

"They have ways of making sure that doesn't happen again."

"Then probably," Rob said. "But wait until I talk to Rex first. This is way the fuck out my jurisdiction, but I want to make sure we have all the information we need to keep Bella safe." A pause. "Once that's done, I'll call my contact at the FBI, and he can advise the department from there."

"Henry?" Justin asked.

He nodded, eyes locked on Bella, memorizing every detail, promising himself he would never take another moment with her for granted.

"He's with us," Justin translated for him to Rob and then hung up.

They'd driven another fifteen minutes, the sun firmly behind the hills, the sky an ever-deepening navy, when Bella finally stirred.

Her head rolled from side to side, she stretched, and then went ramrod straight.

She jerked, eyes flashing open, mouth parting as though to scream.

Then she saw Henry.

And burst into tears.

Huge gasping sobs that absolutely broke his heart. "It's okay," he told her, repeating the words over and over again. "You're safe now. I'm here."

Her arms wrapped around his neck and she crawled into his lap, tears soaking into his shirt. "I thought—" Her breath caught. "I thought—" But she couldn't finish the sentence.

"I know," he murmured. "I know, sweetheart. You're home now. You're safe." He whispered the mantra over and over again, until finally her spine softened, her breathing slowed.

Finally she nodded, as though hearing the words for the first time and burrowed into him.

"Sleep now," he said. "I've got you."

———

LATER THAT NIGHT, Bella woke with a start, lurching against him, panicked for long, heartbreaking moments until his voice finally penetrated.

Henry held it together until she fell back to sleep, the terror of the last few days clearly taking its toll on her. He slipped out of bed and moved quietly into the bathroom.

There he opened the medicine cabinet, pulled out the little black box hidden on the top shelf.

Above Bella's sight. So she couldn't stumble on it.

Henry had bought it five years before.

Had planned on giving it to her then, had intended to give it to her only a few days ago.

And now?

Henry shoved it back on the shelf.

How could he?

He stared at himself in the mirror, wondering all over again why he'd left Bella alone.

He should have known.

Yet, how *could* he have known?

But dammit, he fucking hadn't protected her five years ago, and he hadn't protected her now. He was fucking useless and—

The door slid open on a quiet squeak, Bella's eyes peering at him through the gap.

She hesitated, and he put out a hand. "Come here, sweetheart."

Then she was in his arms. The guilt abated, for the moment, anyway, because the relief that they'd somehow found their way back to each other was so great.

"Every time I close my eyes, I keep thinking of them. I keep worrying they'll—"

She clamped her mouth closed, biting back the rest of her words.

Henry cupped her cheek and tilted her head back so he could see her face. Dark circles still ringed the skin beneath her eyes, and she was very pale. But she was alive and in his arms. That was enough for now.

"I know, baby. But it was traumatic. You have to give yourself time to heal."

They'd talked to Rex, now knew that it wasn't just Sergio who'd kidnapped Bella, that her father had an equal, or worse, hand in it.

"I don't want time to heal!" she snapped, pushing out of his embrace and pacing away. "I'm so tired of my father trying to ruin my life. I'm so tired of being a pawn that he doesn't want and yet can't let go. He absolutely despises me, but because I chose to leave, he had to punish me."

He watched her stride across the bathroom, back and forth, back and forth. The fire in her eyes, the first sign he'd seen since her return, settled the gaping wound in his heart.

Oh, it was still there, would probably never completely go away, same as the wound from his dad, but the guilt and worry weren't so all-encompassing.

He could finally breathe, could focus on being what Bella needed.

"I know."

"He hates me." She shook her head. "I don't know why he wants to control me. Why can't he just let me go? Forget I existed."

"Men like him can never let it go, not when they feel like they've been bested."

She swallowed hard. "I know. That's why I'm so worried about Rex. He took a huge risk in helping me. I don't even know how many people he paid off—officials, security guards."

"Rex will be okay," he assured her. "He can afford to hire security."

"But—"

"And there's also the fact that Justin's friends visited your father and Sergio."

Bella frowned. "Why would it matter if Justin's friends visited?"

"Because he has some friends in very high places. Friends that can make you disappear without a trace, but also friends that can make your father's business prospects dry up." Henry shrugged. "Justin just told me they found evidence of your father participating in some unsavory, and decidedly illegal activities. If he or Sergio or one of their lackeys gets within even a hundred miles of you, that information will be passed along to the proper authorities."

"Oh."

He smiled for what felt like the first time in a century. "Yeah, oh."

"And we'll keep some security around for a while. Install a system here and at the diner, have some guys keep watch on the house until you're comfortable."

Bella laced her fingers with his. "So, if you've done all that, then why are you in here beating yourself up?"

Henry froze. "I'm—"

"Don't deny it." She tugged him into the bedroom and over to the bed. "I know you, love. I know you're beating yourself up because you have some notion that you should have protected me."

He shook his head. "I shouldn't have—"

"Don't." She lay down, coaxed him to cuddle up next to her. "Don't say you shouldn't have helped Tilly. I love this town. I love the way everyone looks after one another." She rested her head on his shoulder. "I love you."

"I love you, too."

"Hold me while I sleep?"

"Always."

Her voice, when it came a few minutes later, was gentle. "I know you're going to feel guilty for a long time. Because you're a good man and because you care about me, but you need to come to terms with the fact that this wasn't your fault."

"I—"

"No," she said, firmer now. "No. You don't get to shoulder this. My father and Sergio were at fault. Not you."

"Sweetheart—"

She sat up then glared down at him. "Do you blame *me* for being kidnapped?"

"Fuck no," he growled.

"Then you can't blame yourself, either."

He opened his mouth, found it covered with her hand.

"I know it will take you time to believe it, so I'm going to be patient." One half of her mouth curved. "For the moment."

He touched her cheek. "I love you."

A full smile now. "And I love you, but you want to be here for me? I need you to be present, not sneaking off to mentally berate yourself. I need us to live the future I dreamed of for five years." She turned her head, pressed a kiss to his palm. "I need the diner and a bakery. I need you in my bed every night. I need babies and puppies. And I"—she pressed her mouth to his—"need you."

"You have me." A kiss to her forehead, each cheek, her nose. "Forever."

"I can deal with that."

And then as they drifted off to sleep, the sound of their laughter echoing in the air around them, Henry thought that he might just be able to give her that ring after all.

CHAPTER TWENTY-TWO

She'd finally completed a wedding cake.

Or nearly, she thought, adding one last flower to the grouping of red and white blooms cascading down the side of the cake.

"That's beautiful," Melissa said.

Bella bumped her shoulder against her friend's. "I think you're just glad that I didn't get out of making the cake this time."

Melissa's eyes twinkled. "Oh, definitely. Kidnapping as a way to get out of commitments, totally solid plan."

"Takes one to know one."

They fist-bumped and giggled.

It was a relief to be able to laugh with someone about what happened, but also to be able to talk with someone who knew what it was like to go through something so traumatic. Melissa had passed along the name of the therapist she'd spoken to after her own harrowing abduction, a much-appreciated gesture.

Bella knew she would need to eventually talk with someone, but she wanted a little more time to get her legs back under her.

Only six weeks had passed since Rex delivered her safely back to Darlington and while she still had the occasional nightmare, they were coming less frequently. It also helped that Justin's *friends* delivered weekly reports on her father and Sergio's whereabouts. Not the healthiest thing ever, but she took a lot of comfort in knowing where they were . . . though in reality, she didn't give a damn where they were, so long as that was far, *far* away from her.

More importantly, she'd seen Henry relax over the last weeks, going from not being able to stand having her out of his sight, to leaving her alone for hours at a time.

Like today.

Though, she was surrounded by people.

And he'd texted a half-dozen times.

Still, it was progress and she was just happy Henry had managed to put the majority of his guilt behind him.

She'd officially moved her stuff out of the apartment and into his house and was looking for a commercial space to open the bakery, but for now, she continued to take shifts at the diner when she could.

Because the majority of the time was spent filling its cold cases with baked goods that the people of Darlington snatched up in rapid succession.

They'd even written an article in the local newspaper accusing her of making everyone in town fat.

Outwardly, she suggested a 5K to raise money for P.E. programs at the local elementary, middle, and high schools, but internally she'd been thrilled to have her very own news story in the *Darlington Gazette*.

Finally, she'd made it.

But, celebrity status or not, it was time to get this cake out to the venue.

"Ready?" she asked, nudging one more flower into the arrangement. Melissa was going to help her carry it from the small kitchen where she'd put on the finishing touches, out to the cake table in the pavilion.

And it was going to be filmed for the show.

Bella sent up a mental prayer. Please let her not ruin another wedding cake.

"Ready," Melissa chirped, grabbing the other side of the stand. They lifted on three and carefully navigated the space, not breathing until it was safely on the table.

Bella stepped back, wiped her forehead on a towel. "Damn. I did good."

Melissa snorted, but she was smiling. "Hell, yes, you did." A beat. "You now know this will never end, right? You'll be baking Darlington's wedding cakes for all eternity."

Bella grinned over at her. "I can live with that."

Her phone buzzed in her pocket, and she pulled it out to see another text from Henry.

Melissa rolled her eyes. "That man needs to chill."

Bella hardly heard her because the text wasn't checking up on her. Instead, it said:

Our place. Sunset?

She grinned.

I'll be there.

Another buzz.

Will you bring me cake?

But before she could type out a response, he had her bursting out into laughter at a GIF he sent of a puppy with a surprisingly innocent face surrounded by the evidence of his decidedly *not* innocent playtime with a roll of toilet paper.

Funny you ask because I might have made an extra pan.

Her cell vibrated.

I'll bring the forks.

"Okay," Melissa said, "I take it back. The man is good. Too good."

Bella happened to agree and loved him all the more for it. "I think I'm going to take off. Can you—?"

Melissa made a shooing movement. "Get out of here before you miss the sunset."

Bella grinned and waved, stopping only to pick up the smaller cake she'd made for Henry. Then she drove to his spot and carried it up to where he waited at the top of the hill, two forks in hand.

She knew what it cost him to not hover, to give her the space to go about her life without a babysitter when part of him was still always on edge about her safety.

"How'd you get here?" She'd only just gotten her license and had borrowed his car to drop off the cake.

He slid an arm around her waist. "Justin," he said and nudged her down to their rock. She was shocked to see he'd gone through the trouble of laying out a blanket and basket. There was even a candle in the center. "Not the most practical place for a picnic," he told her, pulling the cake from her hands and setting it on top before lifting her up. "But I couldn't resist."

Practical or not, it was both beautiful *and* sweet.

"Please, tell me there's Cobb salad in that basket."

Henry smirked. "We need *something* to counter all the sugar you keep forcing me to eat."

A snort. "Forcing. Ha." But she'd already opened the basket and was digging out a container of her favorite salad. "Oh, thank you. I'm starving." She scooped up a giant bite, shoved it in her mouth—

He lifted a hand. "Wait—"

Crunch.

She winced. *He* winced.

"I was going to . . ."

Bella lifted a napkin to her mouth, deposited the object that had nearly cracked her tooth inside of it.

"I figured you'd see it in the slice of egg."

She stared down at the ring, a simple band with a diamond in its center. "I didn't," she whispered.

"Bella." Her eyes met his. "I wished for this five years ago. And I know it's fast and so much has happened in so short a time now. But what I've learned from my dad, from you, from *us* is that we have to grab on to our chances for happiness with two hands." He swallowed. "Will you marry me? It doesn't have to be today or even this year but—"

"Shut up." Bella laughed at the expression on his face as she wiped the ring clean. "I love you. Of course, I'll marry you. Today, tomorrow, or next year. I just want a life with you, Henry Miller, however we end up making it work." A beat. "Now, put this damned ring on my finger and kiss me."

And for once, he didn't tease her or argue or delay.

He slid the ring on and kissed her until they missed the sunset all together and the sky was dark.

Then he kissed her again as the stars shone brightly in the sky.

DESIRE AT ROOSEVELT RANCH

CHAPTER ONE

Rex

He drove down the dark road, trying to figure out why he was still in Darlington, Utah, almost two months after he'd deposited Bella back with her one true love, Henry.

Barf.

Love was for idiots.

Or pussies.

Or people who were insanely, sickeningly happy.

Ugh.

Rex was jealous. He knew it. He embraced it.

But that didn't change the fact he wasn't the kind of person who fell in love. Or rather, he didn't *allow* himself to fall in love. He'd seen the way his father had loved his mother—a touching Hollywood scene if there ever was one, filled with so much devotion and affection that when she'd died, his father had changed.

Part of him had died, too.

And so, Rex and Justin had lost *both* parents.

That was the troubling part of so-called happily ever afters.

They never lasted.

Rex sighed because the real casualties in those failed or aborted happy endings were the kids. *They* suffered. *They* lost it all. *They*—

"Fuck!" he said and swerved, almost clipping the car barely pulled over on the shoulder.

No hazard lights flashing. No flares. Nothing but a dark shape silhouetted against the moonlight. Were they trying to get themselves killed?

He slowed and turned around, heading back to the parked car.

His tirade about responsibility was on the tip of his tongue and—*ha!*—if anyone even knew that *he'd* thought the word responsibility, they would have keeled over and dropped dead.

Responsibility and Rex Roosevelt did not belong in the same sentence.

He was the screw-up.

He was the bad guy.

He was pulling over behind the car.

Rex parked behind it and turned on his hazard lights before getting out. He'd extended a hand to knock when he saw the woman inside. Spot-lit by his car's headlights, she looked like an angel with pale blond hair and delicate features.

Or at least from the glimpse he caught, they *seemed* delicate.

He only caught hints of a pert nose, plump lips, and a slender jaw because she was spending a lot of time banging her face against the steering wheel.

Rex hesitated and almost turned away, leaving her to whatever sort of mental breakdown she was determined to have, but just as he'd taken a step back toward his car, his conscience pinged.

The annoying bastard had been all too busy lately.

He sighed but knew he couldn't leave her, and so he blew out a breath, raised his hand, and knocked on the window.

The woman inside jumped.

Her gaze shot to his for one long moment before her eyes slid closed, head dropping down to the steering wheel.

But Rex barely noticed.

Because one look from *her,* and he'd felt like he'd been struck over the head by a two-by-four.

Or maybe hit in the ass by Cupid's arrow.

She was . . . different . . . wonderful . . .

And he wanted her.

CHAPTER TWO

Tilly

"Go away, y-you . . . *you!*" she shouted through the closed window of her car.

It was late. It was dark.

Her car had decided it was Satan's spawn again.

And so, no, she wasn't firing on all cylinders when it came to her insult game. Not that her insult game was ever that strong, but circling back to the late, dark, stuck on the side of the road thing—and having watched way too many murder documentaries on Netflix lately—Tilly wasn't about to greet the shadow outside her car with any familiarity.

Especially when all she could discern was that the person crouching to peer into the window of her little sedan was big, with broad shoulders. She grabbed her phone and flicked on the flashlight, shining it in the murderer's—Good Samaritan's—face.

Then almost dropped it in her haste to turn it off.

"Justin?" she asked, identifying her former coworker's husband. Kelly and Justin had been married for a few years, and he was decidedly a good guy.

Think Goody Two Shoes as an alternative to the leading man in a horror flick.

She pressed the button to unlock the car door then popped the handle.

"Sorry," she said quickly. "I didn't know it was you, and I stayed up way too late last night watching this movie, and now it's dark and my car just up and died and—"

Her words cut off.

Because in her haste to exit the car, she'd left the door open and that open door meant that the overhead light was shining, illuminating the space around them.

Illuminating Justin's face.

"I thought your eyes were green," she murmured.

Justin blinked, and it was as though someone had wiped his face clean with a towel, but instead of scrubbing away dirt and grime, her words had rubbed away all traces of emotion.

His expression went blank, blue eyes hardening. "Nope," he said, mouth pressing flat. "In fact, I was born with this pair."

The cadence with which he spoke—arrogant, cool—told Tilly all she needed to know.

"You're not Justin."

"Ding. Ding. Ding." He stepped toward her.

She backed away . . . into the door.

The man didn't stop, just kept moving forward, but just when his chest would have brushed hers, the moment she'd sucked in a huge gulp of air, readying herself to scream, he shifted, nudging her out of the way and dropping down into the driver's seat.

Was he trying to steal her car?

"No," he said with a smirk, nodding in the direction of the sleek sedan that was parked behind her as her cheeks went red-hot with embarrassment at having said that aloud. "I *have* a working vehicle."

What would he want with a dumpy Mazda like hers anyway? It was on the leeward side of two hundred thousand miles, the front seat had a spring that was bent and always poked her as she drove, the radio rarely worked, and . . . well, based on the fact that it was stopped on the side of the road for the umpteenth time in the last few months, it was seriously lacking in the one quality that most people valued in a car this old.

Reliability.

Click.

She jumped, mental diatribe about her vehicle halting. "I tried that—" she said, or rather *started* to say because the not-Justin reached down and tugged on the lever to pop her hood—er, the *car's* hood—then pushed out of the driver's seat. Tilly caught a whiff of his cologne as he went, spice mixed with something earthy.

Her kryptonite.

Sandalwood.

The little *je ne sais quoi* that was the basis for so many scents, both male and female. It rounded out the notes, added depth to something like cinnamon or bergamot, paired well with vanilla and warm black pepper.

A loud banging pulled her out of her mental soliloquy to all things nose-related.

She was Tilly Conner, of the long line of Conners from Darlington, Utah. Who stayed in Darlington, who met their husbands in Darlington, who had tiny humans that grew up in Darlington. Her future was waitressing in Henry's Diner until she met someone she didn't hate—and maybe sort of, even liked—they'd date for the prerequisite one-point-five years, get engaged, get married, pop out some of those tiny humans, then go their separate ways . . . at least in her branch of the family.

And now she was the last of her side.

But regardless of lineage, what Conners from Darlington did *not* do was dream and wish and hope for a different life—especially not one that had her starring as the creator of a line of perfumes and colognes.

Then expanding into hair products. And makeup. And candles.

Nope.

That was exactly what she shouldn't be thinking about.

She *could* go.

But she wouldn't.

"Thinking isn't the problem," she muttered. "It's the hoping that does it—"

A banging noise drove out all imaginings of a different life, in a different place, with different opportunities. She gasped and jumped, clutching the top of the door for balance, shoving all thoughts away, forcing herself to stop acting like a daydreaming child and to focus on the present.

On what was important.

Namely, the fact that she was on the side of the road with a non-Justin, who seemed to be getting very angry with her engine.

"Um," she called over the sound. "What are you—"

"Try it now," the man called, his voice dripping down her spine like honey.

Thighs clenching, fingers still gripping the door, she frowned. "Try what?"

A sigh. Footsteps crunching the dirt and rocks as he rounded the front of the car, slipped around her, and reached over to turn the key in the ignition.

Her engine started up.

And not just the one in her pants, because sweet baby Jesus, his ass in those slacks, the cotton cupping the mounds lovingly, making her fingers ache to touch—

Whoa, girl.

Yes, she'd calmed herself like one of Kelly's horses.

But she'd never been attracted to Kelly's husband. Hell, she'd barely been attracted to *anyone* for the last few years. It was why she *hadn't* made tiny humans, why she was frighteningly single, why—

"Get in the car."

Tilly blinked. "What?"

The man sighed. "I'll follow you home, make sure you get there." When she didn't immediately move, he nudged her again, and this time his fingers brushed the bare skin of her arm.

Sparks.

As in, she felt actual sparks.

Except that was insane.

She was delusional, wrapped up in her bergamot, sandalwood, vanilla haze. She was—

Plunked into the driver's seat, the man's lovely bergamot, sandalwood, and light vanilla scent filling the air around her. He stretched over her, clipped her seat belt in place, put her hands on the steering wheel, then spoke to her like she was the biggest idiot on the planet. "You. Drive. Me. Follow."

Tilly shook her head. "I don't understand how you fixed my car."

A flash of white teeth that threatened to make her stupid. "It's not fixed. It's running. For now." He leaned back, started to close the door. "But you need a new battery and starter."

"Thank—"

The door shut, cutting off her words.

She sighed, used the manual handle to roll down the window. "Thank you for fixing—getting my car started, but I don't need an escort."

He paused, glanced back at her, then shrugged before continuing back to his car.

"What's your name, anyway?" she called as he opened his driver's side and started to climb in.

"Rex," he said, that dripping honey voice now sliding lower. "Rex Roosevelt."

Then, as she was reeling from the confirmation of the truth she'd known deep inside the moment she'd realized he wasn't Justin, Rex started up his car—it purred to life with no protest—and drove away.

The cloud of dust in his wake, the only sign he'd been there at all.

CHAPTER THREE

Rex

"Stupid," he muttered. "Stupid fucking idiot."

What had he expected? For her to jump into his arms and declare her eternal love all because he'd banged on her starter?

He snorted.

Yeah, no. Women didn't work that way.

They were transactional, and it was better for all involved if both sides' terms were hammered out in the beginning.

Rex sighed, shifting slightly in his seat because thinking about hammering and banging the beautiful blonde was not good for his self-imposed celibacy. And why was he doing that to himself again?

What did it matter if he fucked his way around the globe?

Oh, yeah. Because he felt like shit afterward.

It had been nice while it lasted, that pussy fog, the bleak numbness that had enveloped him, not caring about anyone other than himself.

And then Kelly.

And feelings.

And a dick that didn't work.

Or didn't want to work for anyone *except* for Kelly.

But he'd gone and screwed things up between him and Kelly way too fucking long ago. She and his twin Justin had found each other in the wreckage Rex had wrought, and they were *happy*.

His newest curse word.

Because everyone was fucking *happy*.

Except him.

"Stop being so sensitive," he muttered, repeating the words his father had told him way too many times growing up—along with "Be a man," and "Feelings are for pussies," and "Women will only destroy you."

So, yup, baggage, for the win.

He was driving at a snail's pace, not breathing until he saw the headlights pull out onto the road behind him, the silhouette of the pretty blonde barely visible in his rearview. She caught up with him pretty quickly, and he continued driving out of town, trying to watch to see where she'd turn off, to make sure she'd make it home safely.

A few months before, he'd have lied to himself, made up an excuse for wanting to know that fact.

Tonight, he didn't bother lying.

He knew he wouldn't get a good night's sleep unless he saw her home.

Darlington was a small town, but he hadn't seen the blonde around, didn't know her name, wasn't on good enough terms with anyone to find out, but just as he was thinking again that he needed to leave and start fresh, the car behind him turned off.

He braked, waiting to see she'd made it up the winding driveway, the headlights drifting orbs of light as they weaved their way up the hill until, eventually, they parked in front of a mostly dark house.

The porch light flicked on—via a motion sensor or someone waiting inside for her—and she bounded up the steps.

Then stopped.

And turned to face the street.

To face *his* car on the road.

She waved, turned for the door, and disappeared inside.

Gone, just that easily.

"Yeah," he murmured, driving forward again. "That's a familiar feeling."

———

HE WAS BEING A PEST.

But that was Rex Roosevelt's specialty—annoying, pestering, infuriating everyone around him. Luckily, despite the glare his brother was lobbing his way, his rescue of Bella had gone a long way toward thawing the ice Kelly had in her heart where he was concerned.

Well, that and the fact that he'd made it a point to have Abigail and the twins refer to him as Uncle Rex—the twins because he was truly their uncle, and Abigail because while he might have provided one half of her DNA, Rex had never been anything like a father to her.

That was where the infuriating portion of his personality came in . . . or perhaps, disappointing.

Or maybe the best description yet, failure.

And Justin saving his ass, yet again.

Taking care of Kelly, stepping in, falling for the only person Rex had ever felt anything for. But he hadn't felt enough. He knew that now. After he'd returned, thinking he might be able to win her back, he'd seen Justin with Kelly, seen how perfect they were for each other, how they hadn't been trying to take and take and *take* from each other. As opposed to him trying squeeze every bit of satisfaction out of his partners and then never finding it to be enough.

Because he was lacking something inside.

Broken. Missing. Empty.

Jax, Justin's little boy and Jesse's twin, hurtled a toy car off the edge of the table. It clattered to the floor, making Rex wince and focus back on the subject at hand: trading empty, missing, and broken for mischief.

"I just don't see why we can't have ice cream for breakfast," he said, attempting to keep his lips from curving. "We all know that it will be much less messy than Justin making pancakes."

Kelly's eyes twinkled. "True," she said, stooping to pick up the car. "But now you're threatening my stash of mint chocolate chip, and them's fighting words."

Rex lifted his hands in the universal sign of surrender. "Even I wouldn't dare to do that. I know how much you love your mint chocolate chip."

She dropped a handful of cereal in front of Jesse and Jax then a bowl of yogurt in front of Abigail in that easy, efficient way she had. It was the same with the horses, whether it was a handful of them or the several dozen they now housed on the ranch. Kelly could always handle multi-tasking without missing a beat. This horse needed his medication. Another's favorite snack was apples. Still one more never failed to miss an opportunity to nip. She'd been able to rattle that off to him with her arms full of tack while saddling one horse and passing treats to another.

And she was an even better mother.

Abigail looked exactly like her with the exception of having the Roosevelt eyes. The same eyes Justin had but Rex didn't. Lucky, that. No trace of him. And while they might share that DNA, Rex didn't feel anything fatherly toward her. Maybe once upon a time, he'd thought that perhaps . . .

But he'd let that go.

She belonged to Justin.

Abby scooped up a spoonful of yogurt and shoved it into her mouth.

"You're silly, Uncle Rex." Some of the white viscous liquid dribbled down her chin.

He wrinkled his nose and picked up a napkin from the holder in the middle of the table, grabbing the square of paper, then belatedly realizing he'd recognized the painted clay monstrosity from his childhood.

"Where'd you find that?" he asked lightly, wiping Abigail's chin. "I thought Dad had burned it."

Justin's eyes held a note of emotion that Rex didn't like. He held Rex's gaze for a long moment then returned to mixing pancake batter and generally making a giant mess of the kitchen. "Turns out that there was a lot of stuff in storage. Dad sent it over after Abby was born."

"Ah."

Kelly set a bowl of berries, granola, and yogurt in front of Rex, and his heart clenched in regret when he realized she'd remembered his preferred breakfast. "Because it will take Justin an hour to make enough pancakes for all of us."

"Hey! I—" Justin said, but Kelly cut him off with a kiss.

Regret, Rex thought. *Not want.*

He didn't want Kelly any longer, but he sure did regret hurting her.

CHAPTER FOUR

Tilly

HER ALARM CAME WAY TOO EARLY.

She hated working the morning shift, but she hated it all the more when she'd stayed late to cover the evening shift the night before.

"Ugh," she groaned, blearily reaching for her cell and attempting to press the "Done" button. Not "Snooze" because fuck if she wanted to deal with the incessant ringing in nine minutes.

Nine. Not ten. Not five.

Nine.

Her cell slipped out of her hands and fell to the floor with a sickening *crack.*

Hardwood floor meeting glass-covered cell phone was never a good thing, but it was even *less* of a good thing when said cell phone was out of its protective case because the fucking wireless charger didn't charge with the bulky plastic surrounding it. And since Tilly was about as good with technology as a bull in the proverbial china shop . . .

That *crack* meant her brand-new cell phone that she'd splurged for now had a lovely fissure right down the middle of the screen.

Not on the back. On the front. In the middle.

"Fuck my life."

She should have put that money into fixing her car. Instead, she'd splurged and . . . *le sigh.* Because as things had often done in her life, they'd gone wrong.

Since her cell was still incessantly blaring, Tilly shoved her bangs out of her face and slipped out of bed. Two jabs at the screen and she managed to silence the ringing before shoving it back into the indestructible case. Then it was time for her to stop grousing and move.

She was one of those people who didn't like to build extra time into her morning routine. She wanted to sleep as late as humanly possible, then hurtle herself out of bed and into the shower. No washing her hair, because her mane of blond locks took way too much effort to dry for zero-dark thirty in the morning. Rather, she simply waited impatiently for the shower to heat, hopped in, and washed up as quickly as possible, then with slightly more awake hands, fumbled her way into her uniform.

Bypassing her kitchen—it was too early to be hungry for breakfast and Henry would cook something for her that was way better than anything she could cobble together once the morning rush passed anyway—Tilly ran out onto her front porch.

This was the moment she typically ran across the darkened front yard —hello, scary murderers and freezing cold Utah mornings—to her car.

Just not this morning.

She stopped dead—no pun intended—on the second step.

"What the *fuck?*"

Her car was gone.

———

WALKING IN THE DARK, mind full of scary thoughts and images, did not do a girl well.

She'd called Henry to tell him she would be late but would be in as soon as possible. As usual, he'd been understanding when she'd told him that she had car trouble—*ha*, a missing car still counted as trouble, right? He had offered to give her the morning off to deal with her car, but she needed the money from her shift . . . especially if she might need to buy a new one.

Sighing and mentally adding a brand new vehicle to her already stretched budget, Tilly picked up her pace. She lived on the outskirts of Darlington, but luckily her hometown wasn't what one would call big. It would take all of twenty minutes to get to Main Street, where Henry's Diner was located.

By then, the restaurant would be slammed, every booth crammed with Darlington natives, plates piled high with fluffy pancakes and delicious omelets, perfect triangles of freshly baked bread, courtesy of the lovely Isabella.

Henry's better half was beautiful, inside and out, and an amazing baker, to boot. It would be enough to make Tilly hate her, if not for the whole beautiful on the inside thing.

Because Bella was amazing, and nice, and talented . . . and perfect for Henry.

So no hating. Only love and . . . the slightest bit of jealousy.

Because once upon a time she'd believed in happily ever afters. Then reality had struck and she was back home, in debt up to her eyeballs—though she was slowly making progress in paying it off—and, perhaps most depressing of all, she was alone. All alone.

Wrinkling her nose, Tilly wrapped her jacket more securely around her and quickened her pace.

Winter was coming.

A snort, though it was the truth.

The leaves had turned, the nights had come earlier, the days had grown cooler and shorter. Halloween was in a few weeks and then a fresh hell would begin.

The Holiday Season.

Such a fucking pain in the ass when a girl was alone and single.

"Pity, pity party," she muttered, rounding the corner where her car had been an asshole the night before. The sun was still hidden behind the hills in the distance, but it was beginning to rise, making their tops look like someone had run an orange highlighter across their rounded domes.

It was beautiful and also a good reminder for her to keep moving.

The minutes were flying by, and she'd never get them back.

"Don't I know that?" she muttered and trudged on.

CHAPTER FIVE

Rex

HE FELT his phone buzz and pulled it out to check if it was the message he'd been waiting for.

Then felt his cheeks crease when it was.

There was one benefit of throwing money around. People jumped and often jumped high.

Rex still didn't know what had persuaded him to make the call late the night before, the one that had offered an obscene amount of money to the local mechanic to tow the angel's car to his shop to fix it.

But he *had* and, in fact, had paid more than the actual rust bucket was worth to replace the starter, the ignition, several important belts, one engine rod, and a broken spring in the front seat. Expensive, but Dale, the mechanic, had come through. And if Rex were being completely honest, fixing the car was the lesser of two evils . . . especially when his first instinct had been to buy the woman a brand-new car.

Didn't even know her name and yet was willing to spend thirty grand on a new vehicle.

Brilliant thought, Roosevelt.

Rex sighed then typed out a thanks, asking the mechanic to drive the car back to the woman's house. She'd been working very late the evening before and so hopefully would still be sleeping or at the very least, had seen the note he'd instructed Dale to leave behind.

Last thing he needed was the woman reporting her car being stolen.

Despite his role in Bella's return to Henry and Darlington, the sheriff's office still wasn't his biggest fan. The head detective was Kelly's brother-in-law and not quick to forgive Rex.

Not that he could blame him.

Rex's phone buzzed again.

Already dropped off. Note still there and not a peep from the house. The total with parts will be—

To which, Dale added a monetary amount that was obscene, but marginally less than the price of a new car. He typed a reply, promising to drop the payment by in a couple of hours, and then pocketed his phone and forced himself to focus on the task at hand—namely, cleaning up the kitchen mess that was the result of Justin's pancakes.

The happy family of five had taken off for the barn, coaxed out by Rex, three sets of sticky faces and hands trailing their parents. Knowing Kelly, a morning check and feed of the horses had already been completed, but she'd spend several hours assisting the ranch hands with feeding, exercising, and keeping a close watch on their highly valued horses.

She'd turned this operation into something very special.

No thanks to him.

Rex shook his head, shoved the circling emotions down—because he really needed to stop being a pathetic pussy—then got to work on the dishes. It was almost worth it, having to wash the ridiculous amount of dishes, just to have witnessed Justin's face when he had offered.

Pure, unadulterated shock.

Punctuated by pancake batter above his right eyebrow.

Of course, there was karmic intervention for his amusement . . . in the form of a griddle caked with bacon grease that he spent the better part of thirty minutes scrubbing clean, so by the time he managed to escape it was nearly lunchtime.

Kelly and company were making their way up to the front door as Rex emerged from the house. While she offered to make him a matching heart-shaped PB&J sandwich to go along with Abigail's lunch—and really, how the little girl could be hungry after the huge amount of pancakes she'd consumed less than two hours before was beyond him— he turned down Kel's offer and headed to his car.

Justin was chasing the twins around the front lawn, but Rex didn't miss his brother's shoulders relaxing when he announced his impending exit.

"Bye, Roosevelt clan," he called lightly, really good at pretending that he hadn't secretly wanted to stay.

He liked being around Justin and his family, enjoyed the noise and chaos, interspersed with laughter, tears, and the occasional meltdown. It reminded him of when his mom had still been alive.

But as much as he wanted to soak up every moment, Rex knew he was nothing more than a complication—fine, an *annoyance*—to them.

Things would never be the same.

He'd ensured that.

"I'll be heading back out of town soon," he announced to no one specifically. "Let you all get back to your life."

"Rex—" Kelly began, but her words were cut off when Abigail launched herself from the front porch. She sprinted toward him, little legs pumping faster than he would have thought possible.

"Don't go, Uncle Rex!" she said, and he was surprised to see tears in her eyes.

His heart clenched. "I—"

He didn't do kids, didn't know how to respond . . . to someone wanting him to stay. Or at least, not because they wanted *him* to stay and not his money or his father's business connections.

She sniffed and threw her arms around his waist.

"I—" he started again and stopped. "You're probably hungry," he eventually settled on. "You should go eat that sandwich your mom is going to make you."

Green eyes, so like his brother's, narrowed in his direction. "Mommy says you like to run away." Her gaze was penetrating. "Don't."

And now this was getting really freaking weird.

"I'm not going anywhere," he found himself saying. "Except into town for a bit."

A nod.

"Good." She turned to the house. Stopped. "Because you and Daddy need to make up." With that proclamation, she flounced into the house.

Rex turned to Justin. "How old is she now?"

"Four." A beat. "Going on forty."

His lips twitched. "She reminds me of Mom."

Justin nodded. "Yes, she does."

When the silence stretched for a few beats, Rex nodded, propelled his ass into motion, and hightailed it for his car. This time there wasn't a tiny green-eyed cherub to stop him from buckling in and taking off down the driveway.

But that didn't mean there wasn't an angel to stop him in his tracks just around the corner.

CHAPTER SIX

Tilly

HER FEET ACHED, and her hair smelled like eggs.

Scrambled. With a touch of cheddar, sour cream, and bacon.

The perfect combination for an omelet in her opinion, but definitely not her preferred shampoo scent. She shook out her long blond locks as she walked, another crumb of bacon falling to the road. Her house was ten minutes out, her pace much slower than that morning.

Panic and fear had fueled her steps, and she'd made it into town in record time.

Thank her overactive imagination for that small miracle.

Now, she'd worked the morning rush . . . or maybe it had worked *her*. Because besides the omelet hair she now sported, courtesy of a toddler who'd launched her mother's breakfast in Tilly's direction with unerring accuracy in the middle of a major temper tantrum, her shirt was grease-stained, her cell phone had given its final goodbye thanks to an over-turned glass of orange juice, and—

She was tired.

So damned tired of everything.

She hadn't even gotten a chance to call the police department about her car, and seeing as how she didn't have a house phone any longer, she wondered how in the heck she was going to do that without a cell.

Could she Skype them? Facebook message Kelly's sister, Melissa, since her husband was the lead detective in town?

Did detectives even track down stolen cars?

Weren't they supposed to go undercover and arrest people? Or at least, that was what Rob had done several years before—taken down a huge drug ring and corrupt government agents.

Finding her dumpy little car with two hundred thousand miles on it couldn't be much of a priority.

She wasn't much of a priority.

"Enough," she muttered, kicking a rock and watching it roll down the road. "Enough moping and whining and being tired all the time." She kicked another. "Enough being defeated. Enough of this fucking town and its history and enough of—"

Here, two things happened.

First, a tear escaped her eye.

Tilly had been fighting the salty little fuckers, blinking back against the stinging, trying to drum up some mad instead of the sad that had dominated her life for the last years.

Because she was damn tired of sad.

She succeeded in drumming up the mad and it came on rapidly, raging through her with all the fury of a forest fire. With a snarl—or perhaps a full-bellied, furious scream—she kicked another rock.

And then the second thing happened.

The rock sailed through the air, flying up in a perfect arc until . . . it crashed right into the windshield of a sleek black sedan coming around the corner.

Crack.

The car swerved, brakes screeching as it came to a halt on the shoulder.

Tilly had frozen, her hands over her mouth, for one horrible moment before starting to run. To her credit, she ran *toward* the car, rather than away from it. "Oh God," she muttered. "I could have killed somebody. Shit. *Shit.*"

The windshield had a giant divot in it, several cracks already spiraling out from the center, but thankfully the rock hadn't actually made it through the glass. Sun in her eyes, but concern growing as no one emerged from the car, she reached for the driver's door and yanked furiously on the handle.

It didn't open for several long moments, the only noise the car's engine and her labored breathing. She tugged on the handle again—

Click.

The door unlocked and seeing as she was mid-tug, it flew open.

She landed in a heap on the gravel-covered shoulder, barely registering the sting of her backside and palms as they made contact with the sharp rocks.

Because then, he stepped out.

Him.

Justin's brother.

And fuck her life, that was just absolutely perfect.

CHAPTER SEVEN

Rex

THE ANGEL SITTING in the road, covered in dust and tears, probably should have looked much less angel-like, but instead, she was even more beautiful in the light of day than she'd been the previous evening.

He held his breath as he surveyed her, starting at her toes—sturdy, comfortable sneakers—going to her legs—tight jeans with a rip over one knee—and up to her torso—a shirt from Henry's Diner, identical to the one she'd been wearing the night before. She must be going to work.

Rex frowned.

Had her car not started again?

Dale had better not be fucking with him.

But just as he pulled out his cell to give Dale a piece of his mind, the angel pushed herself to her feet, sighed, then straightened her shoulders and sighed again. She came over to him and stuck out her hand.

"I'm Tilly," she said, hazel eyes meeting his. "And I'm so sorry. I'll pay for your windshield. I shouldn't have—" She broke off, cheeks reddening. "Well, I shouldn't have been kicking rocks."

He lifted a brow, amusement curling through him at her contrite words. "Why *were* you kicking rocks?"

She shook her head. "Let me give you my number. I'm happy to pay for whatever damages I—"

"Why were you walking to work?" he interrupted.

Tilly, and for some reason that name seemed to fit her perfectly, froze. "Um . . ." Then she wrinkled her nose, and he had the oddest urge to lean forward and brush his lips across the freckles there. "Well, my car was stolen this morning."

Rex blinked. "What?"

"I know, right?" she said. "I don't know who would want that old rust bucket, but I woke up this morning and it was gone. I was thirty minutes late for my shift because I had to walk in."

Walk in?

He took a closer look at Tilly, saw what he'd missed the first time. The shirt wasn't clean and . . . neither was her hair?

Reaching up before he could stop himself, he plucked a piece of green out of her hair. "Is that an onion?"

She flicked it from his fingers. "Chive. There was this little girl who—" She seemed to shake herself, and Rex found that in that moment, he would have given a whole lot to hear the rest. "Never mind. You don't need to hear about my morning. I've already inconvenienced you twice in as many days. My cell is—"

She'd pulled out her phone and froze, cheeks getting even pinker.

"What is it?" he asked, more than a little intrigued about this woman and her reactions.

A rueful smile curved her lips. "My cell is dead."

"Ah." He smiled back. "How'd that happen?"

"Electronics and orange juice don't mix."

"Ah."

"I—" She broke off. "I can give you my email?"

Amusement boiled up in his veins and Rex smothered a smile. "Email is fine." Not that he had any intention in allowing her to pay to replace his windshield, but he also wasn't going to give up any avenue for contacting her, especially if her cell was dead. He made a mental note to take care of that as well and handed her his phone. "Go ahead and put it in." A beat. "You might as well put your cell in, too. The insurance company might need it."

She winced but spent the next twenty seconds plugging things into his phone before handing it back. "I really am sorry."

He tugged the end of her ponytail. "It's not a big deal."

A nod as she shoved her hands back into her pockets and turned away.

"Can I give you a ride?"

She spun back around. "Oh, no. I couldn't possibly—"

Rex wrapped his hand around her elbow, cutting off her protests and leading her toward the passenger's side of his car. "Let me at least drive you home," he said. "I can't just leave you on the side of the road. I'm not a total creep."

"Just kind of one."

Burn.

But he couldn't deny he'd heard that before, more than once even. "True enough," he said, nudging her into the seat.

Tilly had frozen, cheeks turning bright red, hands over her mouth. Rex simply tugged her right arm down, brought the seat belt across her torso, and buckled her in.

Then he closed the door and paused. Breathed.

Once. Twice. *Enough.*

Rounding the front of his car, he tucked down the biting words he wanted to snap back, shoved away the hurt feelings. Numbing coldness swept through him, cooling the burning sensation in his gut, the warmth that had been steadily filling his heart over the last months.

He tugged open the door, plunked into the driver's seat.

Pressing the button to start the ignition, he kept his gaze forward as the car rumbled to life. But when he reached down to shift it into gear, Tilly's delicate voice filled the air.

"I'm sorry."

He shrugged. "It's fine."

"No," she said fiercely. His gaze shot to the right, locked with her beautiful hazel eyes, and it was hard to hold on to that numbness, so damned hard. "It's *not* fine. You rescued me last night, and I repaid you by ruining your windshield."

"It's nothing."

A shake of her head. "It was something to me, and . . ." She paused, sucking in a breath before the words seemed to burst out of her. "It's just, I know something of what it's like to be judged and found lacking. I shouldn't have—" She broke off and nibbled at the corner of her mouth.

"How could anyone find you lacking?"

An honest question, albeit a blurted one that was based more on instinct than actually knowing her. She was a good person. And considering he *wasn't*, Rex figured he was a good authority on knowing when someone wasn't like him. *Thank fuck* she wasn't like him.

"You should buckle up," she said softly.

"What?"

She shifted, one second in her own seat, the next her blond ponytail was in his face, her breasts against his chest. Her scent was a combination of roses and a multitude of food smells—which should have been off-putting but somehow was intoxicating. He inhaled deeply, felt the *eau de Tilly* sink into his pores.

Click.

She sat back.

He blinked.

"There," she murmured. "Now, you're safe."

Rex didn't believe that for a second.

CHAPTER EIGHT

Tilly

THE DRIVE to her house was only a couple of minutes, but the guilt was eating her alive.

Such an asshole.

As in, *she* was the asshole here.

Rex turned up her driveway, gravel pinging the undercarriage of his expensive sedan. Great. Now she probably needed to figure out a way to budget for a paint job, too.

She turned to face him as they slowed at the top of the hill, another apology on the tip of her tongue.

Then she saw her car.

Her. Car.

Parked exactly where she'd left it the night before, right next to her front porch.

"What the fuck?" she muttered.

Rex pulled to a stop and one brow lifted. "You kiss your mother with that mouth?"

"I would," she said, shock making her lips loose. "If she were still alive." She didn't stay to witness his reaction. Instead, just pushed out of his sedan and walked over to where her beater was parked. Which was the moment she saw the sign on the front porch post.

Don't freak out. I brought it to the shop to fix it up.

—Dale

"What the fuck?" she muttered again.

"Just to be clear," Rex said from very close behind her, the liquid honey of his voice heating her from the inside out, "I'm not opposed to cursing. You do you, sweetheart."

Her breath caught. "Then why bring it up at all?"

"Because hearing the word fuck from your pretty lips is beyond hot." Tilly swallowed hard, but before she could formulate a response to that, he went on. "So, I'm guessing you missed"—he nodded at the piece of paper taped to her porch post—"the note this morning?"

"Unfortunately, it was dark when I left, and I didn't see it."

"That sucks."

A nod. "Though, I guess I don't need to call the police and report my car being stolen."

Half his mouth curved up. "I see it now."

Tilly's brows drew together. "See what?"

"You're a bright side."

"What?"

"You're one of those people who always sees the bright side."

It took a heartbeat for his words to process, but when they did, she couldn't stop the hysterical laughter from bursting free. It ripped out of her, made her eyes fill with tears, chest hiccupping, and knees wobbling. She staggered a few steps forward and dropped onto the edge of her porch. If he only knew. *Oh God,* if he only knew.

One minute, or maybe five minutes, perhaps even an eternity passed before she managed to get herself under control. And the first thing she saw when she glanced up was Rex. He was leaning against a post opposite her, blue eyes swimming with curiosity.

But he didn't ask.

Just extended a hand and held out a handkerchief.

An honest to goodness linen handkerchief.

"Who *are* you?" she asked, taking it and blotting her eyes.

"Funny," he said, a smirk playing at the edges of his beautiful mouth. "I was going to ask you the same thing."

"I'm just a girl," she said quietly. "A stuck, small-town girl."

"Why are you stuck?"

He couldn't begin to understand, this man who was born into obscene wealth, who'd never had to worry where his next meal might come from, who never had to struggle for anything in his entire life.

"Some people aren't free to flit around the world." She sighed. "Some people have responsibilities."

"And by that, you're inferring I don't have any?"

His tone was deadly, quiet with an edge of frost.

She opened her mouth, ready to backtrack her words, but then thought, *Fuck it all.* Because dammit, no. He didn't have any responsibilities. He wasn't Justin. He'd appeared in town, wreaked havoc, and left.

And from what she knew, that was his M.O. "Yes," she said. "That's exactly what I'm *inferring*."

A flash of white teeth. "Well then, angel, I'd say you're right." He pushed to his feet and came close enough that her lungs strained with the effort to keep her breathing steady. His hand lifted, and suddenly she was inundated with the scent of Rex.

That fucking glorious mix of sandalwood and bergamot.

And cinnamon.

It was most definitely cinnamon.

She inhaled, trying to capture it in her memories, holding on to the scent to study later. Why the mix of common ingredients smelled so fucking good on Rex Roosevelt.

Probably the old money.

That was enough for her to snap herself out of the scent fog.

At least until his fingers drifted into her hair, sliding gently through the strands, sending a shiver down her spine, and turning the scent fog into a *Rex* fog. Fingers drifted along her nape, up to the crown of head, and then paused.

"You really are the most beautiful woman I've ever seen." A beat. "Even with chives in your hair." His fingers moved in quick succession, plucking at her scalp several times. He tossed his bounty to the ground, hesitated for a long moment that had her holding her breath, then stepped back. Two seconds later, he was in his car, dust cloud in his wake as he drove down the driveway.

About thirty seconds after he'd disappeared from sight, Tilly reached into her purse for her keys.

She found them easily.

Unfortunately, her orange juice-soaked cell phone was nowhere to be seen.

Even more unfortunately, she knew exactly where it was.

Sitting on the plush leather seat of Rex's car.

Perfect. Just fucking perfect.

CHAPTER NINE

Rex

HE STILL WASN'T sure why he'd done it.

It being doing something not selfish for the first time in his life.

Which was quite possibly an exaggeration, though not by a whole lot, and it didn't do anything to explain why he all of a sudden had emotions and longings and—fuck him senseless—*feelings.*

And *that* was definitely a curse word in his mind.

Roosevelts didn't have feelings.

Except, his brother did. His father had. So maybe it wasn't that Rex didn't have feelings, so much as he preferred to avoid them at all costs . . . because they made him vulnerable.

"I've been hearing too many of those fucking podcasts Kelly is addicted to," he muttered, though not altering his destination. They were filled with all sorts of Millennial bullshit about self-affirmations and embracing one's emotions. There must be some damned good subliminal messages in them.

Or . . . maybe he was tired of being so fucking alone all the time.

Rex paused, hands clenching the steering wheel for a heartbeat before he brushed off the thought and kept driving. He had important things to do.

Fine.

One important thing to do.

He turned into the small strip mall on the edge of town, thinking it was lucky there was only one cell service provider that worked in the area. Made his next task easier.

And easy he was comfortable with.

Doing something nice for someone without expecting something in return . . .

"Enough," he growled, snatching up the cell and marching into the store. He strode up to the counter, plunked the phone onto the counter, and demanded to see a manager.

There.

That was Rex Roosevelt.

A slender man with bright red curls came out of the back. "Is there a problem, sir?" he asked tentatively.

"Yes." He shoved the cell forward an inch. "Got doused in orange juice this morning. I need an exact replacement."

Relief crossed the kid's face. "I can do that." He glanced down at the phone. "Be right back with it." Then he disappeared back through the gray swinging door. It had a porthole like a ship, but not even that idiosyncrasy could distract Rex from the question swirling around his mind.

Mainly, why the fuck was he doing this?

Because . . . Tilly.

Because something inside him told him to pay attention.

Because he'd only felt this way once before.

With Kelly.

Sighing, knowing he was being a fucking idiot, but not able to stop himself anyway, he tapped his fingers on the counter and waited. A woman in the corner kept glancing over at him, lips curved as she tried to catch his eye. But that particular type of interaction could only go two ways—she either wanted to fuck him or she thought he was Justin.

And both possibilities would end in disappointment.

Eventually, she stopped trying to get his attention, and he breathed a sigh of relief. The kid came out from the back—Jeremy, Rex realized was his name. Look at that, he could read a nametag.

Kudos to him.

Kudos?

Fuck him. He needed to get out of this town before he turned into even more of an idiot. *Kudos.* Holy fucking shit. He was losing his damned mind. Jeremy held the box toward him, as though expecting Rex to inspect it.

Rex was too trapped in *kudos* thoughts. He took the briefest glance, saw it appeared to be an identical phone then pushed his own cell with Tilly's number on the screen. "Set it up for this account please, but"—he tugged out his credit card—"pay for it with this—"

"Justin?"

Fuck his life.

He didn't turn until Jeremy took his card and started the ungodly long process at the computer that seemed to accompany any trip to a cell store.

Then, very slowly, he rotated to face the woman. She was beautiful, with a mane of chestnut hair and nice lean legs. And great, now he sounded like Kelly describing her horses. Next thing, he'd be describing her flanks.

"I just wanted to say thank you for helping with Kaycee yesterday. I don't know what I would have done without you." She smiled. "It's only a sprain, like you thought, but this mama hadn't been through that before and . . ." Her lips flattened out. "Are you okay? I didn't mean to interrupt you, I just thought—"

So tempting to snap back, to ruin the perfect image of his perfect brother.

But feelings.

Fucking feelings.

Rex forced his lips to curve. "I'll be sure to let Justin know." He extended his hand. "Rex Roosevelt. Justin's twin."

"Oh." Her jaw worked for a second. "I didn't realize you were still . . . um, that's to say, I didn't know—"

He put her out of her misery.

"I'm in town for a few more weeks." A beat. "I'm glad Kaycee isn't badly injured. I'll let Justin and Kelly know."

Her face paled at the mention of Kelly's name. "*Don't.* I shouldn't have bothered—"

"It's no bother. Abigail and the twins are putting me through my uncle paces this afternoon. They're trying to get me back up on a horse." He kept his tone light, though with a deliberate emphasis on *uncle*.

The woman's face was gray now. "I—uh—"

He put her out of her misery. "I swear they're going to try and get me up on Theo." Theodore was widely known as the most temperamental horse at the ranch, and he'd more than earned his reputation. Hell, the last time he'd been in the barn, Theo had tried to take another bite out of him and had nearly succeeded. The only person he liked was Melissa— Kelly's sister—and Rex was half-convinced that was only the case because Theo had gotten to play hero with her and just liked to play up his prowess.

And now he sounded like Kelly again, anthropomorphizing horses.

Though, even he had to admit that Theo had enough personality for ten people.

Kaycee's mom laughed and it was tinged with panic. "Great. Okay. Well . . . just great." She pointed over her shoulder. "I . . . uh . . . should get back to the phones. Need to pick out a new one."

"That's usually why people come to places like this," he said drolly.

She chucked again, still uncomfortable. "Okay . . . well. Bye."

Rex did her a favor and turned away, watching as Jeremy typed for an inordinately long time on the computer, and by the time the kid had finished with the cell, the woman was gone.

He needed out of this town.

But he'd been saying that for weeks, and still he'd stayed.

Why? For what?

Well, at least that part had now become clear. Because . . . Tilly.

"Here you go, man," Jeremy said, setting the phone down in front of him. "Log into the cloud and your latest backup will download. Do you need a new case?" he asked. "This one is a little . . . sticky."

Since it *was* a little sticky, Rex had Jeremy grab one along with a new screen protector. With the way Tilly was going, he thought she'd probably need it.

Five minutes and twelve hundred dollars later, Rex was out of the store and driving back to Tilly's house, brand new cell in hand. He parked at the bottom of the hill and walked up the winding driveway before depositing it on her porch, propping it up where it would be the first thing she'd see when she came out.

Music blared from inside the house, something pop-tastic that he wouldn't be caught dead listening to, but something that seemed to fit Tilly perfectly.

And then he did something he hadn't done since he was a teenager.

Act like a pervert. Lie, but that was what he was going with.

Rex crept forward and peeked through the window, leaning his head so he could glance through a gap of the white cotton curtains.

The house was small, a tiny living room off to one side with the kitchen right in front of him, a narrow hall with a few doors splitting the two spaces. His heart skipped a beat when he saw Tilly standing there, a tea kettle in her hand and a towel wrapped around her head. She wore a plain gray T-shirt along with pajama pants patterned with unicorns, and he thought it was the sexiest thing he'd ever seen.

That was the moment he really did something he hadn't done since he was a teenager.

Rex rang the doorbell.

The peel was loud enough to cover his steps as he sprinted off the porch and hid around the corner of the house. Inside, the music stopped, and he listened to the little house creak and groan as Tilly made her way to the front door.

Was it even safe if it made that much noise? What if the roof collapsed and Tilly—

The front door opened. "Hello?"

Her voice did that thing again. Feelings.

It swung wider, and Rex was careful to keep out of sight. He heard more than saw her cross the porch, though he did catch a glimpse of her bare feet and the lilac mythical-creature-dotted pajamas.

Still sexy.

Still slowly losing his mind.

But for the moment, he was just going to embrace it.

"What?" she murmured, picking up the phone. "How?" She stood there for a long time, and Rex realized he was too damned old to be hiding along the side of someone's house, crouched in the bushes like some sort of serial killer.

But just as he stood up, ready to announce himself, a whistling sound rent the air. Tilly rushed back across the porch, closing the front door behind her, cutting off the sound of the tea kettle with the panel of wood. A soft click of the lock sliding home was the last thing he heard before the music turned back on.

And Rex stood there, firmly planted on the outside of Tilly's world, but not able to make himself so much as peer in again.

Familiar. That feeling was so damned familiar.

CHAPTER TEN

SHE STARED at the phone like it was a snake.

First the car.

Now the cell.

What the hell was going on?

Her tea was getting cold, that was what, and Rex had simply returned her phone. That was it. Simple explanation. Simple truth.

But if it were so simple, then why didn't he stay and tell her that? Why doorbell ditch? And how quickly had he driven away for his car to be at the bottom of her hill by the time she'd gotten to the door? It wasn't like her driveway was short.

It just didn't make sense.

Or maybe it made perfect sense. Maybe he didn't want to talk to her. See? Simple truth. It just . . . didn't feel simple.

She sighed and poured herself some tea before getting out her box of essential oils and getting to work. She'd had a big order come through on Etsy that morning. One of the people she'd sold her bath products to at the county fair that summer apparently ran a B&B, and they wanted her to supply them with shampoo, conditioner, lotion, lip balm, and more than a few scented candles.

Twelve rooms worth.

The biggest order she'd ever sold.

Tilly couldn't afford to screw this up, knew that she'd lucked out with her car not actually being stolen—which was a mystery she still didn't understand but also didn't have the mental energy to deal with at the moment.

Dale had fixed it.

Why?

And how much did she owe him?

Shaking her head firmly to dislodge those thoughts, she got to work.

Lip balm first because it was so easy, she didn't understand why people would ever buy it off the shelf. Literally four ingredients and done —beeswax, coconut oil, shea butter, and whatever scent she was feeling.

Or, because the B&B had requested her peppermint hot chocolate version, that variety.

Her kitchen was smelling festive by the time she'd moved on to shampoo and conditioner. They always took a bit longer, as the conditioner, especially, had more ingredients, but she'd managed to knock them both out by bedtime.

She still hadn't looked at the cell phone.

Lie.

She'd looked at it because it had buzzed. Because somehow it had turned on. She just hadn't gotten any further than the home screen, to the message displayed there:

Found your phone, obviously. It was buzzing in my seat. Maybe not as bad off as you feared. Text me back so I know you found it on your porch.

-Rex

Candles.

She needed to make the candles.

But her fingers reached for her phone anyway, and she was surprised when it unlocked right away without FaceID or her passcode or—

Weird.

It prompted her to sign into her iCloud.

Case in point, orange juice and technology didn't mix. Tilly spent a few minutes avoiding Rex's message, instead logging in and making sure her phone was set up just the way she liked it. Her apps and their respective folders needed to be just right, otherwise she'd go—

Avoidance.

She was a master at it.

Her phone buzzed again, and she jumped, cell flying from her hands to crash to the kitchen floor.

"Tilly Conner, you are an absolute mess," she muttered, sending good vibes up to the cellular gods when she scooped up her phone and saw it was unscathed.

Small miracles. Sometimes it was the small miracles in life.

I hope this isn't still sitting on your porch. It's supposed to rain tonight.

"Great." Another mutter, this time tinged with guilt because Rex had gone out of his way for her three times now, and she'd been avoiding him. Why? Well, there *was* the embarrassment factor. He'd seen her at her worst twice now, three times if she counted not replying to his act of kindness of returning her phone. But while her gut was twisting with guilt, that wasn't what was waving the caution flag in her mind.

Rex was dangerous.

He'd left Kelly.

But he'd brought back Isabella.

He'd rescued her twice.

Was it possible he'd changed?

And *that* right there was what was giving her pause.

Men didn't change. Her father hadn't. Her ex-fiancé hadn't. Rex Roosevelt, legendary sleaze, most certainly hadn't.

Except, what if he had?

Tilly sighed in irritation with herself, with the reminder of the man who was creating so much turmoil inside her—she wasn't the type of girl who looked on the bright side, okay? She couldn't afford to be.

So, she bucked up and texted back.

Thank you for dropping it by, Rex.

There. That was good enough. A thanks, if a bit on the cool side. He had gone out of his way and—

Buzz.

Her eyes glanced down before she could stop herself.

How'd you know it was me?

BESIDES THE FACT that you signed your earlier text message like an elderly person?

Because I saw your car at the bottom of the hill. Why'd you doorbell ditch me?

A FEW SECONDS passed before his reply came through.

I didn't want to interrupt. You'd had an eventful morning.

Her fingers flew across the screen.

And by eventful you mean I thought my car was stolen, spent way too long attempting to wrestle an omelet away from a very persistent two-year-old and losing, then vandalized your car all before one?

Nothing for a long moment then:

That's a good definition of eventful, yes.

Before she could snarkily reply to that, her phone buzzed again.

How's the hair? Chive free?

Her lips twitched.

Yes. Though you wouldn't believe what I have in it now.
Barely a second before:
Angel, you can't say things like that to me.
Tilly's breath caught in her lungs.
Wax. I was going to say wax. And stop calling me Angel. It's kind of creepy.
Silence in response. She started to set her phone down, knowing that her words were a conversation killer for sure, but just as her case hit the scarred wooden table, her cell vibrated again.
We'll circle back to why you have wax in your hair. Why is calling you Angel creepy?
She wrinkled her nose, decided to leave the candle-making for the following night, and walked down the hall to brush said wax out of said hair.
It just is.
Her brush caught on the wax, and she winced as she worked it through the ends.
At least this time she smelled like peppermint rather than chives and eggs.
Ah. The age-old argument: It just is. I bow to your brilliance.
Tilly rolled her eyes, set the brush on the counter with more force than necessary.
Shut up. I'm not the one using creepy endearments with a woman I barely know.
Buzz.
Fair point. So, how about we solve that problem?
She picked her brush up. Put it down again.
Sure. It's easy. Stop calling women Angel.
A beat before her cell vibrated again.
I meant the getting to know you part of your statement. Not the creep factor.
Her lips twitched. Creep factor?
Well, let's just kill two birds with one stone, shall we? It's creepy and now you KNOW I don't like it.
Tilly had hesitated, her phone in her hand, waiting for Rex's reply for at least a full minute before she realized what she was doing. Waiting on a man. Again. Snorting in disgust, she dropped the cell to the counter and began deliberately brushing the wax from her hair . . . and also deliberately ignoring the message when it came through a little while later.
But eventually she'd brushed her hair until it was wax-free, until it gleamed like one of Kelly's horse's tails.
"Cute analogy," she grumbled. "Thanks, brain."
She picked up her cell from the counter and strode into the bedroom, still ignoring the message, still pretending that she hadn't just been texting with *the* Rex Roosevelt.

But then she saw the words on the screen.

You were like an angel last night.

What the—

Her fingers were typing out a response to that, a demand for an explanation of that bit of nonsense before she realized what she was doing. After quickly deleting the message, she sent the only thing she could.

Thanks for returning my phone.

Nothing then:

Is this where we circle back to the wax in your hair?

Tilly sighed. She knew what she needed to do, and it didn't relate to wax at all.

No, Rex. This is where we circle back to me saying goodbye.

A beat.

How about instead of goodbye, we just say goodnight?

She found that she didn't have the strength to reply to that. Instead, she plunked her phone into the charger, turned off her light, and burrowed under her covers.

Unfortunately, sleep was a long time coming.

CHAPTER ELEVEN

Rex

Two days later, Rex found himself doing something he'd never imagined —striding through the door to Henry's Diner, Abigail holding his hand while Kelly corralled the twins. Justin was running late but was supposed to meet them there, and while Kel could have handled the crew of kids herself, Rex had surprised himself by offering to help anyway.

He'd been at the ranch because it had given him an excuse to drive by Tilly's house when Justin's call had come, and though Kel had told her husband they would just pick another day, the under-five crew was not having it.

Abigail demanded Bella's French toast. The twins banged on the table for, "Muffins. Muffins!"

And like any sane person, Kelly had relented.

Or rather, Rex had caved, promising any manner of baked goods to get the kids to calm down. To which, Kel had sighed then left the room to grab her giant purse and car keys.

"You've got a soft touch, Uncle Rex," she'd said, though her eyes were gentle.

They'd buckled everyone in, and he'd listened to too many renditions of *Wheels on the Bus* en route, and now they were in the diner. He'd stared out the window as they'd driven, pretending to take in the scenery, but really, he'd been focused on not missing their drive by Tilly's house, or the fact that her car wasn't in her driveway.

Two days had felt like an eternity, which was especially ridiculous when he considered the fact that he hadn't even known her three days before.

If her car wasn't in the driveway . . .

Maybe it was parked behind the diner, in the employee lot.

No way for him to check that at the moment, so he had to hope that she was working. Either that or just be content with enjoying some of the fabulous baked goods the kids were looking forward to.

See? He could occasionally ponder the bright side.

They walked over to Kel's booth in the back. As Henry's best friend and a former employee, she had perks, and one of those was a permanent table. Though that table was getting progressively tighter as the kids got bigger.

Henry came over, giving him an even look—infinitely better than the death glares of earlier days, but still not remotely friendly. "Justin coming, too?"

Kel nodded.

"I'll bring the usuals all around then. Rex? What do you want?"

He had no clue, hadn't bothered to eat here before, not when he'd had a housekeeper and cook at the ranch. But he *had* tasted plenty of Bella's food. She'd taken to bringing him her "inventions" after he'd helped her get home, and they were some of the most delicious baked items he'd ever tasted.

"Did Bella make anything fresh today?"

Henry's expression turned incredulous, but his lips tipped up. "Only brioche, cinnamon rolls, apple turnovers, cheese tarts, and five varieties of quiche. Any of that sound good to you?"

All of it.

But he settled on a cinnamon roll and apple turnover.

Rex would get his sugar fix at the very least.

"Coffee?"

He nodded. "Thanks."

Henry left then returned a few minutes later with drinks for everyone. Kelly stopped him before he went off. "You short-staffed again?"

"No," Henry said. "Tilly's just on her break now that the rush is over."

"Good," Kel replied. "You need to hire someone else."

"I need my star waitress back," Henry teased.

Kel scoffed. "You mean Melissa? 'Cause she's a long way out from waiting tables."

"Considering she's on a book tour for another hit cookbook," Henry said, "I'd agree with you." He grinned. "But I *was* referring to you, brat. Tilly's great, but I miss you around here."

"She's way better at waiting tables than me. Plus, she doesn't puke on customers . . ."

Rex tuned them out as they continued to banter back and forth.

Because he'd noticed something, or rather, *someone*. Tilly had come up behind Henry, pad in her hand, eyes warm and smile on her face.

"...but she's not you."

That warmth slipped away, that smile became decidedly more forced.

And Kelly for her part—she didn't have a mean bone in her body, would be distraught to know that her words had hurt someone's situation —misread the situation completely. Maybe it was Jesse almost tipping over her cup. Perhaps it was a lack of sleep.

Regardless, she saw Tilly and instead of ending the conversation, she brought the sweet, blond *angel*—take that, creepy vibes—into their discussion.

"Tilly," Kel said. "You've got to convince Henry that you are a way better waitress than me." She laughed. "I was horrible. I could mostly get the right food on the tables, but I was never like you."

Tilly opened her mouth.

Henry spoke first. "You were great. I loved having you here with me."

Kel rolled her eyes. "You just liked having me somewhere I couldn't get in trouble."

"Didn't work out very well though, did it?" he teased. "Still, I give you my award of Henry's Diner's Best Waitress Ever. Right, Tilly? She's got *all* the skills."

"Tilly is way better than I ever was," Kel said. "I'll remind you that she's never even puked on anyone."

Henry waved a hand. "Meh. It was only Justin."

Kel cackled. "Well, I guess she can work up to that."

"Exactly. I'll put it on her evaluation . . ."

Tongue in cheek. As in, this conversation was *all* a joke, poking fun at Kel's subpar waitressing talents. But the problem with inside jokes, with teasing and laughing in that manner was that if a person didn't understand all the context, if they happened to be on the outside looking in, the joking part didn't matter. They either felt left out or they might take that lighthearted ribbing personally.

Especially, if a soft, vulnerable underbelly had accidentally been punched.

And Tilly seemed to choose the second option.

She whirled away, disappearing through the swinging double doors.

Kel and Henry didn't notice.

But Rex did.

He stood up and followed her into the hall, walking past the bathrooms, the kitchen, Henry's office. No sign of Tilly. But the rear exit was slightly ajar, and he found himself pushing through the metal door, stepping out into the alleyway behind the restaurant.

Tilly was there, clad in faded blue jeans and a white diner T-shirt, black apron filled with pens and notepads slung around her waist.

It would have been good if his perusal stopped there.

Preferable for both of them and significantly less messy.

But Rex found he couldn't stop his eyes from locking onto Tilly's face, from noticing the paleness of her skin, her lips. All except her eyes. *They* were slightly reddened.

She turned to face him when the door closed. "I'm fine, Henry. Just tired—"

Her words cut off.

"Hey," he said, prose-writing genius that he was.

"You're not Henry," she said.

"No." A shrug as he leaned carefully against the wall. "I'm pretty sure he's still teasing Kelly about puking on Justin all those years ago."

Tilly did a valiant job of forcing a smile. "It's a good story."

Rex nodded. "Their meet-cute."

Blond brows drew together. "Their what?"

"The way they met." He shrugged. "Every romcom has one. Saving someone from a car because their heel is stuck, bumping into someone and spilling their coffee on them, accidentally texting the wrong person." Another shrug. "Pick your poison. There are oodles of them."

One of those pretty brows lifted. "Oodles?"

He lifted his own in return. "Better than Angel?"

God, she was cute when she wrinkled her nose. "Yes. But just barely."

"You know what they were saying wasn't about you at all, right?" Rex inwardly groaned because when had he become a fucking therapist? He didn't know the first thing about healthy emotional reactions and sure as shit shouldn't be advising someone else on how to feel.

And anyway, he'd managed to distract her for a moment then had brought up the same thing that had upset her in the first place.

Super smooth.

Fucking moron.

Her eyes chilled. "Of course not. I just needed some fresh air."

He should have let the lie stand, but instead—and see above because fucking moron—he blurted, "I thought you just finished your break."

What the fuck was wrong with him?

Why did this woman turn him into an idiot?

"Never mind," he said. "I just wanted to make sure you were okay."

Tilly's expression was bewildered. "I'm fine."

Well, at least he'd distracted her from whatever had made her sad, even if it had been because he was acting insane. Rex nodded. "Okay, great. Well—"

"I wanted to say something," she murmured, touching his arm and stopping him in his tracks when he turned to go. "I should have said it sooner."

"What?" He rotated back to face her, struck again by how beautiful she was.

But it wasn't just her gorgeous cheekbones or the way her bottom lip was slightly bigger than the top one, nor was it the delicate arch of her eyebrows or the lovely green and gold and brown of her irises. Because while all of those made for a beautiful package on the outside, none of it came close to what he was drawn to on the inside. Vulnerability was normally a turnoff for him—Rex wasn't a rescuer by any means. In fact, usually any slice of weakness made him head for the hills, *a la* him taking off on Kelly.

The biggest weakness of all was attachment.

But though he barely knew Tilly, though he was already feeling more than a little attached, for the first time in his life, he wasn't freaked out by the idea of building those bonds. In fact, he found that every minute with her made him want more—to figure her out, to discover why *her*. Why he was so drawn to this woman when he'd had so many others before and never felt anything like this for any of them.

Tilly worried her bottom lip with her teeth. "I just wanted to apologize and to say thank you for returning my phone. I don't know how you got it working again . . ." She paused, as though waiting for him to confess some mysterious cell phone fixing ability, but Rex wasn't about to push it, wasn't going to lie to this woman who was so different from all the others. Instead, he just studied her, watched her teeth sink into that lip again, the slightest bit of pink creeping along her cheekbones.

"I'm glad you have a working phone again," he said into the silence. There, that wasn't a lie exactly.

Tilly froze, eyes widening. "You didn't." She reached into her apron, pulled out her phone then gasped. "I was so thrown off that I didn't realize before. You. Didn't."

"Didn't what?" he asked carefully.

"You did *not* buy me a new phone, Rex Roosevelt!"

Shit.

"It's not a big—"

"Do not say it's not a big deal," she said, pacing away. "I have insurance. It would have covered it. This phone is stupid expensive. I shouldn't have even splurged for it in the first place and—" She shoved it in his direction. "Take it back. I'll go to the store after my shift and get a cheaper replacement."

He caught it before it tumbled to the ground, shoved it back into her apron. "Keep it," he said. "I can't return it anyway. Save your insurance for a future cell failure. It seems likely that you might need it," he added when she tried to push it into his hands again and he had to scramble to catch it. Her fingers were on his wrist, his hand in her apron pocket as he tucked the phone deep inside when he blew it completely. "Fuck, woman. It's not like I bought you a new car. It's just a phone, accept the damn thing graciously."

So, Rex meant the words.

And though had he not been so frustrated, he might have tried to find a kinder way to say the same thing, he still *meant* the sentiment.

It was just the car addendum he would have skipped.

Her jaw dropped open and she slapped his hands away from her apron.

Since that meant the phone ended up in her pocket, Rex allowed it. And because her poking him in the chest with her finger brought her close enough that he could smell her delicate scent, could see the way her lips flushed bright pink in fury, he allowed that, too.

"Rex. Roosevelt," she gritted out. "You did *not* fix my car."

He shrugged. "According to the note, Dale fixed it."

She plunked her hands on her hips, one foot tapping. "And who called Dale?"

"Does it matter?" he asked.

"Yes, it matters!" she snapped, yanking at the end of her ponytail and pacing away.

He couldn't not follow her, didn't back up when she spun around and nearly plowed into him. "Why?" he said, tone as harsh as hers. "Who gives a fuck? Your car works. Your phone works. I made one stop, one call, threw some money that I could easily afford at your problems and—"

"It fucking matters because I don't know you!"

Rex clenched his jaw tight, biting back the urge to refute that statement because dammit, he *didn't* know Tilly. He knew she wore lilac unicorn pajamas, that she worked her ass off at the diner, and then went home to fulfill products ordered from an Etsy storefront he'd discovered two nights before.

He'd seen her up late in her kitchen, moving back and forth from the stove to the counters, filling bottles, stirring pots—

Fuck, yes. He was still spying on her. A.k.a. Rex was losing his goddamned mind.

But he'd worried. He'd obsessed and—

Fine. He'd made a few calls to some of his favorite luxury bed and breakfasts, all but demanding they start carrying Tilly's line of products. Her stuff wouldn't disappoint, despite his multitude of experience with crap business ventures, he knew at least that much. Now he just needed to talk her into raising her prices and setting up a storefront.

"You don't have to know me," he finally said. "All you have to do is accept that I wanted to do something nice for someone other than myself and move the fuck on."

She stopped, eyes flashing. "You mean accept it *graciously*."

"Well, fuck yes. That would be nice for a goddamn change."

Tilly stepped toward him, that finger digging into his chest again. "People don't do things for nothing." Her words were sharp, like daggers. "There are always strings. *Always*."

That statement made him sad.

He didn't want her to have learned that lesson.

He wanted her protected, for her life to be easy, and maybe . . . maybe he'd done it in a vain hope that she might actually give him a chance.

Despite his reputation in this town.

Despite his royally fucked up past.

Despite—

"I don't have any strings, Angel."

More wrinkles on that cute nose. He wanted to kiss them away. But at least his response seemed to have distracted her from her anger. "I thought we'd cooled the *angel* talk, creeper."

His mouth curved. "If you're pissed at me, I might as well go all in."

Tilly sighed, glancing up at him and reminding his body once more that she was close, so damned close that it would only take the smallest movement to bring their torsos flush, their mouths aligned. A heartbeat passed, and she seemed to sense the same thing he did, freezing in place, voice dropping to a whisper. "All in with what?"

Rex held his breath, considering his options for the first time in his life rather than jumping into the deep end head first.

But that brief hesitation didn't change anything.

Because, in the end, he jumped anyway.

Wrapping his arm around Tilly's waist, he slammed his lips down onto hers.

CHAPTER TWELVE

Tilly

WHAT WAS HAPPENING with her life right now?

She was in the arms of the most beautiful man she'd ever laid eyes on, his mouth was slanting across hers, tongue caressing the crease of her lips, inching inside to stroke along hers.

Tilly Conner, smelling of sweat and eggs and grease, was in Rex Roosevelt's arms, and he was kissing her as though she were the most precious object on the planet.

But only for a moment longer, because the second she rose on tiptoe, the moment she allowed herself to get closer, to feel his chest against hers, to soak in just a little more of his bergamot and sandalwood scent, something in Rex snapped.

His control. His sanity. His—

It didn't matter.

Because suddenly the kiss wasn't soft and sweet and gentle.

It was fucking hot.

His arm banded around her waist, his free hand wove into her hair. He tilted her head back, and Rex kissed her . . . really, *fucking* kissed her. With teeth and tongue and roving hands. With an erection poking into her belly and rough fingers in her hair. With more heat and passion than she'd ever felt before.

She never wanted it to end, just wanted to stay wrapped up in him for an eternity, to feel those flames of desire licking up her skin, sliding through her center, coiling in her stomach, between her thighs.

She wanted him to slip his hand down, to feel how wet she was for him, and—

Tilly needed air.

Gasping, she pulled back, sucking in much-needed oxygen.

Rex let her breathe, though his mouth didn't stop moving. She felt hot breath on her throat then his teeth nipped, making her jump before his tongue darted out to soothe the slight sting.

"Rex," she murmured, not wanting to break the moment but knowing that at any second someone could walk out of the diner and find them.

"Mmm?"

"We have to stop."

"Uh-uh." He tugged the neck of her T-shirt to the side, licked her collar bone. "We don't."

She gasped, fingers coming up to clench his shoulders. Tilly sucked in air, trying desperately to hold on to the one sane thought swirling around the desire and need filling her brain. "But we should anyway."

Rex froze, entire body stiffening as though she shoved a live wire up his—

Before she could finish that thought—which was probably for the best considering its direction—he set her away from him and stepped back. "You go in first."

Cold, cold words from a man who'd been kissing her so hotly only heartbeats before.

"Are you—?"

"My cock is threatening to poke a hole in my jeans, Tilly," he growled. "So, no, I'm not okay." Blue eyes locked with hers. "And you won't be either unless you go. The. Fuck. Back. Inside."

Heat this time. Heat that threatened to make her smile.

But one glance into those baby blues, into the fire roiling just beneath the surface, and she reconsidered. His expression said that he would have her naked and against the diner's brick wall given the slightest provocation, whoever might walk in on them be damned.

She hesitated because, dammit, Rex was sexy as shit and kissed like a dream and it had been so *fucking* long.

"Go," he snapped, jarring her out of her thoughts and startling her into motion.

Tilly hurried through the metal door, emerging into the hallway, heart pounding, lungs sawing, and . . .

Smile on her lips.

Rex Roosevelt.

Hot damn.

———

SHE SPENT a few minutes delivering plates to Kelly's table since her order was ready, and Henry had apparently gotten too invested in his conversation with his bestie to realize the food was growing cold in the pass.

Something Bella would kick his ass for later, Tilly reminded herself with a smirk as she set the plates of French toast down in front of Abigail.

Justin had arrived, and he swiped his finger through the freshly whipped cream piled high on top.

Part of the reason that Bella's food was so popular with the kids.

She knew her audience . . . and fully understood that her freshly whipped cream was like crack. Which was a euphemism that she would not be sharing aloud with the class. And definitely not with Rex, who seemed to take even the most innocuous words to a whole new realm of dirty. What he would do with cream and crack she couldn't even begin to imagine.

Blueberry muffins with freshly grated hash browns went in front of Jesse, while the chocolate chip muffin with scrambled eggs she plunked down in reach of Jax.

"Careful," she told the little boy. "The plate is a bit hot."

Wide blue eyes—so much like Rex's that it took her breath away—met hers. How had she never noticed before? And such an odd twist in genetics that even though Rex was technically Abigail's biological father, she looked nothing like him, but the little boy was his spitting image.

For the first time, she wondered how he was possibly in Darlington, how he was interacting with the family, playing the role of uncle when Abigail was really his.

It had to be tough to step aside like that.

And it wasn't like Abigail's parentage was a secret, Darlington was the epitome of small town, and gossip spread like wildfire—which was to say that everyone knew exactly who Abigail's father was, and it wasn't Justin.

Not fair, she thought, shoving the uncharitable thoughts aside.

Sperm did not make a father, as she so personally knew, and Justin had been there since the beginning. He was a great dad, and she thought highly of Rex for having stepped back and let Justin and Kel build their family.

If someone wasn't ready to be a father, then sometimes it was better for all parties involved if he didn't try to fill that role.

Or maybe she was thinking of herself and her own father.

Of all the times he'd canceled or hadn't shown up or had flaked out because he couldn't *handle* it. *Her.* So, yeah. Abigail was lucky to have two parents who loved her dearly along with a fun uncle.

By the time she'd snagged the final three plates and returned to the table, Rex was back, leaning against the wall as Kel and Henry continued to talk.

Justin rolled his eyes, smiling at her, but Tilly had a hard time focusing on anything except Rex. He was disheveled, his hair sporting tracks from her fingers running through it, his shirt wrinkled, lips swollen.

No doubt hers were the same.

It would be a fucking miracle if no one figured out what they had been doing in that alleyway, she thought, panic seeping up inside her.

Yet, at the same time, would it really be so bad?

Hadn't she just been thinking he wasn't a terrible person?

But he was Rex Roosevelt—love 'em and leave 'em, flighty millionaire, more notches in his bedpost that a fucking wood-carver Rex Roosevelt. She couldn't be attracted to him, couldn't want him.

Not if she wanted to escape with her heart intact.

If he was nothing else, then he was dangerous, and if Kel had illustrated only one thing clearly in her entire life, it was that Rex wasn't a man with staying power. He got what he wanted and he got the fuck out and . . .

Tilly couldn't afford to do that again.

Not for a third time.

Just . . . not ever again.

CHAPTER THIRTEEN

Rex

OUTSIDE LOOKING IN, that was the theme of his life, and it was no different watching his brother with his family.

They hadn't even saved him a seat, for fuck's sake.

Justin had just swept in and taken his spot . . . along with his fucking breakfast. Well, that was nothing new, but that apple turnover looked heavenly. And apparently, his brother thought the same because he picked it up from the plate Tilly had situated at the end of the table and took a giant bite, even though she'd also set a plate with Justin's usual omelet in front him.

Fucker.

Tilly flicked a gaze in his direction that he pretended not to see, even though he noticed everything about her, including the kiss-swollen lips and the way her cheeks went pink when she glanced in his direction, but most especially the way she slipped away from the table as quickly as possible when she noticed him staring.

She disappeared through the swinging doors with barely more than a flash of her blond ponytail.

Rex sighed and pushed off the wall. His brother had moved onto his cinnamon roll, and he barely glanced up when Rex came over to the table, Henry having finally departed the table. Abigail had a whipped cream mustache, Justin was in his seat, and the twins were covered with their respective muffins. Rex crouched next to the table to fist bump Abigail then waved at Jax and Jess, thus avoiding chocolate and blueberry coated palms.

Kel's face clouded. "You don't have to go, Rex—" She nudged Justin. "We'll pull up a chair."

"I've got a few calls to make," he told her. "Enjoy the crew."

"But you haven't eaten your breakfast . . ." Her voice trailed off when she glanced down at the crumbs that were all that were left of his apple turnover and cinnamon roll.

"I'm not hungry anyway."

"Oh, sorry," Justin said, finally coming out of his sugar and carb stupor and staring up at Rex. "Was this yours?" It actually sounded like, "Sho, smorry. Smwas fish hors?" but Rex was well-versed in his brother's full-mouthed speech to deduce the words without an issue.

Kelly rolled her eyes, wiping a napkin across the table to clean up the crumbs her husband had spit on the table. "And they say romance isn't dead," she muttered, but her eyes twinkled as she pressed a kiss to Justin's mouth. "Should I wipe your face for you, too?"

Justin slid an arm around her shoulders. "You love me," he teased. "Even in my Hoover mode."

Thinking that sentiment could definitely be applied in a different way from what his brother was implying, Rex called his goodbyes then walked out the front doors of Henry's Diner.

Main Street of Darlington was probably his favorite thing about the small town. Brightly colored buildings lined both sides of the street, each a different shade of the rainbow, but all of them somehow fitting together. Maybe it was the crisp white trim or perhaps the eclectic mix of architecture, but whatever the magic mixture was, it had a way of relaxing him like no other place on the planet.

Probably why he'd decided to sublet one of the apartments over the empty shop just a few buildings down.

He'd stayed all of one night with his brother and Kelly before making the decision to get his own place, however temporary that might be. And because it had been the peak of summer when he'd chosen to stay on and the B&B had been full, subletting his own apartment had seemed the smartest option.

Today's perk was that he didn't have far to walk to get home.

Though later, he'd have to figure out how to get his car.

Darlington didn't exactly have Über.

There. Maybe *that* was what he should do with his life. He'd played at being the screw-up for so long, stepped right into that image and didn't correct anyone—read: he didn't correct his brother—when they'd assumed he'd failed. He wasn't a great businessman like his father or even the noble, hardworking sod like his brother.

A mediocre, fifty-percent successful man, that was him.

Some of his plans succeeded, some crashed and burned. Same as anyone.

The difference, he supposed as he strolled toward his apartment, was the Roosevelt name. Ubiquitous with success and definitely with old money. And . . . the truth was that for a time, Rex had loved pissing off his dad and brother. He'd *wanted* to be the black sheep, going his own way. So, he didn't tell his family that his production company had a hand in the last four Best Picture Oscar winners, nor did he pass along the information that the small startup he'd invested in had received a patent for a lifesaving blood pressure medicine. He shared the horrible documentaries, the failed cruise line that he had merely loaned a friend a few thousand to help settle debts. He bought a failing ranch on a whim from a rancher who wanted to retire but didn't have the means to.

All because he'd like this little strip of Americana.

Rex's persona had one thing right. He was impulsive.

Dropping several million on a ranch and several million more on the horses, falling for the woman who cared for them, and then when things had gotten too serious with Kelly, bailing.

Well, panicking *then* bailing.

But this thing with Tilly was different. Panic was the least of his emotions—needing, wanting, fucking hard as granite any time she was in the vicinity, they were all infinitely more common.

And more . . . she called to a part of him he'd thought hadn't existed.

The Roosevelt Rescue Gene.

His father had it. Justin sure as shit possessed it as well.

Rex had always figured it had skipped over him. Until Tilly, that was. Because from the moment he'd seen her bashing her head against her steering wheel, the pale blue lights of her dashboard haloing her face, he wanted to both fuck and rescue her.

In equal proportions.

Probably that should have made him run away in terror, but instead he felt calm, at peace with the fact that his soul seemed to resonate with Tilly's. Not love, definitely not that treacherous emotion, but more like . . . a woman he could sleep with and then not immediately want to throw out the front door, one who was sweet and hardworking and who'd refuse all the nice things he wanted to do for her.

One who might make his tough as boots, way overcooked pork chop of a heart not wither up and die further.

Pork chops.

Fuck, he hadn't thought about them in ages. Not since his mother had passed. The one meal she knew how to cook . . . and cook was definitely a loose term for the shoe leather she'd managed to transform those chops into.

It was the reason his father had hired Rosa—the housekeeper and chef that he and Justin had grown up with, who now lived at Roosevelt Ranch —in the first place. His mother hadn't been able to use a stove to save her life, and though she hated what she'd called "a ridiculous expense," her three boys were thrilled to have edible food and a kitchen that didn't smell like whatever she was attempting to burn—*cough*—cook.

Although, Rosa was getting ready to retire and Kel wasn't great in the kitchen either, so perhaps Roosevelt men were only attracted to women whose talents existed outside of the kitchen.

Hmm.

He wondered whether Tilly could cook.

Tilly.

His cock twitched.

Tilly, who'd kissed him back without hesitation, whose fucking incredible breasts had been plastered against his chest, who—

"Rex!"

Was right behind him.

He turned, watched her close the distance between them. She had a gray hoodie slung over her shoulders, a small black purse held in one hand, a box in the other. And fuck, but he might be developing a fantasy for worn-in T-shirts and faded jeans because her diner uniform hugged those incredible curves exactly as his hands longed to. She blushed, that lovely shade of pink creeping into her cheeks as she walked toward him. Probably because his gaze was locked onto her, taking in every inch of deliciousness.

"Hey, Angel."

She stopped, box dropping to her side, hazel eyes sparking fire. "You know what? Never mind." Tilly spun away, ponytail fanning out behind her as she turned, a little flash of gold on an otherwise cloudy day.

"No." He grabbed her arm. "Why'd you come over?"

A huff and he couldn't lie and say he didn't like the thing that sigh did to her boobs, the slight jiggle even beneath the cotton. "I'm leaving, Rex."

"Because of *Angel*?"

She shrugged. "It's creepy," she muttered, but then her voice changed, dropping in volume, becoming laced with something that sounded suspiciously like vulnerability. And they all knew where Rex Roosevelt stood when it came to this woman and anything approximating vulnerability. "And plus, I asked you to stop."

I asked you to stop.

Why did he think there was a bigger story behind that statement?

Probably because of the haunted look in her gorgeous eyes.

"Tilly." He cupped the back of her neck, met her stare straight on. "I'm sorry," he told her. "It won't happen again."

She shook her head, silky hair sliding over the back of his hand. "What'd you tell me before?" A beat. "Oh, that's right. You do you. It doesn't matter what I want."

Rex scoffed. "The fuck it doesn't." He squeezed lightly when her eyes darted away, bringing them back to his. "*You* matter. What you want matters." She swallowed roughly, then shook her head again. "Sweetheart."

A sigh before she slipped from his grip.

He could have held tight, could have kept her close, but they were in the middle of downtown Darlington and already risking a ride on the gossip train. Rex glanced around, surprised they had thus far gone unnoticed, but draw this encounter out any longer, and they'd be the talk of the town.

"What's in the box?" he asked when she merely stood there and stared at him, shadows in her eyes.

"What? Oh." She thrust it at him. "I noticed that Justin ate your breakfast." A shrug. "So, I brought you some."

He lifted the lid, saw she'd packed him two apple turnovers and a cinnamon roll.

"Bella said you could have the last two," Tilly said, cheeks still pink. "Seeing as you saved her and all."

He snorted. "She did as much saving as I did."

"That's not what I heard."

"I need to go," he said quickly, not wanting to get into his supposed heroics. "I should get home."

Tilly paused, and this time it was *her* turn to study him, and though Rex tried to keep his expression placid, he had the feeling this woman saw way too much: how he was drawn to her, the crazy connection he couldn't seem to shake. How he had so much respect for her, despite just getting to know her, and other . . . deeper feelings.

Danger.

Her mouth curved. "Want a ride home?"

Fuck danger.

He tugged the end of her ponytail. "Sure."

CHAPTER FOURTEEN

Tilly

THEY'D BEEN DRIVING for about ten minutes when Rex abruptly broke the silence and said, "Where are you taking me?"

She frowned, had the sugar from those two turnovers he'd pounded gone to his head? "Um. Home? To the ranch," she added when he continued to look confused.

"What?" He glanced out the window. "Oh. I don't live at the ranch."

She turned right down the road leading out of town. They'd drive by her house in just a couple of minutes. "I didn't mean live," she said. "I meant staying. You're staying there with Justin and Kelly."

"No, I'm not."

Tilly glanced over at him, sure he was messing with her. "What are you talking about? Where are you staying if not the ranch?"

She would have heard if he was at the B&B.

"Above the old bookstore."

Now, she did more than glance over. She stopped the car on the side of the road. Conveniently, this was in front of her own driveway, so she didn't mind blocking it.

"You're living downtown?" she asked, incredulous. "Then why in the hell did you let me give you a ride? You could have walked there in two more minutes."

Rex held up the box. "Baked goods."

She lifted a brow.

He looked like he was trying not to smile. "You offered."

Tilly sighed, plunked her head back against the headrest. "How is this my life?" Then when he didn't reply, she tilted her neck so her cheek was against the headrest and her eyes were on him. "Why do you look so amused?"

"What were you doing in your kitchen so late last night?"

The question took her aback—shock before the creep factor sank in. "How'd you know I was in my kitchen late last night?" she asked carefully, wondering if she might be able to execute some sort of throw the door open and speed away maneuver if his reasoning was as weird as his words.

"I drove by late from the ranch. Saw your light was on."

The correct answer, a perfectly reasonable expectation, and yet it seemed a little too pat.

But before she could ruminate on that, Rex bopped her on the nose. "Not a stalker," he reassured her. "Just curious."

"I run an Etsy shop. Basic toiletries and home goods—candles, air fresheners, soaps, and hair products. Nothing super exciting," she said. "Just filling a few big orders that came in recently."

"That sounds promising."

Her hands tightened on the steering wheel. "I hope so," she told him. "I love Henry, but I don't want to be stuck in the diner forever. I want—" She broke off, stifling the rest of that sentence because she was so far away from being able to think about what she wanted that it was almost comical.

Almost.

Rex's fingers grazed her cheek. "What do you want?"

She almost told him, came a heartbeat within sharing the secret desire in her heart. To make her side-hustle something big and profitable and worldwide. How she'd dreamed it would start online and grow to store-fronts. How it might one day allow her to pay off the stifling debts so she could travel or have a house where she wasn't worried if the water heater was going to go out or whether the next big snow might collapse the roof.

But she was lucky. In so many ways.

Thus, as she'd gotten so damned good at over the last two decades of her life, since her seven-year-old's dreams had been so thoroughly shattered, she shoved those dreams down and forced herself to smile.

"Oh," she said, laughing lightly. "I want the same as anyone I supposed. Food, a place to live, some really good, really bad reality TV."

"Really good *and* really bad?"

She shrugged. "It's only really good if it's really bad."

His mouth curved up into a grin that should have been illegal. "And you like things that are bad?"

Since she wasn't going to fall for *that* line, Tilly smirked. "I'm afraid that my enjoyment of bad, bad things ends with scripted reality television."

"Hmm."

Shifting her gaze forward, she prepared to turn the car around. "You can actually just drive me to Kelly and Justin's," he said. "If you don't mind. My car is there since Kel drove me to town."

"Well," she muttered. "Since we're almost there already . . ."

She scanned for cars then pulled back onto the road, heading toward the ranch once again.

"So, a soap-maker and a waitress," Rex said. "Anything you can't do?"

She snorted. "So many things," she told him. "Starting with baking cinnamon rolls that are half as good as Bella's."

"But could you teach me how to make a candle that *smells* as good?"

A pause. No one had ever asked her how she made her products.

"Why would you want to know that?"

He drummed his fingers on the center console, the sharp *rap-rap-rap* drawing her attention to how close his hand was to her thigh . . . and how she wanted it that much closer. *On* her thigh, sliding *up* the inside of her legs, pressing—

"I find that I want to know everything about you."

"*Oh.*"

Not magical prose or a witty response. Just *oh*, after the most beautiful and fascinating man she'd ever met said he wanted to know *everything*.

Perfect.

"But I'll start with your favorite type of flower."

Her hands twitched on the steering wheel. "What?"

"I'll start with the easy questions first."

"Um . . ."

"Do you not like flowers?"

She loved them actually, but the strange turn in conversation had taken her for a loop. "No."

"So, what kind? Roses?"

A shudder coursed through her. That was one scent and flower she couldn't abide by, not when her mother had loved them so violently that it had taken her months to forget the cloying fragrance that had clogged her nostrils in the hospital, that had filled the rooms in her home. It had taken ages to get the smell out of the house.

"Okay, not roses," he said quietly.

"No, not roses," she murmured. "I like sunflowers."

"Yellow?"

"For the sunflowers?" Her shoulders relaxed at his nod. "Yes, I like those. They're cheerful, but I really love the rust-colored ones or the slightly reddened ones you find in the grocery store this time of year. It's so fall and . . ."

"Cheerful?" he supplied.

Surprised, she glanced over at him. "Yes," she murmured. "That exactly."

"Fitting," he said, then spent their last couple of minutes together quizzing her on her favorite food—chocolate, duh—favorite movie—she didn't have one, but was a sucker for superhero films—and her favorite scent—which gave her ample opportunity to wax poetic about her love of bergamot.

And shockingly, he didn't seem bored out of his mind.

In fact, when she talked about how she paired the fragrances together to make her products, he'd seemed genuinely interested and had actually asked a few insightful questions about her process.

It was the best conversation she'd had in ages.

And she hadn't even asked him a question about himself, but when she parked in front of the ranch and opened her mouth to apologize for monopolizing their time, he placed a finger over her mouth and seemed to know what she was thinking before her apology crossed her lips. "I wouldn't have asked if I didn't want to know."

"Well," she said, the slightly roughened skin of his finger making her mouth tingle, "I want to know those things about you, too."

His smile bordered on a smirk, but she liked it anyway.

She also liked when he moved his hand and replaced it with his lips . . . and tongue. He kissed her for ages, mouth working against hers, the slick darting of his tongue slowly driving her insane, but eventually he pulled back, both of them sucking in huge gulps of air.

"Good," he said.

She frowned. "Good, what?" The kiss was more than good, it was fucking off the charts.

"Good, you want to know those things," he said, pressing one more kiss to her lips. "Because I can tell you when I come over to learn how to make a cinnamon roll candle tomorrow." Then, as though he hadn't just dropped a giant bomb, he popped the door handle and slipped from the car.

Dumbfounded, she didn't immediately drive away.

The knock on her window made her jump, but she rolled the pane down when he gestured for her to do so. But by the time she'd cranked it open—this car was from the Stone Age when electric windows were just a pipe dream—he had a scowl on his face.

"Did you really have to do that by hand?"

The gleam in his expression was becoming familiar. "Don't you dare buy me a new car, Rex Roosevelt!"

"It would have automatic windows," he said.

"No." She narrowed her eyes. "This works fine, and you've already done way too much for me. Now I have a reliable car *and* phone, so *no more*." Maybe if she was firm enough, he'd listen because that gleam was calculating, and she didn't need to owe this man any more favors.

He pouted for a moment before his tone went cajoling. "You could have seat warmers."

Oh. Now that would be nice.

No!

She glared. "Stop it, Roosevelt. You will not woo me with seat warmers and automatic windows, or I won't teach you my magical mastery of candle-making."

He grinned, put his hands up in surrender. "I admit defeat."

"Good," she snapped, backing up so she could pull out of the driveway.

"Tomorrow?" he called. "Magical mastery is happening tomorrow?"

She snorted and shifted into drive. "Yes. I get off at six. Come by at seven. I'll make you dinner."

He nodded. "Oh, Tilly?" he asked as she began to creep forward.

She braked, hand on the window crank. "Yeah?"

"I took that ride because you offered," he said, coming close enough to rest his hands on the top of her car, voice rasping, words quiet but no less powerful because of it. "Because you're beautiful and interesting . . ."

Her breath caught.

"And because I can't seem to stay away from you."

She knew the feeling. *God*, did she know the feeling.

It was a miracle she didn't hit anything on the way home.

But it *wasn't* a miracle to see Rex's car pause at the bottom of her driveway, for her to peek through her curtains and wave at him before he drove off, for the text to make her phone buzz.

My favorite flowers are hydrangeas. My mom loved them.

Her heart pounded as she typed back a response. Those things weren't miracles, Rex checking up on her, following her home, texting her before bed . . . none of them were a surprise.

For some insane reason, she'd begun to expect those actions from Rex.

And that was what scared her the most.

CHAPTER FIFTEEN

Rex

He pulled up the driveway to Tilly's house, parked, then walked straight across her front porch. There would be no hiding in the bushes any longer.

Nope.

Rex had decided to put his impulsivity to the test, stop overthinking everything, and to just go with it. Not that he had a snowball's chance in hell in staying away from her anyway.

She whipped open the door, ponytail askew, cheeks flushed red, and still in her diner uniform. "You're early."

The door slammed closed.

"Um."

He knocked again, but the only thing he got in response was another, "You're early," though it was significantly more muffled and trailed by the sound of footsteps. But instead of those steps coming back toward the door, instead of Tilly opening it and letting him in, they moved away.

Rex waited a minute, listening intently. There were more footfalls, a crash or two, and then after a long moment, nothing.

He hesitated, trying to track her movements again, but when after a few more heartbeats, he still heard nothing, Rex tried the knob. It turned, and he pushed the door open, slipping into the house.

Small, was his first thought, but not in a negative way in the least. Her living room held a love seat, coffee table, and bookcase, and while none of the furniture matched and there were more than a few dings, scratches, and worn spots, the whole effect was cozy and comfortable. Not decorated by a designer to be magazine-worthy, to capture that false sense of country chic, but real life.

Lived in rather than put on a shelf.

And everything smelled fucking incredible—cinnamon and earthy with just the hint of something floral that made his mind want to go in and check it out

He turned to study the kitchen but didn't get further than identifying it as the source of the lovely smell and seeing the counter stacked with a variety of bowls and other vessels before he heard a loud *thunk* followed by a pained cry.

Moving before his brain finished processing the noise, he sprinted down the hall, passed an open door leading to the bathroom then burst into Tilly's bedroom. How did he know that it was her bedroom? Well, smart man that he was, Rex was able to deduce it was the place she slept because there was a bed in the middle of the room. Congratulate him now, Alec.

His eyes didn't stay on the bed for long, however. Because while he'd spent the last few days imagining what it might be like to get Tilly into a bed, the sight actually in front of him was much more tempting than a mattress and silk sheets.

What?

A man had to dream, didn't he?

But for now, he had to focus . . . on committing every single one of the details in front of him to memory.

Because Tilly was in her bedroom. Topless.

Fucking gorgeous, tits bouncing as she struggled to get out of her shirt. He couldn't figure out how she'd managed to get stuck, the tangle of bra and cotton completely covering her face, while her arms were somehow bound straight over her head.

Perfect nipples. Deliciously curved waist. Hips that he wanted to—

She yanked at the shirt, a pathetic mewl escaping her lips before transforming into another pained cry as she crashed into the dresser along one side of the room.

Fuck.

He was standing there ogling her, and she was hurt.

Ass.

But that didn't stop him from staring at her for a few moments longer. Fuck, she had perfect breasts. Rex swallowed, tore his eyes from her chest, and affected a casual, "Need a hand?"

She shrieked, making him jump. "Don't look!" she shouted, turning her back on him and managing to catch herself on the corner of the dresser. He caught her before her head collided with the sharp corner. "Don't you dare look, Rex Roosevelt."

"Not a chance in hell, sweetheart," he said, studying the mess that was the tangle of her bra and shirt. "Not a chance in hell of ignoring the most perfect pair of breasts I've ever seen." His fingers lifted, started working at the knot, and he fucking deserved a medal for doing that rather than drifting them lower, stroking over the hardened buds of her nipples, or better yet, sucking one deep into his mouth.

Tilly's sigh was outraged, and she tried to slip away from him. "You're a pig."

"Yep." A beat. "Now hold still. I think I see where you're caught."

"It's my hair," she groaned.

"That and the hook on the back of your bra. Let me just . . . *there*." He managed to release the tiny hook from the T-shirt then set to work on unwrapping the strands of gold silk. "How'd you get stuck?"

If those hazel eyes had been on his, if the cotton was out of the way, Rex had no doubt they'd have been narrowed into a glare. "Because you were *early*."

"Why are you saying that like it's a bad thing?"

She huffed as he worked on the final knot of hair. "Because I was late getting off work and still trying to get set up, and you showed up *early*."

"So, it's my fault because you were late?"

"Yes." Another sigh. "No. I just wanted to get out of these clothes and wash my face. I smell like the diner."

He sniffed. "I love the way you smell." Tilly froze, but Rex kept working on the tangle until . . . *there*. She was free at last. He tugged the shirt up and over her head then placed it in front of her chest before she could so much as blink.

"I—" She clutched the cotton to her breasts then sighed, defeat creeping into her expression. "Why do I always seem to be thanking you?"

He didn't like the direction of her thoughts in the least, so he waggled his brows, a teasing smile on his lips. "If you keep letting me see your tits, you can forgo the *thank yous*." Pink had already stained her cheeks, but his words made them go even brighter, and his dick twitched in response. Naked breasts, fiery eyes, and pink cheeks . . . fucking slayed him.

"Pig," she accused, smacking his chest. However, in doing so, she managed to lose her grip on the shirt and it fell to the floor.

Rex wasn't a fucking gentleman, so he didn't pick it up. He also sure as shit let his gaze drift back down. *Fucking hell.* "You're welcome," he said, mouth curving, still not helping her as she fought to scoop up the cotton for a few moments then attempted to situate it over those luscious curves.

"I wasn't thanking you," she grumbled.

"I know. But my mom instilled a manner or two in this lascivious mind." He tapped his temple, grinned, and turned to leave. "Get dressed. I'll meet you in the kitchen."

"Rex?"

He stopped in the doorway, turned back.

Tilly crossed over to him. "Why were you early?"

He was tempted to lie, to make up some excuse about just hating to be late or running ahead of schedule, but he found that with her eyes on his, Rex *couldn't* lie to her.

"Why?" she pressed when he didn't immediately reply.

"I needed to see you," he said softly.

"Oh." She was close enough that he felt the heat of her breath on his lips. "I was hoping you would say that."

"I—"

But the rest of his sentence was lost because instead of her breath on his lips, suddenly the shirt was gone, her fingers were woven into his hair, and her mouth was on his.

Fuck, her mouth was on his.

And it was *everything*.

CHAPTER SIXTEEN

Tilly

OKAY, so launching herself topless at Rex Roosevelt may not have been the best idea, she realized. But it was too late. She'd leaped, and now she was topless and in Rex's arms because he'd caught her reflexively. But that was it.

He'd caught her. She'd kissed him.

Then hadn't moved.

Not one muscle.

Cheeks burning, mortification tearing down her spine, Tilly started to pull back.

"I'm—"

She'd been about to say she was sorry, but the words didn't emerge because her mouth had suddenly become otherwise occupied.

By Rex's.

His tongue thrust through her parted lips and swept inside, rubbing against hers in a rhythm that had her squirming close. Especially when his hands drifted up her sides, roughened fingertips brushing along the outside of her breasts.

Fuck yeah, that was good.

She arched, shifting and squirming until his palm shifted over, squeezing her, fingers now teasing her nipples.

And . . . nirvana.

He pulled back and she swayed on her feet, head spinning, not fully cognizant that her oxygen had been so limited. Thus was the power of

Rex Roosevelt. One kiss and she got stupid . . . or passed out from a lack of fresh air.

But he tasted like mint and cinnamon, and they both knew how she felt about cinnamon. Spicy, intoxicating—

Any hope of a lucid thought flew out of her head. Rex's mouth moved from hers, drifted along her jaw. He nipped at her earlobe, making goose-flesh break out all over her body and slid lower, kissing down her throat, teeth grazing her collarbone.

Then lower still.

"Oh, God," she moaned when he latched onto her nipple, sucking it deeply as he pinched and rolled her neglected side between his thumb and forefinger.

Desire arrowed through her, spreading through her limbs, making her lips tingle and her thighs press together. Her panties were absolutely soaked, and she wanted nothing more than to strip off her jeans, climb on top of Rex, then take them both for a wild ride. As though reading her mind, he slid his palms down her torso, flicked open the button of her jeans and shoved them down to her knees. But instead of scooping her up and tossing her on the bed as she'd imagined, he leaned in and pressed his mouth to her.

Hot breath through thin cotton.

Damp heat against her pussy.

Her eyes rolled back and before she could think about what he was doing or the fact that she'd worked a full shift and hadn't showered, her underwear joined her jeans and his tongue was on her clit.

"*Oh fuck,*" she said, knees buckling.

Rex guided her down to the rug, yanking off her clothes and shoving his shoulders between her thighs.

And then he got to work.

Glorious, incredible work.

Spreading her wide with one hand, he circled the flat of his tongue around her clit, then slid one finger of the other hand inside, pumping slow and steady and deep. Tilly cried out, hips arching, wanting him closer, wanting more, wanting—

"Rex," she groaned when he added another finger and timed their motion to that of his tongue. Fire pumped through her veins, scorching her limbs, coalescing in her center, coiling tighter and tighter and tighter until finally it exploded outward. She cried out, pleasure coursing through her, lids slamming shut, and when she finally managed to open them, what felt like hours later, Tilly was half-surprised that her body hadn't been reduced to ash.

That orgasm had been—

Holy fuck is what it'd been.

Rex shifted, and she felt a bolt of embarrassment shoot through her when she realized he was still between her thighs, chin glistening, blue eyes molten.

She bit her lip. "I—um—" Clenching her teeth together, she cut off the words, just barely able to stop herself from asking if she'd tasted okay. A little late for that *now*.

He lifted the hem of his shirt and wiped his mouth. "What?"

"That was incredible," she murmured.

A smirk. "Yes, it was," he said and crawled up her body, still fully dressed. He slipped an arm under her shoulders, tugged her against his chest. "But that also wasn't what you were going to say."

Her jaw dropped open. "How do you always know?"

"Because for whatever reason, the universe has decided to throw us together," he said. "And for as different as our lives have been up until this point, I don't think either of us can deny that we have a connection that can only come from shared experiences."

She scoffed.

"Okay, how about similar experiences?" he asked. "Because I have the feeling you know exactly what it feels like to be on the outside looking in."

"I—" She broke off, shock coursing through her. He was right. That— her role as the perpetual outsider—had been her entire childhood. It didn't matter if she was at school or at home, but she'd never felt like she had a place, and eventually she'd begun to keep people at a distance to stop herself from feeling that way.

So much easier, so much *safer* that way.

He brushed back her hair from her forehead. "I see you know exactly what I mean."

She nodded. "I do. I—" She broke off again.

Another strand of hair tucked safely behind her ear. "No?" he asked, when she didn't finish her thought for the second time.

"No," she agreed.

"Hmm." He nuzzled her throat, and she shivered when his voice rumbled against her skin. "So, perhaps we should circle back to the first conversation? To what you stopped yourself from saying?"

"Um . . ."

"No?" he asked again when she trailed off. "Well, I guess I'll fill in the blanks for you then." His mouth found her ear. "You tasted fucking incredible, baby. Sweet like that cinnamon roll with the barest hint of spicy tartness. It was the absolute best meal of my life."

Her pulse pounded, the words colliding with a spot deep within her heart.

But instead of harming her, of knocking a piece of herself loose, of bruising or slicing, they bolstered . . . and frankly, they turned her on.

Turned her into a smoldering pile of mush.

Or maybe just her brain because when he asked, "Who made you feel like you were on the outside, baby?" she actually answered.

"My mother," she said softly. "My father." A long slow breath. "And my fiancé."

"You're engaged?" Rex stiffened, drawing his arm out from beneath her so quickly that her head *thunked* against the floor. Thank God for the thick rug.

Blinking, she sat up, crossed her arms over her chest, suddenly vulnerable and self-conscious. "Was," she said. "*Was* engaged."

"Oh." He sat up, stripping off his shirt and slipping it over her head.

Even though she had a perfectly good drawer full of shirts, she let him. Hell, more than let him. Tilly curled into the warm cotton, drew in a lungful of his spicy scent, crisscrossing her legs so it covered her from shoulders to toes.

"He broke up with me not long after my mom passed."

"Asshole."

Her mouth turned up. "Yes. Yes, he was."

"What happened?"

"To my mom? Or with Steven?"

"Both."

She didn't think she could handle this conversation, naked except for a T-shirt, on her bedroom floor. She needed armor, barriers between her and the past. And this room with its memories of her mother, of her time with Steven . . . it was too much.

"I need to put on pants for this," she muttered. "And maybe a bra."

"Shame that," Rex said lightly, but he stood and crossed to her dresser, opening the top drawer and holding up one of her most-worn sports bras. From the next drawer, he extracted her favorite pair of pajamas, lilac and covered with unicorns. They were threadbare and ready to split at the seams, but they were also so freaking cozy that she couldn't bear to part with them. He seemed to study the waistband for a moment and Tilly wondered if he were checking the size.

Seemed a little nosy if anyone asked her.

But also . . . he'd been nose-deep in her vagina only minutes before, so it wasn't like she had room to be outraged.

He knelt and slipped them over her feet, helped her slide them up to her hips then handed her the sports bra. "Have any alcohol in that kitchen of yours?" he asked. "Seems like you might need it."

Considering the mere thought of her parents and Steven had driven her to drink many times before, Tilly couldn't fault his logic.

"Vodka in the freezer. Sprite and orange juice in the fridge."

"Screwdriver on steroids," he said. "I like it." A kiss to the top of her head. "I'll make yours a double."

"Why?" she asked as he started to walk from the room. "Why are you here?"

What could you possibly see in me?

That was the question running through her head.

And once again, he seemed to be able to read her mind.

He closed the distance between them and kissed her fiercely, one hand cupping her cheek, the other squeezing her hip. "You," he murmured when he broke free. "I see *you*."

He paused in the doorway.

"And that's enough."

CHAPTER SEVENTEEN

Rex

His body radiated with tension as he strode down the hall and into the kitchen.

Only part of it was sexual because his cock was still rock-hard and throbbing. But he barely focused on that as he pulled out the bottle of vodka from the freezer, along with the Sprite and orange juice from the fridge, and *that* was saying something. Rex wasn't the kind of man to forgo his own sexual urges in place of conversation, and he *definitely* wasn't a man who was jealous over an asshole from a woman's past.

Probably because *he* usually was the asshole from the past.

Snorting, he searched the cabinets until he located two glasses and then fixed them both strong drinks. Because the rest of his tension had been strongly from anticipation . . . or maybe dread.

Anticipation because he wanted to know everything about Tilly—the secrets and long-buried hurts, her hopes and dreams for the future.

Dread because he knew that if he wanted to have a snowball's chance in hell of that future possibly including him, then he would need to level with her about his past in the very same way.

Talking and sharing feelings were almost as scary words to him as responsibility.

And yet here he was. Not running but digging in and preparing to stay.

To fight to stay.

Rex couldn't deny that was one feeling he actually enjoyed.

Footsteps and creaking floorboards announced Tilly's arrival before she walked tentatively around the corner and into the kitchen. Eyes landing on the glasses but not on him, she all but snatched one from his hand and downed the contents.

"Um. Okay?" he asked.

She nodded, took his glass and started chugging.

"I don't think—"

"I do," she said. "Because if I'm going to tell you about my parents and Steven, then I need alcohol in my life."

"Well, then." He refilled and held out her glass.

She took it, gulped. Then, cheeks pinkened, though this time not for a reason he viewed as particularly pleasant, Tilly lifted her chin and said, "My mom blamed me for my dad leaving."

His brows drew together. "What? No—" he began.

"I'm not telling you this as some sort of emotional reasoning or baggage or hurt feelings a kid holds on to." She put both glasses in the sink then began returning the bottles to their respective locations. "I'm saying this as an adult woman who is fully aware of her parents' opinions because she *lived* them." A beat. "And also because she told me in no uncertain terms."

Shadows in those hazel depths. "The first time I remember her telling me that was as my dad drove down the driveway before he left us the first time. A dust cloud trailed him, lingering in the air for far longer than his car."

"How old were you?"

"Six? Seven?" she said. "Young enough to not understand what he was doing and too old not to miss him once he'd gone."

"Why did he leave?"

She leaned back against the counter. "I wasn't exactly an easy child. I was a preemie and didn't sleep much at all for the first two years. And I was energetic, needy. I couldn't entertain myself, had to have an adult keep me occupied or I got in trouble."

He frowned. "So you were a normal six or seven-year-old kid."

"I guess."

The silence stretched for a few moments before Rex asked, "You said the first time he left?"

"Oh, yeah." Tilly smiled, but it wasn't a happy one. "My parents were special. They couldn't stay together, couldn't live apart. They were like the most fucked-up drug addicts, but their relationship was their drug of choice." She sighed. "Unfortunately, even though they couldn't stay away from each other for long, they also couldn't make each other happy."

"And you were stuck in the crossfire."

"Happily so," she said, surprising him. Then added, no doubt at his confused look, "It was attention, and I was starving for it."

His heart skipped a beat, and her eyes softened as she took in his face. He was still shirtless and when she placed her hand over his heart, the soft skin of her palm made goose bumps break out on his skin. "You know something about that, don't you?" she murmured. "Know what it's like to feel so lonely and isolated that you'll take any form of attention."

He nodded, sucked in a breath, and just laid his cards on the table. "I was the bad twin, never as smart or talented as Justin, so I stopped trying, and eventually, I learned to love the negative attention, took pleasure in their shock and disappointment."

"Better a disappointment than ignored."

Rex brushed his fingers over her cheek. "Yes. That."

"But it's not healthy."

He shook his head. "No."

"And when I was ten, my dad left for good." Her lips pressed flat for a long moment. "I thought it would only be a matter of time before he came back. It wasn't like that was the first time he'd disappeared for a few weeks to cool off." She swallowed hard, pulled out the vodka bottle and splashed some more in her glass. "I remember getting home from school every day and rushing into their bedroom"—she pointed down the hall—"but he was never there. Then I'd stand here in the kitchen and watch through the window until he came home."

"But he didn't come back?"

"No."

For some reason, the image of ten-year-old Tilly staring through the small window, watching the street for any sign of her father's car coming up the driveway sliced him to the core. Okay, not for *some* reason, because he wasn't a monster and didn't want to see any kid hurt, emotionally or otherwise.

But it hit him harder than normal because it was Tilly.

And he could picture it.

And he wanted to pummel anyone who'd ever so much as hurt her feelings.

"So—" He stopped, shoving the question of what she'd done after her father had gone deep down. They'd drudged up enough tonight and—

"We stayed in this house," she murmured. "On pause for ages. Waiting for him to show back up, waiting for our lives to start again. I think that's why I got into scents so much. I found an old bottle of my dad's cologne and tried to replicate it." Her smile was sad. "I think part of me thought that if I could just make the house smell like him again, then maybe . . . oh God, it's so stupid now."

"You hoped he might come back."

She rolled her eyes. "Unfortunately, yes."

"Shit, baby," he said and took her in his arms. Rex had rarely comforted another person. It wasn't his instinct or nature or . . . style, he supposed, to focus on someone who wasn't himself. Or maybe he'd been so closed down that he hadn't been able to recognize when someone might need something from him.

He definitely hadn't been capable of giving it.

But over the last few years, things had begun shifting. He'd seen his brother and Kelly happy and hadn't acted selfishly for once. He'd helped Bella. And he wanted to do the same thing for Tilly.

No. He wanted to do more.

"It was stupid," she said, burrowing into his chest with a sniff. "To stop living for so long. But after a month had passed then two then more, my mom just sort of shut down, I guess. She stopped picking me up from school, and I started walking home. She didn't cook dinner or buy groceries."

"How did you live?"

"My dad sent money," she said softly. "Enough for me to stretch after my mom stopped showing up for work and lost her job." She shoved out of his arms. "This town never got it. They thought she was lazy, that she was just after a free ride." Tilly paced away. "They didn't understand she was depressed, that she literally could *not* get out of bed. I was fine. I cashed the checks, bought food, cooked."

He snagged her hand as she paced by, tugging her against him, and this time she stayed in the circle of his arms. "Henry's mom and dad were the only ones who understood. They never gave me those judgy looks and when I was old enough, I got a job at the diner."

"How old was old enough?"

She smiled. "Fourteen. Not legal, I know," she added. "But he paid me in food, and it was so much better than anything I could cook up at the time that it was like I'd brought home food from a four-star Michelin chef. My mom even perked up for a time."

"Why do I sense a *but* coming?"

Tilly sighed. "Probably because there is one."

"I was afraid of that."

A shrug. "It's not that unusual. She got sick. Things got even tighter. I made it work . . . and then she died."

"How old were you?"

"Seventeen." She straightened her shoulders, tried to pull away again, but he wouldn't let her. No distance between them. Not in this moment. "Luckily, I was only two months shy of eighteen, so by the time they figured out I was a minor, I was legal."

"But you were alone."

"I got used to being alone long before my mother passed."

Silence stretched between them for a long moment, and Rex would be lying if he'd said he knew how to comfort her. The pain in her words had been acute, but it was also an old hurt, and he thought that harping on it might make things worse. And then there was the fact that she'd now bared her soul, and he probably needed to reciprocate and—

Cool fingers cupped his jaw.

"Too much?" she asked.

Rex slipped his hand behind her neck, held her in place when her gaze would have drifted away from his. "No," he said. "I was just thinking that this meant I needed to tell you everything about my childhood, too, and—"

"It's a lot?"

"Nothing when compared to what you went through, which makes me a giant asshole because I spent so many years acting like—" He sighed. "And you were dealing with all this— And I wasted so much fucking time just being—"

She placed a finger over his lips. "There's a lot happening here, but I think the first thing you need to do is finish a sentence." Her mouth curved. "And know that just because I told you a bunch of shit about my past doesn't mean you have to reciprocate in turn tonight."

He pressed a kiss to her finger then lifted it from his face. "But—"

"Shh," she said and rose on tiptoe to slant her lips across his. Then she dropped back down to the balls of her feet. "Enough," she said. "For tonight, let's just let this be enough."

He hesitated, warring with himself, knowing he should share but fucking terrified to put himself out there. It was easy to fix a car or to buy a phone. Emotions, on the other hand? Scary as shit. But as he watched Tilly, her eyes soft and kind, no trace of disappointment or anger in her expression, he thought that perhaps they weren't so scary after all. Though, it wasn't a thought with one hundred percent certainty, because when she laced her fingers with his and tugged him over to one of the many bowls on the counter, waxing poetic about the scent she'd come up with for his cinnamon roll candle, he didn't put the activity on pause.

Instead, he went along for the ride.

He let himself enjoy the process, soaked up Tilly and spending time with a woman because she was fun and smart and witty.

Soon he'd have to lay it all out there.

But tonight, he'd just take this moment.

And for the first time in his life, instead of throwing it away or treating it as casual and unimportant, Rex clutched it tight, tucked it safe inside his heart.

Where Tilly had already made a permanent place for herself.

CHAPTER EIGHTEEN

Tilly

SHE TAUGHT Rex how to make cinnamon roll scented candles and then he helped her fill her outstanding orders that had come in with sudden, shocking frequency.

"I don't know how she got my name," Tilly said, holding up the paper with the information. "I don't think I ever met her at the couple of craft fairs I go to, and yet she's ordered six dozen toiletry sets. But," she added with a smile, "if this keeps up, I might finally be able to open up my own place."

"Seems to me, it's finally your time to shine," Rex said, tongue poking out in rather adorable fashion as he filled lip balm tubes with her lemon-raspberry concoction.

Maybe it was the way he said it or perhaps it was knowing that he'd been behind her car and her phone, that finally a niggle of something penetrated her thoughts. "Please, don't tell me you have a warehouse of my candles and shampoos somewhere."

"What?" He jerked, overflowing several of the tubes, and glancing up at her with a definitely guilty expression.

"Oh, my God," she moaned. "You do."

She clanked the spoon on the counter, turned off the heat on the wax she was melting, tears filling her eyes, and mortification burning through her. The phone, the car, and now he'd bought close to ten thousand dollars in candles?

Well, candles, shampoos, face wash, lip balm—

Not the point, Conner.

She should have known this wasn't something she'd done on her own. This was another fucking handout.

Rex might like her, might *want* her in bed, but he was just like everyone else. He didn't think she was a fully capable human being, didn't think she could make things work on her own, even though she'd always managed, had clawed and squeaked through tight spots more times in her life than anyone ever should have.

She'd told him everything . . . and he was just the same as everyone else.

Not fair, her brain cautioned her, but it was too little too late. Her temper had sparked, and she was vulnerable and embarrassed and—

"Get out," she snapped, brushing by him and picking up her laptop.

"What are you doing?"

"Canceling the fucking orders," she gritted out. "Refunding your money. I can't believe you'd buy—"

"Why wouldn't I buy it?" he asked. "It's fucking incredible. But I—"

"I told you to leave," she said. "I can't believe I was stupid enough to think that things would be different, that I would finally get out of debt. Or worse, that someone might actually think I could be a fully capable person all on my own."

Rex closed her laptop before she could actually cancel anything. "You are!"

She growled, tried to open it again, but he didn't let her. Instead, he snatched up the computer and shoved it on top of the fridge. And because she was a short motherfucker, she couldn't reach it without getting a stool.

Which she did. Snatching it from the pantry and plunking it down in front of the fridge.

Tilly clambered up, reached on tiptoe and—

Nearly fell.

Nearly because Rex caught her and set her firmly on the floor.

"I don't need a rescue!" she screamed, shoving away from him and trying to sprint from the room. "Just go," she spat, when he snagged her arm to stop her. "Go, like all the rest of them and save me the heartache later."

Rex froze, not speaking for a long moment, then he cursed, yanked her against his chest and wrapped his arms around her in a hug she really wanted to pretend she didn't want.

"What is it, exactly, that has you so upset?"

Tilly huffed, tried to squirm free of his hold.

"You're such a fucking asshole." She glared up at him when he held firm.

"That we all know." One brow came up. "So, care to share?"

"No," she muttered, feeling extremely childish and still not willing to give in.

"Fine," he said and tossed her onto his shoulder. He spent a moment at the stove, and though she couldn't see him since she was getting an eyeful of an attractive ass she didn't want to admit she was staring at, she still heard the *click* of the knobs, the slight whoosh of the gas turning off. "Will they be okay?"

She knew he was referring to the scents she had steeping and while part of her wanted to be touched by his kindness—and all the other kindnesses he'd shown her over the last days—the rest of her was seriously pissed off.

Maybe unreasonably so, but still fucking furious.

"They'll be fine," she snapped. "And I will, too, once you let me down and get the hell out of my house."

"Good."

But he didn't put her down, and he didn't walk out the front door. Instead, he carried her down the hall into her bedroom, dropped her onto the mattress, then crawled in beside her.

Yeah, not happening.

She started to get up, but Rex caught her waist, pulled her against him, and . . . just held her.

Held her.

His hand didn't move up or down to cop a feel, he didn't thrust his crotch against her ass. He didn't try to kiss her or talk dirty or get her naked. He. Just. Held. Her.

Until she stopped fighting.

Until she slowly relaxed against him.

Until her anger peaked and began decreasing infinitesimally.

Only then did he speak. "I don't have a warehouse of your products. I called a few friends, suggested they check out your stuff. *They* decided to order it. They paid for it." She felt him shrug. "I merely suggested it."

Tilly shifted in the circle of his arms, rolling to face him, to see his eyes. "You're not lying."

He shook his head. "I'm not."

"You . . . suggested?"

"Yes." His gaze stayed on hers, but she could read between the lines.

A snort. "I'm guessing you *strongly* suggested."

Blue eyes rolled. "I'm a Roosevelt. All of our *suggestions* are strong."

"Really?"

He smirked. "Should I add large as well?"

Tilly laughed, but it wasn't entirely comfortable. She was feeling a bit stupid for having overreacted the way she had, especially when he'd been nothing but nice and fun and had given her the best orgasm of her life.

The memory of that mouth on her, his tongue flicking against her clit was enough for her cheeks to heat, her thighs to clench.

His thumb brushed over her skin. "Is this from my bad innuendos?"

"No." She sucked in a breath then stifled a moan when she got a whiff of his delicious scent.

"Hmm?" He cupped her jaw, bent to nuzzle her throat. "Then what?"

"Your cock," she blurted. "I was thinking about your mouth on me and how that was fucking incredible and how you'd probably feel even better inside me—"

He froze, pulled back. "Sweetheart, you can't say things like that."

Tilly smiled and cupped his cheek with her palm. "I'm sorry."

"For making my dick hard or for freaking out earlier?"

"Well, definitely not the first." She smiled when he groaned and flopped to his back. "What?" She climbed on top of him, straddling his hips. "I find that I'm rather fine with making this"—a shift of her hips—"hard."

"Fine?" His hands came to her waist. "Just *fine*?"

"Is adequate better? Perhaps satisfying?"

He growled. "Woman, you have to be the most infuriating creature on the planet."

Stilling, the smile dropping from her lips, she stared down at the beautiful man beneath her. "I really am sorry. I tend not to lose my temper, but when I do, I admit that I go a bit overboard. And this wasn't even really about you so much as it was about Steven."

"We'll circle back to that asshole, Steven part," he said, leaning up and pressing a hard kiss to her lips. "Because I like your temper, baby. I don't mind you getting fired up or upset or angry. I just want you to be you. And more than that, I always want you to feel like you can be you with me." He tugged the end of her ponytail. "Even if you think I won't like it. Okay?"

She nodded.

"Now, Steven?"

"It's a small thing, really. No, I don't mean the way it made me feel," she said, hurrying to add when Rex's eyes narrowed and his mouth opened, no doubt to protest her statement. Fair that, since what she was calling a *small thing* had caused such a big reaction. "Because it did make me feel shitty, but more because I didn't realize how much it had upset me until everything hit me in the kitchen."

He touched her cheek. "I want to be following, sweetheart, but I'm a little confused. It seems like a big thing because you had a huge reaction, but you're telling me it's not important."

She plunked her forehead to his chest. "I . . . okay, I guess this is so hard because I thought I was over Steven completely. We were young when we were engaged, and I thought he was my white knight put on the planet to rescue me." She rolled her eyes. "Stupid, I know. But I think I wanted it to be true for so long that I just . . . let it be that way." Ripping out her ponytail holder, she sighed. "Is this making any sense at all? I mean, I thought Steven would swoop in and fill all the empty holes in me, and he was really good at taking care of me. I think he even liked it. The saving part made him feel good."

"But?"

"But at some point, he resented it," she said. "And I get it. I wasn't even eighteen yet, he was barely twenty, commuting to school during the week, seeing me on the weekends. I was a wreck and had no clue what to do and—" A sigh. "Eventually, he couldn't take it anymore, couldn't take how sad I was, how I sometimes forgot to eat or struggled with filling out insurance papers because I didn't want to put pen to paper and admit she was gone. I was depressed and unable, unwilling, to find help and . . . something gave. He left." She sucked in a breath. "I went into a tailspin, didn't get out of bed for a week, didn't eat, didn't sleep. I was heartbroken and alone, but one day it was like the fog cleared. I realized that if I was ever going to get out of this town, then I had to figure my own shit out." A beat. "By myself. Without a man to—"

"So, you think because I fixed your car and got you a phone, because I mentioned—"

"Strongly suggested," she interrupted with a raised brow.

He smirked. "Because I suggested to a friend that she try out your products and maybe roll them out to a few boutique hotels, that I'm going to get resentful of you?"

"I'm—" She started to deny it, but then realized, yes, that was exactly what she was afraid of.

He'd find out about the bills and pay them off.

Her car would break down, and he'd buy her a new one.

Her roof would collapse, and then she'd come home to find it fixed.

He'd swoop in and do the saving, and what could she possibly give in return to him?

Nothing.

Because she *had* nothing, couldn't compete with the Roosevelt wealth or power. She was just a twenty-six-year-old girl trying to figure shit out, had spent the last eight years trying to sort out her shit so she could move on to bigger and better things, and he wouldn't see any of that if he just swept into her life, snapped his fingers, and made everything perfect.

And so, she told him that.

"Rex, you're *you*. Your family is powerful. You're rich, and I know you can fix things in my life that are nearly impossible for me to even dream about mending easily."

"But you don't want that." He seemed genuinely confused, poor thing.

"No," she murmured with a smile. "I don't want a partner who needs to save me all the time."

He tucked a strand of her hair behind her ear. "But isn't that what real relationships are all about? You save each other."

"Each other, I think, are the keys words there. Because Rex, what can I possibly hope to do for you? I can't compete with the money or the influence." Her gaze drifted to the floor, to the spot that had rotted away. She'd repaired it with plywood, thrown a rug over the top, and no one was the wiser.

Except her.

She was the wiser and just like the floor, she was just a patchwork of mismatched pieces, cobbled together to make some semblance of a whole.

How could she possibly be an equal partner with anyone if she could barely keep her head above water?

"Come here."

Her gaze jumped back to his. "What?"

"Come here," he murmured, tugging her back to his chest and covering them both with a blanket. "Let me tell you a story, darling."

"Darling?" She snorted. "And a story?" She clapped her hands together. "Oh my God! Really?"

Fingers on her cheek. "There's my sarcastic girl."

"And you like sarcasm?"

"I like you. So fucking much, sweetheart." His fingers tightened on her arm, not painful, but strong with intention, exactly like the words that followed. "I spent so much of my life in a fog, flitting from one thing to the next, trying to feel something after my mom died. You see?" he said, when her eyes filled with tears. "Instead of doing something important, like trying to build a life for myself, after my mother died, I just shut down. I lived to numb every feeling, pushed everyone away. And . . . I hurt so many people who mattered."

"You were hurting."

"Yes," he agreed. "But I was also an asshole. I know I lost my mom and that my dad retreated into himself for way too long, especially considering that he had Justin and myself to raise, but I chose the wrong path."

"You were young and—"

"No more excuses for me, sweetheart." He smiled at her, a gentle, fragile thing. "They're all true, but what's also true is that I walked, drove like a crazy fucker in one of my ridiculous sports cars down that path for way too long." She laughed, and he wiped the corner of her eye, where a tear had gathered. "Then, I met Kelly."

He paused and the smile she was wearing slipped away.

Because he'd said—

Kelly.

And not her.

Oh God, was he still hung up on her?

"No," he said gently. "It's not her I want. What I was trying to say is I met her, saw her with my brother, and I realized how different things could be. They took a tragedy and tough situation and turned it into something unbreakable."

Tilly's heart settled.

"Then Bella thought I was my brother in Italy and the way she looked at me with such hope—no, not *hope*, exactly, but conviction. Like she knew that Justin would do the right thing. That without one iota of doubt, he'd help her . . . and then I saw the way it faded when she realized I was me." He rolled his eyes at himself. "My ego was bruised, but more than that, I saw in that moment I had the opportunity to change."

"And you did."

He scoffed. "I'm at least trying."

"Well, coming from a stranger you helped on the side of the road, I can vouch for that change."

He brushed a kiss on her forehead. "That wasn't selfless in the least. I saw a beautiful *angel* through the window and had to stop."

"Have X-ray vision, do you?" she teased. "Being able to see into a car in the dead of night." She ran her hands over his chest, stopped at the space above his heart. "You stopped because this is good inside."

"Maybe," he said.

"And the universe rewarded you with me." She chuckled. "A mess of a project with more baggage than the belly of a plane."

"Baggage, I'm happy to help carry, sweetheart."

Her lips curved. "Only if you'll let me carry yours, too."

"Deal, Angel," he said, his eyes dancing. "Deal."

A sigh before she hugged him tight. "I let you get away with the first *Angel*, but I can't let that second one slide."

He laughed, cuddling her closer when she yawned. "Sleep now. We can negotiate tomorrow."

Burrowing into his arms, she soaked in his scent. "You always smell too good."

"So, turn me into a candle then."

Exhaustion swept over her, the emotions of the evening and the late hour catching up with her, but she laughed at his joke, though that laugh transmuted into another yawn.

"Sleep now," he murmured. "We can argue more in the morning."

CHAPTER NINETEEN

Rex

"ARE you sure you can't come?" he asked a few days later, standing near the hostess stand of Henry's Diner, box filled with Bella's delicious baked goods in one hand and Tilly's ass in the other.

Speaking of that, he shifted his hand upward. It was late, so the diner crowd was decidedly older, but they were garnering a fair amount of attention, and he didn't want to scar the odd child that was in the restaurant. Especially when he'd been trying to just give his girl a simple kiss goodbye, and as things were wont to do with Tilly, they'd heated up and almost gotten out of hand.

Pun intended.

He snorted inwardly and placed his hand determinedly on the small of her back.

Reddened lips tipping up at the corners, Tilly brushed one more kiss across his cheek. "Trying to be good, Roosevelt?"

"Attempting to, yes."

She rose on tiptoe, whispered in his ear. "I like you a little bad."

He groaned softly and turned to glare at her. "You're not helping."

"Have a little problem?" She smirked.

"I resent the term *little*," he muttered, releasing her and stepping back, strategically placing the box of baked goods in front of his groin.

"And, yes," she said, regret rather than teasing in her words. "I'm sorry, I can't join you for dinner, but with Sally calling out, I don't want to leave Henry shorthanded."

"I understand. Call me when you're off?"

She nodded, and he turned to go.

"Rex?"

He paused, slanting a look over his shoulder and lifting a brow.

"You know that *this*"—she pointed between them—"will reach Kel and Justin before you do?"

Considering that Esther, the head gossip in town, had her phone out and was recording them, Rex very much knew that. He blew a kiss at Tilly, chuckling when Esther cackled something about great material for Snapchat. "Meh."

"Really?" she asked. "You're that cavalier about this? About everyone talking about what's going on with us?"

He spun to face her, stole one more kiss. "Cavalier?" he said, breaking away once they were both breathing hard. "Not in the least. You're mine, and I'm counting on the gossip train to inform everyone of that fact, sweetheart." He started for the door. "Because I don't share well."

"Rex!"

He turned his head and met her stare.

"Just for the record," she said, eyes hot. "I don't share well either."

He was smiling the entire drive to Kelly and Justin's.

Yeah, he'd most definitely met his match.

———

HIS BROTHER HAD BEEN SLANTING him looks across the dinner table the entire evening.

Kelly had cooked—or rather, she'd heated up a dish that her sister, Melissa, had left earlier that afternoon as a thanks for riding lessons—and they were all chowing down. If not for the looks, Rex would have been relaxed—the kids were eating happily, no plates had hit the floor, and no arguments had broken out.

But Justin kept staring at him, not saying anything, acting completely normal with the rest of the table, and yet with him . . .

Weird.

Rex sighed. Because not *weird*, exactly. He could sense the impending conversation and had been a fucking moron for not recognizing that it would be coming. Justin was worried about Tilly.

And Rex couldn't stop himself from thinking that his brother was right to worry.

Fuck.

They'd all just about finished when there was a knock at the door. He remembered a time when he would have heard the tires on the gravel, signifying any car's approach, like at Tilly's house, but here at the ranch, three kids and three adults chatting and laughing and talking over each other—okay, that was mostly the kids—and the only signal of a visitor was the doorbell.

"I'll get it," Kel said, jumping up. "Melissa is probably trying to make sure she gets her dish back." She bent to kiss the top of Jax's head.

"You're just trying to get out of dishes," Justin teased.

"Cook doesn't clean," she sing-sang as she left the room.

Since Rex was done, he picked up his plate and stood, then gathered some of the carnage from the table and carried it all over to the sink. He'd just started the water when Justin came over.

"What are you doing to that poor girl, bro?"

Rex froze, the ice down his spine colder than the water on his hands. "I like her, Jus," he said, not willing to admit to his brother that he loved Tilly. That was for her ears only, at least the first time he said it.

After that, he could write it in the sky or buy a billboard, but the first time should be special.

Roses—no, sunflowers. Romantic words. Candles—

The thought made him smile.

Justin's sigh didn't.

"She's not for you," Justin said. "You know that. She's . . . fragile, and you'll destroy her."

"Tilly's the strongest person I know."

That sigh again, followed by a tone he knew too well. Disappointment. "Rex."

"What? You think I'm going to break her? Destroy her? You think I'm that much of an asshole?" His brother's hesitation in answering had Rex's gut sinking. "You do. You think I'm the same prick who took advantage of Kelly."

"You don't think of anyone but yourself," Justin said. "That's not your way, bro, and now Tilly is caught in the crosshairs."

"But I'm not the same."

"Who are you trying to convince?" It was a reasonable question considering his past, considering the weak ass declaration Rex had just given.

He tried again.

"I'm not that man," he said. "Not anymore. I've changed."

Justin crossed his arms, eyes not hard exactly, but something inside of them had shifted. He didn't believe Rex had changed, and he probably never would. This was all just a fucking waste of his time. He'd never find his place in this family again. Hell, he wasn't even convinced that he actually *did* deserve a spot. He'd pissed on that honor plenty of times in the past.

"What are you doing here?" Justin asked before his voice softened. "What did you expect to find?"

"Not to fall in love," he snapped. He sure as shit hadn't anticipated that curve ball.

Justin's eyes widened. "Did you say—?"

"No."

But it wasn't in response to his brother.

Tilly stood in the doorway.

Horror coursed through him. She'd heard him say he loved her, and he hadn't made it special. Fuck. She deserved special.

"I'm sorry," he began, walking toward her.

"No." She put up a hand, and he stopped.

"That's twice you said that," he murmured. "No, what?" To the apology? To the sentiment itself? To him?

"You can't mean it," she said, face pale and eyes glittering with tears. "I thought we were . . . different. You made me hope—" She choked on a sob.

"I'm sorry," he said again, pulling her into her arms. "I didn't mean for you to overhear that. I was going to tell you another way."

Her spine went ramrod stiff, and she shoved him hard enough that he stumbled back a step. "Of course, you were."

"Tilly—"

She scooted away, backing toward the door. "J-just stay away from me, Rex Roosevelt. Stay the *fuck* away."

Familiar ice coated his spine, numbed him from the inside out. Nothing. He was better off if he felt nothing. *Wrong. This is wrong to stay away.* But before he could grasp fully on to the thought, Tilly was gone, and he was standing in the kitchen with his brother's family staring at him incredulously.

Kel and Justin both spoke at once.

It was Justin's words that struck home.

"See?" he said. "Tilly doesn't want this."

Rex was too gutted to see Kelly smack him, to watch her rise on tiptoe and whisper in his brother's ear. Too devastated to see Justin's face pale.

He left.

It was better that way.

For everyone.

CHAPTER TWENTY

Tilly

THE LETTER WAS under her mat the next morning.

I'm sorry you feel that way. I'd bought this for you before you changed your before things between us changed. Don't say no until you go and see it.

-R

Below that was an address.

"Shit," she muttered, recognizing it.

Absolutely no way was she going there, even if it was just down the street from Henry's Diner. With the way things were going, it was probably an empty room full of the candles she'd made.

Sighing, she pushed through into the diner, only to stop short.

Henry was at the hostess stand, arms crossed. "What are you doing here, Tilly?"

Her stomach clenched. "What do you mean?"

"I mean, you're not on shift today," he said, dropping his arms to rearrange the stack of menus behind the stand.

"Oh, yeah," she said, remembering he'd given her the morning off after she'd worked late the previous night. Before she'd finished up a few minutes early and had headed to the ranch to surprise Rex. Before she'd had her heart broken again because she was an idiot who'd fallen for the wrong person hook, line, and sinker. "I figured I'd come anyway. I could use the—"

She stopped herself from finishing that sentence because she didn't really need the money anymore. The shop had given her a cushion. She'd be able to pay off the outstanding bills and could easily live on her wait-ressing salary without the added pressure of the medical debts.

Thanks to Rex.

Her eyes burned.

"I'm sure Bella can use prep help."

Henry shook his head. "No, kiddo," he said softly. "You've been working too hard for too long. I missed it before, but you need some time off to reset."

"I'm not a kid," she muttered.

He touched her arm. "I know that's not fair to think of you that way after everything you've been through, but you've been through so much. Plus, now you've got Rex, and it's new and fresh and you seem happy with him." A nudge toward the door. "You should go enjoy yourself." A beat. "With him."

And her heart shattered a little more.

Tilly knew she was moments away from bursting into tears and so she kept her gaze down, nodded, and slipped outside the door, but when she made it to her car, it wouldn't start.

"Perfect," she said, losing her battle with the tears. They streamed down her cheeks, dripped off her jaw, turning the gray of her seat black.

She tried the key again and nothing.

"Fuck!" she said, suddenly so damned furious and upset and . . . hurt.

Alone again, heart shredded.

P.A.T.H.E.T.I.C.

She was absolutely—

No.

Not anymore. Not again. She wasn't weak or fragile or freaking pathetic. Maybe she'd been deceived and naïve, falling for the wrong man in too short of a time, but also . . . maybe she didn't have to let this destroy her.

She pulled the handle to pop the hood, then slipped from her car and spent a few minutes staring at the respective parts.

But she hadn't seen what Rex had done to get it started and so she had to resort to calling Dale. He answered on the first ring and promised to come check it out after he got his morning appointments checked in and underway.

Until then, she would wait.

Fifteen minutes later, she was going stir crazy.

She was up to date on all her shows, none of her favorite YouTubers had released videos, and was out of energy in the one game she played on her phone. And Rex's note kept staring at her from the passenger's seat.

Should she just go and see?

If it *was* candles, it would serve him right if she resold them.

Maybe she should—

"No, you will not, Tilly Conner," she told herself firmly. "Absolutely not.

But when another half hour passed and Dale still hadn't come, she found herself getting out of the car to "stretch her legs." Or at least that was the convenient lie she told herself. Couldn't let those quads tighten up, might get sore and not be able to—

She cut the lie off there and walked down to the end of the block.

To the address on the note.

Brown paper covered the windows, and she sighed at finding the For Rent sign gone. It wasn't a surprise that someone had rented the space. Darlington's downtown was a popular destination for both locals and tourists alike, so empty storefronts didn't stay empty for long.

Tilly had just been eyeing this one because it was perfect. It had been a coffee shop and bookstore before, the walls lined with gorgeous oak shelves, the old worn tables left behind. She'd been able to picture her products on those shelves, candles on one wall, toiletries on other, maybe even makeup or a hairstylist who could come in on special days and give customers a new look—

Sigh.

It wasn't to be.

She'd keep inching her way into success. She'd keep waitressing and working her Etsy shop and craft fairs and—

One day everything would be fine.

See? She could be heartbroken and healthy.

Tilly walked past the front doors and rounded the building. Rex had said he was in the apartment above the store, and she thought the entrance was along the alleyway. It took a couple of tries to find the right door, but eventually she found one that was unlocked—well, slightly propped open with a thin sliver of wood. She pulled it wide, saw a flight of stairs leading up, and with a deep, bracing breath, walked up to the second floor.

The first thing that hit her was the smell.

Oh fuck, the smell. *His* smell was everywhere.

Almost a physical sensation, it crawled up her nose, coated her skin, and her eyes prickled all over again. God, how could she have been stupid enough to fall for him?

To fall in love with him.

Sighing, she stepped further into the apartment, taking in the simple studio that was so different from the house on the ranch. A table was propped in one corner, an L-shaped kitchenette surrounding it. The couch was a pale blue, the curtains a soft gray, the bed stripped of its linens, which were folded neatly at the foot of the mattress.

That neat stack of cotton did her in.

Or maybe everything that had happened did her in.

Hearing Justin warn Rex about her was bad enough. Despite everything she'd been through, everyone still thought she was weak. But worse was hearing Rex say he didn't love her, implying he never would, and the regret on his face when he'd realized she was there had burned like hell, only made worse by the half-hearted apology.

As if he thought they'd just keep going when there was no future.

It was just . . . she didn't get it.

She didn't *expect* him to love her, no matter that she'd fallen hard. It was too much too soon. But Tilly *had* expected him to be honest with her, especially after they'd shared so much of their pasts. Rex knew more about her than probably any other person on the planet and . . .

He'd thrown that away.

Which made this whole situation worse. She'd allowed herself to be vulnerable and—

Never mind. She'd forget him and move on . . .

As soon as she sorted out this wild goose chase of coming to the apartment. It wasn't like she needed to live here. This wasn't any nicer than her house, and it wasn't filled with her products from what she could see, as she'd half expected.

Sighing, she sank down onto the couch.

Maybe she should just sell her house and move. There wasn't really anything here, and it was something she'd considered more than once in the past. She'd never had the courage to pull that particular plug before, but maybe this experience with Rex would change that because the idea of facing the town, of seeing Kelly or Henry or Justin look at her with that sad, pitying look she'd seen on Kelly's face the night before . . .

No. She couldn't live like that.

"Okay," she muttered. "Nothing here. Just another mistake when it comes to Rex Roos—*oh*." Tilly had placed her hand on the cushion next to her to push herself up to her feet, but instead of fabric, she felt paper. Or rather, a manila envelope with her name on the front.

Carefully, she opened the flap and pulled out the sheet inside.

"What?" A key was taped onto the single white piece of paper.

Not here. Downstairs.

-R

Heart pounding, she tugged the key free and before she could overthink it, Tilly pounded down the stairs and out into the alley. There was a locked door right next to the one she just exited. She'd tried it earlier, and though it hadn't budged, she thought maybe this key might work in the lock.

Her fingers shook as she inserted the key, then shook some more when it turned.

"Oh," she murmured, finding it opened to reveal a dim hallway, and she couldn't be sure if she was disappointed to see it was empty or excited that there seemed to be a light on at the end of it. "Hello?" she called, and when no one answered, she felt along the wall for a light switch and flicked it on.

Empty, except for a few items that must have belonged to the coffee shop when Carol had retired to Florida—a tray of ceramic mugs and some cleaning supplies were on the shelf, a mop bucket pushed into one corner.

"Hello?" she called again.

Nothing.

Quiet feet led her fully inside and down the hall, drawing her toward that single light like a moth to a flame . . . or an addict to Rex's scent.

Because she could smell it all around her, and it made her heart ache.

Ignoring her sudden urge to cry, knowing this was a grief that she'd get over given enough time, she kept walking until she reached the front of the store. Then gasped.

The space was the same and yet different.

The shelves had been sanded and prepped for fresh stain, same as the tables. The cooking equipment had been stacked on one side to be cataloged. A trash can, a broom, and a dustpan were in another corner.

And she was focusing on the mundane because she was deliberately avoiding the sight directly in front of her. It was so fucking heartbreakingly perfect that it threatened to take her breath away.

Artfully arranged, better than she could have imagined were her products.

Shampoo and conditioner, face masks and lip balms. Every single item she made was on that table.

Including a cinnamon roll candle.

Sitting on top of another manila envelope.

This time she knew what was inside before she opened the flap, which was a good thing because her vision was so blurry with tears that it was hard to actually read the paper, to see her name on the deed, to see mock-ups of a sign for the storefront—an exact match to her *Tilly's Treasures* logo online.

"Oh, Rex," she said, sniffing as she clutched the sheet to her chest. "How can you be so fucking perfect and leave me so easily?"

"Actually, I found I couldn't leave you."

Gasping, she whirled around, saw that Rex was in the hall. "I thought you'd gone."

His expression was careful. "I did go. Got all the way to the airport but found I couldn't leave. Not without fighting for you, for us. And so, I came back." He stepped toward her, paused with too many feet between them. "I know you don't love me, that it's too soon, because even though I'm in it deep for you, I get that you need time to trust the men in your life and—" He sucked in a breath, came close enough for her to feel his heat. "I just know that I can't just leave the woman I love without trying one more time."

Her throat was dry, her pulse pounding. "I don't understand," she said. "You told Justin you could never love me."

"I said I never expected to fall in love, sweetheart. But then there you were, a perfect angel on the side of the road, knocking me off my axis, making me realize that life is too fucking short to not go after the love of your life." He lifted his palm, hesitated with it an inch above her cheek. "That's you, by the way."

She laughed, and it was watery. "I—uh . . ." She shook her head, trying desperately to clear it. "I don't understand what's happening. You don't want to break up with me? You love me? You're not leaving?"

"God, no. Fuck yes. And hell no."

Tilly dropped her head in her hands. "So—I—"

She burst into tears and perfect man that he was, Rex tugged her close and gave her the words she needed, telling her all the parts of the conversation she'd missed, how he'd been so upset by her words and leaving that he'd decided to move on. But Kelly and Justin hadn't let him go. They'd caught him at the airport, and Kelly had kicked both of their asses on the way home—Justin for being a judging meddling fool who didn't realize that Rex had changed, and Rex for not immediately going after Tilly.

"I didn't realize you hadn't heard it all," he whispered. "Not until Kelly told me what she'd overheard, and I finally clued in to what you thought. I was such a fucking idiot for not chasing you down straight away, but my feelings were hurt, and I was running stupid, and—" He sucked in a breath. "I left you, sweetheart. I'm so damn sorry for that, most of all."

She stuck her face into the crook of his neck and inhaled, letting the scent center her for a moment. "Thank you," she murmured. "For coming back. I should have fought for us, too. I shouldn't have run off. Not when you're so damned important to me."

"It was my—"

"Let's play who was the bigger idiot later," she said, hugging him tightly. "I love you, Rex, you imperfect man. I love you because you're perfect for me. Because you're kind and thoughtful and—"

He kissed her, fierce and sweet at the same time, his tongue stroking along hers, his body hard where she was soft, and that fucking delicious *eau de* Rex making her head spin. Or maybe the lack of oxygen. Or, more likely, it was just Rex because he was loving and considerate, funny, and strong. The only person in all the world who seemed to understand what was going on in her brain and what she needed.

She'd meant what she said.

Neither of them was perfect, but he was absolutely perfect for her.

"I love you," he said, pulling back and crushing her to his chest. He held her tight for a long moment, but when he set her away from him then laced his fingers through hers and said, "Come on. Let me show you around your shop," Tilly stopped him.

"I'd rather you show me the tabletops," she said slyly.

His brows drew together. "What?" he asked. "I sanded them down, so they'd be ready for whatever finish you wanted. Did I ruin—?"

She tore her T-shirt over her head, dropped it to the dusty floor. Then stepped out of her sneakers, shoved her jeans off, and hopped up on a table.

"Careful of splinters—" he started to warn as she jumped up, but the rest of his words never emerged because her bra joined the rest of her clothes. She crooked a finger in his direction.

"Forget the splinters," she said. "Just come over here and love me, Roosevelt."

His mouth curved into a sinful smile. "Now *that* I can do."

EPILOGUE

Rex

Four years later

Rex stood in the doorway of Tilly's shop, cradling their nine-month-old son in his arms. Justin and Jax were having a serious conversation in one corner, while Jesse, her eyes reddened from crying, was getting a hug from Tilly.

Abigail, looking so damn grown-up, was sweeping the remnants of a broken candle from the floor, carefully carrying the full dustpan to the garbage can behind the counter.

"I'm so sorry, Aunt Tilly," Jesse was saying. "I got so mad at Jax, and I shouldn't have pushed him." She hung her head, cheeks glistening with tears.

"Come here, kiddo," Tilly said and hugged her tight. "Thank you for owning up to your mistake. That makes much more of a difference to me than one candle."

Jesse's arms were around Tilly's neck. "But the candles cost money."

His beautiful wife met his stare over Jesse's shoulder. "They do, but I know how you can pay for it."

Jesse nodded and stepped back. "I'll go home and get my piggy bank."

"No, kiddo. I want you to help me break down the boxes in the storeroom. My hands get so tired and I can't fit them in the recycle bin by myself."

"I can do that."

"I'll show you what to do."

Rex trailed Tilly, watching her explain the task to the little girl who'd just started first grade. Not even seven and yet so mature for her age already, so self-sufficient, smart, and capable—like her mama and aunties. She had great role models.

Once Jesse got going on the boxes, Tilly came over to him and hugged him tight. "How are my two favorite boys?"

"Missing you," he said softly, handing over Jordan—because his brother didn't get the copyright on J names in the Roosevelt household, and his son was as crazy about his wife as Kel and Justin's kids were. It was probably why the twins had gotten into a rare disagreement, they tended to get very competitive over their Aunt Tilly.

"It's been a busy time," she said. "I'm sorry I've been working so much."

He tugged her ponytail and went over to help Jesse with a box that was as big as her. "That's what happens when your store is so successful that you need to open up three more locations."

Tilly blushed, and it was as cute now as it had been from the first moment he'd seen her. "I love you," she murmured.

"Meh," he teased and folded the box for Jesse.

"Thanks, Uncle Rex," she said, wrestling it out the back door.

"Should I—?" He started to follow her, but Tilly stopped him.

"She's fine." A cheeky grin. "You forgot to kiss me hello."

"Hmm," he said, tapping his chin. "Do parents do that? Especially very successful, very busy, fairly new parents?"

"Shut up and get your mouth on mine."

He did as commanded, and as things were often the case now that he and Tilly had found their happy, now that they had crept in from the outside and firmly planted themselves into the center of their family, his kiss didn't go as planned.

Right when things began to heat up in all the right ways, he heard,

"Ew, Uncle Rex."

"Yes, ew!"

Jesse and Jax seemed to have finally found their common ground, and that was in the form of ew-ness. Ew-nity, one might say.

Fine. He *did* say, which garnered him an eye roll from his wife, a snort from Justin, fresh "ew"s from the twins, and giggles from Abigail. Then, fresh from the ranch, Kelly joined them, her pregnant belly leading the way, because she and his brother was expecting *another* set of twins. The chaos of the kiddos' greetings for their mother woke up Jordan, who began crying in earnest while Tilly walked and bounced him through the store.

It was insanity.

It was loud and decidedly *not* peaceful.

It was everything he could have ever dreamed of.

Rex crossed to his wife and kissed her soundly on the lips, scooping up Jordan and making silly faces at him until he settled down and demanded to be put down so he could join his cousins.

They watched Justin's brood encourage Jordan until he managed to crawl close enough that Abigail took pity on him and carried him the last bit of the distance.

"I can't wait to make another one of those with you," he murmured.

Tilly's eyes softened. "Funny you should say that," she said, lacing their fingers together. "We might not have had much time for kissing but . . ." She brought his palm to her belly.

Holy shit.

"You're—?"

She nodded, smile huge, and he bravely risked more "ew"s because the most important thing in the world in that moment was kissing his beautiful, incredible wife.

"I fucking love you," he said when they finally had to stop for air.

Her cheeks were pink, her lips swollen, and she glanced around the shop that had gotten suspiciously quiet.

"I think Justin took a hint," she said with a laugh.

"About time," he said, laughing along with her. "Should we go rescue them?"

"Probably." Her mouth curved, her eyes mischievous. "But kiss me once more before we go."

Not one to deny his wife anything, Rex obliged.

And then kept kissing her until the "ew"s returned.

CHRISTMAS AT ROOSEVELT RANCH

A ROOSEVELT RANCH NOVELLA

CHAPTER ONE

Dale

EXPENSIVE SHOES.

Clicking across his floor.

How did he know this when his head was currently under the frame of a car?

Because boots did not make that sound.

And because people around here didn't wear shoes that were not boots. Especially not in the fall when the rain had come, snow was falling at intermittent intervals but not yet sticking to the ground. Dirt had become mud, and mud had become quicksand, and *click-clicking* shoes were definitely a danger.

Especially in these parts.

And now, Dale sounded like a wannabe cowboy.

The Darlington he'd grown up in might have been rough around the edges, but the Darlington of today was a quaint, small town in north-eastern Utah. It was a place he'd spent more hours outdoors than in, trailing through the cattle ranches, the peach orchards, the vineyards. He'd trekked through that mud, had sloughed through the snow, had enjoyed traversing the green hills until they were turned brown by the summer's heat.

And he'd enjoyed *that*, too.

Long summer days, the sun rising early and setting late. So much heat that it was easy to spot, shimmering waves as it rose off the ground.

But he'd stayed out for all of it.

Because it hadn't been *inside*.

Because *inside* had been absolutely unbearable.

Those shoes continued to *click-click* across the garage floor, moving toward him and not away like he'd hoped.

This engine was a bitch to work on, and he'd promised to have it finished by noon for his customer, so he could close up early and get over to his friend Kelly's by one to help her and her husband set up for their annual Christmas party. Which was both too fucking close to now, since the car wasn't fixed, and was still too far away, considering the grief this fucking P.O.S. had been giving him since it had been towed to the shop.

The shoes stopped just next to the driver's side tire, perfectly centered in his line of vision.

And tapped.

Click-click.

Click-click.

Click-click.

When the clicking continued even as he did his damndest to ignore it —or rather, *them*, the pointy, shiny black leather pumps with a flash of red at every tap and mud ringing their perimeter.

Unfortunately, ignoring didn't help.

The muddy shoes didn't disappear.

They stayed.

And clicked.

"Fucking hell," he muttered, pushing with his feet and sliding out from beneath the car. The creeper cart's wheels screeched as they found purchase against the concrete floor, and—

Holy fucking hell.

Long, long legs. Hips and breasts and—

A fiercely beautiful face that was glowering down at him.

He sat up, wiping his hands on the towel he kept in his pocket. "Can I help you?"

Silence, imperious brown eyes staring down at him, and a brow lifted.

Dale stood. "Was the brow-lifting supposed to be an answer to my question?" he asked. "Because I'm not great at interpreting the intricacies of the various eyebrow languages."

"I am looking for the owner of this establishment."

Rich tones of an English accent, the bearing of old—or perhaps *expensive* manners. To go with her expensive clothes and very expensive shoes.

Or maybe he was just a small-town hick.

"I'm the owner," he said. "Your car break down?"

"Precisely." She turned, spun away. "This way."

Click-clicking across the cracked and stained concrete, as though she were the queen traversing across the finest marble tile. All that *click-*

clicking had the side benefit of making that fabulous ass sitting atop those long, long gorgeous legs bounce just the slightest bit.

Not that he was looking.

Nope. No women for him. Give him the rolling hills and the various parts of a car engine. Hell, even give him balancing the books at the end of the month, which was pretty much the only thing he hated about running his own business.

The cars were easy.

Even the customers mostly were.

But he had the feeling this one wouldn't be.

He followed her out through the yard—the small parking lot that was more dirt than asphalt—and currently more mud than dirt due to the most recent rain. He'd saved up his profits, would be able to afford brand new asphalt the entire length, but he was waiting for spring. There was no need to subject his new road and parking lot to a fierce Utah winter right off the bat.

"Uh-hem." A sharp cough drew his focus to melted chocolate eyes . . . filled with disapproval.

"Where's your car?"

The barest narrowing of her eyes before she spun and continued down the short drive. Dale followed her as she turned right and *click-clicked* all the way down the road to a sleek black sedan.

Wouldn't last the winter around here with a car like that.

The problem was easy to spot, the back tire completely flat.

"Engine trouble then?" he deadpanned.

She stopped, spun, face pressed into sharp lines. "It's—" Clarity dawned as she realized he was joking with her, and the lines got somehow sharper. "Hilarious," she said. "Can you fix the tire?"

He nodded. "Pop the trunk."

"Pop the . . . *what?*" An arched question.

"The trunk." He tapped the back. "Open it up, please."

"Ah." She reached into a small handbag, one of her spring-like curls sliding forward to cover her cheek. An annoyed flick of her head had it darting back in place like a soldier out of formation, and a moment later, she had her keys in hand.

Pop.

The trunk opened, and he made short work of loosening the jack and retrieving the spare tire. It was surprisingly hard with these fancy cars— as though the manufacturers had all decided to make a mechanic's life a living hell. Unlike his perfectly sensible truck, this wasn't undoing a couple of screws to gain access to the spare. This was five minutes of frustration and stifled cursing as he fought tooth and nail to loosen the compartment where everything he needed was located.

But eventually—and with no audible curses—he was lifting the tire out and bending to position the jack in place.

As luck—something he'd never had much of, and something he'd really been lacking of late—would have it, when she'd pulled off the road, she'd perfectly positioned the flat tire in the mud.

Perfect.

Perhaps also unfair of him to be further annoyed, as this entire stretch was currently mud. So, he couldn't move the car forward or back to save himself the sludgy bath he was about to take.

Maybe he should have put her off, but he was behind on his work and wanted to be done with this interruption. Plus, based on the clicking, on the impatience in every line of her body, he instinctively knew that any delay on his part would have been met with arguing on hers. So, he figured he might as well get her tire changed and the sexy little priss back out on her way.

"Pretty shoes you got there," he said, giving in to the inevitable and kneeling in the mud.

"They serve their purpose," she replied.

"Maybe," he said, loosening the lug nuts. "If you spend most of your life indoors." A beat. "Or at least on mostly paved roads."

She shifted, and he watched her study her shoes—now caked with no small amount of mud. "I expected the roads to be . . . more road-like."

"You're in the country now."

"Hmm."

Silence followed. Or well, the silence of being outside on a quiet road, the wind rustling through the vegetation, whistling softly through the rocks on the road, and the unobtrusive *wooshing* sound of the water in the nearby puddles.

Unobtrusive until someone was knee-deep in it.

"What's your name?" he asked.

"How long until the tire is changed?"

"Five minutes," he told her. "Your name? If I'm kneeling in the muck, I should at least know who I'm rescuing."

"I am not a woman who needs rescuing."

He snorted. "So you were going to change this yourself?" Pushing back, he went to stand. "I'll just let you get on with it then."

His gaze went to hers, and he saw the fire in those brown depths.

But only for a moment.

"My name is Elizabeth." She lifted her chin. "And if you don't mind, you'll complete your task of changing the tire, so I can be on my way."

He swapped the tires, tightened the lug nuts. "I'm Dale," he said. "Thanks for asking."

"I—"

Standing, he moved back to the trunk, stowed the jack, wrestled the muddy tire into the truck, and slammed the metal lid closed. Then he turned to face her. "All set."

"Thank—"

He spun away, began heading back to the shop.

If he hustled, he might still make that noon deadline.

"Where are you going?" she asked.

"I have work to do," he said, not stopping, not rotating back to face her.

"I need to pay you."

A shrug. "I don't charge for simple tire changes."

"I *must*—"

He trudged through a puddle, ignored her.

"Stop!"

Yeah. Not happening. "Goodbye, Elizabeth."

Then Dale went back to doing what he did best—working, ignoring the rest of the world, and . . . oh, working.

CHAPTER TWO

Elizabeth

HER CELL RANG as she watched the handsome mechanic's stride eating up the path that led back to the garage.

It was a lucky feat that her tire had blown so near the shop.

She might not like to pretend she needed anyone's help, but tire-changing was not one of the skills she considered as hers. Running a business. Yes. Wondering why on God's green earth she was in the outskirts of Utah as a responsibility of that business. Also yes.

Staring after a sexy man giving her serious Idris Elba vibes.

No.

Hard no.

She didn't do men, and she most certainly didn't do men from small towns who didn't have any clue how to deal with a woman like her.

Demanding. Confident. Brusque. Cold-hearted and business-minded.

The company came first.

Always. *Always.*

Which was why she was here when she might very well wish to be anywhere else on the planet.

Mud and wide-open skies. Cool air and rolling hills.

And flat tires. And ruined shoes. And—

Her phone rang again.

Cursing, she lifted it to her ear and answered the call, barking orders into the receiver at her assistant as she attempted to scrape the mud from her heels. Definitely ruined and definitely not suitable for these parts.

But she hadn't spent much time anywhere outside of a boardroom of late, and the heels were a mask.

A painful mask paired with tailored trousers and silk shirts—feminine to the extreme and yet somehow not. Powerful, confident, pure business, she had a closet full of that exact same outfit. In a variety of muted colors, of course, but still a wardrobe filled with . . . masks.

"What happened?"

"Production is down," Francisco, her assistant, said. "All of the new machines are malfunctioning."

"Shit," she muttered. "Have the head of operations call me the moment you're off the phone with me."

"Will do."

"Now, tell me the rest of it."

She listened with growing dread to the rest of Francisco's report.

All of which basically amounted to the wheels falling off the bus.

Perfect.

She'd been gone less than twenty-four hours, and everything was going to hell.

"Schedule a call with the head of finance after operations," she ordered. "And for fuck's sake, if anything else goes poorly, you need to call me immediately. No trying to handle this yourself."

"Got it," Francisco said.

She hung up without another word and turned on the car.

Why was she in the middle of nowhere?

Oh yes, because only *she* could apparently attend this ridiculous event and see to the business that needed to take place.

Her father had been friends with the father of the man she was meeting, and they'd extended this invitation as a way to welcome her into the business circle of the super-rich.

Pft.

They didn't know that she had been running the business for near on five years now, that her father had been merely the face of the company.

And she was the brain.

The engine.

The heart.

Because otherwise, they would have lost it all. Twenty-three thousand employees without jobs, customers without the medical supplies they needed, distributers with channels to ship product but no product to transport.

Their company made one thing—heart valve replacements—and they certainly didn't have a monopoly on the device, but theirs was the best. Their valve could be replaced laparoscopically, and the recovery time was shortened exponentially. This meant they were the preferred brand around the world.

Great for business.

They'd grown from small potatoes to power in just a few years and had undergone the expected growing pains.

Pains that were insurmountable for a CEO who'd just lost his beloved wife.

Pains Elizabeth had shouldered because . . . well, that was what she did.

Head down. Endure on.

Even if that enduring meant that she now had to take the place of her father at this trifling Christmas party.

A broken hip.

It was so cliché a thing to have sidelined her sixty-six-year-old father, a depressing reminder that he was getting older, and that he, for the most part, had seemed to give up.

"I'm ready to join your mother," he'd told her from that hospital bed.

"And what about me?" she'd wanted to ask.

But she hadn't, of course, hadn't wanted to rub salt in the wound, to be selfish when he was clearly still hurting—

No.

She hadn't asked that because she'd known it wouldn't make a difference.

She was capable and strong and used to being on her own.

Growing up with parents who loved each other truly was perhaps one of those enviable characteristics that school children dreamed up. But the reality could be darker, especially when those parents loved each other more than anything else—more than work, than their families, than . . . their own child.

"Enough," she muttered, glancing into her mirror and checking the road for traffic.

Not that there was much of it in these parts. She'd barely seen another car for the last hour, knew she was lucky to have made it to the edge of town and the mechanic's shop on her flat. But she was also skirting that edge of the town, driving beyond it to the ranch Justin Roosevelt currently resided on with his wife and children in blissful happiness.

Or that was what the *Medical Insider* magazine had declared when they'd discussed his taking over the reins of the family business from his father, Vincent.

Distribution.

That was what the Roosevelts specialized in.

That was why she was here. Attending the fucking Christmas party.

With gifts for the children in the back seat of her rental.

The Roosevelts handled the second most important job of *Hjerte*— meaning heart in Danish and referencing how her late mother had been her father's heart. It was a sickeningly sweet and yet somehow still touching show of affection from a man who loved deeply enough to name his company after a woman and to highlight her family's ancestral roots. But she digressed. Because names aside, the Roosevelt operations handled the most critical operation of *Hjerte* after the creation of the actual product: distribution.

Otherwise, their valves would be languishing in warehouses instead of helping hearts pump better in tens of thousands of patients' chests.

She pulled onto the road, navigated the curving street that was grossly pot-holed and surrounded by high muddy embankments. On either side, there were large ditches filled with puddles that were ringed with dirty-looking snow.

A recent rain, or perhaps a spat of warmer weather that had prevented much snow from sticking.

Either way, it was ugly and fit her mood perfectly.

"Just call me, Scrooge," she muttered.

Her cell rang again as she turned left on a road that seemed to be leading her even farther from civilization. And perhaps it was, considering that Justin Roosevelt's ranch was on the outskirts of the town called Darlington.

"Darling to whom?" she asked, navigating carefully and feeling no little amount of resentment at being here.

But that resentment didn't stop her from doing her job.

She shoved her earpiece into her ear and answered the call, taking the next few minutes to speak with her head of operations. The conversation enlightened her to the issue at hand, mainly discovering the problem with production was a software glitch rather than with their actual equipment malfunctioning.

"Rest assured," he said, "we have the entire technical arm on alert and tasked with fixing the error. We'll be back up as soon as humanly—"

"Bypass the new machines," she interrupted.

A beat then, "What?"

"The old production equipment is still in those spaces, correct?" she asked, knowing the area with the issue was one that had been upgraded a bare week before.

"Um . . . yes."

"And how long have we been down?"

"Three hours."

She maneuvered the car around a bend in the road. "And when do the techs have the fix coming?"

"Well, um, they're not sure how—"

"Right," she said. "So set up our old equipment, sterilize it, and we'll be back up within an hour. If the techs get a fix, we can update during shift change or in the night, but we can't miss an entire day of production and still make our orders for the western seaboard."

"I—"

"Can you do it?" she asked in a tone that told him he'd better be capable.

Thankfully, he didn't disappoint her. "We'll get the old equipment up and running within the hour," he assured her.

"Good."

Her earpiece beeped with an incoming call. "I'll leave you to it. Touch base with me in one hour."

Elizabeth hung up without hearing his reply, or rather, switched to the other call. As planned, it was from her finance chief, and she spent the next few minutes untangling an issue with the board and an upcoming share split.

When she hung up, her head was spinning, her brain telling her it was much later in the UK, where she had her flat.

But *Hjerte* was a worldwide operation.

They had production and storage facilities in more than thirty countries. So, she'd dealt with her fair share of operational issues in various time zones. Lack of sleep did not dissuade her, neither did it have her shirking her duties, especially when she was finally getting the company to function like a . . . well, functional company.

Pretty soon, she wouldn't need to do all the handholding she was doing now.

Pretty soon, she might actually be able to have an *actual* life.

"Yeah, well, what are you going to do with that?" she whispered, spotting a heavy metal gate with intertwined R's in the distance.

It was decorated with garland and flashing Christmas lights, even though it was barely noon, and seeing that jaunty gate, that bright blip of season's tidings made her think of her own flat—white and stark and empty of all things garland and Christmas related.

Of course, it was empty of holiday décor.

First, she wasn't ever home for Christmas.

And second, she hated the holiday.

Always had, always would.

So, it was absolutely fitting that she was here for a Christmas party.

"No, not a party," she whispered, after announcing herself at the tiny speaker by the gate and waiting for the large iron barrier to open. She pulled into the driveway and forced herself to focus on the real reason she was here.

"Business," she said stoutly. "I am *only* here for business."

If only she'd known then how wrong she would be.

CHAPTER THREE

Dale

"Whoever decided that Christmas lights should come on strands should be hung, drawn, and quartered," Dale muttered, tossing the tangled mess of lights down on the grass.

"That's the Christmas spirit," Kelly told him, pressing a kiss to his cheek and scooping up the ball of knotted green strands.

"It's too early for Christmas."

"It is after the first of December so, no, it is not, in fact, too early for Christmas." She plunked down onto the grass and began untangling. "Additionally, I would make the assertion that any time after the first of November is acceptable for Christmas festivities."

"Wrong," he said, snatching the ball back and methodically freeing the strand from itself. "Tell me again why your fancy, rich husband can't hire someone to put up these lights?"

"I second this question," Henry, another of their longtime friends and owner of the best restaurant in town, said. From atop a ladder. Where he was stringing another strand of the Devil's illumination—Dale's contribution to the festivities included naming all of the too perky, too happy, too festive items names that would make Kelly sigh and roll her eyes.

Which she did.

Again.

Heh.

"My quote 'fancy, rich husband' offered to have someone come out and decorate the house, but I prefer to do it myself," she said, grabbing the end of the strand he'd managed to unknot and handing it up to Henry.

"And by yourself, you mean the free manual labor of Dale and myself," Henry grumbled, plugging the end in and continuing hanging the lights.

"Precisely," she chirped. "Well, except you two aren't doing it out of the kindness of your squishy little hearts. You're doing it because Melissa offered you her French silk pie as payment."

"For filming our hilarious efforts, you mean," Dale pointed out, nodding to the television crew that was recording a few wide shots that would be used in Kelly's sister's cooking show. "She offered us pie so we'd agree to be on camera." She'd come out mid-decoration, asking if they could tape for a few minutes, and it wasn't like any of them would say no.

Not for Melissa.

Darlington's most famous resident, Melissa, had begun as a food blogger then had caught the eye of a cooking network.

Next thing they all knew, she had cookbooks and endorsements and was all over television and social media and streaming services. And she was *still* one of the nicest people he knew. And a great mom. And an awesome cook. Not one of those who just made things look pretty on T.V.

Pretty fucking cool, huh?

But also part of the reason he was currently untangling Christmas lights for a national broadcast—thankfully, one that didn't include audio of their grumbling. Nope that would be covered by festive music and interspersed with cuts of delicious cuisine.

Probably a good thing, considering the sheer quantity of his and Henry's complaining.

Kelly tapped her foot, tucked her hair behind her ear. "You know, the only reason you're here at all is—"

Henry hopped down from the ladder and hugged her. "Because we love you and can't ever say no to you."

A beatific smile. "Okay, that too." She pressed a kiss to his cheek then bent to pick up more lights. "Well, *that* and the fact that I promised to never *ever* make my onion dip again."

Just the words *onion dip* made Dale shudder.

Unfortunately for Kel, the cooking genes had skipped right over her.

"I saw that," she exclaimed, outrage in her tone. "It's not *that* bad."

"It's bad," Henry told her. "And that much worse."

Considering Henry's chef skills and his status as Kel's best friend, his statement was accepted as truth.

A begrudging truth based on the dark look on Kel's face. "Fine."

"Aw, don't be like that," Dale said, standing up and tossing an arm around her shoulders. "We love you for your horse training skills." He kissed the top of her head. "God knows there's too many damned chefs in this town as it is. You. Melissa. The lovely Isabella."

"Hey!" Henry said, narrowing his eyes.

Isabella *was* lovely. She was also all Henry's.

Kel grinned. "You're right."

"I'm always right."

"I meant about there being too many chefs in this town." She sniffed, tossing her hair over her shoulders.

He opened his mouth to retort, but right then, the director of the episode called out that they'd gotten the shots they needed.

"Be right back," Kel said and walked away, talking with the crew and for their sake, hopefully not offering up that onion dip as it really *was* foul. Luckily, even if she was, her trio of kids descended at that moment, careening down the lawn and grabbing her around the waist. She teetered, but well-used to her daughter, Abigail, and her twins, Jax and Jess, Kel held her ground, listening with attentive ears to whatever important thing the gaggle of young ones was telling her.

"Five-to-one we're about to finish these Christmas lights on our own," Henry muttered.

"I've got it if you want to take yourself off to your lovely Isabella," Dale told him, handing up the next strand. "We're almost done as it is."

Henry checked his watch. "You don't mind? I still need to shower and change then pull my wife from the gloriousness of flour and butter and eggs."

He wasn't sure about the *gloriousness of flour and butter and eggs*, but Dale *did* know that Isabella was a talented baker, and he would eat any of her creations any day of the week. "I'm sure. I brought my clothes, so I'm just going to shower in the bunkhouse and change here before the party. Go on," he ordered. "I've got this."

"Thanks, man," Henry said, stepping down from the ladder and clapping him on the shoulder. "I appreciate it."

"Have your wife make me another chocolate cake and we're square."

"Deal."

With that, Henry was gone, Kel was dragged off by the trio of cuteness —albeit with a shouted out "Be right back!" and he was left alone with the lights.

And the ladder. And the roof.

Ah. Christmas time was his favorite.

Also, yes, that was sarcasm. He hadn't grown up on a farm, one of a trio of siblings with a great mom like Kel. He certainly hadn't grown up with a silver spoon, *a la* Kel's husband, Justin. But . . . then again, neither of them had experienced stellar childhoods either.

Bad parents were one of those things that seemed to transcend class and race.

And his had certainly been an example of that.

Middle class. Plenty of food. A warm house and new clothes. What should have been an easy and bright childhood. Instead, it had been filled with alcohol and yelling, with fists into walls and doors and . . . more yelling.

Good times.

Good fucking times.

Although, speaking of times, he needed to stop thinking about the old ones and start focusing on the ones in the here and now.

The end in sight, he made short work of the rest of the lights, made easier since he'd finished untangling the giant knot and because some gem—read: *him*—had installed hooks on the eaves last winter.

Maybe he was just a man from a small town, one who'd gone to trade school instead of a fancy college, but he could be smart and useful and . . .

Hang Christmas lights.

Aw. A life's dream.

Too bad sometimes dreams didn't work out. Sometimes a person had to make do, had to shrink down their dreams to fit reality. Sometimes even those reduced and shrunken dreams never came to fruition.

Thus was life.

And *now* he'd officially spent too much time in his own brain, thinking about things he'd long since wanted to forget.

Finish the job and move on.

Keep his head and continue working.

Pretend all was good when nothing had been good for a long time.

Most of all, keep working.

Those were some things Dale could do with certainty. He'd perfected pretending everything was great and keeping his head down. He'd perfected . . .

Being alone.

Now *that* was a positive Christmas thought.

That's what everyone wanted, right? To be alone for the holidays, to be unloved and—

And *that* was enough. Really. Just enough.

He climbed down from the ladder, threw the lid on the now-empty light container, and began carrying the supplies back to the storage area.

Kel wasn't in sight after he'd stowed the ladder and stacked the bin, so he headed to his car, grabbed his bag from the trunk, and headed over to the bunkhouse to change.

Shower first.

Because engine grease and formal wear didn't go hand-in-hand.

He dropped the bag in his usual room—the wide-open space of actual bunks had been broken into smaller and much more luxurious rooms for guests. Kelly and Justin's house was large, but with a trio of kids and a niece and nephew who stayed over frequently, there wasn't a whole lot of extra rooms.

So, the bunkhouse had been revamped.

Aside from the odd sleepover from a townsperson, only the occasional business guest of Justin's stayed here if they were visiting the ranch, affording them some privacy from the chaos of kids and family in the main house.

Dale preferred that chaos and usually only crashed here if he'd had a beer too many and didn't feel safe to drive home.

His bed in the bunkhouse still had a pillow monogrammed with a D on it.

Kel.

That girl had a heart the size of a mountain, and she just kept recruiting people into her life, expanding that circle, growing her family.

Which was why he'd spent the afternoon putting up Christmas lights.

And why he'd spend the evening cramming down slice after slice of Melissa's French silk pie.

He had a family, and for the first time in his life, it was a healthy one.

He set his bag down on the bed, began stripping off his clothes. The bunkhouse was quiet, all the lights off except for the ones in his room. Which was why he assumed the space was empty.

Assuming.

That was where he went wrong.

He toed off his boots and tossed his shirt on the bed, turned to grab a folded towel off the dresser in the corner.

The bunkhouse had gotten its revival, but there hadn't been space to add extra bathrooms. There was a set of showers at the end of the hall that had been split in two, each space with a door that locked, and then an additional space attached to each one with a separate toilet and vanity area. The tiling had been completed, the drains and all the finishings installed. Everything, that was, except for the shower glass, much to Kel's chagrin. That had been mismeasured and was slated to be installed in January.

Which was fine.

Maybe a little cold, but close the door, crank the shower on hot, and the room got nice and steamy.

It was a hell of a lot nicer than his apartment, that was for sure.

Still, as nice as it was, it wasn't what most of Justin's clients were used to—in fact, his friend had begun to use it as a tactic to vet the people he worked with.

Couldn't bear to walk thirty feet to take a shower?

Well, maybe they wouldn't hack it when business got tough.

As for Dale, the marble and bronze finishes were still way nicer than anything he'd lived in, so he was more than fine with the thirty feet.

Speaking of which, he needed to get traversing that thirty feet underway.

He pushed down his pants and underwear, wrapped his hips in a towel and strode down the hall.

So. Many. Feet.

Snort.

He was inwardly chuckling at his own joke, so totally in his head that he wasn't aware of his surroundings when he pushed into the shower room.

He was so focused on the shower that he didn't realize the lights were on in the attached vanity space.

He didn't comprehend he wasn't alone until that door opened.

A flash of bright light hit his eyes, just before the words.

"What the fuck are you doing?"

Mid-shampoo, his eyes flew open at the cold words laced with a lilting English accent. He saw curly brown hair, bare feet . . . and miles and miles of gorgeous legs.

Tapping impatiently on the floor.

Assuming.

Fuck.

CHAPTER FOUR

Elizabeth

HOLY FUCKING HELL.

The man was naked.

Exquisitely so.

A rough-hewn strength, the dim lighting only seeming to emphasize the deep lines of his strength. Strong biceps, flat abs, that delicious V at his waist that had her remembering just how long it had been since she'd had any naked fun.

Too long.

Too damned long.

Slowly, he rinsed his hair, not answering her blurted-out question. Probably because it was clear. This God was showering, and it was a sight for her senses.

What?

She blinked, cleared her head.

The only senses she should be focused on were those of the business variety. What she definitely *shouldn't* be thinking about was the very thin robe encasing her naked body.

Her clothes were in her room.

Her silk robe rubbed against her skin, the most sensual tease.

"Did that tire get you here?" asked the man.

No, not the man. *Dale.* The mechanic who'd fixed her flat without complaint and faster than she'd imagined possible. The mechanic who was gorgeous in clothes and a fucking Renaissance statue out of them.

He tilted his head back, continuing to rinse the shampoo from his hair, and she continued to struggle with forming actual words as the rivulets of water trailed down his chest, his abdomen, *lower*.

Beautiful . . . and erect.

Her lips parted, a breath shuddering out, and she stood frozen in place. Why didn't she leave, just turn and walk away?

Because there was something about this man—

No.

No.

Down that path lay insanity.

There wasn't anything about this man except for the fact that he was gorgeous and her body was primed to want his. That was it. They'd spent less than ten minutes together. Nothing more.

And you've seen him naked, the voice in her head chimed in, rather unhelpfully, she thought.

Because shit. There was that.

A naked man.

Meh. She'd seen plenty of those.

So, why was her heart thundering in her chest and her pussy fucking drenched? If he was just a pretty piece of architecture to admire, she should be able to turn away and storm back to her room, affronted that the man had so inappropriately invaded her space.

Except . . . she'd seen the shock on his face when she'd first come in.

He might be calm and collected now, but she'd bet her cell phone—and that was a life or death bet for Elizabeth—that he hadn't expected to find anyone here.

She heard a *creak,* saw that as she'd been lost in thought, he turned and yanked the handle, turning off the shower. The water slowed to a stop, the only sound in the space the drip-drip as the remaining liquid made its way down the drain.

Oh, that and the sound of her breathing.

Because it was decidedly raspy, coming all too fast.

Especially because he'd *turned around.*

She never saw much in men's asses, but holy hell, she could appreciate the one in front of her, nearly groaned in disappointment when he grabbed his towel from the hook and wrapped it around his hips.

Slow footsteps closed the distance between them.

Hot, humid air. A rapid pulse. Feeling way too small without her heels.

But then he stopped a few steps away and smiled, a slow, sexy smirk that filled her belly with fire.

"Like what you see?"

CHAPTER FIVE

Dale

SHE ROLLED HER EYES. "You're pretty enough." A sniff. "But not pretty enough to tempt me."

He grinned.

Fire. Yeah, he liked that.

Her eyes narrowed. "Why do you look like the cat ate the canary?"

A shrug, amusement coursing through him. "Because you said I'm pretty."

"*That's* what you took—" She huffed and shook her head. "Never mind. I'll leave you to your"—she waved her hand before spinning around and heading toward the door, and he had to admit that view wasn't all bad either—"*ablutions*."

He trailed after her. "Oh, I've finished." A beat. "Unless you'd like to watch me shower again?" Dale asked, affecting innocence.

She halted, tossed a glare in his direction.

Another shrug, more false innocence. "Never let it be said I'm not chivalrous."

Elizabeth snorted. "*Sure* you are."

"Look." He slipped past her. "I'll even get the door for you," he said, reaching for the handle.

"I don't *need* you to get the door for me." She shoved him, her hand on the bare skin of his arm. It was innocuous contact, but he might as well have been hit by a taser for the way it sent sparks shooting through him.

And she felt it, too.

Because she froze, lips parting, eyes wide, and—

She dropped her hand, skittered back.

Was that fear in her eyes?

Fuck.

Of course, it was fear in her eyes. She'd stumbled upon him naked in a space she'd certainly figured was safe—or if not safe, then at least empty. And it wasn't like he'd gone through any real trouble to cover himself. Nope. He'd stayed there and continued showering like a creep. A naked stranger who'd intruded.

Real nice.

"Sorry," he said, taking his own step back. "I really didn't know you were in here. I was helping Kel with the Christmas lights and just popped in here to shower and change."

Her chin lifted. "The mistake is mine. I should have locked the door."

"Probably."

Chocolate eyes narrowing, lush lips pressing flat for a moment. "It wasn't like I expected there to be anyone in here with me."

"Seems to be a lot of that going around."

Silence.

Then she tilted her head to the side, studying him closely enough that Dale thought she could read every thought in his mind, plainly, as though it had been written out in a book. "You've always got some sarcasm at hand, don't you? A seemingly lighthearted joke to diffuse the tension."

She might as well have punched him in the gut.

Because she had no fucking idea.

That humor had been his weapon and his shield, as effectively wielded as the outdoors to keep him safe and mentally sane.

"It's getting late," he said. "And if you're here at the farm, then I'm guessing it's because you've got business to attend to with Justin."

She continued studying him.

"And if you're one of those busy business people," he went on, "then time is money, and you certainly don't waste either—unless it's buying champagne or caviar or something equally important for *status.*"

"I happen to abhor champagne *and* caviar."

He happened to like both, but he wasn't going to prolong this conversation, not when she was navigating through a minefield. "The point still stands."

She tilted her head to the side and continued studying. "My business *is* the most important thing in my life."

"Right," he said. "So, I should let you get on with it."

"Precisely." She reached for the doorknob, grasped on to it, and turned—

And it came off in her hand.

CHAPTER SIX

Elizabeth

FOR A MOMENT, neither of them moved.

For a moment, she *couldn't* move.

She was holding the door handle.

The. Door. Handle.

Blinking, she glanced over her shoulder in shock, saw that Dale's expression was equally surprised.

"Um . . ." she began then stopped. "I—"

The handle was in her hand and not on the door, and—oh God! How in the hell were they going to get out of here? She dropped the hunk of metal, lurched toward the door.

Dale was right there next to her, their shoulders bumping.

"Wait," he said, *"don't."*

But he spoke too late, because her fingers were already in the empty space, grasping at the hole, and trying to yank the door open. She hit something, heard a *clink*, something falling to the floor on the other side of the wooden panel.

And a sick feeling wove through her.

Oh. Shit.

"No, no," he said, reaching up and tugging her hand away. He took one look at the handle—or rather, where the handle had been—and froze. Then sighed.

"What is it?" she asked.

"You managed to engage the lock and knock the handle off the other side."

That didn't sound good, but this man had changed her tire in under ten minutes. A lock should be easy pickings, no pun intended. "So, unlock it."

Wide eyes, the deep brown reminding her of the bark lining the trees on her father's property, came to hers. "With what tools?" he asked. "Unless you're carrying a screwdriver in that robe of yours."

"I—" She pressed her lips together. "No, I don't carry tools in my robe pockets."

"Then how do you propose we unlock it?"

"By you doing something mechanical, or perhaps breaking down the door with your shoulder."

He rapped his knuckles against the wood. "It's solid core and opens in. I'd have to be fucking Captain America to bust it open."

"And you can't kick it in?"

His gaze went to hers then dropped to his feet. "I'd rather not end up in a cast for the next six to eight weeks."

"Well . . ." She fumbled for a few moments, struggling to find words. "Shit."

And that was apropos.

"Yeah." Dale stepped away from the door, began moving to the cabinets mounted on the wall next to the shower space. He opened them, searched through their contents. "You know, for an English girl, you sure curse like an American."

She followed him to the cabinets. "My mother was an American." He glanced down at her, expression gentle, and she had the distinct thought he was about to tell her he was sorry for her loss. That had been a look directed her way many times over the last years. Everyone had loved her mother.

Everyone.

It was quite a stifling cloud to live under.

"She taught me a lot," Elizabeth murmured. "In fact, because of her, I can curse in two languages."

"Yeah?" he asked. "Which two?"

"English and American."

He stopped, setting the towels he'd pulled out of the cabinet down on the floor, and the smile he gave her was . . . sexy as hell.

Uh-oh.

"What are you doing?" she asked, deliberately ignoring the heat coiling in her abdomen.

"So, you're not totally uppity," he said. "Just a little stiff."

"Hey! I resent that!"

"Were you not the least bit prideful when demanding I stop so you could pay your underling?" He affected her voice—horribly. "I say there. Stop, I say. I must throw money at you because I do *not* accept charity."

"I do not sound like that," she said, scowling. "And I don't need charity. I can make my own way."

He finished searching the back of the cabinet then bent and lifted the stack of towels, stowing them away. "For the record, it wasn't charity so much as recognizing you had someplace to be." A beat. "Consider it basic human kindness."

Her jaw dropped.

A finger under her chin, closing it for her. Luckily, it also knocked her out of her stupor. "People don't do things—" She shook her head sharply, dislodging that particular train of thought. "There's always a reason. People always want something."

"You must have led a sad life."

It was said so matter-of-fact that she didn't process the meaning for several moments. "Hey!" She whipped toward him.

Palm lifted, he shrugged. "I didn't say mine was any better."

"Who *are* you?"

"I'm just Dale. I own a mechanic shop in a small ass town in Utah." He dropped his palms. "And I'm currently searching for a screwdriver, so we can get out of this bathroom, get dressed, and make it to the party before all of Melissa's French silk pie is eaten."

"What is French silk pie?" A beat. "And who's Melissa?"

"Kelly's sister," he said, opening and closing the three drawers beneath the cabinet, not finding the screwdriver and moving to the toilet and sink area. "And French silk pie is the best dessert on the planet. Chocolate mousse, graham cracker crust, and topped with a silky whipped cream and tiny curls of dark chocolate."

"You have a sweet tooth," she said, following him and joining in the search by opening the cabinet on the far side of the room.

"Chocolate and whipped cream, what's not to like?"

"That sounds like a come-on," she muttered.

He snorted. "If I made a come-on, you'd know it, baby."

"Not your baby." She rose on tiptoe, checking the shelf and finding it disappointingly empty of any type of screwdriver.

"Noted. No kindness. No endearments. No—"

"How about no more being locked in this room?" she said.

"I'd take that." With that, he carried on the search, methodically checking every cabinet and shelf and drawer without further comment.

Good. That was what she should want.

Nothing from this stranger, this man she didn't want to know.

Except . . . he was fascinating.

Why? Was it the efficient way he carried himself or him brazening out the shower or how he'd changed her tire with competent hands? Maybe it was the glimpse of sad she'd seen in those dark brown eyes, a hint of secrets beneath the slightly cocky, totally self-assured man. Perhaps, it was those secrets that called to her—a woman who supposedly had it all —wealth, parents who loved each other, anything she could ever want.

Possessions.

Because she could have any possession she wanted.

Emotionally? That was where the gaps had first appeared.

And she sensed a similar hole in Dale, something missing, some common trauma that only came from people who'd experienced painful loneliness. Who still felt so lonely and isolated that she didn't feel like she'd ever be able to trust someone enough to crawl out of the deep dark pit—

Whoa.

That was too far down the rabbit hole.

She still couldn't stop herself from talking, from finding out about this man. Part of her was desperate to know what made him tick, why he was a mechanic and in this small town. How he'd come to know Kelly and Justin.

But when she opened her mouth to ask him a question, he beat her to the punch.

"What are you and Justin in business together for?"

Suspicion wove through her. "Why?"

"Last I heard, he wanted to do more doctoring and less Roosevelt business."

"Hmm." Was this some sort of corporate espionage? It certainly wouldn't be the first time someone had tried to get company secrets from her.

"So, I'm surprised you're here, talking business when his happy place was the hospital."

That was why she was there. Because the family man was at home in Utah and couldn't leave his patients or children. If she wanted to keep the business running smoothly, she needed to cement that relationship.

Hence, Christmas in Darlington, Utah.

Or Christmas *Eve* anyway, since she was planning on flying out after the party.

Or *had* been.

Now, she was nearly naked and no closer to cementing anything except for her permanent place in this room.

"Elizabeth?"

She paused, going through her cosmetics bag she'd left on the counter, holding out the tweezers she'd extracted. "What do you think?"

He took them. "We can try."

They walked over to the door, that towel around his waist seeming so precarious, but to her relief—or maybe disappointment—it remained in place. He knelt and once again, she admired the lean strength of his back, the rich russet skin that made her fingers itch to touch. Then he began fiddling with the lock.

"You going to tell me what your company does?"

Probably, she shouldn't answer this, but Elizabeth couldn't find a reason to not tell him. She liked talking with him. From the moment she'd encountered him, she hadn't felt the overwhelming urge to be so guarded and closed down.

This wasn't schmoozing or forced small talk during business meetings.

This was just two people talking.

When was the last time she'd had that?

"*Hjerte* specializes in medical devices."

"Ah. And Justin?"

"Roosevelt helps with distribution."

"From what I understand, they're good at that."

A frown. "From what you understand?" she asked. "Aren't you friends with them?"

"I've known Kelly since grade school, but Justin is just her side piece, as far as the rest of us Darlington kids are concerned."

"What's a side piece?"

A pause. "Google is your friend." He glanced back, waggled his brows. "Also, Kel would kill me if you said that to her, so save us both and don't." A grin. "But seriously, Justin is just Justin in this town. He's a dad and a husband and a doctor. We don't see the business side of him."

"Hmm."

"Who sees the *non*-business side of you?"

Great question.

He set down the tweezers, shifted around to face her. "Who, Elizabeth?" he asked again. "Or maybe the reason you have all that sad in your eyes is because no one sees that side of you."

Normally, she would have brushed him off, told him to mind his own bleeping business. But she was jet-lagged and feeling an odd connection to this man, and they were trapped in a room nearly naked and . . . fuck, but she was lonely.

Had been lonely for so freaking long.

And this man didn't see her as a route to her business, didn't want a favor or money.

He . . . was just talking to her, teasing her, asking questions about her.

A Christmas miracle?

Not quite.

But maybe a conversation with this man would fill the bottomless pit inside her?

Or maybe she was insane.

There was that, too.

"Would you prefer silence?"

No. She wouldn't. "Why do you own a mechanic shop?"

A pause. "I never planned to. It was my father's, but he died during my senior year and I worked there to keep it afloat for my mom. Luckily, I'd been an unpaid apprentice for most of my life, so I knew the ropes."

"What did you want to do before then?"

His eyes flared with some emotion. "What do you mean?"

"I mean," she said, "the way you speak, it sounds like you had other plans."

"Everything worked out as it should," he said, turning back to the door. "I enjoy working on cars. It provides me a living."

"And your mom?"

"Gone for five years now."

"I'm sorry."

He didn't look at her, just turned back to the lock. "Thanks."

"My mom died two years ago," she blurted out.

"I'm sorry."

"We weren't close." Another blurt. Something she had never told anyone, least of all a complete stranger.

Silence, then, "Neither were my mom and I." He sighed. "My parents were addicts and my father abusive. It was, frankly, a relief when they were gone."

She inhaled sharply. "Dale."

"But I'm lucky," he said, ignoring her. "I grew up in a small town where people care about each other. I had safe places to crash as needed. I had food in my belly. And"—a sigh and he spun back around and set the tweezers down—"why am I telling you this?"

"Because we're trapped, and there's nothing to do but talk?"

His expression went hot. "There are definitely things we can do that don't involve talking."

Her brows lifted.

"That *was* a come-on," he said. "In case you were wondering."

"Well, it's a come-on that's not going to work," she said.

"Damn. And I put so much effort into it."

She snorted. "You don't often blab your family history to strangers."

"You've seen my diddly bits," he told her. "I think that makes us more than strangers."

Laughter bubbled up in her throat. "You're terrible."

"I'm something."

"How are your lock-picking skills?"

"Lame."

"Damn."

He sighed, leaned back against the door. "Yeah."

"I've flown halfway around the globe, and I'm not even going to get any business done."

A frown as he glanced at her. "What did you do all day?"

Her lips curved despite herself. "Business."

"So, what other business do you need to do?"

"It never stops."

His eyes pierced through her. "Yeah? Or do *you* never stop?"

"I stop."

"Hmm."

"I do!" She picked up the tweezers and tried to pretend to know what she was doing with the lock—which basically meant she jabbed the sharp metal end into any hole she could find, all while not doing anything.

"When was the last time you stopped?"

She whipped around. "I stopped on the plane?"

"Yeah?" His lips twitched. "Or did you just stop long enough to reach the requisite thirty-thousand feet before you could turn on your laptop?"

"That's not the point."

He burst out laughing, and she couldn't resist turning and watching him, seeing the amusement on his gorgeous face. So much strength and yet so much soft—soft eyes drifting up to meet hers, soft lips—

Or they looked soft.

She wanted to test and see if they *were* soft.

Stupid?

Probably.

But he was right about one thing. She didn't stop. She hadn't stopped. Not in the last two years. Not often in her entire life.

"It was always me trying to prove to my parents that I was worthy," she whispered, sinking to the floor, Dale mirroring her action by sitting beside her. "I was always trying to be the best, to do all the extracurriculars, to get the best grades, go to the best schools, earn multiple degrees, understand every bit of the business." She shifted to lean her back against the door, curling her legs under her, fiddling with her robe, making sure it covered as much of her as possible. Then she stopped delaying, and just . . . let it out. Dale was right. She hadn't stopped in a long time, and she certainly hadn't ever given voice to all of the dark things in her heart and soul. "I learned the scientific name for every plant in my mother's garden, wanting her to be impressed."

He rested his palm on her knee.

Just a warm, work-worn palm on an innocent part of her body.

And yet, it was more than her parents had ever given her.

"Was she?"

"No," she admitted. "It wasn't like she was intentionally cruel or mean." A sigh. "My parents were so in love with each other, they didn't have space in their lives for anything but each other. Travel over the holidays and leave me at home?" She shrugged. "Without a second thought. Missed a school performance because they needed to celebrate their anniversary in Fiji? Absolutely. And yet . . . I know I'm lucky. I had a home and food and my health."

"But you felt unloved."

"Gah. That sounds pathetic."

"No, it sounds like something most every other person on this planet has felt at some point."

She made a face.

"What?" he asked. "You think you're immune?"

"I just think . . ." She had no words to express what she was feeling.

"This is too much for Christmas Eve, nearly naked, and with a stranger."

"Yes. That."

Except this man, this *Dale* wasn't exactly feeling like a stranger. He felt like . . .

More.

CHAPTER SEVEN

Dale

THEY SAT for a little while in quiet before he propped himself up and attempted to pick that lock again.

With no success.

Because he had no fucking idea what he was doing.

"I think you can give it up," she said a few minutes later.

"Said no man ever," he quipped, but he did give it up, sinking back down and trying not to flash her. He should grab some more towels, give her something to warm up with, and it wasn't like he was roasting with just the strip of cotton around his waist. Not to mention the chance of flashing.

The shower space was well-heated and still humid from his shower, but it was cold outside, and he knew that would seep into the room pretty soon.

He should move, maybe try to bust down that door.

Except . . . he didn't want to move. He wanted to stay next to this woman and untangle all of her secrets.

She shivered.

And his wants didn't matter.

Pushing to his feet, he was across the room in seconds, opening the cabinet and pulling out the stack of towels. He crossed back to her, passed several over, keeping one to cover his upper body.

"Wh—"

"You're cold."

Her expression went blank.

"What?"

"Nothing," she said. "We've done enough sharing for strangers."

"For strangers trapped in a room together for the interminable future?"

"Yes, that."

He nodded, covered himself with the towel and leaned back against the wall. "So, want to sing your favorite Christmas carol?"

Her eyes shot to his then narrowed.

Probably because he was laughing his ass off.

"Hilarious," she muttered.

"If it makes you feel better, I'm sure someone will miss us sooner or later and come looking."

"It's the later part that worries me."

"We'll be fine. Bundle up in those towels, and we'll work on being patient." He smiled. "And if patient doesn't work, I'll put my foot at risk and try to kick down that door."

She made a face.

"In the meantime, we pass the time."

Wide eyes on his. "Pass the time how exactly?"

"Well . . ." He grinned. "I supposed we'll have to make . . ." There went those wide eyes again, drifting to his face, lips parting. "Small talk."

She groaned.

"Christmas carols?"

Another groan.

"Random trivia quiz?"

"Better."

"Sitting in quiet and fantasizing about the food inside?"

A beat. "Fine."

He tucked the towel around her shoulders, settled back. "Fine," he said. "Let me tell you all about Melissa and her incredible—"

"Do not say French silk pie."

"French silk pie."

She swatted him. He laughed.

And the conversation flowed. No awkward pauses. No hesitations and weird blips. For hours, they just talked. About food and then movies and then TV shows—surprisingly, even though she said she worked all the time, she'd seen a fair amount of them.

Probably plane rides.

But eventually, their conversation lulled from their favorite places to travel into comfortable quiet, their sentences coming few and far between, the odd yawn punctuating a sentence.

"You cold?" he asked.

She'd slumped, her side pressed to his, her chin slipping forward to rest on his chest. That was pretty much all he could see of her, seeing how the rest of her was covered by the towels. "No," she whispered.

"Tell me about London," he said. "I've never been."

"It's a busy city, with such a variable set of buildings and people that it"—she yawned again—"it always seems like something new and . . . um . . ."

She trailed off, slumping against him, as sleep took her under.

CHAPTER EIGHT

Elizabeth

SHE WOKE SLOWLY, her hip aching, her head in . . . someone's lap?

Throat tightening, she stiffened, started to push—

"It's just me," Dale said softly. "We're still trapped in the bathroom."

Me.

One sentence, and she knew immediately who it was. Perhaps, that should have frightened her, but instead it just . . . sanded down a piece inside her she hadn't even known was jagged.

But without that jabbing piece, she could breathe.

And not worry.

"Anyone come in?"

"Unfortunately not," he said. "But I heard a few cars leave not too long ago. Someone has to come looking soon."

Her stomach rumbled.

"Yeah, babe," he said on a chuckle. "I'm with you." He laughed again, the sound sliding down her spine, filling her with heat. "Should I try my lock-picking skills again?"

"Maybe I'll gnaw through the door."

He snorted. "I might join you." His tone went grumpy. "The pie is definitely all eaten by now."

"It'll—"

The door opened.

Not the one trapping them in the bathroom, but one farther away, leading to the outside of the building. How did she know this? Because the hinges shrieked like an unhappy feline getting a bath . . . and because it was trailed by footsteps.

Footsteps.

Dale must have realized the same thing as she, at exactly the same moment because he burst to his feet. "Hello?" he called.

"Dale?" came a female voice, one that Elizabeth thought belonged to Kelly, though she couldn't be a hundred percent sure, since she'd just met the other woman earlier that afternoon.

"I'm here!"

"Where?" The voice came closer.

"Stuck in the shower! The handle broke, and we're stuck."

"The handle—" She stopped then sounded like she was just outside the door. "Who's *we?*"

His gaze drifted over to Elizabeth's, chagrin written across the lines of her face. "Well, it's a funny story," he said, "one I'll tell you once we're free."

Silence.

"Turns out, I'm not a good burglar," he added. "I've been attempting to pick the lock for hours."

More silence.

"Kel?" Dale pressed.

"Sorry, was looking at the handle." The door creaked but didn't open. "Did you try the hinges?"

"What?" he asked.

"Did you try to take off the hinges?"

Dale froze and looked at Elizabeth, lips parting. "Um, no . . . we didn't think of that." He picked up the tweezers, lifted them to the hinge. "You don't happen to have a screwdriver handy, do you?"

"One that will fit under the door?" Kelly sighed. "No, I don't think so, but let me grab the tool kit." A minute later, she was back, and with a little sweat and a lot of cursing, they managed to squeeze a small screwdriver beneath the gap in the door. "While you try that, I'm going to go get Rob."

"Good idea," Dale said, positioning the flat part of the screwdriver at the hinge. To Elizabeth, he explained, "Rob's a cop. Might be able to kick it in."

"If that gets us closer to the pie, I'm all for it."

He grinned. "Besides being starving, I'm not complaining about being stuck in here with you. It's been nice being trapped with you, Beth."

She wrinkled her nose.

"No Beth?"

A shake of her head.

"And no baby, honey, or sweetheart?"

Another shake.

"So, what am I allowed to call you?"

"Elizabeth."

He made a face. "You're talking to a man with one syllable in his name. You've got to dumb it down for me."

"Ridiculous man."

"Probably," he said, stepping closer, tucking a curl behind her ear, fingers lingering and brushing along her cheek, her jaw. "But I'm one who thinks you're a pretty cool chick. One who'd like to know you more."

Her breath caught, heat prickling over her skin.

She thought *he* was cool. In fact, she thought that he might be the first person in a very long time that she wanted to truly get to know, wanted to learn all of the hidden secrets. This was a man who could erase the loneliness.

Except . . .

"I'm leaving tomorrow."

Disappointment drifted across his face. "Right," he said. "Of course. You mentioned that."

"And I live in England."

"Of course." He shifted back, dropping his hand, and turned to the door again to work on the hinges.

Now, she was the one feeling disappointment.

Acute and heavy and weighing her down.

For no reason. She didn't know this man.

Except . . . maybe a piece of her heart did. Maybe it recognized him as a kindred spirit, the same way her body responded to the proximity of his, to his scent, his heat. Everything was telling her this man was more.

And yet, it just couldn't be.

They lived a continent and an ocean apart. He was from a small town. She lived in London. They both had businesses to run and she, for one, had absolutely no time for a relationship.

But while she wanted out of this bathroom, she also didn't want this night to end.

She liked him.

A lot.

After one night.

"Dale—" she whispered.

He rotated to face her. "What's up?"

She stepped close, lifted her palm and rested it on his shoulder. Sparks beneath her palm, heat exploding along her skin. "I—"

His hand covered hers. "What is it, Lizzy?"

Her lips twitched. "I was just going to say, I at least wanted to kiss you before I go."

Hot eyes. Fingers convulsing. A broad chest coming closer.

"Yeah?" A husky question.

"Yes."

"My lucky day. Or night. Or—"

She rose on tiptoe and pressed her mouth to his.

Right as they heard, "Stand back!"

And the door exploded inward in a shower of splinters.

CHAPTER NINE

Dale

ONE HEARTBEAT OF HEAVEN.

Then splinters.

He'd jumped back at the sound of Rob's voice, tucked Elizabeth behind him, and not a moment too soon because the door burst inward, revealing Rob, Kelly, and Justin in the hall.

The two men kept their expressions blank.

But Kel lifted both eyebrows, her mouth dropping open.

"It's a long story," he told them, "starting with the fact that I didn't know Elizabeth was in the guest house, let alone the bathroom." He slanted a glance her way. "And ending with a defective doorknob, no fucking pie, and hungry stomachs. Wait," he added, when she began to slide by him. "Your feet."

The floor was covered with shards of wood and pieces of metal from the broken lock.

"Thanks for the assist."

Rob tapped his boot against the ground. "Gotta put these to use every once in a while."

"I'm so sorry," Kel said. "I can't imagine how hungry you both must be. Let me grab you each some clothes and shoes."

"Thank you," Elizabeth told her.

Kel disappeared down the hall, reappearing a moment later with Elizabeth's small suitcase. Dale reached over and grabbed it, carrying the bag into the vanity area, and leaving her to change, closing, but not actually latching the door shut.

See?

He learned things.

By the time he made it back, Kel had brought his overnight bag, and he made short order of telling his friends to turn their backs or risk a flashing.

They disappeared down the hall, and he pulled on underwear, pants, and a shirt. He was just shoving his feet into his boots when he heard the door to the vanity area open and Elizabeth emerged.

God, she was pretty. He normally didn't go for the businesswoman look, preferring jeans and boots and a clean face, but even in slacks and flats and a simple blouse, her hair pulled neatly back, her makeup understated, she was absolutely gorgeous.

Though he couldn't deny that he preferred her in the robe.

"You okay?" he murmured.

"Fine."

There was a distance to her now that he didn't like. It was a distance he understood, especially with her leaving in the morning. But he still really hated it.

"You kids dressed?" Kel called from down the hall. "Let's get you fed and tucked into bed so Santa can come."

"Right," Elizabeth whispered, starting to pick her way through the debris. "And then I'll be home."

Except, the way she said *home* tore through him.

It was a painful word, a lonely word.

She might as well be saying prison.

But what could he do? She *was* leaving the next day, and they'd only known each other a day. This connection didn't have a chance of going anywhere. All they could do was make their way into the house, join the remnants of the party, and eat some delicious food.

So, that's what they did.

"Come on," Justin said, helping Elizabeth over the debris. "The temperature's dropped. I'll help you up to the house."

"I'm fine."

"Of course you are," Justin said, "but I did want to pick your brain about Brussels. What if we . . ."

His words trailed off as they moved down the hall, Elizabeth's reply barely audible, but Dale didn't have a chance to trail after her, to haul her close—against his better judgment—to kiss her like he wanted.

Because the door squeaked open and closed.

And then Kel was grabbing his arm, tugging him forward. "Dale," she whispered. "Holy shit, I can't believe that happened. When I realized you hadn't come up for dinner, I swore you'd fallen asleep and promised myself I'd bring you a plate later."

"Should I clean this up?" he asked, stepping through the mess.

"Absolutely not," she said. "This was my fault. I thought vintage doorknobs were the coolest thing." A shake of her head. "If I'd known—"

"Hush, you," he told her and slung an arm around her shoulder.

"But—"

"Where's the plate?"

"What?"

"Where's my plate of food?"

"Oh, I . . ." She winced. "I got sidetracked when I realized that Elizabeth was missing, too. I thought something bad had happened and came down and . . ."

"No food," he muttered.

"Sorry." Another wince. "I know Melissa put some leftovers in the fridge though. I saw her doing it when I went up to get Rob."

Rob was in front of them, held the door open, and turned back, nodding. "My wife always cooks enough for an army. There will be plenty of food left when we get back up to the house."

They were probably right. But . . .

"Will there be enough French silk pie?"

That made them both wince and he groaned. "No?"

Kel shook her head, and they made their way up to the house. "Jax"—her son—"devoured the last piece."

"Damn."

She dropped his hand. "I'm so—"

He tugged her ponytail. "Stop," he told her.

"But I feel so bad!"

Dale slipped his arm around her shoulders. "You know the only thing that'll make it up to me?"

"What's that?" Her tone grew suspicious.

"No more antique doorknobs."

A giggle. "Deal."

"Oh and . . ."

"What?" she asked.

"Rummikub."

Kelly groaned long and loud.

"It's the only game that will make this tired, hungry man happy." A combination of rummy and mahjong, they always got extremely competitive.

"Why?"

He pushed her into the house. "Because there's no more French silk pie left." A beat as he closed the door behind them. "And also because those Christmas lights look damned good on your roof."

Another groan, this one paired with a glare.

But he didn't miss the fact that she went to the game cupboard and set the requested game on the dining room table.

"Food first," she grumbled, shoving him toward the kitchen.

That was an order he didn't mind following in the least.

CHAPTER TEN

Elizabeth

SHE SAT with a blue plastic tray in front of her, a giant pile of numbered tiles on the table, and a handsome mechanic to her left. "Why am I doing this?"

Dale leaned close. "For business."

"How exactly is this *business*?" she muttered back.

"Business relationships," he countered. "As in, building them."

Since that was the whole point of this trip and she was just feeling a little pouty because she'd lost the last three rounds, Elizabeth didn't retort. Instead, she narrowed her eyes and declared, "You're going down!"

Thus far, the conversation had been mostly filled with polite conversation about the ranch, about Melissa's work—she'd met Kelly's sister, the cooking show extraordinaire, when Melissa had shoved a plate piled high with food into her hands almost the moment she crossed the threshold—and about *Hjerte*, Justin expounding on their heart valve and his personal experience with it.

But her exclamation made the table go quiet and stare at her.

She felt her cheeks heat.

She was pleasantly full, had her ego stroked by Justin telling everyone how good their product was, and was relaxed, enjoying feeling like part of a family.

This wasn't something she'd experienced before, gathering around a table, belly over-full, kids running in and out, their voices carrying and echoing through the room, hopped up on sugar and excitement, and so sweet.

"Those are fighting words," Dale said.

"You're too damned smug."

"Damn is a bad word," a blond cherub said as she skipped by.

Elizabeth felt her cheeks heat. "Sorry," she told the table at large.

"Meh," Kel said. "They've heard it all and much worse." She nudged Justin's shoulder. "Mostly from this one."

"Hey!" Justin exclaimed.

"No," Henry, the restaurant owner she'd met earlier, said, "he gets it from Isa." His wife was a well-known pastry chef and she glared, equally as affronted as Justin.

"Lies," she said, her voice speaking to her Italian roots. "It's clearly Rex's bad influence."

Rex was Justin's twin and a reformed troublemaker. He also had his arm around his wife, Tilly, who had given Elizabeth a gaily wrapped package earlier when the room had gone around exchanging presents.

"Oh, I can't," Elizabeth had said, trying to hand it back when the other woman had plunked it into her lap. "I don't have anything for you."

Tilly had simply patted her arm. "I'm a sucker for fancy wrapping paper." Her voice dropped. "Plus, it's small and from my shop." Another pat, shoving the present a bit closer. "Humor me."

"Thank you," she'd murmured and had opened the package, revealing the loveliest smelling candle and bath set—citrus and spice and packaged in a sparkling container that caught the glimmers from the Christmas lights. "This is absolutely gorgeous," she'd said and had meant it, touched by her first Christmas gift that year.

Tilly had just shrugged, her cheeks going a bit pink. "I make them, so I had to brag a little." She nibbled her bottom lip. "Anyway, Happy Holidays."

Normally, Elizabeth would have just nodded and said the same in return, but something about the scene in the bathroom—sharing with Dale—and being in this house, surrounded by so much happiness and love and open affection had unlocked something in her.

Yearning.

But also . . . joy.

Like maybe Christmas wasn't just a consumer-driven holiday with nothing redeeming about it. Because there was a lot to say for the way the Roosevelts celebrated.

Hell, there was a lot to say for how this group loved.

And included.

She didn't feel like a weird voyeur, creeping in on the festivities. She felt like part of the group.

Take that, Scroogey heart.

Maybe she didn't hate Christmas so much as she hated what she'd been missing out on.

"Rude," Rex said, pulling her out of her daydreaming. "I happen to be the most responsible one at this table. Dale, on the other hand, is the worst. Just look at that smirk on his face."

"Them's fighting words." Dale scooped up a popcorn ball—some delicious combination of marshmallows, popcorn, and flavored gelatin she'd added to her stuffed stomach not long before—and chucked it across the table. Rex snagged it, saluted, and took a bite.

"You're going down, Buchanan," Kelly declared, stabbing a finger toward Dale.

More catcalls broke out, everyone talking and teasing over each other, declaring they would be the winner—

A tap on her arm had her looking to her right.

And spotting the cutest black-haired boy. He had striking blue eyes that reminded her of Melissa's husband, Rob, the hero-of-the-day with his police door-kicking-in skills.

"Hi," she said.

"Can I play on your team?" he asked, a bit shyly.

"Max," Melissa said. "I'm not sure Elizabeth wants a teammate . . ."

She acutely remembered being on the sidelines like this, wanting to join in, being scared of being rejected. Well, the last was her projecting, especially when Melissa shifted and finished the sentence with, "If you want to play, come be on my team."

"I don't mind," Elizabeth said, meeting Melissa's gaze. "If it's okay with you."

Melissa smiled and nodded, and Elizabeth slid her chair over so Max could sit next to her. "You know how to play?"

His face was a study in determination. "Yup." Max leaned around her and pointed a finger at Dale. "You're going down, Uncle Dale!"

Laughter broke out around the table.

"I hear all this talk," Dale said, moving his thumb and fingers like they were talking, "but I don't see any game to back it up."

More catcalls, this time paired with booing.

Then they began to play.

And it turned out she had a secret weapon on her team.

Because she and Max absolutely crushed everyone at the table, including Dale.

"Yes!" Max exclaimed, placing their last tile and fist-pumping.

Dale groaned. She put her hand up to Max for a high five. The table cheered and then Max was tugging her up, teaching her his Happy Dance.

Something she would have never done in public before.

Absolutely *never*.

But coaxed by a little boy, encouraged by the sweet taste of victory, and filled up with the love in this room, she got up, and she executed that Happy Dance like an absolute professional.

CHAPTER ELEVEN

Dale

HE FOLLOWED Elizabeth into the other room about an hour after his painful defeat at his favorite game.

Max as a secret weapon.

He'd need to remember that.

Though it hadn't only been Max. Elizabeth was brilliant and would definitely give him a run for his money when they played again.

If.

Right.

Because it was an *if*. Elizabeth was leaving the next day, going back to her life, her work.

And he was acutely disappointed, just the thought making him feel as though he'd lost a limb, even though he'd only known her for a day.

The children had disappeared to get into their pajamas and brush their teeth, then they'd each be able to pick one present from beneath the tree to open before getting cookies ready for Santa, carrots for his reindeer.

"I don't envy their parents trying to get them to bed," he murmured.

She stopped, turned to face him, and the sad in her eyes was intense. "They're wonderful," she said. "All of them. I—" A shake of her head. "I've never had that—never had a night like this. It's . . ." Words trailing off, she rotated back around and started for the front door.

"Wait."

He should let her go. Stop this before his draw to her grew to even more absurd proportions.

But . . . he didn't want to.

"What is it?" she asked.

"I—"

His eyes flicked up, saw the sprig of green hanging overhead.

And he stopped thinking, especially when her eyes followed his, when their gazes came together, and he saw the heat there.

She stepped toward him.

Or maybe he stepped toward her.

Then their mouths met—and for more than a heartbeat this time.

Sweet, the taste of marshmallow on her tongue. Tart, the nip of his bottom lip as she moved closer and wound her arms around his neck. Pleasure slid down his spine, coiled in his middle. Winding his arms around her, he tugged her until her breasts were flush against his chest, until her scent was surrounding him like a thundercloud, until . . .

Voices in the hall.

They jumped back, breath coming in rapid gasps.

"I should go," she began.

"Don't." He took her hand. "Just stay a little longer."

Her lips parted, and he could see the protest in the depths of those rich brown eyes.

"Please?"

She released a shuddering breath, nodded. "Just a little longer."

"Uncle Dale," Max called, thundering toward them. "It's present time!"

"*One* present time," Melissa said, hurrying after him.

"Present time!" he yelled, running toward the big family room.

Melissa grinned and shook her head, following him. "You guys staying?"

Dale nodded. "For a bit more."

"Great," she said, her voice dropped to a whisper. "We're having adult hot cocoa in a few. You guys want it?"

"That sounds lovely," Elizabeth murmured.

"Yes, thanks, Miss," he said.

"Anytime." A beat, more laughter and pounding feet heading into the family room. "I'd better get in there before they start demolishing the tree." Then she was gone, and they were alone in the hall.

"Why can't you be a contact of Justin's from northeast Utah?" he asked lightly.

"I know," she murmured. "But maybe—"

"What?" he asked, when she didn't finish the statement.

"It doesn't matter."

"It does," he said, just deciding to bare his soul, to go with his gut and put everything he was feeling out in the open. "Don't tell me that you don't feel this." He cupped her cheek. "Don't tell me this doesn't feel more right than anything with anyone else."

"It can't be, Dale."

"Why can't we decide what it can or can't be?" he asked, stepping closer, brushing his lips across hers. "Why can't we take the time and—"

"Because we don't have time," she whispered. "Because we only have tonight."

His heart sank, but instead of protesting, he walked to the coat rack, grabbed two jackets and handed one to her.

"What are you doing?"

"If we only have tonight," he said. "Let's make it count."

Then he took her hand and led her out the front door.

CHAPTER TWELVE

Elizabeth

He took her to look at the moon.

Traipsing through the hills in shoes that were definitely not designed for hiking.

"Wait," he said, lifting her up onto his back when she slipped again. "Hang on tight."

Then he carried her, piggy-back style, through those hills until they got to the top of one that gave a view of the entire valley.

A few bright lights from the houses below dotted the landscape, but most of the space was wide open, dimly lit from the moon shining overhead.

"I used to come out here when I was a kid," he said in a hushed tone. "Well, not here, exactly, but outside, day or night, trying to clear my head, to find some quiet that wasn't going to be interrupted by yelling or fighting or something worse."

Her heart thudded in her chest.

"Did you do it a lot?"

He nodded, helping her find her feet and slipping an arm around her waist. "Yes, almost every night, and in the summer whenever I wasn't at the garage. It was the only place that . . . I found peace."

She rested her head on his shoulder. "I used to hide in a corner of my parents' garden. There was a wall covered with vines and shadowed by a tree. I would go there and pretend to be a princess locked in a tower, waiting for someone to come free me."

Only they never did.

And she couldn't bring herself to give voice to that thought.

"You didn't need them."

"What?" she asked, glancing up.

"You didn't need someone to come," he said. "You were able to free yourself."

Yes, she had.

"So, why do I still feel so trapped?" She shuddered. So alone. So empty.

"Just because you were able to free yourself doesn't mean you should have."

One sentence, and that jagged hole in her settled, its ragged edges softening. One sentence, and she wanted to forget about the business, about London. She wanted to stay here longer.

But . . . what if she ended up alone again?

She'd worked so hard to be her own person, to not need anyone else, so she couldn't need this man, especially when she was so drawn to him after mere hours.

"I should get back," she whispered. "I have an early flight in the morning."

Fingers on her cheek, a warm arm tucking her closer.

For. One. More. Moment.

Then he scooped her up onto his back, piggy-back style again, and carried her to the bunkhouse. They only had the night, that was why she didn't protest when he kissed her again.

At least, that was what she told herself.

Same reason as why she took his hand and drew him into her bedroom.

Why she kissed him, her fingers working at the zipper of his coat, tugging at the hem of his T-shirt, helping him bring it up over his head. Wanting one more moment is why she reached for her own coat and shrugged it off.

Why she let him kiss every inch of her body and why she returned the favor.

And that moment is why she pulled a condom from her makeup bag then reached for the button on his jeans.

"Are you—"

"Sure," she finished, fingers on his lips. "Yes," she whispered. "Let's be together. At least for tonight."

Hot eyes on hers. Warm hands on her breasts, her torso, between her thighs. Gentle lips trailing their path. Pleasure tore through her, tightening her skin, moisture pooling between her legs, turning her nipples into hard points.

Then he was lifting her onto the bed, tugging her shoes and pants.

And the next moment was perfect.

Holding her close as he slipped inside.

Patient, coaxing strokes, driving her higher and higher . . . until she exploded. Until he followed her, her name on his tongue. He gentled her down, continued to hold her tightly, and then as the moon began to set on Christmas morning, they finally slipped into sleep.

It was the best day of her life.

And also the worst.

CHAPTER THIRTEEN

Dale

IN THE MORNING, he woke up to a silent bunkhouse.

Elizabeth had gone.

Left him while he was sleeping after the best day of his life.

"Fuck," he whispered, throwing his stuff into his bag, making his way through the new coating of snow that had fallen overnight, and stopping by the house to return the coats he'd commandeered. The gaggle of kids were tearing through the mountain of gifts beneath the tree, and he crossed the war zone in order to hug Kel and say goodbye.

"You okay?" she asked.

"Fine," he said, even though he felt anything but fine. He was unsettled, confused, and a little annoyed that Elizabeth hadn't even said goodbye.

She was probably the smart one, cutting off the contact when it wasn't going to ever go anywhere with them.

But . . . he'd wanted a little bit more time.

"I'm sorry again about the—"

"If you apologize for the doorknob again, I'll never fix another car of yours."

"Dale!"

"It was a freak one-time thing," he said, narrowing his eyes. "Let it go."

Kel wrinkled her nose. "I'm still—"

He bopped her on that cute nose. "Hush."

"Rude!"

"Bye. I'll see you later this week." He called his goodbyes to the room and disappeared out the front door before he got pulled into breakfast. He didn't want to be surrounded by all that Christmas joy.

He wanted to be alone and soaking in his misery.

Sighing, he made his way to his car, got in, and started the engine, waving when Kel popped her head out the front door, and maneuvering the driveway and down through the winding road that led back to the shop and his house behind it.

The clouds were dark overhead, hinting at a storm ahead, and that just fit his mood.

"You're being ridiculous," he muttered.

Maybe.

But he was feeling pouty.

Last night had been fun, more fun than he'd had in years, actually, but he really just wanted to be alone and sulking in his apartment, wishing he could teleport or that the distance between London and Darlington wasn't so great.

See? Pouty.

Dale needed to forget about Elizabeth, focus on work and his friends in town.

He'd go back to his life and find a nice girl to date. Maybe one that wasn't so inclined to disappear after the most fantastic night of his life and—

"Shit!"

He swerved, nearly sideswiping the car that was partially blocking the driveway to the shop. He'd been on autopilot, stuck in his morose thoughts, and not paying close attention.

But as he parked and looked closer, he realized it was a car he recognized.

A car whose driver was sitting in the driver's seat, banging her head on the steering wheel.

Or she *had* been.

Because when he put his car in park, got out, and walked to her window, she stopped and looked up at him.

He mimed to roll down her window.

The soft *whir* was the only sound for a long moment.

"You okay?" he finally asked, blinking away the pleasure of seeing her, the urge to close the distance between them.

"I'm—" Her eyes slid closed, and she sighed. Then turned off the car, unbuckled her seat belt, and opened the door.

A second later, she was in front of him.

"I was driving to the airport and I saw your shop and—" Another sigh, her head tipping back, gaze on the clouds overhead. "And I," she said, dropping her gaze back down, eyes fixing on his. "I realized I didn't really *have* to fly home today. I realized I don't really have to be back for a week."

His lungs froze, but when he opened his mouth to reply, she kept going.

"And I thought . . . I haven't stopped working in two years. I haven't lived my life for *me* for much longer than that. And . . . I guess I just wanted to see if whatever this thing between us is . . . real."

"I—"

"And I don't have to stay here. I can get a hotel or ask Justin to stay at the ranch." She bit her lip. "I'm sure I could find plenty of business to keep me busy while you're working, because I know you have a business to run. And—" A long exhale. "I—I know this is crazy, but I'm not ready to let you go yet."

"I—"

"And you can totally say no."

"I—"

"Or that you want me to leave early if things aren't working out, or—"

Since it appeared that he wasn't going to be able to get a word in edge-wise, Dale did what he'd been longing for.

He wove his fingers into her hair, tilted up her chin, and . . . he kissed her.

He kissed her long enough to taste the mint of toothpaste on her breath, to feel the rapid pulse of her heart beating against his chest, lush curves beneath his palms.

He kissed her until he didn't want to ever let her go.

But the skies had other plans. The temperature dropped and snow began to fall, covering them in icy flakes.

Lucky for him, that meant he got to bring her inside.

"A week?" he asked when he was unlocking the door.

"A week," she said. "Or maybe more."

"I guess I'd better read up on squatter's rights."

A scowl, but the effect was ruined when she grinned and wove her arms around him. "Maybe I'll leave early," she threatened.

"And maybe I haven't taken a vacation in years and would love to spend a week with you."

"Yeah?"

"Yeah." He kissed her. "And maybe if you don't get tired of me, my next vacation can be to London," he murmured when they broke apart, chests heaving, blood pounding in his veins.

She touched his cheek. "I think I'd like that."

Her stomach growled. He pulled her close again. "I've got a secret."

"What's that?" she asked, nuzzling his throat.

"Melissa smuggled an entire French silk pie into the trunk of my car."

Elizabeth pulled back, grinned. "Pie for breakfast?"

"Why not?" he asked, stroking a hand down her back. "I think it's time we both live a little." A kiss to her forehead. "What do you say?"

"I say . . ." She paused, eyes calculating. "That I get first dibs on the chocolate curls."

"Not if I get them first!" he said, stepping back, opening the front door, and taking off for his car.

"Hey!" Footsteps pounding behind him.

He turned back, called, "You snooze, you lose—"

A snowball pelted him in the face.

He sputtered.

She bent over in hysterics.

He wiped the snow free, gathered her close, and gave her a snow-filled kiss. *Then* he went to get the pie.

For the record, he also gave her all the chocolate curls she wanted.

And for the first time in a long time, Dale's Christmas morning was filled with laughter and warmth and joy . . . and with a woman who had the protentional of being so much more.

ALSO BY ELISE FABER

Billionaire's Club **(all stand alone)**

Bad Night Stand

Bad Breakup

Bad Husband

Bad Hookup

Bad Divorce

Bad Fiancé

Bad Boyfriend

Bad Blind Date

Bad Wedding

Bad Engagement

Bad Bridesmaid

Bad Swipe (June 28th)

Gold Hockey **(all stand alone)**

Blocked

Backhand

Boarding

Benched

Breakaway

Breakout

Checked

Coasting

Centered

Charging

Caged (April 12th, 2021)

Breakers Hockey **(all stand alone)**

Broken (May 24th, 2021)

Love, Action, Camera (all stand alone)

Dotted Line

Action Shot

Close-Up
End Scene
Meet Cute (April 5th, 2021)

Love After Midnight **(all stand alone)**
Rum And Notes
Virgin Daiquiri
On The Rocks
Sex On The Seats (April 26th, 2021)

Life Sucks Series **(all stand alone)**
Train Wreck
Hot Mess
Dumpster Fire
Clusterf*@k (August 16th, 2021)

Roosevelt Ranch Series **(all stand alone, series complete)**
Disaster at Roosevelt Ranch
Heartbreak at Roosevelt Ranch
Collision at Roosevelt Ranch
Regret at Roosevelt Ranch
Desire at Roosevelt Ranch

Phoenix Series **(read in order)**
Phoenix Rising
Dark Phoenix
Phoenix Freed

Phoenix: LexTal Chronicles **(rereleasing soon, stand alone, Phoenix world)**
From Ashes
In Flames
To Smoke (October 18th, 2021)

KTS Series
Fire and Ice (Hurt Anthology, stand alone)
Riding The Edge
Crossing The Line (March 22nd, 2021)
Leveling The Field (June 14th, 2021)

Stand Alones

Someday, Maybe (YA)

ABOUT THE AUTHOR

USA Today bestselling author, Elise Faber, loves chocolate, Star Wars, Harry Potter, and hockey (the order depending on the day and how well her team -- the Sharks! -- are playing). She and her husband also play as much hockey as they can squeeze into their schedules, so much so that their typical date night is spent on the ice. Elise changes her hair color more often than some people change their socks, loves sparkly things, and is the mom to two exuberant boys. She lives in Northern California. Connect with her in her Facebook group, the Fabinators or find more information about her books at www.elisefaber.com.

facebook.com/elisefaberauthor

amazon.com/author/elisefaber

bookbub.com/profile/elise-faber

instagram.com/elisefaber

goodreads.com/elisefaber

pinterest.com/elisefaberwrite

www.ingramcontent.com/pod-product-compliance
Lightning Source LLC
Chambersburg PA
CBHW032106110726
47902CB00003B/495